HOLD ME LIKE A BREATH

Also by Tiffany Schmidt

Send Me a Sign
Bright Before Sunrise

ONCE UPON A CRIME FAMILY

HOLD ME LIKE A BREATH

TIFFANY SCHMIDT

BLOOMSBURY
NEW YORK LONDON NEW DELHI SYDNEY

First published in the United States of America in May 2015
by Bloomsbury Children's Books
www.bloomsbury.com

For information about permission to reproduce selections from this book, write to Permissions, Bloomsbury Children's Books, 1385 Broadway, New York, New York 10018
Bloomsbury books may be purchased for business or promotional use. For information on bulk purchases please contact Macmillan Corporate and Premium Sales Department at specialmarkets@macmillan.com

Library of Congress Cataloging-in-Publication Data
Schmidt, Tiffany.
Hold me like a breath / by Tiffany Schmidt.
pages cm
Summary: Penny Landlow, seventeen, the overprotected daughter of a powerful crime family, has rarely left the family estate due to a blood disorder, but when tragedy strikes and she is left alone in New York City, she must prove she is not as fragile as everyone believes.
ISBN 978-0-8027-3782-3 (hardcover) • ISBN 978-0-8027-3810-3 (e-book)
[1. Organized crime—Fiction. 2. Self-reliance—Fiction. 3. Sick—Fiction. 4. Family life—New York (State)—New York—Fiction. 5. Transplantation of organs, tissues, etc.—Fiction. 6. New York (N.Y.)—Fiction.] I. Title.
PZ7.S3563Hol 2015 [Fic]—dc23 2014019262

Book design by Amanda Bartlett
Typeset by Westchester Book Composition
Printed and bound in the U.S.A. by Thomson-Shore Inc., Dexter, Michigan
2 4 6 8 10 9 7 5 3 1

To this book's "fairy godfather," Joe Monti,
for choosing door #3.
And to Emily and Courtney, for giving me the courage
to step through it.

HOLD ME LIKE A BREATH

Once upon a time—nine years ago, to be exact—I didn't know anything about the Family Business. My parents wanted it this way, and since my father was the head of the Family, his wishes were obeyed without question. My childhood was spent being loved and coddled by members of my family and members of *the* Family—I was taken for walks by Father's second-in-command, flew kites with his enforcers, and played board games with my older brother, Carter. I was constantly told I was the most precious person on the estate . . . and the most fragile. These were the twin truths that governed the first eight years of my life.

My innocence and ignorance ended on a day that started like so many others, with me skipping down the hallway that connected my family's house with the Family clinic. This story became part of family lore, and even the parts I couldn't possibly remember feel vivid and full of Father's storytelling details.

But I remember the beginning. I remember spotting a girl sitting cross-legged on the floor outside a closed door. She had red hair, a frilly blue dress, and a smile. She was holding a picture book, and even though she was older than I was, she struggled to sound out the simple words and read them aloud.

I approached the girl, curious. The only children I ever saw were the kids of other members of the Families, but they were all boys, except for Magnolia Vickers. And she was "too wild" to be my playmate.

"Can you help me?" the girl asked, and so I did. After looking up and down the hallway to make sure no one could catch me sitting on a hard floor—I sank down next to her and read the book about a raven-haired princess who ate a poisoned apple and fell into an enchanted sleep. It was one of my favorites.

The girl squeezed me tightly in a sideways hug and looked at the pictures over my shoulder.

Even back then I knew I should tell the girl to let go, but it was so nice to be hugged. I just smiled and turned a page.

When the door opened and two tall, suited gentlemen emerged, we beamed up at them and I asked, "Daddy, do you know Kelly?"

As usual, Father's first reaction was to scan me from head to toe, taking a visual inventory of my well-being. On this day, his eyes focused on the arms twined tightly around my neck. His posture stiffened with alarm.

"Yes, I do. Kelly, please be careful with Penny."

"She's fine," I said.

"Careful" was my least favorite word. I leaned defiantly into Kelly's embrace.

"Penny's my friend," insisted Kelly, tugging a little harder on my neck, hard enough that I must have winced or flinched, done something that made both men spring into action and untangle Kelly's arms from me.

The other man hugged her to his side. "You can't touch Penelope. She's . . . easy to break."

I scowled. "What is Kelly doing here? Can we keep her?"

The men laughed and shook their heads.

"We were in that room discussing Kelly. She needs a kidney," Father answered.

I sucked on my finger while I considered this. "She *needs* it?"

"Yes," said the other man. He bent and kissed the top of Kelly's head. "Very badly."

"Can we give her one?" I asked Father.

"We can," he said.

"Then you'd better or I'll never talk to you again." I punctuated my threat with a small wet finger pointed at him, and both men laughed again. I failed to see the humor. My world was still simple back then, I still believed in black-and-white logic: if Kelly needed a kidney, she should have it—just like when I "needed" a new dress or unicorn statue, all I had to do was tell my parents and one would appear in my room.

"Then, Bob, I guess your daughter's getting a kidney." Father held a hand out for the other man to shake. "It shouldn't take me long to locate a match. I'll be in touch."

"Thank you," Kelly's father said. Then he bent to look at me. "Thank you too. I owe you . . ." He trailed off, swallowed, then managed a smile.

"You're welcome, Bob," I answered.

"Oh, no, missy," scolded Father. "That's Senator Forman to you."

"You're welcome, Senator Forman," I corrected, but mouthed the word "Bob" behind Father's back, earning a less-sad smile and a wink from the other man. "Have fun with your kidney, Kelly!"

Our dads stopped Kelly when she reached for another hug. They insisted we say good-bye by blowing kisses and waving. Then Father steered me down the corridor.

"Come on, Penelope. You're late for Dr. Castillo." He gently tugged at the collar of my shirt and frowned at the purple marks emerging on my neck. "And I want him to take a look at these new bruises."

I twitched my shirt out of Father's hand and sighed. I loved Dr. Castillo but hated his needles.

There were far too many needles in my life. Far, far too many bruises.

CHAPTER 1

Mother had the ability to switch from serene to terrified much faster than any of Father's sports cars could go from zero to sixty.

It wasn't the Business that generally spooked her, it was me; my blood, my skin, the color purple. She clung to those fears—held them tighter than she'd ever be able to hold me. Today I planned to ask her to loosen her grip.

I timed my entrance to the dining room with the exit of Father and his entourage. I saw the back of my brother's blond head bend down an inch or so as he spoke in Father's ear. As usual, Garrett Ward was with Carter. I always noticed Garrett—especially when he noticed me. This time he did, pausing at the edge of the room to lean one broad shoulder against the wall's ornate molding and throw me a wink from his gray-green eyes. Then he disappeared along with the other Wards; Father's second-in-command, Miles Banks; my tutor, Nolan; and the half-dozen Family members buzzing around Father like flies over a carcass.

"Good morning, Penelope. Tea?" Mother lifted the pot from the table as I slid into my chair.

Father and Carter gulped coffee by the gallon, I was an orange juice drinker, but Mother was all about the antioxidants and whatever other healthy things made tea taste like hot water plus dirty sticks.

I'd stopped drinking it years ago, when I outgrew tea parties and the excuse to eat sugar cubes, but Mother never stopped hoping and today I wanted the brownie points.

"Sure." I flipped my cup over on its saucer and slid it toward her.

In a khaki shirtdress with a navy cardigan she looked effortlessly elegant. Her blond hair shone with highlights, some she'd picked up on the tennis court and some she'd paid for at a salon. Her makeup and nails were classically understated, and she arched one sculpted eyebrow as she filled my cup. She handed it back, then placed a vitamin tablet directly over the *L* imprinted on my napkin ring.

I served myself some eggs and fruit, smiling as innocently as I could, pretending everything about this breakfast wasn't strategic, from waiting until the others had left the room to the fact that it was a Wednesday, when Mother had an early-morning massage and tended to be most relaxed.

"How are you today?" she asked. "What's in the folder?"

Beside me on the table was an inch-high stack of papers in a bright red folder. It was all the research, data, and support for an idea I knew she'd hate.

But what choice did I have? No white knight was coming to rescue me. At seventeen I was too old to believe in fairy tales, was sick of waiting for a miracle, and knew the only person who could save me from death by boredom on the estate was *me*.

I took a deep breath. "Mother, I've been tracking my latest platelet counts." I flipped open the folder and reached for the pages that displayed my blood test results in five different types of graphs.

"Sweet pea, please do not start this." She sat back in her chair, her mouth turned down and her forehead creased in disapproval. I'd overheard her talking with other Family wives recently; the topic was Botox and who had and hadn't gotten it. Mother had pointed to these wrinkles and called them her "Penny lines."

She was married to the head of a crime family that trafficked in illegal human organs and *I* was her biggest source of worry?

"But, Mother, my counts have been good. If you would just listen," I said. The "Penny lines" deepened, as if her soul-weary sigh or my request to be heard had pressed more fatigue into her face. I fought the urge to roll my eyes. "I'm not asking to go hang gliding! I'm asking—"

"Hang gliding? Don't even joke about that. Any head trauma could cause—" Instead of finishing the statement, she pressed a shaky hand to her lips and shook her head.

"Fine, no joking. I want *more* than this." I knew the irony of my gesture—that my hands sweeping in a circle indicated the enormous dining room with its table for fourteen and two chandeliers. Outside the row of soaring windows was a magazine-worthy patio, grass as green and lush as any golf course. A hint of the pool was made visible by the reflection of sun off its infinity surface and the glass of the solarium—built just for me so I'd have an indoor paradise year-round.

"What is it you want, Penny? Whatever it is, buy it. You know you don't have to ask."

"That's not the point!" I stood up so quickly my chair tipped over and crashed to the ground.

The noise made our cook, Annette, poke her head out of the kitchen. "Everything okay?"

"Did you hurt yourself?" asked Mother, the color draining from her face.

"I'm fine." My words were forced through clenched teeth as I fixed my chair and sat. I closed the red folder. That conversation would have to wait until Mother wasn't quite so panicked and I wasn't quite so angry.

Mother nodded at Annette, who vanished into the kitchen; then she turned back to me. "Sometimes I forget you have your father's temper under that deceptively sweet face. Darling, your safety, your health, have to be our first priority."

"I feel like I'm suffocating. What about *one* day off-estate? I understand your concerns, and I promise to be extremely—careful," I spit out that word like a mouthful of spoiled food. "I'll bring whatever security you want. I'll bring Caroline or another nurse if it would make you feel more comfortable. But I need to get off-estate. Just . . . *please*?"

She stood and tapped one fingernail on the back of her chair as she thought. "I'll make you a deal: How about a picnic? I'll set it up—"

I dropped my fork. It clattered against my plate and made her flinch. "You will?"

"—while you go see Dr. Castillo and get your ABC." She walked around the table and touched my dark-blond hair, running her fingers through it in her no-chance-of-bruising-Penny caress. I hated it; it made me feel like a dog.

ABC. My childhood name for a Complete Blood Count, since I'd insisted that "CBC" was *not* how the alphabet went.

It was a name I hadn't used in ten years, and I wasn't in the mood to be infantilized, but . . . *picnic*.

My head danced with visions of checkered blankets, sunblock, and sand. Or, if the ground was deemed too hard, restaurants with outside tables beneath colorful umbrellas. And once the whole outing went well, I'd add that to the evidence inside the red folder when I presented my argument. Tomorrow. I'd do it tomorrow.

"Thank you, thank you, thank you!" If kissing were a thing we did, I would have given her a kiss And if hugging were allowed, I would have squeezed her tight. Then again, if hugging were allowed, I wouldn't have *needed* permission to live a normal life beyond the estate's walls. It's not that hugging me was *always* dangerous—just that the same embrace that would be fine if my counts were good would band me with arm and handprint bruises if they'd had a dramatic drop. My parents had decided to order everyone to "err on the side of caution" and made all physical contact with me verboten. No one disobeyed my parents. Ever.

Despite the eleven years I'd had to absorb the fact that I was "breakable," "fragile," "untouchable," . . . I still missed hugs. I still missed a lot of things.

I said "thank you" one last time and bounced out of my seat.

"Yes, yes. All right now." She hid her smile by feigning interest in a flower arrangement. "Run along to the clinic and I'll arrange everything. Come find me in the front parlor when you're done."

It took less than a minute to get from the dining room to the clinic if I went the direct route: past Father's office, straight through the double oak doors at the rear of the library, down the white tile hallway, and through the second set of doors—stainless steel this time. The clinic was made up of five rooms and a storage closet: two for patient stays, a surgery, Dr. Castillo's office, and the consult room where Father, doctors, and other members of the Family met with VIP patients.

When I was little, I thought Dr. Castillo lived on the estate—I remember being shocked to learn he had a house fifteen minutes away and a family I'd never met. In my mind he *must* live in the clinic, because he was always there when I needed him. For 80 percent of the year, I was his lone patient. Only the elite of the elite—like the daughter of a former senator turned current vice president—were allowed to have their transplants here instead of at one of the six "spa" locations. As a child I'd resented those other patients—he was *my* doctor—now I welcomed anything that took attention off me and my platelets.

As usual I paused outside the dark paneled door to Father's office, wishing I were allowed to sit in on his meetings, or still small enough to hide in the cabinets and eavesdrop. He was yelling—not super unusual—but what *was* unheard of was another voicing shouting back: Carter's. I wished the door was thin enough to give me answers, or that my brother wasn't too busy to give them to me himself. Too busy to give me the time of day lately.

I left my red folder in the library under a coffee-table book about castles. For weeks I'd been planning to bring it up with Dr. Castillo, to ask his opinion on its contents, to ask for his endorsement, but I kept wimping out. If *remission* was a possibility, a word strong enough to hang my wishes on, wouldn't he have said it by now?

Dr. Castillo was waiting for me in one of the exam rooms. It was Wednesday after all, and *my* Wednesdays meant blood tests, not massages.

"There's my favorite pincushion!" He'd been making this joke for a decade, since before his dark hair had grayed at his temples. And despite the number of times he'd poked me with needles, he was one of my favorite people.

"To your throne, my lady." He pointed to the blood-drawing chair while he readied his supplies on a tray. I rolled up the sleeve of my pink pinstriped shirt. Opened and closed my fist to get my blood flowing.

Over the past ten years we'd perfected our medical

choreography: tourniquet, *squeeze your hand, quick pinch, open your hand, almost done, press here,* bandage, *you're all set.*

I fixed my sleeve and fished a lollipop from the jar he held out. I was much too old to need a reward for "quick pinches," but I wasn't going to turn down sugar.

As usual, he'd gotten one for himself too.

"Any new bruises, petechiae, etc.?" He pulled off his gloves and the candy wrapper, then examined my ankles for the pinhead-sized red dots that showed up on my lower legs whenever my counts started to drop.

"None," I answered. "And guess what? Mother's taking me off-estate for a picnic!"

Between the lollipop and that statement, I sounded about five, but he didn't mock me. "Really? That's great, Penelope. With the way your levels have been lately, I support the idea of loosening your restrictions. Unless this platelet count comes back low, you still don't need an infusion and there's nothing here to give me pause. Just be mindful of your actions. And have fun."

I tried to smile at his encouragement, but it was hard not to get caught on "unless" and his other loaded statements. After "careful," "pause" and "mindful" and "platelet counts" were my least favorite words. And I didn't need his reminders—my life was run by my counts. Had been since I was six and developed the inconvenient habit of turning all shades of purple and spontaneously bleeding. After a year of testing and more testing, I'd finally been diagnosed with idiopathic thrombocytopenic purpura.

Everyone but Carter shortened it to ITP. He liked to joke that

I was *idiot-pathetic*. Not that *idiopathic* was much better—"of unknown cause." My body destroyed its own platelets and no one could tell me why.

Most children outgrew it. I wasn't one of the lucky ones. I was *chronically* idiot-pathetic. I'd likely spend the rest of my life at the mercy of my platelet counts, watching for bruises and other symptoms, worrying that any injury could result in internal bleeding and worse.

The best I could pray for was remission, a word I didn't dare say aloud. I'd only just convinced myself to hope—and like me, hope was a fragile thing that would break far too easily.

"Thanks," I said.

"See you next week."

CHAPTER 2

"Are you ready?" Mother asked. She was smiling as she stood up from her desk, the one where she paid bills, wrote e-mails, and managed the household and its staff.

"Yes! I think? Unless I need to change? Am I dressed okay?"

"Of course." She laughed lightly. "I hope you're hungry."

I practically danced to the foyer as I dreamed of possibilities. Should I ask if we could take a convertible or choose which Ward we brought as a bodyguard? Speaking of Wards, if Carter and his best friend, Garrett Ward, weren't *too* busy, maybe they could be persuaded to join us . . . Maybe we'd picnic on the beach. Or Central Park! Stopping at a little deli along the way to pick up sandwiches and cold drinks. Frisbee! Lying next to Garrett on a picnic blanket and staring up at the clouds . . .

"Where are you going, goose?" Mother asked. "We're set up in the solarium."

My heart and hopes crashed. "The *solarium*?"

I followed her beckoning finger, like I wouldn't believe I'd been duped until I'd entered the room and seen the sunbeams streaming through the glass walls and falling like spotlights on the table set with plates of chicken salad, dishes of strawberries, and a glass pitcher of lemonade.

"But . . . I thought . . ."

She was already seated with her napkin in her lap, smiling up at me with all sorts of expectations in her eyes.

"Mother, it's not that I don't appreciate your effort—I do—it's just . . . This isn't what I expected. I thought I made it clear; I wanted a day *off*-estate. Maybe Central Park? With Carter and Garrett—"

"Why drive two hours when you can have a picnic here? No need to worry about food spoiling in a hot car or paper plates. Now sit down. Don't these strawberries look divine? Annette got them fresh from the farmers' market this morning."

"You're not—you're not listening! You never—" It was hard to fight off my anger *and* tears. One or both was going to come spilling out. "I can't do this . . ."

I let the solarium door slam behind me, let out my breath, let the tears leak down my face.

"—so much potential in partnering with crematoriums and morgues. It's not like anyone *needs* those bodies. Putting a corpse in an urn doesn't help anyone."

I'd been running down the hall, but as soon as I heard Carter's voice, I tried to freeze. Instead I stumbled over the edge of a Persian carpet.

He was standing in the middle of the library, illuminated by squares of light streaming down on him from the windows that alternated with dark paneled bookshelves on the narrow balcony ringing the room. Garrett Ward lounged against the wall beneath the gilt frame of an antique map, his fingers absently tracing the carvings on the side of the marble fireplace. My movement caught both their glances, and Garrett lunged forward as if he would catch me, even though I'd already caught myself. He raised his hand to steady me, then halted with a look of horror. He'd almost touched me.

Oh, how I wished he could.

All I'd wanted was a trip off-estate. A simple picnic. Not to be sent to the solarium like it was a time-out. Not to get caught crying like a five-year-old by Carter, who used to be my best friend but now was off living a life full of adventures and experiences I couldn't be part of. Not to have Garrett, the guy who played the role of prince in all my childhood make-believes and all my current daydreams, stare at me as if I were as delicate as spun sugar.

"You okay, princess? What's wrong?" Garrett's nickname for me was usually more affectionate than judgmental. He wielded it like an unintentional weapon—one word capable of filling my stomach with swarms of butterflies and leaving me incoherent. He was still standing catch-me close and his eyes were sweeping back and forth across my face. I wanted a redo, to have his attention like this at a time when my cheeks weren't wet with tears and dark with embarrassment.

"Nothing. I'm fine." I wiped at my face and faked a smile.

He nodded slowly, allowing me the lie. He clenched his hand as he lowered it and took a step backward, then another. Until he was halfway across the room, gripping the back of the chair he'd put between us.

"What's the matter?" demanded Carter, who was not nearly as tactful or sensitive as Garrett but made up for it in loyalty and humor. "Why were you crying?"

"I had a fight with Mother."

"Trade you. I've been fighting with Father all week." He turned to Garrett. "When *we're* in charge of the Family, remind me not to be a—"

"Person who doesn't think about where he's standing when he speaks?" Garrett tilted his head at the doors to Father's office, clearly visible across the long room. The gesture made his reddish-brown hair flop forward into his eyes. Garrett wasn't a person who spoke before weighing his words or acted without calculating the effects—his hairstyle was equally deliberate. The rest of his brothers copied their dad and wore their hair cropped short. I loved how his had personality, how it emphasized he *wasn't* like the rest of them. Al Ward didn't tolerate rebellion, so I knew Garrett had paid some consequence for skipping the buzz cut. Despite this, he'd come home from college with it longer, not shorter.

"What were you fighting about?" I asked. Perhaps it wasn't the best choice of question, but I was desperate to keep their attention.

Carter exhaled his frustration and sank onto one of the leather chairs, thumping his blond head against its high back.

"Everything. Things are changing. It's not just H.R. 197—though if the Organ Act passes, we're so . . . No, it can't pass. No one is going to vote to allow people to sell their body parts." He paused and shook his head, then resumed banging it again. "But everything else. We've got to keep up, and Father refuses to adapt. Do you know how close the Zhus are to perfecting artificial organs?"

Actually I did. People didn't tell me much, but I was really good at listening. And on our estate, there were lots of opportunities to eavesdrop on interesting conversations. "The Vickers are too. Aren't they?"

These were the other major Families. And while there wasn't a Landlow-Zhu-Vickers softball tournament or campfires where our Families shared trade secrets, there were enough whispers, leaks, and rumors to keep us fairly informed about one another's developments. When we were younger, the other Families' kids had come to visit our estate. But they hadn't in years. Not since Carter broke his arm on a dare from Magnolia Vickers; not since Ming Zhu sat miserable and sniffling through an endless afternoon, staring silently at me through crooked glasses. I think Father still talked with the other Families' heads pretty regularly, but the only information I had about them was what I'd overheard—and I'd heard Miles mention "Vickers" and "liver prototype" last week.

"Supposedly." Carter sighed. "So, Pen, why are you and Mother fighting?"

"Because she never takes me seriously! There are important

conversations I need to have with her that she won't even let me start."

"Conversations about what?" asked Garrett, then ducked his head and added, "Unless it's too personal."

"It's not," I said quickly, swallowing down the way my heart had leaped to my throat with his question. "And actually, I do want your advice . . . you guys just haven't been around to ask."

They'd come home from their freshman year of college two weeks ago, yet I'd barely seen them besides at meals. Carter was always sequestered with Father and the council or off the estate. Where my brother went, Garrett followed. I'm not sure if it was loyalty or duty.

"I'm not avoiding you," said Carter. "Don't give me that look; I'm really not. Things have been insane. I *do* feel bad about it. I was just telling Gare we should do something with you."

"Prove it," I challenged.

"What?"

"If you miss me, prove it." At five feet three inches tall there weren't many chances for me to use height to my advantage, but my giant of a brother was seated, so I glared down into eyes as blue as my own. My medical ID bracelet jingled as it slid down my wrist, settling like a shackle. "Take me off-estate. Now. Not next week, not when things are less busy."

"You think I'd put off spending time with my favorite sister?"

"Twenty percent of your summer vacation is already over and this is the longest conversation we've had, so, *yes*, yes, I do."

Carter laughed. "I know when I'm beat. Let's go."

He stood and headed toward the hall, but neither Garrett nor I moved. I was too busy mentally cycling through *Really? Is he serious*?

Garrett was frowning. "We can't." My brother and I turned to him. "We have *that thing* we have to do."

"Ohhh." Carter drew out the word, then sucked an inhale through his teeth. "Right."

"Can't I come?" I begged. "I don't care if *that thing* is boring. At least it would be a different kind of boring."

"Sorry, Pen." Carter carefully tugged my sleeve—it was what passed for a playful sibling gesture between us since he *couldn't* give me wedgies or noogies or even poke and pinch me like the siblings I saw on sitcoms. "It's just . . . there's some stuff happening. Big stuff. But it doesn't mean I don't want to hang out with you."

"I am so sick of excuses I could scream!" My voice actually *did* get rather close to screaming by the end of the sentence.

A door opened and Mother called, "Penny? Why are you yelling? Come back into the solarium so I can talk to you."

"You can't leave me here," I hissed at my brother.

"Maybe—"

"No," said Garrett. "Don't even think about it."

I glared at him, but he was giving my brother a look of raised-eyebrow warning and didn't even notice. It was a very Ward look, square-jawed, narrow-lipped, so menacing you forgot how handsome he normally was. I'd seen this expression on the faces of his older brothers but never him. It erased my annoyance and replaced it with shivers.

"What about this? I'll try and get back early enough to do something. I can't make any promises, but I'll do my best. Okay?" Carter tugged my sleeve again.

"I don't have a choice, do I?" I pulled my shirt out of his grip and crossed my arms.

"Well, you *could* turn down your two favorite guys . . . but why would you want to?"

"Favorite guys?" I reached over and pinched him.

"Ouch, Pen!"

"Strange. I thought you must be dreaming, but you're actually awake."

Garrett tried to hide his smile.

"If you're done beating me up . . ." Carter made a show of rubbing his arm. "I could really go for some Korean barbecue later. How's that sound?"

"I wouldn't know; I've never had it," I muttered.

"Penelope Maeve!" Mother's voice sounded less patient this time, and closer. "I know you can hear me."

"Well, I'm thinking of a great place in the city . . ." He trailed off and raised his eyebrows.

"New York City?" I squealed. It was my weakness, my favorite daydream. And, curse him, he knew it.

"Yup. So go make nice with Mother, and I'll call you with an update later. Gare, let's roll." Carter strolled out of the room all confidence and swagger. For a moment, I hated him: that he was allowed to come and go as he pleased; that he didn't see the gates surrounding our property as a cage; that he didn't have to go smile, apologize, beg for a night of *maybe* freedom.

Garrett paused for a second after Carter was gone. He stepped around the chairs and couch and tables to stand in front of me. So close I could touch him, or he could touch me . . . except, he *couldn't*. He grinned in a way that made his almost-green eyes glow, in a way that made my years-old crush swell in my chest, my cheeks flush, and heart race. "Just so you know, I want to work on that favorite-guy thing . . ."

I nodded and bit down on my tongue so I didn't confess how lonely I was when they left for school without me.

Mother appeared in one doorway as Garrett slipped out the other. "I've been calling you. Have you calmed down enough to be reasonable yet?"

"Calm" was the last word I'd use to describe the emotions cycloning through me—but I needed to "make nice" if I wanted to go off-estate with Carter—NYC!—*if* he had the time to take me.

"Yes, Mother," I said meekly. "Is the picnic still set up? I'd love to try some of those strawberries."

It's not like time ever moved quickly on the estate, but while waiting to *maybe* leave, it ceased to move at all. I gritted my teeth while Mother showed me swatch books for new library curtains. I tried on dozens of outfits, creating a mountain of discarded dresses and tank tops on the floor of my closet. I resisted the urge to text Garrett and Carter every five minutes—once an hour, however, was completely reasonable.

And when Carter responded: Pick U up @ 6, I shrieked with

glee—causing Mother to rush into my bedroom, breathless with alarm. I begged, pleaded, called Carter and made him talk to her, and finally went limp with relief when she said, "Yes, as long as . . ."

Her list of rules and warnings was endless, but I pretended to listen as I second-guessed my appearance and watched out the window for Carter's car.

When I caught the first glimpse of the black Mercedes, I blew Mother a kiss, grabbed my purse, and ran outside.

Garrett got out to open the car door for me. I studied him while I went down the steps and walked across the driveway. The sun was reflecting off his hair, making it look more red than auburn. It was long enough that the ends curled. I wanted to keep staring and list the ways his first year at college had changed him—sharpened the line of his jaw and filled out his neck and chest so he mirrored the muscular bulk of his older brothers—but I was out of footsteps.

I caught him watching me too. Making me so glad I'd enlisted Caroline's help in selecting an outfit. She was a nurse but also the closest thing I had to a friend, and she'd teased me about my brother tagging along on my "date." She'd vetoed my capris and skirts and thumbs-upped the yellow sundress with white eyelet trim. The sundress that made Garrett exhale slowly as I stepped close.

"You look . . ." He swallowed. "Really nice."

I smiled, and he did too. The smile I remembered from days of board game marathons and crossword puzzle races. From the times when he'd sneak away from games of manhunt with his brothers and Carter to come tell me about his day and ask about mine. From before he was too busy. Back then, his smiles were innocent—they hadn't made my blood run hot—and his eyes weren't so intense.

Carter beeped the horn, and we both jumped. "Let's go," he shouted.

Garrett dropped his gaze and patted the car's roof. "Your chariot." He waited for me to slip into the backseat and click my seat belt before shutting my door.

CHAPTER 3

There was always a moment as I rolled down the long driveway toward the high fence surrounding the estate when my breath caught in my chest and I doubted my decision to leave. *Anything* could happen to me outside the perimeter of our property.

Carter interrupted my thoughts. "I told Mother we're going to see a musical. You know what's playing and can pick one, right?"

Of course I did. I spent hours on NYC websites, blogs, and forums. Someday I'd go into a long remission. Someday I'd live there and walk the streets of promise, freedom, and opportunity they sang about in *Annie,* a play I'd seen with Father on Broadway right before my life turned purple and red.

"Really?" It made sense that Mother would agree to a play. It would be safe, a seated activity. The chairs would mark out defined personal space, and I'd be perfectly cocooned between the two guys. It made a whole lot *less* sense that Carter would voluntarily attend the theater.

He lowered his window and called a greeting to Ian, the guard on gate duty. Once his window was closed and the gate was shutting behind us, he snorted. "No, not really. That's just what I said to buy you some extra time."

"You should at least listen to the score then," I countered. "You know she's going to want to discuss it. Or, if she doesn't, Father will. He'll probably perform it if I ask."

"Then don't ask," said Carter. "Fine. Pick a show and Garrett can download the soundtrack. We'll listen to it *once,* then I get the radio for the rest of the drive—no complaints."

It was more than I'd expected; he truly felt guilty about being so MIA. "There's a revival of *Once Upon a Mattress* that's getting great reviews."

They snickered.

"*Once Upon a Mattress*? That sounds like—"

I cut my brother off. "Don't go there! It's a fairy tale, gutter-brain."

"Of course it is," laughed Garrett.

I'm pretty sure the subtext of that laugh was *you're such a child.* I swallowed a retort. Freedom was too rare a thing to waste arguing. And I'd never had Korean barbecue. I'd never even heard of it. There were so many things I'd never seen, tasted, experienced . . . Tension melted into giddy anticipation, bubbling in my stomach like giggles waiting to escape.

"So, how'd your super-secret errand go?" I asked. "Was it something exciting? Something illegal?"

Garrett met my gaze in the rearview mirror and shook his head.

But it was too late. Carter's expression darkened. "*Everything* we do is illegal. It's not a game where you get to pick and choose which crimes you're okay with."

"So it didn't go well," I muttered under my breath.

I knew it wasn't a game, and I knew the Family Business was against the law. I'd known it for so long it was easy to forget. Or remember only in a vague way, like knowing the sky is blue without paying any attention to its blueness.

Only in those moments when things went wrong—when lazy clouds were replaced by threats and storms, when someone got hurt or killed—only then did I stare down the reality of the Business through a haze of grief and funeral black. My fingers tensed on the edge of the seat.

"Ignore him," said Garrett. "He's just pissy because the people we were supposed to meet with stood us up."

"Someone *dared* to no-show for a meeting with the mighty Carter Landlow?" I teased, hoping to break the gloom settling in the car like an unwelcome passenger. "I assumed it was a Business errand, but if someone stood you up, it must be a *girl*."

"No offense, Pen, but you don't have a clue what's going on in the Business."

"*No offense,* Carter, but you're being a—"

"Who wants to hear some songs about mattresses?"

interrupted Garrett. He reached for the stereo, but Carter swatted his hand away.

"I'm not an idiot," I said. And wishing for things that had been denied for so long was idiotic. No less so than repeatedly bashing your head against a wall or touching a hot iron. I knew the answer was *no,* was always going to be *no,* so asking to be included in Family matters was like volunteering to be a punch line for one of the Ward brothers' jokes.

But I knew the basics. It wouldn't be possible to live on the estate, spend so much time in the clinic, and *not* know. The first person to explain it to me had been my grandfather; fitting, since he was the man who'd reacted to the formation of FOTA—the Federal Organ and Tissue Association—by founding our Family.

The same day I'd demanded a kidney for Kelly Forman, he'd sat me down and demonstrated using a plate of crackers and cheese. "When donation regulation was moved from the FDA to FOTA, they added more restrictions and testing." He ate a few of the Ritz-brand "organs" on his plate, shuffled the empty cheese slices that represented humans who needed transplants. "This, combined with a population that's living longer than ever before"—he plunked down several more slices of cheese—"created a smaller, slower supply and greater demand." He built me an inside-out cheese-cracker-cheese sandwich. "It was a moment of opportunity, and when you see those in life, you take them."

This felt like a moment of opportunity. And not to prove that I wasn't an idiot by listing all the facts I knew—about how the Families provided illegal transplants for the many, many people rejected from or buried at the bottom of the government lists. How more than two-thirds of those who made it through all the protocols to qualify for a spot on the official transplant list died before receiving an organ. Or to recite the unofficial Family motto: *Landlows help people who can't afford to wait, but* can *afford to pay.*

"Fine, tell me what I don't know," I said. "Tell me what's going on, why you and Father are fighting, and what's keeping you so busy. Tell me *everything*."

Garrett muttered something that sounded suspiciously like "Don't do this," but since my brother ignored him, I did too.

Carter's eyes met mine in the rearview mirror. "None of this leaves the car, Pen. I'm trusting you."

"I understand." I sat a little straighter. "And I promise."

"Wait," said Garrett. "Before we drag her into this, let's just hear what she wanted to ask us. There *was* something you wanted, right, Penny?"

I thought about my red folder. Underneath the blood count charts were stacks of glossy brochures, a pile of completed applications. Which did I want more: a future with school, a normal life, friends, or one that included the Family Business?

"Pen?" prompted Carter. "Is everything okay?"

"Everything's really good actually." I took a deep breath—maybe the two futures weren't incompatible. Maybe I could have both. "My platelet counts have been decent since mid-May. I've gone more than seven weeks without needing an immunoglobulin infusion. That's my longest in . . . *years*. I think I'm heading into another remission."

"Serious, Pen? That's amazing!" Carter slapped his fist against the horn and matched its blaring noise with his own *whoop!*

"Wow." Garrett's celebration wasn't hand-waving and yelling. He'd gone still, except for a slight nod of his head and cautious grin. "What does Dr. Castillo say? Your parents?"

"Dr. Castillo hasn't said anything yet, not beyond, 'your numbers still look good.' But last week's count was around eighty-five K—and that's without any treatment for forever! While that's not impressive for you guys with your several *hundred* thousand platelets, it's significant for me. And if this is another remission, I want to take advantage of it."

When I was twelve I'd had ten months of steady, healthy, treatment-free counts. It had been a time of tentative parental hugs, nibbles at normalcy, and minutely planned trips off-estate.

It was during one of these that everything came crashing down. During a fitting for my first bra, the clerk said, "You sure do bruise easily . . . and quickly." She'd pointed to the purple stripe her measuring tape had created around my torso. I'd responded by bleeding from my nose and gums. Mother had screamed and screamed. Our driver, Dylan, had broken every traffic law rushing me back to the clinic, which I didn't leave for a full week.

One CBC later—platelet count four thousand—and I'd been back in lockdown.

"Take advantage of it *how*?" asked Garrett.

I gulped. This was my most cherished daydream, and I was handing it over for scrutiny. "I want to go to school in the fall."

"You hate Nolan that much?" joked Carter. "Though, after dealing with him in Business meetings this summer, I get it."

I gritted my teeth at the mention of Nolan. "Isn't he the most frustrating man on the planet? But no. It wouldn't matter who my tutor was. It'll be my senior year and I haven't been in a classroom since first grade. I just want . . . school, freedom. Friends! People my own age, so maybe you'll stop teasing me for being a baby *and* talking like I'm sixty. I know I can do it, but Mother and Father . . . Say you'll help me?"

"Like, a *school* school?" One of Garrett's hands gripped a handful of his jeans, the other clenched the side of Carter's seat. He twisted so far around he was practically in my lap.

"Why couldn't she? Pen, I think it's a great idea."

Garrett turned to glare at my brother. "Maybe because there's a million things that could hurt her there? Plus, people. Lots of people. Your parents would have to hire her a guard."

"Carter didn't have one," I said.

"He had—*has*—me."

"Gare." Carter's voice was a warning. "Don't ruin this for her. There's got to be a Family member somewhere that's either her age or can pass for it. Doesn't Glen from the South Carolina clinic have a son?"

"Leo, who was caught trying to steal painkillers?" The knuckles on Garrett's hand turned white as he clenched them tighter. "He's not going anywhere near her."

"Eh, I'm sure my father had yours teach him a lesson. But hey, I know, let's send *you* back to senior year. Maybe you'll learn something this time and be able to keep up in college."

Garrett's jaw locked, and he swallowed hard. "I'm not trying to ruin anything. I'm being realistic and playing devil's advocate. Isn't that why you told us, princess? So we can come up with the arguments your parents will use?"

"Something like that," I said softly. Though I wouldn't have minded his support before he tore the idea apart.

"Have you given any thought to a splenectomy?" asked Carter. "If they cut yours out, there's a chance that would fix you, and you'd be good to go, right?"

"Are you insane?" Garrett slapped his palm against the dashboard and looked as if he wanted to slap my brother. "You want her to have elective surgery to *remove part of her body*?"

"Um . . ." I wanted to point out the irony of his statement: his salary, his schooling, his life were funded by people who chose elective surgery to sell parts of their bodies, but all I could do was laugh.

"Well, she'd have a heck of an experienced medical team," Carter said before he gave into his own laughter.

Garrett's anger deflated into a chuckle too. "But you're not going to?"

"Right," I reassured him. "My parents won't even okay steroid treatment because of the side effects. A splenectomy definitely isn't an option. And it's not as simple as cut it out and all better. The results are mixed, and Dr. Castillo doesn't think it would work for me."

"Okay," he said. "And I really am happy you're doing so well. If you want to go to—"

A phone beeped with a text alert, almost immediately

followed by a ringtone that cut through his words and made them jump. Carter picked up his cell, swore, showed the screen to Garrett, then swore again. All the buoyancy of freedom seemed to evaporate from the car.

"Now? They blow us off earlier and expect us to answer *now*?" said Garrett.

"Well, it's not like these things can be scheduled," replied Carter, jabbing the screen of his cell. "Hello?"

He muttered low and furious into the phone while Garrett tried to distract me: "Did you pick a school? It'd have to be a day school, and one close to the estate." He even went so far as to fix me with one of his heart-stopping grins and suggest, "Carter might've been on to something; I could still pass for a senior. I'll have Jake go to college with him, and I'll come hang out with you."

Carter hung up, still cursing. "We have to do the pickup."

Garrett's grin disappeared. "No one else can do it?"

He shook his head.

"Pick up *what*?" I asked.

Carter opened his mouth, but Garrett put a hand on his arm. "She's *seventeen*, she wants to go to school. Let her be seventeen. There's plenty of time to get her involved later."

"When *we* were seventeen we were already sitting on council, visiting the clinics, meeting with patients. She can't even tell a kidney scar from a skin graft—she needs to catch up."

"*She* can make her own decisions, *she* is sitting right here, and *she* is coming along to whatever this mysterious pickup is, so she's already involved," I snapped.

"You are *not* coming," said Garrett.

"We don't have a choice, unless you want me to leave her on the side of the highway. This is our exit." Carter was clutching his cell phone, shaking it as if that could erase whatever the text instructed him to do.

Garrett groaned. "You're staying in the car."

I hid my smile by looking out the window. It had gotten dark while we were driving, the dusky purple of summer evenings. On the estate these nights buzzed with a soundtrack of cicadas and crickets, but there was no nature outside the car. Nothing but concrete and pavement and cinder-block industrial construction. We pulled into a parking lot. A poorly lit, empty parking lot.

"Where are we? What are we picking up?" I examined Garrett's stiff posture and the bright gleam in my brother's eyes. "Does Father know about this Business errand?"

"No, and you're not going to tell him," Carter answered.

"Oh, really? So what am I going to do?"

"Stay in the car. Lock the doors. Keep the windows up." Carter turned around to look me in the eye. "This isn't a joke, Pen. If I'd known this was going to come up, I would've left you at home."

"Please, princess," added Garrett in a soft voice, but his eyes didn't leave the windshield, didn't stop their scan of the parking lot.

"Fine, but when you're done, you're filling me in. Then *I* can decide if I want to be part of it or not." It was all false bravado.

Each one of Carter's statements tied another knot in my stomach; Garrett's plea pulled them tighter.

Carter dumped a half-dozen mints from the plastic container in his cup holder into his mouth—like his breath mattered, like this was a date not a disaster. He waved the container at us, but we shook our heads. He crunched the candies and said, "Gare, you're hot, right?"

I blurted out, "You can turn on the A/C, I'm not cold," before I caught on: Garrett pulled a gun from a holster below the back of his shirt.

They laughed, but it wasn't funny to me. I'd been to too many funerals—they'd been to more. I wanted to ask how long he'd been "hot." If he always had a gun on him. Had he when we went mini-golfing at Easter? Or the time last summer when I slipped on the pool deck and he'd carried me to the clinic? No. He couldn't have then. He'd been wearing a swimsuit too—there's no way he could've hidden a gun.

So what had happened in the past year, and why was he carrying one now?

Garrett was Family, he was a Ward, but he wasn't supposed to follow his brothers' footsteps. Or his father's. They were enforcers, but he didn't belong in their grim-faced, split-knuckles ranks. That was why he was in college with Carter—Garrett was going to be his right-hand man when my brother took over the Business.

Not a thug with a gun.

"Stay here, Pen," Carter said again, then slipped out into the night. His keys still dangled from the ignition, the engine still hummed.

Garrett lingered an extra moment. "This shouldn't take long. And everything's okay. I don't want you to worry."

"I'm not." I would've sounded believable if my voice wasn't quivering. If I weren't clutching fistfuls of my dress.

"You're cute when you're worried." Garrett winked, and then he too was out in the darkness and humidity and I was alone.

I tried to lower my window—just a crack, enough to let in voices but not even mosquitoes—except Carter must've engaged some sort of child lock. I stared out the tinted glass, watched as their shadows grew gigantic on the wall as they approached the warehouse, then disappeared around its corner.

No matter how hard I concentrated, my eyes couldn't adjust enough to make sense of the dark. Maybe it was the placement of the parking lot lights—how I had to peer through them to see the warehouse beyond.

After they'd left this afternoon, I'd rushed to the clinic to model different outfits for Caroline. She'd teased. We'd laughed. I'd blushed and daydreamed about the lovely combination of me, Garrett, and NYC.

But in my daydreams, Garrett hadn't been wearing a gun.

And now we were parked somewhere made of shadows and secrets and fear that sat on my tongue like a bitter hard candy that wouldn't dissolve.

The car still smelled like them. Their seats were still warm when I leaned forward and pressed my hands against the leather.

But I couldn't see them. What if the dark decided never to spit them back out again?

This wasn't the Business as I knew it: secret transplant surgeries that took place at our six "Bed and Breakfasts" and "Spas" in Connecticut, Vermont, Maryland, Maine, Massachusetts, and South Carolina, where we saved people like Kelly Forman. She'd been ten when she needed a kidney transplant, but her chromosomal mutation—unrelated to her renal impairment— earned her a rejection from the Federal Organ and Tissue Agency's lists. According to them, Down syndrome made her a "poor medical investment." FOTA wrote her a death warrant. We saved her life.

She graduated from high school a few weeks ago. The past nine years since we'd met—she wouldn't have had those without the Family Business.

That was enough. That was all I needed to know. Illegal or not, that was *good.*

I heard something. A crack so sharp it echoed and seemed to fill the spaces between my bones, making me shiver. I prayed it was a car backfiring.

Then it happened again.

My stomach jumped to my throat, crowded out my lungs, and made it impossible to breathe. I tried the door handle, but it wouldn't open. Not the first, second, or eighth time I jerked on it. Not even when I pulled hard enough for it to bite into the insides of my fingers.

Terror was a thing with claws that squeezed my throat and demanded I keep yanking and yanking on the handle. It whispered my worst memories in my ear, flashbacks to my tenth birthday when we'd gotten news of an FBI raid at the Nantucket clinic. The local police on the Family payroll had failed to tip them off, so the staff hadn't had time to activate the spa facade. Things had escalated quickly, badly: handcuffs, gunshots.

A second call had come in while my family was singing "Happy Birthday": Keith Ward had passed away from bullet wounds. The candles melted all over my Empire State Building cake; I'd been too busy gasping for air to blow them out. And what was the point? It was far too late to wish Garrett's oldest brother would be all right.

Keith had been a thug with a gun. Garrett . . . he couldn't be.

They had to be okay. They *had* to be.

I was so focused on that noise and looking out the front of the car, it was perfectly reasonable that I jumped and screamed when I heard a thump behind me. The trunk opened. Something heavy thudded inside. The trunk shut. Carter and Garrett got back in the car, still laughing at me.

"You scare too easily," said Carter.

I refused to let my relief escape in a sob or declaration that I loved him. "Yeah, well . . . not all of us make a habit of skulking around in shady places," I finished lamely.

"Skulking?" Garrett grinned. "Nice vocabulary. What're you, fifty?"

"Nope, she's Nolan Jr. None of that hooligan teen-speak for our Penelope."

"Maybe I'd speak more like a teen if I ever got to spend time with any." I'd tried for defiant, but it came out as wistful. I ground my teeth. "Stop distracting me. Were those gunshots? And were they yours? Did you just put a *body* in the trunk?"

"A body?" scoffed Carter. "This isn't *The Godfather,* Pen. We're not a mafia out whacking people . . . although I'd kinda love to hear you say 'fuhgeddaboutit' in your prissy little voice." His eyes were too bright, his forehead beaded with sweat, his smile stretched wide and smug.

"I didn't shoot anyone." Garrett hit my brother on the arm. "Sorry we scared you."

"What you guys are doing—this thing you can't tell Father—it's really dangerous, isn't it?"

Carter gave me a quick grin as he glanced over his shoulder and reversed out of the parking lot. The tires squealed as he threw the car in drive and sped down the street. "If I say it is, will that scare you off?"

"No," I said through gritted teeth.

"I wish it would." Garrett turned around in his seat. "I'm not going to let anything happen to him or you." Which was the exactly wrong thing for him to say when he was still holding a gun in his lap.

"And who's going to protect you?" I locked eyes with Garrett, each of us daring the other to look away first. I wasn't going to back down, not even if my gaze laid bare how much I cared about his well-being.

"Hungry?" Carter asked, and we both jumped. "I'm ready to get my B-B-Q on."

"Stop. No. Just stop. We're not going to dinner right now," I said. "We're not going to a restaurant where you'll use 'public place' as an excuse to ignore my questions. I'm not leaving this car until I get some answers."

"But I'm starving," Carter whined.

"Fine. We can eat. Drive-through. No one is getting out of this car."

"I have to pee." Carter was way too self-amused, and Garrett snickered.

If I could have kicked the back of their seats without Garrett insisting we pull over so he could check for bruises, I would've. I settled for narrowing my eyes. "You're not funny," I told Carter.

"I'm hilarious. Your sense of humor is broken."

We both looked to Garrett. "Oh, no. I want no part of this. *Stay out of Landlow infighting* is the first rule of being a Ward."

Was the second about carrying a gun? Seeing him holding it so casually made my stomach clench and my appetite disappear. I shivered in the A/C.

"What did you shoot?" I asked. "And can you put that away, please?"

"Car tires," he answered.

"Bet they won't be late again," Carter said. His eyes were on the road as he merged onto the highway. He didn't see the way I watched Garrett's hands on the gun or the way Garrett was watching me in the rearview mirror, his mouth forming an apology. He leaned forward and tucked it back in its holster.

"So you don't want to go to the city, Pen? You'd rather do drive-through and head home?" Carter put on his blinker and moved into the right lane.

Not fair. He *knew* about my NYC obsession. He *knew* I rarely saw it on anything other than TV and computer screens. "Fine. Let's go get dinner."

"Sure thing." He accelerated and merged left, exchanging a look with Garrett that was far too smug.

"So, did tonight's errand have anything to do with *Everly*?" I threw out the word like a challenge, and they both froze.

"What do you know about the Everlys?" asked Garrett.

The answer, not that I would ever admit it, was *nothing*. I didn't even know to add a "the" in front. It was just a word I'd overheard a few times lately. Always in hushed tones and always with serious expressions.

But where Garrett looked horrified, Carter grinned like I'd just invented electricity.

"The Everlys?" I prompted. "Answers?"

Carter shrugged. "They're an upstart. A wannabe Family."

"And?" I'd eavesdropped enough to know new Families never succeeded. They didn't have the influence to buy off/blackmail law enforcement and government officials. They didn't have the pharmaceutical companies in their pockets, so they lacked a steady supply of antirejection meds, steroids, antibiotics, etc. They had a shortage of skilled doctors and were too reckless with recruiting donors. My grandfather had had to deal with all these obstacles when he'd started the Family, way back before Father was born, but he'd had some advantages: money; a family with influence and connections; a half-dozen established spas that could be transformed into clinics without raising suspicion; a wife who was a transplant surgeon and fed up with the days she *wasn't* performing surgeries because there weren't organs available. But, most important, he was *first.* Not that he hadn't encountered raids and setbacks, but he'd been able to get up and running, establish safeguards and cover stories, before the Feds even knew the Business existed. Or maybe that wasn't most important. Maybe the most important thing was a character trait he shared with Father—they were fastidious. Grandfather had had incredible attention to detail, and he demanded it from everyone around him.

Father said all the upstarts were sloppy—too focused on making a quick profit and ignoring both the minutiae and bigger picture. He said *this* was why they inevitably got themselves arrested—which actually benefited the real Families because it kept the FBI busy and away from us.

"The Everlys use cadaver tissue, Pen," said Carter, "and most of it comes from crematorium or morgue connections."

"Like you were talking about earlier," I said, "in the library."

"No! Not at—they're nothing like that. We're, we're nothing like—we would never be like them."

Carter was almost incoherent with horror, so I turned to Garrett. "Explain."

"There are some . . . questions about where they get their organs and their clinic conditions. Like, they told this one guy he was getting a teenager's heart and it was actually a sixty-five-year-old's. The guy needs another transplant already and he's DQ'd from the government list. And there have been rumors of patients getting hepatitis from organs. Hep C, I think."

"They're using diseased and misrepresented organs," said Carter. "I'd never do something like that!"

"Well, of course not," I agreed. "Are they a threat?"

He shook his head. "They shouldn't be. They should all be arrested or out of the Business soon enough."

"So why were you talking about crematoriums earlier? Our Family only does live-donor transplants. Or donors who signed over their bodies while still alive." I swallowed a "right?" but the statement still sounded like a question.

"Pen, I'm talking innovations. If Father wants to compete, he's got to change things up, or we'll be swallowed by the Zhus and the Vickers."

"The Zhus are on the West Coast, the Vickers are in Texas—I hardly feel like they're about to raid New England and steal our patients."

"True," said Garrett. "But if the Organ Act passes and donation becomes legalized, what's going to happen to us? We need a backup plan."

This might've been a time when I could've explained *exactly* what I thought would happen if H.R. 197—aka the Organ Act—miraculously managed to become a law: we'd become a legal industry. Yes, we'd lose significant money per surgery because of the proposed price regulations, but we'd also be able to slash our overhead, cut costs on security and payoffs.

But that conversation would be endless, and I wanted more answers. "The Organ Act has been stuck in subcommittees for forever. That's not an immediate threat."

"Fine," said Garrett. "But the Everlys are doing their best to poach our client list, which is dangerous for everyone and another reason we need to innovate."

"But Carter just said they weren't a threat! And what's the *innovation* that's in the trunk?"

There was a long silence. Garrett played with the stereo; he even turned on the *Once Upon a Mattress* score . . . which lasted a whole thirty seconds before Carter changed it. I stared at the back of their seats. Standing, they were the same heights, but Garrett's shoulders were broader, and Carter was built like Father, all long legs, so seated he looked shorter.

"Is anyone going to answer me? Don't stop now, it was finally getting interesting."

There was another silence, an exchange of looks. It ended in Garrett swearing under his breath and Carter changing lanes a little too aggressively.

"Let's make a deal," he said. "I'll drop you and Gare off to pick up dinner, then park and use the bathroom. You guys can meet me, and I'll tell you what I can."

"Meet you *where*?"

He grinned. "Remember in middle school when Gare and I had that clubhouse and you were desperate to come in? Well, here's your chance to see our latest hideaway—we've upgraded a bit since then. So . . . deal?"

It wasn't like I really had a choice, but at least he was pretending I did. "On one condition," I said. "I want pizza. The greasy, delicious kind you see in every NYC movie."

CHAPTER 4

Carter said he had the "perfect spot," and I expected somewhere in Little Italy or one of the restaurants I'd seen on a Food Network show, but he dropped us outside a narrow pizza place in Harlem, a couple of blocks past the Apollo Theater. It was loud, busy, crowded with customers—and corners: on the tables, freezer cases, counters. The type of chaos that made Garrett extra-vigilant and me hyper-aware of the distance between my body and all potential bruisers while we waited for our slices to be heated, tossed on paper plates, and slid into a brown paper bag.

I exhaled my relief when Garrett opened the restaurant's door and we stepped into the night. I pulled out my phone and opened my favorite NYC map app, adding a flag to mark our spot.

"I'm dying to see your 'secret clubhouse'—does this one have Spiderman posters too?" As I skipped down the sidewalk, the toe of my shoe hit a piece of broken bottle and sent it tinkling off into the shadows.

"Put your phone away." His expression was tight. "Stay close to me."

I understood that order. We walked past cracked windows and graffiti, around split garbage bags and the huddled shapes of the homeless. It was very different *being here* versus playing with virtual maps—marking walks I hoped to take in some distant, healthy future and planning someday visits to landmarks and museums. Although those walks and places weren't in this neighborhood.

Garrett was at my side, one hand not quite touching my elbow, the other clutching the brown bag that was growing grease stains. His eyes were alert and darting but also pointing out things.

"See that alley? It goes all the way to the next street. That one, the one with the tattoo parlor on the corner? It's a dead end. Don't go in that bodega. It's just a cover for a drug operation. You know how to work the panic button on your phone, right? And how to tell if someone's following you?"

"Of course. I might not be 'hot,' but I'm not helpless. My father taught me some things too." I saw him wince, his hand involuntarily patting the back of his shirt.

"This is a bad idea. I don't agree with Carter. I don't think dragging you into any of this is smart or safe."

I narrowed my eyes. "Too bad it's not your decision."

"Yeah. Well, I guess it's too late now anyway. We're here."

I pulled out my phone and added another location flag. This

was something big, something important, and I was being included. I felt my eyes go wide with anticipation as he ducked into a dingy doorway. Just a few square feet of dirty gray tile and mangled mailboxes. The inner door was propped open with a container of mints, the same brand my brother had offered us earlier. Garrett picked it up and slid it in his pocket. "Good, Carter's already here."

Passing through the door, we faced another small area. Not even a proper lobby. It smelled of mold and spoiled food. Garrett pointed to a staircase, and we began to climb. Four flights later he knocked on 4B.

There were sounds of something dragging in the apartment, something slamming.

Then there were the slides and clicks of locks being turned, and my brother's face appeared in the doorway. "Hey, come on in."

"Your clubhouse is an apartment? Since when do you even *like* the city? I thought you were all anti-noise or bustle or whatever it was."

"You mean back when you were eleven and every time you didn't get your way, you threatened to run away here so we'd never see you again? People grow up, Pen. You stopped throwing tantrums, and I changed my mind about the city."

Except I still threatened that in my head, all the time. And daydreamed about it through every immunoglobulin infusion. How nice of Carter to go ahead and realize my dream *for* me. "So why are we here? Whose place is this?"

"It's *my* apartment," Carter stated proudly. "I own it."

"No way." I'd watched far too many real estate reality shows to fall for that. "Nice try. You couldn't even afford a shoe box in New York City. Not unless you've dropped out of school and taken up a lucrative career as—"

"What would you know about real estate?" The tips of his ears were red, the way they got when he was angry or embarrassed. Or both. "Or money for that matter. You sit behind your computer screen with Daddy's platinum cards, but when was the last time you even held a dollar bill?"

Since I couldn't remember I couldn't contradict him, so I just glared.

"Who's hungry?" asked Garrett, stepping between us and rubbing his hands together. That had to be instinct honed in *his* family, because there wasn't any chance Carter and I would actually come to blows.

"As I was saying,"—Carter gestured around him—"welcome to my place. It's completely off-grid. No one but Garrett, and now you, knows about it. No Family bugs. No enforcement waiting in the hall. This is my safe space to do whatever I want."

"Like what?" I asked. "Like tell me what's going on? Let's start with what was making so much noise before you opened the door."

"Okay, wee impatient one. Sit. Eat. We'll fill you in."

"Is this a hold-your-questions-till-the-end type of presentation? Or am I allowed to interrupt?" I asked. Garrett was pulling the pizza out of the bag, so to him I said, "Mine's the pepperoni."

"Does that work for Nolan? Because I didn't think you were

capable of not interrupting." Carter laughed, and I knew I was forgiven.

I reached for the plate Garrett was holding out to me, but he froze. Then flung the pizza on the coffee table. He stepped toward me, eyes narrowing, mouth tightening. "What happened to your hand?"

"What?" I glanced at my fingers, then curled them toward my palm, hid them behind my back. My bracelet slid down my wrist to land just above them and mock my next words, "It's nothing."

"You didn't have those bruises earlier. What happened?"

Carter's smile was gone now too. Erased by the purple stains on the inside of my fingers. "How bad is it, Pen?"

"I'm fine. It's really no big deal, just from . . ." I mentally connected some dots. "From the car door earlier." Except that made it sound worse—like my counts were so low, closing a door could cause this. "*Normal* people bruise too. I might have gone a bit ballistic when I heard the gunshots and tried to claw my way out. Which reminds me, child-locking my door is not cool, Carter."

"Neither is leaving the car after I told you to stay put." There was no joking warmth in his eyes. "You couldn't even follow that simple request?"

"I-I was worried about you. I heard the gunshots. Is that really a bad thing?"

"Yes," they snapped simultaneously.

"How can I trust you?" asked Carter with a shake of his head. "You really would've disobeyed and run directly *toward* gunshots?"

"Garrett, back me up, please?" I reached a hand for his arm, but all he did was gently flip my palm and sigh over the purple lines that marred my fingers.

"Princess, you don't get it, do you? And you got *hurt*. You can't—" He turned to Carter. "We can't. Don't you see that? We can't involve her in this."

I snatched my hand away. "These are just regular bruises. The kind *anyone* could get. My counts are *good*." That was supposed to be the magic sentence that unlocked all the doors in my life.

"Are they?" asked Carter, pointing to my purple fingers, pointing to the inscription on the bracelet right above them:

PENELOPE LANDLOW
BLEEDING DISORDER/LOW PLATELETS/ITP

His question shattered every one of my arguments and retorts, replaced them with all-consuming doubt. Were they? They could flip in an instant, my body suddenly deciding it liked destroying platelets more than being healthy. Maybe this wasn't the cusp of a remission, but a lull before a big crash. Was he thinking of my worst periods? When I was ten and my counts had been so low we could draw smiley faces on my skin, the lines we traced showing up immediately in purple? Dr. Castillo had *not* been amused by our ingenuity. Neither had my parents. At the time, my platelet counts were below a thousand. Not much had broken through their wild terror, but I can still remember the way they'd yelled at him, the way he'd radiated guilt and apologies and "I just wanted to make her smile."

The expression Carter wore now wasn't much different. He studied me as if he was in pain, as if looking at me was painful. "Eat your pizza, Pen, then we'll head home. Unless . . . do we need to leave now? Take you right to the clinic? Let me see your hand again." Garrett exhaled a sound of relief and palmed Carter's keys off the counter.

"I'm really okay." I bit back tears and retrieved my plate from the coffee table.

It was quiet for several minutes. Garrett and Carter frowned and watched me like I might spontaneously bleed all over the apartment. I tried to convince myself that all I'd lost was some Business secret I hadn't known I wanted when I woke up that morning. My numbers could still be good. How easily and quickly I bruised *could* be an indicator of lower counts, but it wasn't like every bruise meant disaster and danger. They were like a smoke alarm—sometimes they meant *fire!* and sometimes they meant burned toast. These had to be toast.

Carter cleared his throat and forced a smile. "So, what do you think of the apartment?"

The pizza rasped like sandpaper when I tried to swallow. "It's nice."

It wasn't quite a lie. Nothing in the apartment was new or top-notch, but it had a look. Things went together to create a style. It showed an eye for design that I'd never imagined my brother had.

Carter, who mocked me every time I tried to watch a home makeover show, had chosen a deep purple for the walls. There were accent colors: teal and lime used on throw pillows, curtains, and an afghan draped on the navy couch. There was a rug the color of paprika, and the chair where I sat to eat my pizza was huge. Big enough for three of me. It had once been a deep chocolate color—before use and age had faded the leather into a series of comfortable wrinkles.

If I hadn't been trying so, so hard to make myself chew, swallow, and hold back tears, I would have teased him for it.

I gave up on my pizza and wandered into the kitchen, feeling their eyes tracking my moves. It was a small room, separated from the main living space by a breakfast bar with two stools and dominated by a freezer that took up the whole wall between the fridge and trash can.

There were coffee mugs in the sink. "Were you guys here recently?"

"No," said Garrett at the same time Carter said, "Yeah . . . I mean, no."

I'd had a decade to accept that people often told me lies to spare my feelings. This one hurt more than most, because it was pointless and transparent.

"This thing is massive. What's in it?" I tugged on the freezer's lid, but it was either locked or iced shut.

"It came with the apartment. It's empty. Broken. I just haven't gotten rid of it yet," Carter said.

But it was plugged in. It hummed with electricity, and there were spots of water on the floor at its base. Like melted freezer frost—the kind knocked off if the lid was slammed quickly because you were hurrying to open the door.

I gave Carter a *you're-full-of-it* look, which he chose to ignore, and tugged on the lid again.

"Princess, stop," said Garrett. "Don't make your hand worse."

I stepped away as if it might burn me. Not that I'd been doing anything remotely bruise-worthy. At least not if my counts were still where they'd been seven days ago.

Carter balled up his plate, uneaten pizza and all. "You done, Gare? Let's go."

If they kept this place a secret, there must be a reason, and I was running out of time. Maybe they wouldn't let me see what was in the freezer, but not everything was locked. I grabbed the fridge door and opened it triumphantly: nothing but pickles, cheese, jam, and tiny plastic packets of soy sauce and mustard.

I left the kitchen and turned to go down the hallway, but Garrett was out of his seat in a flash, standing between me and the three remaining doors.

"It's time to go."

"Don't I get the rest of the tour?" I asked.

"I think that's enough for tonight."

"But . . ."

"We're leaving, Pen," Carter said. "If you're up for it, we'll take you off-estate again soon—maybe even actually see a play next time. Or Korean barbecue. Right now I just want to get you home without further damage."

I didn't want to be placated. I didn't want Carter to suffer through musicals or feel guilted into letting me tag along to dinner. I wanted him to respect me, *include* me. And while I may have gotten in the front door of their nineteen-year-olds' version of a boys' clubhouse, I still wasn't good enough for their secrets.

"I'm fine." The words sounded like a prayer—they were a prayer.

On the ride home, Carter chatted nonstop about the area, naming the cross streets, the distinguishing characteristics of the building, the apartment number. He told me where he had keys hidden—two keys, two different locations. The one for the main door was taped inside the top of the mailbox for apartment 5F. The mailbox itself could be popped open if you pressed on the bottom left corner. To access the apartment key, you had to go behind the staircase, get down on your stomach, and feel around on the bottom of the third stair to find the spot where it was magnetically attached.

It was chatter I normally would've loved and recorded on my map app, but it was also noise to prevent me from asking questions—pointless pity information, since I'd never be able to use any of it without him. And after tonight, who knew when I'd get off-estate again.

"Though, with your map obsession, you probably know New York better than I do. Bet we could drop you anywhere in the city and you could find the apartment."

"Why don't we try it and see?" I suggested.

"Not funny," said Garrett with a groan. He reached around his back, pulling up his shirt to expose muscles and skin . . . and the black lines of his holster. "Can't sit comfortably with this thing." He pulled out the gun and placed it in the glove box.

Carter laughed. "Better?"

"Much."

They relaxed and I tensed up. It was another unwelcome reminder of how they'd changed and I was still me. I cradled my hand in my lap and stared at the bruises. Hated them. Hated my skin. Hated the blood beneath it and the platelets within that.

CHAPTER 5

When Carter turned on the musical score I shut my eyes so I wouldn't have to see the pity in his. With the quiet music and smooth motion of the car, going from faking sleep to actually sleeping was effortless.

I woke because Carter was saying my name. Or maybe it was Garrett. Their heads were bent close as they debated in tense whispers with words and phrases that seemed as foreign as Mandarin. The music was off. It was just past eleven, and we'd traded the highway for the slow roads leading to the estate.

"Who's dead meat?" I stretched, covered a yawn, and rubbed the spot where the seat belt had pressed against my shoulder when my head lolled in sleep. "Besides both of you if I had my way. Jerks."

Carter didn't even have the good sense to look guilty as he snorted. "It's not a who, it's a what."

"Shut up." Garrett glared at my brother. "Go back to sleep, Penny."

"Make me," I whispered through gritted teeth. Either they didn't hear my lame retort or they pretended not to.

Conversation dropped to a taut silence until we reached the estate. Carter waved to Ian in the guardhouse. He did a flashlight sweep over the interior of the car before hitting the button to open the gates. As usual, when they closed behind us my throat constricted, my skin felt tighter, and I had a moment's sympathy for every zoo animal everywhere.

Carter parked outside the garage. "Gare, can you walk Penny back to her room? I need to deal with—" He nodded his head at the back of the Mercedes.

"Need any help with that?" I asked. Garrett opened my door and I tried to maneuver around him, but he was faster and bigger. More than capable of blocking my view of the trunk.

Carter sighed and ran his fingers through his hair. "Pen, I know you're disappointed, and I'm sorry."

"Not as sorry as I am," I snapped.

He pushed Garrett out of the way and bent so his eyes were level with mine. "I *want* to include you—let me just figure out a way to do it. A way that keeps you safe."

I hissed my answer from between clenched teeth. "Has it ever occurred to you that if whatever you're involved in is too dangerous for me and has to be kept secret from Father, then *maybe you shouldn't be doing it?*"

"Yeah, actually, it has." He scrubbed at his face with both hands, looking suddenly exhausted.

And then *I* was the one feeling guilty for pushing him too far, searching for a way to make him smile. "You still owe me Korean barbecue. And it better be the best thing I've ever tasted after all this hype."

"Good night, Pen."

"Come on," said Garrett, and I followed him up the walk to the side door.

"Will *you* tell me what's in the trunk?"

"At this point, nothing. Some empty coolers and leftover dry ice. Let it go, okay?"

"Were there organs? And if so, why in the world were you transporting them like that instead of through the regular channels?"

"Penny, it's late, I'm tired. Please, just go in the house."

I sighed and punched in the unlock code. "You know, if I were a regular girl, a guy walking me to my door at the end of the night would be a date."

Garrett raised one reddish eyebrow in a look that made my pulse jump. "Oh, yeah?"

I let him enter first, his gray-green eyes scanning all corners of the rooms that lit up automatically as we passed through. I liked the estate best late at night. There were still security at the gate and patrolling, but there weren't Family members and staff around every rounded corner. This was the only time of day it felt more like a house and less like the headquarters of the Business.

In the foyer I paused beneath the chandelier. Its crystals seemed to drip down and form the abstract sculpture displayed on the marble table that stood between the dual staircases that curved up to the second floor.

I put one hand on my hip and pointed a finger at him, at the muscles visible through the navy cotton of his shirt. "Though *he'd* take me on a more romantic evening than clandestine parking lot shadiness and a rat-infested apartment."

"Don't let Carter hear you call his place rat-infested. And don't forget dinner—that was good pizza." Garrett followed me up the left branch of the stairs. His hand on the railing right beside mine, his breath and voice in my ear.

I stopped at the top and turned to face him—our eyes, noses, mouths were almost level from my vantage point two steps above him. "On my date, we'd eat dinner off real plates, not ones made of paper."

Garrett's smile changed from amusement to something warmer, something that touched his eyes and made him look younger, less intense—more like the boy I'd grown up crushing on than the duty-focused man who'd come home from college with a gun.

"And would you let this guy kiss you at your door?" He stepped around me and into the hallway that led to my bedroom.

"That's for me to know." I dropped my voice so it wouldn't carry down the opposite hallway toward the light that crept out from under my parents' bedroom door. My heart was pounding so loud, I had a hard time believing they couldn't hear its drumbeat.

Though maybe they could, because the door cracked open and

Mother stepped out, all regal elegance with her hair down and curling around the shoulders of her satin robe. I froze where I was, half in her hallway, half in my own.

"How was your night, sweet pea? How are you?"

"Fun. Great." With my bruised hand behind my back, I made a *stay put* gesture to Garrett. He was close. So close I could feel his body heat and all I wanted to do was lean into it. "Thanks for letting me go, but can we talk in the morning?" I yawned.

"Of course. Get some rest."

"You too."

Before her door was even completely shut, I was turning to Garrett, hoping the interruption hadn't killed the flirtation and energy of the moments before. He was waiting, eyes on me with an intensity that made me need to fill the silence. "Where were we? Oh, right. I was knowing things." I could feel my cheeks warming with blushes, but I still added, "Kissing things."

"And I was going to ask if I could find them out," Garrett whispered, his voice deep. "May I?"

"That depends." I continued down the hall to my bedroom. He followed. "Not if you're going to treat me like I'm not old or smart enough to make my own decisions."

"You can't ask me not to care about you. I'm always going to want to keep you safe." He reached for my doorknob, and for a moment he was all stiffness and attention as he pushed it open and scanned my room.

It was a moment I needed. To catch my breath. To convince myself that this was reality and not a fairy-tale fantasy.

He turned away from my room and looked at me in a way he

never had before. This was not the look he'd given me when he'd lost a bet at eleven and Carter had told him to kiss me as punishment.

It was a gaze of fire and flames and like he wanted to devour me whole—and something else too . . . *fear*? Like maybe he was as nervous as I was. It was a combination so intimidating and thrilling that even as I edged closer and tilted my chin up, I couldn't help but use my least favorite word. "You'll be careful? My counts *are* good, so you can touch me, just be gentle."

"I'd never hurt you, princess." His voice was low, vibrating with emotion, and his hands were in my hair, the tips of his fingers barely skimming my skin. He leaned down—

"Pen? You still up?" Carter's footsteps padded up the carpet of the stairs, smashing the moment before it had truly begun.

Garrett let go of my hair and stepped backward, but not fast enough. Or maybe too fast. Maybe the sight of Garrett and me framed in the doorway to my bedroom wouldn't have tipped off Carter if we hadn't been so frantic to put space between our bodies.

"No," he growled.

"Carter—" We said it in unison—which made it worse, made us both fall silent.

Finally I swallowed. "Did you want something?"

"Never mind. Penny, go in your room and go to sleep. Garrett, you forgot your piece in the car."

I'd never hated anything as much as the hunk of metal in Carter's hand. The way it had scared me in the parking lot, the way it had poisoned this moment, the way my brother looked comfortable holding it, and the way Garrett was turning pale.

"You're not gonna tell your dad I forgot it, are you?" He cursed under his breath. "Or *my* dad? My brothers?"

"No," said Carter. "But you'll be lucky if I don't shoot you with it."

I squeaked and grabbed the hem of Garrett's shirt.

"Don't touch her," Carter snapped when Garrett moved to put his hand on mine. "I *was* joking, but if you bruise her, I won't be."

"Hey!" Garrett sounded, if possible, angrier than Carter. "If you think I'd leave so much as a mark on Penelope—"

"Stop it!" I stepped between them.

Once, when I was ten, Carter had whacked me instead of Garrett when they were "roughhousing"—I'd missed the fireworks of Father's wrath, but even from the isolation of my bed in the clinic, I'd known the consequences were severe. Just the fact that neither of them was allowed to visit me proved that. They'd learned the lesson well, and now both of them practically leaped backward to give me space: Garrett into my room and Carter farther into the hall.

"You're both being ridiculous. Just stop."

Carter curled one hand into a fist, but he reached past me and handed Garrett the gun.

Garrett tucked it in the holster beneath his shirt and edged around me into the hall. He drummed his fingers on the wall before giving me a weak smile. "I'm sorry, princess."

A quick nod to Carter and he was leaving. Walking away.

I ducked my head so they wouldn't see that those words hurt more than any physical bruise.

"Pen?" Carter's pity was like a thumb pressing on a sore spot. Good thing I had plenty of experience hiding pain.

I turned around to face him, eyebrows raised, face blank. "What's up?"

He snorted. "You're something else, kid."

"I'm not a kid."

"I know." He sighed and rubbed his forehead, ruffling the front of his blond hair. "You're this crazy mix of too-old-for-your-age and too innocent."

I shook my hair out of my face and glared at him. "Don't even start with me. I *almost* kiss Garrett and you throw a fit? My nonexistent love life is *none* of your business. If anyone should be mad, it's *me*—your timing is awful. Couldn't that mystery thing in your trunk have kept you busy just two minutes longer?"

I could see the arguments swirling in his eyes, in the clenching of his jaw, but he exhaled slowly. "Fine. It's not a big deal. I guess. I don't know. That's not why I wanted to talk to you."

"No? Well, if you're not here to play some sort of purity police, what do you want? To lie to me some more?"

"I get it. I'm a jerk. I'm the world's worst brother—" He banged a hand against the wall. "But if you'll listen for a minute, I came up here to apologize. You have a right to know what's going on and make your own decisions."

"Oh." I'd reached for my door, planned a rageful slam in his face, but instead I leaned against the frame—it was rounded.

When I'd first been diagnosed Mother had hired a team of architects to smooth out all the corners of the rooms I used most. Reduce the sharp edges, pad the hard surfaces, hide the marble stairs beneath cushioned carpet. I looked up at Carter and in a voice squeaky with surprise, I asked, "Really?"

"Sorry I freaked out over your bruises—and if you want to go to school, I'm on your side. I'll help you convince Mother and Father."

"You think it's possible?" My whisper was a desperate plea for reassurance.

"Yeah, I do. You've got to pick your battles, Pen, but then fight to the death for the ones that matter. *This* matters."

"That sounds like it should be my screen saver." A bit of confidence was creeping back into my voice, back into my veins.

"Oh, I'm full of motivational clichés: *Go, fight, win; Ask forgiveness, not permission; If you want respect, demand it; 'No' is never the final answer,* and something about doors, windows, and a rocking chair."

"Remind me to get you some pom-poms for your next birthday." I tugged on his sleeve. "You're a good guy, Carter Landlow."

His smile disappeared. "I hope so."

"Although good guys aren't usually the ones shooting out tires." I'd been aiming for a joke, but his face went pale. "Carter? What really happened tonight?"

"Something I'm starting to think was a mistake." He shut his eyes and rubbed his forehead. "Ask me something else, Pen. I'll tell you anything else about the Business."

"Okay . . ." I was torn between wanting to help with whatever was stressing him and wanting answers before he changed his mind. "What about the Everlys? I get that they're amoral slime, but are they really a threat to our Family?"

"You mean besides the fact that Nolan's using them as reason eight hundred we should support the Organ Act? He gave a two-hour presentation on it yesterday morning. Two hours of explaining why we should support a law that would make it legal to pay organ donors—and pretty much put ourselves out of business. Two hours."

I didn't necessarily agree that the Organ Act would ruin the Business, but this wasn't the time for a political debate. "Yeah . . . that doesn't surprise me. It's Father's fault for giving him an audience—but no one listens to him. He's my tutor, and *I* barely listen to him."

This earned me a quick grin and an "I know," before he lapsed back into seriousness. "They might listen to him this time. A couple of the guys seemed interested. Miles and Frank especially. The bill's getting some traction. The FBI is facing a ton of public pressure and salivating to shut someone down. On top of that, the Everlys had someone die on the table this week."

"How horrible." It had only happened to us once—that I knew of—a fifty-eight-year-old man had died during a heart transplant at the Hilton Head clinic. It was a tragedy for sure, but there was always a risk. The waits to reach the top of the government transplant lists were so long; sometimes people didn't contact the Families until it was too late. "But the FBI is *always* salivating.

Are we worried our payoffs aren't getting to the right people? Or that one of the clinics isn't secure?"

"No, you don't get it—it was the *donor* who died. A twenty-six-year-old kindergarten teacher who was going to use the kidney money to pay for her wedding. And after she died, they harvested all her usable parts without asking her next of kin.

"It's turned up the heat on all the Families—the donor's fiancé is talking to the press, and there was a group of senators on the news today demanding answers." Carter tugged on his hair again, shut his eyes. "I don't know, maybe Nolan's right. If the industry was legalized . . . We'd lose profits, but maybe it would be better, you know?"

"Money is not more important than morals. If it keeps scum like the Everlys from killing donors, giving people diseased parts, or lying about corpse pieces—yeah, I think that'd be better. And no more fear of FBI raids; no more people like Keith Ward getting killed; or worrying about you or Father ending up in jail or worse—sounds heavenly to me."

Carter flinched repeatedly during my rant, though these truths couldn't be news to him. "You worry about all that?"

"Constantly. Every single time you or Father leave the estate, and that's the bulk of my prayers every night. I think it's part of being a Family."

"I don't want you worrying about me, Pen."

"Then maybe it's time to support the Organ Act," I joked, waiting for him to say *Okay, mini-Nolan* like he did whenever I brought up H.R. 197 or used a big word. Instead he turned away from me.

"Maybe. Yeah, maybe . . ." He wasn't really answering me, just thinking out loud. His gaze was out the window, down the drive, and on something that either I couldn't see or that wasn't there. "Listen, Pen, I've got to go. There's something I've got to do."

"Go where? It's midnight, and I have more questions."

"We'll talk again soon. Promise."

"No, wait." I grabbed his arm and he was stuck. He couldn't leave unless he pulled away forcefully—and that would hurt me. It was a cheap trick, but an effective one. "*When* will we talk?"

I could practically feel the impatience skittering down his arm. "Let me go now—so I can do this thing before I change my mind—and you can name the place and time."

"You realize my first question is going to be *'Do what?'*"

He nodded.

"Followed by *'How'd you pay for a New York City apartment?' 'What was in the trunk?' 'Whose tires did Garrett shoot?'* And a million other things."

"Can't. Wait." He stretched out the words like rubber bands of sarcasm.

"Fine. Go on your hot date or secret mission or whatever, but don't stay out too late; you're taking me out for breakfast."

"Sounds good. Doughnuts? Eight?"

"Deal." I let go of his arm, giving his sleeve one last tug. "Have fun."

He took a step down the hall, then turned around and bent to kiss my cheek. "And if you do hook up with Gare, don't let him break your heart—I'd hate to have to kill my best friend."

"What if I break his?" I taunted.

"Serves him right." Carter's laughter drifted down the hall to be joined by the pattering of his tan loafers on the stairs. Then both noises and my brother disappeared behind the leaded-glass panes of the front door.

CHAPTER 6

The sunlight was slanted wrong, creating shadows instead of a glow. A glance at my clock confirmed my apprehension—10:47. A glance in the mirror heightened it—I had a new bruise.

It was on the side of my neck, a two-inch-wide, inch-long stripe—from the seat belt. Probably from when I'd fallen asleep on the drive home. Probably no big deal.

Just like there was probably no good reason for me to get the shivers when I called Carter and it rang and rang and went to voice mail. No good reason for me to continue shaking when I stood in a scalding-hot shower.

He'd changed his mind—again.

He was busy.

He was pissed I'd overslept and stood him up.

I was healthy.

I was healthy.

I was *still* healthy.

I exhaled a reassurance on each step as I walked past his empty bedroom and headed downstairs.

As I passed the parlor, Mother put down her tablet. "Good morning, sleepyhead. Are you just getting up?"

"A little bit ago."

"How was the play? I still can't believe you got those boys to sit through a musical."

I gave her a sharp look, but she wasn't suspicious, just amused. "It was good. Carter fell asleep—speaking of, where is he?"

"I haven't seen him. I had an early session with my trainer, and by the time I got back they were already in your father's office. I'm sure he'll be at lunch."

I frowned.

"Are you that bored, sweet pea? I could ask Nolan to set up some lessons."

"It's summer." Even the homeschooled were entitled to a break. Especially when faced with a tutor like mine. Nolan was Family. He'd been fresh out of college when Father put him in charge of my education. He had wanted in the *business* aspect of the Business, but Father said he needed patience and leadership . . . skills that *I* was supposed to teach him in return for biology and world civ. I'd thought his lack of experience would make him a pushover. He'd assumed having only one pupil would be easy. We were both wrong. Five years later, our school days were still battles of will and stubbornness.

Nolan was big on structure, drills, and memorization. I craved novelty and creativity. Preferred writing and reading fiction to his research projects; geometry over his favored calculus. Our only overlapping interest was a shared addiction to C-Span and a quiet support of the Organ Act, which aimed to legalize compensation for organ donations. It would allow payment for both live donors who gave things like kidneys or a portion of their livers, as well as families who chose to donate the bodies of their deceased.

"Mother," I said, trying another tactic, "don't you think Nolan deserves a break from me? Carter says Father has him working on some 'big, important projects.'" I added air quotes, but if it had been Nolan I'd been quoting, it would've sounded more like "prestigious, imperative endeavors."

"He was just saying the other day how much he misses you. I'm sure he could find time to come up with a summer curriculum if I asked." She paired her threat with a twinkle-eyed smile. I couldn't tell if this meant she was joking or serious.

I needed Carter *now*. Needed his help strategizing my argument for school so I never had to endure another of Nolan's lessons.

And maybe if I went to school, if I had more in my life than what fit between the gates of our property, then I wouldn't have fallen for his best friend. I'd have options. I'd have friends of my own, and not just Caroline, who was paid to jab me with needles.

"That won't be necessary," I said. "Please don't bother Nolan. I'll find something to do."

"Good girl." She patted my hair. I bit down the urge to bark and beg for a cookie.

Pick your battles, Pen, but then fight to the death for the ones that matter.

I wanted more of Carter's advice, more of his answers.

Ask forgiveness, not permission.

I didn't go back to my room or toward the solarium, pool, library, or game room. I headed for Father's office. I didn't knock, and I didn't ease the door open quietly. I also didn't see my brother among the startled faces on the couches and chairs.

"Where's Carter?" I'd spoken over someone. Interrupted what was probably a serious, important discussion, but I was too anxious to be embarrassed. Not even Nolan's disapproving sniff, Al's frown, or the Ward brothers' snickers mattered.

"Off with Garrett, I assume," said Father with a touch of indulgent amusement, like I was still eight and looking to tag along on the boys' latest adventure. "I haven't seen them today—but it's their summer break. I'm not a tyrant, sweet pea."

"Summer break . . . must be nice," scoffed Jacob Ward and his brother Mick cuffed him.

I didn't pause to roll my eyes at them, apologize for interrupting, or do more than nod at Miles Banks's "Good morning, Penelope."

I ran to the garage. His car was gone. So Father was right: he and Garrett had gone out. Maybe for doughnuts, or maybe they'd gone for Korean barbecue without me. For all I knew, they were bonding over Garrett's lapse in brain activity when he'd mistakenly considered kissing me.

And here I was worried about the jerk.

So. Worried.

"Hey, princess." I turned at the voice, at the noise of a car door opening. But it was only *one* door. Garrett's car was parked in the driveway, and he was the only one getting out. His long legs made short work of the pavers between us, then he was standing there, head bent, shuffling his feet.

I realized I hadn't returned his greeting, but to do so at that point would be adding awkward on top of awkward.

"Have you seen Carter?" we asked at the same time, then both looked up. Our eyes met, and I'm sure mine broadcast alarm—Garrett's did too, for an instant, before he forced a smile.

"He's not answering my calls. He must be *really* pissed at me," said Garrett.

"You think that's it?" Carter hadn't seemed that mad when he said good night. Distracted, yes, but not mad at Garrett.

"What else can it be? I've been waiting around all morning for him. And I've texted and called him a dozen times. I feel like a jilted girlfriend."

"He's never supposed to go off-estate without you, right?" I asked.

"Not unless he wants to hear about it from your dad *and* mine."

"Because his car's not here."

Garrett swore under his breath. "I hate when he pulls a Houdini. We *both* get in trouble, but guess whose dad is less forgiving."

I flinched. Father had an impressive temper, but it flared hot and extinguished fast. Al Ward's anger burned cold. "They don't know. They think he's off with you."

"I'll go track him down. Can you cover for me?"

"Of course." I mentally replayed my last conversation with Carter. There had to be something useful I could add to Garrett's search. "He went out last night. After . . ." My words trailed into a blush, and I looked at the pavers beneath my feet. "Didn't you go with him?"

"What? No. Where'd he go?"

"I don't know. He just said he had to do something—that he needed to do it right away, before he changed his mind."

"Changed his mind?" Garrett said slowly. His face had gone grim.

"Could it be the people you shot at?"

"I didn't shoot at people. I shot the tires on a hea—a car. And no, they're not a threat."

"Okay," I said, but it lacked conviction.

"Hey, princess, look at me. He's fine."

I shivered despite the July humidity. If Carter were here he'd tease, *Someone walk over your grave, Pen?* I shivered again.

"Find him quickly, okay?" I whispered.

Garrett touched my cheek with the tip of his pointer finger, tracing the curve from chin to ear. The touch was so light it shouldn't bruise and all I wanted was for him to do it over and over and over again. Make me forget I'd woken up in a day that felt wrong. Father would kill him for these caresses—another reason that it was better to *find Carter* than explain what made him so angry that he'd left Garrett behind.

"No worrying," he ordered.

I nodded; it was a nonverbal lie.

"*We'll* see you soon," he promised.

I nodded again and stood on the driveway as he drove away.

I'd promised Garrett I'd cover for him, but it would probably be wiser to hide. I headed to the clinic. I couldn't find answers about Carter there, but I'd ask some about myself.

CHAPTER 7

Dr. Castillo was watching a video of a surgery on his computer when I knocked on the open door of his office. It looked like something laparoscopic—a liver maybe, or intestine? Something gray. He paused and minimized the screen. "Back so soon?"

"I have some bruises."

"How are you feeling?" He stood and pulled his glasses from the pocket of his white coat, fitting them on the bridge of his wide nose and magnifying his brown eyes.

"Fine. I'm sure it's nothing." I wished, hoped, prayed.

"Your mother sent you." He exhaled into a smile.

"No. I came on my own. She already worries too much, so please don't say anything."

"Let's see what we've got here before I make any promises."

He apparently also knew better than to pick sides in Landlow infighting—maybe that was a Family rule, not just a Ward one.

I offered my left hand, used the other to brush my hair back, and tilted my neck. He inspected both bruises while I compared his healthy bronze skin to my bone-china pallor.

"Unknown cause? Or trauma?"

"Trauma." If they'd been nontraumatic discolorations he'd have marked the boundaries with pen—like I was some human game of connect the dots—then checked later to see if they'd grown. "Car door and seat belt."

His lips twitched slightly. "Who knew Carter's driving was so dangerous? Those are the only ones? Any nosebleeds? Gums bleeding? Petechiae?"

"None. Just these." And an increasing feeling of dread and panic. I fought back a shiver.

Dr. Castillo gave me a measuring glance. "Are you worried about something, Penelope?"

"My counts . . ." I swallowed and attempted to forge the question despite the desert dryness of my throat.

"Yes? They've been good lately." He pointed to one of the clinic whiteboards where the latest were always displayed: PL-84,000µl. "Oh, I guess I didn't update that yet. The results from yesterday's draw showed a slight reduction in platelets, but still around seventy thousand."

"They've dropped?" The word "remission" popped like a bubble on my tongue, dissolving dreams of school and normalcy.

My body was never going to stop destroying its platelets, but the rate at which it destroyed them was key. When my counts dipped to thirty thousand it was as well known throughout the estate as the daily forecast. If they dropped lower than that, or I got cut and bled excessively, or if I managed to majorly bruise myself—not that this took much effort—I needed an infusion of immunoglobulin, aka IVIg. Until recently, I'd also needed one every two to three weeks.

"Before you get upset, think about this: we've been pushing your body lately. You've gone more than double the amount of time you usually go between infusions and your counts are still quite acceptable. I'm comfortable waiting for the results of next week's CBC before deciding if you need some IVIg to stabilize you, but if you're concerned or feel off, we can check your counts again today."

"We can wait," I whispered. I knew it would be a week of worry, but possibly also my *last* week of hope. Carter better have his pom-poms ready, because when he reappeared, I needed a pep talk.

"There's always going to be some fluctuation in your numbers, but you're doing well," he reassured me. "Now, Caroline's counting supplies in the surgical closet. Tell her to take a break. The two of you can go watch *America's Next Top Fashion Project* or whatever that show is."

He waved off my thanks and resumed his surgical video.

I could hear Caroline counting under her breath before I opened the door to the closet. She held up a finger and continued. "Seventy-eight, seventy-nine—you make me lose count and I'll kill you—eighty, eighty-one. Eighty. Two." She dropped the last whatever triumphantly back into the bin, wrote the number on her clipboard, and stood up.

"Killing me might be a bit of an overreaction."

"Fine, then I'd *accidentally* miss your vein a few times during your next blood draw." Caroline looked like she could be my sister: her hair was only a shade lighter than mine; she was only an inch or two taller; and we wore the same size clothing, down to our shoes. But we weren't family. She wasn't even *Family*. She'd been hired nine months ago, straight from nursing school, probably chosen because she had no relatives or significant other. No one to ask her questions about what went on in the clinic, or why the estate needed a whole medical staff to deal with one sickly daughter who was currently (hopefully) not-so-sickly.

"Dr. Castillo said you could take a break." But I wasn't sure I wanted her to. I wasn't sure I was up to chatting, smiling, and doing anything but checking my cell for messages from Garrett or Carter.

"So, how did your adventure with your brother and the stud muffin go? Did we pick a good outfit? Spill!"

No. I definitely couldn't do this.

"Oh, that's my phone," I faked a vibration and pretended to read something on the screen. "My mother. She wants me for lunch."

I typed Update please and sent it to Garrett, then echoed Caroline's pout. "Sorry."

"I still want details, so if you have time this afternoon, come back over."

"Sure." And as soon as I knew where Carter had gone, as soon as I gave him a piece of my mind, as soon as I shook off this cape of dread and unease, I'd gladly rush back to ask her opinion on almost-kisses, blurred boundaries, and Garrett-Carter-Garrett-*me*.

CHAPTER 8

Garrett and Carter didn't follow Mother, Father, and his second-in-command, Miles Banks, into the dining room as we assembled for lunch. Garrett's older brothers, Mick, Hugh, and Jacob, were there. His father, Al, too. And Nolan, his hair flopping onto glasses I suspected were purely cosmetic, part of his "academic costume" like his sweater vests and tweed, elbow-patched jackets. He looked, as always, like he was about to moderate a spelling bee or launch into a debate. At least he was seated by Mother's left and not mine. Why had he been in so many meetings lately? Maybe if I was lucky Father would decide he was invaluable to the Business—freeing me up for school. Based on the way Father clapped Nolan on the back and smiled at him, I might be onto something. Now I wished I was sitting closer so I could eavesdrop. I frowned as Jacob pulled out my chair.

Business had been spilling into meals more and more often.

I rarely saw Father without a flanking of Family members. Lately it felt like he belonged more to them, to big *F* Family, than to *us*, his little *f* family. I didn't like the way that creased his face—wrinkles in the corners of his eyes and across his forehead instead of laugh lines around his mouth.

When Father picked up his fork, everyone began eating and chatting. I played with my food.

"You're awful fidgety, Penny-Pea. Is something making you nervous?" Al Ward paired his question with a slow grin, and I shivered. He had been the center of my childhood nightmares. It didn't matter how many times Father reassured me that his job was to *protect us*, Al was the wicked dragon, the evil sorcerer, and all the villains from my fairy-tale bedtime stories. He'd only gotten scarier since Keith died and his wife left him.

But I'd promised Garrett I'd cover for him, so I laughed like the idea was ridiculous. "No. Of course not."

I hacked at my salad like it was the toughest bark, or like my knife was made of paper. It wasn't until I put a mangled bite in my mouth that I noticed Garrett's brothers were watching me too. And in between their speculative glances, they looked at each other and raised their eyebrows. They knew *something*, but which something: the almost kiss? That Carter was AWOL? Garrett's forgotten gun? The secret errand?

The questions made it impossible to swallow my food or participate in conversation.

Mother clucked over my lack of appetite, then turned to Father. "Penny said they all enjoyed *Once Upon a Mattress*. Should I get tickets for us?"

He frowned at his plate. "I'd like to, but it's not a good time."

"Oh?" said Mother.

"Why?" I asked.

"Things are a bit tense right now," said Miles Banks with a gentle smile. It was the same expression he always used with me. Whether he was inviting me to join him and his basset hound, Thumbelina—I named her—for a stroll around the property, or complimenting my haircut, or asking about my classes.

"Tense because of the Everly incident?" I tossed the question at them and waited for the reaction to their porcelain doll not being as ignorant or complacent as they wished.

The silence stretched like taffy, gluing people's eyes to their plates.

Finally Father demanded, "How do you know about the Everly incident?"

"Nolan may not be the best tutor in the world, but I do know how to watch the news and use Google."

"Penelope Maeve!" exclaimed Mother, while Nolan coughed into his water glass.

Hugh didn't even try to cover his laughter. Jacob choked on a mouthful of bread. Mick whacked him on the back—probably harder than necessary, since his brother's eyes widened with each blow. Miles was suddenly fascinated by his napkin, and Father's face was turning pre-fury red.

"I apologize. That was rude," I muttered.

"You're quite forgiven," replied Nolan with a magnanimous nod that made me want to insult him again.

My phone buzzed in my pocket. Mother absolutely forbade

anything electronic at the table, so I let my butter knife slip from my fingers. It clattered against the edge of my plate and then continued its free fall to the floor. Manners dictated leaving it—ignoring it—but being impolite provided a moment of privacy. I bent over, using the split-second I fumbled beneath the tablecloth to read the screen.

Can't find him. U?

Mother graciously covered my faux pas by saying, "The whole Everly thing is tragic. But I'm not clear on the connection to us seeing a play."

Al Ward raised a finger. Father nodded at him. "The Feds can't ignore this, ma'am. I don't want you all out in public more than absolutely necessary."

There went Korean barbecue, doughnuts, and all my opportunities for summer freedom. Al had just given Mother the perfect excuse for all her *no*s.

"May I please be excused? I'm not hungry." I stood, and the men did too.

"But Penny, you didn't eat breakfast . . ."

I waved off Mother's concern. "I have a headache. I need some air. I'll eat later."

"Do you want company?" she offered.

"Oh. Um, no. I'm going to call Kelly." And once I was outside, I *did* make phone calls, but not to the vice president's daughter. I called Garrett.

When he said he still hadn't found him, I dialed Carter again.

I walked toward the gate as I called, nodded to Frank, the

guard on duty, then continued inside the perimeter. My phone rang against my ear—the noise joined by a faint song in the distance. One that grew louder as I walked up the lawn's slope toward the blind spot Father had been complaining about during breakfast two days ago. A tree limb had taken out a camera during the last summer storm. It dangled on wires, its lens pointed at the sky.

"Pennies from Heaven." Carter's not-as-funny-as-he-thought ringtone for me.

And then I saw his shoes. The loafers he'd been wearing last night. Saw the soles of them through the fence.

They were attached to a body. There was blood.

And then I was falling to my knees, crawling across dirt and rocks to reach him. And there was my blood. My ineffective arms pulling and yanking on the sharp iron scrollwork that separated me from Carter. The red tips of my fingers clawing at the gravel. My tongue bitten as I screamed some wordless howl that meant both *this isn't real* and *get up, get up now, Carter.* It did nothing. Changed nothing.

And then I saw nothing. Nothing at all.

CHAPTER 9

There was a delay between the moment I woke up and the instant I remembered. Not a long delay. Just the length of time it took for me to realize I was in the clinic. *Why* hit like a collision—dwarfing the pain in my body with mental screams of anguish.

When Dr. Castillo, Caroline, and Hugh Ward rushed into my room, I realized they weren't mental screams. I was screaming.

"No!"

There was a needle in Dr. Castillo's hand.

"Carter!"

An IV line in my arm.

"Please, please, please!"

My parents weren't there.

"Tell me he's okay. Tell me!"

Caroline's eyes were wet. Her lips were white. She shook her head.

"No. Lie to me. Just lie to me. He can't be—"

Then whatever was in that needle entered my bloodstream and erased truth and delusions along with consciousness.

In my dreams, I was swimming through blood. It filled my mouth, ran into my ears, blurred my vision. It was my blood. Carter's. Kelly's—and every other transplant recipient's. It was the donors' blood: the ones the Family recruited to sell a kidney for a retirement fund, or trade part of their liver for a year of college tuition. The ones who sold their blood and marrow as often as we'd allow to pay their mortgage, and the ones who lived with one cornea because they'd rather keep gambling than see through both eyes. The families who sold the cadavers of their loved ones for living expenses or for a memorial service. Or the ones with big-time debt who paid by donating skin—Carter had told me once that with skin grafts it was more painful for the donor than the recipient.

Carter.

He was with me sometimes. Always too far away to reach. And the closer I got to the surface, the farther he slipped. Sometimes it seemed as if I would escape, breathe air instead of blood, but then there'd be a flash of silver, a burning in my veins, and I was pulled back by a crimson undertow.

When I finally broke through it was with a gasp so powerful it propelled me into a seated position. I was still in the clinic. My arms from the elbow down were invisible beneath thick swaths of bandage. One of them was cradled in a large hand. I traced this past a starched cuff and up an arm clad in a white button-down shirt. Garrett was seated in a chair beside my bed wearing a tie. The hand not under mine held a bag of frozen corn to his face.

"Princess?" He dropped the bag to reveal an eye ringed in watercolor shades of pink running into purple darkening to navy blue.

"He's dead."

Garrett swallowed and pulled his chair closer. Swallowed again. "I couldn't find him. I couldn't find him anywhere . . . I should've been with him. I could've . . ."

Garrett had seen me cry dozens of times over tantrums and imagined tragedies, but I'd never seen him cry. Not even when his mother left. Now he carefully lowered my bandaged hand and dropped his head in his palms. There was a weight to his grief, to the shaking of his shoulders. This was real. I wasn't going to wake up and forget the sounds of Garrett's pain.

And it broke me.

Carter would never walk through the clinic door with a bouquet of lilies and make a joke about me being "idiot-pathetic." He was never going to Skype in to say good night and complain that his business classes were useless for the Business or that the girl in his French seminar was immune to his charms. He wouldn't run interference with Mother or sneak me out for midnight drive-through. He wouldn't be here today. Tomorrow. Ever.

My tears started as a whimper. It was too inadequate a sound, too insignificant. Grief felt like it should be roared, screamed, bellowed.

I reached with bandaged hands for Garrett, my movements clumsy but demonstrating what I couldn't say: hold me so I don't fall to pieces. So I don't drown in the memories of all that blood. I wanted to be held tightly, gripped so I knew I was still something solid to cling to.

But of course he couldn't. That he touched me at all was testament to his pain. Gentle hands went around my waist, and his face leaned lightly against my stomach as he cried on the stark white sheets. My tears dripped onto his hair. My bandaged hands rested on his back.

"Please let go of my daughter."

Father's words may have expressed a request, but his voice didn't allow for any disagreement. It was a tone of steel and blood and threat.

Garrett's reaction was instantaneous. I barely had time to snatch my hands off his back before he was ramrod-postured with a mask of professional alertness. A horrible, flawed mask of splotchy skin, tear tracks, and a black eye.

Mother was beside Father, but he stepped away to lean out the door. "Darius, I need you to examine Penelope for new damage." His face hardened as he turned back toward the room. "Garrett, join me in the hall."

Dr. Castillo's typical white coat was replaced by a black suit jacket. I looked at Father's back—suited. At Mother's black dress. At the jacket Garrett had left behind on his chair. He'd been wearing a tie.

"The funeral," I said. "You were at the funeral."

Mother nodded. Her lips pressed so tightly I didn't know if she'd ever speak again.

I'd missed it. I'd missed *days*. I'd missed my chance to say good-bye.

I could hear snatches of conversation through the door; I listened between Dr. Castillo's directions to sit up and raise my arms so he could unfasten my hospital gown and inspect my back and abdomen. *Vigilance. Threats. Security. Failure.*

"Does this hurt?" he asked as he examined my skin.

"No." I could've told him that Garrett hadn't bruised me, but they needed to see for themselves. Right now I wouldn't argue. Especially since, once the sheets had been drawn down, I could see the damage I'd done. My knees and calves were buried beneath gauze. Wrinkling my forehead, I felt a bandage I hadn't noticed before and had a blurred recollection of banging my face against the fence.

I wished it were worse. Bad enough to obliterate the pain in my head, heart, stomach. An ache like I'd never experienced before—but Garrett had.

Garrett's brother died.

I didn't know I'd spoken the words aloud until Mother stepped closer, straightened my blankets, and retied my gown with soft fingers. "Yes, he did." She touched my hair and turned to Dr. Castillo. "She's okay?"

"Yes," he agreed. "She's not in any danger. The cuts on her fingertips and knees, and the one on her forehead, have all clotted. The bruises have stopped expanding, and she's had an infusion, so her counts are well above a hundred thousand. I'll take another blood sample tonight to see if she's maintaining that level or needs more."

I flinched. While I'd been sedated and stabilized, she'd had to fear for one child while mourning her other.

"I hadn't eaten, Mother. Nothing the whole day—and the shock . . ." I shut my eyes and forced those images away. "That's why I fainted. Please don't worry about me. I'm okay." I looked to Dr. Castillo for agreement.

He patted my pillow. "Rest up, Penelope, and you can sleep in your own bed tomorrow." Then he left the room, letting in more of Father's lecture.

"How could you be so irresponsible *again*?"

"Dear, please stop." Mother's voice was enough to make Father pause, put out a hand, and catch the door before it swung shut. He and Garrett were framed by the opening and backlit by the hall lights. "He didn't harm her. And before you say anything else you might regret, remember security on the clinic is four layers thick—that *I* counted—which means it's probably more. Personally, I'd rather Carter's best friend be in here comforting Penny than standing guard outside her room so she woke up grieving and alone."

Father's posture changed in ways it hurt to watch, the muscles of his shoulders and neck rearranging from a tight line of threat to a slump of sorrow. "You're right. Garrett, my apologies. Thank you for being there for Penelope."

"Always, sir." His injured eye looked puffier. I couldn't tell if it was swelling or crying—and didn't know why no one was asking him how he'd gotten hurt. Protecting me?

No. If so, the red lights above all the rooms would be illuminated. Dr. Castillo would be commencing evacuation procedures if there was *any* hint of a security threat.

Mother placed a hand on Garrett's shoulder as she passed him his jacket and the bag of frozen corn. "You should go get some rest, and make sure to keep ice on that eye."

"I can stay." He wrapped his fingers around the metal side rail on my bed.

If I spoke up Father would consent. But did I want him to? Garrett told me he'd find Carter. He hadn't. I had. And I'd been too late.

I looked away from him.

"The service is over. Mick will be coming shortly. You can stay until he arrives, then go." Father's voice was still stern but laced with exhaustion.

"Dear." Mother's eyes skipped from me to my father to Garrett and back to me. "I think, since Garrett will need a new assignment now, I'd like him to be placed with Penny—as much as possible."

"We can talk about this later, Abigail."

"Yes, it's simply that . . . I know he'll look after her." She turned impassioned eyes on Garrett. "You would look after my little girl, wouldn't you?"

His voice was thick with emotion when he answered, "Of course."

"You've always protected Penelope—sometimes been more careful with her than . . . than *he* was."

"Abigail, this is a Business decision—"

She ignored Father. No one ever ignored him. "And you've been through this before. Having lost Keith, you know what she's feeling. I think you'd be good for her."

She finally turned back to Father, her voice and posture breaking. "I think he'd be good for her, and I don't know how to do this. I don't know how to be there for her when I can't—"

Her voice muffled as he put his arms around her and she buried her head in his shoulder. He was holding her tightly—as tightly as I'd wished to be held. Patting her back, squeezing her shoulder. And looking haunted, like at any moment he might break down too.

"Garrett, for now we'll follow my wife's suggestion: you'll be assigned to Penelope. You and I will meet to discuss this further, but for the rest of the day, *go*."

Garrett gave each of us a nod. His eyes lingering on me for an extended second before he nodded again.

I heard him exchange terse greetings with Mick in the hallway and then it was quiet. The quiet of my parents having no idea what to say to me. Or each other. The quiet of a grief so thick it was like a fog that settled and separated us, creating three people each suffering alone.

CHAPTER 10

I wished I could do karate. Or wrestle. Work out with a punching bag. Something. Anything that involved taking all these too-large emotions inside of me and turning them into physical violence that left me too exhausted to feel. Too exhausted to hurt in any way but sore muscles.

My soreness was confined to the pinpricks of the daily CBCs Mother requested. My results were no longer posted on the clinic's whiteboards, and Dr. Castillo stopped smiling, joking, or letting Caroline handle my blood work.

Mother fussed over every bite I put in my mouth, every new shadow that ringed my eyes. Fussed and fretted—then abruptly excused herself to go break down in private.

Father holed up in his office surrounded by the Wards and Miles Banks. Nolan. Anyone. Everyone. His demands of "how" and "why" shook the house to its foundation. His anger scared me. He was never around, except for the moments when I woke up at night to a soft kiss on my forehead or him readjusting my blankets, humming "Tomorrow" or "Any Dream Will Do" or other show tunes lullabies, whispering a quiet, "Go back to sleep, sweet pea, you're safe."

Garrett was *always* around. I wondered if he slept outside my bedroom door because that's where I found him every morning and left him every night. He was constantly in some part of my peripheral vision, following me like a ghost. Both of us were silent and haunted.

We sat on different couches in the den and I turned the TV to C-Span. People were debating something, their names and credentials displayed below them on the split screen, but I couldn't be bothered to read them or listen. The television provided an excuse not to talk, an excuse to stare straight ahead and not look at the person who'd shared Carter's last night with me. The person who was supposed to protect him. The person I'd wanted to kiss—still wanted to kiss—and now wanted to punch. The person whose voice and eyes and company made me wistful, resentful, angry, and so, so lonely.

Our head gardener leaned in the doorway. "Penelope, there are two officers here to see you." There were grass clippings in his hair and he had work gloves on, but I also knew he had a gun strapped under his jacket. Father insisted most everyone be armed these days. "Should I show them in?"

"I guess." I looked to Garrett for confirmation, letting my eyes rest on him for a half second before I had to turn away. Father was off-estate this morning. He, Miles, and Al were at

Turtle Island Spa in Connecticut looking into a security breach. It was the first time he had left since the funeral three days ago, and nerves had driven Mother to a bottle of Xanax and her bedroom.

The officers looked like bookends; they were both around Father's age, both slightly bald and going soft around the belt. They had the same stride, the same direct eye contact, and they said in near unison, "We're sorry for your loss, Miss Landlow."

They held out hands to shake, but Garrett intercepted these with a gruff "Hey." He shut off the television. "We were about to head over to the clinic. Penelope needs some blood work. If you have to ask her questions, do it there."

I raised my eyebrows but didn't say anything. Typically my blood work took place after a meal, and Mother had been too distraught to demand I have a CBC today. I'd been looking forward to giving my veins a break.

My brain may have been spinning with questions about Garrett's motives, but Mother's etiquette training was ingrained deeper than my confusion. "Welcome, officers. I'm sorry my parents are unavailable to meet with you today, but I'll be glad to answer your questions if you don't mind accompanying us to the clinic."

The officers exchanged a look. Now that they were closer I could see they weren't quite mirror images. One was about three inches taller than the other. He spoke, "Mrs. Landlow had told us this would be a good time."

"I apologize; she's indisposed at the moment." I aimed my gaze over Garrett's shoulder. "Who did my father leave in charge?"

"Nolan."

I made a face.

"Do you want to reschedule?" asked the shorter cop. "You're a difficult girl to question, Miss Landlow. This is our third trip out here."

No one had mentioned this to me.

Garrett snarled. "It's hard to question someone when she's unconscious."

"Now is fine," I reassured them. "I want to help." I held the door to the library so the two men could follow me through it to the clinic. Garrett had stridden ahead and emerged from Dr. Castillo's office with the doctor in tow.

"Make this fast," Garrett demanded. His face was stone and anger. "You've said it's just a formality, and we've told you she doesn't know anything."

I expected them to snap back, to threaten to drag me down to the station if I wouldn't cooperate—that's what always happened on TV when cops' actions were questioned.

But they didn't; they shuffled their feet and apologized again. "We'll try and make this as quick and painless as possible."

They were on the Family payroll. They must be.

"In here, please." Dr. Castillo put the materials for a CBC on a metal tray. I sat in my usual place, pulled up my sleeves, and tried to remember which arm I should offer today.

"Left," the doctor prompted, and I held it out for the rubber tourniquet.

"Miss Landlow." The officer's eyes were on the needle Dr. Castillo was assembling. "You were the one to find your brother, correct?"

"Yes," I whispered.

"Around what time?"

"A little after noon. It was during lunch."

"Why were you by the fence?"

"I was going for a walk. I called him, and I heard his phone—his ringtone for me. I followed it and found . . ."

I felt Garrett's eyes on me too—his anguished gaze heavier than the policemen's.

"When did you last see him alive?"

"Around midnight. He said he had to go somewhere."

"Where?" The cops were taking turns asking the questions; it left me uneasy, not quite sure where to aim my answers.

"I don't know. Sorry. We made plans to meet for breakfast—I was going to ask him then—but he never showed up."

The shorter cop steepled his fingers and pointed them at me. "Miss Landlow, it seems you were the last person to talk to him—we don't know what happened in the twelve hours before you found his body. I need you to think. Did he seem agitated at all? Worried?"

"I-I-I don't know," I sputtered, shaking so much that Dr. Castillo paused and pulled the tip of the needle back from where he was about to plunge it through my skin. I hadn't been paying enough attention that night, hadn't known it would matter. Hadn't known it was the last time I'd see him, the last conversation we'd have.

Garrett took over. "Carter would never have willingly exposed his baby sister to any danger. Or to this either." He paused to point slowly between the two men.

The cops swallowed and looked chastised, but it didn't stop them from asking, "What about the Zhu family—had he mentioned them to you recently? Said anything that would lead you to believe he perceived them as a threat?"

"The Zhus? No. What do they—"

Garrett put a hand on my chair, the backs of his fingers grazing my shirt. "Penelope Landlow is a very sick girl. She doesn't leave the estate. She has no contact with the Zhus or anyone outside these gates, and she doesn't know who killed her older brother. Finding those answers is your job. It's been six days; why don't you have any? You're not going to find them in here."

I'd stilled enough for Dr. Castillo to insert the needle in my vein. Blood flowed into the test tube and everyone's eyes were on the red. Were they picturing the crimson of Carter's blood on the ground, the way it pooled around him, seeped into his shirt, and stained the ends of his blond hair, or was that just me?

I whimpered.

An officer reached for my hand, probably in apology or comfort.

Garrett lunged in front of my chair. "Don't touch her!"

"Hold this, please, Penelope," Dr. Castillo said as he placed gauze on my arm. He turned to the officers with a face of calm fury. "A simple touch like that will harm my patient, causing her platelets to degrade and contusions or ecchymosis to form. I cannot stress how fragile Penelope is, so do your job, but do it quickly, sensitively, and there is absolutely no reason grown men like you need to be touching this girl."

I understood his words were deliberate, that Garrett's had

been too—chosen to make me seem as young and delicate as possible and make the officers' sympathy and duty seem inappropriate. I understood they'd been effective, because the cops squirmed and apologized and handed over cards and more apologies along with requests that I call them if I thought of anything and even more apologies and sympathy for my loss. I understood the logic and intelligence of Garrett and Dr. Castillo's words, but they still stung. Maybe I'd wanted to answer questions, maybe I *could* be helpful. It hurt that only strangers thought this plausible.

Garrett left to show them out, and there was a tacit agreement that I'd stay with Dr. Castillo until he returned.

This would've been the ideal opportunity to ask about my counts. To question the empty whiteboard . . . but next to it on the wall was a calendar.

Tomorrow I'd be brotherless for a whole week. Seven days. And that would grow to a month, multiply to two. I couldn't stop time from pushing me farther and farther from Carter.

It was hard to look from the calendar to the blank space where the ghost of "PL:" could still be read, and to care about the numbers that should be after it.

Hugh, Garrett's oldest living brother, banged through the exam room door, swearing and demanding, "What was the idiot thinking? Bringing cops *in the clinic*? And you agreed with it? Letting her be questioned *here*?" He ended with another snarl of swears aimed at his brother, Nolan, and the world at large.

"Excuse me, Hugh?" I stood up. He was nearly a foot taller

than I was, but he hadn't had Mother's lessons on posture and diction. "I must have misheard you. Your brother was brilliant, Dr. Castillo too. I doubt the officers will be bothering us again."

The doctor chimed in agreement and reassurances—but Hugh shrugged us off. "None of this would even be happening if Garrett had done his job and stayed with Carter. It's his fault your brother's dead."

"Get. Out." I wasn't sure if the words were Garrett's or mine. I tasted them on my gritted teeth, but he was standing in the door to the exam room, glaring flames and hands balled in fists.

"Oh, did I hurt little Garrett's feelings? Is that what they teach you at your fancy schools? How to be all sensitive and in touch with your inner girl?"

"Excuse me?" I said. "Inner *girl*?"

"I apologize for my brother," growled Garrett. "He's probably too ignorant to understand why that's offensive."

"Whatever," snorted Hugh. He did a mock bow in my direction on his way out the door. "I don't have time to play babysitter anyway. Some of us have real responsibilities."

"A few words to my father and that can be remedied." I enjoyed the heartbeat's worth of panic my threat brought to Hugh's face before he covered it with a scoff and disappeared down the hall.

Garrett had always been different from his brothers. He was smarter, better—he'd been set apart to rise above the role of enforcer, to be my brother's second-in-command. It never occurred to me that they might resent him—blame him for Carter's death.

My own deliberate distance, avoidance of eye contact and conversation weren't any kinder. In fact, they might have been crueler. My throat tightened with guilt.

"What do you want to do now? More TV or go sit in the solarium?" he asked.

"What do you want to do?"

"What I *want* is for you to find something to keep yourself busy so I can call your father and update him on what just happened." The frustration in his words wasn't directed at me, so I shrugged it off. Dr. Castillo was less understanding, clearing his throat and raising his eyebrows. Garrett's cheeks flushed. "Please."

I wondered if he ever hated me for seeming helpless, hated Carter for dying, hated my father for estranging him from his family, hated his brothers for resenting that, hated the Family for dictating all our life choices.

"What are my counts?"

Dr. Castillo hadn't expected me to pivot toward him, hadn't expected that question. He kept his poker face in place but clicked a relentless rhythm with the pen in his hand. "I'm afraid I don't remember off the top of my head, and I'm already late for a phone call, so if you'll excuse me."

Before he shut the door to his office across the hall, I caught a glimpse of his whiteboard. Also blank.

Pity rolled off Garrett. It hit the skin on the back of my neck and my bare arms, bruised at the crook of my elbows for the results Dr. Castillo couldn't, or wouldn't, tell me.

I rushed away from it. Down the clinic hallway and into the library.

There were three things waiting on the other side of the oak doors: Mother, Father, and my red folder.

CHAPTER 11

Garrett was a half step behind me, catching the door from my hand. "Penny, can we talk? I—" and then he saw my parents. "Hello, ma'am, sir. Did your trip to Turtle Island go well?"

Father waved off the question. "Could you excuse us for a minute? We need to speak to Penelope." His face was only a half shade less intense than the folder he gripped between both hands.

Mother's face was wet, splotched with sadness, tight with exhaustion.

I saw Garrett taking this all in. Confusion, fear, duty, and reluctance all fighting for command of his face. "Of course, sir. I'll wait for you in the solarium, Penny."

In another world, I would have asked him to stay. In a better world, Carter would be by my side for this conversation, interrupting to argue my case or whisper encouragement under his breath. *Go. Fight. Win.*

In *this* world, I'd have to stand on my own two feet and face the consequences of my hope.

Mother sniffled. She looked so broken, and I fought the urge to apologize for every tear, every "Penny line," every thought or feeling that would make her worry.

"How was Turtle Island?" I asked with all the innocence I could fake. "I didn't expect you back until later."

Father ignored me. He threw the folder onto a table and the contents spilled out, glossy brochures and application essays mixed with blood count charts and bullet point lists of arguments. I winced as my careful organization was annihilated beneath the fist he pounded on the table, paper clips flying and pages tearing. "Penelope Maeve, what *is* this?"

"I was going to talk to you about it, before . . ."

"You want to leave me too?" Mother asked.

Her "too" crushed my heart. I should have promised to never leave the estate again, to never even *want* to leave the estate again, but Carter's voice echoed in my head, *This matters.*

"I'm not trying to leave you, but attending a school for my senior year is something I—"

"You can't. It's not safe. If he . . . And *you* . . ." She was wringing her hands, shredding the tissue she clutched between fingers that were gnawed and raw instead of manicured. "Please, excuse me. I—" She left the room before finishing that sentence, before we could see her cry.

Her sniffles creating an audible trail that I tried to follow, but Father stepped in front of me. "I'll check on her as soon as we're done with this conversation," he said. "Now, explain."

"I know I'd need protection. But my counts—" I plucked up a graph and turned to him. "They've been really good. Or they were. I can't get any answers on what they are now. Is that your doing?"

"Now is not the time to be taking risks, Penny. You will not be going to school in the fall. This topic is closed." Father slid the papers off the desk into a trash can and reached for the page I was holding.

"I'm not okay with that." I held tight to the chart and Carter's advice, *"No" is never the final answer.* "I understand if I can't go in the fall, but I'm not okay with the topic being closed. This is important to me. Maybe by spring semester things will be more settled and I could go then."

"Don't you realize how important *you* are to this family?"

I wanted to ask if the *f* on that word was upper- or lowercase. Did he mean the damaged trio of remaining Landlows, or the greater group of the Business? As the sole remaining heir, had he decided to let me have a role?

"I'm important?"

"Essential." He leaned over and kissed the top of my head, prying the paper from my distracted fingers. "Now more than ever. I'm sorry if I haven't made that clear."

"How about a compromise?" I suggested. I needed to walk away from this confrontation feeling like I had a meager amount of control, some say in my future.

"Like?" Father's voice was both amused and wary.

"No more Nolan. Get me a new tutor."

"Done." His laugh boomed in the quiet room. It startled us both. Laughter was a foreign sound on the post-Carter estate. "Sweet pea, I promise you will never have to endure another one of Nolan's lectures. I have plans to inflict him on some other Family members instead."

"Wow. Thank you."

He returned my smile. "Perhaps I'll start teaching some of your lessons. Would you like that?"

I could only nod. Only imagine the Family things he could and would be teaching me.

"Then that's settled." He folded the graph in half before dropping it in the trash.

Father followed me to the solarium. "Wait here. I need to speak with Garrett about what happened in the clinic this morning. Then I need to go calm your mother."

I tried to determine if there was anger in his voice, if Hugh's insults were a reflection of the Family's opinion of Garrett, or just the Wards'.

I touched his arm, gripping his sleeve. He froze with his hand on the doorknob and gave me his full attention. "Father, I've been meaning to thank you for assigning Garrett to my protection."

He looked at me with raised eyebrows. "This is unexpected. I thought you hated having a shadow, sweet pea? Or people carrying guns? Garrett tells me you've barely acknowledged him all week."

"He makes me feel safe." I almost choked on my guilt. Because he did, and I'd never told him. I hadn't thought about whether or not it felt like blame when I excluded him from my cocoon of grief.

Father's face softened. "You will always be safe here, Penelope. I will never let anything happen to you." He kissed the top of my head. "Now wait here a moment."

I watched through the glass in the solarium door as he moved to Garrett, placed a hand on his shoulder, and spoke. Whatever he said made Garrett's face crumple with relief and emotion.

The solarium truly was a stunning room; sparkling glass walls supported a soaring glass ceiling. Carefully cultured flowerbeds bordered a soft path of wood chips dotted with cushioned chairs and benches and tables. There was a fountain in the center where koi splashed and swam like fragments of sunshine.

The only thing I focused on was the beautiful boy standing in the middle, looking both lost and found as his eyes met mine. Once the door closed us in a bubble of glass and sun, plants and privacy, I asked, "What did my father say to you?"

"Thank you," said Garrett. He crossed the room and gestured to a bench. I moved a computer tablet to the side so we could both sit. "He thanked me for making you feel safe. And I should thank you for saying that. I . . . I thought you hated me too. Princess, you never talk to me. You don't even look at me if you can help it."

"I don't hate you. It's just—I—" My voice broke and broke again. "It hurts to see you without him."

"I know," he whispered. "I'm sorry. And I'm sorry about school. Your dad told me."

I shrugged off that topic. I wasn't sure if the library showdown had been a victory or a defeat. No school—for now—but no Nolan either. And more Father, more importance with the Family.

"Why did the police ask about the Zhus?" I asked instead.

"We think it was them. And that they were behind the security breach at Turtle Island too."

I tried to form a mental picture of them. Stern, silent father; gentle, graceful mother; and Ming, their short, sniffling son who failed to make eye contact or conversation and had hidden away in the library for most of their visit. I'd only met them once, a half-dozen years ago. *They* were responsible for Carter?

It was unfathomable that a Family would attack another. Upstarts, maybe. But *the* Families? No.

"Why the Zhus? Why not the Ever—" But then the last time I'd seen Carter filled my mind. The whole image. Parts I hadn't thought about until now. Things I hadn't processed. "His shirt was—his chest was . . ."

I bent over and tried to breathe. My throat closed up to the diameter of a pea, then a needle. I needed so much air and there wasn't a way to get it to my lungs.

Garrett was instantly kneeling on the wood chips at my feet. "Princess? Penny? Breathe." His hands kept reaching for me and stopping. They hovered near my hands, near my knees, near my feet. Rested like a question on the toes of my shoes. "That's better. Look at me. Breathe with me. In. Out. In."

The fog forming around the edges of my vision began to clear. My throat gradually unclenched. Garrett stayed at my feet, watched me with eyes of panic and grief. "We should get you to the clinic."

"He was carved up," I whispered. "They wrote something on his chest. It wasn't English. Was it in Chinese?"

Garrett nodded. Stood. "I don't think we should talk about it anymore."

"What did it say?"

"Let's go find Dr. Castillo."

"He was my brother." I stood, wished I had something I could break, a way of shattering something other than my heart. "Tell me!"

"It said 'Warning.' "

"Warning?" I let the word sink in deep, as if it were carved into my own chest. The pain made me cross my arms over it, hug myself as tightly as I dared.

"I should've been there. Whatever he was doing, I would've gone with him. If I'd been there . . ." He stormed over to the wall, pressed both hands flat against the glass, and bowed his head. "They still haven't found his car. And I have no clue how he spent those hours. How could I not know? How could he not tell me?"

I crossed the room to stand near him, wishing he'd turn around and look at me. I could share this burden. "I wouldn't have let him leave if I'd known. I assumed he'd pick you up on the way, but—"

But they'd just fought. They never fought. And they'd fought about *me*. Guilt made my body heavy, like my veins were filled with mercury. I sank into the mulch of the flowerbed, ignoring that its dampness was seeping into my white pants. "Your eye—who hit you? I've been thinking it was Carter, but he *couldn't* have. It happened the day I woke up, not that night . . ."

He finally turned, revealing a face ravaged by grief and guilt. "This," he pointed to the fading green and yellow around his eye, "had nothing to do with you. Jacob hit me. He was . . . insensitive at the funeral. To be fair, I punched him first."

"I haven't seen him."

"He's been on gate duty." His tone was clipped. "Though I doubt he would've been punished if he didn't do it publicly."

"What did he say?"

"You don't need to hear this." Garrett sat next to me. He placed his hand on the ground in the space between my waist and my arm. It wasn't quite the same as putting his arm around me, but it was close. If I leaned backward I could rest my head against his shoulder. I almost dared. Almost.

But he and Carter had fought over me. And because of that Carter had gone out unguarded.

"What did Jake say?"

He gritted his teeth, then spoke in a rush. "He asked how it felt to be responsible for the death of my best friend."

My throat tightened again, and I found myself doing exactly what I'd just promised I wouldn't, leaning against him for support. If it was his fault, it was mine too.

"I hope you hit him hard." I tilted my face up to his.

"I did. Broke his nose. He had *two* black eyes."

"Good."

"Ha, has our little pacifist developed some blood lust?"

Garrett's head bowed slightly, his nose just grazing mine, sending shivers down my spine.

I sat up, pulled away. "I think I'm growing out of my beliefs in fairy tales and any sort of absolutes."

His eyes measured the space between us, growing more serious with every centimeter I added to the distance, lingering on the air, my face, my eyes, my lips. Finally he spoke. "I hope not. That would be another tragedy."

I stood and strolled back over to the bench, wiping off wood chips and picking up the tablet. I hid behind it for the rest of the afternoon.

Right before dinner, I made a trip down the white corridor of the clinic, leaned my head in the door of Dr. Castillo's office, and asked, "Are my results back yet?"

He looked up and blinked. "Have they recruited you to double-check our efficiency? I assure you, everything here is running smoothly and on time." He smiled, but it didn't reach his eyes.

"What are my counts?" *Ask a direct question, demand a direct answer.* That was actually a piece of my grandfather's wisdom, but I felt that Carter would approve.

"You had an infusion six days ago; your counts are good. Please, let this go. You have more than enough on your plate right now." He forced another smile, then stood and slipped off his white coat, hung it on the back of his door. "Now, I need to head home or I'll be late for dinner. My family won't wait, and it's tamale night."

I smiled at him, pretended to acquiesce. But if no one was going to tell me my counts, I'd get them myself.

I was quiet during dinner, but no one noticed. Mother had the glassy-eyed look I associated with her new medications. Miles and Father were too involved in a hushed debate to acknowledge anyone else. Mick was flouting Mother's lack of alertness by texting at the table. Nolan was telling Garrett, Al, and me about a poll a lobbyist had shared with him—it showed the percent of people who supported the Organ Act, the percent who thought they'd be able to make contact with a Family if they needed an organ—the smaller percent who thought they could afford it, and the percent who knew someone waiting for a transplant.

"The most common comparison made by citizens was equating the clinics to speakeasies. When H.R. 197 passes, it will be fascinating to observe if the transition out of Prohibition will provide a model for legalizing our industry."

Normally, I'd find this interesting too, or be amused by Al's struggles not to smack Nolan. But I was too busy thinking about my secret counts. Too busy planning.

I waited several hours after dinner, until Garrett was yawning and subtly checking the time on his cell phone. "Going to bed soon, Penny?"

"Actually, I wanted to watch a documentary on Regency ballroom etiquette."

"Ha!" He paused. "You *are* joking, right?"

"No. I can't wait to watch it." I blinked innocently. I'd seen it before with Mother—she loved historical romances, but even she had been bored by the monotone narrator, nondescript background music, and lackluster photography. "It looks really good."

"Oh. Okay. Sure."

A pang of guilt hit me as I watched him swallow his disappointment. "It's on the DVR, if you want to pull it up. I'm going to get popcorn. Want anything?"

"Coffee," he said, covering another yawn. "A big mug, please."

I filled the biggest mug we had with coffee. Black, like he liked. *Decaf*, like he did *not*.

I set one of Mother's sleeping pills on the counter, crushed it with the flat of a knife blade. Then stood in front of that pile of powder and wondered if that was a line I was willing to cross. Torture through documentary boredom, yes. Lies, yes. Caffeine deprivation, yes.

But drugging him?

I swept the powder into my hands and then washed it down the sink.

No.

I wasn't willing to betray his trust on that level.

The smile he traded for his mug twisted in my stomach. Especially when he patted the couch next to him and spent the opening credits paying more attention to my hand than the screen. I'd placed my palm flat on the cushion between us, fingers splayed, and he traced around these, just outside the perimeter of my skin. The lines seemed like they should be carved into the couch's leather, like they should be glowing on my hand, because even without any skin-to-skin contact, I felt warm all over.

I pulled away, crossed my arms. He sank back with a barely audible sigh and switched his gaze to a thin-lipped historian droning about how the waltz was once considered too scandalous for unmarried women.

In his reflection in the window, I watched Garrett's chin sink toward his chest. He startled and jerked awake once, twice, but I pretended not to see the sheepish *did-you-notice* glances he sent my way. Using the remote, I gradually dimmed the lights, lowered the volume, and increased the room temp.

The third time his eyes shut, they stayed closed. His head lolled backward, rested comfortably on the couch instead of in a cramped angle against his chest.

I leaned toward him and whispered, "Garrett?"

He looked younger in his sleep. The tension erased from his eyes and forehead, the angles of his jaw relaxed. His mouth was parted and his bottom lip shivered slightly with each inhale and exhale. I wanted to touch it. I wanted to bend over and kiss him. I wanted to snuggle against him and have a night where I wore his security and scent like a blanket.

"Garrett," I whispered again. "You awake?"

He stirred, pressed his lips together, then exhaled and relaxed further into the couch cushions. I *could* kiss him. He was sleeping deeply enough that it probably wouldn't disturb him. And if it did, I could pretend I was leaning over to nudge him awake. I *could,* but that was a violation akin to sleeping pills. I'd deceived him enough tonight—and I needed that deception to be worthwhile.

I shrugged off his temptation and padded out of the room and across the house.

The sudden brightness of the clinic's hallway made me blink as I eased the door shut behind me. After the cozy dimness of the den and the tiptoe darkness of the library, the stark lighting of halogens on white tile made me feel exposed, as if my hopes were being examined and might crumble from the scrutiny.

I'd had the clinic's network password for weeks, since before Carter. Getting it had been as simple as waiting until Caroline's hands were busy labeling a vial of my blood and saying, "I want your opinion on a dress. What's your login? I'll pull it up."

She hadn't hesitated to tell me or even looked away from the syringe she was putting in the sharps container.

The clicking sound of keystrokes never seemed loud during the day, but at night I flinched as each reverberated in the exam room like a gunshot. While the edges and corners of the estate were rounded, the clinic hadn't had the same architectural renovations. Lit only by the computer screen and the spilled glow from the hallway, all I saw were shadows made of points, angles, and threats.

And the *numbers* on the screen. Disappointment shaped into digits. My CBC results from the past six days read like a countdown: Infusion, less, less, less, less, less. Today's numbers were above forty K, but not by much.

"Don't move."

It was hard to obey once I realized what was poking me in the back.

My voice quivered as I said, "It's *Penny*."

The response was a rush of gold-medal swearing, which allowed me to identify the Ward brother behind me.

"Mick, could you move the gun, please?" The pressure lifted from my spine, but I didn't feel any less panicked. "Thank you."

Mick gripped the back of the office chair and spun me around to face him. "*You* are not supposed to be here."

All the Ward brothers had the same auburn hair and greenish eyes, but Mick looked the most like Garrett. It was like staring at a distorted copy: a little less handsome, a little more mean; a little less humanity, a little more muscle.

He kicked the base of my chair. "Well?"

"I-I forgot my cell phone?"

"And you were hoping Google would help you find it?" He tapped the muzzle of the gun against the computer monitor. "Does Garrett know you're here?"

I started to shake my head, then froze, not sure which answer was *less* incriminating.

"He's assigned to you for a *reason*, you know."

Guilt was a fist around my heart, making me all too aware of how he'd feel if he woke up alone. If anything happened to me while he wasn't there. Sleeping pills or stolen kisses were nothing compared with my real betrayal—leaving him behind, just like Carter had.

My panic wanted me to beg, *Please don't tell him; please don't tell my father.* My rational side knew I lacked bartering chips.

Or . . .

"If you don't tattle to our fathers about catching me here, I won't tell them how you bruised me by shoving a gun in my back."

He swore under his breath.

I stared him down, eyes narrowed as I bluffed. "It's probably going to be a *bad* one. You really pressed hard. So, I could wear a low-backed sundress to breakfast . . . or I could cover it up with a T-shirt."

He raised his eyebrows as he chuckled. "So that's how you're going to play it? Good for you, kid. Go. I never saw you."

I slid from the desk chair and into the hallway, feeling his eyes on my back all the way to the library doors, where I paused and turned.

He saluted me with the hand still holding his gun.

I tiptoed back to the couch in the den. Curled up next to another Ward brother.

I leaned down and kissed the air just over his left cheek.

CHAPTER 12

Garrett sat across from me at breakfast and watched with resigned eyes as his family exited. Nolan trotted at Father's side like a pet dog, and Miles wished us a good day as he left.

We had become the proverbial "kids' table." I was used to it, he wasn't. I could see his stir-crazy building. His tolerance for my boring routines of swimming, stretching, clinic, reading, online shopping, and television was evaporating. These ways of filling my days seemed so much more pathetic when he was beside me sighing, fidgeting, and casting long glances at the closed door of Father's office.

When the only things remaining at the table were us and the other leftovers, he asked, "Is today another *Project Runway* marathon, or some other NYC reality show?"

"Neither."

He sighed. "C-Span?"

"Come with me." I followed a trail of invisible breadcrumbs, taking the path the others had just walked. If Father had been serious about my being important to the Family, then it was time I acted serious too.

"Good morning, sweet pea." Father looked up from his seat behind the massive mahogany desk he'd inherited, along with his position, from my grandfather. "Did your mother send you with a message for me?"

"No. Um, I just thought—" I swallowed and squared my shoulders. *If you want respect, demand it.* "I'd like to attend this morning's meetings."

Like the clinic, Father's office hadn't been included in the architectural remodel that had curved the edges of the main parts of the house. The walls in here had angles, the furniture had corners. There were shelves and filing cabinets, a floor of unforgiving travertine instead of soft cork or plush carpet. The office made me feel unsafe, unwelcomed, and that was before I considered the men inside and their hard judgment.

"Oh." Father's voice was surprised, but I couldn't tell if he was pleased. He nodded at Garrett, who was standing beside me looking confused. "Well, find some seats, we're starting."

It seemed like there were more Family members than usual; almost two dozen men fitting themselves on the chairs and couches—but maybe there were always this many. Or maybe it was a post-Carter thing. From my perch on a chair beside a corner bookshelf I identified Miles's doctor sons, the director of the spa in Maine, plus plenty of unfamiliar faces.

"Penny-pea!" Al Ward's smile made my skin crawl. He turned

to the gathered men. "Remember when she used to come in here and sing and do little dances for us? Adorable."

The Family members exchanged nods and indulgent glances. Garrett's hand gripped the back of my chair; I gritted my teeth.

"Is that why you're here today? I assume you've mastered that M-N-O-P part by now." He laughed and grinned. "Wasn't she the most precious thing?"

Inwardly I seethed and thought, *And aren't you the most vile?* But I refused to let him know he'd gotten a reaction out of me; it would please him far too much. "Sadly, I've retired my dancing shoes. I'm here for the meeting."

"How nice. Did you bring a magazine or something to keep you busy?" he asked.

I raised an eyebrow and held his gaze. "No. Did *you*?"

Garrett coughed to cover a snort.

I slowly made eye contact with each of the Ward brothers. Hugh first, with an arch of my eyebrow, then I met Mick's gaze briefly, but I held Jacob's until the angle of his mouth twitched from sardonic to irritated.

I saved the non-Ward Ward brother for last. Tipping my head back, I looked up at Garrett, pleased to see he was amused and proud. Then he blinked and looked past me, his face turning anxious. I followed his gaze back to his father, whose expression promised consequences.

There didn't seem to be any big gesture that called the meeting to order, just two dozen pairs of eyes focusing on my father and him beginning to talk.

"It's a numbers-heavy morning, men. Clinic financials, patient census, and donor recruitment reports."

Jake's eyebrows and the corners of his mouth twitched up as he glanced at me and mouthed the word Father had used, "men."

I ignored him and settled back in my chair.

Money had always seemed abstract to me. I rarely handled bills. Rarely had transactions that weren't point and click and a shipping box arriving at the gates. I knew the Family made *a lot,* but didn't know how to quantify or comprehend it beyond that.

"Five of the six clinics continued to bring in at least seven-figure profits last year," reported Miles. "Kilney's continues to be our best earner, with fourteen million gross."

"And the sixth?" prompted Father.

"Sky and Light. It's struggling to stay in high-five-, low-six-figure range. The overhead and payoffs are neutralizing most of their profit."

The graphics projected on Father's wall showed patients and donors on double bar graphs—I half expected Nolan to stand up and assign a word problem. There were about a thousand patients per clinic, almost *six thousand* total last year. Six thousand people we'd saved.

I smiled at Garrett, then let my attention wander. Six thousand people was a happy thought to hold on to—and much more interesting than listening to Al speculate about the negative effect the Organ Act was having on donor recruitment. Or Nolan's counterargument on the "practically inexhaustible" supply we'd have if the industry were legalized.

"Your opinions are noted, gentlemen," Father finally said.

"Let's take a break. I've got some calls and then we'll resume in twenty." He pushed his way to me as Family members' attention shifted from focused to idle chatter and trips to the kitchen for coffee.

"It was nice having you here." Before I could reply, Father kissed the top of my head. "I'll see you both at lunch . . . or maybe dinner. We might work through lunch—pass that along to your mother, okay?"

The dismissal caught me off guard. He was gone before I'd processed it, and Garrett was standing, forcing a path through the clusters of men. I stomped after him.

Miles stopped me at the door. "You're a good girl, Penny. It was thoughtful of you to sit through that for Garrett." He always had a kind word for me. A kind word or pint of my favorite ice cream from the creamery by his house. But it hadn't occurred to me—until this very minute—that he still treated me the same way he had when I was seven. I wasn't a "good girl"—I wasn't still a girl at all.

"For Garrett?"

He chuckled lightly and patted Garrett's shoulder. "Though I daresay you've probably made him sit through enough fashion shows or soap operas; it's only fair for you to return the favor and spend some time being bored."

"If Garrett's watching soap operas, it must be on his own time. I don't believe I've ever seen one. And as for boredom—that meeting *wasn't*." At least most of it wasn't. And mine weren't the only eyes I caught glancing at the clock or out the window. "Is this because—"

"Pen!" I froze at Garrett's use of Carter's nickname. It was deliberate. He widened his eyes, shook his head. "Let's go swim. I need to cool down. Too many people in this office."

By *I* he meant *you,* but he wasn't wrong. Better for me to take my frustration out in laps than say something that confirmed Al's depiction of me as immature and decorative.

I nodded.

CHAPTER 13

I swam until my anger cooled and my curiosity crystallized into questions. I climbed out of the pool, asking, "Do they have proof it was the Zhus yet? I heard Mother signing for *another* delivery of flowers from Mrs. Zhu; do you think that's odd? And last night when Miles came to get Father from dinner because Mr. Vickers was on the phone, what was that was about?"

I'd been trying to remember everything I could about the other Families. Mr. Vickers was a short man with a manicured beard. His wife was a blond-haired, tanned Texan with a soft voice and sweet smile. Their daughter didn't take after either of them; she was neither short nor quiet.

"Remember Magnolia?" I asked.

Garrett gave up pretending to ignore me. He looked up from his magazine and handed me a towel. "Yeah. Were you there the time she made Carter drink hot sauce?" His mouth pulled into a nostalgic smile, but I shook my head. "She was wild. You probably weren't allowed out to play when she was over."

"Only once. Mother set up a tea party for us in my room while they had their own." Maggie had eaten all the sugar cubes, poured the tea in my unicorn bank, made a tower of the cups and saucers, then used my Cinderella snow globe to bowl them down. "It did not go well."

"You've got to remember the time she dared Carter to jump from the tree to the pool—or at least the result. He was miserable in that cast—he used to hit me with it when he got mad. Did he tell you we saw her this year? In the fall. She was on campus for a cross-country race. I thought *he* was going to run away. Carter is still terrified of her."

Carter. He wasn't *still* terrified of her. He wasn't *still* anything, except a hole in our lives and an ache attached to every breath and memory.

In moments like this, it was too hard to look at each other. I studied the lawn, and Garrett turned back to his magazine. Once I could inhale and exhale without it catching in my throat, once I'd stopped blinking to clear my eyes, I flipped the cover up: *Gun World*. The address label said "Hugh Ward." At least it wasn't his subscription.

"You're dripping," he grumbled.

"Whatever, you're not even reading. Put it down and talk to me. Tell me what you know." I touched his shoulder, softly, hesitantly, then couldn't bring myself to pull my hand away from his warm skin.

He scoffed. "What I know? Do you think my dad or brothers

tell me *anything*? And despite that, they're still convinced your dad will pick me to replace him."

"Oh." I hadn't thought about that.

"I don't know if I want to. Lead *with* Carter, yeah. But without him . . ."

I squeezed his shoulder, back to blinking and swallowing against tears. "Why would anyone kill him?"

"I don't know. I really don't." He rolled the magazine into a tight cylinder.

"Then tell me something you do. What really happened the night we went to NYC? What's happening with the Everlys? What's dead meat?"

His face had been carefully blank throughout my assault of questions . . . but the last one made him swallow.

"What's dead meat, Garrett?"

I counted to ten while he stared at me. Ten, with Mississippis in between. And when I got to *eleven Missi*— I retracted my hand, ready to give up, but he groaned and patted the cushion next to him.

"You can't talk to your dad about this. Promise."

I nodded, wrapping my towel tighter to prevent the goose bumps that were chasing up my arms.

He studied me for another five Mississippis before he spoke. "Dead Meat was the code name for Deer Meadow—you know how all the spas and B&Bs have code names, right?"

I nodded. *Sky and Light Day Spa* up in Maine was *Skin and Liver; Kilney's Bed and Breakfast* down in Hilton Head specialized in *Kidneys. Turtle Island—Tissue.*

"I've never heard of Deer Meadow—and *dead meat*? Wait!" I jumped up. "Does that mean it's cadaver tissue?"

"Listen before you start judging. Please." I sat back down and chewed my lip. "Dead Meat was Carter's baby. It's a new spa—in Manhattan. Your dad doesn't know. It's not cadavers the way we normally get them—with families signing them over or with the donor filling out all the forms prior to dying."

He looked away from me, stared out through the gate. "We have a connection with a morgue; we get calls when they have bodies coming in. We pay a fee—way less than the 250K your dad pays donor families—and we have a whole body to work with."

"Carter did this?" Forget goose bumps, I was trying not to vomit. I knew he'd talked about it. But hypothetical discussion was different than learning it was happening. "And that night? Was it a whole body in the trunk or just the valuable parts? Were they *in the kitchen freezer* while we ate pizza in his apartment?"

"Don't sound like that. It's not just a money thing—yeah, the profits are good, but we can do transplants for way cheaper. So many more people can afford them. Not just the super-rich. Our clients *aren't* like Mr. Pyle—who's currently drinking his way through his third liver and already gave your dad the down payment for his fourth."

"Who have you fixed?" I wanted Garrett to be able to look me in the eye and convince me to support Carter's last project.

"Lots of people. We still do all the testing—nucleic acid, you know, the good kind—we're not the Everlys using diseased parts. But, like, this one kid—sixteen years old, a baseball star. He was in a car crash and wrecked his knee. We did a ligament transplant for him. He should be able to play again. Or we did a heart valve transplant on a two-year-old girl."

"Is she going to be all right?"

He finally turned back toward me, his face tense. "Yeah, she is. And it was a single mom, she never could have afforded what the Zhus, Vickers, or even what your dad charges."

"Is this—Dead Meat—is this why Carter was killed?"

"No, I don't think so. I've checked up on the spa and it's all secure, nothing's changed there. And I had security review the tapes from that night. Wherever Carter was, it wasn't Deer Meadow."

"It's still functioning?" I whispered.

"It's Carter's legacy. The Family may not be letting me do much around here these days, but I'll do anything to protect this." He clenched his jaw and flipped the edge of my towel between two fingers. "So . . . what are you thinking?"

"I don't know," I said slowly. "Nolan's always talking about the need for price control. It's part of why he supports the Organ Act—if the industry was legalized, there'd be set prices and better quality control. I hadn't ever thought about it this way. When are you going to tell my father and the Family?"

Garrett's fingers stilled. "When I think they're ready to listen. Maybe after the Zhus are punished and people calm down. This is all I have left of Carter—I can't screw this up, Penny. Do you get it?"

I wasn't sure. I wanted to, but I just wasn't sure. I'd opened and closed my mouth a half-dozen times, each one to give a different answer, when Mother appeared through the french doors behind the library.

She had a tray of food and an indulgent expression as she looked at Garrett and me sitting together.

"I thought you might be hungry, so I fixed up a snack for before your CBC." She set down the tray on a patio table: glasses of orange juice and bowls of chickpeas, raisins, almonds, and dates. She ruffled his hair affectionately, smiled at me.

"Thanks," we said, but she didn't leave.

"How are you doing, Garrett?" Her eyes turned sad, her smile faded. "I keep meaning to make time to ask you that, and to tell you that if you ever want to talk, I'm here."

"Thank you, ma'am." Garrett ducked his head and resumed playing with the edge of my towel. I thought I heard him sniff.

"I know your father's not the most . . ." She reached out and stroked his hair again. "And your brothers—I know it can't be easy, that it couldn't have been easy growing up as much a part of *our* family as *yours*. I want you to know I'm here for you."

He stood and hugged her. Mother was tiny compared to his height and bulk, but he was the one that looked vulnerable as she rubbed his back and murmured soothing things.

I curled my legs up under the towel, as if wrapping myself in terry cloth would help me contain my jealousy. I wasn't even sure who or what I jealous of. A hug from either of them? Both of them? The fact that Garrett was letting Mother be there for him in ways he hadn't let me?

It didn't matter, because entwined with my jealousy was so much self-reproach for feeling jealous. Why shouldn't Garrett, whose own mother had walked out on him when he was twelve, borrow mine when he was mourning his best friend?

"I feel like my shadow is gone . . . ," he said through quiet sobs. "Or, like, I'm the shadow left behind and the person I'm supposed to be following is gone. I just keep *looking for him.* It's instinct. And I'm never going to find him."

He hiccupped, and Mother rubbed his back in calming circles, the way she'd rubbed mine for the first six years of my life.

"I'm never going to find him," Garrett repeated. "But I can't—I can't remember to stop looking."

I stood up, planning to walk away and give him privacy, but he let go of Mother with one hand and held it out to me. I squeezed his fingers, he flexed them against mine. It wasn't holding hands, he couldn't squeeze back, but it was enough to let me know I was included. It was enough of an invitation that I stepped closer, put my hand on his back above my mother's, and leaned my head on his shoulder.

We stood this way for a long time. It was Mother who pulled back first, with a reluctant glance at her wristwatch.

"I love you, dear children." She kissed both of our foreheads. "I have to go make sure Annette has sent in lunch trays for the men. Oh, and dinner tonight will be a little earlier—six thirty. Wear something nice; your father's invited the whole Family. Apparently there's going to be an announcement."

CHAPTER 14

Father stood at the head of the dining room table surrounded by all the members of the Family who could be gathered on short notice. His hand was on Nolan's shoulder. And Nolan beamed like a five-year-old who'd been given a puppy. Except it wasn't a puppy he'd been gifted, it was the Family.

"What?" I breathed it out. Choked on the word. Then said it louder—in a voice I wished was a demand but was little more than a whimper. *"What?"*

"Sweet pea, we can talk later." Father scarcely glanced at me before turning back to Nolan and lifting his wineglass high. "I know you'll all agree that this will be the beginning of another long reign of success for our Family. And that when my time ends, you'll pledge your loyalty to Nolan in the same way you've always given it to me."

"Thank you, Malcolm." Nolan took a deep breath, like he was preparing for a speech, but I cut him off.

"I don't understand." I was on my feet. My glass was in my hand, but at an angle now. The splash of wine Mother had allowed Miles to pour for me spilled onto my plate and the tablecloth.

Jacob was seated next to me. He muttered quietly, "Yet your lack of understanding explains so much to the rest of us." If there'd been anything left in my glass, I'd have thrown it in his face.

The rest of the Wards, the rest of the table, looked as shocked as I felt. Al's face was turning the same color as my spilled merlot. But they were raising glasses. Forcing neutral expressions and stiff nods of support.

I dropped my glass so I could brace myself against the table with both hands. It broke off at the stem and I heard Mother's sharp intake of breath. "But . . . how? *Nolan?*"

"We'll discuss this *later,* Penelope." I'd never been on the receiving end when Father used that voice. It bit like a whip, making my eyes fill from the sting.

Through tears, I saw Garrett move. He pushed his chair back and stood, shook off Mick's restraining hand. Hugh grumbled, "Don't bother, Mick, he's more Landlow than Ward these days. Didn't you see the group hug by the pool?"

Garrett's mouth pressed into a hard line, but he kept walking around the table.

"Carter's dead, and he's *still* not their favorite son," Jacob muttered under his breath, adding a few curses in front of Nolan's name.

I glanced at him in horror. I couldn't have heard him correctly. If Garrett had, Jacob would be sporting two new black eyes over the ones that'd mostly faded.

"Princess, let's go get some air," he whispered when he reached my place.

I knew naming Nolan as successor was a Business decision, but it still felt *personal*. Father's whole *"I promise you will never have to endure another one of Nolan's lectures"*—he'd known . . . and hadn't told me.

"Is this because I broke into the clinic?" I whirled from Father to Mick. "You said you wouldn't tell. They're my counts—it's my blood."

Mick's eyes widened and he shook his head, but the actions didn't register until Father thundered, "What?"

"I . . . I . . . it's my blood," I repeated lamely.

"Penelope," Father's roar continued, "you are excused." The men at the table stood to mark my exit, eyes averted. He nodded at Garrett who moved to put a hand on my shoulder until Mother called out, "Don't touch her"—reminding everyone just how flawed I was.

He dropped his hands to my chair, pulling it out.

Jacob scoffed and said, "Babysitter," and Father threw a warning glare his way. I stepped on his foot as I stood up.

It was too late, though. That word hit his brother the same way Mother's outburst had struck me. Garrett's cheeks burned as brightly as mine when he gestured for me to precede him out of the room.

I didn't run until we were out of sight. Garrett was right

behind me. I wanted our footsteps to clatter in the hallways, to show our anger and frustration in resounding echoes. But the original polished marble floors had been ripped out in the same remodel that rounded the estate's corners and softened the edges. The cork that replaced it absorbed most of the noise. How had I possibly thought Father would trust me with news about the Business when he didn't even trust me to walk without breaking myself?

In the solarium I carefully sat on a cushioned chair. Just once I'd like to throw myself down and weep with abandon—without worry that post-weeping, I'd spend a week in the clinic.

Garrett turned the lock before coming over to me. He crouched in the wood chips beside my chair, placing his hands on either side of my legs with just a whisper of space between his fingers and the bare skin below the hem of my dress.

I hiccupped. "Nolan's not even a Landlow. If I can't run it—and why can't I? Then it should go to *you*."

Garrett looked down; the tips of his ears were red. "I'd kinda thought—well, hoped really—that someday it would be *ours*—all three of us. Carter and I always joked you and I would end up together. Only neither of us was really joking."

I blushed and looked down too. Watched his pointer finger move closer until he was touching my leg, tracing small, soft circles across the front of my thigh. The touch made my head spin, sensation battling all my contradictory thoughts. Though Carter had given me plenty of grief about my infatuation, he'd never kept us apart.

"But he was so mad when he saw us that night . . . And you said you were sorry about it."

Garrett flinched. "I wasn't sorry about *us*, I was sorry about the scene he caused." He brushed a fingertip below my chin, telling me to look at him without actually exerting any pressure. "I don't think he was really mad, just shocked."

"He did say it wasn't a big deal," I was thinking aloud, replaying the Garrett-parts of my last conversation with Carter. "In fact, his last words to me were 'Serves him right,' when I joked about breaking your heart."

I was seeing through tears; Garrett was swallowing and blinking. "I only backed off because you needed space. And now everything's gone wrong. Nolan? I can't believe . . . *Nolan*?" He groaned. "My dad's going to be so pissed. And blame me. I know it." His jaw tightened slightly, his finger pressing down on my leg for the barest fraction of a second before it resumed caressing. "Jacob's right, I'm a glorified babysitter. They're never going to take me seriously. They'll never stop blaming me. Carter's never coming back . . ."

His voice was thick. His eyes dark and far away, looking up through the glass ceiling as if there were an answer to be found in the night sky.

I reached out a trembling hand and touched his face, turned it back toward me. "Sometimes I really wish I could run away. Live in a shiny New York City apartment with a smiling doorman and forget all about life on the estate."

Garrett placed his hand on top of mine, cupping my palm against his cheek, nuzzling into it in a way that made my pulse skip and my skin flush. "Sounds good. Is there room in this fantasy for me to come too?"

"Yes." I was breathless. Could he feel my hand go clammy against his face? This wasn't romance, it was grief and guilt and rage, but my head and heart and body were reacting like this was the stuff of fairy tales.

"Can I kiss you?" he asked.

I swallowed. And swallowed the urge to correct his *can* to *may*. Then cursed the voice of Nolan for running through my head at a time like this. Cursed everything about Nolan.

"I'll be gentle. You know I'd never hurt you, right?"

I nodded, tugging down the hem of my dress to cover the fingerprint bruise he'd left on my thigh when he was talking about Al. But that was an accident, it *shouldn't* have left a mark—which meant I needed to see Dr. Castillo.

His hands left the chair's cushion and settled on my neck, working their way up into my hair and tilting my head toward his—

There was a rattling of the door handle. A banging on the door.

"Penelope Maeve Landlow, open the door this instant or I'll have it broken down."

We were across the solarium, obscured by a fountain. Father couldn't have seen us. We both exhaled, mine a sigh, his a grim chuckle as he walked to the door.

As soon as the lock was flipped, Father stormed into the room.

His rage was impressive, but so was mine. I stood up, putting my hands on my hips and straightening to make use of every one of my five feet three inches.

"Father, I can't believe you."

"*Me*? Don't start. Don't you even start. You embarrassed me in there. And you ruined what should have been a triumphant moment for Nolan."

"Good," I spat. "Why Nolan? Why not Garrett? Why not *me*?" My stupid voice quavered on the last word, and Father's face softened. "You said I was *essential* to the Family."

"You are essential to *our* family—because your mother and I love you." He sat down on a cushion and patted the seat next to him. "Come sit, Penny."

"I wanted you to *fire him,* not promote him. And you said you were going to teach me how to run the Business."

"No, I said I wanted to teach you. As Nolan learns my role, I'll be able to turn some responsibilities over to him and have more time for you. I was thinking classic literature—our own father-daughter book club."

I shook my head. "Is this because I'm a girl?"

"Do not—do *not* imply that I am sexist."

"Have you heard the Wards talk about women? Or some of the other Family members?"

"Don't mistake their opinions for mine. I have no problem with the idea of a female heading up a Family, but you are no Magnolia Vickers."

"I'm not claiming I'm ready now, but you could train me. Why not name Miles for now and then train me?"

"Miles is older than I am. He's looking to retire soon."

"But he'd only be a placeholder until I'm ready. It's hardly like *you're* retiring anytime soon."

"Oh, Penelope." He dropped his chin; sadness crept in to add lines on his face. "Who knows how long I have? The Family needs to know whom I've chosen as a successor. They need to know I have someone ready to take my place. Otherwise it leads to infighting, bloodshed. Nolan's got a vision for the future of the Business, and I think it's a valid one."

"The Organ Act?"

Father didn't answer. He leaned over and kissed the top of my head. "I want you to have a life, sweet pea. Leading the Family is no way for you to spend it."

"Shouldn't that be my choice? How I spend my life—and who I spend it with?" I looked for Garrett. He'd moved to stand by the windowed wall, giving us some space and the illusion of privacy, though I knew he could hear every word. "Maybe I couldn't lead alone. But I could with help."

"You wanted me to co-name you with Nolan?" Father laughed. "Just yesterday you were begging to get away from him."

"Not Nolan." I paused and held a hand out in invitation, but Garrett must not have seen it because he didn't move. "Father, I could marry Garrett. You could name him your successor, and he and I could lead together."

"*Marry?* Garrett!" The word was a summons and did what my hand had not, drew him away from the wall to come stand before my father. "Is there something I need to know about you and my daughter?"

Garrett shook his head emphatically. "No, sir." And I choked on the breath I'd been holding.

"Good. Keep it that way." The fire went out of Father's eyes, moving to heat my cheeks with humiliation. "Penny, you're still such a child—dreaming of marriage and unicorns and rainbows. It's not a job you could handle—it's dangerous. With your delicacy, you'd be a liability."

I swallowed past the sting of his words. "I see."

"Sweet pea, life is not one of your storybooks. I've already lost one child to this Business. After what happened to Carter, how can you expect me to allow you anywhere near it? You're all I have left." He looked down, swallowed twice, then looked back up with flint in his eyes. "This discussion is over. I expect you to congratulate Nolan the next time you see him. And when he does succeed me, you will offer him your loyalty and obedience. Understand?"

My cheeks burned with anger and embarrassment, but I had seen the pain flash through his eyes when he mentioned Carter. "Yes, Father."

"Now, about the clinic, I've already questioned and dealt with Mick. Can you think of anything he might have left out?"

I raised my chin and tried not to feel guilty about Mick being punished. "I have a right to know my counts."

"Were you aware Penny broke into the clinic on your watch?" Father asked Garrett.

I had to turn away from the betrayal in his eyes, the shame in his voice when he answered, "No, sir."

"I see." The look on Father's face made it clear that discussion was far from over. "Bring Penny to her room, then join me and the others in the library and raise a glass to Nolan."

"Of course, sir."

I stared at Garrett, but his eyes were fixed on my father's retreating back. I knew the moment Garrett judged him to be out of earshot, because his shoulders relaxed ever so slightly.

"Ballroom etiquette, huh?" he asked in a voice full of false humor. "I should've guessed you were up to something. Your taste in movies is normally less torturous. Except for *Enchanted*—I know, it's New York and fairy tales, pretty much custom made for you—but the chipmunk . . ."

"I'm sorry," I whispered.

"I get it." He dropped the fake grin. "I'm not happy you left me behind—don't *ever* do that again—but I get it."

"Why did you—with Father, you implied we aren't . . ." I shrugged, muted by hurt and confusion. What should I accuse him of, denying there was anything between us? Was there?

"The first rule of being a Ward is not to take sides when the Landlows are infighting," quoted Garrett. When he saw my stormy face, he smiled gently. "It wasn't the right time. He's all wound up by Nolan, and he's still mourning Carter."

"But . . ."

"He'd reassign me. I'd never see you again without a room full of chaperones. He still might because of the clinic thing."

"No! He can't." Except we both knew he could.

"Remember when we were little and playing Go Fish? And you always wanted to show me your whole hand?"

I nodded.

"Now's the time for us to keep our cards tipped up. You know Malcolm Landlow as a father, but I know him as a businessman." Garrett held out his hand. "Trust me."

I slowly placed mine inside and watched his fingers fold gently over, swallowing it up.

My hand in his—it was my daydreams made reality. Father may control most things, but he didn't command them *all.*

CHAPTER 15

Over the next four days Garrett got several scathing lectures about duty and vigilance, I got another infusion, and Nolan started appearing at *all* our meals. And wherever Nolan was, there was an entourage. The Wards, Miles, Frank, and every other Family member within a hundred-mile radius seemed determined to either suck up to the new successor or make a fool of him in front of Father.

Except no one had any luck agitating Nolan. This didn't surprise me; I'd had years and years of trying to irritate the man.

"I'm afraid that's incorrect," Nolan said calmly in response to another one of Al's jabs at the Organ Act. "Prior to the creation of FOTA, back when tissue transplant was regulated by the FDA, there was no national registry or tracking system whatsoever. There *was* serological testing done, but nucleic acid testing wasn't required and there's a window—"

"I don't want a history lecture; I'm not your pupil." Al's white linen napkin was crushed between his scarred and scabbed knuckles. "I just want to know how you think you can get in bed with politicians *and* lead the Family at the same time."

"If H.R. 197 were to pass, the two roles wouldn't be incompatible," answered Nolan. "And if the industry were legalized, not only would we have a steady supply of prescreened donors but we wouldn't have to worry about raids or tragic acts of violence." He gave Mother a cloying look of sympathy, and I put down my fork.

Whenever his presence threatened to make me gag, I turned and looked at Garrett. His tight smiles made it easier to resist stabbing Nolan with Mother's silver.

It was unbelievable that four days ago our Family hadn't been divided; fourteen days ago Carter hadn't been dead.

"How long will you be in DC?" I asked Nolan.

"My best estimate is two to three weeks, but, like we've discussed in your history classes, politics is a game of patience, influence, and strategy. I've received word that the House of Representatives will be bringing H.R. 197 to the floor for a vote soon, and I want to be in town when this happens."

"It's out of subcommittees? I didn't know this."

He nodded. "And while we know that there are no guarantees in politics, I've been informed that it should have enough support to pass."

Which meant it would go to Congress for a vote. Then the president. It wasn't a sure thing, not even close to one yet, but if it passed in the House, it was a huge step closer to happening. "Wow."

Nolan lifted a haughty eyebrow. "Wow, indeed. Once I've had preliminary meetings with these lobbyists, I'll be able to more accurately project the duration of my sojourn."

Jacob and Hugh rolled their eyes. They did whenever he spoke, which was just stupid. They'd make themselves dizzy long before Nolan stopped using his word choice to demonstrate that he was the smartest person in the room.

"Will you see Vice President Forman?" I asked this follow-up question even though the Wards—except Mick, whom I hadn't seen since the announcement dinner—were shifting their frowns in my direction. "If so, can you pass along my love to him and Kelly?"

Nolan blinked. Then removed his glasses and wiped them on a napkin. Nothing made him squirm like talk of emotions. "Of course I'll see him. He's been an ally of this Family, and he's one of the strongest supporters of this bill."

"So he's paying back our help by working to destroy us," grumbled Hugh.

"Malcolm, you can't possibly agree with Nolan's idiotic opinions about legalizing donors, set prices, and regulations," said Al. It wasn't the first time someone had asked Father how he felt about the bill—so far he'd refused to state an opinion—but it was the first time someone had asked with such contempt. "Dirty politicians having their hands in the Business and controlling you like a dog on a leash—you want that?"

Father wiped his mouth and turned to Mother. "You know, Abigail, perhaps it's time we had fewer guests at meals. I find the company and conversation are ruining my appetite lately."

"Just like *he's* going to ruin the Family." Jacob pointed toward Nolan with the tip of his butter knife. Al smiled at his son's insolence, but everyone else at the table inhaled a collective gasp. Jacob had never been good at judging when he was going too far, but when he opened his mouth to continue, I wanted to slap my hand across it—even if that meant hitting his recently broken nose. "Man, even naming the glass princess would've been better." He nodded in my direction as if this were a compliment. "She wouldn't have lasted long, but at least she'd be a pretty little puppet before she broke."

I glared at him and pushed my temptingly sharp fork farther away.

Garrett's lips were white, his eyes thin lines of fury. Mother dropped her spoon and didn't seem to notice it splashed granola and yogurt onto her blouse. I didn't get any further in my examination of the diners' reactions because Father threw his mug across the room—it shattered on the wall behind Jacob's head.

"Wards, *get out of my sight*. I'll let you know when you no longer sicken me, but until then, you're not to step foot on the estate."

Al gaped and slammed down his fork. Right before he stormed out, he pointed a finger at Garrett. "This is *your* fault. Remember that."

Jacob hesitated for a moment like he might apologize, but then he tightened his jaw and copied Hugh's hasty retreat. Garrett shifted his weight but remained seated. His gaze followed his family out of the room, so he saw Al's look of disgust, but not my father's nod of approval.

Mother paused for just a second, then turned to Nolan. "What time is the car coming to take you to the airport?"

The meal ended abruptly after that. Everyone scattered, stumbling over themselves to get out of Father's sight. Everyone but Garrett and me. We looked at each other down the length of the long, now-empty table, then sighed and wandered into the solarium.

"Nolan is a disaster. No one's happy Father picked him. Your dad and mine—I've never heard them fight like that."

"They've both got pride and tempers. Emotions are running high right now—everyone's frustrated the police haven't arrested anyone. It's Jake I'm worried about—he's not funny, and one of these days . . ." Muscles along his jaw clenched. "I'm sorry, Penny. I can't even think of an excuse to give you—he was so out of line."

"Don't apologize for them. But . . . why did your dad blame you? You didn't do anything."

"According to him, I did *everything* wrong. I didn't protect Carter, I didn't get named successor."

"That's not your fault. I'm so sorry you got caught in the middle." I put a hand on his arm and squeezed lightly. "When it comes to choosing between family—little *f*—and the Family, you should always choose little *f*. But I'm so glad you stayed with me."

"Do you mean that?" he asked. "Really, seriously mean it?"

"Of course I do." Garrett kept studying me, so I felt the need to elaborate. "Maybe we should tell them about Dead Meat. That should prove pretty clearly you're good at the Business. Your dad would respect that."

"Princess—"

"I could talk to your father. Make him see what an impossible position—"

He exhaled deeply and said in a rush, "Run away with me."

"What?"

"I think you were right the other day. We should leave. Let's run away." He'd started to do this thing where he *almost* touched me. Holding his hand so close that I wondered sometimes if he had. He at least stirred the air around my skin so it felt like a caress.

"Are you serious?"

He nodded solemnly.

"What would we do?" Life beyond the gates. Not an hour or an afternoon, but a *life*.

"Anything we wanted." He grinned at me. "I've got plenty of Dead Meat money."

"Glass princess." "Puppet." Jacob's words weren't creative or new insults, but I couldn't shake how useless they made me feel. But if we left . . . outside these gates, I could be anyone.

"I can't live like this, Penny. Trapped on the estate, and with the way my brothers and my dad . . . since Carter—" He swallowed and met my eyes with a piercing gaze. "It's been bad."

I wanted to ask "Bad how?" but the look in his eyes scared me. It was a look he'd worn too often as a child on days when it felt less like he was keeping me company and more like he was hiding, jumping every time a door opened and moving in stiff, skittish ways.

Only once had I seen bruises. Right after his mom left, which was right after his brother Keith died. Carter had pushed Garrett in the pool in his clothes, and the purple across his ribs had been visible through the wet cotton of his white shirt. Even without seeing them directly, I could tell they were as dark and painful as any I'd ever had. And it explained why he'd been so slow and awkward all morning.

He'd grabbed a towel and wrapped it around himself, saying, "You can't tell," to wide-eyed Carter and wet-cheeked, ten-year-old me.

"I'll kill him," my brother had said, but Garrett shook his head.

"And then I'll have *no* parents. Just forget you saw it. It won't happen again. Promise. If it does, I'll tell. Promise you won't tell."

We'd agreed. Because we were kids and wanted to believe him. Because we'd been raised to see police as enemies, not allies. Because we worried that if we told, they'd take Garrett away—and if anyone looked too closely at the Family, they'd take our father as well.

I've always hated myself for that promise.

I put a hand on Garrett's chest, just lightly—and wondered if the reason he hadn't joined me in the pool lately was lurking beneath his T-shirt. He shut his eyes and dropped his head. His heart beat beneath my palm, his chest rising and falling in shattered breaths.

"I can't stay, princess. If you don't want to come, I understand. But I *can't.*" He skimmed a finger down my cheek. I could feel the blush creeping along the line of his caress. He traced it over to brush my bottom lip and tilted my chin up.

"Where would we go?" My voice was breathless.

"Where do you want? New York City? I promise I'll take care of you. We could use Dead Meat doctors if you need anything."

Maybe it would be better if we left. Our fathers could work things out without us in the middle—and Nolan would be gone too. In fact, our being missing would give them a unified goal—to work together to find us.

"When will we go?" My mind skipped from "would" to "will" as soon as I considered what life *here* would be like without him. I could feel the heat rise off his skin as he noticed the change.

"Now. Today. Before you lose your nerve or someone suspects."

"Today?" My stomach tightened. "But I need time to pack."

"You can't. We can't tip anyone off. Just bring whatever fits in a purse. I'll get you anything you need." He grinned, and his hand reached out, his palm skimmed over mine. The nerves in my stomach melted into butterflies.

"We're really going to do this?" I asked.

"We're really going to do this." He leaned his forehead to just barely rest on mine and breathed out a sigh of soul-deep relief. "Thank you."

❦

Lunch and an afternoon. That was how long I had to play-act at normal. Pretend every glance I shot at Garrett wasn't full of thrills and doubts. With Nolan gone and the Wards banished there was too much of my parents' attention focused on me.

"Sweet pea, you are all fidgets. Are you sleeping enough?" Mother asked. "I think you should go lie down after you eat."

"That's a good idea," said Father. "You do look a little tired, and I might need Garrett and Ian to cover some duties this afternoon."

I shot Garrett a panicked look, but he was calmly eating dill potatoes. "Of course, sir."

"*You* could use a rest too," admonished Mother. "You're working too hard. There's no need to train Nolan overnight. I was hoping with him being away, you'd have some free time."

Before Carter died she never would have criticized Father. But before Carter died he didn't work twenty-five hours a day. He lifted his eyebrows and I could practically see him debating his response.

"I miss you," she breathed out with a quiet dignity.

"Garrett, go tell Darius to push the meeting with the VIP up to one thirty. I'll be wrapping up early today so I can have a glass of wine with my wife." Father picked up her hand and kissed her knuckles; she blushed and smiled at him as if he'd gift-wrapped the universe and presented it to her with a bow.

"Yes, sir." I wanted Garrett to look at me that way, but he didn't glance in my direction as he left the room.

I cleared my throat. "I'll just go lie down and give you guys some privacy." I was only half-embarrassed they were being affectionate, maybe less than half. It was good to see her happy, it was good to see him notice things outside his office.

"Love you, sweet pea," said Mother, turning to flash me a radiant smile. Father tugged my sleeve as I walked by. I offered a tremulous grin, then headed upstairs, feeling like Rapunzel about to be released from her tower and terrified of everything that lay beyond.

CHAPTER 16

I stood in my room: a half-full purse in one hand and fingers twitching with indecision on the other. I'd spent my life collecting all these *things*, ways to bring the outside world in, and now I was leaving them all behind and going out.

"Hey."

I gasped. I hadn't heard the door open or Garrett cross the room to stand behind me at my bureau. And because my eyes had been on the contents of my jewelry box, I hadn't seen his approach in the mirror. I looked up at his reflection, slightly aware that a strand of pearls was slipping from my fingers and clattering onto the glass top, but more aware of the way his eyes glittered as they met mine in the mirror. And the warmth radiating from his arms as he circled them around me to rest on the edge of the dresser.

"Just wanted to check on you. Any second thoughts?" He bent down so the question raised goose bumps on my neck.

"No. Of course not," I stammered. "You?"

He shook his head, his nose grazing the skin below my ear and making me shiver. "You almost ready?"

"When" had become "now" and I didn't feel ready at all, but I swallowed, nodded, managed a smile. "I need a few more minutes."

"Sure. Meet me behind the pool shed in ten." He pressed his lips quickly to the top of my head.

"We are coming back, right?" I almost didn't dare ask because if he gave the wrong answer I couldn't go. And he couldn't stay. I didn't know what went on in the Wards' house, but his joy and relief about leaving made my heart ache.

"Whenever you want, princess. Promise. But for now, don't be late. We want to go before the gate shift change—Mick's on duty and he'll let us leave without telling. We need that head start."

I nodded. Right answer. I could do this.

He skated his fingers down my arm, then left.

I took a deep breath and shut my jewelry box. I wouldn't need anything from there. This was temporary. I'd go with Garrett, we'd have adventures, establish that I was fine outside these curved walls without twelve zillion layers of protection. We'd get a break from Family politics and our fathers' pissing contest. He'd get a reprieve from his family's bullying . . . or worse. Then, in a week, maybe two, we could come home. Triumphant.

So why did it feel so much like good-bye? Why did I want to go downstairs to kiss my parents' cheeks and tell them "I love you both"?

It wasn't the unicorn statues I minded leaving. Or the closets full of clothes. Or my makeup table. It was the photos. The dollhouse I hadn't played with in years, as tall as I was and custom-ordered to look just like our house, complete with dolls: Mother, Father, Carter, and a seven-year-old Penelope. It was the teddy bear Father had given me when I was six and my platelets first started rebelling—the one I'd named Rumpelstiltskin, called "Rumpel" for short, and gripped tightly through so many blood draws and nightmares. The nightlight Mother brought back from Venice with the blue-and-green glass that reflected like rainbows on my wall. The crown of dried roses, which had been alive and gorgeously pink when I wore them on my head on the day of my First Holy Communion. The Bible Grandfather had given me that same day, my name and a benediction scratched in his wavering handwriting on the first page. The large illustrated treasury of Hans Christian Andersen fairy tales Father, Carter, and Mother had taken turns reading at my bedtimes.

These were the pieces of my life—and they wouldn't fit inside the lining of my purse.

I took the Carter doll. I took some cash. Took a deep breath.

I kissed Rumpel and left him on my pillow.

I shut my closet. I shut all my drawers. Shut my eyes.

Exhaled slowly.

And stood in front of my door trying to gather the strength to step into the hall.

Don't be late.

A knock made me jump. I swallowed a scream.

"Penny? You in there?" a familiar voice asked.

"Hey, Caroline." I shielded my purse behind the door as I opened it. "What are you doing over here?"

"You know how you're always saying I can raid your closet? I wanted to borrow a dress. I have a first date tonight—do you mind?"

"Of course not." I still had six minutes to kill—and being early might be more conspicuous. "Did you have one in mind?"

"Not really. Maybe that white eyelet one? Or the blue pleated? What do you think?" Caroline flounced into my room and pounced on my closet door. "It's so quiet in your house today. Where is everyone? It's dead in the clinic too. Dr. Castillo is entertaining a VIP, but there's nothing for me to do. I could play fashion show for hours and he wouldn't even notice."

Hours? Normally that wouldn't be a problem. "Um, why don't you try on the blue one," I suggested. "I think that'd be perfect."

I watched the clock while Caroline wriggled out and into clothing. "Zip me?" she asked. And, "What do you think?"

Four minutes. *We need that head start.*

"Gorgeous," I said.

"You're not even looking." She laughed. "Why are you so distracted? And where's your hot-stuff shadow and his creepy family today?"

I gulped.

She laughed harder. "What aren't you telling me? Is something going on with Garrett?"

"No." I said it a little too quickly. "He's in a meeting with Father."

Caroline's forehead wrinkled. "No, he's not. I just saw your dad. He's sitting on the patio with your mom—"

"I think you should try the green seersucker dress—that would be so pretty on you."

Three minutes.

I stood. "I'm thirsty. I'm going to run and get a drink. Want anything?"

"Sure. Lemonade? And when you get back, you have to tell me what's going on. I *knew* you and Garrett would get together."

I nodded and fled. Grateful she'd gone back in my closet and hadn't seen me pick up my purse.

If Mother and Father were on the patio, I didn't need to creep down the stairs, but I did anyway, doing my best imitation of a spy based on what I'd learned from watching Bond movies with Carter and Garrett. Quiet and caution seemed doubly unnecessary, because I could hear loud voices outside. The shouting would more than cover any sounds I made.

Poor Mother, she got to see so little of Father lately—and if a Business phone call had interrupted their time he'd be furious and she'd be silently annoyed. Had Al called to apologize? If so, it wasn't going well. The shouting escalated. Something smashed—probably Father breaking his glass. He did that when he was mad—he and Carter both liked to take their frustration out on glassware. At least he hadn't thrown it through a window this time.

With my parents on the patio, I couldn't go out the back door. I'd have to go the roundabout way—through the library's french doors and approach the pool house from the back.

There was a sharp crack and a shattering. Maybe Father *had* thrown something through a window. Except . . . that was a scream. A high-pitched scream. Father's temper wasn't fun to witness, but it had never scared me, not like the fear I heard in that voice. My fingers froze on the handle of the library door.

It was wrenched open from the inside, pulled from my hand by Dr. Castillo. He was wearing a look I'd never seen before—not during any of my medical emergencies—panic.

"Penelope." He breathed my name out like a prayer. "Thank God."

"Something's wrong."

"Shh." He cut me off with a finger to my lips and a tense whisper. "You have to come with me."

"I can't." I had to get to Garrett. *You can't be late.* I had to get to him, and then I had to see who was screaming.

"No, you have come to with me. Now." He propelled me down the hallway and into an exam room with a bruising grip on my arm. That alone was jarring enough to make me obey. That plus the shouts getting louder on the other side of the clinic doors.

Spread out.

Check upstairs.

"Penelope, do you trust me?" Dr. Castillo asked—his voice was barely a whisper but thick with tension.

I nodded, listening for more words, more voices.

"Good." In a swift motion he swabbed my arm and uncapped a needle. "Hold still."

The needle wasn't attached to an empty test tube waiting for my blood. It was a full syringe. Whatever was in it burned. And the effect was instantaneous. A distancing from myself. An iciness in my veins. A detachment that made sounds echo and my fear turn hollow. Just before I gave into the urge to shut my eyes I noticed the light above the exam room door. It had turned on. Red.

Warning red.

Blood red.

CHAPTER 17

My mouth was dry. Like someone had swabbed up all my saliva with paper towels, leaving behind dust and fibers and not even enough spit to swallow or wet my lips. I coughed.

"Penelope. It's Dr. Castillo, can you open your eyes?"

I managed it for a moment. Barely long enough to confirm what the voice had said—yes, Dr. Castillo, but also a stranger—before they shut again. My brain worked slower, memories clicking into place one puzzle piece at a time.

Screams. Dr. Castillo. A syringe. Blackness. Garrett.

Don't be late, princess.

"Penelope."

My eyes flickered open again, looking for the clock that hung across from the beds in the clinic. They met twilight. Sky. Trees. Telephone poles. Fences. And sunset glare on glass and—I shut my eyes again.

This was not the clinic.

"Wh—" I tried to swallow. My tongue was too big, filling my mouth like an uncooperative, floppy, dead thing. "Wh-where?"

"Penelope, open your eyes, little girl."

I did. Blinking and pausing, I traced the lines of the walls up to a low ceiling. To double doors and their small rounded windows. Followed the lines back to where Dr. Castillo sat on a bench beside me with a stranger. In an ambulance.

When I focused on him, he smiled at me. "Good girl. Welcome back."

The stranger was a distinguished Asian man with gray hair and a suit. His face tugged at my memory, but I couldn't place him.

"How about some water?" Dr. Castillo held out a cup with a straw.

I wanted it. Desperately wanted something to cool the fire in my throat and unglue the parts of my mouth that felt like nearly set cement. But I'd never been in an ambulance. This wasn't right. It wasn't where I was supposed to be.

"You . . . drugged . . . me."

Dr. Castillo looked down, his eyes falling on a spot on my arm. "I'm sorry I had to do that."

I wanted to press up off this table. React to the threat of the situation. Dig my cell phone out of my pocket and hit the panic button. It would trigger a GPS tracker, and I'd have a Ward here within . . .

I didn't know where "here" was. I didn't know how long I'd been unconscious or how long it would take a Ward to arrive.

I didn't know what would happen in the meantime.

Why was that stranger staring at me with such concern and fear?

And my fingers were clumsy. Struggling to even open and close, never mind dig around in my pocket to retrieve the phone.

Dr. Castillo held out the water again. "You'll feel better if you drink. And it's good you're moving your fingers. Can you move your toes too? The sooner you can do that, the better. We need to start driving again."

I'd always thought the panic button was ridiculous—I never went anywhere. The only time I'd ever pressed it had been a mistake, when I was trying to wriggle it into a too-small pocket on tight pants. Al and Mick had thundered into my bedroom with such force that the knob on the backside of the door had been embedded in my wall.

I hoped it was Al who came to rescue me. I could get consoling words from my parents later. Garrett could almost touch me and reassure me I was okay after that, but first I wanted Al, with all his intimidation and not an ounce of humanity. His ruthlessness would get me home, wouldn't pause or hesitate just because my betrayer was Family . . . had been practically *family*.

I managed to close my hand around the square shape of my phone through the fabric of my jeans. Clumsy fingers grasped for the round button on the lower right side. I needed to hold it in for five seconds. Five seconds and alarms would ring back at the estate.

Dr. Castillo put his hand on mine. "Don't worry, I turned it off. If we'd had time to stop, or could've done so inconspicuously, I'd have thrown it away. Do so tonight, please."

"Don't. Worry?"

He was still trying to press the cup in my other hand. I took it, then threw it weakly back at him.

He flinched as the cup landed harmlessly on my leg. The plastic lid popped off and water and ice chips sprayed across my jeans; some bounced into the stranger's lap.

"Take me home." I wanted to add a "please." Mother's etiquette training practically commanded it. But Father would never request something of a kidnapper, he'd *demand* it.

"Penelope, I can't. I know you're confused and scared, but I need you to trust me. I'm keeping you safe. I did this to save you. I promise."

"Save me?"

"I'm so sorry, Penelope, about everything that has happened. That I have to be the one to tell you. That I couldn't save you all."

The stranger shifted uncomfortably. Looked away from me and out the window.

Save us?

"Carter?"

Dr. Castillo opened and closed his mouth a few times. Finally he shook his head in resignation. Reached over and turned on a radio. Thumbed it to a satellite news station and turned it up.

"Maybe I should wait outside for this." The man opened the back door of the ambulance and climbed out. I devoured every inch of the landscape. It was an anywhere road. An anywhere field. An endless line of phone poles pointed each direction without revealing which way led home.

Where and why? I should've been asking that. I should've been asking a million questions and distracting him while I maneuvered the panic button into my grip, turned my phone back on, and called in a rescue party.

But I was too busy holding my breath. Listening.

—receiving reports of bodies found on the Landlow estate. You may remember that their eldest child, Carter, was murdered just two weeks ago. His death remains unsolved. His body was found outside the gates of the family's estate with two bullets in his head and Chinese characters carved into his chest.

The reports we're getting off the police scanners suggest there were three new bodies found today. Malcolm and Abigail Landlow—

It no longer mattered that my mouth was glued shut, because I could no longer breathe. I'd gone to pieces. I'd dissolved and couldn't be whole again. I couldn't possibly be whole, not when the radio was telling me my world was irreparably broken and gone.

The third body was found in an upstairs bedroom and is believed to be their only remaining child, seventeen-year-old Penelope.

"I'm not dead?"

These were important words. Maybe they shouldn't be a question, but they were.

"No," Dr. Castillo agreed. "No, you're not. That was why I

drugged you: you were fighting me and I didn't have time to argue; I needed to get you off the property as fast as possible and undetected."

Malcolm Landlow was heir to the Landlow spa fortune, though he and his father before him were rumored to be involved in the illegal and controversial process of trafficking in and transplanting human organs and tissue—a topic that is becoming increasingly heated with Vice President Forman championing a bill that would legalize the buying and selling of organs for transplant—

"They're not—they can't be. Father, Mother . . . they're fine."

He used the sleeve of his white jacket to wipe the ice and pooled water off my jeans. Then pulled a blanket from some compartment and tucked it up around me. I realized I was shaking.

"I'm so sorry, Penelope, but they're not."

"No. You're wrong. The report is wrong. I'm not dead. They're fine."

He shook his head.

"But—" I managed to move, enough to slap blindly at the radio, succeeding only in turning the volume to blasting levels.

—bring you further details about the gruesome—

Dr. Castillo turned it off. "Penny, they're not okay. I wish I could say differently, but I heard the gunshots. I saw part of it on the clinic's security monitors. The warning light went on—your father must have triggered it—and I had to get you out."

"You called me Penny." It was a stupid thing to say. An idiotic, nonsensical thing. There was so much my brain should be processing right now, how could *this* be what I fixated on?

He put a hand on my wrist, checking my pulse. "We can't keep the ambulance parked here any longer without drawing notice. It's not safe. Can you sleep any more? Would you like another shot?"

"No."

I was fighting so hard to stay awake. Stay in this moment and make it make sense. I could feel the pain. Practically even see it. It was just away from me. Just shy of settling in my mind and on my skin and making me realize what this all meant—

I started to scream.

CHAPTER 18

I screamed until my voice gave out and Dr. Castillo flashed another needle like a threat. The stranger climbed into the passenger seat and the doctor drove. Alone in the back of the ambulance, alone in the world.

I was still screaming; it just wasn't audible. Inside my head was a chaotic orchestra of wails and whimpers and sobs.

Words like "orphan," "forsaken," "defenseless," "murdered" drifted across the front of my mind. They were nonsensical, detached from all meaning. The world itself had lost its meaning. This was not the way my story went: *Once upon a time Penelope lived and they did not.*

The invalid did not outlive her vivacious brother. The powerful father and gracious mother did not get gunned down in their own home. The gregarious nurse—because it must've been

Caroline—did not get killed because she wanted to borrow a dress to impress a date.

Home. The place we'd celebrated seventeen Easters and Thanksgivings, Christmases and New Year's Eves. The place where I'd left my first tooth under my pillow and later found it in Mother's jewelry box nestled beside diamonds and pearls like it was equally precious. Where my and Carter's heights were marked on the inside of his bathroom closet door. Where Garrett and I had spent the afternoons after rainstorms rescuing worms from drying up on the patio. Where the three of us had played epic games of hide-and-seek. I'd been so good at hiding that sometimes I fell asleep before they found me curled up beneath Father's desk, or behind the racks of evening gowns in Mother's closet.

I wanted to hide there now. Behind that row of silks and satins and sequins, my cheek brushed by the slippery fabric and my nose tickled by the ghostly traces of her perfume.

The home I was fleeing.

The home where I left Garrett waiting behind the pool shed. He had to be okay—he *had* to be. But did he know *I* was?

Because home was also where Caroline was being zipped into a body bag with my name on it.

The ambulance stopped in a parking lot in an industrial area. It was too similar to my last outing with Carter, when the air had also been full of secrets and gunshots.

I looked out the window with wild eyes. The only other vehicle was an idling town car. I flinched when the ambulance doors opened and Dr. Castillo and the stranger stepped back in.

"This is Tom Tanaka, I should have introduced him earlier. He's one of your father's—" He paused to swallow and seemed to lose his train of thought.

"I was at the estate for an incision check," the man said gently. "We met briefly a few months ago, before I had my transplant."

"Of course. You're looking very well, Mr. Tanaka." The words were automatic. A script. A very inappropriate script.

But as a VIP client he had the breeding or money to recognize and ignore it, nodding briefly before saying, "I'd like to help you if you'll let me."

He and Dr. Castillo began to outline a plan: car/driver, a hotel room they'd reserved under a fake name, cash—they pulled this from their wallets. My credit cards and cell must not be used—get rid of them. Get rid of all forms of ID. I must be—for all intents and purposes—dead.

But sedative drugs and grief don't lend themselves to comprehension. I blinked against the mental fog. "But what do I *do*?"

They didn't have an answer. Their plans and aid would end once I stepped out of this ambulance and into the other car.

I stared at Dr. Castillo. "Alone?" This was as taboo as bungee jumping or hang gliding. I was never alone. Alone was forbidden. Father would have a fit—

I doubled over, wrapped both hands around my stomach so the sob threatening to tear me in half couldn't escape.

"Penelope, you have to understand. I love you like you were my own daughter—but what about my children? My wife? If they realize I smuggled you out in the ambulance with

Mr. Tanaka . . . *No one* can know I helped you escape. And they can't know you're alive."

"Who are *they*? Who did this?"

He shook his head. "I wish I knew. And until we do, you have to hide. Stay in the hotel, order room service, and be safe. I'll be in touch as soon as I can."

His answer turned my whole world into a boogeyman. Anyone could be the bad guy. Anyone could be coming for me with a gun. And if *they* knew I was alive—then I wouldn't be for much longer. Goose bumps surfaced all over my body, and I wished I could scoot into the corner. *Keep your back to the wall. Face the entrances. See everyone before they see you.* Father's advice. I'd never get to hear him say it again.

With autopilot acceptance, I thanked the men for their rolls of cash. I smoothed them and added them to the inside pocket of my purse where they nestled next to the fat stack of bills I'd plundered from my unicorn bank this morning.

I let Dr. Castillo help me down from the ambulance and hand me my purse. I nodded at Mr. Tanaka's good luck wishes and when Dr. Castillo opened the town car's door for me, saying, "Be brave. I'll come for you as soon as I can."

"Wait!" I said. "My counts? Before Carter, I thought I might be heading into a remission—" I saw his face and didn't bother to continue.

"You don't need to worry about your counts right now. They're . . . okay. It's been less than two days since your last infusion. I'm sure this will be . . ." He couldn't finish that sentence. It wouldn't ever be "better" or "resolved" or "over." And the driver was watching us, listening. "I'll see you before you need more."

He kissed the cheek I tilted toward him, accepted my flat-voiced "Thank you," and was gone.

It was only after the door shut behind me—after the engine started and the tires began to put distance between me and everything I'd ever known—that my veneer of mannerly obedience cracked and reality started to filter in.

I was shivering, shaking, and they were gone. All gone. I couldn't think about it. Not with a hawk-eyed driver who kept offering to turn down the A/C and asking me what type of music would cheer me up. His words were probably friendly, but all I felt was the edge of danger, the unknown threat that hung like a mystery over my whole life.

What would Father do in this situation? What would he tell me to do? This was the stupidest of questions, and it tore at my throat, trying to unlock the sobs trapped there. If Father were here, I never would be. I'd be home protected, coddled—or would I be running away with Garrett? His plan now seemed idiotic edging toward reckless—my parents would have worried so much and all it would have proved was our immaturity, our lack of leadership ability.

Garrett . . .

He'd been waiting behind the pool house. He wasn't near the fighting. He couldn't be hurt. The radio said *three* bodies. And if he'd heard—but no, Caroline's identity would be cleared up soon and then he'd come for me. He'd come and he'd get me and he'd tell me he could keep me safe and he would.

He would.

But Father . . . he'd never approve of *this*. An overly concerned stranger bringing me to a hotel—knowing where I was. When I was most vulnerable.

"You okay, miss?" The driver turned around at a red light to ask. "You sick? That guy was talking about infusions. My cousin had to get something like that. He had the big C, ya know?"

Outside my window twilight was descending, suburbia was bleeding into the urban. We were heading toward the city. I wanted to open a map app, trace our route, predict our destination, orient myself with all the landmarks that were familiar from computer screens and daydreams. But I couldn't use my phone.

"How long until we reach the hotel?"

"At least twenty minutes. Maybe more if there's traffic on the bridge. I'm doing my best."

"Thank you." I broke his gaze in the rearview mirror by turning to stare out the window, willing the skyline to appear sooner and the wheels to turn faster.

But nothing was easier when the skyscrapers loomed closer. When my windows lit up with lights from buildings and billboards, and the air was filled with horns, conversations on the sidewalks, music.

The car pulled over in front of a hotel. It was all gleaming windows, crisp black awnings, and immaculate facade. Clean, expensive, safe. Except I didn't feel safe.

It was simpler to allow the driver to open my door, carry my purse, follow me into the overly air-conditioned lobby, and hand me his business card than it was to resist—and I needed to save my energy, stockpile it for the sobs and grief that threatened to break through my survival numbness at any moment.

"I'd be happy to be your driver again. Anytime. I wrote my personal number on the back of the card in case you need anything." His eyes were too interested. He moved to touch me, clasp my hand, invade my personal space.

I slipped around the other side of the marble table that stood in the lobby—its shiny black circle looking like the center of a bull's-eye topped with a vase of blood-red flowers.

The color made my throat clench.

"Thank you for your assistance," I said in a thin echo of Mother's voice, the one she used for dismissing event staff or gossipy wives of other Family members.

The one I'd never hear again.

But it was Father's voice bellowing in my head right now—demanding I attend to my safety first, foremost, manners be damned. Safety, then tears. I wasn't safe in a hotel where this creepy stranger of a driver could locate me. Had eavesdropped on a conversation that included the words "Carter" and "infusion," and might be able to piece together the rest as soon as he watched the news. And what did I know about Mr. Tanaka other than that he happened to be the VIP who was on the estate the day my life detonated?

I couldn't stay here. I had to get out. Get off-grid. Out of sight. Until Garrett came.

I exited the lobby, ducking behind a couple pushing a stroller and wrangling way too many kids. I had a good mental picture of the apartment on a map, but where was *I*? I'd kept track as best I could during the drive and thought there was water to my left and a park to my right. Which meant I was probably on the Upper West Side facing north. But I could also be on the Upper East Side facing south. I walked to the closest corner and exhaled a shaky breath when I read the street signs—Upper West Side, good. I did the mental math of blocks-to-miles; the apartment was walkable, about two miles. And all I'd need to focus on was watching the street numbers increase, watching traffic and walk signals.

I took one last look over my shoulder at the hotel's friendly brightness.

And then I walked. Putting each foot down with a mental chastisement—*Not yet. A little longer. You can fall apart soon. But you're not quite there yet.*

A few more minutes of focusing on the directions and cross-streets Garrett and Carter had mentioned on our last night together. A few more blocks of real estate prices falling and crime rates rising. A few more shadows that made me jump as people detached themselves from walls or alleys, melted in and out of the night—ignoring me like I ignored them: a see-no-evil agreement that clung to these streets.

The building was both a relief and more run-down than I remembered. And I couldn't go teary-eyed because it made it so much harder to locate the key attached to the top of the mailbox and let myself through the door. The stairwell's floor was cold against my skin and tacky with grime, but I could focus on that. I *should* focus on that, on the size of the dust balls and the sticky green spill that glued them to the tile. Those were good things to think about while I fished around for the second key below the steps. Not the fact that this apartment—Carter's "clubhouse"—would save my life but not his—not my parents'.

And the stairs, I thought about each one, about the strength it cost to lift my feet and find the next riser.

Finally I was standing in front of the apartment door, the last barrier between me and everything I promised myself I could feel when I arrived.

CHAPTER 19

I opened the door to a hushed place. A place that felt hollow in the absence of Carter and Garrett: the space they occupied, the air they breathed, the noise they made as they banged and stomped and claimed this world as their own.

Now it seemed near sacred. This was Carter's. He'd shared it with me the night he died. It felt wrong to touch anything, to move anything. I locked the door and leaned against the back of it, trying to picture him here. Bring to mind a ghost or shade of a memory.

I wanted it to feel like a shrine, a place where his presence and memories were stronger—strong enough to protect me from the truth.

But it's hard to make relics of a coffee table and a couch, a takeout menu from a Chinese restaurant. A cardboard coaster from a bar. And in the end, I was as sturdy as a house of cards.

I put my purse on the counter and glimpsed the Carter doll inside. I'd been so wrong not to bring Mother's and Father's too. And Rumpel—I craved the familiar security of his fur and smell. I folded in on myself, curled up on the floor like that could protect the parts of me that were broken and would never heal.

I watched the hours move through tear-swollen eyes from my place on the throw rug. Shadows crept, lengthened, shrank. And nothing changed. Nothing could. Mine wasn't a reality that could be reversed or corrected. I had nothing left.

Except to breathe and make sure they didn't get me too.

Garrett would come for me. On a white horse, through an enchanted forest guarded by dragons, wicked witches, FBI agents, or murderers—it didn't matter what the obstacles were, as soon as he learned I was alive, he would come. He would.

It took a few more hours, but then I found the energy to begin to look around.

Energy that turned from respectful worship to heretical frenzy as I tore open the fridge door—the same few bottles of jam, pickles, block of cheese, mustard and soy sauce packets. I searched through all the cabinets: mismatched mugs; piles of paper plates and individually wrapped plastic cutlery; the packs of crackers that come with soup; a box of sugary marshmallow cereal; a bag of Carter's favorite dill pickle chips; cups, beer steins, bottle and can openers.

I pulled and pulled on the locked freezer until I worried my fingertips would bruise, which made my frustration change to helpless fury. Except I wasn't a helpless thing: I grabbed the fire extinguisher from beneath the sink and bashed the lock. The impact vibrated up my arms, but I kept going. Hitting, and hitting, and hitting, and hitting, until the latch lay in pieces around my feet. I didn't pause to second-guess or gag over what *could be* inside, I threw open the lid, pulse racing and panting for the answers.

It was empty. Nothing but ice crystals. I slammed the dented lid and left the kitchen; collapsed sideways onto the thronelike chair and cried. Sobbed. With my face buried in my knees and my shoulders shaking. All the emotions inside felt bigger than me, and letting them out felt dangerous—like I'd deflate.

Carter.

Mother.

Father.

Caroline.

I mourned for each one separately because the collective grief was too all-consuming to even consider.

I was alone. And feeling too small in this chair that felt too large. But since I'd sat here last time, it seemed like where I should stay. Where I was allowed to stay. With a gulp and a last blubber, I shut my eyes and stopped fighting against the easy oblivion of sleep.

I woke up stiff and disoriented. Sat, stretched, and banged my wrist on something in the dark. A bruise I could ill afford and which caused new tears—or provided an excuse to cry again.

I stood and carefully edged across the room, fumbling for a light switch or a lamp. Finding one, I turned it on and then went around the living room and kitchen, turning on *all* the lights.

Then I went a step further: opened the three closed doors at the end of the hall. The doors that had been off-limits during my last trip here. I don't know what I was expecting, but it wasn't a bathroom, a bedroom, and a room that was half office and half twin bed.

It didn't matter that it was eleven p.m., that I'd been gone more than twenty-four hours, or that I had no clue what was happening on the estate—there would be answers in those rooms. That was enough to kick my exhaustion into frenzy. I started in the bedroom. The closet contained clothing for Carter and maybe Garrett too, clothing for me. But not my typical style—usually I stuck to pastels. At least lighter colors, smaller prints. And never, ever anything purple. Nothing that would emphasize bruises. The clothing Carter had bought me was bright patterns, bold colors. Accessories that weren't dainty. Jewelry that wasn't pearl or diamond. Shoes with heels and prints and pointy and open toes. Apparently in my life outside the estate I was to be trendy. Brave. Noticeable.

There was little else in the room that made sense or told me anything about Carter's life here. A few of his favorite novels on a bedside table. An untouched book of Sudoku puzzles on the dresser, a half-finished one left in the closet. Nothing personal, nothing identifying. No mail beyond catalogs addressed to "current resident." No photographs.

There had to be answers in his office. I wanted a laptop with a password of "password" and a file called "Everything Pen Needs to Know." A manila folder with a list of the bad guys and a second list that told me what to do next. An instruction manual for grief annotated with his comments and provisions.

No. I needed more than this imaginary list or manual. I didn't know how to live without my family. And if I didn't have a family, I didn't know who I was anymore.

But the desk was pure decoration. It had a calendar with days *X*'d and circled . . . with no explanation for either. It had a bank mug with a few pens, a handful of tangled rubber bands and paper clips, and a small key topped with a silver stag's head . . . probably to the lock on the freezer I'd smashed. Two blank notebooks, and a third whose spiral binding sprouted a few of the spiky strips left behind when a page is torn out. I tucked this under my arm and prayed the remaining pages were full of . . . something helpful.

And in the bottom left drawer nestled beside a roll of cash the size of my wrist: a gun.

My fingers continued to reach for it. Not getting the message from my brain because my brain was too horrified to process this properly. My fingertips brushed the metal before I gagged and shuddered backward. Slammed the desk drawer, backed out of the room, and slammed that door too.

No.

Carter should not own a gun. Not Garrett either, but he *was* a Ward, no matter how much I tried to forget it. He had guns and bullets in his DNA. But not Carter. Not my brother.

I dropped the notebook in the hall, ran into the bathroom, and retched. Spitting out sour saliva and making my stomach muscles ache with the spasms.

As I leaned my cheek against the wall, I couldn't swallow the worst thought of all: And if he'd owned a gun, why didn't he have it with him? Why hadn't he used it? Why wasn't he alive? If Father had carried a gun, would he be?

I rinsed my mouth and washed my hands. Carter's soap smelled like tangerines, which made no sense. He hated scented soap—said if he wanted to smell like vanilla, he'd rub himself with cookies, and if he wanted to smell like fruit or flowers, he'd douse himself in teenybopper body splash.

Or was that Father?

I couldn't remember, and there was no one left to ask.

I retched again.

Was I really forgetting my family? Already?

What was the last thing each of them had said to me? That I'd said to them? What were they wearing? What did I give them on their last birthdays? What were their last presents to me? I needed to know so those items could become that much more precious, but I couldn't remember and couldn't retrieve them from the estate even if I did.

I stumbled back into the hall and grabbed Carter's notebook. Yanked the mechanical pencil from its binding and flipped it open to find only blank, blank, blank pages.

I labeled three in a row: *Mother, Father, Carter.*

I was the last Landlow. If I forgot anything, then it was gone forever. I couldn't forget—I couldn't fail at this.

I scrawled lists—

- *Mother's favorite perfume: Hermès, 24 Faubourg*
- *Father's favorite musical: Guys and Dolls*
- *Carter's favorite teams: Giants, Mets, Celtics, Devils*

- *Carter hated getting his hair cut and would put it off until Father threatened to do it for him. His reasoning: the clippers tickled.*
- *Mother had a cleaning staff at her disposal, but when she was stressed she liked to vacuum. "It drowns out my thoughts—sometimes it's good to not be able to hear yourself think."*
- *It was really Father who hit the golf ball through the solarium roof. He'd been showing off his range with a new driver. He blamed Mick, but Mother knew and indulged his cover story.*
- *Carter was afraid of heights—they made him vomit. He'd thrown up on Ferris wheels and over the side of the Grand Canyon.*
- *Mother collected tea sets—she had beautiful ones, even a Revere Silver—but her favorite was chipped ceramic from a department store, because her godmother had bought it.*
- *Father sang in an award-winning a cappella group in college, but never told his family because Grandfather thought singing was "soft." And he ate mustard on everything: pretzels, salads, seafood, steak, toast.*

All these and more, pages more. When I paused, my fingers ached from gripping the pencil and my back complained about my stooped-over posture on the hard hall floor.

It wasn't enough, not nearly enough, but it was a start.

CHAPTER 20

For two days I added to my memory log and watched the door. Waited for Garrett to walk through it and whisk me away to safety. I expected him with every tick of the vintage black-and-white cat clock whose eyes and tail twitched away seconds of my life. I held my breath and listened for knocks or keys in the lock, but they never came.

He never came. The only place he appeared was in the memories on the pages of my notebook. His childhood was knotted up with my own, as tangled as my old Slinky, which he and Carter had used to play tug-of-war. He'd been the fifth person in my stick-figure, crayoned family portraits. The one who taught me to tie my shoes. The one who cheated to help me find more eggs on Easter.

He would come for me. He had to come for me.

But after the cheese, cereal, chips, and oyster crackers were gone, I was faced with making a meal out of soy sauce or leaving the four walls that were crowding in on me. I hadn't followed Dr. Castillo's advice and thrown away my cell, but I hadn't turned it on either. And while I couldn't bring myself to toss my license or credit cards, I hid all forms of ID behind a gift card in my wallet.

I had no similar hesitation when it came to my medical ID bracelet. I removed that shackle and tossed it in the bottom of Carter's trash can.

I flipped over a take-out menu and scrawled a note.

G,
I'm here. Please wait, I'll be back soon.

I centered it on the coffee table, slipped the keys onto a paper clip and into my pocket, and tiptoed out. I slunk down the stairs and reminded myself to breathe with every step that took me farther from the building. I skipped the bodega Garrett had warned me about and went into one on the next corner.

Bread, peanut butter, milk, and a smile from the clerk—these were the things I took back to the apartment with me.

Seeing the untouched note threw my claustrophobia into overdrive. A quick sandwich and I was back out the door, down the stairs, and burying myself in the foot traffic.

New York City had a rhythm, but I couldn't quite master it. I couldn't figure out the pattern for merging into the streams of pedestrian traffic. When to chance crossing during a blinking signal and when to pause. How to purchase an umbrella from a street vendor during a quick summer storm, then manage it and my purse without becoming a liability to myself and everyone around me.

They were the same numbered streets and avenues from the maps I'd studied through so many infusions. The same districts I'd dreamed about—but they were different in reality than on a screen. My theoretical knowledge of the city didn't translate.

The steps of the crowds hit like a metronome, but I never could match their beat. Others looked forward, at phones, at buildings in the distance. They smoked cigarettes, juggled packages, strollers, dog leashes, conversations. I looked sideways, skipped and skittered in diagonals. Dodged and danced and did everything I could to avoid elbows and heels and shoulders and purses.

The brush-against, the casual collision. It was a part of city life. To the extent that stopping to say "excuse me" was irrelevant and unnecessary. But I couldn't afford those bumps. Not without a steady supply of immunoglobulin. I didn't need a CBC to tell me that if my counts had started at "okay," they were only getting worse with every day that passed.

I didn't fit in. Nothing about me did. Not my steps. Not my clothing—neither the clothing I would have worn if I had access to my pastel wardrobe, nor the brightly patterned dresses left for me in the closet. Everything here was black. Black on black. Black as an accent. In accessories. Always somewhere. But not on me.

And I talked too much. To strangers at crosswalks. To dog walkers. To nannies and parents. To the man standing between me and the trash can when I went to throw away a gum wrapper. To the person handing out flyers on a corner.

I knew I was supposed to be keeping my head down. I knew it. I understood it. I woke wet-eyed several times each night from nightmarish reminders.

Still, I couldn't stop myself from having conversations with everyone. Conversations that validated I still existed; I was still here. Conversations with the clerk at the drug store where I bought hair dye—after I'd already consulted with three different shoppers about color selection. With the businessmen lining up in front of and behind me for morning coffee. The harried baristas who could barely keep up with the chaos of latte, double-shot, extra-dry, nonfat, half-caf, soy milk, almond milk, no milk, medium-in-a-large-cup. With the nannies in the park where I sat on a bench and drank mine as slowly as possible—in no rush to return and see the apartment empty and my note to Garrett still unread. I toed the line between friendly and flirty with the guys who played Hacky Sack in front of a private school, then practiced the art of polite rejection when they tried to slip me phone numbers. I offered extra smiles to the waitress at the diner where I stopped for orange juice and toast. She looked like she wanted to shuffle through the remainder of her shift and go home and bury herself in a pack of cigarettes, an afghan, and a romance novel—but when I asked for honey, using the name on her tag, "Shanice," she paused long enough for me to launch into an explanation of how Mother always buttered my toast, spread it with honey, sprinkled it with cinnamon, then cut it into fourths with the crusts removed to look like hearts.

"That's a lot of work for bread," she said with a grudging smile.

"She only did it when I was sick," I admitted, twirling a strand of my newly dark-brown hair. "Homesick counts as sick, right? Because I really crave that today."

She took my plate and I added this detail to Mother's pages in the notebook, finishing just before Shanice came back with it exactly as I'd described. Her hearts might not have been as perfect as Mother's and she was a little heavy-handed with the cinnamon, but if I closed my eyes while I bit I could pretend I was back home in my bed with a breakfast tray and Mother seated in a chair beside me.

My teary-eyed "thank you" earned me a pat on the cheek. Even with her cigarette and bacon-grease-and-coffee smell, she felt like a mom. I needed that, and told her as much.

"I needed it too." She wiped her eyes. "My youngest just moved out. Do you think he calls home? Never. You be a good girl and call your mama, okay? Tell her you need her. Tell her you love her."

I sucked on the inside of my cheek and nodded, wishing oh so badly that I could.

I should have been lying low. Waiting. But there were only so many times I could pace the dimensions of the apartment without going crazy. Only so many times I could imagine Garrett walking through that door armed with answers and comfort. Only so many times I could reread the anecdotes and lists in my notebook without panicking when I couldn't come up with anything new to add. Without dissolving into a mush of memories and grief and missing.

When I was moving, when I was out in the city with its heartbeat and its energy and its demands and promises, then I could pretend this was all some elaborate game. My parents weren't dead. Neither was Carter. I wasn't exiled awaiting who-knows-what, with an unnamed, unknown threat hanging above my head.

This wasn't really my life. This couldn't really be my life.

So it all must be a dream.

And as long as I kept moving, I could believe it.

CHAPTER 21

It took me five days to realize my major mistake: if Garrett wasn't coming, Dr. Castillo was my only way out—and I'd left the hotel where he knew how to reach me. I didn't even know the name I was supposed to check in under—it had been written on a scrap of paper I'd torn and tossed in various trash cans on my walk from the hotel to the apartment—so I couldn't call to see if there were messages left for me.

Instead I went to a random street corner—one as far from my building as I'd dared to venture. With stress-stiffened fingers, I turned on my cell phone, panicking through the moments it took to load, and then jotted down Dr. Castillo's number. I jammed my thumb on the Off button, already moving and putting space between myself and the corner. Looking around with fear-wide eyes, like *if* the mysterious "They" were monitoring the GPS on my phone, they had the ability to teleport and become an immediate threat.

Fifteen minutes later I finally located a pay phone, punched in the doctor's number, and prayed while it rang. Voice mail—but not his usual message.

"You've reached Doctor Darius Castillo. At the *pause,* leave a *careful* message. You can *count* on a response at my earliest convenience. Please be patient."

I didn't leave a message. I could hear his warning in the awkward cadence, his desperately inflected words—words he knew I hated, words he knew I'd notice. I wondered how much it had cost him not to say, "Penelope, be careful!" at the end. How long until the last bit of patience I was clutching like a kite string flew away?

On the walk home I did something I'd vowed not to: I bought a newspaper. I would *not* bring it back in the apartment—where there was no audience to keep me from falling to pieces or obsessing over the photos and articles—instead I sat on a bench and unfolded it with shaking fingers.

I stared at the pictures on page seven: grim-faced officers standing beside the estate's fence, which was decorated with police tape and also flowers and teddy bears. From clients? I couldn't hold the paper steady enough to read the article, but I caught headlines and quotes and pieced together some of the horror.

Mick Ward was still in the hospital with a head injury and a gunshot wound. He'd been found in the gatehouse, knocked unconscious and shot through the arm.

Mother—dead on the patio. Killed first.

Father—dead in the hallway outside the library. The

gunshots and blood patterns indicated he'd crawled inside the house while the killers continued to shoot.

Caroline—killed with a single bullet to the back of the head in my bedroom.

They still hadn't identified her—she was still listed as *me*. She'd been buried as me—the funerals had been yesterday—there was a photo from that as well: Garrett in front of a gravestone. His face a shattering portrait of unchecked sorrow. Al standing behind him, a tight-knuckled grip on his shoulder, his head bowed.

I wasn't dead.

I wasn't.

That night I left the chair in the living room and slept in the bedroom—not the spare with the gun, but in the bed that had been Carter's. It was also the first night my nightmares weren't just blood and grief, but also choking panic and tinted bruise-purple. It had been almost a week; what if no one ever came for me?

I needed a plan. An ally. I couldn't do this on my own. Around five a.m., when the pale pinks and buttery yellows of a new day began to seep through the blinds, I thought of one. It required a repetition of yesterday's risks: random corner, turning on my cell, retrieving a number from my contacts, shutting it off, and wandering until I found a pay phone.

I dialed, bit my lip harder with each ring.

"Hi."

I knew the number was correct, but the voice on the other end was wrong.

"Um, is Kelly there?" I held my breath and imagined the worst: she'd changed her number, lost her phone.

"Sure, hang on," said the girl's voice, "I'll go get her." I heard the garbled sound of someone covering the mouthpiece and a holler of "Kelly! Where are you? You left your phone in the kitchen again."

Caleigh. It had to be Kelly's sister, Caleigh. She was my age, but my only connection to her was through Kelly's stories. I breathed out a wish for a life like hers: school, friends, health, safety. In every political ad and campaign stop she'd practically glowed with happiness. Even the media hadn't found a way to pick her apart.

"Hello?"

I let go of stupid wishes and smiled. Kelly's greeting was all sunshine and innocence and unlimited friendliness. "Hi! It's Penny."

"You can't be Penny." All the excitement drained out of her voice, leaving her sounding pinched and sad. "Penny died."

"No, wait—" but the line was dead and she didn't answer when I called back. I slammed the phone down, catching my palm on the hook of the receiver and cursing with frustration, pain, and fear. I couldn't get hurt right now, couldn't be careless. Yet my skin was already splotchy red.

I vowed to call Kelly again the next day and the day after that. As many days as it took. I *had* to make her listen, had to get her father on the phone. I had no other options.

Day two of my calls landed me at a pay phone in the lobby of a hospital. I badly wanted to go up to the desk and ask if they'd give me an infusion. Or a CBC. It had been nine days since I'd had either, and my dropping counts were depicted all over my body—the daily bumps and contacts of city life transforming my skin to abstract art in shades from lilac to indigo.

I wasn't at the stage where I could draw on skin with the slightest pressure, but I was close. The seams of my pants were imprinted in purple on my legs. And I was exhausted. The drenching fatigue of grief compounding and exaggerating the toll of my body fighting against itself.

If things weren't dire yet . . . they were close.

I dialed. "Hi, Kelly. It's really Penny Landlow. Please let me talk to your father."

"No," she said in a voice that cracked. "He says you *can't* be Penny. Stop being mean. Stop calling."

My emotions crossed from desperate impatience to guilt. I wished I could stop being mean, stop torturing the girl I considered a friend, but the next day I hunted down yet another pay phone—this time in a subway station—and pressed each number with regretful fingers.

"Kelly, please listen—"

My explanation was cut off midsentence by an angry voice from the phone's speaker. "I don't know who this is, or how you got this number—"

"Vice President Forman, it's me, Penelope."

"Penny is dead." His words seemed to echo despite the

footsteps, the turnstiles, the beeps of MetroCards being swiped, the coughs, the conversations.

"I can prove it," I whispered urgently. "My full name is Penelope Maeve Landlow."

"That's public record, and I'm hanging up."

"Would public record show *you* were the one who told me Maeve might mean "delicate," but it's also the name of a warrior queen?" I spit the words out in a rush, expecting to hear nothing—the empty sound of an empty line. And the line was silent—except for a sharp intake of breath. "Or how every time my father sees you—saw you—he'd ask Kelly if she was enjoying her kidney?"

"Penny?"

"Or how, just to annoy him, I 'forgot' to call you by your title. Even though you've told him and me a thousand times—"

We finished the sentence together, "She can call me Bob."

"Penny, *how*?"

"It was a nurse. Did you ever meet Caroline? She looked like me, but not enough to fool anyone for more than a second."

"How has this not been discovered?"

My heart sank. "I don't know, sir. I was hoping you'd have some insight." Caroline might not have been part of my family, but she deserved so much more than this. I'd spent hours lying awake, wrapped in guilt, and wondering how long her date had waited before deciding he'd been stood up, and whether friends, neighbors, or anyone had noticed her disappearance yet.

"I'll get people on it," said Bob. "But the fact that—" He

cleared his throat. "There are more immediate issues: Where are you? Are you okay?"

"I-I can't tell you where I am. I don't dare."

"Yes, that's probably best. How are you calling? Not your cell, I hope."

"No, a pay phone. I've only used pay phones."

"Those still exist?"

"A few. They're not easy to find."

"What do you need? How can I help?"

I leaned against the dirty metal surface of the phone. Relief unhinged my knees, made my voice go thin, filled my eyes with tears. In any other setting, people might have worried, they might have intervened or asked if I was okay. Here, no one noticed. I wasn't worth a second glance—less interesting than the person with the patriotic-colored Mohawk, or in an eighties prom dress, wearing a chain-mail shirt made from safety pins, the immaculate businessperson holding hands with a Goth, the homeless man toting bulging garbage bags, the guitarist pouring her heart into folk songs, the toddler screaming for a lollipop. I was part of the scenery; we were *all* part of the scenery.

I took a deep breath and answered his question. "Immunoglobulin. My platelet count is getting low—" I'd had a nosebleed that morning; it had taken forever for it to clot. And petechiae were spreading like poison ivy from my feet to my calves. "I need an infusion when my count drops below thirty thousand, and it's got to be under that, but I don't know what to do. It's not like I can walk into a hospital and give them the name of a dead girl."

"I'll figure out a way to get some to you. Are you safe?"

"I think so." I paused and considered this, then modified my answer. "I hope so."

"Do you want me to come get you? You know you're welcome to stay with my family. The girls would love to have your company."

Kelly would. But his second wife, Imee, whom I'd never met, and Caleigh, the spitting image of all-American perfection—I'm not sure they'd enjoy having their lives turned upside down for a criminal's daughter. Then there was the damage a connection with me would do to *him*.

"It would ruin the Organ Act. You having ties to the Landlows. Especially now." It was why Kelly's transplant had always been the most sacred of secrets. He could only be the public face of the movement to legalize the trade of human organs if no one knew about his daughter's black market past. "It would destroy your whole career if anyone found out."

"If you're not safe . . ." His hesitation answered all my questions. "Penny, I'd . . . I can't bring you to the vice president's residence, but maybe my house in Connecticut? Kelly's in DC with me, but Caleigh's there whenever she's home from school. We could attempt to keep you off radar."

"I don't want to put you in that position—not unless I absolutely have to."

"But you must let me help you."

This I would agree to; though beyond the medical, neither of us had a clue how. As I pumped the last of my change into the slot, he promised to assign more FBI resources to my parents' case. Then he hesitated again. "I wouldn't ask this if I thought I could get a trustworthy answer any other way—but Kelly's antirejection medicines, should I go to one of the other Families for more? I don't even know who's leading your Family now; do you?"

"It should be Nolan, but . . ." That wasn't safe to assume. Not with how the others regarded him. Not with his priorities being ideals first, Family second. Had he even returned from DC to attend the funerals? Or had he seen the murders as an opportunity to further his cause?

Maybe he'd even . . .

I choked on the idea. "Have you see Nolan Russell?"

Bob laughed. "The man's stuck tighter than a barnacle. He's a bit of a lost soul without your father. I'm not sure if he's turning to me for mentorship or just pouring his grief into a cause, but every time I turn around he's got new Organ Act literature or events for me. He says he hasn't talked to your Family at all. I don't think he has any plans to lead it."

I considered Bob's question. Could he trust what remained of my Family with his secret? Miles? Al? Frank? Ian? Could he trust the other Families at all? Kelly needed those drugs; all our patients did and *would* for the rest of their lives. "What's your supply?"

"Six months, like your father always insisted. I've heard rumors the Everlys are sniffing around some of your Family's former clients, and the Zhus."

That couldn't be true—the client lists were confidential. Other than Kelly Forman and Tom Tanaka, even I didn't know any of their real identities. And that's *if* Mr. Tanaka was his real name.

"Call Dr. Castillo directly. Talk *only* with him. He should be able to get Kelly's meds. And tell him I'm okay, please. He'll be able to give you specifics about what I need too."

"It'll take me a few days to coordinate the logistics of procurement and delivery. Can you wait?"

I swallowed a bitter laugh; waiting was all I could do lately.

"Yes," I answered, hoping it was true.

"Call me in three days; that should be sufficient." The vice president gave me his direct number. I wrote it on the inside cover of my memory journal. Thanked him. Hung up the phone, relieved some of the responsibility and fear had been lifted off my shoulders.

Three more days and I'd have immunoglobulin, but how many more days until my identity was mine again? Until "Penelope Maeve Landlow" wasn't a name on a gravestone or a walking target? Until I could figure out who she was in my post-family world.

CHAPTER 22

Routines are dangerous.

This was Family Facts 101. It was why Carter had changed up the route he drove back to college, and the ones he took across campus to his classes. He'd varied the restaurants he ate in, the cars he drove.

Don't form favorites. Don't develop habits. Don't get attached.

These had never applied to me before. There were only so many ways to walk from the house to the clinic. My lifestyle made me immune to most of the Family rules; it had been built on structure and routine—useful for surviving years of monotony, but I was having a hard time giving it up.

I went back to the diner to get updates on Shanice's son and his no-good girlfriend. Byron, the manager of my favorite coffee shop, teased me as I sipped through his list of flavors—so far my top pick was iced coffee with butterscotch syrup. I had a favorite dog park where I liked watching the pups scamper and play—and watching the dreadlocked and trendy owner of a dachshund and the librarian-chic owner of a Pomeranian fall for each other while holding leashes and lattes. And I loved taking the longer walk down to the Museum of Natural History in the mornings when the crowds were at their thinnest and it felt safe to be engrossed in the dioramas and displays.

Maybe routines were dangerous, but so were unpredictable environments. The whole city felt like a threat, so I forgave myself for carving out pieces of normal.

On day two of my wait, the dachshund's owner let the Pomeranian's enter her number in his phone. I left the park smiling. They'd started talking last week because I'd seen her practically drool as he flipped his neat dreads out of his face, and I said, "I'm not sure who's cuter, guy or dog. What do you think?" When I caught *him* checking her out, I'd been more blunt. "She's interested. Go talk to her."

It had taken nudges and encouragement, but they'd exchanged numbers, then both turned toward the bench where I sat with my cinnamon coffee; he winked, she mouthed "OMG."

So maybe I was too busy self-congratulating my matchmaking skills. Or too distracted by the feelings they stirred up—how much I missed Garrett, my MIA knight in shining armor. Or too caffeinated. Or too careless.

The excuse didn't matter as much as the result—that when

I saw my parents' picture on a TV in the window of an electronics store, I ran toward it.

I ignored the city noise: the beeping the yelling the conversations and steam and buzz and clip of shoes on sidewalks—I tuned out everything but the screen. It was a photo from a Family wedding last spring. One that hung framed above the mantel in the den. Who had given it to the media? Shouldn't they have had to ask permission before turning Mother's favorite family photo into something sandwiched between garish headlines—NEW LEADS IN THE LANDLOW MASSACRES—and a scrollbar of sensationalized facts?

But whom could they ask? Everyone in the photo—Mother, Father, Carter, me—was dead.

The photo changed, the headline too: THE BODYGUARD SPEAKS above a candid shot outside a hospital. Jacob was helping Mick into a car. His head was bandaged, his arm in a sling. Garrett stood alone by the driver's door, his expression so lost it made me ache.

I ran—desperate to get close enough to read the smaller print before the news changed to selling someone else's tragedy. And then—in an instant—I wasn't running, I was reeling from a collision.

My forehead smacked into a chin, my face slammed into collarbones, chest to chest. I'm sure Nolan taught me the physics that explained why the guy kept moving forward like a teenage Asian wrecking ball, and why I ricocheted off him and would have fallen if his hand hadn't shot out to grab my shoulder. Something about forces, objects in motion, momentum.

He'd hit me. Hard. But when the guy reached out to steady me by cupping my elbow with his other hand and I met his eyes, I swear it wasn't just dizziness caused by the impact. I'd known plenty of guys in the Family—the ones that weren't truly *my* family—and they were not unattractive. But looking up at this guy, my breath was literally stolen.

"Are you okay?"

I blinked a few times. Trying to clear my head in the moments my eyes were shut and then swooning anew each time they opened.

"That was some hit. I'm sorry." His fingers on my elbow slid around my arm, became a circlet of sensation as he tugged lightly, pulling me out of the crowd and against the building. Through the thin cotton of my red T-shirt, I felt rough brick at my back. He'd let go of my arm; was leaning one shoulder against the wall, shielding me from the crowd. "I've been hit like that before—in sports. It knocks the breath out of you. If you drop your chin a little, it will make it easier to breathe."

I obeyed. Dropping my chin meant not looking at him. It made it easier to breathe. Easier to think. And, *oh,* I hurt. From shoulder to stomach was a flaming line of pain. Inhaling deeply made me gasp. And the ache was radiating in larger and larger circles. This was not good. This was days-in-the-clinic-with-Dr.-Castillo-hovering bad.

I looked up at this stranger and my head swam again. It was the light. The contrast of the sunlight on his black hair. The way it played across his golden skin, the ridges of his cheekbones, and the depth in his eyes.

"You're not okay, are you? I'm so sorry. I really should've been paying attention where I was walking. What can I do?"

"I'm . . ." I coughed, shook my head, tried to chase away the dizziness. "I should get home."

"Let me take you."

"I'm fine, really." Except when I tried to straighten, I stumbled, scraping my elbow and forearm on the rough wall.

My blood was nearly the same color as my shirt.

"I'm sorry, but you don't look fine." He crouched slightly, peered into my eyes as if he were looking for a mystery. His irises were the rich color of coffee beans. At least I thought they were? It was getting harder to concentrate. Things were kaleidoscoping in and out of focus. "I wonder if you have a concussion. Did you hit your head? Maybe I should take you to the hospital?"

"No." My thoughts crystallized for a moment, long enough to concentrate on what that would mean. "I just need to get home. I'll be fine . . ." I tried to stand again. Still couldn't. The blood was dribbling down my arm, dripping off my wrist. ". . . in a minute."

"Can I get you something? Water?"

"Orange juice." It was my favorite, reminded me of home and Mother, but more than that, the errand would buy me a few seconds to get myself together. To escape before he returned, before we attracted the notice of concerned passersby.

"Stay here. I'll be right back." He touched my shoulder. A tentative squeeze so reassuring I didn't care about the bruising consequences. At that point, what did one more matter?

I laughed. Or maybe sobbed. It was a sound that made a businesswoman turn and frown.

I couldn't stay there, not vulnerable and exposed, drawing attention to myself with blood and uncoordinated movements. And just a few yards from where my family picture had been featured on the news. Brown hair dye and a bright outfit were hardly a disguise.

I waited until his broad shoulders had been swallowed by the blur of people, then tried to straighten for a third time. Orienting myself was hard; the buildings seemed to sway more than I did. If I leaned a hand against the wall for support, I could stay upright, drag myself a few steps, then pause to rest.

I was tougher than this. Stronger. I wouldn't let myself collapse on the street. I couldn't let myself be caught. I pictured the headline: LIVING DEAD GIRL FOUND BLEEDING IN MANHATTAN. Took another step. Two.

A few more and brick wall gave way to the smooth glass surface of a store window. I was striping it red with the tips of my fingers. Were they bleeding too? Or was it runoff from the scrapes on my arm, which were refusing to clot, refusing to stop spilling blood I needed to keep inside my arteries and veins.

"Wait. Hey, wait!"

There was so much noise around me, but this cut through it. And then there was the softest brush of a hand around my back. Under my arm. Holding me up. There was a bottle of orange juice being held in front of my lips, tilted to the perfect angle so I could sip it.

"Where do you live? If you won't let me take you to the hospital, at least let me get you home."

My answer was supposed to be *no*. It should have been automatic, as easy as an exhale. But exhaling hurt and nothing was easy anymore. I nodded and gave him an address on the street next to mine.

"You're really bleeding—are you sure I can't take you to a doctor?"

"It'll stop." I hoped.

He didn't disagree, but he did peel off his outer T-shirt. He wrapped it carefully around my arm and secured it by crossing the long sleeves in an *X* on each side, then knotting them together. I let him touch me, let him do this. Then let him hail me a cab, help me in, and climb in beside me.

I was dimly aware of the cab driver asking if I was "on something," slightly more aware that this guy was asking what else he could do, offering me an assortment of candy: Starburst, a crushed chocolate bar, a roll of Lifesavers that he pulled from pockets—asking for my cell phone the same way the Pomeranian's owner had asked for the dachshund's, pulling it out of my purse, turning it on, punching buttons, putting it back. Holding the orange juice to my lips, encouraging me with, "Take another sip. Good. One more."

"Please call me if you need anything," he said. "Please call me and let me know you're okay."

I think I nodded. Mostly I focused on keeping my eyes open, keeping my chin from lolling onto my chest, and keeping Father's voice from echoing in my head.

Be on your guard. Stay alert. Focus, Penelope, focus like your life depends on this.

The cab stopped and I stumbled out, pressed a useless hand on the outside of the door when the guy tried to follow me.

"Here?" I was too tired to lift my head and read his expression, but I didn't need to, his surprise, concern, and dismay all bled into his voice. "You're sure this is the right address?"

He was already so much closer to the apartment than I liked. No way I was letting him compromise my location any further.

"I'm sure. Thank you for seeing me home." Mother's tone of dismissal poured from my throat. "That was kind of you."

And I turned. Cut down an alley, swayed around a corner, in a side door and out the front of a bodega—the bodega I promised Garrett I'd never enter. They may have reacted to my stumble steps, but I wasn't looking up, wasn't caring. I was making deals with myself: a hundred more steps. Then a hundred after that. Then just one more set of a hundred and I was at the apartment building.

I shook as I inserted my key in the lobby door. I only made it one flight of stairs before my legs refused to cooperate and I had to crawl on my knees. I had no plausible explanations to give if any of my neighbors—the anonymous people behind the other doors—had come into the hall.

But none of them did. Not one in the hours, days, months, lifetimes it took me to reach my floor.

I got blood on the door frame when I used it to pull myself up to the lock. I used the stranger's shirt to swipe at it, but there was more blood seeping through its fabric. I had a moment of guilt about this.

Just a moment, then I was lurching, stumbling, falling forward—the couch was a few feet away and I didn't think I'd make it. The ground was coming toward me so much faster than I wanted, but when my face hit, it was on a cushion. The rest of me was more floorward, but that didn't matter. All that mattered was closing my eyes.

CHAPTER 23

I dreamed of him. Over and over.

They started as my normal Carter nightmares—the blood, all the blood—stirred into a storm of waves and wind and pain that gagged me and flattened my lungs. And then the dreams changed. Carter was gone, and the stranger was there.

"You're my reason for breathing," he said, and I found *I* could, I was no longer choking. I wasn't in blood anymore. Wasn't drowning. I was inhaling the sweetest air and staring at his sweetest of smiles.

And then I didn't need to breathe. I only needed to kiss him.

I stumbled in and out of consciousness. Being awake felt like being shipwrecked, drenched in agony, and cut off from the oblivion of dreams. I needed to do something, save myself, but could never gather up enough strength before I was dragged back into unconsciousness by the undertow of pain and disaster.

My eyes finally opened. This time being awake was different. I hadn't drifted there on my own. This time it was an insistent rhythm letting me know something was amiss, demanding I connect the pieces and pay attention. I didn't want to. I wanted to shut my eyes and float away, but the noise wouldn't let me. I located its source: the door was throbbing. The wall was throbbing. My head too. And my legs, which were still folded under me on the floor. My arm—the T-shirt bandage felt too tight. I made a feeble attempt to undo the knotted sleeves, then gave up and shut my eyes.

The throbbing stopped. The throbbing in the room, that is. My head threatened to explode when I turned to see why the throbbing had stopped.

The door was open. Men. In the apartment. I tried to sit, to push myself into a posture slightly less defenseless. To suck in a breath and scream. They were speaking, but I couldn't hear them over the drumming in my head.

They cornered me against the couch. Three of them. One of me. Less than one since the portions that remained didn't make up a functional whole. A man leaned down, extended his hand, and held something to my face. I tried to turn away, tried to take a deep breath before he covered my nose and mouth. If I could've, I would've bitten him, but even that was far beyond what I was capable of. It had to be chloroform—that was how it was going to end. And I wasn't even going to manage a fight or a whimper or a sob.

Except, it wasn't a rag. He didn't cover my nose or mouth; he held something against my ear.

"Penelope Maeve, are you there?" said the voice from the cell phone. "It's Bob."

They'd gotten to the vice president. It was my fault. I'd made a mistake. Exposed him. "I'll cooperate," I rasped at my abductors. "What—whatever you want."

"No. Penny. Penny—listen to me." Bob's voice was calm in my ear. "You're safe. No one's going to hurt you. The man holding the phone is my physician. The other men are part of my security detail. I trust them all implicitly. You are safe."

I'm not sure how many times Bob had to repeat this before I believed him. Before I let the doctor cut the stranger's shirt from my arm and clean and bandage those scrapes. Examine the bruises that covered the front of my body like an apron, and settle me in bed with two IVs—fluids and glorious immunoglobulin.

Through it all, the vice president's voice was in my ear. "We tracked you through the GPS in your phone—you can't have that on, Penny. If I can track you, so can others."

The stranger. I'd let him put his number in my phone. He'd left it on. I hadn't had the energy or awareness to think through the consequences. But maybe that was a blessing.

Bob continued. "My men have a new phone for you. It's secure. You can call me anytime. You are not alone. If I have a say, you will never be alone. But you need to be careful."

It was a paternal lecture, full of affection and sternness and requiring nothing from me but agreement at intervals.

"Yes. Okay. I understand. Thank you."

He sighed. "Are you sure you won't come stay at my Connecticut house?"

Agreeing meant surrendering all hope Garrett was coming. All hope of regaining any of my old life and all promise of autonomy. It would be another estate-prison without the comfort of family or the familiar.

"I'm sure, but thank you."

"You should know, I talked to Darius Castillo—"

"Can I see him?"

"Not yet. He doesn't want to know where you are. Doesn't think it's safe if he knows."

"But—"

"Penny, we need to trust him on this. If they could get through the security on your father's estate—if they had no qualms about their actions there—they're not going to hesitate to torture the doctor to get to you. The less people who know about you, the better. I'm debating moving you myself. If not to Connecticut, at least somewhere more secure."

But Garrett. But the freedoms I'd just gained. But the fact that this place was *Carter's*—all I had left of him—and he'd told me it was safe.

"I'll be more careful, I promise."

"I won't force you . . . *yet*. Call if you change your mind. Just call me, period. I want to know how you're doing."

After good-byes I turned what remained of my attention to the men in the room. Maybe it wasn't just fluids in the first IV because my exhaustion had a medicinal tint—I hated that no one ever consulted *me* before plying my body with drugs. I needed to be awake. Alert. Ask questions.

"How did you know . . . *my* apartment? Not the building—GPS—but which . . . was . . . mine . . ." My words were slowing into breathy things, the letters dragging and distorting.

"Door wasn't closed all the way," said one of the men. I had an impression of graying buzz cut and square jaw, but I couldn't stop blinking long enough to make eye contact or form clear memories. "And there was a smear of blood on the frame."

"And it's steel. Reinforced. Has a full seal. It's not the same door as the other apartments in this building." This was the other nondoctor. A smudge of black clothing, dark hair, dark skin. A voice like music. I bet he laughed a lot. I liked his explanation, what it said about Carter's foresight, I wanted to tell him . . .

"Sleep now, Miss Landlow. You need rest."

CHAPTER 24

It was eerily quiet when I opened my eyes. My muscles were stiff, joints tense and achy—weighted with the hours (days?) I'd spent in a drugged, motionless sleep. My temples were tight with my usual post-infusion headache. I walked gingerly from room to room, testing my body, measuring the differences in the apartment with addition and subtraction.

Gone: The men. The IVs. My cell phone. The stranger's shirt. The pain that had consumed me.

Added: A constant ache from head to navel that demanded careful movement and limited rotation. A new cell phone with a single contact: *Bob.* A new key on my table and new dead bolt on the door—how could I have slept through the drilling? A pill bottle with a note: "Take one every four hours as needed for pain." A loaf of bread. A neat row of apples and bananas. A fridge full of milk, juice, butter, yogurt, hummus, and all sorts of healthiness that had never before rested on those shelves. A sense of calm, security—a memory of the vice president's voice in my head: *You aren't alone.*

It was enough to make me smile as I took a careful shower, dressed in a bright yellow sundress printed with clocks, and blow-dried my bangs to cover a fading chin-shaped bruise on my forehead. With the dress's Peter Pan collar and a light cardigan, I could hide most of the damage. The scrapes on my arm were healing behind bandages and the petechiae on my ankles were disappearing. I could pass for healthy, and thanks to all the new antibodies infused into my body, I was.

For now.

"Garrett, where are you?" My question made the silence feel louder, made typing his number into this new phone and pressing send so dangerously tempting. I hit send on a different call instead.

"Penny, I have to ask you something." The vice president had barely taken the time for social niceties. Only inquiring how I was feeling and if I needed anything, accepting my answers and gratitude without seeking more details or pressing me to come stay with him. These, combined with the tone of his voice, made my arms break into goose bumps and soured the last sips of my orange juice.

"Go ahead."

"Your father—how did he . . . The past couple weeks, did he seem . . ." Bob cleared his throat. "Since Carter, had your father seemed depressed?"

"What?"

"I mean, more than what would be expected. Or violent?"

"Is there a *normal* amount of grieving?" I asked. "He was busy with work and sad—but not violent. Why?"

"There's some evidence that suggests this might have been a murder-suicide. We need to consider all possibilities."

"What evidence? My father would *never*—"

"But he *did* send away his security that morning, right? Which was atypical. And he even told your personal guard to leave you alone, even though you'd had constant surveillance since—"

"No!" I wanted to throw the phone out the window, bleach his words from my head. "That makes no sense."

"And he was training a successor, planning for someone to replace him."

"It's not possible. And I can prove it! Father would've known in an instant that Caroline wasn't me. Besides, she was shot *last*. She was alive when I left my room. And the shots started on the patio where Mother and Father were sitting. There were voices yelling—male, plural. I could hear them from the clinic."

"You're sure?"

"Positive!"

"I need to figure out how we can use your information to influence the investigation without revealing you're alive."

"How *hasn't* that been revealed?"

"At this point it's safer if you're secret. If it wasn't your father—"

"It wasn't!"

"I don't want to believe it either—but I wanted you to be

prepared. You're going to see it in the news. We're trying to suppress the story until more is known, but it'll leak. Tomorrow, day after at the latest."

I was tearing a paper towel into pieces with edges as ragged as my breathing. "They need new theories *now* because while they waste time on this, the real murderers are still out there."

"Penny, calm down."

"Calm down? You just asked if Father—" I paused to swallow against the tightening of my throat, gulp air that burned into my lungs with all the fury of my emotions. "Have you looked at Nolan? He could have orchestrated the murders to win support for the Organ Act—he was the one who stirred up the fight at breakfast, the reason Father sent the Wards away. Or the Zhus—they're suspects for Carter—"

"Nolan was on an airplane at the time. We're following *all* leads. I probably shouldn't be telling you any of this, but maybe you can help. Mick Ward suggested the Zhus too—he's having a rough recovery from his head injury, but he thinks he recalls—"

It was probably illegal to interrupt the vice president, but I did it again. "He *thinks* he recalls? Where are the cameras? We have security!"

"The hard drives were erased and smashed, the online backup server wiped clean."

"How?"

"We don't know. The ID logged into the system for the wipe was your father's."

I shook my head, trying to clear these images. I needed a hug or someone to hold my hand. I needed my parents, Carter. I needed everything impossible or I'd lie down sobbing and never get up. "Have you talked to Garrett Ward?"

"He's the youngest? He was away from the site of the shooting. He said he was waiting to meet you."

"He was."

"When he heard the sounds, he ran toward the gunfire. He's the one who called 911."

"Is he okay?"

"Physically, yes." Bob cleared his throat. "That's enough questions, Penny. I've already told you too much. They're following up on everything, I promise."

"What about Tom Tanaka? He's the VIP who was on the estate that day—if Mick thinks . . . If he's having trouble remembering . . ." Bob's new wife was Korean, I didn't want to offend him or imply *I* thought all Asians looked the same, just that it was entirely possible an idiot-Ward might assume Tanaka was a Zhu.

"But Tom was with Castillo in the clinic when the shooting began, and then with *you* in the ambulance. Surely you don't think Darius is in on it?"

"No, of course not. Can I talk to him yet? Or Garrett?" Please. Please please please please.

Bob sighed. It was the type of sigh Mother used to make whenever I asked to go off-estate. It expressed, *Why do you ask these questions and force me to give you disappointing answers?*

"I know it's hard, but it's safer for everyone if you don't. You're going to have to trust the professionals to do their job—sometimes these things take time."

"I-I need to go." I couldn't handle the dead ends and nonanswers. The accusations and implications and the horrible thought that some crimes were *never* solved.

"Yes, of course. I'm sorry I upset you."

I didn't tell him it was all right, because it wasn't.

"Call me *anytime* if you need to talk. Need anything," said Bob. "There's unlimited minutes on the phone and it's secure."

"Thank you."

"And be careful, Penelope Maeve."

"Always." The word was as weary and worn as the oversized chair I was sitting in.

I stared at the cell phone's screen after we hung up. Based on the date displayed, it had been three days since my last trip out of the apartment. I'd guessed as much based on the color progression of my bruises—the greens, yellows, and browns.

I needed to get out. Get sunlight. Distract myself from the fears and images looping through my head. See if the dachshund and Pom's owners were coupled yet, try the blueberry coffee, check on Shanice's son. Find a pretty view and a sunny bench where I could sit and update my notebook. I wanted to add stories about the times I'd injured myself over the years and my family's various bedside manners. I'd taken them for granted: Father's balloon bouquets and Broadway serenades. Mother's attempts to teach me to cross-stitch and crochet—though her own skills were limited. We'd made one lumpy, unraveling afghan and never finished our stitchery. Carter brought comic books, lilies, video games, frappés. He made "idiot-pathetic" jokes that somehow always made me *less* self-conscious. He'd bring Garrett too, who was always his own brand of distraction.

Garrett. *Physically okay* . . . but thinking I was dead. Thinking we were *all* dead. That would wreck him. My guilt and desire to console him made me pick the phone back up. My fear of placing him in danger made me put it back down.

He wasn't coming. I was alone. And probably *should* stay pinned within the walls where I was safest, but I needed to try street pretzels and the peanuts that were roasted and sugared and smelled like ice-cream cones. I wanted to watch the carriage riders in Central Park, see the Statue of Liberty. All those touristy things I'd daydreamed and bookmarked back when my biggest problems were boredom and blood counts. I needed to enjoy freedom, because there were no guarantees I'd have it for long. I put my new cell phone in my purse, added the new key to the paper clip with the others, and left. Shutting the apartment door Bob's people had wiped clean of my blood, I skipped down the stairs I'd painfully crawled up.

I stepped into the sunshine of a perfect morning and gulped a breath of outside air—then choked on it. He was there. The Asian guy who'd run into me and haunted my dreams. My stranger.

Standing on the sidewalk across the street, his dark pants, gray shirt, and messenger bag looked far too pristine against the grimy backdrop of the neighborhood. His eyes were on my building, on me, and he was crossing the street, running toward where I stood frozen on the step.

My dreams hadn't done him justice. He was gorgeous. The most attractive guy I'd ever seen. Period. Exclamation point.

His black hair lacked any sort of part or order. It was long enough to be pushed back when he shoved his sunglasses to the top of his head so he could look at me with eyes that were intensity-brown under eyebrows that arched in shivery, come-hithery ways. Except they weren't purposely come-hither—they were raised in concern. For me.

"How are you feeling?"

"I'm fine."

He beamed. Beamed. No one had ever smiled at me like that. Like just by walking out the door I'd made his life better. It punched holes in my caution, made me feel off-balance.

But I stuck to my script anyway. "What are you doing here?"

"You didn't call, and I was worried."

"Do girls always call you?" His lips distracted me as I waited for him to form them into an answer . . . An answer to the wrong question. "Why are you outside my apartment?"

"I wanted to see that you were okay. You just—you seemed so disoriented. I should've insisted on taking you to the hospital. I was worried you were diabetic and had gone into insulin shock."

This wasn't the apartment building where I'd left him. My back and palms glossed with a panic-sheen of sweat.

"You followed me. In what world is it okay to follow a girl you don't know home and wait outside her building?" There was so much of my father in my voice. If I'd had a Ward here, I would have nodded at him to step closer and crack his knuckles. But I didn't need the extra menace; the guy looked nervous enough. Shifting his weight, staring at my shoes.

"I . . . I wanted to see you again. I was worried. I felt responsible. I—" His eyes swept across my face and he frowned. "Did I do this?"

He brushed my bangs aside with a finger, revealing the grayish bruise. "I'm so sorry."

I wanted to lean into the touch. Instead I jumped backward and smoothed my hair into place. This was the *correct* reaction, and the correct words would be some enraged version of "Don't touch me" or "Who do you think you are?"

What came out of my mouth was, "And I thought rock-hard jaw lines only existed in romance novels."

He chuckled and some of the guilt eased out of his expression.

I raised my eyebrows in a silent *your move*. I wanted him to continue our conversation, to give me an excuse for not saying the word I should: "good-bye."

He didn't. He fidgeted with the flap on his messenger bag, shifted his weight. Opened and closed his mouth. Licked his lips. Sighed. He let the pause stretch beyond the point of uncomfortable till I was rocking back on my heels to pivot and walk away.

Then he opened his mouth again and said in a rush, "I know you must think I'm crazy for being here. I'm not sure I disagree. It's probably some strange post-adrenaline, serotonin, or dopamine overload that's causing a momentary hero complex, but . . . I'm so happy to see you." He lifted his eyes from the sidewalk, and his expression was as transparent as glass—hope balanced on his slightly parted lips; nerves drew lines between his eyebrows.

These changed to doubt as he studied my face. I'd adopted a practiced mask of neutrality, and he couldn't tell I was hiding the same emotions behind it. It was agony watching his courageous vulnerability turn into flushed-cheek humiliation. Especially after he'd given what had to be the most scientific, least romantic declaration of I'm not sure what.

Probably he'd lived a life where he didn't *have* to hide his feelings. I forgot sometimes that not everyone was raised with gates and guards and guns. Maybe he'd been blessed with an ordinary life. One without all the posturing and duplicity. One where a reaction of silence meant disinterest, not self-preservation.

"Um. Yeah. Okay. Never mind. Sorry for disturbing you . . . and for that." He pointed at my forehead.

"It was really unnecessary for you to come check on me, but thank you for bringing me home. I don't know if I remembered to say that."

It was a polite exit line. It didn't reveal I'd spent three days dreaming of his lips on mine. That I was equal parts thrilled and mortified to see him again. That it hurt me to take the first step away.

"Wait." His hand shot out and grasped my wrist. "Is there any chance you'd want to see me again?"

I looked at his fingers on my skin, loving the contrast of his pigment against mine. But they needed to not be there. I needed to not be wasting precious antibody-protected platelets on this.

Yet . . . as his fingers rearranged into a lighter grip, skating across the skin on the inside of my wrist, the feeling made me want to sigh or bite my lip.

I pulled away. "What?"

"Look, I don't want to come on too strong." He paused and gave a self-deprecating grin. "Probably too late for that, huh?"

I nodded. "Stalking isn't really on my list of attractive qualities."

"What *is* on this list?" he asked. "Are there copies I could obtain and study?"

I raised my eyebrows. "Persistence *was* on it, but I'm rethinking it."

"What can I say? You really made an impression on me." The corner of his mouth twitched as he tried not to smile at his own joke.

It was lame . . . and endearing. It caught me off-guard and I laughed. "Actually, *you* made the impression on me."

His laughter was rich and thick like melted chocolate. It seemed to pour slowly over me, erasing so much of my foreboding and replacing it with the sweetest sensation. Like smiling through a blush. Both of which I was doing.

"Now I've exposed my cheesy side too." He peeked at me with a sheepish grin. "I don't suppose there's any recovering from being the cheesy, persistent stalker who made you bleed?"

"Well, when you put it like that . . ."

He was going to give up. I could see a regretful good-bye poised on the bow of his lips—which were so full and tempting and so much more attractive when smiling. And delicious to kiss— No. Wait. I hadn't ever *really* kissed him. Those had been dreams. Illness dreams. A manifestation of my body breaking down and falling apart and for some reason releasing euphoric brain chemicals—probably the same ones he'd just listed.

But could it possibly feel as good in real life?

"I was going to get coffee and go for a walk. I guess some company wouldn't kill me." I bit my tongue on the last words. *Kill me*. There were people in this world who wanted to. Somewhere. Anywhere. And I'd been flirting.

And not with Garrett. His name felt like an obstruction in my throat when I tried to swallow.

But the killers would be looking for a blonde. By herself. Not a brunette with a guy whose shoulders would make anyone second-guess an assault.

"Yes, please." And that smile. That beaming smile from my dreams—where he'd said, "You're my reason for breathing." I *wanted* to be that reason. I *needed* to make my brain stop replaying that image and my cheeks stop blushing.

"What's your name?" he asked. "With the amount of time I've spent thinking about you, I can't believe I don't know it."

"Maeve." I'd hesitated for a fraction of a second, but I hesitated so much around him, he couldn't attribute it to anything but not having won me over yet. He would. I knew he would. It terrified me how much I wanted to yield to his charm and smile. "Yours?"

He hesitated too. Maybe not trusting I cared. Like this was a test he needed to pass in order to walk the next block with me. Then he relaxed back into his smile, held out his hand and said, "Charlie. It's so nice to finally meet you, Maeve."

"Charlie? No." It was the touch of his fingers that caused

the unguarded reaction. I'd been so busy concentrating on not gasping when his palm slid across mine in the light grasp of a quick handshake that I'd forgotten to police my thoughts.

It wasn't fair. Other people touched all the time. They were immune to the electricity of skin plus skin, but I'd never had a chance to build up a tolerance. He probably didn't feel the same thrill of energy, his pulse probably wasn't racing.

Something shifted in his face. Not anger or fear, but something. Something guarded. Something I couldn't read. It bothered me. I wanted to know all his expressions. I wanted them all to be smiles. "Why *no*?"

"Charlie is someone who's five years old. Or a dumpy-looking cartoon with persistent pessimism and poor coordination. *You* do not look like a Charlie."

"What do I look like then?" He'd figured out the compliment and his smile was back. A smolder more than a smile, like he was making up for its lapse by burning hotter.

"Um . . . How about Char?"

I needed to get a grip. So he was an attractive guy. A very attractive guy. So what? I'd seen plenty of attractive guys on TV. Garrett was attractive.

Garrett. Whom I'd promised to run away with two weeks ago and who I'd thought would come and rescue me. He wouldn't. He couldn't. And fair or not, the thought made me angry. He'd *promised* to protect me.

"Char. I'll take it." He continued to smolder at me. "Hmm, you've invited me on a walk and given me a nickname. This is a pretty good morning."

"It is," I agreed. I owed myself a good morning. A reward for the three days I'd just endured. One morning.

"Would it be pressing my luck to ask to hold your hand?"

I glanced down at mine. So far there was no sign of a handshake bruise. I should've asked Bob for my counts; I should have asked when they'd next be checked.

There were so many reasons my answers should've been *No. Never.* Turning and walking away.

Platelets. Murderers. Secrets. Crimes. The lies I'd have to tell and remember. The danger I'd put him in.

If I'd been a better person I would've said no. Never. Run.

"Not yet," I answered. "Patience *is* on my list of desirable qualities. I'd like to see if you have it."

CHAPTER 25

We walked a ribbon-candy pattern, down one block and back the next. Back and forth through a section of the city.

"Where are we going and why like this?" I wished I had my map app so I could track our progress, create a record of the magic of the day.

"Nowhere. It's the perfect way to wander without getting lost."

That made sense, and it meant I didn't have to pay attention to our setting beyond counting: three blocks from the apartment, four. I could focus on him. His gaze was skipping from the buildings to me and back again. His smile brightened each time his eyes hit mine and dimmed at the stone and brick and glass. I wanted to tell him to forget manners, forget social mores; he could have my permission to stare, because I certainly was and had no intention of stopping.

"Oh, watch out." Char touched my arm to get my attention and pointed at a pair of men carrying a couch from a truck toward an apartment building.

While we paused on the sidewalk to let them pass, I fluttered my lashes, pressed the back of my hand to my head, and simpered, "My hero."

He moved my hand out of the way and touched my forehead again, outlining the shape of the bruise with the lightest caress. "Some hero. I'm really sorry, Maeve."

My heart was too busy thudding for me to do more than nod.

"You're probably wondering why I'm coming on so strong."

I was, but not as much as I was wondering why I wasn't running, why his statement made me lean toward him and nod in a way that meant *go on*.

"Believe it or not, I'm not usually this . . . aggressive." He shook his head. "That's not really the right word. I'm not really a pursuer. Is that any better?"

"I believe you." His self-conscious jokes and unguarded grins made me think "earnest" not "player." He didn't have the practiced smoothness of guys on TV shows or the swagger of the older Ward brothers. "So why now? Why me?"

He paused on a corner, taking a step out of the foot traffic and waiting for me to follow. I did, watching his mouth as he swallowed and licked his bottom lip while choosing the right words. "I recently lost two . . . opportunities because I didn't speak up. They were things that mattered to me and . . ." He shook his head. "I decided when I got on the plane to New York that I wouldn't do that anymore. That I wouldn't be so passive or wait for things to come to me. That I'd be better at communicating—asking for—the things I want."

He reached out and gently placed a hand on my sleeve. "I want to spend more time with you."

I noted his choice of vague words: "opportunities," "things." Clearly whatever he'd missed out on was personal—but I wanted to know him well enough that he'd confide them. And I'd recently lost something as well: my family.

Stupid. Rash. Whatever adjective I pinned on it, it didn't change that his words resonated with sincerity and my reaction was to open my dry mouth and whisper, "I want that too."

Morning melted into afternoon. My resolve melted too. And my caution. I ignored the passersby. I even let myself be seated in a restaurant with my back to the door. Char was dangerous for my well-being, not because of the collision, or because I wanted more—more bruises if it meant he'd touch me—but because he made me distracted, he made me breathless, he made me reckless.

"What are you drawing?" he asked, sitting back down and leaning forward to see the napkin I'd been idly doodling while he'd been in the bathroom.

My stomach dropped. Before I could wad it up, Char reached across the table and spun the napkin around. "Wow. Where'd you come up with this?"

The only answer I could think to give started with a kernel of the truth. "My brother once teased me that all girls ever doodle are hearts and flowers—so I came up with this." I took the drawing back and folded the napkin to hide the anatomical heart made out of daisies and tulips and other simple flowers. It was pretty much the only thing I ever doodled, so I guess Carter had been right.

"Ha!" Char laughed and leaned forward. "How'd he react?"

I'd put it on his birthday card that year—the year he turned thirteen—and he'd loved it. It was framed in his room. Father had often said we should adopt it as a Family crest, have it put on letterhead and the gates. I swallowed. Lies hurt, but the truth hurt more.

"Oh. He just said I was weird or something."

"Well, I think it's fantastic. May I have it?"

I studied his face. There was no suspicion, no scrutiny. And why *would* there be? It was a strange thing to doodle, but since Father had never gotten around to making it into a crest, it was hardly incriminating.

I slid the napkin across the table.

"Thank you," he said, folding it and putting it carefully in his pocket. "Now tell me something else. Tell me, I don't know, your favorite constellation."

I laughed and my fear evaporated. "I don't think I have one. But, by all means, tell me yours."

The afternoon dissolved into an endless conversation, an exchange of information that was carefully guarded on my part, but also felt effortless and honest.

"—And *that*'s why, even though I'm seventeen and it makes me ridiculous, my favorite movie is still the cartoon of *Sleeping Beauty*." And *Enchanted*, but that reminded me of Garrett and I couldn't think of him while sitting here. Not without my smile cracking and my mouth turning sour with the taste of betrayal.

"You know, I don't think I've ever seen it," Char confessed.

"You have to! I love fairy tales. There's something so charming and comforting about the idea of fairy godmothers and magic and happily ever afters." I touched his wrist and we both froze, blushed, smiled. When he moved like he might cover my hand with his own, I pulled back and put mine in my lap. "So what's yours?"

"Um, I like documentaries more than movies. I know. It makes me weird. I've never really been a magic, or fantasy, or even fiction person. Give me a good biography or science journal any day."

"Really?" Carter would've had such a field day with this moment: his head-in-the-clouds baby sister on a date with a data junkie.

Our waitress stopped by to refill our waters again and drop off my dessert.

"Should you eat that?" Char asked, then immediately looked contrite. "I know it's not any of my business."

I looked down at the brownie, then back up at him. "Are you calling me fat?" This would be a deal-breaker. I knew I wasn't, that I needed to gain back the weight I'd lost post-collision, but even if I was, he had no right to comment on my diet.

"No." He leaned away from me, palms up, eyebrows too. "Are you kidding? Not at all. It's just . . . You're diabetic, right?"

"Why do you keep asking me that?"

"When I hit you, you asked for orange juice, not

water—because you needed the sugar, I assumed. And even before we crashed into each other, your eyes—they were so unfocused, it was like you didn't even notice I was there."

"You saw me? And still hit me?"

"I didn't see you until it was too late; I was distracted by the TV in the store window. When I looked up, you were right there and I couldn't stop in time. I've known a few diabetics, and that's what you looked like, unfocused eyes, the shaking—like you were having a hypoglycemic episode."

"Oh." I weighed the value of this lie in my head, debated whether trading one vulnerability for another made sense—but then again, Penelope Landlow was known for being idiot-pathetic, *not* diabetic. "What was so interesting about the TV?" I asked.

His gaze slid down and away. "Oh, just an old rerun of one of my favorite sitcoms."

I'm not sure why he'd lie about watching the news, maybe because it was too macabre to mention on a first-date-type thing, but if he could lie, I could too.

"Yes, I'm diabetic." I pushed the brownie away with a pout. "It's a new diagnosis. I'm still trying to figure out what I can and can't do and how to get my blood sugar right. I miss chocolate."

"Do you need to check it? Do you have a monitor with you? The brownie probably isn't even good. It looks dry, definitely not worth throwing your insulin levels off. Never mind the long-term eye, kidney, nerve damage stuff . . ." He trailed off. "Sorry, I'll get off my soapbox. I'm sure you know this. You don't need a lecture from me."

I might have been too hasty with this particular lie. "How do you know so much about diabetes?"

He shifted in his seat. "It interests me. One of my best friends has it—type 1. Last summer we designed an app—well, with help from some other people—but it will keep track of your blood sugar and help with diet planning and exercise and stuff. Do you want me to download it for you?"

I'd *definitely* been too hasty with this particular lie. "My phone's not 'smart' enough for that." I smiled apologetically and sent a silent prayer of thanks to whatever government tech guru had told Bob I'd be safer and more off-grid with a no-frills phone. "You can have the brownie if you want, at least then it won't go to waste. And it won't be sitting on the table tempting me."

"I can go throw it away."

"No, please eat it. Unless you don't—" but he'd already picked up the fork and taken a large bite.

"So, were you low that day?" he asked. "When I walked into you?"

It was time to follow one of Mother's best conversational tactics—perfect for nosy, non-Family women who asked too many questions—and turn the topic back on him. "Wow, you're really into this. Are you premed?" He'd mentioned college earlier, that he'd be a freshman at Georgetown in the fall.

His face fell. It was the first time since the sidewalk outside my apartment that I'd seen it slip from hopeful and happy to something defeated. Even his shoulders seemed less square. "No. I thought for a while I might be. Undergrad I would've focused on biochem, or bioengineering . . . but I'm not."

"Why not?"

"My father didn't even want me to go to college. He wanted me to stay home and work for him."

"I know a bit about family businesses and expectations," I said bitterly. The sour mood joined our table like an uninvited guest.

"You do?" he asked, leaning forward. I wondered if he could read the panic on my face or see the shape of my heart as it pounded against my ribs. "What's your family like?"

"Where are you from?" The question was far too loud, the words blurring together in my rush to change the subject. I forced myself to take a deep breath before continuing. "There's no New York in your accent, and you mentioned an airplane earlier."

"West," he said. "The Midwest." He shifted back in his chair, rubbing his fingers through his hair in a way that pulled his shirt tight across his muscles.

It was the movement of someone relaxing; the topic change had worked, had brought a smile back to his face. I wanted to know what he was thinking about: his Midwestern home, or here, now, me?

I looked at his shoulders again. What would it take to get shoulders like that? Wide and square and defined. They looked as if they could carry the weight of the world. Or at least hold up the drama of my crazy life. And the way they tapered down to his waist . . . Mick and Hugh and Jacob were big, muscular, but they were big everywhere. This wasn't weight-lifting muscle.

I wanted to trust him, but I didn't know nearly enough about him.

"Do you help out on a farm?" I asked.

He snorted his water. "What?" I loved his laughter. It was unguarded, infectious. It made people turn; it made people smile. "Now that's a random question."

"Well, Midwest, your shoulders . . ."

"My shoulders?" He laughed again and I wanted to crawl under the table, except not really. There wasn't any mocking in the laughter. More than crawl under the table I wanted to drag him under it with me.

"You've got . . . muscles."

Now he was blushing. It looked good on him. Almost as good as his T-shirt would look *off* him. I was blushing too.

"I swim," he said.

"Oh. Like on a team?"

Char nodded, and I wondered what that would be like. To have a team, a group of friends working toward a common goal—not all that different than a Family, but *my* age? And to race? Not just swim aimlessly back and forth. Competition was an unfamiliar idea—no one had ever viewed me as potential adversary. No one ever saw me as anything but fragile.

"So your family doesn't have a farm?" Apparently I'd swallowed the stereotype that all Midwesterners were farmers. Then again, *he* didn't fit the American farming stereotype—on TV they all had blond hair, blue eyes, cowboy boots, hats, Wrangler jeans, and plaid shirts. But if TV was to be believed, then, depending on which Lifetime movie you were watching, the Families were all mafia thugs or medical Robin Hoods, and I was either a blond bombshell or a bedridden invalid.

"Sort of a small ranch," he answered.

"Why are you in New York?" It was starting to feel like Twenty Questions—but also starting to feel like he didn't want to play. He was sitting up again, folding a straw wrapper. Looking away from me, around the restaurant, at the door.

I wanted his attention. All of it. I hadn't realized this was what I'd had all day until it became divided.

"In some Aboriginal cultures, when a man comes of age he goes on a walkabout." His answer was aimed at the door, his eyes and mind on something faraway, something other than me. "It's a sort of journey alone to prove his manhood."

I looked at him skeptically; reached out to touch his hand, get his attention. "You're Australian Asian American? That's a mouthful."

He laughed, but it wasn't honeyed this time. "No. Chinese American. That was just the closest example I could come up with. I think my parents expected me to call them my first night in New York, crying and begging to come back home."

"And because you didn't, you're a man?"

"Something like that. My father is big on me proving my independence. It also doesn't help that he can't stand to look at me right now."

"Why?" I asked, then, watching his face grow stonier and stormier, I wished I hadn't. "Never mind."

He cleared his throat and poked a fork in the last few bites of my brownie. "What do your parents do?"

"My parents . . ." I swallowed. Talking about them in present tense felt dangerous, like given any chance, I might convince myself they weren't actually gone.

Char leaned forward, smiling again, nodding, encouraging a charade that was far too tempting.

"My mother's a housewife. She's stayed home since she had my brother, then me, but before that she was an administrative assistant. My father's, actually—how cliché is that?"

This was all true, all real. And it felt *good* to talk about them with someone who could talk back. To think about them outside the pages of my notebook.

"My father . . . he's in, um, acquisitions? I don't actually know all that much about his job—something my family likes to tease me about." I forced a careless shrug. "He works in an office. He travels a bit, but not a ton. And I'm really lucky because he's home for dinner most nights, so it's not like he's a workaholic."

"What's your brother like? Besides someone who clearly doesn't recognize your artistic talent? I'm jealous. I always hated being an only child."

My make-believe was shattered like a blow to the stomach. *Carter.* I couldn't pretend he was . . . Not when I'd seen . . .

I gagged and tried to cover it with a cough.

"You're not close?" Char guessed.

If I nodded it would be the end of this conversation, but that was a lie I wasn't willing to tell.

"I want to hear more about your ranch," I said instead. "What do you raise? Is that the right word? Do you 'raise' animals? Herd them? Keep them?"

"Raise works." Char wasn't looking at me. He pointed at the clock above the bar, which had gotten crowded while I wasn't paying attention. "It's getting late. I should probably let you go—otherwise I'm going to be that guy who beat you up, stalked you, kidnapped you, and held you hostage through boring farm tales."

I was going to protest that he *hadn't* told me any boring farm tales. Or that I held equal blame in the beating up of myself, but what was the point? The subtext in his statement was he wanted to go. And this was probably for the best. Dancing along the line between truth and fiction was going to lead to a misstep. Either revealing too much or getting caught in a web of deception too tangled to keep straight.

And since I liked *him*, I didn't want to see if he liked the invented girl I was only pretending to be.

Disappointment crawled across me, clinging to my skin, climbing in my ears to change the way his voice sounded, and over my eyes so that I only saw his detachment. It wanted in my mouth, down my throat, so it could curdle in my stomach, spoil the day, and spill out over my lips with words of dismissal and farewell.

"Fine. You're right." Stiff. Sharp. Short. It matched my posture. Matched the angles and jerkiness of my movements as I shoved my phone in my pocket and threw down cash to cover my half of our check.

I was out of my seat, out of the restaurant, out of my mind with frustration that I cared this much. He was scratching at all the cracks in my composure.

"Maeve! Maeve! Wait!"

I heard him but didn't stop walking. My steps still didn't match the rhythm of the city, but I'd gotten good at dodging and weaving through crowds. I was putting people between us, distance, so that maybe he wouldn't catch up, or I wouldn't cry. One or the other. Not both.

But it wasn't okay that my first tears that weren't mourning would be for a guy. One I'd just met. One who couldn't mean this much to me. He couldn't mean anything to me. There was no place in my life for a romance.

He disappeared from sight, or I did. I was the one moving away, so maybe I was the one who disappeared. My choice. A painful choice, but a necessary one.

CHAPTER 26

Before I opened my eyes the next morning, I made a wish that it wouldn't be raining. I needed to get out from between those walls, out of that building, and outside of my wallowing. I needed to get back into the something-like-normal I'd established before I'd been thrown off-course. Coffee. Dog park. Breakfast. Museum. Maybe some window shopping. Maybe some actual shopping. A cheap laptop or tablet or some way of connecting with the world wouldn't be a bad idea. Except it would need Wi-Fi, Bob would disapprove, and it would use up most of my dwindling cash supply. Okay, it *was* a bad idea, but my new cell phone wasn't web-equipped and there wasn't even a TV in the apartment—not all that surprising given that Carter could only be pinned down to watch sports, and he'd preferred watching those in a pub with drinks courtesy of his fake ID.

The night before would have been a million times more

bearable if I'd been able to distract myself with fashion blogs, YouTube cat videos, or CNN's newsfeed. Even infomercials or Spanish soap operas. I would've welcomed any outside noise that competed with my racing thoughts. If Carter owned a vacuum I would've tried Mother's coping method.

I refused to think of Char. I'd left all that longing on the other side of midnight, and in this new day where sunshine turned the wall shades of pink and possibility, I wasn't letting him invade. But still, when I walked out the door of my building, I couldn't stop my eyes from skipping over to where he'd waited yesterday—

Where he was waiting today.

"So here's the thing—" Char stepped off the sidewalk, barely even glancing to see if there was a car coming, hurrying toward me at nearly a run. "I'm not a creeper, I promise. If you tell me not to, I'll never wait outside your apartment again—" He paused on the edge of the street, the toes of his gray shoes touching the curb of the sidewalk in front of me. "That sounds like a creeper sentence, doesn't it? I've been out here for an hour, and I was up pacing my hotel room all night. You'd think with all that time I'd be able to come up with a better line than that. And after . . . On the plane I vowed I'd be better at taking chances and going after the things I want . . . Not that you're a *thing*." He clenched his eyes shut and pinched the bridge of his nose. "I hope "smooth" wasn't on your list of desirable qualities, because I'm *not*."

I shook my head. Nodded. Not sure what I was agreeing with or if I should be disagreeing. I covered my mouth with both hands, trapping a near sob of relief and a smile.

"You never have to see me again. I just wanted to—I don't know—see *you.* Yesterday, wandering and talking with you, I felt more like myself than I can remember. Like who I am and who I want to be had finally met. I don't know why you ran away, Maeve, but you are the best thing about this whole city. I'm sorry if that's too much . . . It's too much, isn't it?" He sighed and hung his head. "I'm sorry. I'll go."

"Stay." My word was soft—like a cotton ball dropped in the middle of his maelstrom, but it had the effect of a blanket on a fire—extinguishing his outpouring and leaving me wondering what had happened to all the oxygen on the street. We stared—measuring honesty and fear and surrender in each other's gazes.

Carter had said, "Fight to the death for the ones that matter." Char was following my brother's advice. Would I? Should I?

"Why did you run?" he asked.

"We were saying good-bye anyway." It was a cheat of an answer; he'd given me honesty and I couldn't bring myself to admit the truth. *Because you scare me. No, that's not it: because I scare myself around you.*

"For the day, not forever." He looked at the ground, then at the roof of the buildings. Inhaled so his shoulders climbed toward his ears, then exhaled a sigh that settled them back to normal. "No, that's not quite true. I *was* pulling away. I thought I could. I wanted to see if I could . . . Maeve—"

"I know," I said. Because I did. Because this guy was the only thing that numbed the hollowness left behind when my life imploded. Because I couldn't stop thinking about him, even while unconscious. And because even standing in front of him, I could already feel the ache that would descend the moment we said our next farewell. Because seventeen years of being treated like a princess and reading gilded fairy tales hadn't prepared me for the happiness I felt when he said my name—which wasn't even really my name at all. "I *know,* Char."

His smile felt like an embrace. His actual embrace felt like heaven. The place where his hands rested in the center of my back felt as if it had been molded just for him. I could feel all ten of his fingertips mirroring each other on either side of my spine. He pulled me to him, but not too hard—just enough that the soft fabric of his slate-blue T-shirt whispered against my cheek and I got a hint of his smell. I might have a set of fingerprint bruises, but maybe not . . . He was holding himself back, trying not to hug me with an eagerness that matched his voice in my ear. "Are you real?"

I wondered the same thing. Was anything about my life real anymore?

I let my hands flutter up for a quick squeeze, but when I let go, he released me instantly. It took me a moment to find my breath and manage a "good morning."

Nothing in my life had readied me for the intoxication of casual touch. The fact that I could reach over and run a fingertip down the back of his hand. And that when I did, he'd light up and twist his palm, making his hand available for mine to hold.

I didn't. That seemed like too much.

Like greediness or self-indulgence. Or like it would overwhelm me completely, making it impossible to walk and talk or even just remember how to inhale and exhale.

It was the perfect promise of a moment.

"I have a surprise for you," he said.

It shattered in a shiver that left my voice frosty. "No. No surprises."

On the estate I'd lived for surprises. Just the word had made me smile. Anticipation of something that Carter, Mother, or Father had devised to amuse me was enough to make hours pass with borrowed sweetness. They'd been great about coming up with various unexpected treats. Mother left paths of rhyming riddles that ended with a handbag or new nail polish. Father just hid things and played hot/cold. Carter's surprises had been the best. They almost always involved passing through the gates.

I didn't want to be surprised now. Not just because of the memories, but because surprises didn't feel safe. Surprises meant letting someone else control my life, and that wasn't acceptable. Not even a Midwestern rancher's son. Not even for a moment.

Char may not have understood the *why* of the emotion in my voice, but he clearly heard its panic. "Sure. No surprises. No big deal."

He stepped in front of me, held both of his hands up like he was making a vow—like we weren't standing on a filthy street being watched by curious eyes of people going about their daily routines. "I keep scaring you off. I don't mean to. Is there anything I can do or say to make you less skittish?"

"Let me lead." It went against the relationship dynamic my parents had modeled; it went against seventeen years of obedience to others' orders. I didn't care.

"Sure," said Char. "So, what do *you* want to do today?"

"Ever tried caramel pecan coffee?" I asked. When he grinned and shook his head, I held out my hand, held my breath.

Even bracing myself didn't stop the sensation of his fingers sliding through mine from sending shivers across my skin. Didn't stop the smiles from spreading across both our faces as he swung our entwined hands and said, "Lead the way."

Words I'd never had directed at me.

I liked them, quite a bit.

Coffee first, which I ordered with sugar-free raspberry syrup while cursing my fake diabetes. I saw Char sneaking longing glances at the cake pops and glazed muffins. "Go ahead," I said. "I don't mind."

He shook his head, smiled. "No, it's fine. My sweet tooth is out of control; this is good for me. *You're* good for me."

Next the dog park and watching the Pom-hund couple cuddle like I'd missed weeks of furious courtship instead of just a few days.

Their happiness at seeing me: "So you're not just a matchmaking fairy godmother! We were worried you'd disappeared."

Their grinning welcomes to Char: "He'd better be a dog person."

And the way he didn't flinch at the level of commitment that implied. Instead, he raised the hand he hadn't let go of yet—not through ordering coffee, paying for it, adding his milk and sugar, or walking through the streets—and brushed the back of my fingers across his lips. "I'm allergic to cats, but anything else: dogs, fish, turtles, hermit crabs, these pet pigs I saw a documentary on once—they're really smart. Pretty much any other animal is fine with me."

"No worries. There are no cats, or any other animals, in the apartment," I said. But more and more, I kept imagining *him* in there. In my life as more than a temporary injection of bliss. As a permanent fixture. As someone who knew me. Someone I could confide in, talk to. Someone who understood.

He made me feel alive—reminded me that despite the fact I'd had a funeral and had a gravestone beside my parents' and Carter's, I *was* alive. And that I should spend the time I had *living,* not cowering and waiting. Carter had said as much: *Fight to the death for the ones that matter.* My grandfather's version had been, *When you see an opportunity, take it!*

These past few days were my nod of agreement; I just wished I could hear Carter say, "I'm proud of you."

CHAPTER 27

Char and I spent the day in conversation, in another walk, like a lazy game of Ping-Pong, drifting back and forth down streets. Finally, we parted in front of my building after dinner.

We'd exchanged numbers, me fumbling with how to locate mine or enter his, especially after he commented, "That's a different phone."

"I, um, dropped the other one. In water. In the sink. I was doing dishes. And watching TV. And talking on the phone with my aunt. She told a joke and I laughed. The phone slipped and *whoops*."

Liars always included too many details; Al Ward had taught me that. I hoped no one had told Char.

He just smiled. "Is the lesson you shouldn't multitask or I shouldn't tell you jokes?"

"I guess we'll have to try both and see."

"Good night."

Upstairs in the apartment, I frowned at the note for Garrett that still sat on the coffee table. Each time I saw it my chest tightened and I froze for a moment—trying to remember what it felt like when *his* eyes had made me flush and stammer, how I used to feel safe and proud with him by my side. Out of habit I poked the note with the tip of one finger. I'd spent days nudging it this way and that, as if its angle would make a difference. Now I picked it up and crumpled it in my fist. He wasn't coming. And maybe that was a relief. Maybe he'd be a cruel reminder of my life before. Seeing him would shatter my current charade and be a painful reality check.

I dropped the note in the bathroom trash. Scowled at the fading bruises I saw in the mirror as I changed into my pajamas—try as I might, there were aspects of my old life I couldn't escape.

My phone rang as I was brushing my teeth. "Miss me already?" I teased.

"I did." Char stated it as a simple fact, unashamed, unembellished.

I climbed into bed and pressed my giggle into a pillow before I took a deep breath and said, "So, tell me about your day."

"Not going to lie, it was kind of surreal. I spent it with the most gorgeous girl I've ever met and she's not bored with me yet."

"Not at all," I replied. "She'd walk the whole city as long as you were next to her."

"Likewise. Though I need to remember to wear different shoes tomorrow, because *ow,* blisters."

I quickly learned I didn't *want* to multitask when his was the voice in my ear. I was too busy collecting his words and cheesy jokes, weaving them into a web of facts and connections that bound us together.

"Fears," Char challenged around midnight. "Tell me one from your childhood and one from now."

I rolled over onto my stomach and propped the phone on a pillow. "As a child? I was terrified of dragons."

"Wait, there's a dragon in *Sleeping Beauty*! I, um, might have watched it last night."

"Really? And, yes, my fear and that movie were definitely related. My brother and his best friend used to build these elaborate 'dragon traps' in my closet and in the hall outside my room. The problem was I couldn't leave my room or get dressed in the morning until they came along and unassembled them."

Char burst into laughter and the sound made me brave enough to add, "And now, my big fear is being useless."

"I don't know what you mean. Can you explain?"

"Like, no one expecting anything of me. Never achieving anything that matters. I want to matter." These were the type of things I could only whisper at the darkened ceiling, never say to his face.

"You matter to me," he said softly.

"Thanks." I flushed from his words, though that wasn't what I meant. "Now tell me yours."

"As a kid? Bullies. I was a nerd in a community that wasn't all that nerd-friendly."

"You, a nerd?" I teased. "This coming from the guy who

just spent twenty minutes explaining how caffeine affects the nervous system, and how decaf coffee isn't really caffeine-free? I'm shocked."

"Sorry," he said. "You were probably bored. You've got to just tell me to shut up."

"I wasn't bored at all. I love your nerdiness—"

I dropped the phone on my bed and squeezed my eyes shut. Too much, too soon. I hadn't meant to imply anything so serious. Still wincing, I picked the phone back up.

"Thank you," he whispered.

"Um, what's your *now* fear?" I asked, wanting to put so much distance between myself and that accidental four-letter word.

"I guess . . . that I'll change without realizing it. Wake up one morning and be the person my dad wants me to be instead of who I want. I feel like I keep getting pushed farther down that road, and there's got to be a point of no return, right?"

"I hope not." I'd been thinking about that idea lately, knowing full well I was getting dangerously close to a point of no return with Char, a place at which it would hurt so much to have to let him go . . . even though I knew I couldn't keep him.

We spent the whole night talking, taking turns drifting off to sleep, then startling awake with "Don't hang up, I'm still here."

It was the first night I hadn't cried myself to sleep. The first I hadn't crashed from one nightmare to the next.

And despite the lack of closed-eye time between sunset and sunrise, I felt more rested.

And guiltier.

I stared at the window, watching the glow change from

garish nighttime signs to sunrise clear, and listened as Char told me about working in the garden with his mother, accidentally weeding an entire row of mint plants and trying stick them back in the ground before she noticed.

"Char, I've got some things I need to do." Showering was one, and I desperately needed to use the bathroom—I hadn't figured out a romantic way to request a pee break—but after that I needed to spend some time with my notebook. Reassure myself grieving wasn't any less painful or important, and making new memories with Char didn't mean I was forgetting my family.

"Oh, okay."

"Thanks for keeping me company all night."

"I feel like I should be saying that to you." He laughed.

"Breakfast?" I asked. "Want to meet outside my place at ten?"

"Perfect. Good-bye, Maeve."

I was already opening my notebook as I said good-bye. Skimming my last words before I set down the phone and planning my next ones while I took a quick shower and got dressed. When I sat back down with the notebook, my hand flew, a flood of memory pouring out as my shower-damp hair dripped down the back of my sundress.

Carter ran away once when he was twelve. It was during a bad spell, when my body was destroying platelets as fast as we infused them. He'd tried cheering me up by drawing smiley faces on my skin—and had been rewarded with a thunderous reprimand. He was feeling ignored and angry—and Magnolia

Vickers had dared him to during an ill-fated visit. The same visit where she broke my tea set and he broke his arm because of another one of her dares. In fact, I think it was her <u>*last*</u> *visit to our estate. So he was in a cast—which made it easy for Al Ward to track him.*

"Have you seen a tall, blond boy with a camouflage-print arm cast?" is a pretty easy yes/no question. And it's not like the townspeople didn't know who he was or who our Family was—he was probably more supervised in town than he was on the estate. They quickly ratted out his escape route from the ice-cream shop to the comic book store to the bakery where Al found him halfway through a box of doughnuts.

After he finished puking up his sugar overload, I expected Mother to hug him and cry and Father to yell, but it was Mother who went frosty and Father who intervened in her lecture. He led Carter outside for a man-to-man talk. I watched through the window as Father put his arm around Carter's shoulder and they strolled around the property.

Carter never would tell me what Father said, or how he got past the guards and gates and all the way into town.

I guess now I'll never know.

I felt better after writing down that memory. Sadder, but that's how I was *supposed* to feel. I wiped tears from my cheeks, fixed my makeup, braided my damp hair, then watched the swinging tail of the cat clock. Ten a.m. was when we'd agreed to meet, but I headed out my door at 9:45 and wasn't even a little surprised to see Char already waiting on the sidewalk spot I'd started thinking of as *his*.

I couldn't prevent my smile—a face-stretching grin that made it nearly impossible to mouth the word "hi" against his neck when he curled me into a greeting-slash-embrace.

"Hi, yourself."

I inhaled his smell, then made myself step away from him, from his potential bruises. "Coffee? Maybe coconut?"

"Actually, may I meet your parents?" He looked over my shoulder at the apartment building, and I was grateful for that half second because I needed it to compose my face.

"What?"

"I know it's old-fashioned, but it's how I was raised. If they're home, I'd like to meet them, let your father know you're in good hands. Honorable intentions and all that."

It was probably Midwestern values. I could imagine him sitting down in some other girl's family room, talking to her father before taking her out on a date—I wondered if he drove a truck. I wondered where he took other girls. If they had felt about him the way I did. But I couldn't afford to wonder—I needed to lie.

"They don't live here," I said. "I'm apartment sitting for my aunt—the one from the whole phone-dishes caper. She's out of the country for the summer. In, uh . . . London. For business."

"Wow." He shook his head. "You've got to have the most trusting parents in the world. Who lets a seventeen-year-old apartment-sit by herself?"

The question hung open-ended because it would take too

many lies. But it's not like he'd really offered anything about his family either, not the first time I'd asked, not in any of our conversations since.

"Almost as big a show of trust as a walkabout." I'd intended it as a tease, but it came out as a challenge. I met his eyes with searing contact. "Why are *you* in New York? Really?"

"This is my father's grand concession." Char's face changed, the smile dropping like petals off a flower—leaving an expression as vulnerable and naked as a bare stem. I fought the urge to look away, study graffiti, boarded and barred windows, weeds growing between buildings, and cigarette butts, gum spots on the sidewalk—anything ugly, anything less painful than the look on his face.

I didn't want to ask. And I could have pushed him back to grins and glow with a snuggle or a safe comment, but I slid my fingers between his instead. He squeezed them, but this truth, this moment, was worth a bruise.

"Tell me." The words might press him farther from happy, but if he shared this story—his pain—it would take *us* someplace deeper.

"He's not really one for compromise, my father. We had an argument at my graduation party—I was stupid enough to say something about med school to a friend's mom and he overheard. It was ugly. Like, he got so angry, he thought he was having a heart attack. This month of go-to-New-York-and-sow-your-wild-oats-or-do-whatever is a bribe. I get thirty days of freedom, time and space to let go of my dreams, and he gets the rest of my life."

Char touched my wrist. Dragged a finger down the blue lines

of my arteries, making the blood inside rush and tumble back to my heart, which was skipping beats and breaking with my inability to fix this.

"Was that one of the opportunities you missed out on? Premed?"

He nodded. "I kept thinking he'd come around, but I let him shut down the topic whenever it came up and I never talked about it directly with him. I was scared and stupid—and his face when he overheard me at the party . . . His heart's not great. I could've killed him." Char's face was pale; drops of sweat stood out around the edges of his hair. "If I'd just sat down and had a conversation with him—anytime this year—things wouldn't have blown up like that. And how can I possibly ask him to change his mind now?"

"I'm sorry."

"Thanks, but can we change the topic? I don't want to be thinking about that right now. Not when I'm here, happy, with you."

I nodded. Wondered what the *other* missed opportunity was, then allowed the question to be swallowed by a bigger concern. He only had thirty days. Thirty minus six since we'd met. Minus however many days he'd been in New York before then. I wasn't brave enough to ask for the difference.

"I believe you mentioned coconut coffee," Char said. "I don't think I'm courageous enough for that combination, but I could use some caffeine after last night, what about you?"

"*Coconut* scares you? Then I guess you won't even consider kiwi. Byron will be so disappointed."

I thought we were safe. Away from conversational land mines. Especially when Byron pulled out a new case of fall flavor syrups for us to "taste test." Even I had to admit that sugar-free caramel apple and pumpkin pie sounded more appealing than tropical fruits.

But while we waited for our order, my eyes caught on the back page of the newspaper a man in a Yankees cap was reading and I was trapped by the headline and photo—the same one from our collision day. Mother's favorite. But with bull's-eyes superimposed over everyone but Father.

GRIEVING FATHER OR COLD-BLOODED KILLER?

I flinched when Char touched my arm, getting my attention so he could hand me my cup.

"It's so sad." He nodded at the paper. I'd only just pulled my eyes away and now they followed his gesture back. One small part of me was grateful to this salt-and-pepper man for covering my face in the photo with his pointer finger, but most of me was just trying not to cry. "I don't believe that for a second," Char said.

"What? Why?" His were magic words, cutting the paper's hold on me so I could turn full attention to his explanation.

"I don't know, just a feeling. I mean, he already lost his son, right? That's what they were saying on the news this morning. I may not have the greatest relationship with my father, but no guy who knows the pain of losing one kid would then kill the other one. That kind of tragedy would make you appreciate life *more*, not less."

I put my coffee down on the condiments bar and hugged him.

He had no idea how much I need to hear someone else say he believed my father's innocence.

"Oh, okay. Hello, hug." He kissed the top of my head, then rested one hand on my back while he doctored our coffees with his other. "Plus, look at him—or maybe don't, so that man doesn't think we're checking him out—but Malcolm Landlow doesn't look like the kind of guy . . . I don't know, I guess there's not really a *look*. It's not like I have facts or anything, I just don't want to believe it."

Nestled against Char's chest, I inhaled. Despite the buzz of the bean grinder and cinnamon aroma of a tray of scones being pulled from the oven, I could make out *his* smell and each breath loosened the knot in my chest.

"He looks like he'd sing show tunes and read bedtime stories," I whispered.

Char laughed. "I don't know if I'd go that far. He *was* part of one of those transplant mafias."

I wanted to ask what he thought of them, but I didn't dare, not with my picture a few feet away. So I stepped back and accepted my coffee. "Let's go watch the dogs."

On the sidewalk, Char said, "So, tell me about *your* future. I know you're here for the summer, but where do you live usually? You'll be a senior, right? Have you thought about what you'll do after?"

I ignored all the questions but the last one, which was really the only one that mattered. *After*.

I was already in *after*. Maybe not the after he'd intended, but this, and all days since Carter died. They were all my *after*.

"I've never really thought about college. Maybe? It never seemed like it was for me."

It never seemed like a future my parents would allow. But if I could survive New York City, college couldn't be more dangerous.

"What do you want to do? What do you like?"

I liked the friction of his thumb on my inner wrist. I liked the way he was looking at me, as if the words about to cross my lips would be the most captivating thing he'd ever heard. Except I didn't know which words to use.

These were questions that shouldn't be seventeen years in the asking. I should have ready answers.

"I like . . . politics." The answer surprised me more than him. "Maybe I'll take a post-school year and work on campaigns. Then decide."

"That sounds amazing," he said.

And it did. I could see myself working on the Organ Act. Not like Nolan did, where a single cause became an obsession, but maybe making campaign phone calls, updating a political blog, tracking poll numbers, editing flyers. I loved talking to strangers. I loved reading about policy. I loved watching C-Span.

I fingered the phone in my pocket. It's not as if I lacked for political connections—

There was a crack. A loud one. Like the soundtrack of my worst memories exploding into reality. I flung myself around a corner, pressed flat against a building. Char threw himself after me. I wasn't breathing. I don't think he was either.

The silence was suffocating.

"A car," he whispered. "It was a car backfiring."

I tried to nod. Panic was shaped like an elephant and perched on my chest. My blood was electric, carbonated. It sizzled in my veins and pounded in my temples.

I pushed against it. Fought to be rational. Measured the damaged I'd done—my hands, elbows, knees had all made contact with the brick wall. Knees and elbows were cushioned behind capris and a shirt—hopefully the bruises wouldn't be horrible.

And Char's hand. The one that he had curved protectively around me as he'd shielded my body with his. I'd have a bruise from that—a handprint across my stomach.

But I wasn't broken. I wasn't bleeding.

I wasn't shot.

No one had been shooting.

There'd been no danger.

Char was taking deliberate breaths. "Are you okay, Maeve? I'm sorry I overreacted. I didn't mean to scare you."

It took a few attempts before I managed to say, "Fine," but the picture from the newspaper burned in my mind. *My* face beneath a bull's-eye. I didn't want to be on the sidewalk anymore. I didn't want to stand in a park. Didn't want to feel exposed.

I wanted my mother. I wanted safety. I wanted the impossible.

"I'm hungry," I lied, kicking my foot to shake spilled coffee off my toes. The cups we'd dropped were leaking sluggishly onto the concrete, creating a moat around my sandals. "Let's skip the dog park and get breakfast."

I relaxed in stages. I remembered how to breathe first. Then my pulse slowed. My palms dried. I stopped shivering. I thawed. Began to feel the warmth of Char's arm around my shoulders, felt the security of him holding me close as we walked to the diner.

The smells of burned coffee, frying grease, and bacon soothed me too. And the slightly tacky, slightly waxy feel of the fake-leather padding on the booths when I slid in across from him. The new familiarity of Shanice's greeting and her admiring appraisal of my dining companion.

He let me order for both of us. Didn't even comment about the glycemic index of honey.

We were safe.

I pressed my toes against the inside of his bare calf—needing the contact, needing to feel my skin on his and ground myself in *this* moment, not in the imagined danger replaying in my head.

"Maeve—" Char kept finding reasons to say my not-name. Kept finding reasons to touch the back of my hand. He traced a faint line of mauve there. "Is this from today? The wall? I'm sorry."

It could be. Or from holding his hand any one of a dozen times. Or neither, some other minor unknown cause.

"I'm fine."

I needed to examine my elbows, my knees. Maybe after I'd done that I'd be able to let this go. Forget and focus on Char. Convince him, convince myself I wasn't lying.

"I'll be right back," I said.

I locked the bathroom door. Someone had written "Never Promise" on the wall in red marker. It stood out among the faded black ink of lewd drawings and initials + initials. The girl reflected in the scratched and smeared mirror was paler than I liked. She chewed her lip. I made her stop. I pushed up the three-quarter sleeves of her green-and-yellow-striped shirt, pulled up the hem. Unbuttoned the pants her brother had left for her in an apartment that would never be her home, and pushed down the waistband to examine her knees.

It wasn't bad. It wasn't worth being this upset. Sixteen days ago it would have meant a CBC and probably pushing up the timing of my infusion by a week. Now, it meant being a bit more careful. Cautious. Monitoring my energy level and calling Bob if I felt off. It wasn't ideal, but I wasn't out of options.

I fixed my clothing. Finger combed my hair. Practiced smiling in the mirror.

Shanice was carrying two plates of heart-and honey toast when she pulled me aside on my way back from the bathroom. "Babydoll, *I approve*! And is his father single?"

I laughed. And with the laughter, forced myself to let go of the last piece of me that was still tied in a knot. I could fixate on nothing—on a car backfiring—and let it ruin one of the fewer-than-twenty-four days Char had left, or I could enjoy this moment. Enjoy him.

Shanice winked as she set down our plates and walked away humming.

It was a choice; happiness and caution weren't incompatible, but happiness and fear were.

"Wait until you try this toast," I said, sliding in beside him. "It's way better than those candy bars whose wrappers are always crinkling in your pockets."

I loved his sheepish smile. "You noticed those?"

I poked his shorts pocket to demonstrate. "Crinkle, crinkle. So do you feed your sugar habit *before* you meet me in the morning, or after we say good-bye?" He ducked his head and I laughed. "Both?"

He nodded, and I slid two of my hearts onto his plate. "Good thing *you're* not the diabetic."

Two bites and a toast-heart had disappeared behind his lips. He nodded his approval. "Can I make a cheesy joke about 'You're so sweet, you don't need any extra sugar'?"

"Yes." I leaned my head against his shoulder. "Please do."

CHAPTER 28

"Want to go to the library?" Char asked as we paid the bill. His tone was neutral, but he looked away from me and crinkled the wrappers in his pocket as he pushed open the door to the diner.

"You remember I hate surprises." It was hard to take that first step back outside. Hard to forget the newspaper article, hard to forget the car backfiring, hard to forget that safety was a lie I was telling myself.

Char smiled at me from the open doorway, where air-conditioning rushed to mingle with muggy air. "I remember everything you say."

I took a deep breath and stepped outside. "Then why do you want to go there?"

"I promise, it's just a library. There's a book I want to find."

I opened my mouth, but he smoothed a hand along my cheek, tapped his thumb against my lips. "Before you ask 'what book?'

can I say wait and see? It's not really a *surprise,* just that I want to . . . Okay, *the book* is a surprise, but—"

I moved his hand from my face and tried to think of ways I could suss out whether this was a trap without looking like a freak in case it wasn't. "Is it a biography?"

"What? No." His forehead wrinkled in adorable confusion.

"A book about science? Medicine? Current events?" There was no way to be more specific, and the highly specific details wouldn't be in print yet anyway. Or maybe even ever. It's not like the Zhu or Vickers Families were going to sit down for candid interviews about their work on artificial organs. The thought of Garrett writing a book about his and Carter's double life almost made me smile. Actually, now that I thought about it, Nolan would probably love to pen some unreadable erudite tome about his struggles to work *within* a Family while promoting the Organ Act.

Char interrupted my musings with a laugh. "No. Nothing like that. Nothing that would bore you, I think. It's a children's book."

I studied his face; it was earnest, concerned, eager. And this was *Char.* I trusted him. "Now you've got me intrigued." I looped my hand around his arm, loving the way his pulse beat beneath my fingertips. "Let's go."

We separated in the entryway, promising to meet back up in fifteen minutes. He turned left to enter the Children's Room; I turned toward the stairs that spiraled up to a reading room. After a quick stop at an info desk for directions on how to log on to the Internet, my fingers were flying. Pulling up a half-dozen tabs on the Organ Act, googling mentions of the vice president, Nolan, conspiracy blogs about the murders, my own name. There was so much I needed to know, and I couldn't stop ping-ponging between topics, skimming, gulping down bolded text and diagrams, bracing myself against the romanticized characterization of me as a tragic princess cursed with fragility. Pausing at a picture of Nolan walking down a Capitol hallway with a senator from Utah. Freezing on a blog that featured a re-creation of the crime scene so realistic I had to blink and blink and gasp before I recognized it as a Photoshop mash-up of other pictures from the media. That wasn't the dress Mother had been wearing the day she died, and her hair was shorter in the picture. Our foyer was no longer that shade of gray. Father wasn't that tan. It wasn't possible there had been that much blood.

The honeyed toast threatened to climb back up my throat. How could anyone spend their time creating something so gruesome? For fun? I jammed a finger on the power button, ignored the protest of the man next to me, "Hey, you need to shut it down first!" and staggered out of my chair.

Char found me halfway down the stairs. It was as far as my legs had carried me before I'd needed to sit. To think about anything, *anything*, but my mother's face beneath a mask of blood.

"Hey. Maeve?" He sat down next to me and settled his arm around my shoulder. The warmth and weight of it was an anchor, holding me in the present. "You okay? Is it your blood sugar? Have you tested it?"

I leaned my face against him and nodded. "I just did. It's fine."

"Then what are you doing sitting here?"

"These stairs are beautiful, aren't they?" They were. The walls and the curves, the column they created, and the gilt paint on the domed ceiling at the top of the spiral. I needed to focus on beautiful things right now. Safe things. Innocent things.

"Yeah, they really are. I love how you notice things like this." His face was so close to mine. Then closer. His hand moved from my shoulder, slid up my cheek and into my hair. I turned toward him, and my own hands crept out to tentatively settle on his arms. My face tilted up as his eyelids drifted shut and his lips parted . . .

Footsteps echoed on the steps below us and we both jumped. Laughed nervously, then pulled on smiles.

He stood first, then held out a hand to help me up. "I found the book I wanted to show you, but let's find somewhere more comfortable to read it."

An older woman with a large-print edition of a romance novel smiled as she passed by. I wanted to frown at her, blame her for ruining what was almost our first kiss, but I didn't. When I kissed Char, I didn't want it to be so I'd forget bloody pictures and nightmare memories. I wanted it to be about him, *us*.

Leaning against floor pillows in the Children's Room, Char pulled out a book with a yellow cover. "They're Chinese fairy tales," he explained. "I didn't know any. I wasn't really a fairytale kid. I called my mother and asked if she could tell some, but she only remembers fragments of a few and couldn't keep straight who'd been turned into a carp and who had the magic pot. I thought we'd read some together. What do you think?"

There were times my heart seized up with terror, times it

sprinted from nerves. Then there were those times it seemed to climb upward and block my throat. The moments when I felt so much but couldn't say a single word. Probably because I was feeling *too* much, and would say far, far more than what was acceptable about my feelings. Words with four letters. Sentences with three words. Emotions that couldn't be taken back at the end of a month, would change every day until he left, and cloak him with guilt as a parting gift.

"I just thought . . ." Char lowered the book, glanced at my panicked face, then hastily put a hand over the red dragon that curved across the cover. "Sorry! I didn't see that. You said you liked fairy tales . . ."

I swallowed down my heart and the feelings behind it. Picked up his hand and kissed his fingertips. "Would you read me one, please?"

CHAPTER 29

That night ended not with a kiss, or on the phone with Char, but with a call from the vice president.

"It's my, uh, aunt," I said when my cell rang a few steps from my building.

"See you tomorrow." He raised a hand like he might touch my face, then hesitated and waved instead.

I stood on the other side of the apartment building's door and watched him walk away. I hated the idea of him being out of my sight. Too many people had disappeared from my life, their absences echoed with the good-byes I never got to say. I couldn't handle adding his name to that list.

"Hi, Bob," I said, juggling the flowers I was holding and catching the last notes of his ringtone.

"Hello, Penelope Maeve. How are you holding up?"

"I saw an article about Father," I admitted. "Sometimes I hate freedom of the press."

"I know, Penny, I know. Today is one of the few times I wish I could cut the First Amendment right out of the Constitution."

"Can't you?" I teased. "As a little vice presidential prank? You should at least call the IRS and make sure those reporters get audited this year."

"Consider it done." He chuckled, but it trailed to an awkward pause before he cleared his throat. "I'm going to ask again, and I'll probably ask every time we talk—are you sure you don't want to come to Connecticut?"

I couldn't quite manage an automatic *no* this time. In less than a month Char would vanish like smoke, and I'd be left alone, burned by his absence and too aware of how empty and lonely my life had become.

"Maybe. Not yet. But I'll think about it."

"Please do. I'd love to have you. Kelly and Caleigh would love to have you. Imee too."

When he'd finished asking how I was and I'd finished promising to be careful, I hung up, plugged my phone in to charge on the bedside table, and curled up in the living room's big chair with my family notebook.

I started by documenting everyone's favorite movies.

Father: Braveheart
Mother: You've Got Mail
Carter: The Hangover

Then I settled into some more narrative memories.

When Carter was ten, he desperately wanted a dog. Al and the other security guards used to have a German shepherd that patrolled the perimeter of the estate, and Carter was constantly getting in trouble for trying to play catch with Trigger or sneak him cookies. One time he even tried to hide the dog in his bedroom while Al was in a meeting, and Trigger just about scratched the door down to get out. If there'd been any chance of him getting a dog, that would've ruined it, but it was already hopeless because Mother "didn't like things that shed." Father took pity on Carter and bought him an ant farm instead. Only it got knocked over when he, Mick, and Garrett were playing something that involved hockey sticks and soccer balls and was definitely against the rules. The escaped ants drove Mother into near hysterics . . . and Carter too. He climbed on his bed and shrieked, while Garrett and Mick howled with laughter and I tried to herd up and rescue as many ants as possible before Father brought in the vacuum.

I bought him sea monkeys for his birthday that year. We named them all after different types of soda: Pepsi, Sprite, Dr Pepper, 7UP, Sunkist. Dr Pepper was obviously the smart one. Sunkist and 7UP were the rejects, since neither of us liked those flavors. We totally pretended we could tell them apart.

Carter always said that the first thing he was doing after college, once he had his own place, was getting the biggest, sheddingest dog in the world . . .

I put down my pencil and looked around the apartment. Would he have moved here full time in three years when he graduated? Would he have gotten a dog? Should I, since he couldn't? Questions like these drained all the energy from my limbs, drained all the color from the room.

I hugged a pillow for a long time before getting up to brush my teeth.

There was a text waiting on my cell when I climbed into bed:

Call me if you get lonely. Or if you need someone to come build you a dragon trap.

I smiled weakly, briefly—but it was enough to stop the tears. I tapped out a quick Thank you, then fell into a mostly nightmare-free sleep.

"What do you want to do today?"

I liked that I could roll over and call Char before I got out of bed. Liked that I could ask this and assume his answer included me. At home I had fit into the cracks and gaps in other people's lives. *If I have time, maybe later, I guess you can help me.* Or there were those last few weeks when Garrett was my companion—by Family order, not choice. He'd chafed miserably under the arrangement, bored by my life and by my company. But Char made space for me. I made space for him. It was effortless; it felt both natural and necessary.

I tried not to think about how he'd have to end his "walkabout" and go back home. I tried not to think about the dangers and uncertainty of my own life. Or even the dangers of *him*—that he'd tickled me yesterday afternoon and I had V-shaped bruises up the sides of my ribs in addition to my car-backfiring injuries.

I blocked out all thoughts of my counts and pretended I wasn't feeling more sluggish, that an increasing percentage of my skin wasn't painted in shades from lavender to aubergine. I *should* have said something to Bob last night. I *would* call him later and set up a CBC and infusion.

I rolled the other direction, so my bruises weren't pressed into the mattress and so I could see the plastic toothbrush holder on the dresser—it was filled with roses Char had bought from a street vendor who'd set up on the corner across from my apartment. The vendor had winked at me when Char asked for *all* his roses, one dark caterpillar of an eyebrow arching up with his grin. I'd giggled.

I arranged them while talking to Bob last night. They were also in mugs on the kitchen counter and in Carter's pint glasses on the coffee table. Despite the smell of flowers in the air and Char's breath through the phone at my ear, I knew this wasn't permanent. But I wanted to savor every second.

"Good morning," he answered. "What do you want to do?"

"Let's go to the Natural History Museum—last Tuesday it

was pretty empty." I could practically hear Father screaming about risks and schedules.

"I've never been," said Char, and Father's voice was crowded out by the excitement of showing it to him.

"It opens at ten, so where do you want to meet?" I'd never seen the hotel where he was staying. I hadn't invited him into my apartment. Those were boundaries we weren't crossing. Not yet. And possibly not ever. It was harder and harder not to touch him. Not just holding hands or occasional brushes against his arm, or leaning my leg against his as we sat in the back of a cab or on a park bench.

"I'll come get you," he said.

I wanted more and I think he did too. And it was such a temptation.

I sat up in bed, lifted my shirt, and looked at the plum-colored Vs like bird tracks up my ribs, across the darker purple line from his arm during the nonshooting. It had gotten worse overnight, deepening into an angry midnight color with five distinct fingers. I pulled up my hair and turned toward the mirror, assessing the thumbprint bruise on the back of my neck from when he'd squeezed my shoulder in reassurance yesterday. Kicking off my blankets, I glanced down at the indigo stripe on my ankle from when he'd returned my game of footsie with a little too much pressure. And was that petechiae on my other foot? I stuck it back under the blanket so I didn't have to see. I didn't want to waste any of our time being sick, but I didn't have a choice; my counts were definitely dropping. I would *have* to call Bob today.

"Maeve?" he was asking in the phone. "Is that okay? When will you be ready?"

"No." I shouldn't have him here. It was too easy for that to slip into *come on up*. Too tempting. "I'll meet you there. Out front in an hour?"

It wasn't him I didn't trust, it was me. It was my idiot-pathetic body and the way it warred with my please-touch-me mind.

I knew I'd made the right decision when I saw him waiting on the museum stairs, his eyes looking up from the map he must have gone inside to snag.

All I wanted to do was run up those steps and bury myself in his arms. Let him swing me around like a couple in a romantic comedy. Fit my face against his shoulder and then tip my lips up to—

"Hello!" The anticipation on his face mirrored my own shivery Christmas-morning feeling.

He was going to hold out his arms. Was going to move in for an embrace. So I offered him my hands instead, let him grip them and squeeze.

It wasn't enough, it would never be enough—but those would be insignificant bruises, just new smears of color joining the others on the back of my hands—and the sensation . . . it was reflected in the dewy quality of my voice when I said, "Hi."

"Hello," he repeated, squeezing my hands for one more beat before letting go. "Let's head inside."

I took him in through the Asian Mammals exhibit. It was where I always started, staring at the elephants, amazed that anything could be that big and strong.

Standing in front of them made me feel incredibly small and vulnerable, but also resilient and brave. I didn't have strength on my side. Or size. Or tusks, claws, or teeth like the animals in the cases on either side. But I'd made it. I'd survived.

Char came to stand behind me. Putting his hands lightly on my shoulders and resting his chin on my hair. This wouldn't mark, these light touches. And leaning back against his chest, I felt the safest I had in ages.

"Amazing, isn't it?" he asked.

"Yes." Whether he meant the elephant or the sensation, the answer was true.

We wandered through the animals, never straying too far from each other. It was as if there were a string tethering us together, and it was getting shorter and shorter.

"Asian Peoples?" Char asked, pointing at the sign that led to the next exhibit. His voice went dry as he added, "My father will be so proud that I'm learning about my ancestors."

Though probably not if he'd seen the way Char's eyes glossed around and over the dioramas and displays, and how our conversation veered farther and farther from the content on the informational signs.

"Do you ever feel like if people cared a little more or tried a little harder, they would see the real you?" Char asked as he stepped around a sculpture on a pedestal in the middle of the exhibit hall. I don't think we were even in Asian Peoples anymore; it's possible we'd gone through multiple continents and cultures. I didn't even glance at the sculpture. He didn't either. His eye contact was a magnetic thing, the pull to look at him so strong.

I was scared that if I glanced away—if I even blinked—our polarities would reverse, and we'd never get this moment back.

We stepped through a doorway and up a ramp. He continued, "Like, if they tried, they could see through all the posturing and pretending and reputation and who you're supposed to be and see the true you underneath? The person you are and who you want to be?"

I nodded. These were thoughts I'd had, things I'd felt every day, every hour, every second of my life at the estate. I was more than my illness, more than my last name. I wanted more than doctors' limits and the spectator role my family assigned me. I'd just never been able to put these needs into words or had someone who would listen.

I didn't notice the display in front of me. Char's eyes hadn't left mine, but he somehow knew. And crossed to step between me and the model tree, preventing my collision with its buttressed trunk—it looked tropical, draped with vines, spotted with mushrooms and moss.

I stopped walking, just inches short of making that collision with his chest instead.

He stepped closer, erased those inches.

"You see me," said Char.

Then he kissed me.

It started as a whisper of a caress. Fingers light on my hair, lips light on my lips.

Tingles, but I wanted lightning. And I could practically taste it, just a breath away. A dangerous breath away.

But Char didn't know the danger, didn't know I was breakable, untouchable.

His fingers slipped to my neck, to my back, pulled me toward him. Past the tree and into an alcove. A dark room with flickering light. Touching. Touching. Skin on skin in a way that I could *feel.* In a way that meant something. That meant he wanted me closer, needed to hold me. I needed to be held. Needed to know how it felt to have fingertips press with desire, not skirt away with restraint. Needed them to be *his* fingertips.

His mouth demanded, and mine was more than willing to comply.

Lightning.

And then a cough. A throat clearing. An indignant "Excuse me! I was trying to watch this."

Blinking and breaking apart, but only at the lips, I felt Char's chin trace the top of my head as he also swiveled around to take in our surroundings.

It was a small theater. A burgundy room with a wall-mounted screen. A male voice narrating images of jungle green. There were two rows of benches, but just a single occupant. The woman who had been coughing, clearing her throat, and glaring up at us. "This is not a nightclub. Go canoodle somewhere else."

The word "canoodle" made me giggle. Or maybe it was just *everything* that made me giggle. The post-kiss high. The texture of Char's shirt against my cheek. That he tasted like sugar and smelled like clean air and open spaces, like the city hadn't managed to touch him. The shape of his shoulders and the ways his arms felt around my back. That the reality of this moment was greater than all the times I'd imagined it.

Char apologized to the woman, and I giggled. Kept giggling even after we'd backed out of the room and reoriented ourselves: South American Peoples. Distracted by Char, I'd managed to ignore half the peoples of the world.

And for the rest of the afternoon I ignored so much more. Dinosaurs, the giant whale, meteors. I think we went through all these exhibits, but all I was aware of was his hand curled around mine. The way my lips still tingled. And the heat of his voice in my ear as he whispered commentary that rarely had anything to do with the display cases in front of us.

CHAPTER 30

"Have you ever taken a guided tour?" Char asked when we crossed the street into the muggy haze of late afternoon and Central Park. "I think I'd like to. It would have been a waste today"—he paused just long enough to kiss me quickly—"today I was paying more attention to you than to the museum. But sometime, would you want to?"

One touch of his mouth left me too breathless to speak, so I nodded.

"I bet the biodiversity exhibit is fascinating. Have you ever thought about the incredible number of species we've already hunted or polluted out of existence?"

"Um, not really."

"From a medical standpoint, I've always wondered if the earth was once stocked with all the things we'd need to combat every disease—like a jungle plant that could cure cancers. A seaweed that could be used on skin grafts. My mom's really into gardening and herbal medicine. The healing properties of plants are amazing—do you know all the research that's going on with diabetes and plant-based medicines?"

I shook my head, my eyes going wider with respect and with curiosity. Not necessarily about medical uses for undiscovered seaweed, but about Char and his intelligence, his passion. I wanted to hear his theories. I wanted to know what he would study if he were allowed to be premed, and what life was like on his ranch; his mother's gardens and his father's expectations. I wanted to know the shape of each of his fingers and exactly how they felt on my skin. I wanted to learn the limits of my skin's tolerance, and I wanted to test those limits thoroughly.

"I think we'll have a cure for diabetes in your lifetime, Maeve. I just worry we're so busy cutting down and polluting the planet that we'll destroy these species before we ever find all their potential . . ." He trailed off and blushed. "Anyway, that's enough of that. I'm so busy boring you with my nonsense I didn't even notice the sky turning dark."

"I like listening to you. I don't think it's nonsense at all." There'd been an undercurrent to the way he'd said the word; I could tell it wasn't the first time it had been used to describe his thoughts. I waited until his face relaxed into relief, then tipped my head back to look up at the sky. It was ominous. The color of a fresh bruise with clouds crowding on top of one another and adding darker and darker layers.

We'd been strolling toward my place, but we traded a

meander for a brisk walk. Char reached for my hand to pull me around a nanny trying to pack up a baby and I held on tight.

The first drops of rain hit us when we were still four blocks away. I felt them, but was paying far more attention to my thoughts than the weather. I should invite him in. I should let him wait out the storm with me.

That was polite.

But he was eighteen, on his walkabout or whatever. Going to college in the fall.

I was seventeen and felt like a child. I spent most nights longing for my parents and wishing I'd packed my teddy bear.

If he were in my apartment—with no parents or interruptions—anything could happen. I mean, I could *let* anything happen. Or *choose* it—that was probably the most appropriate word.

But—I needed to tell him. If not everything, I needed to show him the birds'-tracks tickling bruises, the blotches from today's brushes against elbows and exhibit cases. Explain the dark lines on the backs of my hands, one of which he was currently lifting to his lips. "This looks much worse than it did yesterday. How hard did you hit the wall? I'm sorry."

I just smiled and shrugged, but I'd have to tell him to be careful with me and explain why. It wasn't safe not to and it wasn't fair to either of us.

And maybe if he took that news well, I'd tell him more. Learn the answers to whether or not he'd have liked me if he'd met me as I was before: a dishwater blonde in pastel clothing trapped inside a gilded cage. And was I worth the risk once he found out who I was, who my parents were, and how that all factored into my very uncertain future?

While I'd been consumed by internal debate, he'd been handing bills to a street vendor with thick eyebrows and a dark coat turned up at the collar. Char opened an umbrella, holding it more above my head than his own.

It was hot, sticky, standing so close, crowded by my thoughts and the humidity that the rain didn't seem to be breaking.

"I can't go back." His voice was so quiet I wanted to shush the pattering of raindrops on the vinyl above our heads. "I thought I could do this—go home, go get the degree my father picked, live the life he's chosen for me. I appreciate the advantages he's given me and the sacrifices he's made, but . . ." His confessions sounded as if they were being ripped out one by one. His eyes were dull with pain.

I didn't dare say anything. Just curled my fingers over his on the umbrella handle and prayed he'd continue.

"He's never even considered the future I want—or how ill-suited I am to follow in his footsteps. Most people would be proud to have a son who wants to be a doctor. But it's not *his* plan for me, so he rejects it. My whole life he's been telling me everything I *am* is wrong because I'm not like him."

"I'm sorry." I wanted to say something more profound, prove I was listening, that I understood and meant so much more sympathy than seven letters could convey.

"I can't go back. And *you*. You're seventeen and on your own. You're figuring out how to live with your medical limitations."

I stopped walking. Pulled my hand away from him. Felt the chill of raindrops down my collar as he continued forward before realizing I wasn't following and turned around with a confused look on his face.

"What are you talking about?" I demanded.

"This summer. You're here alone—so soon after being diagnosed with diabetes. If you can be brave like that . . . and I swore I'd take chances. I did *with you*—I never would've had the guts to go up to a girl like you—imagine if I hadn't? No! I need to find the courage to tell my dad what I want. Which is to stay here. I'll go to Columbia instead of Georgetown. I'll be a doctor. It's just that my father . . . , he—"

"Want to come in?" I asked. We were outside the building. I'd let myself get all the way to the door without having my keys in hand, a piece of dangerous laziness that would've earned lectures from any Ward. Even Garrett would call that unforgivable.

But it didn't matter. What mattered were the conversations we'd have once we climbed a few flights of stairs and shut out the world. When I listened to the rest of his plans and asked more about what had brought him to New York—what was the second lost opportunity that inspired his take-chances vow? What could I do to help?

When I told him who I was. When I told him what that meant. And that if he was staying in New York—and wanted to stay a part of my life—what that could mean for him and his safety.

He nodded.

I reached for the door handle, but it swung out to meet my hand. Followed by a pixie haircut on a tall, thin girl.

"There you are!"

I didn't know my neighbors. They were anonymous people with heads and eyes kept down when we passed each other in halls and stairs. They treated my greetings and attempts at conversation like they were alien and dangerous, responded in exhales and monotones.

I didn't know my neighbors, but I knew this girl.

"I've been waiting for you all morning," she drawled in her Texan accent, coming out to stand on the step, and frowning up at the sky. "Come in, you're getting wet."

Char had been lowering his umbrella when the door opened. I reached back and held it there, horizontal, blocking his face. He reacted to my movement with a stiffness of his own. "I didn't know you had company," he said. "I should let you go."

"Yeah," I managed. The back of my throat itched with panic. I wanted to beg him to take me with him, keep me safe. Instead, I would just keep *him* safe—get him away.

I stepped around the umbrella, using it as a screen to grab a kiss, this one fierce. Fearful.

Char touched my cheek.

"I'll call you later," I said.

He nodded. Kissed me again. So quickly he didn't notice my lips were trembling. "Good-bye," he whispered.

Then he left, twirling away so he was just a boy beneath an umbrella disappearing down the block. And I was left alone with a face I recognized from Christmas cards.

I was weak with fear, with relief. No matter what happened next, Char was gone. Char was safe.

The girl cleared her throat. "Still waiting here. And those shoes are going to be ruined if you get them much wetter."

"Hi, Maggie," I said.

CHAPTER 31

Magnolia Vickers pivoted and opened the door, holding it for me. I considered not going inside. Maybe I could run for it. Catch up with Char. Get away.

But every second I kept her here was a second he could get farther from us. I didn't want her to think of him, I didn't want her to remember I'd had a guy with me. If this was it—if it was not the Zhus, or Nolan, or Mr. Tanaka, but the Vickers, and this was *it*—I needed to know I'd saved Char. He was innocent, not a part of this lifestyle of blood and bodies and black market; he didn't deserve to die for me.

"There's this concept called "inside"; shall I demonstrate it for you?" She flitted in and out the door, stepping around and behind me with the grace of a long-legged bird. "Now let's see you try it."

Her hands were up, like she might push me, prod me, damage me. I darted forward to avoid the bruises, through the doors, the second propped open with her purse.

"What do you want?" I asked.

"Just a minute, we'll get to that. First"—she leaned close enough for me to smell her spicy perfume, tilted her head, whispered—"is cross-pollinating, like, a trend now? Just remember who started it."

I'm sure this was some sort of riddle. Perhaps I was supposed to respond with a coded answer, provide some words that demonstrated I was in the know.

I was never in the know.

I was the most peripheral of people. Even in my own life. And even if the answer to that riddle would save me, no one had ever bothered to clue me in.

This knowledge slumped my shoulders, brought the weight of everything pressing down on me.

"What are you doing here?"

"Walk with me," she said, tucking my hand over her arm. She squeezed it against her side—not quite bruising-tight, but the threat was there. Maggie had always been a voice that refused to be shouted down by the narrow-minded Family males. Not even the Ward brothers could tell her what to do.

And now she was towing me toward the stairs.

"The keys weren't where they should be." Her voice was still that lilting, throaty song I remembered. "I assume you have them? And the one to the new lock?"

Everything was inverted again. The safe gone from my haven. How long had they been watching me? What else did they know? Char—

I'd been selfish to pretend I could have him; that he wasn't in danger every time he stood next to me. People willing to gun down my family would hardly stop and spare a rancher's son who got caught in the crossfire.

My steps felt heavy. I'd slowed, and Maggie tugged impatiently for me to keep up. On the fourth floor she knocked the rounded toe of her black lace-up boots against the door. It left a scuff on its surface.

"The keys?" she prompted, releasing my hand to cross her arms.

I dug them out of the bottom of my purse. Sheer carelessness. A testament to how dangerous it had been to participate in the fairy tale I'd been playing with Char. My keys should've been in my hand long before I approached the building. I should have been more aware. Not of his kisses or how good he smelled, but of the girl standing in my vestibule watching my approach. I should have seen her first and circled around, circled away.

I squeezed my fingers around the keys. What would Carter have done in this situation? What would Garrett? Not the Garrett who'd asked to kiss me a lifetime ago—I couldn't picture him clearly anymore—but the Garrett who wore a gun, shot tires, fought back.

They'd say going in that apartment meant never coming out again. They wouldn't go down without a struggle.

I pulled my arm back and threw the keys—sending them arching up and onto the steps above us, then I spun to flee.

Maggie was already blocking my path, a wry smile on her lips. "Really? Is that the best you can do? Don't disappoint me. Your brother spoke so highly of you, I don't like thinking he was wrong."

Carter. When had she spoken to him? *How* had she extracted information?

"Let's go get the keys," she said evenly, circling her hand back around my elbow. "Then we'll go in the apartment, have a seat, and you can tell me what you've been up to for the past few weeks and how you ended up with a lovely piece of rival on your arm."

"Lovely piece of rival" was a rather appropriate way for her to describe herself. But the Vickers hadn't been our rivals. They hadn't ever been our rivals. The least contentious of the inter-Family relationships had been between my father and hers. When had that changed? Why?

"I don't want anything to do with all of this." I held my hands up, signifying my lack of weapon with my empty palms.

"That's sort of disappointing, Pen. I was really hoping you were more than a pretty-faced puppet." She dragged me up the stairs. This grip would leave a mark. "Actually, it's more than *disappointing*. It's disappointing our mothers let themselves be just painted figureheads. It's downright unacceptable you'd consider playing that role too."

She may be here to kill me, to make a clean sweep of the

Landlows, but I wasn't going to make it easy for her. She bent to snag the keys, and I wrenched my arm out of her grip.

"Carter always said you were nothing but trouble and you were going to get someone killed . . . I guess he was right."

The keys dropped from her fingers, the animation dropped from her face, leaving behind something that looked like it might have been pain.

Maybe.

It was hard to tell because I'd taken the opportunity to push past her and run down the stairs.

CHAPTER 32

A couple seconds of surprise bought me a few stairs. But not many. Not enough.

Maggie caught up before I'd hit the third floor. "Do not make me hurt you, Penelope," she warned. "We're going in that apartment, and we're going to talk. I'd rather you be focused on *me* and not on the bruises I've given you while pushing you through the door."

"I have nothing to say to you."

"That's okay—you can *listen*. I have plenty to say to you. I've got all sorts of things Carter made me promise to tell you, and I've got questions. So many questions. Like, why didn't you call me sooner? How could you go to the Zhus and not me? And why did you add another lock on our apartment?"

She reached in her pocket and pulled out a second set of keys.

Two of them. Banded with the same colored rings as the ones Carter left behind.

"*Our* apartment?" I asked.

"Pen." She sighed in exasperation. "Don't even tell me you thought Carter painted a room purple and picked out those curtains."

"You're not here to kill me?"

She laughed. Maggie had always had the best laugh. It was loud and carefree, wild and throaty. I couldn't imagine ever feeling uninhibited enough to make a noise like that.

"I'll be lucky if your brother doesn't haunt me for that mark on your arm . . ." Her laughter choked to a halt, her gaze dropped to the keys in her hand. Her voice was quieter when she raised serious eyes to my face. "I wish he'd haunt me. I wish I could see him again."

Her implications made me narrow my eyes. Whatever game she was playing, I wasn't going to participate. "What do you want from me?"

"Inside." She herded me up the stairs, slid the right keys into the right locks, turned them, pushed the door open, and entered. She didn't wait to see if I followed, but crossed the room and claimed the big chair. Hooking her toes under the rim of the coffee table, she pulled it closer and propped her feet on top. Char's roses wobbled in their beer-glass vases but didn't fall over. Reaching behind her, she fished an afghan out of a woven basket. Pulling it up to her face, she inhaled with her whole body, arching forward, shoulders creeping upward.

Then all of her seemed to melt in defeat. Her eyes sought

mine where I stood in the hall. "It doesn't smell like him anymore. I hoped . . ." She shook her head and dropped her chin.

"You and Carter?" I stepped inside the door, leaving it open, and leaned against the wall. "How?"

"You didn't know? Whose clothing did you think was in the closet—that dress looks good on you, by the way. And did you really think the shampoo and such around the apartment were his?"

I'd assumed—foolishly, selfishly—that they'd been for me. That Carter had set this whole place up for *us*.

"He really never said anything to you—about me?" She leaned forward and searched my face. Then stood, five feet eight inches of bottled energy and compressed stress. She seemed to absorb all the space in the apartment as she paced a lap around the coffee table and into the kitchen. She snorted and called, "Nice job on the freezer." Then opened cabinets and the fridge, helped herself to a glass of something, and came back into the main room.

I was seated on the edge of the couch. Less because I felt comfortable around her—the door was still open—and more because my legs wouldn't support me any longer.

"No one ever tells me anything," I said sullenly. I considered following Garrett's advice about keeping my cards tipped up, but what was the point in flipping them over one at a time just to reveal they were all blank? "Garrett's been in this apartment too, and he never mentioned it being *yours*."

"Ah, you and Garrett; Carter loved the idea in theory—but wanted to kill him when it actually happened. And your timing couldn't have been worse; those two did not need something else to fight about." She sat down on the coffee table. "Garrett didn't know about me."

"Impossible. Carter told Garrett everything. He brought him with him everywhere."

"No," she corrected. "He didn't."

Maggie reached in her purse, then handed me an envelope. My name was on the front in Carter's slash-and-dash handwriting. On the back he'd drawn a cube over the seal—something he and Garrett had done with their secret club messages when they were little. It hadn't been opened. "I got an envelope in the mail from Carter the day of his funeral. This was in it."

"Why am I only getting it now?"

"Because I was a little distracted by mourning, and then, sugar pie, you were dead."

"Your mom used to call me sugar pie."

"My mother calls everyone sugar pie. It saves her from having to learn their names." She arched an eyebrow and answered my unasked question, "I only use it when people are being dumber than a box of hammers."

"So he knew?" I wanted to tear this envelope in half. Burn it. Shred it. He'd known he was going to be killed and he hadn't done anything to stop it. He hadn't told me.

Maggie lowered her head. Her shoulders shrugged, and the rest of her seemed to slump with their descent. "I don't know. I didn't get a letter or explanation. I got a sticky note: *Take care of Pen. I love you.*"

I looked at the envelope again. It was a paper betrayal.

I hated it.

I cherished it.

"How did you figure out I wasn't? Dead, I mean."

"The electric bill gets paid automatically from my account every month—this month's bill was crazy higher than last's. I didn't know it was necessarily *you*, but it was clear someone was using the apartment."

"He brought me here, showed me the keys, and told me it was safe. How could he know he was in danger and not do anything to stop it?"

"Why are you asking me?" Her voice wavered. "Why can't *you* have any answers? Why did I come all this way if—"

She put down the cup and walked toward the bedrooms. There were the thuds of drawers opening and things banging. A choked, broken sound of sob and triumph, then she reemerged. A sweatshirt draped over one arm and a letter in her hands. She held it up. This one was addressed to *Mags*.

"I bought this for Carter." She slipped the University of Texas sweatshirt over her head and burrowing into the collar to inhale whatever bit of him was left behind. "But we'd fight over who got to wear it whenever we were here."

She wasn't lying. I wasn't sure why an orange piece of clothing with frayed cuffs and a hem that hit her midthigh demonstrated that better than keys to the door or her presence here, but it did.

"How long have you been dating my brother?" I demanded. When she didn't look up from the envelope in her hands, I snatched it away. "Hey!"

"Excuse me?" She was on her feet, towering over me with a thunderous expression, bringing flashbacks of the time she'd kneed twelve-year-old Garrett in the crotch for putting a spider in her hair.

"You said you wanted to talk. To ask me some questions. Well, I have some too. Answer mine and I'll give this back." I was under no delusion I could really keep it away from her. But I could crumple it. I could tear it. And I didn't think she'd take that risk.

"I wasn't *dating* him. I wasn't some high school groupie. We were in love."

Love? Carter?

Something jealous and acrid was crawling up the back of my throat; it settled sour on my lips, curving them into a bitter smile and coming out as a disbelieving laugh. "My brother—sleeping with the enemy. Why not? Everything I thought I knew about my life is wrong, why not that too?"

Her own disbelieving laugh was twice as acidic, twice as loud. "How's the view from your high horse, Penelope? And does Zhu Jr. think hypocrisy is an attractive trait?"

"I have no idea what you mean."

"Ha. Nice try." She stepped closer, snatching the letter from my hand and pausing at the apartment door to say, "I'm going to go find a quiet place to read this. I get you're mad—I'm mad too—but don't lie to me. I saw you with Ming Zhu earlier. If you say *my* Family is your enemy, then how do you categorize the guy attached to the lips you were kissing?"

"Ming? No. He's shorter than me. He has glasses. Char can't be . . ."

But Ming wasn't still eleven or however old he'd been when I last saw him. He wasn't frozen in real life like he was in my mind, at the cross section of awkward and adolescence.

"No." I breathed it out as a whisper, a single word, a lie I desperately wanted to be true.

"Yes. Oh, so very much, yes! I saw him two weeks ago at *your* funeral. He was a mess—looks like you've cheered him up."

She didn't wait for me to respond before she left, slamming the apartment door behind her, which was good, because I was speechless.

CHAPTER 33

I could have chased her down. I probably should have. But I wasn't ready for any more secrets. I didn't want to handle the implications of what she'd said.

I didn't want to stand. I wanted to sink. Sink into the couch, and sink below the level of thinking required to prevent my mind from connecting the dots.

I didn't know Char's last name.

His reaction when I told him he didn't look like a Charlie. He *wasn't* a Charlie, he was a *Ming*. Ming *Zhu*. Or Zhu Ming, actually, if I remembered Mother's lessons correctly. And no wonder he didn't look like a Midwestern rancher. He lived in California, and the only thing his family harvested was organs.

I pressed my hand over my eyes, wanting to reach behind them and claw this out of my brain. Unlearn it. Forget it. Scramble my neurons until everything made sense, or until I no longer cared that nothing did.

Heartbreak was for another time. A time when it wouldn't crush me. A time after I was safe. A time when I knew which end was up and where I belonged.

If I ever belonged anywhere again.

Now was for Carter. For grief. For his need to have the last word—always. And my gratitude for whatever was in this envelope.

I couldn't stay here. Not anymore. Not when Maggie had keys and Char wasn't Char.

I counted the bills in my wallet and swallowed. I hadn't been planning long term. Stupid. Even after I realized Garrett wasn't coming, I hadn't slowed my spending. There was enough cash left for a few nights at a hotel, but not forever. Not even a week. I hoped I liked Connecticut, because I didn't see any other option.

But I couldn't call Bob yet. I wanted one last night of independence and space to read Carter's letter.

I took off Maggie's dress and put on the clothing I'd worn when I left the estate: my favorite jeans and a pale-blue cotton shirt. I packed up Carter doll, my notebook, and the few things that were mine. My purse wasn't even bulging when I put the letter on top and stepped out the door, locking only the lock Maggie had the key for.

There were several hotels within a ten-minute walk. I'd mentally mapped routes to and from them, just in case. I knew their prices and which accepted cash. I'd done all the proper planning except for budgeting, except for believing I'd really have to stay there. It was like I thought the preparation was enough, thought that by knowing the information, I'd never have to use it.

It was a humbling thought as I stood in front of the counter and traded bills and a fake name for a plastic keycard and information about checkout times and a question about my lack of luggage.

"The airline lost it," I answered, cutting off further questions with, "I'll let you know if I need anything, but right now I need a nap. Jet lag. You said the elevator was over this way?"

My apologetic smile was halfhearted as I accepted a city map and quashed any other niceties by crossing the lobby and jamming the Up button.

Room 1306 had windows, curtains, a bed, bedside table, chair, TV, bathroom, generic art print, and an air conditioner that rattled loudly. I noticed these things as I swept the room for "danger"—the kind that was unnamed, came in quotation marks, and could be just about anything, anywhere.

The kind I knew existed but had never been trained to identify or defend against. So I looked under the bed, checked the closet and behind the shower curtains. Stupid, waste-of-time, elementary gestures that didn't make me feel even slightly safer.

I locked the dead bolt, slipped the chain into place, dragged the chair in front of the door, and sat in it with my bag in my lap. I held Carter's letter in both hands. If I didn't open it, I could tell myself there was still one more point of contact with him. If it stayed sealed, I could imagine it saying anything. And I'd never be proven wrong.

My hopes were so sky high I knew the envelope could only contain disappointment, but he wouldn't have mailed it if it weren't important. I stuck a finger under the flap and pulled it open, ripping the cube into two jagged halves.

The sheet I pulled out looked like it had been torn from a notebook similar to the one I'd been filling with memories. It was folded crookedly, and the handwriting started rushed and sloppy and became almost illegible by the postscript.

Hey Pen—

I've only got a minute. I've got to do this now before I lose my nerve or get caught. And maybe this note is straight-up paranoia, but I don't know . . . Things don't feel right.

I'm about to go torch my clinic. MY clinic. Yeah, I have one. Father doesn't know. It's a cadaver clinic—like the Everlys. It's a mistake.

But if things go wrong, then I need you to RUN. Get off the estate and go. Go to the place I showed you tonight. Trust no one but Maggie Vickers. I wrote her number on the back.

I wish I had time to write more. Hopefully I will. Hopefully we'll be eating doughnuts soon.

I love you, kid. More than I ever told you.

Carter

P.S. In September I want to be the one to drop you off on your 1st day of senior year. You're not too cool to be seen with me, right?

I ran, Carter. Now what?

CHAPTER 34

Carter's letter was full of too-late warnings and empty of answers. All I could do was hold it and think of him and Char.

Three a.m.

That's how long it took for my emotions to drain away one at a time: despair, disappointment, confusion, shock, betrayal, grief, desolation, loneliness, longing.

All that was left was hardened rage that sat in my stomach like the last glowing ember in the middle of a forest fire's destruction.

And enough energy to pick up my phone and dial Char's number, determined to deliver a razor-tongued speech. I'd scribbled a draft on hotel stationery with pen that had punched through the paper. I would make him hear I wasn't fooled by him anymore. That he hadn't shattered me.

I may be splinters and fragments, but it wasn't because of him. I hadn't given him that much power.

The pieces of me he'd received had never been whole to start.

And when he'd pretended—

He'd pretended.

We're sorry. The number you have dialed is no longer in service.

The automated message brought a flood of exhaustion and helplessness. Why? Was he scamming me? Did he recognize Magnolia? Was this some new trick to unbalance me in a world where everyone already felt like a threat?

I made a nest in the bathtub and slept there. If anyone *did* find me in this no-name hotel, they'd enter the room and go right to the bed—passing the bathroom door. It wouldn't buy me much, but maybe those seconds could be used to slip out unobserved. Tomorrow I'd go on the offensive. Tonight my mind needed to shut down, shut out the all questions and uncertainty. Forget Carter's postscript and the life we could've had if things had gone differently that night.

It seemed like I should fall apart. Like when I woke up stiff and sore in a bathtub with my head full of fresh grief and betrayal, that all that was left to do was fall apart.

And if I'd truly cared for Char the way I thought I had—I should be immobilized by this, trapped in bed by a box of tissues and a broken heart.

My heart still beat within my chest. Each pulse a painful

reminder of what I thought I had, what I'd thought was real. No, it *was* real, at least my part of it had been.

But I was alive. I'd survived so much worse than heartache, and I wasn't going to dishonor my family by letting Char be the thing that broke me.

If he was in New York to kill me, why had he waited? Why had he kissed me and held me and wrapped his life around me? Why had he shared about his father and defended mine? Was that whole conversation in the coffee shop some sort of cruel test to see if I'd react?

What had he wanted?

My gaze fell on the map the clerk had given me. I grabbed a pen from the bedside table and started tracing our walks. Maybe they weren't mindless. Maybe we weren't weaving back and forth without a purpose. Maybe Char was looking for something.

We'd taken three walks. If it hadn't started raining, we might have taken a fourth yesterday—and I'd bet all the cash in my purse, the fourth would have included some portion of 95th Street, because the first three all overlapped there.

I picked up my phone and dialed the digits Carter had written on the back of his letter.

"Hi, Maggie."

"Thank God! Are you okay? Where are you?"

"I'm fine. What's on 95th Street between Columbus and Broadway?"

"No idea. You? Do you need me to come get you?" Either she was a good liar, or, if my hunch was correct, there was something Carter hadn't told her. An address.

"No."

"You can't disappear. Not again. Is this a number I can use to reach you? I'm writing it down, hang on. The one Carter gave me goes to a full voice mail." I practiced feeling numb, determined, whole, for the seconds she was gone. "Okay, I'm back. Come home, okay? We should talk. I'm sorry if I shocked or scared you yesterday, but we should really talk."

"It's not safe at the apartment anymore."

"Of course it is," she said. "No one will bother us here. Just come back."

"Don't you get it? Char—er, Ming tracked me down in New York City—he knows where the apartment is." I paused to take a breath, to steady my voice. "If he killed the rest of my family, I've got to be next."

"Ming did not kill your family, Penny. Come home."

"Fine, *he* didn't." Even now I couldn't see the hands that had held mine being the ones holding a gun or a knife. "But his Family did."

"What possible reason could the Zhus have for hurting your family?"

I'd thought about this a lot last night while listening to the shower drip. "Artificial organs."

"In that case, why would they be going after *your* Family? No offense, but you haven't even entered the artificial organ race. Mine is the one to beat there, and no one in my Family's been threatened."

"But if mine had come out in favor of the Organ Act, that would tie up everything."

"Look, I've been in every one of my Family's council meetings, I know what I'm talking about. No one was really concerned about that," said Maggie.

"It has to be them." Because if it wasn't, then why had he . . . "No! It does. Carter's body was carved with the Chinese characters for 'warning.' "

"Penelope, stop. Just stop. That was *tattoo Chinese*—the type of thing a drunk spring breaker gets inked on his body. Then, when they're sober, someone tells them it's not a real word or that it says 'mountain sister green.' It's not the Zhus. Believe me. My dad and Mr. Zhu have been in daily contact since your parents' murder."

"Then who?"

"Come back. We'll talk."

CHAPTER 35

"Here's the thing, Maggie, I'm glad my brother was happy with you, and I'm so grateful you brought me his letter, but . . ." Despite the number of times I'd rehearsed this speech during my walk back to the apartment, I couldn't quite finish it now that she was in front of me.

"But you don't know me? We're not friends?" she prompted. She put her hands on her hips, but it was hard to take her seriously with bed head and while wearing a hot pink and black zebra-print pajama shorts set.

"Yeah, kind of. And I don't have time to sit down and make new friends. It's not that I don't want to, or I don't like you, or we can't ever do this . . . it's just, I need to figure things out first."

"Like what? You need my help."

"Like if the guy I thought I loved was really trying to kill me." Char's roses were still everywhere. Blood red, police-tape yellow, tombstone white.

"Which one? If you're talking about Ming, he thinks *you*, as Penelope Landlow, are already dead. He attended your funeral, we both did. And he didn't have anything to do with your family's murders, so let's move on, m'kay?"

But that didn't change the fact that his phone was disconnected and he'd disappeared.

"So . . . it's about Dead Meat, isn't it?"

"Thank you for catching up! See, you *do* need me." Maggie sat on the coffee table, crossing one long leg over the other and taking a sip of something from the travel mug I'd bought at Byron's. "I just wish he'd actually gotten to burn the place down."

"So who was it? The Everlys?"

"What? No. Catch up, Penny. Haven't you been watching the news?"

"Um, no. Been a little busy trying not to die."

"The Everlys are DOA—not literally, but between the dead teacher case and a clinic raid all their power players are behind bars. There's not anyone left to be a threat."

"Then who?"

Maggie opened her mouth, but I was already turning away, both from her and the idea forming in my head. Not the Zhus. Not the Vickers. Not the Everlys.

Dead Meat.

It all came down to this. My brother's legacy according to Garrett. The cause of his murder, according to Maggie. A mistake, according to Carter.

"Go take a shower and get dressed," I told her. "We're going to visit Deer Meadow."

"I don't know where it is."

"I do." And I was going to get some answers.

But first I got his gun.

It was right where I'd left it, in the bottom drawer of his desk. My reaction was the same too: revulsion, the contents of my stomach wanting to crawl out my throat, my fingers wanting to slam the drawer shut, my feet wanting to back out of the room.

Instead I picked it up, felt its weight on my palm, the heaviness of its capabilities on the tips of my fingers. I flipped the safety off, then flipped it back on. It was loaded. I didn't even have to check. I'd heard Al Ward say it enough times, "The only dangerous gun is an empty one," and "There's no safety in a gun without bullets."

I grabbed the wad of cash too. Who cared if it was blood money—my whole life was blood-soaked.

I slid both into my bag and left. Carter had kept this address from Maggie and kept her a secret—instinct told me not to bring her there. And there wasn't time to hesitate. There wasn't time to second-guess or talk myself out of this. Or answer whatever question Maggie called from behind the bathroom door, her words drowned out by the pounding of my pulse in my ears. The pounding of my feet down the stairs, and then the crash-dash-stumble of almost slamming into a man as I flew out the front door.

A man who wasn't Char.

Ming.

Whatever.

It wasn't a repeat of our once upon a time, not-such-a-fairy-tale-after-all meeting.

And I didn't hit this man. At least, *I* didn't hit him. My bag did. Mints and keys and wallet went flying. The gun didn't. But did he feel it? Could he tell from its shape or weight that there was danger and illegality sitting in the lining of my designer purse?

I scrambled to shove things back in my bag, needing to be gone before Maggie caught on, to not be noticed, and thus not noticing when he followed me for a few yards.

"Wait! Wait! These are yours too."

I didn't want to make eye contact, barely let my glance flicker from his Yankees cap to his palm before I grabbed the lip balm and piece of paper he held out and shoved them in my pocket. My "thanks" was a mumble over my shoulder as I kept walking. Pausing felt like stopping, and I needed to do something for once. Something. Anything that felt like it was helping my brother or avenging him or anything but waiting around in a life without purpose. Without anything but waiting.

And hoping they—the "they" that wasn't Zhu/Vickers/Everly and had to be internal, the "they" that must have sat across from me at dinners, walked the halls of my house, seen all my moods, and known all my weaknesses—didn't kill me first.

CHAPTER 36

It could have taken hours to search the block and try to figure out which building was Deer Meadow; Maggie could have remembered my mention of 95th Street and tracked me down; I could have been wrong about the goal of Char's walks.

It didn't. She didn't. I wasn't.

The facade of the building was exactly what I'd expected: elegant stonework set with arched windows, graceful iron railings trailing down immaculate steps. But no sign with DEER MEADOW in classical calligraphy. Instead, in light blue on a gold background, the same stag's-head emblem as the key I'd found in Carter's apartment. So, not for the freezer.

I was debating going back to the apartment to get it, knocking, or doing the smart thing and calling Bob, when I looked up and saw Garrett shutting the leaded glass doors behind him and walking down those steps.

"Penelope?" His face was ghastly white. I wanted to tell him to sit. Put his head between his knees. Breathe into a bag. Wondered if he would benefit from a platelet infusion. Questioned my own lack of reaction and whether I could be in shock.

Slowly he closed his gaping mouth and reached out to touch me. His fingers brushed my sleeve lightly and he inhaled with a gasp, seizing my arms and crushing me to him. "Is it really you?"

"You're hurting me." My words were flat, dead things. My head buzzed with white noise. Shock was likely. Shock, or I'd already used up my entire supply of the brain chemicals that caused emotions. Char would've been able to name them and tell me if that were even possible, but he'd abandoned me.

The thought made me sob—just once—before I fell back into numb.

Once was enough, Garrett's fingers released immediately. "I'm sorry. I'm so sorry. Are you okay?"

"Yes." I'd learned more about my limits these past weeks, and the two handprints already blooming on my arms no longer had me scrambling for the clinic.

"Look at those bruises. I'm so sorry, princess. I just—I just can't even believe it's you. I thought . . ." He paused to swallow and swallow again. Ducked his head and passed a hand over his eyes. "They told me you were dead."

"Who did, Garrett?" Dozens of people should have been able to identify that body as not mine.

He glanced over his shoulder up at the door. "Let's walk and talk."

We headed into Central Park. It took him a block to find his voice again. A block plus a few minutes of staring at me, mumbling incoherent things like, "Your hair— I can't believe— It's really—" And another hug, a gentler hug, with a broken, "Oh, princess."

I couldn't push him. He wouldn't talk until he'd processed this—lessons from our time tethered together that grated at my impatience.

"How have you . . ." Garrett looked around the sidewalk, crowded with strollers and joggers and dogs on leashes and people on cell phones. He stepped back so we were out of the flow of traffic and gestured to a park bench, but I didn't sit. I didn't like the idea of him leaning on a lamppost, towering above me. "It is so good to see you. It's taking everything in me to not keep hugging you, just so I can believe you're real. Where have you been? And how have you been surviving? Penny, you're . . . *you.* Just the idea you were out here—alone—makes me feel sick."

The story of Rapunzel flashed into my mind. The gorgeous illustration in my anthology, and Carter's voice reading it to me while Garrett waited impatiently out in the yard to play catch. I couldn't remember how old I'd been, but I remembered Carter warring with his desire to be a good brother and keep me company and his need to go out in the sunshine and enjoy the day. At some point during the reading he'd slipped up and said, "Penelope, Penelope, let down your long hair."

I'd hated the story ever since. Seen my own face in the illustration. My own golden-brown hair reflected in the coil the princess spilled over the bone-colored stones of her tower.

My hair wasn't gold anymore. I'd escaped my tower, and I'd never let anyone lock me up again.

"I've been fine."

"You don't belong out here. Penny, you've got to come with me. I can keep you safe. I promise I can keep you safe."

He knew better to reach for me with his hands, but his eyes did. His gaze wrapped around me like manacles. The word "safe" was a lot like "careful," felt a lot like "prison."

Did he notice my eyes had narrowed? That I'd exhaled a very loud, barely controlled breath? I ran my tongue over the back of my teeth. It had words it wanted to say—words my jaw wasn't willing to unleash quite yet.

Instead I asked, "I thought you wanted me to run away?" Carter had wanted this too.

"But I was supposed to be with you."

"Turns out I don't need you." The last words he'd said to me jumped into my head: *Don't be late. Mick'll let us leave. We need that head start.*

Mick had been shot—he was the only one of the Wards to have been injured, because he was the only one on the estate. He hadn't been banished because he hadn't been at breakfast. He was already being punished for his part in my clinic break-in. He'd been on duty . . . in the gatehouse.

Every one of my senses was screaming "danger" when I asked, "Garrett, why *that* morning? Why decide to run away then?"

"What do you mean?" But he knew. He knew exactly what I was asking. His jaw had tightened, and his eyes had become shrouded.

I took a step backward. "Who's running the Family now?"

He studied the pavement. "It's chaos. There were FBI everywhere. It's not anything like . . . *before*. The whole estate is closed. Everyone's scattered and trying to stay off-radar. Sky and Light had to shut down for a while because the Feds were circling. It's looking like Kilney's might have to—"

"What about the patients who need those organs? And are we making sure all the clients have the meds they need? Where's Nolan?"

"He—he's been busy in DC. He was never a leader. Maybe a politician, but not a leader of the Family. Your dad made a mistake. But it'll get better soon."

He'd lifted his chin with the last statement in a look so completely Ward it crushed what was left of my heart. I didn't want to ask my next questions, didn't want to think them, or shape them into sentences, but I had to see his face.

"Why? What's going to happen?"

His face paled again, except for two circles of anger on his cheeks. "The Zhus are going to pay for what they did to Carter. My dad, he—*we*—we're gonna strike against their Family. Like *tonight*. It's all planned. We're avenging your brother."

"The Zhus?" I wanted to vomit.

"And once we show the Family that sort of leadership, people will fall in line. They'll get behind Deer Meadow, and we'll rebuild the Family from there. My dad has it all planned."

"Your dad? He's involved in Deer Meadow?"

"Of course. It was his idea to start it." He reached out a hand.

"Penny, you look sick. Let me take you back there—the doctors there can do your blood test and get what you need."

"Carter wanted to shut down Dead Meat." Maybe I should've kept my cards tipped up, but I've never been good at that.

Garrett's Adam's apple bobbed as he swallowed and swallowed, before setting his jaw and answering. "He would've changed his mind. He'd changed it like twelve times already. You remember how excited he was that night."

"Before or after he went back off-estate to burn it down?"

"What are you talking about?" His voice was pinched with panic. "Burn it?"

I took a step backward. Shaking my head. Shaking.

"Princess. Talk to me. Let's go somewhere and you can explain."

I took another step. And another. I held my palms out to Garrett. "Stay there. I will scream. I will make so much noise that every person within a block will turn to look."

He froze. "I'd never hurt you. Don't you know that?"

I pushed up my sleeves, displaying handprints that looked as if they'd been tattooed on my arms in indigo ink and watched his face fall.

"Carter left me a letter. He didn't mention you in it at all." I should have noticed this sooner. This should have screamed from the page. Echoed in the fact that my brother left the letter in Maggie's care, not Garrett's. That if things went wrong, Carter wanted me to run away from the estate and all its well-trained, well-armed security—that he thought I was safer *without it* than I was there. I let Garrett absorb this for a moment before adding a second accusation. "My parents thought of you like another son."

"I know." His voice was so quiet I almost couldn't hear it from across the width of the jog path.

"Your family?" Mine was quieter. He couldn't have possibly heard me, but he must've read my lips because he gave a white-faced nod.

"I didn't know what they were planning—honest. I knew Dad was furious about Nolan, thought it should be him . . . or *me*, but I didn't know they would kill them. I just knew my dad was already close to snapping that morning and then *your* dad made things worse by kicking them out. I just knew I had to get *you* to safety."

"Because you'd already failed Carter."

He recoiled, like the words were the slap I wished I could give him. "I thought I could save you—I tried." His voice broke. "But—but I was too late. You were all dead."

I wouldn't vomit. I wouldn't black out. I wouldn't cry. I'd freeze my heart the way they froze those cadavers at Dead Meat—maybe then this news wouldn't kill me.

"Your family murdered mine—and you're still *helping* them? You didn't turn them in?" My eyes, my voice, every childhood memory with him in it, they were all pleading with him to disagree with me.

"You've got to understand, I didn't know. And you said it yourself—little *f* family comes first. And once it was done, what would telling the Feds help? What would it change? I didn't have anyone else left." He was crying now, and I couldn't make myself feel anything but fury. "You were dead. And not Carter—they didn't—that was the Zhus. The Zhus started this."

"You can't possibly believe that."

"They didn't"—he wiped clumsily at his face—"my family *didn't*. Not Carter."

"Not Carter," I echoed his delusion. "But *me*? You could live with that? With any of this?"

When he took a step forward, I turned and ran.

CHAPTER 37

I ran along the park, in and out of paths, over a field, interrupting a game of Frisbee and almost tripping over a staked dog leash. Then I was back out of the park. On the sidewalk, trying to blend in with a crowd crossing the street.

The Museum of Natural History was right in front of me. Without thinking, I ducked inside. This was not the entrance I normally used, where the doorway to the left led to the elephants. I paused to reorient, and then I heard it: "Penelope, wait!"

I ducked into an elevator, took it down to the level with the meteors display and where the floor was dotted with scales that would measure my weight on other planets. But they were all behind signs that read TICKETS REQUIRED BEYOND THIS POINT.

The gift shop? No, that wasn't a real hiding spot. Not one that would stand up under any scrutiny.

I looked at the lines for the ticket kiosks and despaired. Then a dark-skinned man was stepping in front of me. "Miss, I've got an extra ticket. Why don't you take it?" His voice was deep and musical. I didn't argue, didn't question.

"Thank you so much!" I grabbed the rectangle of paper and ran toward the entrance, scanned the ticket, and slipped through the gate and into the display.

Stairs. I had to find stairs.

And after I'd found them, I needed to climb them faster than the couple trying to coax their toddler. Bribing him with raisins and applause. I ducked and pushed my way around them and the others and dashed into another exhibit. Found myself facing a large bear, teeth exposed, claws extended. His partner bent over a bloody fish.

I was running so fast I almost tripped over the shin-high barrier, almost flew into the glass display case that separated me from the claws and teeth and all those natural weapons—ones animals had, but I did not.

I needed to get lost.

And so I did. Weaving up and down floors. In and out of displays until I was disoriented. And I realized how ineffective this was. Staying in motion when Garrett was also in motion only increased my chance of an encounter. And I couldn't think of him without it squeezing all the air out of me. Did he *truly* believe his family hadn't killed Carter, or did he just desperately want to? The same way I desperately wanted to throw blame and blood at everyone around him. Every Ward *except* him.

I was getting strange looks from the other patrons because of the sounds I was making. Sobs. I was crying. A fact brought home when I tried to pretend I was reading a plaque and couldn't see it through my tears.

I wiped my eyes.

TO SURVIVE: INDIANS OF AMAZONIA

I was outside the theater. Standing next to the same tree where Char and I had had our first kiss.

It was as good a place as any to hide. And since I was already crying, I might as well add a few tears for Char into the mix.

I don't know how many times I watched the documentary. Over and over until the narrator's voice stopped sounding authoritative and blended into a background hum. Until I started to be aware of how hard and uncomfortable the bench was and that there was a rip in the wall covering beside me.

A piece of paper wedged into it. Not a museum map, ticket, or receipt from the gift shop. Not a snack wrapper. A letter. With my name on it.

Or Maeve's, rather.

I didn't hesitate to read this like I had Carter's. I unfolded it with desperate fingers, devoured it with hungry eyes.

Maeve,

I'm trying to convince myself this isn't a coward's note, but I'm not having any success. I'm not who I said I was. Magnolia—that girl at your apartment—she's not just any girl either. She's not safe. I don't know how you know her, but I wish you didn't. Seeing her was an unwelcome reminder of what my life is and the risks that come with it. I don't expect this to make any sense, but I've put you in more danger than I want to think about, so the safest thing for me to do is leave. Leave you.

I'm going home. I'm going to stop running from my future.

I've left these notes everywhere I can think. Shanice has one. Byron. The couple at the dog park too. I don't know if you'll get any of them, or if it will change anything if you do, but I'm sorry.

My life isn't normal. It's not . . . good. I can't really say any more than that. Except I shouldn't have pretended it was, or been selfish enough to think I could have someone as wonderful as you in it.

I know I've lied to you so often that I can't expect you to believe me when I say this much was real: what I felt for you.

Char

I folded his letter and put it in the envelope with Carter's. They were both fragments of my heart shaped into farewells.

Both were also things I should've noticed sooner: Char's lies; Carter's love life and secrets. It was the omissions, the things that had been left out that should have haunted me.

I flipped the envelope over and made a list beneath Carter's cube. A list of things I knew in pluses and things I didn't in minuses.

+ The Wards are truly evil.
- How long have they been planning this? Why?
+ Al's involved in Dead Meat / Carter wanted to torch it
- Is this why they killed him?
+ Garrett admitted they killed my parents.
- Because of Nolan? Organ Act?
+ They're attacking the Zhus tonight.
- Why? To impress the Family? Shift blame? Artificial organs?
- Is Char there?
- How can I stop them?

A list of the contradictions:

Carter: Trust Maggie // Char: Magnolia's not safe.

And a list of questions with a list of the answers.

Did Char lie to me? Yes.
Did he kill my family? No.
Would he have still cared for me if he knew who I was?
Will I ever get the chance to tell him?

Do I love him?
What do I do now?

When I ran out of room, I searched my pockets for more paper—I was not defiling my memory notebook with this. I came up with two more pieces. The museum ticket given to me by a stranger and the folded card handed to me by the man on the street.

Those were answers. Those had always been answers. I just hadn't been paying attention.

CHAPTER 38

Garrett was waiting outside the building when I returned. I'd expected this. I'd already called Maggie, told her to stay in the apartment, lock the new dead bolt, and not let him in no matter what he said.

It felt strange to think of him as a threat. But he was. The guy who'd watched over every breath I took after Carter's death. Every breath I took . . . until my screams when I woke up orphaned.

I set each foot down with precision, each step measured, solid, and taking me closer to him. I thought I could stare him down, manage a glare that matched my marching, but I couldn't. My eyes darted away when they met his, full of apology and regret and sadness.

But in shifting my gaze I noticed something else. The man I'd almost run into earlier. He was still standing on the corner just past my apartment. This also wasn't a surprise, not after playing connect-the-mental-dots in the museum.

I'd seen him before. He'd sold me gum once from a sidewalk kiosk. And he'd sold Char roses. Was he the umbrella vendor too? I couldn't be sure, but probably. He'd stood near me on the subway during my one and only ride—it was because he'd managed to catch a drunk before she'd fallen on me that I escaped the trip unscathed. He'd been reading the newspaper in Byron's cafe. Yet the first time I'd seen him, he'd been a graying buzz cut in the apartment's bedroom. He'd been with the dark-skinned man who'd handed me a ticket at the museum today.

I slid my hand into the pocket of my jeans and pulled out the folded piece of paper he'd given me earlier. It was thick, creamy, expensive. Still taking steps toward Garrett, I flicked it open in my palm, glanced down.

An eagle holding an olive branch and a clutch of arrows. Set on a white background.

You are not alone. If I have a say, you will never be alone.

I should never have underestimated the vice president.

I stepped up on the sidewalk.

"Hi, Garrett."

"Penny. Princess. Please, let me explain."

I shook my head. "That can wait. There's someone I want you to meet."

"Can I just have—"

I grabbed Garrett by the hand. There was no marveling in this touch. No blushing shyness or giddy schoolgirl tingles. "This way, please."

The man was leaning against a building with a cell phone to his ear. I doubted he was really having a conversation, but even if he was, I didn't think he'd mind interrupting it for this.

"You like hats a lot," I told him. He lowered the cell and put it in his pocket. To his credit, his expression didn't change; neither one of his caterpillar eyebrows lifted in surprise, the square line of his jaw remained neutral. "I should've pieced it together sooner, but . . . the hats. And I wasn't paying nearly enough attention."

The man nodded.

"How'd you find me in the museum?" I asked. "Well, not *you,* but your partner or colleague or whatever the correct term is."

The corner of the man's mouth shifted in the slightest show of amusement, but his eyes didn't leave Garrett. "Your phone. We track it. And you're a creature of habit. Though I don't think Antoine expected to be jogging through the park today."

"My father would not be happy about the routine thing, but what I can I say? I like the dinosaurs." The moment was so surreal, joking when I should be crying, when I was holding hands with someone who dealt in murder. But there would be so much time for crying later, so much time for mourning the person I'd thought Garrett was, and could be. There were things I needed to do first.

"I'm Penelope Landlow, by the way. We've met so many times, and I've never introduced myself."

"Whitaker."

I nodded and turned back to the baffled boy I was still clutching in a death grip. "Garrett, this is Whitaker. He's an FBI agent. Or maybe Secret Service? That doesn't matter right now; we can sort all that out later. Whitaker, this man and his family were responsible for the deaths of my brother and parents."

The color drained from Garrett's face. His hand went limp in my grasp as he turned away from Whitaker and toward me. "Penelope, I didn't hurt any of them. I wasn't involved. You know I'd never hurt you. Or Carter."

I tried not to flinch at the names he'd omitted. "I hate you."

"No. You don't under—" Garrett paused midsentence and yanked his fingers from mine. He might have run, but I'd pulled something else from my bag.

"Do. Not. Move."

"Princess . . ."

I'd thought Garrett looked pale earlier. But now his eyes were horrified-wide, his mouth gaping and his lips devoid of color. He'd stopped moving though, all of him focused on the object in my hand.

The gun didn't feel as heavy as it had in Carter's guest room or while carrying it in my bag around the city streets. It felt much lighter; *I* felt much lighter.

I laughed. "This is what it takes for you to take me seriously?"

Whitaker cleared his throat. "Ms. Landlow, I've got it from

here." In one movement he reached around Garrett, grabbed the wrist I'd been holding, and wrenched it up behind his back. "Mr. Ward and I are going someplace private and having a good, long talk, but before we do, why don't you give me the gun?"

I looked at the empty palm he was holding out to me and gripped the gun tighter.

"Penelope," he said. "Think about this. The safety is off, that's not a toy."

"I know." I turned to Garrett and quoted his father, " '*Safety on is for morons*'—that's pretty much what passes for a nursery rhyme in your family, isn't that right? I guess with an upbringing like that, none of this should be a surprise. You know the ironic thing—after your family killed mine, I spent days waiting for *you* to come and rescue me. Literally afraid to leave the apartment because I *knew* you'd be coming soon."

"I didn't know you were alive. I would've come! You have to believe me."

"No. I don't." I flicked the safety back in place and let the weapon drop into Whitaker's waiting hand. "I really wanted you to be more than a thug with a gun."

He flinched, then flinched again when Whitaker used the opportunity to pull his wrist tighter.

"Thank you," said Whitaker. "And you'll go—where you're supposed to?" He nodded toward the piece of paper I was still crushing in my hand.

"Yes," I agreed. "I'll go exactly where I'm supposed to."

I walked away.

And it wasn't a lie really, it was just, with my last tie to the

Family severed, I didn't owe allegiance to anyone. I wasn't anyone's puppet. Bob and I might disagree on where I was supposed to be, but I wasn't going to pause to debate it with him.

I hailed a cab.

Directed it to the airport.

Called Maggie to get an address—*Topanga Canyon.* Called and bought a ticket. I didn't know if Garrett had told his father or the Family that I was alive, but even if he hadn't, it wouldn't stay secret for much longer. It's not like Al was *ever* fooled by Caroline's body; he'd always known I'd survived. So it no longer mattered whether or not I used my credit cards or shuffled my license back to the front of my wallet. Now that I'd identified her killer, Penelope Landlow could exist again.

It wasn't nearly as satisfying as I'd imagined.

With nothing but a purse containing my wallet, cadaver-cash, phone, gum, Carter doll, memory notebook, and an envelope with letters from the two boys I cared about most, I boarded a plane to Los Angeles.

I could still save one of them.

CHAPTER 39

I fought against claustrophobia the whole trip. Since I'd never had a problem with enclosed spaces before, I knew it had to be more than just the plane. It was the feeling that my whole future was caving in and there was nothing I could do to make this flight go faster. Nothing I could do to erase the bruises from my skin or go back in time and have the infusion I knew I needed.

"Why don't you try sleeping?" suggested a flight attendant after I picked up then put down the airline magazine for the fifth or sixth time.

I laughed. Like sleep was possible. Like anything but counting seconds, tapping my foot, and praying was possible while I endured those hours and miles that separated me from him.

My nose started to bleed. I blamed it on the elevation. I blamed it on the dry cabin air. Even after I'd soaked my eighth tissue, I refused to blame my platelet count, despite all the evidence inked on my skin.

I couldn't afford to be vulnerable until after I'd seen Char. After I'd told him who I was. And he'd processed what that meant. That he didn't need to run away to protect me. That he didn't need to fall into his father's plans for his Business future. That the Wards had killed my family; that they planned to target his. That even with Whitaker taking the Wards into custody, they needed to be vigilant and cautious. And that with the scrutiny and public outcry Dead Meat was sure to cause, they needed to be careful Businesswise too.

When the bleeding finally slowed to a stop, I reached in my bag to grab my memory notebook and found something else. I don't know how I missed it packing for the hotel and it was a little squashed—probably from the gun—but it was a candy bar.

I pulled it out and studied the unfamiliar wrapper: not just a candy bar, one that boasted: "Designed for Diabetics." And there was a note rubber-banded to it.

Because you miss chocolate, and so your pockets can crinkle too.

I didn't know whether to laugh or cry. So I opened it and took a bite—then spit it back out in my hand. The note was sweeter than the chocolate, which left my mouth tasting like waxy chalk.

In my fairy tales, princes did the rescuing and princesses danced, cleaned, slept, and waited, but I would slay any dragon that stood between me and a waxy, chalky thank-you kiss, quickly followed by a warning about the Wards, hopefully with some IVIg immediately afterward.

I didn't realize I was broadcasting my impatience until the man in front of me in the LAX taxi line offered to let me go ahead of him. The family in front of him waved me forward as well. Normally I'd defer, apologize for my loud sighs or fidgets or whatever had cued them into my frenzy. Tonight I said "thank you" and continued to work my way through the line until it was my turn and the porter asked for my destination.

"Topanga Canyon," I answered.

He hesitated. "Lady, that's more than a hundred-dollar taxi ride."

"That's fine," I said.

"There are buses, and a shuttle that will get you there. It'll take longer, but that'd be like ten bucks."

"I'd like a taxi, please," I said. "And I'm in a rush."

The taxi driver insisted I pay half up front. I agreed and handed over the bills. I would have paid it all. Extra if I thought I could convince him to speed or get me there sooner.

I flipped on my phone and watched the voice mail count climb.

"Pen? It's Maggie. Where are you? Where's Carter's gun? What's going on? I'm supposed to be on your side. Please let me. Call me."

"Penelope Maeve, it's Bob. Whitaker said you'd be checking in, coming to see me. Everything is prepared for you in Connecticut. Where are you? It's imperative you call me back."

And again from the vice president, "Penelope, things have gotten complicated and dangerous. I need you to call me immediately. We need to get you somewhere secure. Garrett's escaped—we don't have *any* of the Wards in custody. Do you understand? Call me."

Goose bumps spread down my arms. Escaped? Then the Wards were coming. I hadn't stopped them.

There were more voice mails, more of the same, but all they communicated was that Char was in danger—and I could warn him. I texted Maggie, Got your messages. Will check in soon. Bob got the same, with the additions of In CA. The Wards plan to attack the Zhus and My counts = bad. Then I shut off my phone.

I was a Landlow, the Wards were *my* Family—and preventing their actions was *my* responsibility.

It started to rain. I wouldn't have lingered on that for more than a blink, but the taxi driver said, "Whoa," flipped his loud jazz to a news station, and then proceeded to talk over the weather. "It never rains here. Not during the summer. Not unless it's a monsoon or something. We're a desert, you know. But I didn't hear anything about a monsoon thunderstorm, did you?"

"I'm from the East Coast. I haven't been following your weather."

"Stupid El Niño." A clap of thunder punctuated his statement, and lightning lit up the sky. "Sit quiet back there so I can listen. This isn't good weather for canyon driving. The roads around here, they get slick when wet—oil accumulation and such."

I had been sitting quietly, so continuing to do so wasn't an issue. I folded back in on myself, trying to figure out what I would say to Char when we had our first moment face-to-face with all our lies peeled away.

The drive should have taken around forty minutes, but from the moment the first raindrops hit the windshield, it felt as if we were crawling. I couldn't see the speedometer, so I wasn't sure if it was in my head or if our speed had truly slowed. But it didn't seem like we sped up, even after we traded the city lights for a highway headed north, curling through the mountains. Neighborhoods appeared again, and we exchanged one highway for another. Light was fading from the sky prematurely, the storm clouds and mountains making it feel later than seven p.m.—except for when blasts of lightning illuminated everything with stark clarity, leaving me blinking blindly afterward.

The cabbie continued to curse the weather, and I continued to curse my inability to figure out what I would say.

"This is the canyon boulevard. I need the specific address now—and it better not be one of those ones down a dirt road, because I'm not doing muddy canyon roads in this weather. Cabs aren't four-wheel drive, you know. So is it?"

"I don't know," I answered.

He groaned and cursed some more. "Gimme the address. Maybe I will."

I recited the street number Maggie had given me; he pulled over with a screech of wet wheels on the pavement.

I hoped he was just pausing to put it into GPS, or maybe we'd gone too far and needed to make a U-turn, but it was neither of those things.

He put the car in park, unbuckled his seat belt, turned around, and stared at me. "Who are you?" he asked, then shook his head. "No. Don't tell me. I don't want to know. You sure that's the address? You didn't, like, mix up some numbers or get the street wrong?"

"That's the right address."

"I can't take you there." He was shaking his head and gripping the steering wheel—even tighter than when it started to rain. "Not without permission. I'll take you back to the airport. I won't even charge you extra."

"No. I need to get there. It's important."

"I . . ." He sighed. "You're putting me in a tough spot."

"I'll pay you. Another hundred." I saw him waver, his hand started to reach for the keys, and I pressed my case. "Look, I don't know your name, I don't know your license plate or cab number. The most information I could possibly give was that a male cabbie drove me, and the inside of the car was black."

As I was speaking he was flipping over an identification card on his dashboard and canceling out the transaction on the meter "An extra hundred and I'll take you to the turnoff to the street. It's probably another mile from there, dirt road, and it'll be slick in this weather. It's not gonna be a fun walk, and I'm not coming back to get you, understand?"

"I understand." Eavesdropping had taught me there were similar restrictions on the Landlow Estate. Cabbies were paid well to have no knowledge of my address or those of the clinics. These were accessible only via private cars—ones the Family arranged. Last time I'd checked, the estate's address produced a 404 error on direction websites and appeared as an empty field on map apps. "Thank you."

He tried to talk me out of it for the rest of the drive and didn't even pull over when we arrived, just paused on the highway and pointed to a dark cross street down a slope. "I hope you know what you're doing."

"Me too."

I shut the door, and he was gone. His headlights disappeared, making me aware of how much darker things felt without their glow—how much colder the air was now that the sun was beyond the mountains and with the rain seeping through my clothing.

And how very, very alone I was.

CHAPTER 40

I skidded and slid down the steep canyon road. Mud clung to the bottom of my jeans and water soaked into the fabric, making them stiff and heavy. My bangs were pasted to my forehead, getting in my eyes, making poor visibility worse. I lost count of my falls. The rain increased, from drizzle to downpour, steady and soaking. And this time there wasn't a government security agent lurking to sell me an umbrella.

The walk was hellish in ways that made me think Dante was right—hell was a place of cold and shivering instead of burning hot. I held my breath each time I placed a foot. The rain was too loud to hear anything but thunder, but I imagined wild animals, mudslides, trigger-happy security guards. Did I need to worry about flash floods? Those happened in canyons, right?

I didn't notice the wall at first because the stucco blended in with the scrub brush and the rain was confining my visibility to barely beyond my feet. But there was a wall. Tall, topped with elaborate iron points that looked both fanciful and sharp. It gave me something to follow, and if I stretched my arm to its limit, I could keep my fingertips on its surface while keeping my feet on the edge of the road.

There was no reaction as I approached the gate. I'd expected lights to flick on, or a guard to step out.

The Zhus couldn't be this lax. Father never would've allowed someone to come right up to his gate, stick a sandaled foot on the crest where the two halves met, and haul herself up.

But then again, Father had been guarded and murdered by someone he considered a friend.

The thought made me slip. I hit the mud with bone-jarring intensity and wanted to stay there. Quit. Shut my eyes and give up. Instead I thought of all the impossible adrenaline stories I'd heard: mothers pulling cars off trapped children, people surviving a week in earthquake rubble or lost in the wilderness.

All I needed to do was climb a fence.

I tried again. My hands were wet, the skin wrinkled and soft. They slid across the metal at the top of the gates, snagging on imperfections in the paint and welding, splitting with small cuts that bled and tinged the rain on my hands the color of weak tea. I hooked one arm under the top bar and one arm over, pushed up on the tip of my toes and swung one foot up—stretching until its arch just barely cleared the top of the gate. I was grateful to be wearing long pants, for the slight protection jeans provided against the press of metal down the inside of my leg.

Except the crest was only affixed to one side of the gate—it was just the difference of the width of the bars, but that was significant enough. My foot couldn't catch on it as I slid down the opposite side. And I'd over compensated for the balance shift, underprepared for momentum and the slipperiness of metal. Been startled by a blast of lightning.

It was less of a slide, more of a fall. My body clanged against the gate; the motion dislodged my hands so I fell heavily to the ground.

I lay wheezing on the cold. Wet pebbles that made up the driveway. Damning the Zhu security and starting to agonize—not only that I wouldn't physically be able to deliver the message, but that I was already too late.

The hail started as I lay there. Pinpricks of cold on my face, neck. I rolled over and pressed up onto hands and knees. I crawled a foot or two before managing to get up on my feet. Realizing much too late my purse had slipped off my shoulder as I'd fallen and landed on the far side of the gate. Carter doll, my letters, my notebook—all out of reach. And once the leather of my bag was saturated, the paper wouldn't last long. I'd lose all the memories written on those pages—and what if I couldn't remember them again?

I wanted to stay there, lean my face against the gate, and cry.

My nose began to bleed again; another liquid hurt in a world of wet pain. At least the blood was warm as it ran down my chin;

the rest of me was so, so cold. So cold that when I finally reached the sanctuary of the porch, my fingers wouldn't clench into a fist so I could knock on the dark wood door of the Spanish mission–style mansion.

But this wasn't necessary because simultaneously the rain stopped and Mr. Zhu's security finally noticed me.

CHAPTER 41

My arm and a shoulder. This is what the man chose to grab. But he grabbed them from behind, so all I could see was his mammoth shadow, twisting and storming along the walls of the porch.

I cried out in pain, called, "Wait, please. I need to see Mr. Zhu," but he didn't talk or loosen his fingertips. He was dragging me backward.

"You don't understand. I need to talk to him!" I kicked at the door, the windows, trying to make as much noise as possible. "Mr. Zhu! ZHU!"

The guard picked me up, my legs flailing against empty air, making brief contact with the door, and then I was back off the porch.

The front door opened. "What is this?" asked a man in a beige bathrobe. He'd clearly been preparing for bed. The wire frames of his glasses were balanced perfectly on his nose, the sash on his robe was belted in a straight line, cinching in his impressive girth.

"Sir, Mr. Zhu, I have to talk to you. You're in danger."

"The only danger I'm in is having my sleep interrupted by teenage intruders. Find out what she's doing here, then get rid of her."

The grip on my arm tightened. Bruises layered over bruises over bruises.

"Please," I protested. To the man attached to the meaty grip I said, "You're hurting me."

"Let go of her!" At first it was just his voice. Then footsteps too, flying down a set of stairs I couldn't see. And then he was there. Coming through the door. On the porch. He still stole my breath. He still made my lips twitch into a smile, even though this time both reactions were accompanied by a twist in my stomach and a clenching of my heart.

The grip on my arm loosened slightly as the man waited for direction.

"You know this girl?" asked Mr. Zhu.

"Yes. I think so. Her voice—" Char blinked at me from behind glasses I'd never seen before, and I realized that drenched, mud-splattered, and half-drowned, I barely looked like the smiling girl he'd kissed good-bye in New York. "Bring her in here."

Mr. Zhu nodded his consent, stepping back inside. The guard didn't put me down, which was for the best, since I wasn't sure I could stand on my own. Char stayed at the door, so close I could have leaned over to kiss him as I was carried past.

I didn't.

He didn't lean down either. After shutting the door behind us, he went to stand at the bottom of a lavish staircase that curved down a stucco wall set with pointed windows. I dripped onto an oriental rug, catching my first glimpse of the man behind me in the mirror across the foyer. I looked like a doll in his grip. Or a puppet. Someone he could make dance in pain. He caught me watching him, caught my fearful expression, and grinned. He was the Zhus' version of Al Ward. I shivered.

Mr. Zhu cleared his throat and steepled his fingers beneath his many chins. "Ming, explain yourself. How exactly do you know this girl, and what is she doing on our property?"

"From New York." Char removed his glasses and rubbed his eyes, put them back on and blinked as if he didn't trust his vision. I was drinking in the sight of him: worn T-shirt, low-slung, gray-and-black-pinstriped pajama pants, bare feet, those glasses. Healthy. Safe.

He curled his fingers around the post of the ornate banister. I hoped it was to prevent himself from coming to me. I hoped he still wanted to.

"Who is she?" his father demanded.

"Maeve. A friend."

"I'm not." I tugged against the man's grip. His touch made my skin crawl, worse now that Char was in the room. I wanted *his* hand on my arm, in embrace, in support. I turned toward his father. "I'm Penelope Landlow."

"How dare you?" Mr. Zhu stepped directly in front of me,

blocking my view of his son. His eyes blazed with anger, and his palm twitched like he might slap me. "Penelope Landlow is dead."

"No. She's not . . . *I'm* not. It was a mistake. One of our nurses was killed—everyone thought it was me."

"Next time you try a con, do a little more research—even if Penelope Landlow had survived the attack, she would never survive life outside her bubble. The girl was an invalid, basically a minute away from dying under normal circumstances." He gripped my chin and turned my face away from Char so I was looking at him. "Her parents' and brother's deaths were a tragedy, but for Penelope, it was probably a mercy."

The words were like darts, finding the most sensitive parts of me to pierce. I sucked in a breath, and the ache went even deeper. Is this what other people thought of me? Is this what Char had thought of me? Right now, aching from head to toe, it felt like it might be true.

Mr. Zhu took a handkerchief from his pocket and wiped his fingers. He threw it down on a side table and turned to leave the foyer, raising a hand in dismissal and saying, "Take her away."

"Wait." Char finally took that last step down. He reached toward his father, not quite putting his hand on his shoulder. "Father, wait."

"What is it, Ming? What possible reason do you have for extending this interruption?"

"Father, I know this girl."

"We've established that. You believe her to be a friend from New York. Unsurprisingly, you were deceived by a pretty-faced con woman who was probably pumping you for information the whole time. In the morning you and I will be having a discussion to determine the full of extent of the security breach you've created."

"No." We said it in sync—our eyes meeting for an instant then fleeing before we could broadcast or read what the other was feeling.

"One of these days your ineptitude is going to destroy us, Ming."

"If you think she might be a risk, keep her overnight and we'll figure out what she knows in the morning." His words might be strategic, but his voice was desperate.

"Surely you don't intend to send the girl out now? Even if the rain stopped, it's got to be a mess out there. Flash floods and downed trees and who knows what else." It was a new voice, a new presence on the scene. She was beautiful—I could see where Char had inherited his grace and smile and dancing eyes. His height was all his father's, because this woman was tiny, shorter than me. And wrapped in an exquisitely embroidered red silk robe with coordinating slippers. "No one will be able to get back up to the main roads until the storm passes."

"Stay out of this, Mei."

"She's just a child; she looks exhausted. Kun, put her down." He set me on my feet. I wobbled, and her hands steadied me. "Are you okay? Ming, bring me a chair."

"She's no *child*." Her husband's words were saturated with scorn. "She's a spy of some sort. Or intended to be."

"That may be true tomorrow, but tonight she is our guest."

She helped me sit on the brocade chair Char dragged over. He hesitated for a second, then backed away.

"My mother, Abigail Landlow, always spoke so fondly of you," I whispered. "Thank you."

She nodded thoughtfully. "I'll see about making you up a room. You look like you could use some rest."

"No, not sleep. There's going to be an attack. My Family is—"

"She's broken into the estate to deliver threats," Mr. Zhu said. "And you think she should be treated as a guest?"

"For goodness' sake, the girl is nearly dead on her feet. She probably doesn't know what she's saying."

"That's right!" said Char, looking instantly more alert. "She's diabetic—I bet this whole thing is a hypoglycemic episode. She's disoriented, talking nonsense—"

"Stop. I'm not diabetic. I've never been—it was just . . . an easy lie."

He flinched, fell silent.

"She admits to being a liar; I've heard enough," said Mr. Zhu.

"Not this! They're coming!"

"Hush now," said Mrs. Zhu. "There's nothing you have to say that can't wait a couple hours."

"It can't wait," I mumbled at the same time Mr. Zhu said, "There's nothing she has to tell me."

Char just stared at me—still too far away. Much too far, and it was a distance of more than just the marble between our feet, it was a distance defined by our mutual deceptions and agendas.

Finally his father chided him. "Why are you acting like

you've never seen a female before? Either make yourself useful or go to bed."

"He can help me make up a guest room," said his mother. "Why don't you rest a moment while I get you some dry clothing? Rain during the summer is unusual; it's unfortunate you got caught in it. I'll send someone with tea. Unless you want a shower?"

I shook my head. Showering would require standing. I could barely sit upright. Char and his mother left and it was only me, Mr. Zhu, and that silent hulk of a man, Kun.

"I'm not lying." I paused to gulp the pungent tea that had been delivered. Even with the warm cup in my hand and hot liquid coursing down my throat, I couldn't stop shaking.

"There has never been an attack by one Family on another. Never. Whatever remains of the Landlow Family is in no position to attack anyone." He turned his back and left.

I put my head down on the arm of the chair, caring very little about the water that was streaming off me onto the ornate wood. "You've . . . got to . . . ," I insisted.

And then I blacked out.

It was Kun who woke me. Carrying me not so gently up to a bedroom and setting me on unsteady feet inside the door where Mrs. Zhu stood with a smile and Char waited with eyes of questions.

"A fairy tale. *She* is why you wanted a fairy tale," his mother said, and Char just ducked his head in agreement. She seemed amused as she turned to me, "Can we get you anything else? Did you drink the tea?"

"He won lissin." My words were slurring, my hands felt heavy when I rubbed my eyes.

"Perhaps in the morning. Things always seem clearer in the morning."

"It'snot safe."

"My father's security is the best there is. No one's getting in." It was the first time Char had spoken directly to me. His voice sounded different here. More formal. Sharp enough to cut through my mental fog.

At least, just long enough for me to meet his eyes and say, "I did."

"Yes, but I watched on security monitors. You fell the whole way—you were no threat, no reason to go out in that weather," said Kun. His voice reminded me of the snick of a knife or the edge of a razor.

"No one else will get in," said Char with a frown.

"Promise?" I whispered.

"You're safe," he answered. Which wasn't my concern at all.

"I'll be at your door," said Kun.

It wasn't a comforting statement; it made Char flinch. "Get changed and I'll come sit with you . . . if that's okay."

I nodded.

"Sleep well," said his mother.

They left. And sleep was my only option. Not really optional at this point. My vision blurred. My mouth tasted thick with herbal tea and blood, either because I'd bitten my tongue or my gums were bleeding.

There was dry clothing on a chair. I stumbled as I shucked off wet jeans and my painted-on shirt only to wince at the bruised horror that was my skin. I fumbled with sleeves and pants and had to pause and rest my eyes but finally managed to get into the cotton pajamas.

I could see why Mrs. Zhu had needed help preparing the guest room. The bed started with a standard box spring and mattress, but then a foam topper. A feather bed? It was hard to tell through the thick weave of the fleece sheets. And two blankets. A down comforter, a quilt, and a fluffy throw on top of that, then a crocheted afghan. The bed frame was tall to begin with, but with the towering confection of layers, it would have been impossible to get into it without the step stool waiting beside it.

Just crossing the room was hard—staying upright, keeping my eyes open, figuring out the coordination required to lift my feet and climb from the stool onto the bed.

I skipped all the covers. I was alternating between teeth chattering and sweltering. The idea of climbing under them was too much effort. I lay on top, sinking into the softness, drowning in a froth of bedding. Drowning in exhaustion.

There was a light knock and the lock disengaged with a click, the knob began to turn. The door slid open, the hall lights illuminating the silhouette of a male as he slunk into the room.

"Maeve?"

Relief came in a wash of fatigue and dizziness. It made my eyes fill and my fingers unclench.

"Do you swear you're . . ." I thought he might say "Penny."

It looked like his mouth started to form my name, but he swallowed the word down and after a pause, finished with, ". . . not diabetic?"

I nodded. Just enough of a head tilt up / head tilt down to count as a nod. I could feel the adrenaline fading from my system. My heartbeat slowing, my fingertips going cold. It left me feeling off-kilter, disoriented, intoxicated. My vision was warping, my mouth tasted like blood. Sleep pulled at me like a riptide, and I ached. Everywhere. Like I'd been run over, like I was being buried alive under the pressure created by the bruises.

"I'm not lying," I whispered. "Not anymore."

"I know we have so much we need to talk about—"

"You've gotto make your father . . ." The slurring was back, the aggressive pull of sleep.

"I will. I promise. Can you rest? You're so exhausted it's painful to look at you, my Maeve."

I tried to smile at his "my," but was too tired to make it convincing. "I—you—" My words were interrupted by yawns, by long blinks where I shut my eyes and forgot to open them again.

At some point I reached out and he'd sat on the edge of the bed beside me. I opened my eyes to see my head on a pillow in his lap and a crocheted afghan wrapped around me. He stroked my hair. It was still wet. I closed my eyes.

"Maeve?" Char was saying things. Asking things. But I couldn't remember them. Couldn't remember how to open my eyes.

"Maeve! Wake up. Please."

It felt a journey of miles to raise my eyelids, to look up at his bowed head, his gentle eyes. He whispered, "Your nose is bleeding, you're shaking. I need to get you to the clinic."

"I need to warn them." I tasted blood on my lips.

"But . . . are *you* okay?" he asked.

I didn't answer. We didn't need another lie between us.

CHAPTER 42

"What did you do?"

The door opened so suddenly that I heard the words before I registered the three people crowding into the bedroom. Char's parents and Kun.

Mr. Zhu whirled on his wife, "How long until your sedative tea wears off? We need answers."

"Oh, now you want them?" I'd been aiming for attitude, but only managed yawning and pathetic. Char offered me his hand, but I ignored it and struggled into a wobbly sitting position on my own. It wasn't that I didn't want the comfort and support of his touch, it was that I needed to be taken seriously. If I looked like a lovesick girl, I endangered us all. "You drugged me?" The slurring suddenly made sense. The weight and demand of that sleep.

"It wasn't a drug," said Mrs. Zhu. "Just a soporific herbal mixture to help you get some rest. You looked like you needed it."

Mr. Zhu cleared his throat. "Explain why I'm getting calls from my men, telling me US Marshals are gearing up and heading here. Why are we being raided?"

"You're not," I said, swallowing down the coppery taste of blood and blinking back dizziness. "You're being protected—because you're going to be attacked by my Family. The Landlow Family . . . or what's left of it."

"If you truly are Penelope Landlow, prove it."

This was easy enough. The proof was painted on my skin. I pushed up the sleeves of my borrowed shirt and held out my arms for inspection. I didn't look. I didn't want to see how bad it was. I was running on borrowed time, already starting to crash, and crash hard. Seeing the proof of my decline could crack the last of my strength and send me unconscious to the floor.

But when I heard the gasps, the "My dear girl" from Char's mom, and his own "Maeve—" in an exhale of panic, I let my eyes fall on my arms.

Pea-sized hail had left Ping-Pong-sized bruises. Handprints, nearly black, wrapped around my wrist like manacles. And over all this, like lace stenciled on my skin, was the pattern of the crocheted blanket—every stitch visible.

Mr. Zhu smiled at me. A sincere smile, and in it I saw I'd been appraised and passed some sort of test. His laugh reminded me of a crow's caw and gave me the shivers. "It seems I've underestimated you, Penelope. Kun—go alert the clinic; we'll be right there."

"But the . . ." Whole sentences were too much effort. My head felt as weak as my body.

"Can you walk? Should we get a gurney?"

I shook my head. To one, both.

"I can carry her," said Char.

I wanted to protest. Wanted to stand on my own feet and demand Mr. Zhu listen to me, but I could barely manage to stay conscious when Char's arms came around me. His mother leaned over to wipe my face with a tissue that came away saturated with red. My foggy mind remembered all of Mother's dire warnings about internal bleeding and intracerebral hemorrhage—all of Dr. Castillo's gentle lectures. A gurney would've been safer, but Char's arms were warm and strong and I felt so cold and weak.

"I've got you," he whispered.

We were moving, going down stairs, Mrs. Zhu hurrying ahead to turn on lights as we entered a long hallway beside a dining room. The walls on both sides were nearly all glass—displaying security lights focused on a manicured rock garden, fading out on the slope down to a small bit of lawn, and beyond that, darkness where scrub brush bled into mountains. The view from the dining room was similar, but with a pool glowing blue against the dark sky. Parallel to those windows was a long sleek table of thick wood with edges that looked angular. Dangerous.

Mr. Zhu walked beside Char, studying me with curiosity and confusion. "Why did you come here? Why risk yourself? Why would you care what happens to my Family? Why side with mine over yours?"

"I know what it's . . . like to . . . lose loved ones. Because . . . I care for . . ." I let my head fall against Char's shoulder, let my gaze finish that sentence.

Mr. Zhu nodded thoughtfully, like I'd passed another test. "We retrieved your handbag, from beside the gate. Your cell phone was destroyed, but your . . . *diary* should be salvageable. I've had it set on a heater to dry."

"Thank you." I wanted to explain just how much I meant that, but the two words had already cost so much effort.

Then there wasn't time for any more discussion, because Kun was running down the hallway. "Sir! There's been a breach."

A single terra-cotta tile slid off the roof to shatter on the rocks outside the hall.

And then there were flashes. The windows burst inward, glass slivers reflecting in the lights as they exploded into the room like lethal tears. Making my cheeks and hands sting, then bleed.

Boots followed glass through the window frames. Landed with hard thuds and crunches on the wood floor. Immediate gunshots—and a row of holes in the ceiling. Yells, commands, people running.

The arms holding me tightened, pulled me back against a firm chest, pulled me into the dining room and below the table. I didn't have the strength to do anything but keep my eyes open and breathe.

It was Char's scent in my lungs and his voice in my ear, "I've got you."

But it was Garrett's voice across the room yelling, "Dad, stop! Wait! I thought we agreed we don't have to kill them—just get the tech."

It shouldn't be him. I'd left him with Whitaker. They let him escape, and now he was here. Not arrested. Not safe. Here.

Al's curses told his youngest to "shut up and obey."

"But this wasn't the plan."

Laughter. Goose-bump-raising laughter. "When have I ever told *you* my plans? Jake, Hugh, spread out. Find them."

There were footsteps, more shots. Screams. Somewhere away from here others were returning fire. In some other room of the mansion, the battle was escalating. I hoped not wherever Kun and Char's parents had escaped to.

There were still two pairs of boots in the room. And our two pairs of bare feet. It wasn't odds I liked.

My vision began to flicker. Distorted like light through a prism. Like light through the shattered crystal of the chandelier that lay beside my feet.

Which were bleeding from either ten or a hundred small cuts.

My head was heavy. So heavy. I'd tipped it back against Char's chest, but gravity didn't like that. It wanted to fall forward, loll on my neck like a yo-yo.

"Stay with me, Maeve. Please."

There were boots approaching my feet. Boots crouching. A gun. In my face.

And then panic. Scrambling. Char pushing me away. Behind him. Punching.

And Garrett. Garrett who shouldn't be here. His nose was bleeding and his eyes were shell-shocked, horrified. "Penny! Are you okay? Dad, hold your fire. They've got Penelope."

There was an instant of quiet. Unnatural quiet where gunshots still echoed in my ears and dust and plaster and debris seemed suspended in the air.

"She's *here*? *This* is where she's been hiding?" the narrator of my nightmares asked. "How convenient. Shoot her."

Garrett's crouch fell into knees down, his face nearly level with mine and so white. "You *knew* she was alive?"

"You want to be a Ward, act like one. Shoot her!"

"Please. Don't," begged Char.

Even Garrett's lips looked bloodless beneath his nosebleed. Mine was bleeding too. Maybe. Everything had taken on a hazy red tint. He shook his head. "I won't. This is *Penny*."

I couldn't see Al, but I could imagine that snarling smile when he said, "If you won't, I'll make it a clean sweep of the Landlows. Never guessed the most useless would be the hardest to eliminate."

Char was pushing me behind him, trying to communicate something with frantic gestures, but I couldn't focus on anything but Garrett and the heartbreak in his voice as he *had* to accept the truth. "Clean sweep? Carter? *You*? But—"

"All that money the Landlows wasted sending you to fancy schools with Carter and you're dumber than an empty bullet shell. He showed up at Deer Meadow with gasoline and lighters, of course we killed him. Now. Shoot. Her."

Garrett's face wavered, I thought he might vomit or faint; then his expression settled in lines of stone fury. He put his gun down and slid it across the floor away from his father. "No!"

There was a pop, and a chunk of wood struck Char's shoulder. I followed this backward to find a bullet hole in the table by my head. I rolled my eyes forward again to measure the blood. Had Al shot him, or was it just the ricochet? Char wasn't holding still for me to see, and my vision was so red. My hands too heavy to lift. He was pulling me backward, out the other side of the table. Maneuvering on his knees around a tangle of chair and table legs, pieces of plaster. One hand on me. The other on Garrett's gun.

Everyone was moving. So fast. So blurry. We were free. Char was flipping the table on its side. Aiming a gun at Al Ward, who was aiming a gun at us. Garrett was standing. Yelling, "Get down."

Triggers were being pulled. And Garrett was diving. Hitting me. Hitting Char. Knocking us down. He was screaming. Bleeding.

We'd fallen like pick-up sticks. Me, against the sideways table, my back pushed into the underside of the tabletop, which served as a wobbly barricade. The impact stole my breath and made the spots in my vision explode. I was seeing through pinpricks. Tilting and turning my head to try and make sense of what I saw. Garrett, gasping and curling into a ball, but trying to pick himself up to crawl toward me, leaving smears and streaks and splashes of crimson in the layer of white plaster on the floor.

Char had been pushed outward. Toward a doorway. Toward safety, but totally exposed.

He should've crawled backward. In two seconds he could've been through that door. Safe. But he stood. Drew Al's attention to himself. "Take me, leave her alone."

"It's not an either/or," laughed Al, tapping his gun against the edge of the table a few inches above my head.

"Princess." Garrett's hand was on my ankle, but I kicked off whatever protection he wanted to offer.

Bracing my bare feet against the floor, the broken glass, I threw myself backward against the underside of the sideways table with all the strength I had left.

I felt the table teeter on its edge, then the bottom legs lifted from the floor; all four were parallel with it for a blink before continuing their arc upward. I felt the impact when the tabletop hit Al's waist as it flipped. I fell backward with it, experienced its uneven landing as the heavy table settled upside down with his body beneath it. I heard his scream of pain, a satisfying, high-pitched sound like a hurt rodent. All I could see, taste, or smell was blood.

I shut my eyes against the sting of it and couldn't open them again.

CHAPTER 43

Waking up in a hospital bed wasn't a new experience for me.

But waking up in an unfamiliar clinic was. With Char disheveled and crumpled in a chair beside me. His head had fallen back at an angle that made my own neck muscles ache in sympathy. Behind the frames of his glasses, his eyelids were closed, black lashes resting on under-eye shadows as dark as bruises.

As dark as the bruises that peeked out from the edges of the bandages that covered so much of me.

I sucked in a breath, a breath full of pain but also so much gratitude. He was okay, I was too. My next breath was a prayer for everyone else.

I was attached to an IV and a pain-medication pump—and it was tempting, but before I let myself succumb to relief and its accompanying medicinal spaciness, I wanted answers, reassurance. I wanted to hear Char's voice.

I reached over and touched his face, tilting his neck to a more neutral position.

"Hey, Maeve. You're awake!" He stretched and blinked owlishly at me, rolling his neck and shoulders. "How are you feeling?"

I'd wanted to hear his voice, but now that I had, I was inexplicably angry. Angry to be back in a hospital. Angry at Garrett for his family's betrayal. Angry at Whitaker for not stopping the Wards after I'd gift-wrapped and handed him an informant. Angry at Char for all his deception. Angry at my own lies and the ways they tainted everything.

"Why are you even here?" I asked.

"What do you mean?" He reached out to touch my cheek, but I turned my head away.

"You said I was special. You said I *saw* you—"

"You do! Mae—Penelope."

My anger collected speed, weight, pushed its way past my lips in sharpened words. "Since everything you told me was a lie, how did I not see you were a liar? The person I fell for doesn't exist. It may be who you wish you were, but it's not who you *are*."

"So now we're defined by our parents?" He looked angry too. "No. You saw *me*—not who my father is or what people expect from *his* son. Want to know the true reason I went to New York? Yes, I made a scene at my graduation party about med school. Yes, my father said he couldn't stand to look at me and sent me away. That was all true. But want to know why New York?"

I crossed my bandaged arms across the stiff fabric of the pale-blue hospital gown. "Sure."

"I heard my dad talking to Mr. Vickers about Deer Meadow and how they thought it was connected to the murders, but they didn't know where in New York—"

"And you thought finding it and confronting murderers was a good idea?"

"No!" He stood and rubbed two fisted hands down his thighs. "Okay, yes. But not really. I just wanted to find it—then turn the address over to the FBI—like, an anonymous tip. And I came close. I followed one of the Wards to the right street, but I missed seeing which building he went in."

"But *why*?" I asked. This conversation felt like a sucker punch to all my bruises. "To impress your father? I thought you didn't want to be part of the Business?"

"I don't. Not as anything but a doctor—I did it for your family. I needed—I need—to believe people can do what we do, what our Families do, and still be good people. Your parents were. Your mother made everyone in the room feel welcome and appreciated. Your father cared more about patients than profit. And *you*—"

"You hadn't seen me since we were kids," I protested.

"I know. Not since that visit when we were twelve, thirteen. And I was so shy and awkward. I didn't know what to say to you, so I was hiding in your library, reading. My father caught me. He was yelling, 'What's wrong with you? Why can't you—' "

"I remember that." I tried to dredge up details from that day. He'd been short. He'd had crooked glasses—that hadn't changed. He'd been horrible with eye contact, too busy studying the floor as if he were searching for a trap door or escape hatch.

"You walked in looking like something from a movie screen and I wanted to die, but you just turned to me and said—"

" 'There you are, I've been looking for you everywhere!' " And he'd looked up and given me a smile so sincere and heartfelt I'd wanted to hug him . . . if hugging were a thing I'd been allowed to do.

"And you spun a story about hide-and-seek, and how much fun you were having. We were way too old for playground games, but my father bought it, thought we were flirting, was *proud* of me. I think I fell a little bit in love with you that day."

"We were just kids," I protested again. "It was just . . . a day. Any day."

"I know. But you were kind. Your whole family was. And if I'm going to spend my life doing this—if this is going to be my future—I need to believe I can be like *your* family—and they deserved justice. That's why I chose New York."

"Your father, do you hate him?" I asked.

"There's no point in that anymore . . ." Char shut his eyes and exhaled slowly. "I don't know how much you remember, but the Wards, the attack . . . There were casualties."

I swallowed a mouthful of guilt and misplaced priorities. This wasn't the time to blame and point fingers. "Your dad? Was he shot? Is he okay?"

"No. Not shot." He stood and walked over to the window. I wanted to see the expression on the other side of his bowed head and slumped shoulders, but I was tethered to my bed by bandages, wires, and IV lines.

"Char?"

"He had a heart attack." His voice was hoarse, the type of dryness that occurs when your face is wet with tears. He sniffled, and I started to take an inventory of what I'd need to unplug and detach in order to get to him, but then he started talking again, palms flat against the window, head down.

"The irony is, he *knew* he needed heart surgery . . . He *knew* it, knew it even back before the scare at my party. But he's been putting it off . . ." His hands turned to fists, and he banged them against the window in time with his words. "The stupid, stubborn, proud idiot wanted to be the first recipient of our artificial heart prototype. It's not quite ready yet—hadn't been tested enough, but he insisted. He had a stroke midtransplant. He hasn't woken up . . . I don't think he's going to."

"I'm so sorry." Those weak, empty words not doing a thing to touch his pain. I held my breath and braced myself. "And your mother?"

"Fine. Well, not fine. Her husband's in a coma, her house is destroyed, and the FBI have been . . ." He waved a hand to indicate something. "But she's not injured."

I exhaled my relief and studied him more closely, doing an inventory of the parts I could see and forcing away the memory of the last time I'd seen him: standing, exposed, with Al's gun pointed at his chest and Garrett's gun in his hand.

The sleeves of his gray button-down shirt weren't lying the same. "Your shoulder? How bad are you hurt?"

"Just a few stitches. Nothing serious. Nothing like—" He turned around again, coming to stand and rest his hands on the metal railing of my bed. "I'm so sorry no one listened to you sooner. I'm so sorry I couldn't protect you."

"It's not your job to protect me."

The words fell like stones between us. There were people whose job *was* to protect me. They were the same people who'd tried to kill us. And one of them was shot trying to save me, but I couldn't bring myself to ask Char about Garrett—not in the same conversation where he'd shared his father's condition.

My left hand wasn't entirely bandaged. And even my right had individual fingers and knuckles wrapped. I reached out with both of them, placing them on top of one of his. He lowered his eyes from some invisible spot on the ceiling; I raised mine to meet them. Our linked gaze was heavy with apology and sympathy and fear and concern. All the things we couldn't say out loud just yet.

It was hard to turn away from him when the door opened.

"How's my favorite pincushion?"

My eyes filled so quickly I couldn't make out the figure coming in the room, but that was okay because I'd know his voice anywhere.

"Char—how did you? How did you know I needed him?" I squeezed Char's hand before reaching my arms out. "Hello, Dr. Castillo. Hello!"

And maybe the doctor knew how badly I needed it, or maybe

now that we were off our estate, the same rules no longer applied, because he hugged me—gently—rocking me slightly like a child.

"It is so good to see you, Penelope. So good to see you awake."

"I didn't—I didn't bring him. I would've if I'd known how happy it would make you, but it wasn't me." Char was edging toward the door. "I'll give you some privacy."

Dr. Castillo nodded to him. "I'll stay with her; you go see your father. I'm sorry I couldn't be more help there, but he's in very capable hands."

Char nodded. "Thank you for trying. I'll come back soon?"

"Please," I answered before I hugged the doctor again. "If not Char, who?"

"Vice President Forman called. I was on the next flight. Penelope, you have *not* been being careful."

I laughed through tears. "No, I really haven't. But it's so good to see you."

"You too, little one. You too."

There was another knock on the door, and the man standing there cleared his throat. "Ms. Landlow, this isn't where I expected to see you. I can't say I'm happy about it either."

"Hello, Whitaker," I answered. "You were supposed to stop this."

"Things didn't go according to plan. The youngest Ward wasn't quite as influential or in-the-know about his father's intentions as he thought. We lost track of them, and they got the jump on us. It shouldn't have happened."

"Is he okay?" I remembered his blood on the floor. The smear his thumb had left on my ankle before I shook him off. The bullet that had hit him instead of me.

"He's expected to make a full recovery."

"Can I see him?"

"No. I'm sorry, but that's not going to be possible."

My forehead wrinkled in confusion. "But you just said he's going to be okay." I turned to Dr. Castillo. "Didn't he? Why can't I see him?"

"He's gone," said Char from the doorway. When I gasped, he quickly added, "No! He's not dead, but gone. He had some surgery in our clinic. It went well, but when the doctors came to check on him post-op, he . . . wasn't there."

"I don't understand. Did his father get to him? One of his brothers?"

Whitaker shook his head. "You don't need to worry about Garrett. Or the other Wards. Al and Mick are in custody."

"Hugh? Jacob?"

Whitaker's jaw tightened, Char lowered his eyes, and Dr. Castillo pressed my cheek back into his white coat. I nodded, my mind flashing to dim memories of Mrs. Ward at Keith's funeral and my collection of black dresses. I wouldn't be attending these two, but I hoped someone found her and told her so she could.

"You should rest," said Whitaker. "And when you're ready, we can move you to a private hospital. There are some questions we need to ask you."

"Can't I stay here?" I didn't want to go out in public. The idea of being resurrected from the dead was exhausting. And answering questions. Putting my life back together or building a new one on the ruins of the old.

"There are people who would like to come visit you," said Whitaker.

"I'd really rather she wasn't moved," said Dr. Castillo. "At least not yet. I'd like a few stable counts first, and time for her to recover."

"And isn't this location more secure than any hospital would be?" I asked. I knew who Whitaker was implying, and I wanted to see Bob too—but the media circus would be less if the meeting occurred here.

"That's possibly true," Whitaker conceded. It looked like it pained him to do so. "Ming, who should I talk to about security matters?"

Ming. Not Char. I hadn't made that transition yet, and I didn't know if I would.

"Kun was . . ." His jaw tightened. "Now it would be Delun. If you ask my man just down the hall, he'll take you to see him."

"Thank you," said Whitaker. "Rest up, Penelope."

"Is your father okay?" I asked.

"No change." He stepped into the room as Whitaker exited. "My mother's sitting with him. She wanted some time alone."

"Please let me know if I can do anything," said Dr. Castillo.

"Thank you," said Char.

"I'm going to get Penelope something to drink. Would you like anything?" The doctor waited for Char to shake his head, then left.

"I'm in charge now," Char said once the door shut again. "I—that hadn't occurred to me."

"You're a good person. This won't change that."

"Thank you. And I'm sorry about Garrett . . ." He shoved his hands in the pockets of his pants. "Were you close?"

"Not as close as I thought." I wished he would hold my hand, hold me. I sighed. "After . . . *this,* I don't even know what's left of my Family. I should probably get Nolan on the phone, or Miles, not that they need me, but . . . I'm not useless."

"What?" He wrinkled his forehead. "I don't get why this is your fear. Of course you're not useless. Who said you were?"

"Every person in my life ever."

"I've never said that. I never will. You do realize you saved my life, right? If you hadn't flipped that table onto Al Ward, I would've been shot. You bought us the extra thirty seconds so that the US Marshals could come in and break things up."

"They should have been there sooner."

"And my father should have listened when you showed up on my doorstep. We can't live in the should-haves and what-ifs, Maeve. There are too many of them; it'll drive us crazy."

"Will you keep calling me Maeve? *Can* I keep calling you Char?"

"You can call me anything you want; I just want to hear your voice. When you went unconscious—and I couldn't wake you up—that was the scariest moment of my life." He shut his eyes, shook his head, like he was trying to clear away the memory. "They did your CBC twice, and the platelet count was too low to even register. The doctors were worried about brain bleeds, and you wouldn't wake up. You wouldn't."

"Look at me." I put my hand on his arm and waited until he did. "I'm okay. I'll be okay." I thought of the people I'd lost so far, the people I had left to lose. "You are not optional. You are essential to me. To my life. Do you know what I mean by that?"

He leaned down and his lips barely brushed my forehead, the same spot he'd first left his mark on me. "Yes. Yes, I do. Now sleep. I won't go anywhere. I promise."

CHAPTER 44

Time does heal all things. Days passed, my counts stabilized, my physical injuries mended, and Dr. Castillo took one last CBC, kissed my cheek, and then headed back to New York and his own family. "You call me. I won't demand daily, but at least two, three times a week. And I'll be checking in with these doctors, pincushion, so you be caref—*behave.*"

His exit, my healing, served to sharpen the focus on all the other aspects of my shredded life. The pain receded to be replaced by panic, the type that clawed me awake with worries half-formed on my lips.

"I don't know anything. I don't know what I'm going to do. I don't know where I'm going to live—"

"I thought Vice President Forman offered you a place at his house," Char said from his spot beside my bed. He never seemed to need context for my fears, no matter how random or interrupted our conversations were by sleep, medicine, his new Family responsibilities, his dual vigils at his father's and my bedsides, or Whitaker's endless questions.

"He did. But . . . can I live there? With Bob and his family?"

"I don't see why not." He pointed toward a stack of newspapers Bob and Whitaker had brought earlier. The headlines told my story, or told the version we'd agreed upon. They included words like "hero" and "brave." Told how "The Last Landlow" or "The Lost Landlow" had been working undercover with the vice president to catch the bad guys who killed her family and to end illegal corpse transplants. I was officially—and publicly—pro–Organ Act.

Char fiddled with the sheet beside my hand. His fingers so temptingly close to mine, but since he was holding back, I felt like I needed to.

"You think I should move in with them?" I'd already had this conversation with Dr. Castillo and Bob . . . so many times with Bob.

"Yes, I think you should," he reassured me. "You'd be safe—I have to admit, that's what makes me happiest."

"Whatever, you're just glad I'd be in DC—and really close to Georgetown."

He tried to look serious for a minute before relenting and letting his sheepish grin escape. "I've already Google-mapped a dozen routes from my dorm to Number One Observatory Circle."

If I agreed, I'd be close to Char, I'd get to see Kelly and Bob. And, who knows, maybe Caleigh could become a friend. Also,

I'd be in a place where I could be useful—working to change policy.

I couldn't imagine going back home to the estate. I didn't want to deal with the Family, not that there was a Family left. Miles had told me a couple of the clinics were operating autonomously, but most had shut. He was enjoying early retirement but said he'd help with whatever I needed and bring Thumbelina when he came to visit me in DC if I moved.

Of course Nolan was also in DC and calling and sending the most clichéd bouquets and chicken soup with get well cards on which the sole writing beyond the preprinted sentiment were my name and his. Oh, and "sincerely." No doubt if I moved in with Bob, Nolan's and my paths would intersect—but at least now we weren't stuck in a teacher-student dynamic. Maybe, just maybe, he'd be more tolerable as an acquaintance.

"I can pretty much walk away from the Family Business forever," I mused aloud. Except for him. Except for Maggie, who'd called and given me a scathing lecture before bursting into tears and telling me, "Next time you do something stupid, at least *bring me with you.*"

"I kind of am too. I feel so guilty about it," said Char.

"Hey, your mom is *insisting* you go to school. I was there, I heard her."

"But I don't know how this will work—me being across the country at school and my mother in charge of the day-to-day decisions for the Business and my dad's care—but she doesn't seem daunted at all. She's already drawing up plans for shifting more capital to research . . . and I don't know what else I could do."

"It's only for—" I looked at him with a smile. "How many years is med school?"

He grinned back. "Say yes to the vice president. Come to DC with me."

I traded a grin for a bitten lip and new worries. It sounded great in the hypothetical. Too great. "If I say yes, and I probably will, that's not even my biggest fear."

"What is?"

"*Us.* Is that lame? With everything else that's going on, I'm worried about you and me."

The corners of his mouth twitched, and he looked down, trying—and failing miserably—to cover the fact that he was beaming. "Whatever the opposite of lame is, that's what that is."

"I'm serious. I don't know you. I barely know you at all."

"You will."

"But I *don't* right now. And how can I have feelings for someone I don't know?"

"You know the parts of me that are the truest. The parts that no one else but you has ever gotten to see."

"You don't know me either," I whispered.

"I know you're scared of dragons . . . but not coconut-flavored coffee." His lips twitched in a self-amused smile before settling into an expression much more solemn. "I know you spent so much of your life being told to sit on the sidelines, yet you were brave enough to make it on your own in New York, brave enough to fly across the country to save me.

"I know you make friends everywhere you go. That your smile melts my heart. That you love your family so much. That you doodle anatomical hearts and flowers. That you eat your toast with honey and are *not* a diabetic. That you sigh in your sleep.

"Most of all, I know I'm in love with you." He stated it firmly. Without hesitation.

"I—" Everything inside me felt calcified. Everyone who loved me most was dead. And my own emotions were scattered like a handful of sand held up in a breeze. "How do you know?"

"What?" He blinked. Swallowed. This wasn't the reaction he expected.

"How do you know you love me?" My true question was trapped beneath my tongue: *How do I know if I love you?* So I asked a lesser version, "And what if you change your mind?"

"I won't." His gaze was a caress, roving over all of me, making each part of me ache with a desire for his fingers. But he was holding himself back, gripping the arms of his chair, and saying each word clearly. "I've fallen in love twice in my life. Once with a girl during a pretend game of hide-and-seek, and once with a girl who swept me off my feet on a New York City sidewalk."

"I believe *you* swept me off my feet, actually."

"Semantics." He smiled. "I know I'm going to fall in love a million times in my life." I was too surprised to form the word "what?" or remember how to exhale. "Maybe more than a million . . . but it will always be with *you*."

Garrett had claimed to know me, but he hadn't loved me. Not really. He wanted to protect me. He wanted to use me for my connection to the Family. He wanted to save me—and pretend that erased the fact that he hadn't saved Carter.

I looked away from Char while I contrasted my feelings for Garrett with those for him.

It was hard to call them both the same word: "feelings." One set was as ingrained in me as my fingerprints. Garrett's presence in my life predated my memory. He was one of the last parts of my life from *before*.

And he was partially responsible for that. I couldn't forgive him. It didn't matter who his little *f* family was, that he'd been raised by a father who considered shooting Mick and knocking him unconscious acceptable cover-story collateral damage, or with brothers who made him feel like a weak failure, an outsider. I couldn't forget his bystander role in making me an orphan.

Or his face as he crumpled on the ground embedded with a bullet meant for me.

Or the fact that he hadn't stayed around to let me thank him and have the first of so many discussions we needed to have. Maybe he was scared of the things I'd say, the things he would have had to. Or maybe he was scared for his safety. I hated that I didn't know. That I may never know.

That I hadn't gotten to say good-bye.

There wouldn't be a clean break. I could no more sever him completely than I could untangle my DNA and remove whatever combination of nucleotides spelled out my skin's tendency toward purple.

But that *wasn't* love.

At least not in the romantic sense.

"You know me." Char said it like a plea. Like a pledge. Like a prayer. "You know everything that's important. We lied, but we weren't pretending. At least I wasn't. Everything I told you about me and you, everything *we* shared, those were the most real moments of my life."

I heard his chair scrape closer, but I couldn't pull my eyes away from the textured surface of the ceiling tiles. His voice dropped to a hoarse whisper, "I wasn't pretending. Were you?"

The unguarded silliness of teasing him about coffee flavors, his sweet tooth, or his corny jokes. The candid opinions of our all-night conversations. The way he explained and loved all things scientific, but had watched a fairy-tale movie to better understand me. How he believed I could do anything, pushed me to define and pursue my dreams. The way his touch made me feel solid. Reassured me I wouldn't slip away. That I was made of flesh and bone and had words with weight. Words worth listening to. Feelings worth considering. Skin worth touching.

And running through my veins, settled in every cell, was a desire to listen, to consider, to touch. To know and learn, to be surprised and challenged by this guy today and tomorrow and all the days beyond that.

The sensation of tearing my eyes from the ceiling and settling them back on his felt like coming home. I put my hand on top of his, plucking lightly on his fingers until he loosened his grip on the chair and flipped them over to interlace with mine.

"I love you." It didn't come out as the whisper I expected. The hesitation didn't creep in until I added, "But I have no clue where that leaves us. I'm lost."

I tightened my grip on his hand. *Lost,* but not *alone.*

"We'll get to know each other," he said.

Our faces were identical: dopey, love-drunk, smiles of relief and happiness.

"There's one thing you *have* to understand, though," I said.

He sat up straighter. "Okay."

"You don't get to decide if something is too dangerous for me. That's never *your* decision; it's mine. I get why you ran from New York; you thought you were keeping me safe and away from all this, but never again."

His face was as somber as it had been the times he let me join him at his father's bedside. The beeping and clicking of hospital machinery so loud as he stood statue still, and the closest he'd come to accepting comfort from me was to rest a few fingers lightly on the handle of the wheelchair I'd been seated in.

Char swallowed. "I don't know if I can do that."

"I'm not asking, I'm telling you. You don't get to choose to keep me on the sidelines. I'm not saying I want to go rushing into dangerous situations, but trust me enough to make my own decisions."

He nodded slowly.

"And please don't treat me like I'm breakable. You're the only one who ever touches me, and I miss it."

"I miss it too."

I held my hands out, eager for a clasp and a kiss. They didn't come.

"But you're in the clinic, and you're here because of something you did to save my life. I feel like I'm responsible for every spot of purple on your body."

"No. You don't get to take responsibility or guilt for my decisions."

He lowered his chin and studied the floor—for the first time I could see shades of the painfully shy boy he'd been. I knelt up on the bed, taking his face in both my hands and turning it to look into mine. "It was worth it. You are worth it. And I want to be touched, does that count for anything?"

"Of course—" He quickly, lightly brushed the tips of his fingers across the back of mine before folding his hands in his lap. "But I bet I've left bruises before."

"Nothing major. At least not after the whole meeting-by-full-body-collision."

Char winced. "Can you . . . teach me how to touch you without bruising? How much pressure does it take?"

No one had ever asked me that before. Even with my parents it had seemed easier to avoid physical affection than take a risk. But it wasn't all that risky if we established limits, if I knew my counts—currently over a hundred thousand thanks to miraculous, marvelous infusions. I shifted to the side of my bed and patted the space beside me. "Come here."

He hesitated for just a moment before looking me in the eyes and nodding once.

"Lie back," I said. Char's shoulders took up most of the width of the bed, but sitting up, I fit like a puzzle piece next to his waist. My legs folded up beside him, tracing the line of his outer thigh. "Give me your arm."

He smiled and held it out. I lowered it to rest on my lap and then placed both my hands on top. I loved the way his skin looked against mine. It should have made me feel pale and sickly, but it didn't. He always seemed to radiate vitality, and it felt like I could absorb it, steal it from his pores and the cords of his muscles.

"Don't move," I teased, watching the corners of his mouth tip upward.

"Are you going to tickle me?"

"Are you ticklish?" I didn't know this. It seemed like something I should know already. But we'd get there.

I didn't tickle. Instead I circled one arm around his waist, sneaking my hand beneath the hem of his T-shirt to stroke his skin with my thumb. I used my other hand to trace the pattern of muscle and veins down the inside of his arm—watching my touch raise goose bumps along his warm skin.

He shut his eyes and inhaled deeply.

"Light touch is almost always okay. None of this would bruise me." I bent and kissed the skin at his wrist, where his pulse raced beneath my thumb. Char gasped.

"As for adding pressure—slow is always better." I inched my fingers up his stomach to his shoulders, leaning over him so I was supporting myself with my arms and my hair hung down around both our faces. "As long as my counts are under control, slow, steady pressure shouldn't leave a bruise."

I lowered myself softly onto his chest, nuzzling the line of his jaw with my nose, my mouth. I could feel him trembling. Gripping the blankets with both fists.

"Think you got it?" I asked. "And you can always ask if you're not sure."

He breathed out the word "okay," and I felt his chin drop

slightly until it rested against the top of my head and his fingers relaxed on the blanket and inched closer to my sides.

But they stayed on the sheets.

"Do you need me to give you a countdown?" I teased.

"Maybe," he said, brushing his lips against my hair.

"How much time do you need to prepare? Should I start at ten, or three? Or will a 'ready, set, go' work?"

"Ten," he answered, but I could hear the smile in his voice.

Ten more seconds was too long to delay a hug I'd been waiting my whole life to receive, but I pressed my lips to the skin below his ear and whispered, "Ten Mississippi, nine Mississippi—"

His laughter rumbled from his chest, shaking us both.

"Eight Mississippi, seven Mississippi, six Mississippi—"

And then his palms were tentatively skirting over the fabric of my shirt, sliding down my back, settling on my waist with the perfect amount of pressure to make me feel safe and here.

"I couldn't wait," he said. "Not even one more Mississippi."

Once upon a time I was a seventeen-year-old. In love for the first time. In *life* for the first time. And quite determined to have some "happily" in my ever after.

AUTHOR'S NOTE

While Penny and her family are pulled from my imagination, several aspects of this story are real.

Idiopathic thrombocytopenic purpura, also known as Immune Thrombocytopenia, is an actual platelet disorder. To learn more about ITP, visit: www.pdsa.org or www.itpsupport.org.uk.

Organ and tissue transplant regulation are currently controlled by the FDA (FOTA is an agency that exists only in my imagination and on these pages). The level of oversight and testing varies greatly between tissue and organs, and many of the problems presented in this novel have a basis in reality: There have been cases of diseased tissue infecting a recipient; there is a black market for organs; stolen cadavers have been used in transplants; there are instances where patients have been rejected from transplant lists because they have disabilities.

And, unfortunately, there are far more people who need transplants than there are organs available; far too many people who die before reaching the top of the transplant list.

If you're interested in learning more about organ and tissue transplants, I recommend NPR's fascinating series on the tissue transplant industry: www.npr.org/series/156935894/human-tissue-donation; the documentary *Tales From the Organ Trade*; and the Organ Procurement and Transplantation Network website: http://optn.transplant.hrsa.gov.

And, of course, please consider signing up to be an organ donor—www.OrganDonor.gov.

ACKNOWLEDGMENTS

I loved fairy tales when I was a little girl—I still do. But when I was young "The Princess and the Pea" had to be removed from my bedtime story rotation. Instead of easing me into slumber, this story woke up so many questions.

Seven-year-old me would've told you that Hans Christian Andersen started at the wrong place and focused on all the unimportant things. The story is called "The *Princess* and the Pea," yet it's hardly about the princess at all. We never learn why she was alone on a cold and stormy night. No one asks what happened to her family or if she's okay. We're never told *why* she bruises so easily, or *if* she wants to marry the prince. And then there was the fact that always bothered me most: Why does her ability to bruise make her desirable?

I was a stumble-bumble-trip child—constantly in the ER for stitches or casts. I've had plenty of bruises in my accident-prone life, and they're never attractive. Bruises *hurt*. That the ability to bruise was the basis for the princess's identity—the reason she and the prince could marry—was disturbing and confusing to childhood me.

A couple of decades later, I finally sat down to write the princess's story—because while the fairy tale may have her in the title, the story isn't *hers*. *Hold Me Like a Breath* is my way of reclaiming this fairy tale, giving the princess a voice, an identity that's based on more than her skin's ability to turn purple.

This book is my answer to my childhood questions, but I hope it raises some questions for you.

So, of course the first people who need thanking are my parents. Thank you for reading to me. Thank you for answering my endless questions. Thank you for teaching me that curiosity is a gift and sometimes the only way to find an answer is to create my own. I appreciate you even more now that my Schmidtlets are in their own question phase and I live in their barrage of "whys." Pip Squeak and Wild Imp, I hope you never stop asking—except at bedtime, please go to sleep. And, St. Matt, who brings the logic and reality to our little family, I love you so very much.

This book couldn't have been written without Joe Monti, the first person who said, "This is the story you're writing next. Write it now!" and Emily Hainsworth and Courtney Summers who held my hand, brainstormed, read the drafts, and delivered endless pep talks. E. C. Myers, Katie Walker, and Jessica Spotswood also shared their wise feedback, and I'm so grateful to them and to my online and local book community, including Jonathan Maberry, Nancy Keim Comley, Tiff Emerick, Heather Hebert, Jen Zelesko, Annie Gaughen, Victoria Schwab, Scott Tracey, Susan Adrian, Linda Grimes, Gail Yates, Elisa Ludwig, Kate Walton, Eve Mont, Lauren Stroehecker, Kelly Jensen, and so many more.

To Barry, Tricia, and the whole Goldblatt family, so much of this job is spent by myself in front of my computer, thank you for making sure I never feel alone and for always having my back.

To all the talented people at Bloomsbury, I feel so lucky to continue to work with your magical team. Emily Easton, thank you for sharing my excitement for this project and catching my obsession with the organ trade. Laura Whitaker, I guess we're past the point where I can send "Oh, just one more change" e-mails. Thank you for being so patient and such a great champion of me and this story. Many hugs and much gratitude to Sarah Shumway, Lizzy Mason, Erica Barmash, Emily Ritter, Cristina Gilbert, Amanda Bartlett, Courtney Griffin, Linette Kim, Beth Eller, Jenna Pocius, Patricia McHugh, Jill Amack, and everyone else who's worked to make this book stronger and shinier.

I have so much gratitude for the doctors and patients who answered my questions about idiopathic thrombocytopenic purpura and shared their stories. If there are any mistakes in the way I depict Penny's experiences with ITP, they are entirely my fault and I apologize. I especially want to recognize Dr. Pam Boardman, MPH; Charity Hasty; Jeff Writtenhouse; Christina Pena; Erica Klein; Crystal Lee; and Meredith Jane.

Finally, my heart is full of gratitude for all the teachers, librarians, booksellers, bloggers, and readers who have spent their time in these pages or recommended my books to friends, family, strangers in bookstores or libraries, or on the Interwebs. At the risk of exposing my cheesy side (too late?), you are all a part of my happily ever after and I couldn't do this without you.

W9-CDT-546

THUCYDIDES

THE PELOPONNESIAN WARS

Translated by Benjamin Jowett

Revised and Abridged with an Introduction by

P. A. BRUNT

FELLOW OF ORIEL COLLEGE, OXFORD UNIVERSITY

TWAYNE PUBLISHERS, INC.
31 Union Square, N. Y. 3

Grateful acknowledgment is made to the Jowett Copyright Trustees for permission to revise and publish this abridgment of the Benjamin Jowett translation of *Thucydides.*

We are grateful to Clarendon Press, Oxford, for their kind permission to use N. G. L. Hammond's maps which appear on pages xxxix, xl, xli, and xlii, from *A History of Greece,* © Oxford University Press, 1959.

Contents

CONTENTS

Thucydides:

The Peloponnesian Wars

Introduction[1]

"My history is an everlasting possession, not a prize composition that is heard and forgotten" (I:22). Thucydides meant his history to be instructive, and his proud claim which time has vindicated was not based on the literary merits of his work. Yet it was perhaps those merits that preserved it amid the loss of most of the classical literature of Greece. If some of the narrative is arid, Thucydides always rises to the great moments; no one could tell an exciting story better; he has the same sharp eye as Francis Parkman among the moderns for vivid details; and his dramatic gifts, worthy of the great age of Attic tragedy in which he lived, make us share the hopes and fears of the men whose actions and sufferings he recounts. Macaulay pronounced his seventh book the *ne plus ultra* of human art. In antiquity the crabbed style of the speeches with which his history abounds was justly criticized, yet even here he attains to a monumental eloquence which few ancient authors rivaled.

But Thucydides himself expected immortality only because the accuracy of his researches had enabled him, so he thought, to produce useful guidance for the future. He would have been best pleased with the recognition of some modern critical historians that he was the first of their own kind, or with the recommendation of the philosopher Hobbes, his first English translator, that his work contained "profitable instructions for Noble men and such as may come to have the managings of great and weighty actions."

THUCYDIDES' SUBJECT

An Athenian citizen born in the middle of the fifth century before Christ, Thucydides described the struggle

[1] I have borrowed some passages from an article of mine in *History Today*, 1957.

for supremacy in Greece between Athens and Sparta, which we call the Peloponnesian War; it began in 431 and ended in 404 with the surrender of Athens. Thucydides himself was impressed with the material resources of the belligerents and held that it was the greatest war yet fought. But by modern standards the numbers engaged were small and the modes of fighting primitive.[1] A detailed military record might be thought of little interest today. But this would be a misapprehension of the true significance of his subject. The Greek was a political animal, and much of his life was spent in war; Thucydides describes for us conditions in which his Athenian contemporaries, Sophocles and Euripides, Aristophanes, Phidias and Socrates, worked and thought. The Parthenon itself was built from the profits of the Athenian empire. Thucydides' pages are the background to some of the greatest achievements of the Greek genius in literature, art and thought. And his own work is among those achievements. Moreover, the war itself was of even graver importance than he could know. We can see in retrospect that it was to weaken fatally the Greek cities and embitter their relations, so that there was no more hope of their uniting by force or agreement, and that they were ultimately bound to succumb to foreign conquest and lose the freedom which seems to have been essential to the vitality of Greek civilization. But, though Thucydides was no prophet, his own experience did lead him, as I shall show later, to penetrate deeply into the motives of political behavior and to see the war not simply as a clash between states but as a conflict of two ideals—Athenian imperialism and the Greek passion for autonomy—and between two ways of life—the Athenian, democratic and adventurous, and the Spartan, disciplined and conservative.

To understand this, we need to know something of the contemporary state of the Greek world; Thucydides presupposes familiarity with much that is not so well known to the modern reader. That world comprised not only the mainland of Greece but colonies scattered over southern

[1] See General Note 2 (p. 336).

Italy and Sicily, the islands and shores of the Aegean and even the Black Sea, a population of perhaps seven millions. Except in the backward parts of central and northern Greece, which took little part in the war and where the people were villagers loosely grouped in ethnic leagues, the unit was the *polis,* a term which it is often convenient, though misleading, to translate by "city." Though each *polis* had a civic center, which might be a town of note, the *polis* was not the town but the community of citizens, most of whom often lived in the country. The official name for Athens or Corinth was simply "the Athenians" or "the Corinthians." Most cities were small; the island of Lesbos was divided among five; Athens, with a territory of 2,350 square kilometres and probably over 50,000 adult male citizens, was exceptionally large, and rivaled only by Syracuse (VII:28). But every city, however small, was passionately attached to its freedom or autonomy; each desired to be fully sovereign and to enjoy laws of its own choice.

The political and social systems of the cities therefore differed widely, but the forms of government were always, despite much divergence in detail, oligarchic or democratic. Oligarchy meant rule by men of high birth or, more usually, by men of property; in a democracy all the citizens had equal political rights, and in effect this gave preponderance to the poor. Most cities were deeply divided by class conflict; Plato even said that in each there were two cities, one of the rich and another of the poor. Athens was the model democracy, while oligarchs looked to Sparta; and the war between the two most powerful cities precipitated internal revolutions throughout Greece (III: 82-84).

At the outbreak of the war, Athenian policy was guided by Pericles, an aristocrat by birth who had placed himself at the head of the democratic party; and in a famous judgment Thucydides says that in his time Athens was a democracy only in name and was in fact coming to be ruled by her first citizen (II:65). This is a forceful way of putting the fact that the Athenians generally took Pericles' advice. Taken literally, it is false. Even if his advice prevailed, decisions were made by the assembly, sometimes after prolonged discussion (I:139; cf. 44); and in 430 he was actually deposed from office and fined, though soon restored to power (II:65). It is evident that he was no monarch; sovereignty lay with the popular assembly.[1]

This system was both more and less democratic than any known today. Women, slaves and resident foreigners, who were rarely naturalized even if they were domiciled at Athens for generations, had no political rights; and they constituted a majority of the adult population. But all citizens, however poor, had the same rights in an assembly, which controlled policy and administration even in minute details. The people, in a rather restricted sense, thus governed themselves more directly than is now possible. It is obvious, of course, that a large mass gathering could not initiate policy; it needed guidance. This could not be effectively supplied either by the council which prepared business for the assembly or by most of the officials, for they were ordinary citizens, chosen by lot. Many have supposed that policy was largely directed by the ten annually elected generals. They were often men of political importance, and they could be returned year by year. Pericles himself is said to have been general for about fifteen years in succession. But essentially the generals too were executive instruments of the popular will. Nicias as general advised against the Sicilian expedition of 415, yet he was appointed to command it. Pericles was deposed from the office when the people lost confidence in his conduct of the war. A general had important duties, and election doubtless added to a politician's prestige, but he could not direct policy in virtue of his office.

In fact, guidance was provided by the demagogues. The word originally meant no more than "leaders of the people"; it acquired a bad sense only because many were charged by critics of democracy with financial dishonesty and with pandering to the caprices of the mob. True

[1] General Note 3 gives some details (p. 337).

or false, such allegations come mostly from biased sources and must not obscure the fact that demagogues were essential to the working of democracy. They did not need to hold any office: they were simply men with the interest and leisure to devote themselves to politics and with the eloquence to sway the assembly. Leisure presupposes wealth; though they found their chief backing among the poor, they were not themselves poor men, even when they had ceased to come from the aristocracy, like Cleon, who owned a tannery. And they had to be more than good speakers; no politician could retain his influence unless he talked sense; he had to have some knowledge of affairs, or he would soon be discredited by the failure of his schemes. The demagogue's position depended on his constant ability to convince council and assembly. They were not irresponsible. Like modern politicians, they sought power; and they stood to lose it, not at four-year intervals, but at every meeting of the people; it was they who were blamed for errors made by the people on their advice (VIII:1), and they might even suffer death or exile. In some degree every demagogue of note had to possess eloquence and a grasp of the city's resources which helped to explain Pericles' ascendancy (II:65), though none rivaled him in manifest integrity and in the prestige that came from the long success of his career. Thucydides asserts that he even had the authority to oppose the popular will. This can only have been true within limits. The Athenians were ready on occasion to accept unpalatable advice from Pericles because they knew that, in general, he stood for the policies they desired, because he had been the architect of democracy and empire.

Democracy at Athens was intimately connected with naval power and with empire. Everywhere in Greece it was the class on which a city depended most in war that came to exercise political power, and at Athens this class was the poor who manned the ships. Athens had first built a great fleet with the proceeds of the state-owned silver mines in Attica. This fleet saved Greece from conquest by the Persian armada in 480 and liberated most of Persia's Greek subjects across the Aegean in the next few years. The liberated cities formed a league under Athenian leadership (I:96); to an increasing extent they furnished money for the common cause against Persia, and their contributions went to maintain and augment the size of the Athenian navy until in numbers and efficiency it had no match in the eastern Mediterranean. After 449 Athens was at peace with the Persian king; but she compelled the allies to go on paying their contributions, which now amounted to "tribute"; superior at sea to all, and by land to their divided forces, she converted the league into an empire. Secessions or revolts were repressed; democratic governments loyal to Athens were usually established; and Athens ceased to consult the allies in the common councils which had once been held; and she used their resources for her own purposes and at her own will.

This aggressive and imperialist policy enured to the benefit of the poor at Athens. A high proportion of the citizens found employment in the fleet, in public works, in the paid juries and in the numerous paid offices; and some of the indigent were allotted lands abroad in the empire. It was no wonder that the poor were imperialists. Not only did they gain materially from the empire; it may be doubted if, but for the empire, democracy would have become a reality at Athens. For popular rights would have meant little unless the principle of pay for all public services, which was alien to oligarchy, had enabled the humblest citizens to take an active part in the government and acquire some political and administrative experience. It is true that the system survived the fall of the empire; but when Athens lacked imperial revenues, the system imposed an almost intolerable financial strain; and we may question whether it would have been adopted on such a scale, had not tribute been available at its inception.

Thucydides ascribes the greater wealth of Greece in his day to increased maritime activity. Many cities were now exporting wine, oil and manufactures, and importing the grain, timber, metals and other supplies which they lacked. None had a more extensive commerce than

Athens. Her harbor, the Piræus, was the chief emporium in Greece; she bought much of her grain from south Russia and exported olive oil and silver as well as industrial products. In modern times it has been assumed that her imperialism had a commercial motive and that the Peloponnesian War itself was inspired by the deliberate policy of Athens and Corinth to secure control or monopoly of foreign markets. For this view there is neither evidence nor probability. Even at Athens most of the trade was in the hands of resident foreigners, who had no votes. Athenian imperialism, like all ancient imperialism, was directly predatory: empire meant tribute. When the Athenians tried to conquer Sicily, they hoped that they would acquire a perpetual source of pay (VI: 24). Of course, the more tribute came in, the more goods and services Athens could buy from abroad. But, so far as we know, no wars were fought for directly commercial reasons; most conflicts indeed sprang from quarrels over a few barren acres of borderland.

Thucydides puts forward the view in speeches—I take it to be his own—that Athens owed her strength to her democratic institutions and manners (II:36, 41; VI:89). Athens belonged to her citizens; her profits and glory were theirs, and it was for this reason that they were so restless and daring in her service (I:70), and so resolute in fighting on amid growing difficulties (VII:28). But Athenian imperialism challenged the traditional Greek attachment to autonomy. Thucydides repeatedly asserts that, deprived of liberty, all Athens' subjects were passionate to revolt, while the other Greeks feared to come under her rule (e.g., II:8; IV:108; VIII:2). Numerous revolts seem to confirm these assertions. Yet Thucydides goes much too far. Athenian democracy was a pattern to others (II:37), and all over Greece democrats looked to Athens for support (III:82). While Thucydides often makes Athenian speakers avow that her empire was despotism based on force and injustice, he allows others to point out that among the subjects the masses were loyal to Athens (III:47; VIII:48). In almost all cases where we have details of revolts, we find that they were engineered by such oligarchic governments as

Athens had tolerated in the empire, or by oligarchic conspirators. Athens' subjects had, in fact, lost freedom in the sense of independence, but most of them had gained it in the sense of popular control of their own local affairs (cf., IV:84-88); by supporting democracies in the empire, Athens secured to the poor in the subject cities equality before the law and in political privileges rights similar to that which the humbler Athenians enjoyed, rights which they might have been too weak to win for themselves.

Though Thucydides was profoundly concerned with the moral problem of Athenian imperialism, and though he emphasizes to excess the hatred felt in Greece for the empire, he never says that the empire fell because it was iniquitous or unpopular. But he does lay the blame on democracy, which was at once the source of Athens' strength and fatal to her final success. Or rather, he lays it on the demagogues who followed Pericles (II:65). Greedy and ambitious, they sought popularity and power for themselves at the expense of the city's interests; they departed unnecessarily from Pericles' far-sighted prudence. Their rivalry promoted factions; policy fluctuated; and defeats abroad combined with the discontent of the well-to-do at home, who bore enormous financial burdens, to bring on revolution and to subvert Athenian power from within.

It is not easy to contradict this verdict. In the Athenian democracy there were no organized parties, no whips, no government secured of power for a period. A primary assembly controlled everything, and dangerous oscillations in policy could be avoided only if the people had leaders of wisdom in whom they would place continued confidence. After Pericles' death in 429, such leaders did not appear for the rest of the war. Yet, if grave errors ensued, what other political system has insured against equally serious mistakes? Certainly the Athenians themselves never accepted the view that democracy was "acknowledged folly" (VI:89); they retained it long after 404, at all times when they had the choice; and it was widely adopted in Greece. It was in the city "stuffed with freedom," as Plato contemptuously called it, that

Greek comedy and oratory flourished—both were inconceivable where free speech was denied—and that even philosophers hostile to democracy were least inhibited in "following reason wherever it led."

But, however attractive Athenian democracy may appear to us, it was odious to most men of high birth and property in Greece; they detested government "by the rabble" all the more because the rabble were apt to impose heavy financial burdens upon them. This class was dominant in most cities of central Greece and the Peloponnese, where military strength rested on the peasantry who could equip themselves as hoplites (heavy-armed foot soldiers) and who were ready to follow the political leadership of their "betters." Moreover, these cities felt themselves menaced by Athenian imperialism. Between 460 and 446 Athens had won over or subdued many cities in central Greece and the Peloponnese; and though she had been forced to surrender these gains under the Thirty Years' Peace of 446, the treaty which was broken in 432-31, the restless temperament of the Athenians made it likely that they would resume aggressions on the mainland whenever they had the power. Everywhere, the enemies of Athens looked to Sparta for protection.

Sparta had long been the most formidable land power in Greece. From a group of villages in the upper Eurotas, the Spartans had expanded in all directions till their territory had come to embrace two fifths of the Peloponnese, the largest in Greece (I:10). Only a minority of the inhabitants enjoyed full civic rights, but these citizens, the Spartiates, were supported by serfs (Helots) who worked their estates. The Spartan army, which also included second-class citizens (Periœci) and even freed Helots, was one of the largest in Greece; and it was incomparably the best; the Spartiates, who formed the kernel of it, were trained from boyhood in military exercises—they had no other occupation to divert them—and were in effect professional soldiers, whereas the peasant infantry elsewhere was nothing but a militia. Moreover, the Spartans had, as early as the sixth century, organized a confederacy under their hegemony, which by 431 comprised almost all the Peloponnesian cities except Argos, and many in central Greece, notably the Bœotian league. (Dominated by Thebes, that league was hostile to Athens, partly because Athens protected Platæa from it.) The members of this confederacy met in congresses and decided on common action for mutual defense by a majority, each city having one vote (I:125). So far as we know, these congresses met only at Sparta's summons; and whether or not she had a veto, she could usually get her own way by pressure on the smaller cities. Spartans, too, commanded the confederate armies and fleets and conducted negotiations in the name of her allies. In practice the confederacy was often a mere tool of Spartan policy. With her allies Sparta was no less superior to Athens on land than Athens was superior on the sea. While few of the members of the confederacy had ships or trained rowers, and while there was not enough money to build or maintain a fleet which could rival the Athenian, in land fighting the Bœotians alone proved equal to the Athenians; and Athenian manpower was far exceeded by that of Sparta and her allies.

The Spartans professed that unlike the Athenians they respected the "autonomy" of their allies. In fact, membership of the confederacy was in itself a limitation of full independence; and Thucydides avers that Sparta took care that her allies should be governed by oligarchies friendly to herself (I:19, 144). The charge was not quite true; Elis and Mantinea, for instance, had democratic governments. Still, it was precisely these cities that proved least loyal to Sparta. The political system at Sparta itself was believed to be of hoary antiquity (I:18); certainly, it was narrow, harsh and secretive.[1] But its conservatism and the discipline imposed on the citizens aroused general admiration in the upper classes of Greece and even influenced Plato's *Republic*, and the community of oligarchic institutions and ideals undoubtedly cemented the confederacy and won Sparta adherents all over Greece (III:82).

There was another reason why cities remained loyal

[1] See General Note 4 (p. 338) for some details.

to Sparta. Unlike Athens, she had ceased to be aggressive. Thucydides justly observes that Spartan policy was mainly determined by the danger of Helot revolt (IV:80). Though the Helots of Laconia, the original Spartan territory, seem to have been fairly content—it was probably they who served in Spartan armies—those in Messenia had never forgotten their independence, and would seize any opportunity to recover it. Argos, too, refused to recognize Sparta's rights to land conquered by the middle of the sixth century (V:14). Sparta always had to fear a Messenian insurrection backed by Argos and perhaps by Athens. It was for this reason that Sparta accepted an internal discipline which had turned into an "armed camp" what had once been a center of art and poetry. The precarious nature of their rule at home also made the Spartans abjure further expansion. Their allies knew this. Moreover, among her allies Sparta kept the peace so far as she could, protected the weaker allies, and gave them more stability and order than they would otherwise have enjoyed.

Sparta and her allies had formed the nucleus of Greek resistance to Persia in 480-79 and had done most to beat the invading forces by land. Athens had then accepted Spartan leadership; and though in 477 the Athenians had made themselves leaders in the continuing naval war against Persia, it had been with Spartan consent (I:95). But good relations did not long continue. By 465 Sparta was secretly planning to support a secession from the Athenian league, and was only restrained by a Messenian revolt. She then actually invoked Athenian help, only to repudiate it because she feared the revolutionary spirit of the Athenians. There could indeed be no mutual confidence between the Athenians, democratic, innovating and aggressive, and the conservative Spartans. Athens' attempts after 460 to extend her power in the mainland inspired lasting apprehensions at Sparta. They were checked by a Peloponnesian invasion of Attica in 446, but not all Spartans were satisfied with the peace settlement in that year; the king who negotiated it was banished for taking bribes; and it was probably Sparta which desired to intervene in 440 on behalf of Samos against Athens, and was prevented by Corinth (I:40). When Corinth in turn, embittered by Athens' policy towards her own colonies, demanded war, she was knocking on an open door. Thucydides says that the Spartans were reluctant to go to war except in necessity (I:118). But he also says that in 432 the Spartans were under such a necessity (I:23, 88); they feared the growing power of Athens. This last judgment has been disputed, but without good reason. In the fourteen years of peace since 446, Athens had consolidated her hold on the empire, founded great colonies in Amphipolis (IV:102) and Thurii (VI:104 note), augmented her revenues and latterly secured the alliance of Corcyra; her fleet and strategic situation made Corcyra a valuable accession to Athenian power, especially because as an island she was likely to fall under complete Athenian dominance.

Thucydides depicts what he believed to be an inevitable conflict, a conflict not only between two cities which had brought under their control most parts of the Greek world, but between two different ways of life, and one which involved the sympathies and interests of all Greeks; it was to end, thanks to Persian intervention as well as Athenian errors, with Athens' total, though temporary, eclipse.

THE HISTORIAN

Very little is known of Thucydides except from the few references he makes to his own life. By birth he was apparently connected with prominent aristocrats opposed to Pericles, and he was certainly a rich man, with mining concessions in Thrace (IV:105). He says that he was of mature years when the war broke out (V:26), perhaps a man of about twenty-five. In 424 he was a general and was banished because he had lost Amphipolis. From his own laconic report we cannot measure his culpability, but we know that the Athenians were prone to treat mere failure in a general as a crime (IV:65). He only mentions his banishment to explain that for the rest of the war he had excellent opportunities for getting information from the enemies of Athens, among whom he spent part of his time (V:26). He survived Athens' fall in 404 (II:65) but probably not for long; and though he returned to Athens, he did not die there; his memory was preserved by a cenotaph.

He began to write the history at the outset of the war (I:1) and lived to its end, but he did not finish his work; it breaks off abruptly in the narrative of 411, and some parts are manifestly unrevised. His history must have been published posthumously by an editor; it was continued by three other historians, including Xenophon, whose inferior sequel survives. We do not know why he had progressed no further. Perhaps his passion for accuracy and the difficulty he had in ascertaining the exact truth (I:22) ever delayed him as he wrote and rewrote in the quest for perfection.

It is natural to suppose that Thucydides' thinking deepened with experience. He set out simply to describe a war in which great material resources would be deployed; before his death he knew that the war had ruined Athens, and much earlier he must have seen that the survival of her empire was at stake. What had been commenced as a military record—and this his work never ceased to be—grew into something much more, an analysis of the strength and weakness of Athens and her enemies, of the moral and political problem which the Athenian empire constituted, and an interpretation of the permanent factors which influenced or determined men's political behavior. Modern scholars have tried to distinguish late and early drafts in his work and to trace the evolution of his ideas. The project is fascinating, but no agreement has been achieved in the ingenious speculations of a century.

Thucydides stands near the beginning of European historiography, and he had not much respect for his few predecessors. He brushes aside the chronicle of his elder contemporary Hellanicus as "jejune and chronologically inaccurate" (I:97). He does not even name Herodotus but corrects him on some errors of detail (I:20), and may have him in mind when he refers with contempt to "the tales of chroniclers who please the ear rather than speak the truth" (I:21). Still he admits that the Persian war, Herodotus' subject, had been adequately treated (I:97).

Thucydides' problems in the greater part of his history were, in fact, quite different from those of Herodotus or of most later historians. He was writing contemporary history, and most of his evidence came from eyewitnesses whom he could cross-examine; he did not depend on oral tradition like Herodotus or on earlier written accounts or documents like most modern historians. From his excursus on early Greek history (I:2-21) and from a few other digressions into antiquity (e.g., II:15), we can see how he thought that the remoter past should be reconstructed. He used the meager evidence that existed —traditions and legends, the old poetry, inferences from monuments and archaic institutions which had survived —but he interpreted it in a critical and rationalizing spirit, bringing the experience of his own time to bear on it; geographical conditions, the human tendency to exaggerate, the motives by which men are always guided are criteria for checking the old stories and producing an account which is intelligible and therefore relatively trustworthy. Modern scholars may differ from his conclusions on archaic Greek history (though not often), but their methods are essentially the same. No other historian in antiquity followed these methods with so much success.

Even when he came to his proper subject, Thucydides confesses that he found it a hard task to establish the exact truth (I:22). He was not satisfied, as perhaps Herodotus often was, with what "the chance informant" told him; he needed eyewitnesses—probably he preferred men who could supply "inside" information—and he collated different accounts, not even trusting his own memory when he had been present; he had to allow for bias and forgetfulness. It was of advantage that in exile he could more easily check Athenian reports against those of their enemies (V:26). His zeal for accuracy is evident in many ways. Though averse to digressions, he sometimes paused to correct vulgar errors. He inserted documents in his work, a practice that later historians in antiquity, in order to preserve unity of style, usually avoided; documentation reappeared with Jewish and Christian writers, whose veneration for the Scriptures inspired them with a wider respect for documentary truth. He was at pains to observe an exact chronology. We are transported from one scene to another so that each event may appear in its proper order.

Dating presented Thucydides with some difficulty. Each city had its own calendar; the year began at different times in different places but usually in the middle of the summer, and events were officially dated by annual magistrates. Thucydides was careful to correlate the beginning of the war and the peace of 421 with the best known of these systems (II:2; V:25), but he thought that they were inaccurate and confusing for fixing the time of military operations; he divided each year into summer and winter and dated each event in such and such a season of such and such a year of the war (V:20).

When Thucydides believed that he had found out the truth, he wrote it down authoritatively, without giving the evidence. Only rarely (e.g., II:5) does he record divergent accounts, as Herodotus had often done. In a score of cases, he says cautiously that something was reported, without assuming responsibility. He will not try to describe a night battle in detail because none of the combatants could give him a clear account (VI:44). For the rest we have to take his own judgment on trust. Nor can we often confirm or refute what he says from other independent sources. It is an act of faith to rely on Thucydides, yet no modern scholars have (except over a few matters) refused to make it. We believe him because he creates the impression of a man earnest after truth and critical in discovering it and because his narrative is coherent and intelligible. There are supporting reasons. Other ancient writers who still had access to independent information were content to copy or continue his account. A single exception to this rule only strengthens our confidence in him. *The Constitution of Athens,* a work commonly ascribed to Aristotle, gives a very different story of the revolution of 411. But this work is unreliable elsewhere and, unlike Thucydides' history, patently biased; in this instance its version of events is self-contradictory. And scraps of evidence from inscriptions or Aristophanes' comedies generally confirm Thucydides, or dovetail with his story. A few minor errors can be detected, some of them topographical and therefore excusable, for there were no maps.

It is less easy to condone, or even to explain, his omissions. He stresses that Athens' power depended on financial strength, and he surveys her finances in 431 (II: 13). But he tells us hardly anything of the gradual dissipation of her funds, of which we happen to know something from inscriptions. In the last stage of the war, Persian intervention was important, as he knew; it began in 412, but he has told us so little of Athens' relations with Persia that we can hardly understand them. He himself thought that party factions at Athens were the fundamental cause of her ruin, but he gives little attention to them until in 411 revolution was imminent. Here there are not only gaps in the factual record but failures of interpretation, and they do not stand alone. He describes military operations in minute detail, but he sometimes fails to elucidate their strategic purpose. Why, for instance, did Pericles try to take Epidaurus in 430 (II:56)? He does not say, though it was the greatest Athenian enterprise of the war before the Sicilian expedition (VI:31). So far as he attempts an explanation of Pericles' strategy, he leaves the impression that it was more purely defensive than the facts reveal it to have been.

In one respect Thucydides confessedly fails to observe his own standard of accuracy. At important junctures statesmen or generals are given speeches in which they advocate or explain what should be done. It is patent that these speeches contain the words of Thucydides; all are written in the same highly individual style, one which no Greek orator could have used on the platform. Thucydides himself admits that neither he nor any other auditor could recall exactly what had been said and that, while keeping as closely as possible to the general purport of the actual speeches, he has invented what each speaker should have said on the particular occasion (I:22). The partly fictitious nature of the speeches is clearly contrasted with the accuracy which he claims for his record of actions. There is an apologetic overtone.

Why did Thucydides insert speeches? Probably it never occurred to him not to do so. He was following the example of Herodotus, in whose work speeches and dialogues occupy an even larger place, and who in turn had probably adopted the pattern of the Homeric epics, the only model for a large-scale narrative which the "Father of history" had. Herodotus had been criticized for pure invention in the speeches he wrote; to meet similar criticisms in advance, Thucydides does not indeed defend the practice but explains how he intends to use it.

Artistically it had much to commend it. In the conditions of Greek political life, as Polybius was to observe, "a single well-timed speech by a trustworthy man often turns men from the worst courses and incites them to the best." The general's allocution on the battlefield corresponded to the Orders of the Day which the modern commander may distribute. The speeches in Thucydides' work not only diversify the narrative but bring out vividly the conditions of actual life. Moreover, they make us feel that we are, as it were, in direct contact with the speakers. Where a modern historian would say that on Pericles' advice the Athenians rejected a Spartan ultimatum for such and such reasons, Thucydides makes Pericles himself give reasons, and then adds that the Athenians followed his advice. His method preserves more of the appearance of objectivity, but the appearance is an illusion. This would be so, even if the speeches were fully authentic. There were, after all, other speakers besides Pericles, and in selecting his speech alone and suggesting that the arguments he deployed were decisive, Thucydides is already interpreting.

But more than this, Thucydides' own candor lets us see that the speeches are partly fiction. It can hardly be believed that he means only that the words are his own; that was so obvious that it did not need to be expressed. His claim to have kept as closely as possible to the general purport of the real speeches implies that he has in some degree departed from it; he has given at best what could be remembered, perhaps years later, and he has added what *he* thought appropriate. Many of the speeches seem plausible enough in their content, but even here we cannot be sure that they are historic; for in so far as Thucydides' inventions were dramatically true to the speaker and the occasion, we cannot hope to distinguish them from "what was actually said."

Thucydides was writing from the very outset of the war, and we can assume that when the importance of a speech was immediately evident, he will have written down a version of it while recollection was still fresh. In this category we may put most, if not all, of the speeches recorded on the eve of the war or of the Sicilian expedition. Even here his memory might unconsciously have selected those parts of a speech which *he* thought most cogent, and he may have added or elaborated arguments which reflected his own turn of mind.[1] But in other cases the relevance of certain speeches to his theme may have dawned on him long after memory had faded. The plausible suggestion has been made that only after the end of the war did he feel it necessary to recreate for a dispirited generation the vigor which had once characterized the imperialist Athens of Pericles' day and that he chose as his vehicle the Funeral Speech which Pericles had delivered over the men who fell in the first year of fighting. It is a speech of unsurpassed nobility, and as we can see from comparison with other extant Funeral Speeches, it corresponds in its arrangement and choice of themes to what Pericles is likely to have said. But the themes are worked out in an unusual way. In other Funeral Speeches Athens appears as the champion of liberty and the oppressed, and we know from Herodotus and contemporary plays of Euripides that in the fifth century, too, Athenians liked to see themselves in this beneficent role. Thucydides disregards this theme, which did not fit his interpretation, and makes Pericles extol his city for her *power*. Again in Pericles' last speech (II: 60-64) it is out of harmony with his intention of restoring Athenian morale that he should predict that in the course of nature the Athenian empire must one day

[1] Cf. notes to J:70 and J:72.

decline; indeed the speech too aptly illustrates Thucydides' own judgment on Pericles, which was explicitly written over 25 years later (II:65). Another anachronism in Hermocrates' speech in 424 (IV:60 note) confirms the suspicion that it was only in the light of Athens' failure in Sicily in 415-13 that he saw the significance of Hermocrates' earlier appeal to Sicilian patriotism. The Melian dialogue too can hardly be true reporting (note on V:84 and p. 186).

These speeches and some others[1] have common characteristics; they bear on the moral and political issues of Athenian imperialism and are replete with abstract ideas, while often containing little that relates to the concrete situation. Though the speakers are not simply Thucydides' mouthpieces, for they advocate opposed policies and utter contradictory maxims, the way of thinking as well as the style is distinctly his own; with discretion, ideas in the speeches may be used to explain or amplify hints of his own views which he gives elsewhere and to reveal a fairly consistent body of doctrine about human behavior which can be ascribed to Thucydides himself. It is significant, for instance, that so many Athenian spokesmen concede that the Athenian empire is universally hated. Even had this been wholly true, they would hardly have avowed it so candidly. But Thucydides generally believed it to be true; he could not conceive that even in public utterances men would have been less cool and objective than himself in recognizing and stating facts; in inventing their words, he makes them disclose their real thoughts and motives, or what *he* took to be such. For him, as for Bishop Butler, "things and actions are what they are, and their consequences will be what they will be, why then should we desire to be deceived?"

In interpreting events, Thucydides was no doubt assisted by the fact that, unlike Herodotus, he had that practical knowledge of war and politics which Polybius and Clarendon declared essential to a great historian; he had himself held high office. Still more important, he lived in an age when for the first time men were pre-

[1] See Notes on III:9 and 36.

pared to question and investigate everything by the light of reason. The speeches prove his familiarity with the new ideas. His description of the plague shows that he knew medical terms (II:49-51), and its purpose fits the ideal of contemporary medical science; the Hippocratics sought to describe the course of a disease accurately in order to facilitate prognosis, whenever it recurred. They believed that by exact observation natural causes of disease might be found; and they explicitly rejected the old notion that their origin was divine, except in the Newtonian sense that everything was divine; every phenomenon, they thought, had a natural cause accessible to human discovery. Thucydides has the same passion for accurate recording of facts; and he too, unlike Herodotus, excludes divine intervention from human affairs, an epoch-making innovation in thought which was to be temporarily reversed only in the ages of monkish piety. He does indeed allow a large place to the effects of chance, but chance is not a supernatural power; it is coincidence or anything that we cannot explain or predict. Medical writers used the term in the same way and so did the contemporary philosopher Democritus, who invoked it to account for the formation of the world from the whirl of atoms in the void; he believed that its formation was the necessary consequence of the nature of atoms and the void, but he could not explain the process in detail.

Just as the medical writers held that the doctor must be capable of prognosis, so Thucydides regarded the chief quality of the statesman as foresight, the virtue which Pericles possessed in the highest degree (II:65). In a passage omitted from this selection (I:138), he says of Themistocles, the founder of Athenian naval power, that "by native sagacity, not augmented by preliminary or subsequent study, he was the best judge after the least consideration of immediate action and had the greatest ability to guess what the future would hold after the longest period; whatever he put his hand to, he could explain, and where he lacked experience, he did not lack adequate judgment; when the right course was obscure, no one saw further than he; and to sum up, natural ability accompanied by little training made him the best man at improvising the proper policy." Thucydides clearly has in mind the question which was much debated in his time: the relative importance of natural ability and training. In his view the genius of Themistocles enabled him to transcend the limits that his lack of training might have imposed. Other men would do well to equip themselves for politics by study. Thucydides claims that the study of history will be useful when it is written with accuracy (I:22). It is perhaps an unfashionable view today; yet we all think that men become wiser by experience, and history enlarges our own experience by that of others; moreover, economic or military planning, for instance, would be unthinkable if no account were to be taken of the past.

What did Thucydides think that we learn from history? It may be deduced from numerous texts that the statesman would learn to allow a large margin for the unpredictable and that he could profit by study of past failures and successes in all kinds of ways. But Thucydides stresses something else. He affirms (I:22) that *in the order of human nature* future events would resemble those which had occurred. Of course he did not mean that history exactly repeats itself. Not knowing the cause of the plague, he does not venture to predict that it must recur (II:48); yet no war could be quite the same as the Peloponnesian, which did not include this "vicissitude." He says that the calamities of revolutions "will always occur, so long as *human nature* remains the same," though "they are more or less aggravated and differ in character with every new vicissitude of circumstances" (III:82). Apparently, human nature is a constant, and history will reveal the springs of human behavior.

Thucydides traces the revolutionary struggles to mutual fear, greed and ambition, or more literally, the love of honor (III:82); Athenian speakers explain Athenian imperialism by the same triad of motives (I:75-76). It is echoed by Hobbes, whose translation was his earliest work and perhaps formative of his own ideas: "In the nature of man we find three principal causes of quarrell.

First, Competition; Secondly, Diffidence; Thirdly, Glory. The first makes men invade for Gain, the second for Safety; and the third for Reputation." Such are the motives that Thucydides himself imputes to men's actions. Considerations of justice may be mooted; in his view, however, they are never really decisive but, at best, pretexts. Self-interest makes the Athenians accept the Corcyræan alliance (I:44) and intervene in Sicily (III:86; VI:1, 6, 24). The Spartans make war avowedly to liberate Greece but really out of fear of Athens (I:23, 88, 118). They condemn Platæan prisoners, not for their supposed deserts, but to cement the Theban alliance in their own interest (III:68). Personal and egotistic reasons determine Cleon and Brasidas in favor of war, Nicias and Pleistoanax for peace (V:16). It is quite exceptional when Thucydides allows that the Corinthians helped Epidamnus "because they thought it right"; but he adds that they acted from enmity to Corcyra (I:25). In the speeches, allusions to fear, profit and the love of glory and power are too numerous to count.

The last motive has a prominence which may surprise the modern reader, though it is common in Greek thinking. For Pericles Athenian power and glory are the crowning justification of the empire (II:64), and he adjures the Athenians to gaze daily on the power of the city and fall in love with her (II:43).

But this is not all. Athenian spokesmen are made to avow that in acquiring and keeping their empire, they acted under "necessity," or "as *human nature* always will, constrained by the powerful motives of honor, fear and profit" (I:76), or again that there is clear evidence that by a necessity of nature men will rule wherever they have the power (V:105). Even an opponent of Athens, Hermocrates, acknowledges that it is pardonable for Athens to be aggressive—in Greek thinking pardon is due to acts done under necessity—and that it is the nature of mankind to rule wherever no resistance is offered (IV:61). The admission does not help his case; is it not the historian speaking? The concept of necessity reappears in other speeches (e.g., I:32, 124; II:63; III:40; VI:87, 92), and everywhere it is surely Thucydides' own concept, for it recurs in his narrative. The Spartans fight Athens under the necessity of fear (I:23; V:25). The Athenian allies were responsible for their own subjection: it is implied that their weakness made it inevitable that Athens should subdue them (I:99). In archaic Greece "love of gain made the weaker willing to serve the stronger and incited the more powerful to subjugate the lesser cities" (I:8); this is Thucydides' interpretation of the past, based on his view of human nature. The concept of *ananke* (necessary causation) was used by contemporary philosophers, such as Democritus, and Thucydides could regard human nature as a constant because he thought it was subject to such causation.

It does not follow from this that Thucydides held that men had no freedom of choice at all. The contrary is implied when he suggests that *at times* men are subject to "necessities which allow them no choice" (III:82). It is clear that he saw that they could act with more or less passion or circumspection and that he disapproved of irrational acts prompted by anger or fallacious hope. But their choice was always more or less restricted by their own nature, which compelled them to act from self-regarding motives. His theory should exclude moralizing. Many Greeks had thought that power produced *hybris*, an arrogant disregard for divine and moral law, and that *hybris* led to ruin. Some have read this view into Thucydides; Athenian injustice and cruelty met with retribution. This cannot be right; in fact he expressly ascribes the fall of Athens to acts of imprudence, which were indeed prompted by the greed and ambition of the leaders (II:65). He sometimes praises a man for *arete*, a word which in some Greek writing may correspond to our *virtue* or *goodness*. But one such man is Antiphon, on Thucydides' own showing a bloody and treacherous conspirator (VIII:68). In fact *arete* has not always the same moral connotation as *virtue;* a Greek could define it as "the ability to carry on the city's business and to help one's friends and injure one's enemies, while suffering no harm oneself" (cf. IV:63). The Athenian doctrine in the Melian dialogue (V:85-113), with which I believe Thucydides fundamentally agreed, has been described as "might is right." Contemporary thinkers did propound such views, but in fact the Athenian position is rather different. "The question of justice only enters where there is equal power to enforce it"; otherwise "the powerful exact what they can and the weak grant what they must" (V:89). That is the way the world goes; might does not create right but excludes it.

Thucydides' interpretation of human behavior may in part explain his remarkable impartiality. If men were bound to act in their own interest, he could not condemn cities or parties that did so. He portrays the merits and defects of Athens and Sparta with equal sharpness. The Athenian verdict on the Spartans, that they were most conspicuous in identifying expediency with justice (V:105), corresponds with all that he tells of Spartan policy. He exaggerates Athenian unpopularity, but we know this almost entirely from the candor of his own narrative. His error can hardly be ascribed to moral disapproval of Athenian imperialism. The man who wrote Pericles' last speech with so much eloquence must have partly shared the belief that imperialism was justified by the glory that accrued to Athens. Probably he was misled by the hatred expressed for Athens by the upper class circles in which he is likely as an aristocrat himself to have moved, especially after his banishment. He could free himself from their prejudices only when his attention was concentrated on the prevalence of party factions, which revealed that the masses generally supported Athens. His famous analysis of these factions (III:82-84) shows that he stood above them and knew that neither democrats nor oligarchs were really guided by the principles they professed.

Certainly he was no democrat. He despised the "rabble" for its volatility (II:65; IV:28; VIII:1), and he bitterly censured the demagogues who succeeded Pericles. Perhaps he was less than fair to Cleon (see IV:28 note). But in his judgment it was men like Cleon who had helped to dissolve the internal unity of Athens and to bring about her fall. Yet the oligarchs were no less responsible; their leaders were men of talent but self-seekers and even traitors (VIII:68, 89, 91). He approved most of the balanced constitution set up after the oligarchy was overthrown in 411 (VIII:97). Yet in the Funeral Speech he expounds the democratic ideal with sympathy, and he can praise the oligarchies of Sparta and Chios (I:18; VIII:24), the former tyrants of Athens (VI:54) or a king of Macedon (II:100).

In each case the test was power. He probably accepted the view that Athens owed her imperial greatness to her democratic system, and he expressly says that Syracuse was her most efficient enemy because she too was democratic (VIII:96; cf. VII:55). He praises the balanced constitution of 411 because it revived Athenian power, commends the Chians for prudence and prosperity, connects the strength of Sparta with the stability of her institutions, and notes how the Athenian tyrants were successful in war and how Archelaus of Macedon improved the military resources of his country. Individuals too earn his approval for courage, foresight, prudence, moderation—the qualities that could make men successful in the struggle for power, fame, security and profit.

Not indeed that he is consistently amoral. He clearly regretted the moral disintegration at Athens which followed the plague (II:53). He deplores the disappearance in revolutionary times of "the simplicity which is so large an element in a noble nature" (III:83). The term *justice* is sometimes found in contexts where, if the doctrine of the Melian dialogue were right, it could have little or no meaning. Older ideas and human sentiments probably struggled in his mind for supremacy against the harsh convictions that experience forced upon him. His description of the massacre of the schoolboys at Mycalessus, an incident of no military or political importance, suffices to prove that he was a compassionate man (VII:29); and there was nothing in his views to suggest that men should use power with cruelty; he approves of moderation.

We may indeed regard his inconsistencies as an indication that his usual account of human behavior is itself defective. If men were as he describes them, how could social solidarity ever have arisen *within* a city? There are hints of his answer, chiefly in speeches. The city's interest and renown are the interest and renown of the citizens; they may even be expected to contribute their lives to her glory because it is their own (II:43). An individual cannot prosper if his city is ruined (II:60); this was a matter of bitter experience in days when the capture of a city might entail the massacre or enslavement of its people. There were also the sanctions of the laws and the fear of the gods (II:37, 53; III:82). But when such restraints broke down, human nature showed itself in its true light, "ungovernable in passion, uncontrollable by justice and hostile to all superiors" (III:84). And the mutual trust that normally prevailed among fellow citizens was apt to conceal the truth that, as between states, the law of the jungle operated (I:68; III:37).

Thucydides lived in an age of war which "by stealing away the means of providing easily for men's daily lives, is a teacher of violence and assimilates the passions of most men to their circumstances" (III:82). If his vision was narrow and made too little allowance for duty or religion or natural benevolence, it penetrates deeply into the irreconcilable conflicts of states and classes in his own time and remains fresh and relevant in every age of war and revolution. Thus we may read how propaganda perverted the meaning of words (III:82) and be reminded of "democracy" in our own time. If his history has any lessons, as he thought, they bring little comfort. In the same way, the case histories that contemporary medical scientists accurately recorded usually end with the patient's death. They taught the physician to predict the end but not to avert it.

In antiquity Thucydides was often admired but never imitated with success. He taught his successors to probe into the real motives of men; but they did not equal his penetration, impartiality or passion for exactitude. The great historians of modern times have honored him, but they have seldom had to solve the same problems of research as he, and the practice of interpreting the past through speeches has been wisely abandoned. In the annals of historiography, he remains isolated.

TEXT, TRANSLATION AND BIBLIOGRAPHY.

The Greek text of Thucydides, first printed in 1502 by the Aldine press at Venice, is now most accessible in the Oxford edition of H. Stuart-Jones, revised by J. E. Powell (1942), or in the Loeb edition of C. V. Smith (1919-23), where it is accompanied by a translation. In revising the present translation, I have consulted various editions and, where any doubt exists over the true reading, followed my own judgment.

Complete translations by Richard Crawley (Everyman edition, 1910) and Rex Warner (Penguin edition, 1954) are readily available. The translation I have used is basically that of Benjamin Jowett (Oxford, second edition, 1899), which is now out of print; but the Jowett Copyright Trustees have generously given me a free hand in revision.

No one can adequately represent Thucydides' style to English readers. His narrative is indeed generally simple, rapid, and often graphic, and its character can be revealed, but in the speeches and other highly wrought passages, he abounds in antitheses, sometimes forced, violent changes of construction and attempts at a pregnant conciseness which may obscure quite uncomplicated ideas. The structures of the Greek and English languages are so dissimilar that this manner cannot be fully reproduced. I believe that Jowett was right in trying to render the Greek into clear, vigorous and dignified English and that his translation is the best. But his style is sometimes too archaic for modern taste and his rendering often rather inexact. I have therefore made many changes and in some places virtually translated the Greek anew. The selection comprises about two-thirds of the whole work, with books VI and VII complete, and should give a fair picture of Thucydides' methods and manner. In view of the importance of the speeches for understanding the author, I have omitted very few of them, and they therefore constitute a rather larger proportion of this selection than of the history as a whole.

A. W. Gomme's *Historical Commentary on Thucydides*

(Oxford University Press, 1945-56, 3 volumes) goes down only to V:26; it is to be continued by A. Andrewes and K. J. Dover. There is no full, comprehensive and satisfactory treatment of Thucydides in any language, though there are good books and articles on aspects of his work. I may mention here J. B. Bury, *The Ancient Greek Historians* (reprinted as a paperback by the Dover Press, 1958); C. N. Cochrane, *Thucydides and the Science of History* (1929); and J. H. Finley, *Thucydides* (1942). A fuller bibliography will be found in the excellent article by H. T. Wade-Gery in the *Oxford Classical Dictionary* (1949). Naturally all works on Greek history of the fifth century rely on Thucydides and interpret his work; Grote's great history of Greece is still worth reading.

This edition has been provided with maps. If more detailed information is desired, see Westermann's *Atlas Zur Weltgeschichte,* vol. 1, 1956.

P. A. Brunt.

CHRONOLOGICAL TABLE

480-79	Persian invasion of Greece.
477	Formation of league under Athenian leadership to carry on war at sea against Persia.
c. 460-46	Athens at war with Sparta.
c. 456	BIRTH OF THUCYDIDES.
449	End of Persian War; by now the Athenian league has become an "empire."
446	Truce for 30 years between Athens and Sparta.
435	Epidamnus affair.
433	Athenian alliance with Corcyra.
432.	Congress at Sparta decides on war with Athens.
431-21	The first "ten years war" between Athens and Sparta.
430	First outbreak of plague at Athens; Thucydides then or later a victim.
424	THUCYDIDES EXILED FOR FAILURE AT AMPHIPOLIS.
421	"Peace of Nicias."
420-14	Athens involved in hostilities with Sparta without being formally at war.
415-13	Sicilian expedition.
414	Sparta again declares war on Athens.
411	Revolution at Athens.
	THUCYDIDES' HISTORY BREAKS OFF.
410	Democracy restored at Athens.
405	Destruction of Athenian fleet at Ægospotami.
404	Surrender of Athens to Sparta.
	THUCYDIDES RETURNS FROM EXILE AND DIES NOT LONG AFTERWARDS.
404-03	After a second period of oligarchic rule, democracy is again restored at Athens.

SICILY AND ITALY

GREEK MAINLAND

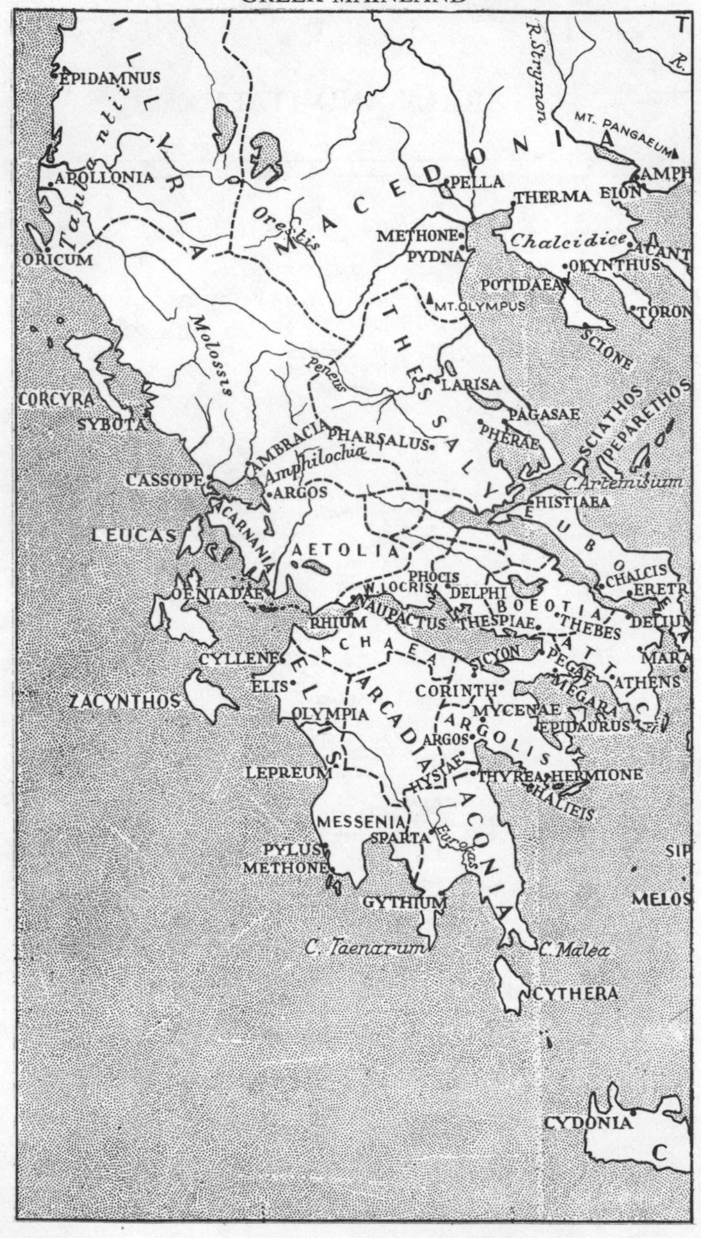

IONIA AND THE GREEK ISLANDS

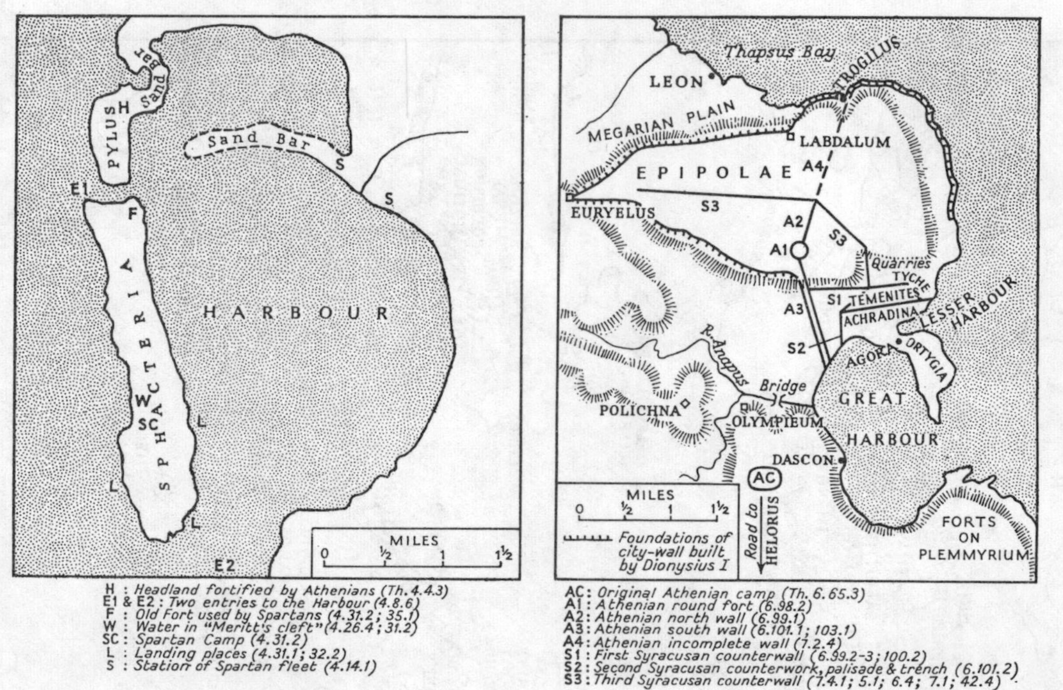

H : *Headland fortified by Athenians (Th. 4.4.3)*
E1 & E2 : *Two entries to the Harbour (4.8.6)*
F : *Old Fort used by Spartans (4.31.2; 35.1)*
W : *Water in "Meritt's cleft" (4.26.4; 31.2)*
SC : *Spartan Camp (4.31.2)*
L : *Landing places (4.31.1; 32.2)*
S : *Station of Spartan fleet (4.14.1)*

AC : *Original Athenian camp (Th. 6.65.3)*
A1 : *Athenian round fort (6.98.2)*
A2 : *Athenian north wall (6.99.1)*
A3 : *Athenian south wall (6.101.1; 103.1)*
A4 : *Athenian incomplete wall (7.2.4)*
S1 : *First Syracusan counterwall (6.99.2–3; 100.2)*
S2 : *Second Syracusan counterwork, palisade & trench (6.101.2)*
S3 : *Third Syracusan counterwall (7.4.1; 5.1; 6.4; 7.1; 42.4)*

Thucydides:

The Peloponnesian Wars

BOOK I

The Early History of Greece

1. Thucydides, an Athenian, wrote the history of the war in which the Peloponnesians and the Athenians fought against one another.[1] He began to write when they first took up arms, expecting that it would be great and memorable above any previous war. For he argued that both states were then at the full height of their military power, and he saw the rest of the Hellenes either siding or intending to side with one or the other of them. No movement ever stirred Hellas or some of the barbarians more deeply than this; it might even be said to affect the world at large. The character of the events which preceded, whether immediately or in more remote antiquity, owing to the lapse of time cannot be made out clearly.[2] But after carrying the inquiry to the furthest point at which any trustworthy evidence can be obtained, I believe that former ages were not great either in their wars or in anything else.

2. It is apparent that the country which is now called Hellas was not regularly settled until recent times. The people were migratory and readily left their homes whenever they were overpowered by numbers. There was no commerce, and they could not safely hold intercourse with one another either by land or sea. The several peoples cultivated their own soil just enough to obtain a subsistence from it. But they had no accumulations of wealth and did not plant the ground; partly because they had no walls, they were never sure that an invader might not come and despoil them. In the belief that they could anywhere obtain a bare livelihood, they were always ready to migrate, so that they had no great cities nor any considerable resources. The richest districts were most constantly changing their inhabitants; for example, the country now called Thessaly, Bœotia, the greater part of

the Peloponnese with the exception of Arcadia, and all the best parts of Hellas. For the productiveness of the land increased the power of some; and this was a source of quarrels by which they were ruined, while at the same time they were more exposed to attacks from foreigners. Certainly Attica, where the soil is poor and thin, enjoyed the longest freedom from civil strife and therefore retained its original inhabitants. And a most striking confirmation of my argument is the fact that no other region increased in population so much through the migrations. For the leading men of Hellas, when driven out of their own country by war or revolution, withdrew to Athens for its security; from the very earliest times they were admitted to rights of citizenship and so greatly increased the number of inhabitants that Attica became incapable of containing them and later sent colonies to Ionia.

3. The feebleness of antiquity is further proved to me especially by the circumstance that before the Trojan War Hellas evidently took no united action.[1] And I think that the very name was not as yet given to the whole country and in fact did not exist at all before the time of Hellen the son of Deucalion; the different peoples, of which the Pelasgian was the most widely spread, gave their own names to different districts. But when Hellen and his sons became powerful in Phthiotis, their aid was invoked by other cities; and the several peoples who associated with them were now more apt to be called Hellenes, though a long time elapsed before the name prevailed over the whole country. Of this Homer affords the best evidence; for although he lived long after the Trojan War, he nowhere uses this name collectively but confines it to the followers of Achilles from Phthiotis, who were the original Hellenes; in his epics he refers to Danaäns, or Argives, or Achæans. Neither is there any mention of barbarians in his poems, I suppose because there were as yet no Hellenes distinguished from them by a single contrasting name. Thus, those who successively acquired the Hellenic name, which first spread among the several peoples speaking the same language and afterwards became universal, were so weak and isolated that they were never united in any collective enterprise before

the Trojan War. And they only made this expedition after they had gained considerable experience of the sea.

4. Minos is the first to whom tradition ascribes the possession of a navy. He made himself master of a great part of what is now termed the Hellenic sea; he ruled the Cyclades and was the first colonizer of most of them, expelling the Carians and appointing his own sons to govern in them. He cleared the sea of pirates, so far as he was able, probably in order to augment his revenues.[1]

5. For in ancient times both the Hellenes and those of the barbarians whose homes were on the coast of the mainland or in islands, when they began to find their way to one another by sea, had recourse to piracy. They were commanded by powerful chiefs, who took this means of increasing their wealth and providing for their poorer followers. They would fall upon the unwalled and straggling towns, or rather villages, which they plundered, and maintained themselves chiefly from this source; for, as yet, such an occupation was held to be honorable rather than disgraceful. This is proved by the practice of certain tribes on the mainland, who, to the present day, glory in such exploits, and by the testimony of the ancient poets, in whose verses the question is invariably asked of newly arrived voyagers, whether they are pirates, which implies that neither those who are questioned disclaim, nor those who are interested in knowing, censure the occupation. On land also, communities plundered each other; and there are many parts of Hellas in which the old practices still continue, as, for example, among the Ozolian Locrians, Aetolians, Acarnanians, and the adjacent regions of the continent. The custom of wearing arms among these continental tribes is a relic of their old predatory habits. For in ancient times all Hellenes carried weapons because their homes were undefended and intercourse was unsafe; like the barbarians, they went armed in their everyday life. And the continuance of the custom in certain parts of the country indicates that similar modes of life once prevailed everywhere.

6. The Athenians were the first who laid aside arms and adopted an easier and more luxurious way of life.

Quite recently the old-fashioned refinement of dress still lingered among the older men of the richer class, who wore undergarments of linen and bound back their hair in a knot with golden clasps in the forms of grasshoppers; and the same fashion long survived among the older men of Ionia, having been derived from their Athenian ancestors. On the other hand, the simple dress which is now common was first worn by the Lacedæmonians; and they in other ways too did most to assimilate the life of the rich to that of the people. They too were the first who in their athletic exercises stripped naked and rubbed themselves over with oil. But this was not the ancient custom; athletes formerly, even when they were contending at Olympia, wore girdles about their loins, a practice which lasted until quite lately, and still prevails among some barbarians, especially those of Asia, where the combatants in boxing and wrestling matches wear girdles. And many other customs which are now barbarian might be shown to have been like those of old Hellas.

7. In later times, when navigation had become more general and wealth was beginning to accumulate, cities were built upon the seashore and fortified; peninsulas too were occupied and walled off with a view to commerce and defense against the neighboring peoples. But the older towns both in the islands and on the continent, in order to protect themselves against the piracy which so long prevailed, were more often built inland; and there they remain to this day. For the piratical tribes plundered not only one another but all those who, without being seamen, lived on the seacoast.

8. The islanders were even more addicted to piracy than the inhabitants of the mainland. They were mostly Carians or Phœnicians. This is the evidence: when the Athenians purified Delos in this war and the tombs of the dead were opened, more than half of them were found to be Carians. They were known by the fashion of the arms buried with them and by their mode of burial, the same which they still use.

After Minos had established his navy, communication by sea became more general; for he expelled the marauders when he colonized the greater part of the islands. The dwellers on the seacoast began to grow richer and to live in a more settled manner; and some of them, finding their wealth increase, surrounded their towns with walls. The love of gain made the weaker willing to serve the stronger and incited the more powerful, who now had wealth at their command, to subjugate the lesser cities. This was the state of society which was beginning to prevail at the time of the Trojan War.

9. I think that Agamemnon succeeded in collecting the expedition, not so much because the suitors of Helen had bound themselves by oath to Tyndareus, as because he was the most powerful man of his time. Those who possess the clearest traditions about the Peloponnese say that originally Pelops gained his power by the great wealth which he brought with him from Asia into a poor country, whereby he was enabled, although a foreigner, to give his name to the country; and that still greater fortune attended his descendants after the death of Eurystheus in Attica at the hands of the Heraclidæ. Atreus was the maternal uncle of Eurystheus, who, when he went on the expedition, entrusted the kingdom of Mycenæ to him as a kinsman. (Atreus had been banished by his father on account of the murder of Chrysippus.) But Eurystheus never returned; and the Mycenæans, dreading the Heraclidæ, were ready to welcome Atreus, who was considered a powerful man and had ingratiated himself with the multitude of the Mycenæans and Eurystheus' subjects. So he succeeded to the throne. Thus, the house of Pelops prevailed over that of Perseus.

And it was, as I believe, because Agamemnon inherited this power and also because he was the greatest naval potentate of his time that he was able to assemble the expedition, not so much from good will as from fear. Of the chiefs who went to Troy, he evidently brought the greatest number of ships himself, besides supplying the Arcadians with them; Homer has made this plain, if his evidence is sufficient. In the "Handing down of the Sceptre"[1] he is described as "the king of many islands, and of all Argos." But, living on the mainland, he could not have ruled over any except the adjacent islands (which would not be "many") unless he had possessed some naval force. From this expedition we must form our conjectures about the character of still earlier times.

10. The fact that Mycenæ was but a small place or that any other city which existed in those days seems inconsiderable in our own, need not be a certain indication to justify belief that the expedition was not as great as the poets told and as is commonly related. Suppose the city of the Lacedæmonians to be deserted and nothing left but the temples and the foundations of buildings; distant ages would be very unwilling to believe that their power was at all equal to their fame. And yet they control two-fifths of the Peloponnese and are acknowledged leaders of the whole, as well as of numerous allies in the rest of Hellas. But their city is not continuously built up and has no costly temples or other edifices; it rather resembles a group of villages like the ancient towns of Hellas, and would therefore make a poor show. Whereas if the same fate befell the Athenians, the ruins of Athens would strike the eye; and we should infer their power to have been twice as great as it really is. We ought not then to be unduly skeptical. We should examine the real power of cities rather than their appearance. And we should suppose the Trojan expedition to have been greater than any which preceded it, although, according to Homer, if we may once more trust his testimony, not equal to those of our own day. He was a poet, and may therefore be expected to exaggerate; yet, even upon his showing, the expedition was comparatively small. For it numbered, as he tells us, 1,200 ships, those of the Bœotians carrying 120 men each, those of Philoctetes 50; and by these numbers he may be presumed to indicate the largest and the smallest ships; else why in the catalogue is nothing said about the size of any others? That the crews were all fighting men as well as rowers he has made clear when speaking of the ships of Philoctetes; for he tells us that all the oarsmen were also archers. And it is not to be supposed that many who were not sailors would accompany the expedition, except the kings and principal officers; for the troops had to cross the sea, bringing with them the materials of war, in vessels

without decks, built after the old piratical fashion. Now if we take a mean between the crews, the invading forces were evidently not very numerous when we remember that they were drawn from the whole of Hellas.

11. The cause of the inferiority was not so much the want of men as the want of money; the invading army was limited, by the difficulty of obtaining supplies, to such a number as might be expected to live on the country in which they had to fight. After their arrival at Troy, when they had won a battle (as they clearly did, for otherwise they could not have fortified their camp), even then they evidently did not use the whole of their force, but were driven by want of provisions to the cultivation of the Chersonese and to pillage. And in consequence of this dispersion of their forces, the Trojans were better able to hold out against them during the whole ten years, being always a match for those who remained on the spot. Whereas if the besieging army had brought abundant supplies and, instead of betaking themselves to agriculture or pillage, had carried on the war persistently with all their forces, they would easily have won a battle and taken the city; since, even divided as they were, and with only a part of their army available at any one time, they held their ground. Or, again, they might have regularly invested Troy, and the place would have been captured in less time and with less trouble. Poverty was the real reason why the achievements of former ages were insignificant and why the Trojan War, the most celebrated of them all, when brought to the test of facts, falls short of its fame and of the prevailing story to which the poets have given authority.

12. Even in the age which followed the Trojan War,[1] Hellas was still in process of migrations and settlements, and had no time for peaceful growth. The return of the Hellenes from Troy after their long absence led to many changes: quarrels too arose in nearly every city, and those who were expelled by them went and founded other cities. Thus, in the sixtieth year after the fall of Troy, the modern Bœotians, having been expelled from Arnè by the Thessalians, settled in the country formerly called Cadmeis, but now Bœotia; a portion of the people al-

ready dwelt there, and some of these had joined in the Trojan expedition. In the eightieth year after the war, the Dorians led by the Heraclidæ conquered the Peloponnese. It was with difficulty after many years that Hellas came to enjoy peace and security and that migrations ceased; then colonies were sent out. The Athenians colonized Ionia and most of the islands; the Peloponnesians, the greater part of Italy and Sicily[2] and various places in the rest of Hellas. These were all founded after the Trojan War.

13. As Hellas grew more powerful and the acquisition of wealth became more and more common as the revenues of her cities increased, in most of them tyrannies were established; they had hitherto been ruled by hereditary kings, having fixed prerogatives. The Hellenes likewise began to equip navies and to take more to the sea. The Corinthians are said to have first adopted something like the modern style of ships, and the oldest Hellenic triremes are said to have been constructed at Corinth. A Corinthian shipbuilder, Ameinocles, apparently built four ships for the Samians too; he went to Samos about three hundred years before the end of this war. And the earliest naval engagement on record is that between the Corinthians and Corcyræans which occurred about forty years later.[1] Corinth, being seated on an isthmus, was naturally always a center of commerce; for the Hellenes within and without the Peloponnese in the old days, when they communicated chiefly by land, had to pass through her territory in order to reach one another. Her wealth too was a source of power, as the ancient poets have made plain, who speak of "Corinth the rich." When navigation grew more common, the Corinthians, having acquired a fleet, were able to put down piracy; they offered a market both by sea and land, and the power of their city increased with the revenues. Later, in the time of Cyrus, the first Persian king (559-29), and of Cambyses his son (529-22), the Ionians had a large navy; they fought with Cyrus and were for a time masters of the sea around their own coasts. Polycrates, too, who was a tyrant of Samos in the reign of Cambyses, had a powerful navy and subdued several of the islands, among them Rhenea,

which he dedicated to the Delian Apollo. And the Phocæans, when they were colonizing Massalia,[2] defeated the Carthaginians on the sea.

14. These were the most powerful navies, and even these, which came into existence many generations after the Trojan War, apparently consisted chiefly of fifty-oared vessels and galleys of war, as in the days of Troy; as yet, triremes were not common. But a little before the Persian War (480) and the death of Darius (521-486), who succeeded Cambyses, the Sicilian tyrants and the Corcyræans had them in considerable numbers. No other maritime powers of any consequence arose in Hellas before the expedition of Xerxes (480). The Aeginetans, Athenians and perhaps a few more had small fleets, and these mostly consisted of fifty-oared vessels. It was quite recently (482), when the Athenians were at war with the Aeginetans and expecting a barbarian attack, that Themistocles persuaded them to build the ships with which they fought at sea;[1] and even these were not completely decked.

15. So inconsiderable were the Hellenic navies in old times and later. And yet those who applied their energies to the sea acquired the greatest strength from revenues and empire. For they attacked and subjugated the islands, especially when they had not sufficient land. Whereas by land, no war which brought increase of power occurred; what wars they had were mere border feuds. Foreign and distant expeditions of conquest the Hellenes never undertook; for they were not as yet combined as subjects by the great states, nor did they make common expeditions on an equal footing. Their wars were rather the wars of neighbors with one another. The conflict in which the rest of Hellas was most divided, allying itself with one side or the other, was the ancient war between the Chalcidians and Eretrians.[1]

16. There were different impediments to the aggrandizement of the different states. The Ionians had attained great prosperity when Cyrus, the Persian king, having overthrown Crœsus[1] and subdued the countries between the river Halys and the sea, made war against them and deprived the cities on the mainland of freedom. Some

time afterwards, Darius, strong in the possession of the Phœnician fleet, conquered the islands also.

17. Nor again did the tyrants of the Hellenic cities extend their thoughts beyond their own interest, their persons and the aggrandizement of their own house. They were extremely cautious in the administration of their cities and never effected anything considerable, except in wars with their neighbors, as in Sicily, where their power attained its greatest height.[1] Thus, for a long time everything conspired to prevent Hellas from uniting in any great action and to paralyze enterprise in the individual states.

18. At length the tyrants both at Athens and in the rest of Hellas (which had been under their dominion long before Athens), at least the greater number of them, and with the exception of the Sicilian, the last who ever ruled, were put down by the Lacedæmonians. For although Lacedæmon, after its settlement by the present Dorian inhabitants, suffered from internal struggles longer than any country which we know, nevertheless she enjoyed good laws at an earlier period than any other and was never subject to tyrants; she has preserved the same form of government for rather more than four hundred years, reckoning to the end of this war.[1] It was this which gave her power and enabled her to regulate the affairs of other states. Not long after the overthrow of the tyrants by the Lacedæmonians,[2] the battle of Marathon was fought between the Athenians and the Persians (490); in the tenth year thereafter, the barbarians returned with the vast armament which was to deprive Hellas of freedom (480). In the greatness of the impending danger, the Lacedæmonians led the Hellenes who joined in the resistance, in virtue of their superior power, while the Athenians, as the Persian forces advanced, resolved to forsake their city, broke up their homes and, taking to their ships, became seamen. The barbarians were repelled by a common effort; but soon the Hellenes, those who had revolted from the King as well as those who formed the original confederacy, took different sides and became the allies of the Athenians or of the Lacedæmonians;[3] for these were now the two

leading powers, the one strong by land and the other by sea. The league between them was of short duration; they speedily quarreled and, with their respective allies, went to war (*c.* 460-46). Any of the other Hellenes who had differences of their own would now resort to one or other of them. So that from the Persian to the present war, the Lacedæmonians and the Athenians were perpetually fighting or making peace, either with one another or with their own revolted allies; thus they attained military efficiency and learned experience in the school of danger.

19. The Lacedæmonians did not make tributaries of those who acknowledged their leadership, but took care that they should be governed by oligarchies in the exclusive interest of Sparta.[1] The Athenians, on the other hand, after a time took over the ships of their allies and made all of them pay a fixed tribute, except Chios and Lesbos.[2] Athens' own resources at the beginning of this war were greater than those of Athens and Sparta together had ever been while they had remained allies.

20. Such are the results of my inquiries into the early history of Hellas, though it is hard to trust every particular of the evidence. Men are too ready to receive ancient traditions, even about their own countries, without investigation. For example, most Athenians think that Hipparchus was actually tyrant when he was killed by Harmodius and Aristogeiton; they are not aware that Hippias was the eldest of the sons of Peisistratus and was the ruler, and that Hipparchus and Thessalus were only his brothers. At the last moment, Harmodius and Aristogeiton suddenly suspected that Hippias had been forewarned by some of their accomplices. They therefore abstained from attacking him; but, wishing to do something before they were arrested, and not to risk their lives in vain, they killed Hipparchus, with whom they fell in near the temple called Leocorium as he was marshaling the Panathenaic procession.[1] There are many other matters, not obscured by time but contemporary, about which the other Hellenes are equally mistaken. For example, they imagine that the kings of Lacedæmon in their council have not one but two votes each, and that in the

army of the Lacedæmonians there is a division called the Pitanate division; whereas they never had anything of the sort.[2] So little trouble do men take in the search after truth; they prefer to accept whatever comes first to hand.

21. Yet anyone who, upon the evidence which I have given, arrives at some such conclusion as my own about those ancient times, would not be far wrong. He must not put more reliance in the exaggerated embellishments of the poets, or in the tales of chroniclers who composed their works to please the ear rather than to speak the truth. Their accounts cannot be tested; the lapse of ages has made them in general unreliable, and they have passed into the region of romance. At such a distance of time one must be content with conclusions resting upon the indications that can be had. And, though men will always judge any war in which they are actually fighting to be the greatest, but, after it is over, revert to their admiration of ancient wars, still, if estimated by the actual facts, this war will certainly prove to have been the greatest yet known.

22.[1] As for the speeches made on the eve of the war or during its course, it was hard for me, when I heard them myself, and for any others who reported them to me, to recollect exactly what had been said. I have therefore put into the mouth of each speaker the views that, in my opinion, they would have been most likely to express, as the particular occasions demanded, while keeping as nearly as I could to the general purport of what was actually said. But when recording men's actions in the war, I did not think it right to recount them after inquiry from the chance informant, nor in accordance with mere opinions of my own; whether I was present myself or drew on the reports of others, I examined every point with the utmost possible exactness. The task was laborious because eyewitnesses of the same occurrences gave different accounts of them, varying with their recollection and partiality. The lack of romance in my work will perhaps make it seem less agreeable to the ear. But if anyone desires to examine the clear truth about the events that have taken place, and about those which are likely to take place in the future—in the order of human things, they will resemble what has occurred—and pronounces what I have written to be useful, I shall be content. My history is an everlasting possession, not a prize composition that is heard and forgotten.

The Origins of the War

23. The greatest achievement of former times was the Persian War; yet even this was speedily decided in two battles by sea and two by land. But this war was a protracted struggle and attended by calamities such as Hellas had never known within a like period of time. Never were so many cities captured and depopulated—some by barbarians, others by Hellenes themselves, fighting against one another; and several of them, after their capture, were repeopled by new settlers. Never were exile and slaughter more frequent, whether in the actual war or in revolutions. And traditions which had often been current before, but rarely verified by fact, were now no longer doubted. Earthquakes were of the greatest extent and fury, and eclipses of the sun more numerous than are recorded to have happened in any former age; there were also, in some places, great droughts causing famines, and lastly the plague which did most harm and destroyed numbers of the people. All these calamities fell upon Hellas simultaneously with the war, which began when the Athenians and Peloponnesians broke the thirty years' truce concluded by them after Athens reconquered Eubœa.[1] I have first recounted the grievances and differences which led to this breach so that, in time to come, no one will inquire what was the origin of so great a war. The truest explanation, though it was least avowed,[2] I believe to have been the growth of the Athenian power, which terrified the Lacedæmonians and put them under the necessity of fighting; but the grievances publicly alleged on either side were as follows.

24. Epidamnus is a city situated on the right-hand side as you sail up the Ionian Gulf. The neighboring inhabitants are the Taulantians, barbarians of Illyrian race. The place was colonized by the Corcyræans, but

under the leadership of a Corinthian, Phalius son of Eratocleides, who was of the lineage of Heracles; he was invited, according to ancient custom, from the mother city; and the Corinthians and other Dorians joined in the colony. In process of time Epidamnus became great and populous; but (it is said) there followed a long period of civil commotion, and the city suffered in a war against the neighboring barbarians and lost much of her power. At last, shortly before this war, the notables were driven out by the people; the exiles, joined by the barbarians, invaded and plundered the remaining inhabitants both by sea and by land. These were hard pressed and sent an embassy to Corcyra as the mother city, begging the Corcyræans not to leave them to their fate but to reconcile them to the exiles and end the war with the barbarians. The ambassadors profferred their request, sitting as suppliants in the temple of Hera; but the Corcyræans rejected their plea, and they returned without success.

25. The Epidamnians, finding that they had no hope of assistance from Corcyra, could find no way of settling the crisis, and, sending to Delphi, inquired of the god whether they should deliver up the city to the Corinthians as the original founders and endeavor to obtain aid from them. The god replied that they should do so and accept Corinthian hegemony. So the Epidamnians went to Corinth and, informing the Corinthians of the answer which the oracle had given, delivered up the city to them. They reminded them that the original leader of the colony was a citizen of Corinth and implored the Corinthians to help them and not leave them to their fate. The Corinthians took up their cause because they thought it right (they considered that Epidamnus belonged to them quite as much as to the Corcyræans), partly too because they hated the Corcyræans, who were their own colonists but slighted them. In their common festivals they would not allow them the customary privileges of founders, and, at their sacrifices, denied to a Corinthian the right of receiving first the lock of hair cut from the head of the victim, as the other colonies did. In fact, they despised the Corinthians, for they were more than a match for them in military strength and as

rich as any state then existing in Hellas. They would often boast that on the sea they were very far superior to them and would appropriate to themselves the naval renown of the Phæacians, the ancient inhabitants of the island. Such feelings led them more and more to strengthen their navy, which was by no means despicable; for they had a hundred and twenty triremes when the war broke out.

26. Irritated by these causes of offense, the Corinthians were only too happy to assist Epidamnus; accordingly, they invited anyone who was willing to settle there, and as a garrison they sent Ambracians and Leucadians[1] and their own men; they went by land as far as Apollonia, a Corinthian colony, fearing that the Corcyræans might oppose their passage by sea. The Corcyræans were vexed when they discovered that the settlers and garrison had entered Epidamnus and that the colony was being given up to the Corinthians. They immediately set sail with twenty-five ships, followed by a second fleet, and, in insulting terms, bade the Epidamnians receive the exiled oligarchs, who had gone to Corcyra and implored the Corcyræans to restore them, appealing to the tie of kindred and pointing to the sepulchers of their common ancestors. They also bade them send away the garrison and the new settlers. But the Epidamnians would not listen to their demands. The Corcyræans then attacked them with forty ships, along with the exiles whom they were to restore; they also obtained the assistance of the Illyrians. They sat down before the city and proclaimed that any Epidamnian who chose, and the foreigners, might depart in safety but that all who remained would be treated as enemies. This had no effect, and the Corcyræans proceeded to invest the city, which is built on an isthmus.

27. When the news of the siege reached the Corinthians, they equipped an army and proclaimed that a colony was to be sent to Epidamnus; all who wished might go and enjoy equal rights of citizenship; anyone who was unwilling to sail at once but wished to share in the colony, might remain behind if he made a deposit of fifty Corinthian drachmæ. Many sailed, and many de-

posited the money. The Corinthians also requested the Megarians to assist them with a convoy in case the Corcyræans should intercept the colonists on their voyage. The Megarians accordingly provided eight ships; the Cephallenians of Palè, four; the Epidaurians, of whom they made a similar request, five; the Hermionians, one; the Troizenians, two; the Leucadians, ten; and the Ambraciots, eight. They asked the Thebans and Phliasians for money and the Eleans for money and ships without crews. On their own account they equipped thirty ships and three thousand hoplites.

28. When the Corcyræans heard of their preparations, they went to Corinth, taking with them Lacedæmonian and Sicyonian envoys, and required the Corinthians to withdraw the garrison and colonists, telling them that they had nothing to do with Epidamnus. If they made any claim to it, the Corcyræans were willing to refer the cause for arbitration to such Peloponnesian states as both parties should agree upon; and the colony was to be subject to the city to whom it was adjudged; or, they were willing to leave the matter in the hands of the Delphian oracle. But they deprecated war and declared that if it occurred, they would be compelled by Corinthian violence to discard their present friends and seek others whom they would rather not for help they must have. The Corinthians replied that if the Corcyræans would withdraw the ships and the barbarians from Epidamnus, they would consider the matter, but that it would not do for them to be litigating while the siege went on. The Corcyræans rejoined that they would consent to this proposal if the Corinthians on their part would withdraw their forces from Epidamnus; or, again, they were willing that both parties should remain on the spot, and that a truce should be made until the decision was given. The Corinthians turned a deaf ear to all these overtures.

[*The Corinthian attempt to relieve Epidamnus was defeated and the town fell (435).*]

31. For a whole year after the battle and for a year after that, the Corinthians, exasperated by the war with

Corcyra, were busy in building ships. They took the utmost pains to create the finest armada: rowers were collected from the Peloponnese and from the rest of Hellas by the attraction of pay. The Corcyræans were alarmed at the report of their preparations. They had no allies in Hellas; they had not enrolled in the league either of the Athenians or of the Lacedæmonians. They determined to go to Athens, join the Athenian alliance, and get what help they could from them. The Corinthians, hearing of their intentions, also sent ambassadors to Athens, fearing lest the combination of the Athenian and Corcyræan navies might prevent them from bringing the war to a satisfactory conclusion. Accordingly, an assembly was held at which both parties came forward to plead their respective causes; and first the Corcyræans spoke somewhat as follows:

32. "Men of Athens, those who, like ourselves, come to others on whom they have no prior claim because of a great service rendered or an alliance and ask help of them, are bound to show, in the first place, that the granting of their request is expedient, or at any rate not hurtful, and, secondly, that their gratitude will be lasting. If they prove neither point, they have no right to be angry at a refusal. Now when they sent us here to ask for an alliance, the Corcyræans were confident that they could establish both these points to your satisfaction. But, unfortunately, we have had a practice no less inconsistent with the request which we are about to make than contrary to our own interest at the present moment: Inconsistent; for hitherto we have never, if we could avoid it, been the allies of others; and now we come and ask you to enter into an alliance with us— Contrary to our interest; for through this practice we find ourselves isolated in our war with the Corinthians. The policy of not making alliances which might endanger us at another's bidding, instead of being sound sense, as we once thought, has now unmistakably proved to be weakness and folly. True, in the last naval engagement we repelled the Corinthians single-handed. But now they are on the point of attacking us with a much greater force, which they have drawn together from the Pelopon-

nese and from all Hellas. We know that we are too weak to resist them unaided, and the danger is great if we fall into their hands. We are therefore compelled to ask assistance of you and of all the world and to ask pardon if we venture to adopt a policy at variance with our former love of peace, which was not a crime but an error of judgment.

33. "There are many circumstances which will justify your compliance with our request. In the first place, you will assist the injured party and not the aggressors; secondly, you will admit us to your alliance at a time when our dearest interests are at stake and will certainly lay up a treasure of gratitude with us by unforgettable proof of your good will. Lastly, we have a navy greater than any but your own. Reflect; what good fortune can be more extraordinary, what more annoying to your enemies than the voluntary accession of a power for whose alliance you would have given any amount of money and thanks? You are to incur no danger and no expense, and in coming over, we bring you a good name in the world, gratitude from those who seek your aid, and an increase of your own strength. Few have ever had all these advantages offered them at once; few when they come asking for an alliance are able to give as much security and honor as they are to receive.

"And if any one thinks that the war in which our services may be needed will never come, he is mistaken. He does not see that the Lacedæmonians fear you and are eager to take up arms, and that the Corinthians are influential with them and hostile to you, and that they are subduing us first with a view to assailing you in order that we may not stand united against them in the bond of a common enmity, and that they may not miss the chance of weakening us or strengthening themselves. And it is our business to strike first; we should offer and you accept alliance, and forestall their designs instead of waiting to counteract them.

34. "If they say that we are their colony and that therefore you have no right to receive us, they should be made to understand that all colonies honor their mother city when she treats them well but are estranged from

her by injustice.[1] For colonists are not meant to be the slaves but the equals of those who remain at home. The injustice of their conduct to us is clear: for we proposed arbitration in the matter of Epidamnus, but they insisted on prosecuting their quarrel by arms, not equity. When you see how they treat us, their own kinsmen, take warning: if they try deception, do not be misled; and if they make a direct request of you, refuse. For men pass through life most securely when they have least reason to reproach themselves with obliging adversaries.

35. "But again, you will not break the treaty with the Lacedæmonians by receiving us: for we are not allies of either party. The treaty provides that any Hellenic city which is the ally of neither party may join whichever league it pleases. And how monstrous if they man their ships, not only from their own confederacy, but from Hellas in general, especially from your subjects, and debar us from the alliance open to us and from every other source of aid, and denounce it as a crime if you accede to our request. We shall have far better reason to complain if you refuse and repulse us, when we are in danger and not your enemies, while they suffer no restraint, hostile and aggressive as they are, but are actually allowed to strengthen themselves from your empire. That will not be just. You should either prevent Corinthians from hiring mercenaries in your dominions or send to us too such help as you may think fit, but it would be best of all if you would openly receive and assist us. As we intimated at the beginning, the advantages we offer are numerous. Above all, our enemies are your enemies, which is the clearest guarantee of fidelity in an ally; and they are not weak but well able to hurt those who secede from them. Again, when the proffered alliance is that of a maritime and not of an inland power, it is a far more serious matter to refuse. You should, if possible, allow no one to have a fleet but yourselves; at worst, secure the friendship of the strongest naval power.

36. "Some one may think that the course which we recommend is expedient; but he may be afraid that if he is convinced by our arguments, he will break the

treaty. He must understand that for all his apprehensions, he will inspire more alarm in his adversaries with strength on his side, but that confidence combined with weakness, if our offer be rejected, will be less formidable to enemies who are strong. He is now deciding on the interests of Athens rather than Corcyra, and he is not showing as much foresight as he should if, when war is imminent and almost at the door, he is so anxious about the chances of the hour that he hesitates to win over a place which cannot be made a friend or enemy without momentous consequences. Corcyra is conveniently situated for the coast voyage to Italy and Sicily; it stands in the way of any fleet coming thence to the Peloponnese and can also facilitate a voyage westwards.[1] In other ways Corcyra offers the greatest advantages. One word more, which is the sum of all and everything we have to say and should convince you that you must not abandon us. Hellas has only three considerable navies: there is ours and there is yours and there is the Corinthian. Now, if the Corinthians get hold of ours and you allow the two to become one, you will have to fight against the united navies of Corcyra and the Peloponnese. But, if you make us your allies, you will have our navy to reinforce you in the conflict against them."

37. The Corinthians replied to the Corcyræans somewhat as follows:

"Since these Corcyræans have argued not only that you should accept them as allies but also that we are acting unjustly and forcing an unreasonable war upon them, we too must touch on these two points before we proceed to our main argument, that you may appreciate our claim upon you with more certainty and may have good reason for rejecting their petition. They say that they have hitherto refused to make alliances from sound sense; but they adopted this policy not honorably but in order to injure others; they did not want an ally to witness their crimes and put them to the blush whenever they called him in. Their city is from its position self-sufficient; this makes them judges of their own offenses against others, and they can dispense with judges appointed under treaties;[1] for they hardly ever visit their neighbors, while foreign ships are constantly compelled to put in at Corcyra. And all the time they screen themselves under the specious name of neutrality, not to avoid complicity in the crimes of others, but to commit them by themselves: to use violence wherever they have the power, to aggrandize themselves wherever they escape detection, and to make whatever gains they can without shame. If they were really as honorable men as they say, the greater their immunity from attack, the more clearly they might have made their honesty appear by submitting differences to arbitration.

38. "But they have not shown themselves honorable either towards us or towards others. Although they are our colony, they have always stood aloof from us; and now they are fighting against us on the plea that they were not sent out to be ill used. But we rejoin that we did not send them out to be outraged by them but to be recognized as their leaders and receive proper respect. Our other colonies do honor us; no city is more beloved by her colonies than Corinth. That we are popular with the majority proves that the Corcyræans are wrong to dislike us; and there is nothing improper in our going to war with them, for they are doing us an unexampled injury. Even if we had been misled by passion, it would have been honorable in them to give way, though dishonorable in us to use violence if they showed moderation. But they have wronged us over and over again in their arrogance and the license that comes from wealth; and now there is our colony of Epidamnus, which they did not claim in its distress; but when we came to the rescue, they seized it and are now holding it by force.

39. "They pretend that they first offered to have the matter decided by arbitration. The appeal to justice might have some meaning in the mouth of one whose actions corresponded to his professions before he entered on the struggle, but not when it is made from a position of security and advantage. These men began by laying siege to Epidamnus, and only when they thought that we would not be indifferent did they put forward their specious offer of arbitration. And as if the wrong which they have themselves done at Epidamnus were not enough,

they now come here and ask you, as of right, to be not their allies but their accomplices in crime and would have you receive them when they are at enmity with us. But they ought to have come when they were out of all danger, not at a time when we have been wronged and they are in danger. You have never derived any benefit from their power, but they will now be benefited by yours; and, although innocent of their crimes, you will equally be held responsible by us. If you were to have shared the consequences with them, they ought long ago to have shared the power with you.

40. "We have proved that our complaints are justified and that our adversaries are violent and aggressive; we will now show you that you have no right to receive them. Admittedly, the treaty allows any unenrolled cities to join either league, but this provision does not benefit those who have in view the injury of others but only those in need of protection—and not as a result of forsaking their allegiance. It does not apply to those whose reception is against sound sense because they bring war instead of peace, as the Corcyræans would do now if you do not listen to us. For if you were now to help the Corcyræans, you would be no longer at peace with us, but our enemies; and we must, if you take their part, in defending ourselves against them, defend ourselves against you. But you ought in common justice to stand aloof from both; or, if you must join either, you should join us and go to war with them; to Corinth you are bound by treaty, but with Corcyra you never even negotiated a truce. And do not establish the custom of receiving the rebellious subjects of others. At the revolt of Samos,[1] when the other Peloponnesians were divided upon the question of giving them aid, we voted in your favor and expressly maintained that every one should be allowed to punish his own allies. If you mean to receive and assist offenders, we shall assuredly gain as many allies of yours as you will of ours; and you will establish a custom which will tell against yourselves more than against us.

41. "Such are the grounds of right which we urge, and they are sufficient according to Hellenic customs. But we

have advice to give and a claim on your gratitude; not being your enemies to do you harm nor friends engaged in frequent intercourse, we hold that this is the time to repay it. Before the Persian invasion when you were in want of ships for the Aeginetan war, we Corinthians lent you twenty;[1] the service which we then rendered gave you the victory over the Aeginetans, as the other service, which prevented the Peloponnesians from aiding the Samians, enabled you to punish Samos. Both benefits were conferred on one of those critical occasions when men in the act of attacking their enemies are generally regardless of everything but victory, and regard whoever assists them as a friend, though he may have previously been an enemy, and opponents as hostile, even though they are really friends; they will often neglect their own interests in passion for victory.

42. "Think of these things; let the younger be informed of them by their elders, and consider it your duty to render us like for like. Do not say to yourselves that this is just but that something else is expedient in the event of war; expediency generally consists in avoidance of wrongdoing. The war with which the Corcyræans frighten you into an unjust course lies in the future; it is not yet clear that it will occur; and it is not right to be so carried away by the prospect of it as to bring upon yourselves the hatred of the Corinthians, which is both manifest and immediate. Would you not be wiser in seeking to remove the suspicion which your treatment of the Megarians[1] has already inspired? A later kindness done in season, though small in comparison, may cancel a greater previous offense. And do not be attracted by their offer of a great naval alliance; for it is a surer source of strength to do no wrong to your peers than, under the inducement of immediate and apparent gain, to aggrandize yourselves at the cost of dangers.

43. "We are now in the same situation in which you were when we declared at Sparta that every one so placed should be allowed to punish his own allies, and we claim to receive the same measure at your hands. You profited from our vote, and we ought not to be injured by yours. Pay what you owe, knowing that this is our

time of need, in which a man's best friend is one who does him a service, his opponent an enemy. Do not receive these Corcyræans into alliance in despite of us, and do not support them in injustice. In acting thus, you will act rightly and will consult your own true interests."

Such were the words of the Corinthians.

44. The Athenians heard both sides and held two assemblies; in the first they were more influenced by the words of the Corinthians, but in the second they changed their minds, not so far as to make an alliance both offensive and defensive with Corcyra; for then, if the Corcyræans had required them to join in an expedition against Corinth, the treaty with the Peloponnesians would have been broken; but they concluded a defensive league, by which the two states promised to aid each other if an attack were made on the territory or on the allies of either. For they thought that in any case the war with the Peloponnese was inevitable, and they had no mind to let Corcyra and her great navy fall into the hands of the Corinthians. They desired to embroil them more and more with one another; and then when the war came, the Corinthians and the other naval powers would be weaker. They also considered that Corcyra was conveniently situated for the coast voyage to Italy and Sicily . . .

[*A small Athenian squadron saved the Corcyræans from decisive defeat off Sybota in the autumn of 433. Anticipating Corinthian hostility, the Athenians ordered Potidæa, a Corinthian colony in Thrace subject to them, to raze its walls on the seaward side and to cease admitting annual magistrates sent from Corinth. This action precipitated the revolt which Athens feared; Potidæa was encouraged to resist not only by Corinth but by Sparta, which promised to invade Attica if the Athenians attacked Potidæa. Some other cities in the same region revolted, all were encouraged by Perdiccas, king of Macedon, who, however, soon made peace with Athens again. The Corinthians sent out a force of volunteers to protect Potidæa, but the Athenians were able, in the spring of 432, to invest the town.*]

66. Such were the grievances which at this time existed between the Athenians and Peloponnesians: the Corinthians complained that the Athenians were blockading their colony of Potidæa, and a Corinthian and Peloponnesian garrison in it; the Athenians rejoined that the Peloponnesians had excited to revolt a state which was an ally and tributary of theirs and that they had now openly joined the Potidæans and were fighting on their side. The war, however, had not yet broken out; the truce still continued, for so far the Corinthians had acted alone.

67. But they did not acquiesce in the siege of Potidæa. Corinthians were shut up within the walls, and they were afraid of losing the town; so without delay they invited the allies to meet at Sparta. There they inveighed against the Athenians on the ground that they had broken the treaty and were wronging the Peloponnese. The Aeginetans did not venture to send envoys openly in fear of Athens but secretly they acted with the Corinthians and were among the chief instigators of the war, declaring that they had been robbed of the autonomy which the treaty guaranteed them.[1] The Lacedæmonians themselves then proceeded to summon any of their allies or any one else who claimed to have been wronged by the Athenians and, calling their own ordinary assembly, told them to speak. Several of them came forward and brought charges; the Megarians alleged, among many other grounds of difference with Athens, that they were excluded from all harbors within the Athenian dominion and from the Athenian Agora, contrary to the treaty.[2] The Corinthians waited until the other allies had stirred up the Lacedæmonians; at length they came forward and spoke somewhat as follows:

68. "The spirit of trust, Lacedæmonians, which animates your own political and social life, makes you distrustful of us when we bring charges against others; you derive from it your calmness of temper; yet it too often leaves you in ignorance of what is going on outside your own country. Time after time we have warned you of the harm which the Athenians would do to us; but instead of learning the truth of what we told you on each oc-

casion, you chose rather to suspect that we spoke from interested motives. And this is the reason why you have brought the allies here to Sparta, not before, but after the injury has been inflicted. Which of them all has a better right to speak than ourselves, who have the heaviest accusations to make, outraged as we are by the Athenians and neglected by you. If the crimes which they are committing against Hellas were being done in a corner, then you might be ignorant; and we should have to inform you of them; but now, what need of many words? Some, as you see, have been already enslaved; they are at this moment intriguing against others, notably against allies of yours; and long ago they had made all their preparations in the prospect of war. Else why did they seduce Corcyra in defiance of us, and why did they blockade Potidæa, the latter a most advantageous post for the command of the Thracian region, the former a city that might have furnished the Peloponnesians with a very large fleet?

69. "And the blame of all this rests on you; for you originally allowed them to fortify their city after the Persian War and afterwards to build their Long Walls,[1] and to this hour you have gone on defrauding of liberty not only the peoples they have enslaved but now your own allies as well. For enslavement is really the work of those who could bring it to an end but have no care about it; and all the more, if they enjoy the honorable claim of being the liberators of Hellas.

"We have met at last, but with what difficulty! And even now we have no definite object. By this time we ought to have been considering not whether we are wronged but how we are to resist. The aggressors have made up their minds while we are resolved about nothing; they are attacking without hesitation. And we know the path by which the Athenians gradually encroach upon their neighbors. While they think that you are too dull to observe them, they are less venturesome; but when they see that you are consciously overlooking their aggressions, they will strike and not spare. Of all Hellenes, Lacedæmonians, you are the only people who never do anything: you defend yourselves against an assailant, not by using your power, but by giving it out that you will; you alone do not destroy your enemies when their strength is beginning to grow, but when it is doubling in size. And yet it used to be said that you were trusty. The report exceeded the truth. We all know that the Persians made their way from the ends of the earth against the Peloponnese before you went out to meet them as you should; and now you look on at the doings of the Athenians, who are not at a distance like the Persians, but close at hand. Instead of attacking your enemy, you prefer to await attack and take the chances of a struggle that has been deferred until his power is much increased. And you know that the barbarians miscarried chiefly through their own errors and that we have more often survived against these very Athenians through blunders of their own than through any aid from you. Some have already been ruined by the hopes which you inspired in them, for so entirely did they trust you that they took no precautions themselves. These things we say in no spirit of enmity—let that be understood—but by way of expostulation. For men expostulate with erring friends but bring accusations against enemies who have done them a wrong.

70. "And surely we have a right to find fault with our neighbors, if any one ever had. There are important interests at stake to which, as far as we can see, you are insensible. And you have never fully considered what manner of men these Athenians are with whom you will have to fight, and how utterly unlike yourselves.[1] They are innovators, equally quick in the conception and in the execution of every plan; while you are careful only to keep what you have and uninventive; in action you do not even go as far as you need. They are audacious beyond their strength; they run risks which policy would condemn; and in the midst of dangers, they are full of hope. Whereas it is your nature to act more feebly than your power allows, in forming your policy not even to rely on certainties, and when dangers arise, to think you will never be delivered from them. They are resolute, and you are dilatory; they are always abroad, and you are always at home. For they think they may gain something

by leaving their homes; but you are afraid that any new enterprise may imperil what you have already. When conquerors, they pursue their victory to the utmost; when defeated, they give as little ground as possible. They devote their bodies to their country as though they belonged to other men, and their minds, their dearest possessions, to action in her service. When they do not carry out an intention which they have formed, they seem to themselves to have sustained a personal bereavement; when an enterprise succeeds, they think they have gained a small installment of what is to come; but if they suffer a reverse, they at once conceive new hopes to compensate and supply their wants. For with them alone, to hope is to have, as they lose not a moment in the execution of an idea. In all these activities they wear themselves out with exertions and dangers throughout their entire lives. None enjoy their good things less because they are always seeking for more. To do their duty is their only holiday, and they deem peaceful repose to be no less of a misfortune than incessant fatigue. If a man should say of them, in a word, that it is their nature neither to be at peace themselves nor to allow peace to other men, he would simply speak the truth.

71. "In the face of such a rival city, Lacedæmonians, you persist in doing nothing. You do not see that peace is best secured by those who use their strength justly yet show their determination not to submit to wrong. Justice with you seems to consist in giving no annoyance to others and in escaping harm in self-defense. But this policy would hardly be successful even if your neighbors were like yourselves; and in the present case, as we pointed out just now, your ways compared with theirs are old-fashioned. And, as in the arts, it is necessary that new inventions should always triumph.[1] In a city at peace, undisturbed traditions are best; but when it is necessary for men to engage in numerous undertakings, much inventiveness is required. The Athenians have had a wide experience and have therefore introduced far more novelties than you.

"Let your procrastination end here; assist your allies, especially the Potidæans, to whom your word is pledged,[2] by invading Attica at once. Do not betray friends and kindred to their worst enemies or drive the rest of us in despair to seek the alliance of others; in taking such a course, we should be doing nothing wrong either before the gods who are the witnesses of our oaths or before men whose eyes are upon us. For treaties are not broken by men who, when forsaken, turn to others, but by men who forsake allies whom they have sworn to defend. We will remain your friends if you choose to exert yourselves, for we should be guilty of impiety if we deserted you, nor should we easily find allies equally congenial to us. You must come to a wise decision on these questions and try to ensure that you exercise the leadership of the Peloponnese, transmitted to you by your fathers, no less honorably than they."

72. This was the substance of the Corinthian speech. Now an Athenian embassy happened to be staying at Lacedæmon; they had come on other business; and when they heard the speech, they felt bound to go before the Lacedæmonian assembly, not to answer the accusations brought against them by the cities, but to put the whole question before the Lacedæmonians and make them understand that they should take time to deliberate and examine it more fully. They also desired to set forth the power of their city, reminding the older men of what they knew and informing the younger of what lay beyond their experience. They thought that their words would make the Lacedæmonians incline to peace rather than war. So they came and said that if they might be allowed, they too would like to address the people. The Lacedæmonians invited them to come forward, and they spoke somewhat as follows:[1]

73. "We were not sent here on an embassy to argue with your allies but on other public business; observing, however, that no small outcry has arisen against us, we have come forward, not to answer the accusations which the cities bring (for you are not judges before whom either we or they might plead), but to prevent you from lending too ready an ear to their advice and so deciding wrongly about a very serious question. We propose also, in reply to the wider case which is raised against us,

to show that it is natural for us to hold what we have acquired and that our city is not to be despised.

"Of events in the remote past recorded by tradition, which no eye of any one who will hear us ever saw, why should we speak? But we cannot avoid speaking of the Persian War and other events which you yourselves remember, although it will be rather disagreeable to repeat what we are always bringing forward. When we faced those perils, we did so for the common advantage: you shared in the solid good, and we would not be wholly deprived of any advantage that accrues from the glory. Our words are not designed to deprecate hostility so much as to set forth in evidence and proof the character of the city with which, if you are ill-advised, you will soon be involved in war. We tell you that we, first and alone, dared to engage the barbarians at Marathon and that when they came again and we were too weak to defend ourselves by land, our whole people embarked on shipboard and shared in the victory of Salamis. This prevented them from sailing to the Peloponnese and ravaging city after city; for how could the cities have helped one another against so mighty a fleet? The Persians are our best witnesses; for when once defeated at sea, they felt that their power was impaired and quickly retreated with the greater part of their army.

74. "The circumstances of this event proved clearly that the fate of Hellas depended on her ships. And the three chief elements of success were contributed by us: namely, the greatest number of ships, the shrewdest general, the most unhesitating enthusiasm. The ships, in all, numbered four hundred, and of these, our own contingent amounted to nearly two-thirds.[1] To the influence of Themistocles, our general, it was chiefly due that we fought in the strait, which was most clearly our salvation; and for this service you yourselves honored him above any foreigner who ever visited you. Thirdly, we displayed far the most audacious enthusiasm; there was no one to help us by land, for the peoples up to our frontier had already submitted; so we left our city and sacrificed our homes. Even in that extremity we did not think it right to desert the common cause of the allies

who still resisted, or by dispersing to become useless to them; but we embarked and faced the danger, taking no offense at your failure to assist us promptly. We maintain, then, that we rendered you a service at least as great as you rendered us. The cities from which you came to help us were still inhabited, and you might hope to enjoy your lands; you feared for yourselves and not so much for us; at any rate, you gave us no support while we had anything to lose. But we had no city when we went out to fight and faced danger for one for which small hope was left, and yet we bore our part in saving you as well as ourselves. If, in fear for our land, like other states, we had at first gone over to the Persians, or had afterwards not ventured to embark because our ruin was already complete, it would have been useless for you with your weak navy to fight at sea; but everything would have proceeded without trouble for the Persians as they desired.

75. "Considering the enthusiasm and sagacity which we then displayed, do we deserve to be so bitterly hated by the other Hellenes merely because we have an empire? That empire was not acquired by force; but you would not stay and finish the Persian War, and the allies came of their own accord and asked us to be their leaders. It was by reason of this very fact that we were placed under the necessity from the first of advancing our empire to its present state, chiefly for fear, then for honor and lastly for profit. And when we had incurred the hatred of most of our allies, when some of them had already revolted and been subjugated, and you were no longer so friendly to us but suspicious and ill-disposed, it no longer seemed safe to take the risk of relaxing our hold. For as fast as the cities fell away from us, they would have gone over to you. But no one is to be reproached for providing for his own interests in the greatest of dangers.

76. "At all events, Lacedæmonians, you, as leaders, manage the Peloponnesian cities to suit your own advantage; and if you had persevered in the command of the allies long enough to be hated like ourselves, you would have been quite as unpopular with them as we are

and would have been under the necessity of ruling with a strong hand or incurring danger yourselves. An empire was offered to us; can you wonder that, acting as men will, we accepted it and now refuse to give it up, constrained by the most powerful motives: honor, fear and profit? We are not the first who have aspired to rule; it has always been the practice that the weaker is kept down by the stronger. And we think that we are worthy of power. There was a time when you thought so too, but now calculations of your interests make you talk about justice. Did justice ever divert any one from aggrandizement when he had the chance to gain anything by force? Men deserve praise who in obedience to human nature exercise dominion over others and yet show more justice than the extent of their power requires. We think our moderation would be soon apparent if others took our place; indeed our very fairness, which should be our glory, has been unfairly converted into a reproach.

77. "Thus, in suits with our allies arising under treaties,[1] even when they are decided in our own courts, where we have ensured that judgments are delivered under impartial laws, we come off less well than we might; and yet we are reputed litigious. None of our opponents observe why others, who exercise dominion elsewhere and are less moderate than we are in their dealings with their subjects, escape this reproach. Why is it? Because men who are free to practice violence have no need to go to law. But we are in the habit of meeting our allies on terms of equality; and, therefore, if they suffer ever so little because we make some decision or exercise our imperial power contrary to their own ideas of right, they are not grateful for our moderation in leaving them so much but are far more offended at their trifling loss than if we had from the first openly plundered them, laying aside all thought of law. For then they would themselves have admitted that the weaker must give way to the ruler. Mankind apparently resents injustice more than violence because injustice seems to be an unfair advantage taken by an equal, while violence is the irresistible force of a superior. They were patient under the yoke of the Persians, who inflicted on them far more grievous

wrongs; but now our dominion is odious in their eyes. Of course subjects always resent their present condition. And should your empire supplant ours, you would soon lose the good will which you have obtained from fear of us, at least if you now adopt the same kind of policy of which you gave a specimen when, for a short time, you were the leaders against Persia.[2] For the institutions under which you live are incompatible with those of other states; and, further, when any of you goes abroad, he respects neither these nor any other Hellenic customs.

78. "Do not then be hasty in deciding a serious question; and do not, by listening to the judgments and complaints of others, bring new trouble upon yourselves. You should realize the incalculable nature of war in advance before you are involved in it and how, when protracted, it ends in becoming largely a matter of chance, over which neither of us can have any control, the issue being equally unknown and equally hazardous to both. The misfortune is that in going to war men begin with blows, which should come later, and have recourse to words only when a reverse comes upon them. But neither you (as we see) nor we have as yet committed such a mistake; and therefore while both of us can still choose the prudent part, we tell you not to break the peace or violate your oaths. Let our differences be determined by arbitration, according to the treaty. If you refuse, we call the gods, by whom your oaths were sworn, to witness that you are the authors of the war; and we shall try to follow your guidance and strike back."

79. When the Lacedæmonians had heard the charges brought by the allies against the Athenians, and their rejoinder, they ordered everybody else to withdraw and deliberated alone. The majority were agreed that the Athenians were now doing wrong and that they must fight at once. But Archidamus, their king, who was held to be a man of shrewdness and sound sense, came forward and spoke somewhat as follows:

80. "At my age, Lacedæmonians, I have had experience of many wars; and I see several of you who are as old as I am and who will not desire war, as men too often do, because they have never known it or in the be-

lief that it is beneficial and safe. Sound calculation would discover that the war about which you are now deliberating is likely to be a very great one. When we encounter our neighbors in the Peloponnese, their mode of fighting is like ours, and they are all within a short march. But when we have to do with men whose country is a long way off and who are most skillful seamen and thoroughly provided with all other resources: wealth, private and public, ships, horses, arms, and a population larger than is to be found in any single Hellenic territory, not to speak of the numerous allies who pay them tribute; is this a people against whom we can lightly take up arms or plunge into a contest unprepared? What are we relying on? Our navy? There we are inferior, and to exercise and equip ourselves until we are a match for them will take time. Our money? In that we are much weaker still; we have none in a common treasury, and we are never ready to contribute out of our private means.[1]

81. "Perhaps some one may be encouraged by the superior equipment and numbers of our infantry, which will enable us regularly to invade and ravage their land. But they have much other land in their empire, and they will import necessary supplies by sea. Or, again, we may try to stir up revolts among their allies. But they are mostly islanders, and we shall need a fleet in their defense, as in our own. How then shall we carry on the war? For if we can neither defeat them at sea nor deprive them of the revenues by which their navy is maintained, we shall get the worst of it. And having gone so far, we shall no longer be able even to make peace with honor, especially if we are believed to have begun the quarrel. We must not for one moment flatter ourselves with the hope that if we ravage their country, the war will be soon at an end. Rather, I fear that we shall bequeath it to our children; so unlikely is it that the Athenians in their pride will be slaves to their land or be terrified like novices at the sight of war.

82. "Not that I would have you shut your eyes to their plots and abstain from unmasking them, or tamely suffer them to injure our allies. But do not take up arms yet.

Let us first send and remonstrate with them: we need not let them know positively whether we intend to go to war or not. In the meantime our own preparations may be going forward; we may seek for allies in Hellas and among the barbarians,[1] wherever we can find any to supply our deficiencies in ships and money. Those who, like ourselves, are exposed to Athenian plots cannot be blamed if in self-defense they seek the aid not of Hellenes only but of barbarians. And we must mobilize our own resources. If they listen to our ambassadors, well and good; but, if not, in two or three years' time we shall be in a stronger position, should we then determine to attack them. Perhaps, too, when they see that we are getting ready and that the tenor of our words corresponds to our actions, they may be more likely to yield; for their fields will be still untouched and their goods undespoiled, and it will be in their power to save them by their decision. Think of their land simply in the light of a hostage, all the more valuable in proportion as it is better cultivated; you should spare it as long as you can and not reduce them to despair and make their resistance harder to overcome. For if we are stung into action by the charges of our allies and waste their country before we are ready, we shall only involve the Peloponnese in more and more difficulty and disgrace. Charges brought by cities or persons against one another can be arranged; but when, in order to satisfy private grudges, we have all together undertaken a war of which no man can foresee the issue, it is not easy to terminate it with honor.

83. "And let no one think that there is any lack of courage in cities so numerous hesitating to attack a single one. The allies of the Athenians are not less numerous; they pay them tribute; and war is not an affair of arms so much as money which gives arms their use and which is needed above all things when a continental is fighting against a maritime power: let us find money first, and then we may allow our minds to be excited by the speeches of our allies. We, on whom responsibility for the consequences will chiefly fall, whether for good or evil, are the people who should calmly foresee some of them.

84. "Do not be ashamed of the slowness and procrastination with which they principally charge us; if you begin the war in haste, you will end it more slowly because you took up arms without preparation. Further, we have always been citizens of a free and most illustrious state; and the qualities which they condemn amount to good sense and discretion, which have saved us, unlike other men, from growing arrogant in success or giving way under disasters. We are not stimulated by the allurements of flattery into dangerous courses of which we disapprove, nor if goaded by accusations are we any more likely to be provoked into compliance. Our habits of discipline make us both warlike and prudent: warlike, because sound sense is generally accompanied by feelings of honor, which go with courage; prudent, because our education gives us too little learning to despise the laws, while its harshness makes us too sensible to disobey them; it teaches us not that useless overintelligence which makes men eloquent in depreciating enemy resources, with no corresponding capacity for action but the belief that the wits of our neighbors are as good as our own and that the blows of fortune cannot be determined by argument. We assume that our opponents have common prudence, and our preparations are in deeds. Our hopes ought not to rest on the probability of their mistakes but on our own caution and foresight. We should remember that one man is much the same as another and that the best is one trained in the school of the strictest necessity.

85. "These are practices which our fathers have handed down to us and which we keep up to our lasting benefit; we must not lose sight of them, and when many lives and much wealth, many cities and a great name are at stake, we must not be hasty or make up our minds in a few short hours; we must take time. We can afford to wait when others cannot because we are strong. And now, send envoys to the Athenians about Potidæa and about the other wrongs of which your allies complain, especially as they say that they are willing to have the matter tried; against anyone who offers to submit to justice you must not proceed as against a criminal with-

out hearing his cause. In the meantime, prepare for war. This decision will be the best for yourselves and the most formidable to your opponents."

This was the substance of Archidamus' speech. Last of all, Sthenelaidas, at that time one of the Ephors, came forward and addressed the Lacedæmonians somewhat as follows:

86. "I do not know what the long speeches of the Athenians mean. They have been loud in their own praise, but they never denied that they are wronging our allies and the Peloponnese. If they behaved well in the Persian War and are now behaving badly to us, they ought to be punished twice over because they were once good men and have become bad. But we are the same now as we were then, and we shall not show good sense if we allow our allies to be ill-treated and put off helping them, for they cannot put off their troubles. Others may have money, ships, and horses; but we have brave allies, and we must not betray them to the Athenians. If their sufferings were nominal, their wrongs might be redressed by words and legal processes; but now there is not a moment to be lost, and we must help them with all our might. Let no one tell us that we should take time to think when we are suffering injustice: those who mean to do injustice should take a long time to think. Therefore, Lacedæmonians, prepare for war as the honor of Sparta demands. Do not let Athens grow stronger. Do not let us betray our allies; but, with the gods on our side, let us march against the wrongdoers!"

87. When Sthenelaidas had spoken in this way, as Ephor he himself put the question to the Lacedæmonian assembly. Their custom is to decide by shouting and not by voting. But he said that he was unable to tell on which side was the louder cry, and wishing to call forth a demonstration which might encourage the warlike spirit, he said, "Any of you, Lacedæmonians, who thinks that the treaty has been broken and that the Athenians are in the wrong, should rise and go to that place (pointing to a particular spot) and those who think otherwise to the other side." So the assembly rose and divided, and it was determined by a large majority that the treaty had

been broken. The Lacedæmonians then recalled the allies and told them that in their judgment the Athenians were guilty but that they wished to hold a general assembly of the allies and take a vote from them all; then, if they approved of war it might be undertaken by common consent. With this success the allies returned home, followed by the Athenian envoys, when they had completed their business. Thirteen years of the thirty years' peace which was concluded after the recovery of Eubœa had elapsed and the fourteenth year had begun when the Lacedæmonian assembly decided that the treaty had been broken.[1]

88. In arriving at this decision and resolving to go to war, the Lacedæmonians were influenced not so much by the speeches of their allies as by the fear that the Athenian power might grow further; for they saw the greater part of Hellas already subject to them.

The Growth of Athenian Power

[Thucydides now gives a very brief and probably unrevised sketch of the rise of Athenian power between 479 and 439, ending with the suppression of the revolt of Samos (chapters 89-117). The following passage describes the origin of the "Delian League" in 478-77 and its subsequent conversion into an Athenian empire. The Spartan regent, Pausanias, had been sent across the Ægean in command of 20 Peloponnesian and 30 Athenian ships to fight in defense of the Greeks there who had rebelled from Persia.]

95. Pausanias had already begun to be oppressive and the Hellenes were offended with him, especially the Ionians and others who had been recently liberated from the Persian king. So they went to the Athenians and begged them as kinsmen to be their leaders and to protect them against Pausanias if he attempted to oppress them. The Athenians accepted their overtures and prepared to interfere and to settle matters at their discretion. In the meantime the Lacedæmonians summoned

Pausanias to Sparta, intending to investigate certain reports which were reaching them; for he was accused of numerous crimes by Hellenes who went to Sparta and appeared to exercise his command more like a despot than a general. His recall occurred at the very time when the hatred which he inspired had induced the allies, with the exception of the Peloponnesian force, to go over to the Athenians. On arriving at Lacedæmon, he was punished for the wrongs which he had done to particular persons; but on the principal charge, that of conspiring with the Persians, which was believed to be proven, he was acquitted. The government however did not continue him in his command but in his place sent Dorcis and certain others with a small force. The allies refused to accept them as commanders; and, seeing the state of affairs, they returned home. The Lacedæmonians sent out no more commanders, for they were afraid that those whom they appointed would be corrupted, as they had found to be the case with Pausanias; they had had enough of the Persian War, and they thought that the Athenians were fully able to take command, and at that time believed them to be their friends.

96. Thus the Athenians took over the leadership by a voluntary act of the allies, who detested Pausanias. They fixed which of the cities should supply money and which ships for the war against the barbarians, the avowed object of which was to compensate themselves and the allies for their losses by devastating the King's country.[1] Then was first instituted at Athens the office of Hellenic treasurers, who received the *phoros*, the name given to the contributions in money.[2] The first assessment was 460 talents. The island of Delos was the treasury,[3] and the councils of the allies were held there in the temple.

97. At first the Athenians were leaders of allies who were autonomous and deliberated in common councils.[1] In the interval between the Persian and this war, the Athenians gained great successes in war and policy against the barbarians, their own rebellious allies and the Peloponnesians who came across their path from time to time. I have gone out of my way to write of this period

because all writers who have preceded me have omitted it and treated either the Hellenic affairs prior to the Persian invasion or that invasion itself, with the exception of Hellanicus; and where he has touched upon it in his Attic history, he is brief and inaccurate in his chronology.[2] The narrative will also serve to explain how the Athenian empire grew up. . .

99. The causes which led to the defections of the allies were of different kinds; but the most important was their neglect to pay the tribute or to furnish ships and, in some cases, failure to perform military service. For the Athenians were exacting and oppressive, using coercive measures toward men who were neither accustomed nor willing to make the necessary exertions. And in various other ways they began to prove less popular leaders than at first. In the joint campaigns their position was superior, and they had no difficulty in reducing allies. For all this the allies themselves were responsible, for the majority of them shirked military service to escape absence from home, and so they agreed to contribute their share of the expense, instead of providing ships. The Athenian navy was increased as a result of their contributing to its cost while they themselves were always untrained and unprepared for war when they revolted. . .[1]

118. In this period the Athenians acquired a firmer hold over their empire, and the city itself became a great power. The Lacedæmonians saw what was going on but did little to prevent it and during most of the time remained inactive. Even before, they had not been prompt to take the field unless under necessity; and at that time they were also embarrassed by wars at home.[1] But now at last Athenian power was plainly rising and entrenching on their own confederacy; they could now bear it no longer: they made up their minds that they must put out all their energy and destroy Athenian strength if they could, and so they began this war. They had already voted in their own assembly that the treaty had been broken and that the Athenians were doing wrong; they now sent to Delphi and asked the god if it would be for their advantage to make war. He is reported

to have answered that if they did their best, they would be conquerors, and that he himself, invited or uninvited, would take their part.

The Preliminaries to War

119. The Lacedæmonians again summoned the allies, intending to put to them the question of war or peace. When their representatives arrived, an assembly was held; and the allies expressed their wishes, most of them complaining of the Athenians and approving of war. The Corinthians had already gone the round of the cities and entreated them privately to vote for war; they were afraid that they would be too late to save Potidæa. At the assembly they came forward last of all and spoke somewhat as follows:[1]

120. "Fellow allies, we could no longer find fault with the Lacedæmonians; they have themselves resolved upon war and have convened us to confirm their decision. And they have done well; for the leaders of a confederacy, while not neglecting the interests of their own state, should be the first to look to the general welfare, as in general they are first in honor. Now those among us who have already had dealings with the Athenians do not require to be warned against them; but those who live somewhat inland and not on a trade route should clearly understand that if they do not protect the seaboard, they will find it more difficult to export their produce or to receive in return goods sent inland from the sea. They should not lend a careless ear to our words, which nearly concern them; they should expect that if they desert the cities on the seashore, the danger may some day even reach them, and that they are consulting for their own interests quite as much as for ours. And therefore no one should hesitate to accept war in exchange for peace. Men of sound sense refuse to move if they are not wronged, but brave men go to war as soon as they are wronged and make peace again when there is a good opportunity. They are not intoxicated by military success, but the pleasure that comes from peace and inactivity does not make them tolerate wrongs. If pleasure makes a

man timid, he would very soon lose by inactivity the enjoyment of the ease from which his timidity arises; while if good fortune in war incites men to aggression, they have failed to realize how unreliable is the confidence which elates them. Many schemes which were ill-advised have succeeded by chance through the still greater folly which possessed the enemy; and yet more, which seemed to be wisely contrived, have ended in dishonorable disaster. The execution of an enterprise is never equal to the confidence with which it is conceived; men form plans in security, but when the time of action comes, fear makes them fail.

121. "We, however, are now urging war upon the Athenians because we are being wronged; there is ample justification, and when we obtain redress, we will put up the sword in due time. For many reasons we are likely to succeed. First, because we are superior in numbers and in military experience; secondly, because we all obey as one man the orders given to us. They are strong at sea, but we too will equip a navy for which the means can be supplied partly from the resources of each state, partly out of the funds at Delphi and Olympia.[1] A loan will be granted to us, and by the offer of higher pay, we can draw away their foreign sailors; the Athenian power consists more of mercenaries than of their own citizens.[2] Ours would suffer less in this way; we are stronger in men than money. Let them be beaten in a single naval engagement and they are likely to be finished; but if they were to hold out, we too shall have more time in which to practice at sea. As soon as we have brought our skill up to the level of theirs, our courage will surely give us the victory. For our courage is a natural gift which they could not acquire by instruction, but their superior skill is something we must overcome by practice.

"Money for this purpose we will contribute. What! Shall their allies never refuse to contribute to their own enslavement, and shall we not give freely in order to save ourselves and be avenged on our enemies, or, rather, to prevent their taking our money from us and actually using it to our harm?

122. "There are other means too by which the war

may be carried on. We may induce their allies to revolt—a sure way of cutting off the revenues in which their strength consists, or we may build a fort in their country; there are other expedients which no one can now foresee. For war, least of all things, proceeds by rules; it generally brings to birth its own inventions as chance offers occasion. It is safer to engage in it with calm; nothing is more apt to cause a man's fall than his own passion.

"If this were merely a quarrel between one of us and our neighbors about a boundary line, it would be tolerable; but reflect on the position: the Athenians are a match for us all, and much more than a match for any single city. And if we allow ourselves to be divided, or are not united against them heart and soul—the whole confederacy and every people and city in it—they will easily overpower us. It may seem a hard saying, but you may be sure that defeat means nothing but downright slavery. It is a disgrace to the Peloponnese that this possibility has even been the subject of debate and that so many states suffer at the hands of one. Men will think that we deserve our fate or that we are too cowardly to resist, and we shall seem a degenerate race. For our fathers were the liberators of Hellas, but we cannot even secure our own liberty; and while we are proud of overthrowing the rule of a single man in this or that city, we allow a city to be set up in the midst of us with despotic power. Are we not victims of one of three most serious misfortunes—folly, cowardice, or carelessness? For you surely have not escaped these imputations by taking refuge in that sense of superiority which has in fact injured so many and which, from the ruin it often causes, has instead been described in the very opposite way as inferiority of sense.

123. "But why should we dwell long and reproachfully upon the past, except in our present interests? You should, rather, look to the future and protect your present position by yet further efforts; it is your tradition to win honor by exertions, and you should not change your character because you are now a little better off in wealth and power, for men should not lose in abundance what they gained in want. There are many reasons why you

may enter into war with confidence. The god has spoken and promised to take our part himself. All Hellas will fight at our side, from fear or interest. And you will not break the treaty—the god, in bidding you go to war, pronounces it to have been violated—but you will be upholding it against infractions; it is not broken by men acting in self-defense but by aggressors.

124. "On every ground you will be right in going to war, and we advise it for the common good; identity of interests is the surest tie for cities and individuals. Send speedy aid to the Potidæans, who are Dorians and now besieged by Ionians (a reversal of former conditions), and pursue the freedom of the rest. We cannot wait any longer: some of us are already suffering, and if it is known that we have met but do not dare to defend ourselves, others will soon share their fate. Acknowledging then, allies, that there is no alternative and that we are advising you for the best, vote for war; do not be afraid of the immediate danger, but fix your thoughts on the durable peace which will follow. For war gives more stability to peace, but it is not equally safe to keep quiet and refuse to fight. The city which has been set up with despotic power in Hellas is a standing menace to all alike; she rules over some of us already and plans to rule over others. Let us attack and subdue her, that we may ourselves live safely for the future and deliver the Hellenes whom she has enslaved."

This was the substance of the Corinthian speech.

125. The Lacedæmonians, after hearing the opinions of all the allies, put the question to them all, one after the other, great and small alike; and the majority voted for war. But although they had come to this decision, they could not act at once for lack of preparation; so they determined each to provide what was required with the least possible delay. Still, nearly a whole year passed in the necessary arrangements before they invaded Attica and commenced open hostilities.[1]

126. During this interval they sent embassies to Athens and made various complaints so as to have the best excuse for going to war in case the Athenians refused to listen.

[The Spartans alleged that Athens was polluted by the existence there of families under an old curse. Their aim was to discredit Pericles, the dominant Athenian statesman, who belonged to one of these families. Athens retaliated by telling the Spartans that they should purify their own city of pollutions. Thucydides recounts the origins of these pollutions. The relevant chapters (126-38) are omitted.]

139. The Spartans went again and again to Athens and told the Athenians that they must raise the siege of Potidæa and restore Ægina to autonomy. Above all, and in the plainest terms, they insisted that if they wanted to avert war, they must rescind the decree which excluded the Megarians from the Attic agora and the harbors in the Athenian empire. But the Athenians would not listen to them nor rescind the decree, alleging that the Megarians had tilled the holy ground and the neutral borderland[1] and had received their runaway slaves. Finally, there came from Sparta the last embassy, consisting of Rhamphias, Melesippus and Hegesander, who said nothing of all this but only, "The Lacedæmonians desire to maintain peace; and peace there may be, if you restore autonomy to the Hellenes." The Athenians then called an assembly and held a debate; it seemed best to them to consider and reply on all points. Many came forward to speak; and much was said on both sides, some affirming that they ought to go to war, and others that the decree about the Megarians should be rescinded and not stand in the way of peace. Above all, Pericles, the son of Xanthippus, who was the first man of his day at Athens, and the ablest speaker and man of affairs, came forward and gave advice of this kind:[2]

140. "Athenians, my policy is always the same, not to yield to the Peloponnesians, although I know that men are subject to different passions when they are persuaded to fight and when they are engaged in action, and that their policies change with circumstances. But I see that I must give you the same, or nearly the same, advice as I gave before; and I claim that those who are convinced should stand by what they all decided, even if we

should suffer some reverse, or else, in the event of success, that they should take no credit for their sagacity. The outcome of events can be as irrational as the plans of men, and this is why we commonly blame chance for whatever belies our calculation.

"For some time past, the hostile designs of the Lacedæmonians have been clear enough, and never more than now. The treaty says that when differences arise, the two parties shall refer them to arbitration, and in the meantime both are to retain what they have. But for arbitration they have never asked; and when we offer it, they refuse it. They want to redress their grievances by arms and not discussion; and now they come to us, using the language no longer of expostulation but of dictation. They tell us to quit Potidæa, to leave Ægina independent, and to rescind the decree respecting the Megarians. These last ambassadors go further still and announce that we must give the Hellenes independence. I would have none of you suppose that he will be fighting for a small matter if we refuse to annul the Megarian decree, of which they make so much, telling us that its revocation would prevent the war. You should have no lingering uneasiness about this; you are not going to war for a trifle. For this trifle tests your whole policy and puts it to the proof. If you yield to them, they will think that you are afraid and will immediately dictate some greater concession; but if you are firm, you would prove to them that they must rather treat you as their equals. Therefore, make up your minds, once for all, either to give way while you are still unharmed, or, if we are going to war, as in my judgment is best, not to give way at all on any plea, small or great, and not to enjoy our possessions in fear. Any claim, the smallest as well as the greatest, imposed on a neighbor and an equal when there has been no legal award, can mean nothing but slavery.

141. "That our resources are equal to theirs and that we shall be as strong in the war, I will now prove to you in detail. The Peloponnesians cultivate their own lands, and they have no money either public or private. Nor have they any experience of long wars in countries beyond the sea; their poverty prevents them from fighting,

except for short periods in person against each other. Such men cannot man fleets or often send out armies. They would be at a distance from their own properties, upon which they must draw; and they will be kept off the sea by us. Now wars are supported out of accumulated wealth, rather than forced contributions.[1] And men who cultivate their own lands are more ready to fight in person than to find money for war; they do not despair of their lives, but they are not sure that their money will last out the war, especially if it is protracted beyond their expectation, as may well be the case. In a single pitched battle the Peloponnesians and their allies are a match for all Hellas, but they are not able to maintain a war against a power different in kind from their own; they have no single council and therefore cannot execute a plan with immediate speed. The confederacy is made up of many races; all the representatives have equal votes, and press their several interests. There follows the usual result, that action is ineffective. For some desire the greatest revenge on an enemy; others, to get off with as little loss as possible. They meet at intervals, and give little time to the consideration of any common interest and more to action in their own. Every one thinks that his own neglect will do no harm but that it is somebody else's business to keep a lookout for him; and so they do not notice that this idea, cherished alike by each, is fatal to the common advantage of all.

142. "Their greatest hindrance will be want of money, which they can provide only slowly; delay will thus occur, and in war opportunity waits for no man. Further, no fortified place which they can build against us is to be feared any more than their navy. As to the first, even in time of peace it would be hard for them to construct it against a city of equal strength; and how much more so when they are in an enemy's country and our walls are a counter-fortification![1] If they raise a fort in our territory, they may do damage to some part of our lands by sallies, and slaves may desert; but that will not prevent us from sailing to the Peloponnese and there building forts against them and defending them with our navy, which is our strong arm. For we have gained more experience of

fighting on land from warfare at sea than they of naval affairs from warfare on land. And they will not easily acquire the art of seamanship; even you yourselves, who have been practicing ever since the Persian War, are not yet perfect. How could they do much, when they are not sailors but tillers of the soil? They will not even be permitted to practice, because a large fleet of ours will constantly be lying in wait for them. If they were watched by a few ships only, they might run the risk, trusting to their numbers and forgetting their inexperience; but if they are kept off the sea by superior strength, their want of practice will make them less skillful, and therefore more timid. Seamanship involves as much professional skill as any other occupation; it cannot be cultivated by the way or at chance times, but, rather, excludes any competing activity.

143. "Suppose, again, that they lay hands on the treasures at Olympia and Delphi and seduce our foreign sailors with higher pay. There might be serious danger if we and our metics, embarking alone, were not still a match for them. But we are a match for them; and, best of all, our pilots and other officers are taken from our own citizens, and there are none so good or so numerous in all the rest of Hellas. And in the crisis none of our foreign sailors would choose to fight on their side for the sake of a few days' high pay from them, when he will be an exile and will have less hope of victory.

"Such I conceive to be the position of the Peloponnesians. But we ourselves are free from the defects which I have noted in them, and we have other great advantages. If they attack our country by land, we shall attack theirs by sea; and the devastation of part of the Peloponnese will be very different thing from that of all Attica. For they, if they want fresh territory, must take it by arms; whereas we have abundance of land both in the islands and on the continent; such is the power which command of the sea gives. Reflect, if we were islanders, who would be more invulnerable? Let us form our plans as if we were, give up land and houses, but keep a watch over the city and the sea. We should not give battle to the Peloponnesians in irritation at the loss of our property, for they far outnumber us. If we conquer, we shall have to fight over again with as many more;[1] and if we fail, our allies, from whom we draw our strength, will also be lost to us; for they will not keep quiet if we are no longer capable of making war upon them. Do not mourn for houses and lands, but for men; it is men who acquire property, but property does not provide men. If I thought that you would listen to me, I would say to you, 'Go out yourselves, destroy your possessions, and prove to the Peloponnesians that you will not submit, simply to save them.'

144. "I have many other reasons for believing that you will come through, but you must not be extending your empire while you are at war, or bring upon yourselves dangers of your own choice. I am more afraid of our own mistakes than of our enemies' designs. But of all this, I will speak again when the time of action comes; for the present, let us send the ambassadors away with the answer: 'That we will not exclude the Megarians from the Agora and harbors if the Lacedæmonians will cease to expel foreigners, whether ourselves or our allies, from Sparta, for the treaty forbids the one no more than the other; that we will concede autonomy to the cities if they were autonomous when we made the treaty, as soon as the Lacedæmonians too restore to their allies an autonomy not merely convenient to them but in accord with the wishes of each city; also that we are willing to offer arbitration according to the treaty; and that we will not begin a war but defend ourselves if attacked. This answer will be just and befits the dignity of the city. We must be aware, however, that war is inevitable; and the more willing we are to accept this, the less hard will our enemies press us. Remember that the greatest honors are to be won by men and states where dangers are greatest. Certainly, when our fathers withstood the Persians, they had no such power as we have; what little they had they forsook: by policy rather than chance and audacity rather than strength, they repelled the barbarians and raised us to our present height of greatness. We must not be behind them, but resist our

enemies to the utmost so that we may hand down our empire unimpaired to posterity."

145. Pericles spoke in this way. The Athenians approved, voted as he told them, and on his motion answered the Lacedæmonians in detail as he had suggested, and on the whole question to the effect "that they would do nothing upon dictation, but were ready to settle their differences by arbitration upon fair terms, according to the treaty." So the ambassadors went home and no more came.

146. These were the grievances and differences on either side before the war began, originating from the affairs of Epidamnus and Corcyra. But the contending parties still kept up intercourse and visited each other, without a herald,[1] though without entire confidence. For what was happening tended to nullify the treaty and to supply an excuse for war.

BOOK II

The First Year of War (431 B.C.)

1. And now the war between the Athenians and Peloponnesians and the allies of both actually began. Henceforward, the struggle was uninterrupted, and they communicated with one another only by heralds. The narrative is arranged according to summers and winters and follows the order of events.

2. For fourteen years, the thirty years' peace which was concluded after the recovery of Eubœa remained unbroken. But in the fifteenth year, when Chrysis the high priestess of Argos was in the forty-eighth year of her priesthood, Ænesias was Ephor at Sparta, and Pythodorus had four months of his archonship to run at Athens, in the tenth month after the engagement at Potidæa, at the beginning of spring,[1] about the first watch of the night, an armed force of somewhat more than three hundred Thebans entered Platæa, a city of Bœotia, which was an ally of Athens, under the command of two Bœotarchs, Pythangelus the son of Phyleides, and Diemporus the son of Onetorides.[2] They were invited by Naucleides, a Platæan, and his partisans, who opened the gates to them. These men wanted to kill certain citizens of the opposite faction and to make over the city to the Thebans, in the hope of getting the power into their own hands. The intrigue had been conducted by Eurymachus the son of Leontiades, one of the chief citizens of Thebes. There was a perpetual quarrel between the two cities, and the Thebans, seeing that war was inevitable, were anxious to surprise the place while the peace lasted and before hostilities had actually broken out. This made it easier to enter the city unperceived; no watch had been set. They grounded their arms in the Agora; but instead of going to work at once and making their way into the houses of their enemies, as those who

invited them suggested, they resolved to issue conciliatory proclamations and try to bring over the city to a friendly agreement. The herald announced that if anyone wished to become their ally and return to the ancient constitution of Bœotia, he should join their ranks. In this way they thought that they would easily win over the city.

3. When the Platæans found that the Thebans were within their walls and that the city had been surprised and taken, they were panic-stricken. In the darkness they were unable to see the Thebans, and greatly overestimated their numbers. So they came to terms and, accepting the proposals which were made to them, remained quiet, the more readily since the Thebans offered violence to no one. But in the course of the negotiations, they somehow discovered that their enemies were not numerous, and concluded that they could easily attack and master them. They determined to make the attempt, for the commons at Platæa were strongly attached to the Athenian alliance. They began to collect inside the houses, breaking through the party walls so as not to be seen going along the streets; they raised barricades of wagons (without the beasts which drew them) and took other measures suitable to the emergency. When they had done all that could be done under the circumstances, they sallied forth from their houses, choosing the time of night just before daybreak, lest, if they put off the attack until dawn, the enemy might be more confident and more a match for them. While darkness lasted, they would be more alarmed and at a disadvantage, not knowing the streets so well as themselves. So they fell upon them at once hand to hand.

4. When the Thebans found that they had been deceived, they sought to close their ranks and repulse assaults wherever made. Two or three times they drove them back. But when at last the Platæans charged them, and the women and slaves on the housetops screamed and yelled and pelted them with stones and tiles, the great confusion, which was aggravated by rain that came on heavily during the night, caused a panic; and they turned and fled through the city. Hardly any of them knew the way out, and the streets were dark as well

as muddy, for the affair happened at the end of the month; whereas their pursuers knew well enough how to prevent their escape, and thus many of them perished. The gates by which they entered were the only ones open, and a Platæan fastened them with the spike of a javelin, which he thrust into the bar instead of the pin. So this exit too was closed, and they were chased up and down the city. Some of them mounted upon the wall and threw themselves down into the open. Most of these were killed. Others found a deserted gate; a woman gave them an axe; and while no one was looking, they cut through the bar, but only a few escaped, for they were soon found out. Others scattered in different parts of the city, and perished. But the greater number, who had kept the closest formation, took refuge in a large building abutting upon the wall of which the doors on the near side chanced to be open, thinking them to be the gates of the city and expecting to find a way through them into the country. The Platæans, seeing that they were in a trap, began to consider whether they should set the building on fire and burn them where they were, or adopt some other course. At last they and the other Thebans who were still alive, wandering about the city, agreed to surrender themselves and their arms unconditionally.

5. While the Thebans in Platæa had met with this fate, the main body of the Theban army, which should have come during the night to the support of the party entering the city in case of a reverse and who had heard on their march what had occurred, were coming to the rescue. Platæa is about eight miles from Thebes, and the rain which had fallen in the night delayed their arrival, for the river Asopus had swollen and was not easily fordable. Marching in the rain, and having difficulty crossing the river, they came up too late; some of their friends were already dead and the others captives. When the Thebans became aware of the state of affairs, they resolved to lay hands on the Platæans outside the walls; for there were men and property left in the fields, as would naturally happen when an unexpected blow was struck in time of peace. They meant to keep anyone whom they caught as hostages for their own men, if

any of them were still alive. But before they had executed their plan, the Platæans, suspecting their intentions and fearing for their people outside, sent a herald to the Thebans protesting against the impiety of which they had been guilty in trying to seize their city during peace and warning them to do no wrong to those outside the walls. If they persisted, they threatened, in return, to kill the prisoners; but if they retired, they would give them up. This is the Theban account, and they add that the Platæans took an oath. The Platæans do not admit that they ever promised to restore the captives at once, but only if they could agree after negotiations; and they deny that they took an oath. However this may have been, the Thebans withdrew, leaving the Platæan territory unhurt; but the Platæans had no sooner got in their property from the country than they put the men to death. The prisoners numbered a hundred and eighty, and Eurymachus, with whom the betrayers of the city had negotiated, was one of them.

6. When they had done this, they sent a messenger to Athens and gave back the dead to the Thebans under a flag of truce; they then took the measures in the city which they thought the circumstances required. The news had already reached Athens, and the Athenians had instantly seized any Bœotians in Attica and sent a herald to Platæa, bidding them do no violence to the Theban prisoners, but wait till the Athenians considered their fate. The news of their death had not arrived, as the first messenger had gone out when the Thebans entered, and the second, when they were just defeated and captured; but of what followed the Athenians knew nothing; they sent the message in ignorance, and the herald found the prisoners dead when he arrived. The Athenians next dispatched an army to Platæa, and brought in grain and left a garrison. They conveyed away the least serviceable of the men, together with the women and children.

7. The affair of Platæa was a glaring violation of the thirty years' truce, and the Athenians now made preparations for war. The Lacedæmonians and their allies made similar preparations. Both they and the Athenians meditated sending embassies to the Persian king and to other

barbarians from whom either party might hope to obtain aid; they also sought the alliance of independent cities outside their own dominion. The Lacedæmonians ordered their friends in Italy and Sicily to build ships in number proportioned to the size of their cities, to add to those they had in the Peloponnese; for they intended to raise their navy to a total of five hundred.[1] They were also required to furnish a fixed sum of money; they were not to receive more than one ship of the Athenians at a time but were to take no further measures until these preparations had been completed. The Athenians reviewed their existing confederacy and sent ambassadors chiefly to the places immediately adjacent to the Peloponnese—Corcyra, Cephallenia, Acarnania, and Zacynthus. They saw that if they could only rely upon the firm friendship of these states, they might encircle and reduce the Peloponnese.

8. Both sides entertained great plans; they were both full of enthusiasm for war: and no wonder, for all men are more energetic at the start. At that time the young men were numerous in the Peloponnese and at Athens; they had never seen war and were therefore very willing to take up arms. All Hellas was excited by the coming conflict between the two chief cities. Many prophecies were circulated and many oracles chanted by diviners in the cities about to engage in the struggle and in the rest. Quite recently, the island of Delos had been shaken by an earthquake for the first time within the memory of the Hellenes; this was interpreted and generally believed to be a sign of coming events. And everything of the sort which occurred was investigated.

Men were far more favorable to the Lacedæmonians, especially as they professed to be the liberators of Hellas. Cities and individuals were eager to assist them to the utmost, both by word and deed; and everyone thought that all progress had ended whenever he was not to be present himself. For the general indignation against the Athenians was intense; some were longing to be delivered from them, others fearful of falling under their rule.

9. Such were the preparations and sentiments with which they began. Their respective allies were as follows:

The Lacedæmonian confederacy included all the Peloponnesians inside the isthmus except the Argives and the Achæans—they were both neutral; only the Achæans of Pellene took the Lacedæmonian side at first; afterwards all the Achæans joined them. Beyond the Peloponnese, the Megarians, Bœotians, Locrians, Phocians, Ambraciots, Leucadians and Anactorians were their allies. Of these the Corinthians, Megarians, Sicyonians, Pellenians, Eleans, Ambraciots and Leucadians provided a navy; the Bœotians, Phocians, and Locrians, cavalry; the other states, only infantry. The allies of the Athenians were Chios, Lesbos, Platæa, the Messenians of Naupactus,[1] the greater part of Acarnania, Corcyra, Zacynthus, and other cities, which were tributary, among the following peoples: the maritime region of Caria, the adjacent Dorian peoples, Ionia, the Hellespont, the Thracian region, the islands that lie east of the Peloponnese and Crete, including all the Cyclades with the exception of Melos and Thera. Chios, Lesbos and Corcyra furnished a navy; the rest, land forces and money. So much concerning the two confederacies and their resources for war.

10. Immediately after the affair at Platæa, the Lacedæmonians sent round to their Peloponnesian and other allies, bidding them equip troops and provide the supplies necessary for a foreign expedition, with the object of invading Attica. When the various states were ready, at the appointed time, with contingents numbering two-thirds of the forces of each, they met at the Isthmus. When the whole army was assembled, Archidamus, the king of the Lacedæmonians and the leader of the expedition, called together the generals and chief officers and most distinguished men of all the cities and gave them some such advice as follows:

11. "Peloponnesians and allies, our fathers made many expeditions both within and without the Peloponnese, and the older men here present are experienced in war: yet we never set out with a greater army than this. But then, whatever may be our numbers or our valor, we are now going against a most powerful city. We are then bound to show ourselves worthy of our fathers and not inferior to our own reputation. For all Hellas is stirred

by our enterprise, and her eyes are fixed upon us: she is friendly and would have us succeed from hatred of Athens. Now although some among you may think that because of our numbers there is very little risk of the enemy meeting us in the field, we ought not, on that account, to advance with less caution; but the general and the soldier of every state should be always expecting that his own division of the army will be in danger. War is carried on in the dark; attacks are generally sudden and furious; and often the smaller army, animated by a proper fear, has been more than a match for a larger force which was overconfident and taken unprepared. When invading an enemy's country, men should always show boldness in spirit, but in action preparedness prompted by fear; and thus they would be at once most courageous in attack and least vulnerable in defense.

"The city which we are attacking is not so utterly powerless against an invader but is in the best possible state of readiness, and for this reason our enemies may be quite expected to meet us in the field. Even if they have not marched out before our arrival, they may do so as soon as they see us in Attica, wasting and destroying their property. Invariably, when damage to which they are not accustomed is inflicted on men before their eyes, in the very moment of seeing it, they are transported by anger; the less they reflect, the more passionate they are to fight; above all men the Athenians are likely to act in this way, they who claim imperial power and are more disposed to invade and waste their neighbor's land than to look on while their own is being wasted. Remembering how great is this city which you are attacking, and how you will bring to your ancestors and yourselves the greatest of reputations for good or evil, according to the result, follow wherever you are led; maintain order and caution above everything, and be quick to obey the word of command. It is the noblest and safest thing for a great army to be visibly animated by unity and order."

12. After speaking to this effect, Archidamus dismissed the assembly. His first step was to send Melesippus the son of Diacritus, a Spartiate, to Athens in the hope that the Athenians might, after all, give way when they saw

their enemies actually on the march. But they would not admit him to the city or assembly. For Pericles had already carried a motion to the effect that they would not receive a herald or embassy while the Lacedæmonians were in the field. So Melesippus was sent away without a hearing and told that he must cross the frontier before sunset; if the Lacedæmonians wanted to send ambassadors to Athens, they must go home first. He was attended by an escort in order to prevent his communicating with anyone. When he arrived at the Athenian frontier and was about to leave them, he uttered these words: "This day will be the beginning of great evils for the Hellenes." On the return of the herald to the camp, Archidamus learned that the Athenians were not as yet at all in the mood to yield; so at last he moved forward his army and prepared to enter Attica. The Bœotians sent their contingent of two-thirds, including their cavalry, to the Peloponnesian army, marched to Platæa with the remainder of the forces and wasted the country.

13. While the Peloponnesians were gathering at the Isthmus and were still on their way, but before they entered Attica, Pericles the son of Xanthippus, who was one of the ten Athenian generals, knowing that the invasion was inevitable, and suspecting, because Archidamus happened to be his friend, that in wasting the country he might perhaps spare his lands, either in order to do him a personal favor or by the order of the Lacedæmonians, to raise a prejudice against him as when they demanded the expulsion of the polluted family,[1] openly declared in the assembly that Archidamus was his friend, but not to the injury of the state, and that, supposing the enemy did not destroy his lands and buildings like the rest, he would make a present of them to the public; and he desired that the Athenians should have no suspicion of him on that account. As to the present situation, he repeated his previous advice; they must prepare for war and bring their property from the country into the city; they must defend their walls but not go out to battle; they should also equip for service the fleet in which lay their strength. Their allies should be kept well in hand, for their power depended on the revenues which

they derived from them; military successes were generally gained by a wise policy and abundance of money. The state of their finances was encouraging; they had on an average 600 talents of tribute coming in annually from their allies, to say nothing of their other revenue;[2] and 6,000 talents of coined silver were still left in the Acropolis. (The whole amount had once been as much as 9,700 talents, but from this, expenditure had been incurred on various buildings, such as the Propylæa of the Acropolis, and on the siege of Potidæa.[3]) Moreover there was uncoined gold and silver in the form of private and public offerings, sacred implements used in processions and games, the Persian spoils and other things of the same sort, worth at least 500 talents. Considerable treasures in various temples were also at their disposal. If they were reduced to the last extremity, they could even take off the plates of gold from the image of the goddess; these, as he pointed out, weighed 40 talents and were of refined gold, which was all removable. They might use this treasure in self-defense, but they were bound to replace all that they had taken. By this estimate of their wealth, he strove to encourage them. He added that they had 13,000 hoplites, besides the 16,000 who occupied the fortresses or who manned the walls of the city. For this was the number engaged on garrison duty whenever the enemy invaded Attica; they were made up of the elder and younger men and of the metics who were hoplites.[4] (The Phaleric wall extended 35 stades from Phalerum to the city walls; the portion of the city wall which was guarded was somewhat less than 43, that between the Long Wall and the Phaleric requiring no guard. The Long Walls[5] running down to the Piræus were 40 stades in length; the outer only was guarded. The whole circuit of the Piræus and of Munychia was 60 stades, of which half required a guard.) The Athenian cavalry, so Pericles pointed out, numbered 1,200, including mounted archers; the foot archers, 1,600; of triremes fit for service the city had 300. The forces of various kinds which Athens possessed at the commencement of the war, when the first Peloponnesian invasion was impending, cannot be estimated at less. To these Pericles added other arguments, such as he was fond of using, to prove that they would win through in the war.

14. The citizens were persuaded, and brought into the city their children and wives, their household goods, and even the woodwork of their houses, which they stripped off. Their flocks and beasts of burden they conveyed to Eubœa and the adjacent islands.

15. The removal of the inhabitants was painful; for the majority had always been accustomed to reside in the country. Such a life had been characteristic of them, more than of any other Hellenic people, from very early times.[1] In the days of Cecrops and the first kings, down to the reign of Theseus, Attica was divided into cities with their own town halls and magistrates. Except in case of alarm, the whole people did not assemble in council under the king; but each community administered its own affairs and deliberated separately. Some of them at times even went to war with him, as the Eleusinians under Eumolpus with Erechtheus. But when Theseus, a powerful as well as a shrewd ruler, came to the throne, among other improvements in the organization of the country, he put an end to the councils and magistracies of the other cities and united all the inhabitants of Attica in the present city, establishing one council and town hall. They continued to live on their own lands, but he compelled them to resort to Athens as their one and only city. As all now belonged to Athens, a great state arose which was handed down by Theseus to his descendants; and from his day to this, the Athenians have regularly celebrated the public festival of the Synœcia,[2] in honor of the goddess Athenè.

Before his time, what is now the Acropolis and the ground lying under it to the south was the city. The evidence is this: The temples of Athenè and of other divinities are situated in the Acropolis itself, and those which are not lie chiefly thereabouts; the temples of Olympian Zeus, for example, and Pythian Apollo, and the temples of Earth and Dionysus in the Marshes, in honor of whom the more ancient Dionysia are celebrated on the twelfth day of the month Anthesterion, a festival which is also still observed by the Ionian descendants of the Athenians. In the same quarter are other ancient temples; and not far off is the fountain now called Enneacrounos from the form given to it by the tyrants,[3] but originally, before the springs were covered in, Callirrhoè. The water of this fountain was used by the ancient Athenians on great occasions, and before marriages and at other ceremonies the old custom is still retained. To this day, the Acropolis is called by the Athenians *Polis* because that neighborhood was first inhabited.[4]

Thus, for a long time the ancient Athenians enjoyed a country life in self-governing communities; and after they were united, they and their descendants, down to the time of this war, from old habit generally resided with their households in the country, where they had been born. For this reason, and also because they had recently restored their properties after the Persian War, they were disinclined to move. They were depressed and discontented at forsaking their homes and the temples which had always been their hereditary shrines from the time of the old political order. They were going to change their manner of life, and in fact each of them was leaving his own city.

17. When they came to Athens, only a few of them had houses or could find homes among friends or kindred. The majority lived in the vacant spaces of the city, and in all the temples and shrines of heroes, with the exception of those on the Acropolis, the Eleusinium, and any other precinct which was securely closed. The Pelasgian ground, as it was called, which lay at the foot of the citadel, was under a curse forbidding its occupation. There was also a half-line of a Delphic oracle to the this effect: "Better the Pelasgian ground left waste." Yet even this was filled under the sudden necessity. And to my mind the oracle came true in a sense exactly contrary to the popular expectation; for the unlawful occupation to which men were driven was not the cause of the city's calamities, but the occupation was a necessity because of the war; and the oracle, without mentioning the war, foresaw that the place would be inhabited some day for no good.[1] Many also established themselves in the tur-

rets of the walls or in any other place that they could find; for the city could not contain them when they first came in. But afterwards they divided among them the Long Walls and the greater part of the Piræus. At the same time, the Athenians applied themselves to the war, summoning their allies and preparing an expedition of a hundred ships against the Peloponnese.

18. While they were thus engaged, the Peloponnesian army was advancing: it arrived first of all at Œnoè, a fortress on the border of Attica and Bœotia, which was garrisoned by the Athenians whenever war broke out and was the point at which the Peloponnesians intended to enter the enemy's country. There they settled down and prepared to assault the walls with engines and by other means. But these and other measures took up time and detained them in the neighborhood. Archidamus was most blamed for the delay; he was also thought to have been slack in organizing the war and to have done the Athenians good service by discouraging vigorous action. After the muster of the forces, he had been accused of delay at the Isthmus and of loitering on the march. But his reputation was most affected by his halt at Œnoè. For the Athenians employed the interval in getting in their property; and the Peloponnesians thought if they had advanced quickly and he had not lingered, they could have seized everything before it was conveyed within the walls. Such was the anger felt for Archidamus by his troops during the halt. He is said to have held back in the belief that the Athenians, while their lands were still unravaged, would yield and shrink from allowing them to be devastated.

19. But when they had assaulted Œnoè, and, after leaving no means untried, were unable to take it, and no herald came from the Athenians, at last they marched on; and about the eightieth day after the entry of the Thebans into Platæa, in the summer, when the corn was in full ear, they invaded Attica, under the command of Archidamus the son of Zeuxidamus, the Lacedæmonian king. They settled down and ravaged, first of all, Eleusis and the plain of Thria, where they put to flight some Athenian horse near the streams called Rheiti;

they then advanced, keeping Mount Ægaleus on the right hand, through the district of Cropia until they reached Acharnæ, the largest of the Athenian demes,[1] as they are called; and at Acharnæ they settled down, built a camp and remained a considerable time, ravaging the country.

20. Archidamus is said to have had the following plan in lingering around Acharnæ with his army ready for battle, instead of descending into the plain during this invasion: he hoped that the Athenians, who were now flourishing with a large population of young men and provided for war as they had never been before, would perhaps meet them in the field rather than allow their lands to be ravaged. When, therefore, they did not appear at Eleusis or in the plain of Thria, he tried once more, by settling in the neighborhood of Acharnæ, to induce them to come out. The situation appeared to be convenient for a camp, and the Acharnians, a considerable section of the city who furnished three thousand hoplites,[1] were likely to be impatient at the destruction of their property, and would impel the whole people to fight. Or if the Athenians did not come out to meet him during this invasion, he could henceforward ravage the plain with more security, and march right up to the city. After losing their own possessions, the Acharnians would be less enthusiastic to hazard their lives for the land of the rest; and so there would be a division in the Athenian counsels. Such was the plan of Archidamus in remaining at Acharnæ.

21. So long as the Lacedæmonians were in the neighborhood of Eleusis and the plain of Thria, the Athenians had some hope that they would come no closer. They remembered how, fourteen years before, the Lacedæmonian king, Pleistoanax the son of Pausanias, invaded Attica with a Peloponnesian army, and how after advancing as far as Eleusis and Thria, he came no further but retreated. And indeed this retreat was the cause of his exile, for he was thought to have been bribed. But when they saw the army in the neighborhood of Acharnæ, sixty stades from the city, they felt it was now intolerable. The devastation of their country before their eyes,

which the younger men had never seen at all, nor the older except in the Persian invasion,[1] naturally appeared terrible to them; and the whole people, the young men especially, were anxious to go out and put a stop to it. Knots were formed in the streets; and there were loud disputes, some eager to go out, a minority resisting. Soothsayers were repeating oracles of all kinds, which different people eagerly listened to. The Acharnians, who in their own estimation were an important part of the Athenian state, seeing their land ravaged, were most insistent that they should go out and fight. The city was thoroughly roused; the people were furious with Pericles; and, forgetting all his previous warnings, they abused him for not leading them to battle, as their general, and laid all their miseries to his charge.

22. Pericles, seeing that they were overcome by the irritation of the moment and not showing the best sense, and confident that he was right in refusing to go out, would not summon an assembly or meeting of any kind;[1] if they came together, they might take some false step, prompted by anger rather than policy. He protected the city and took as little action as he could. However, he sent out horsemen continuously to prevent flying parties from the army making incursions into the fields near the city and doing damage.

[*The Peloponnesians left Attica when their provisions were exhausted. Somewhat earlier, the Athenians sent a hundred ships which ravaged some coastal districts of the Peloponnese and won over places in northwest Greece. They also expelled the hostile population of Ægina and settled colonists there. Other minor operations are recorded. The year ended with a public funeral for Athenians killed in the war. Pericles' speech on this occasion is rightly the most famous part of the whole history. In the editor's view it is largely a free composition by the historian, which follows only the general scheme of the real speech; written much later; it is intended to illustrate further the qualities which enabled Athens to hold out so long (cf. I:70) and the ideals of imperial Athens (cf. II:64).*]

34. During the same winter, in accordance with traditional custom, the funeral of those who first fell in this war was celebrated by the Athenians at the public charge. The ceremony is as follows: Three days before the celebration they erect a tent in which the bones of the dead are laid out,[1] and every one brings to his own dead any offering which he pleases. At the time of the funeral, the bones are placed in chests of cypress wood, which are conveyed on hearses; there is one chest for each tribe.[2] They also carry a single empty litter decked with a pall for all whose bodies had not been found and recovered. The procession is accompanied by anyone who chooses, whether citizen or foreigner; and the female relatives of the deceased are present at the funeral and make lamentation. The public sepulcher is situated in the most beautiful suburb of the city; there they always bury those who fall in war; only after the battle of Marathon, in recognition of their pre-eminent valor, the dead were interred on the field. When the remains have been laid in the earth, a man, chosen by the city for his reputed sagacity of judgment and eminent prestige, delivers the appropriate eulogy over them; after which the people depart. This is the manner of interment, and the ceremony was repeated from time to time throughout the war. Over the first who were buried, Pericles was chosen to speak. At the fitting moment he advanced from the sepulcher to a lofty stage, which had been erected in order that he might be heard as far away as possible by the crowd, and spoke somewhat as follows:

35. "Most of those who have spoken here before me commend the lawgiver who added this oration to our other funeral customs, thinking it right for an oration to be delivered at the funeral of those killed in wars. But I would have thought it enough that when men have been brave in action, they should also be publicly honored in action, and with such a ceremony as this state funeral, which you are now witnessing. Then the reputation of many would not have been imperiled by one man and their merits believed or not, as he speaks well

or ill. For it is difficult to say neither too little nor too much when belief in the truth is hard to confirm. The friend of the dead who knows the facts may well think that the words of the speaker fall short of his wishes and knowledge; another who is not well informed, when he hears of anything which surpasses his own nature, may be envious and suspect exaggeration. Mankind is tolerant of the praises of others so long as each hearer thinks himself capable of doing anything he has heard; but when the speaker rises above this, jealousy and incredulity are at once aroused. However, since our ancestors have set the seal of their approval upon the practice, I must obey the law and, to the utmost of my power, endeavour to satisfy the wishes and beliefs of you all.

36. "I will speak of our ancestors first, for it is right and seemly that on such an occasion as this we should also render this honor to their memory. Men of the same stock, ever dwelling in this land,[1] in successive generations to this very day, by their valor handed it down as a free land. They are worthy of praise, and still more are our fathers, who added to their inheritance, and after many a struggle bequeathed to us, their sons, the great empire we possess. Most of it those of our own number who are still in the settled time of life have strengthened further and have richly endowed our city in every way and made her most self-sufficient for both peace and war. Of the military exploits by which our various possessions were acquired or of the energy with which we or our fathers resisted the onslaught of barbarians or Hellenes I will not speak, for the tale would be long and is familiar to you. But before I praise the dead, I shall first proceed to show by what kind of practices we attained to our position, and under what kind of institutions and manner of life our empire became great. For I conceive that it would not be unsuited to the occasion that this should be told, and that this whole assembly of citizens and foreigners may profitably listen to it.

37. "Our institutions do not emulate the laws of others. We do not copy our neighbors: rather, we are an example to them. Our system is called a democracy, for it re-

spects the majority and not the few; but while the law secures equality to all alike in their private disputes, the claim of excellence is also recognized; and when a citizen is in any way distinguished, he is generally preferred to the public service, not in rotation, but for merit. Nor again is there any bar in poverty and obscurity of rank to a man who can do the state some service. It is as free men that we conduct our public life, and in our daily occupations we avoid mutual suspicions; we are not angry with our neighbor if he does what he likes; we do not put on sour looks at him which, though harmless, are not pleasant. While we give no offense in our private intercourse, in our public acts we are prevented from doing wrong by fear; we respect the authorities and the laws, especially those which are ordained for the protection of the injured as well as those unwritten laws which bring upon the transgressor admitted dishonor.

38. "Furthermore, none have provided more relaxations for the spirit from toil; we have regular games and sacrifices throughout the year; our homes are furnished with elegance; and the delight which we daily feel in all these things banishes melancholy. Because of the greatness of our city, the fruits of the whole earth flow in upon us so that we enjoy the goods of other countries as freely as our own.

39. "Then, again, in military training we are superior to our adversaries, as I shall show. Our city is thrown open to the world, and we never expel a foreigner[1] or prevent him from seeing or learning anything which, if not concealed, it might profit an enemy to see. We rely not so much upon preparations or stratagems, as upon our own courage in action. And in the matter of education, whereas from early youth they are always undergoing laborious exercises which are to make them brave, we live at ease and yet are equally ready to face perils to which our strength is equal. And here is the evidence. The Lacedæmonians march against our land not by themselves, but with all their allies: we invade a neighbor's country alone; and although our opponents are fighting for their homes and we are on a foreign soil, we seldom

have any difficulty in overcoming them. Our enemies have never yet felt our strength in full; the care of a navy divides our attention, and on land we are obliged to send our own citizens to many parts. But if they meet and defeat some part of our army, they boast of having routed us all, and when defeated, of having been vanquished by our whole force.

"If then we prefer to meet danger with a light heart but without laborious training[2] and with a courage which is instilled by habit more than by laws, we are the gainers; we do not anticipate the pain, although, when the hour comes, we show ourselves no less bold than those who never allow themselves to rest. Nor is this the only cause for marveling at our city. We are lovers of beauty without extravagance and of learning without loss of vigor. Wealth we employ less for talk and ostentation than when there is a real use for it. To avow poverty with us is no disgrace: the true disgrace is in doing nothing to avoid it. The same persons attend at once to the concerns of their households and of the city, and men of diverse employments have a very fair idea of politics. If a man takes no interest in public affairs, we alone do not commend him as quiet but condemn him as useless; and if few of us are originators, we are all sound judges of a policy. In our opinion action does not suffer from discussion but, rather, from the want of that instruction which is gained by discussion preparatory to the action required. For we have an exceptional gift of acting with audacity after calculating the prospects of our enterprises, whereas other men are bold from ignorance but hesitate upon reflection. But it would be right to esteem those men bravest in spirit who have the clearest understanding of the pains and pleasures of life and do not on that account shrink from danger. In doing good, again, we are unlike others; we make our friends by conferring, not by receiving favors. Now a man who confers a favor is the firmer friend because he would keep alive the memory of an obligation by kindness to the recipient; the man who owes an obligation is colder in his feelings because he knows that in requiting the service, he will not be winning gratitude but only paying a debt. We alone do good to our neighbors, not so much upon a calculation of interest, but in the fearless confidence of freedom.

41. "To sum up, I say that the whole city is an education for Hellas and that each individual in our society would seem to be capable of the greatest self-reliance and of the utmost dexterity and grace in the widest range of activities. This is no passing boast in a speech, but truth and fact, and verified by the actual power of the city which we have won by this way of life. For when put to the test, Athens alone among her contemporaries is superior to report. No enemy who comes against her is indignant at the reverses which he sustains at the hands of such men; no subject complains that his masters do not deserve to rule. And we shall assuredly not be without witnesses; there are mighty monuments of our power which will make us the wonder of this and of succeeding ages; we shall not need the praises of Homer or of any other whose poetry will please for the moment, but whose reconstruction of the facts the truth will damage. For we have compelled every land and sea to open a path to our daring and have everywhere planted eternal memorials of our triumphs and misfortunes. Such is the city these men fought and died for and nobly disdained to lose, and every one of us who survive would naturally wear himself out in her service.

42. "This is why I have dwelt upon the greatness of Athens, showing you that we are contending for a higher prize than those who enjoy no like advantages, and establishing by manifest proof the merit of these men whom I am now commemorating. Their loftiest praise has been already spoken; for in descanting on the city, I have honored the qualities which earned renown for them and for men such as they. And of how few Hellenes can it be said as of them, that their deeds matched their fame! In my belief an end such as theirs proves a man's worth; it is at once its first revelation and final seal. For even those who come short in other ways may justly plead the valor with which they have fought for their country; they have blotted out evil with good, and their public services have outweighed the harm they

have done in their private actions. None of these men were enervated by wealth or hesitated to resign the pleasures of life; none of them put off the evil day in the hope, natural to poverty, that a man, though poor, may yet become rich. But deeming that vengeance on their enemies was sweeter than any of these things and that they could hazard their lives in no nobler cause, they accepted the risk and resolved on revenge in preference to every other aim. They resigned to hope the obscure chance of success, but in the danger already visible they thought it right to act in reliance upon themselves alone. And when the moment for fighting came, they held it nobler to suffer death than to yield and save their lives; it was the report of dishonor from which they fled, but on the battlefield their feet stood fast; and while for a moment they were in the hands of fortune, at the height, less of terror than of glory, they departed.

43. "Such was the conduct of these men; they were worthy of Athens. The rest of us must pray for a safer issue to our courage and yet disdain to show any less daring towards our enemies. We must not consider only what words can be uttered on the utility of such a spirit. Anyone might discourse to you at length on all the advantages of resisting the enemy bravely, but you know them just as well yourselves. It is better that you should actually gaze day by day on the power of the city until you are filled with the love of her; and when you are convinced of her greatness, reflect that it was acquired by men of daring who knew their duty and feared dishonor in the hour of action, men who if they ever failed in an enterprise, even then disdained to deprive the city of their prowess but offered themselves up as the finest contribution to the common cause.[1] All alike gave their lives and received praise which grows not old and the most conspicuous of sepulchers—I speak not so much of that in which their remains are laid as of that in which their glory survives to be remembered forever, on every fitting occasion in word and deed. For every land is a sepulcher for famous men; not only are they commemorated by inscriptions on monuments in their

own country, but even in foreign lands there dwells an unwritten memorial of them, graven not so much on stone as in the hearts of men. Make them your examples now; and, esteeming courage to be freedom and freedom to be happiness, do not weigh too nicely the perils of war. It is not the unfortunate men with no hope of blessing, who would with best reason be unsparing of their lives, but the prosperous, who, if they survive, are always in danger of a change for the worse, and whose situation would be most transformed by any reverse. To a man of spirit it is more painful to be oppressed like a weakling than in the consciousness of strength and common hopes to meet a death that comes unfelt.

44. "Therefore I do not now commiserate the parents of the dead who stand here; I shall rather comfort them. They know that their life has been passed amid manifold vicissitudes and that those men may be deemed fortunate who have gained most honor, whether an honorable death, like the men we bury here, or an honorable sorrow like yours, and whose days have been so measured that the term of their happiness is likewise the term of their life. I know how hard it is to make you feel this when the good fortune of others will often remind you of the happiness in which you, like them, once rejoiced. Sorrow is felt at the want not of those blessings which a man never knew, but of those which were a part of his life before they were taken from him. Some of you are of an age at which you may have other children, and that hope should make you bear your sorrow better; not only will the children who may hereafter be born make you forget those you have lost, but the city will be doubly a gainer; she will not be left desolate, and she will be safer. For a man's counsel cannot have equal weight or worth when he has no children like the rest to risk in the general danger. To those of you who have passed their prime, I say: 'Congratulate yourselves that you have been happy during the greater part of your days; remember that what remains will not last long, and let it be lightened by the glory of these men.' For only the love of honor is ever young; and it is not so

much profit, as some say, but honor which is the delight of men when they are old and useless.

45. "To you who are the sons and brothers of the departed, I see that the struggle to emulate them will be arduous. For all men praise the dead; and, however preeminent your virtue may be, you would hardly be thought their equals, but somewhat inferior. The living have their rivals and detractors; but when a man is out of the way, the honor and good will which he receives is uncontested. And, if I am also to speak of womanly virtues to those of you who will now be widows, let me sum them up in one short admonition: 'Your glory will be great if you show no more than the infirmities of your nature, a glory that consists in being least the subjects of report among men, for good or evil.'

46. "I have spoken in obedience to the law, making use of such fitting words as I had. The tribute of deeds has been paid in part, for the dead have been honorably interred; it remains only that their children shall be maintained at the public charge until they are grown up: this is the solid prize with which, as with a garland, Athens crowns these men and those left behind after such contests. For where the rewards of virtue are greatest, there men do the greatest services to their cities. And now, when you have duly lamented, everyone his own dead, you may depart."

Such was the order of the funeral celebrated in this winter, with the end of which ended the first year of this war.

The Plague

47. As soon as summer returned (430), the Peloponnesians and allies, as before with two-thirds of their forces, under the command of the Lacedæmonian king Archidamus the son of Zeuxidamus, invaded Attica, where they established themselves and ravaged the country. They had not been there many days when the plague broke out at Athens for the first time. It is said to have previously smitten many places, particularly Lemnos; but there is no record of so great a pestilence occurring else-

where, or of so great a destruction of human life. For a while physicians sought to apply remedies in ignorance, but it was in vain, and they themselves were most prone to perish because they came into most frequent contact with it. No other human art was of any avail; and as to supplications in temples, inquiries of oracles, and the like, they were all useless; and at last men were overpowered by the calamity and gave them all up.

48. The disease is said to have begun south of Egypt in Ethiopia; from there it descended into Egypt and Libya; and after spreading over the greater part of the Persian empire, suddenly fell upon Athens. It first attacked the inhabitants of the Piræus so that it was actually said by them that the Peloponnesians had poisoned the cisterns; no fountains as yet existed there. It afterwards reached the upper city, and then the mortality became far greater. Every man, physician or layman, may declare his own judgment about its probable origin and the causes he thinks sufficient to have produced so great a vicissitude: I shall speak of its actual course and the features by which men may acquire some foreknowledge and be most apt to recognize it, should it ever reappear. I shall describe these clearly as one who was myself attacked, and witnessed the sufferings of others.[1]

49. The season was universally admitted to have been remarkably free from other sicknesses; and if anybody was already ill of any other disease, it finally turned into this. The other victims who were in perfect health, all in a moment and without any exciting cause, were seized first with violent heats in the head and with redness and burning of the eyes. Internally, the throat and the tongue at once became blood-red, and the breath abnormal and fetid. Sneezing and hoarseness followed; in a short time the disorder, accompanied by a violent cough, reached the chest. And whenever it settled in the heart, it upset it; and there were all the vomits of bile to which physicians have ever given names, and they were accompanied by great distress. An ineffectual retching, producing violent convulsions, attacked most of the sufferers; some, as soon as the previous symptoms had abated, others, not until long afterwards. The body externally was not so

very hot to the touch, not yellowish but flushed and livid and breaking out in blisters and ulcers. But the internal fever was intense; the sufferers could not bear to have on them even the lightest linen garment; they insisted on being naked, and there was nothing which they longed for more eagerly than to throw themselves into cold water; many of those who had no one to look after them actually plunged into the cisterns. They were tormented by unceasing thirst, which was not in the least assuaged whether they drank much or little. They could find no way of resting, and sleeplessness attacked them throughout. While the disease was at its height, the body, instead of wasting away, held out amid these sufferings unexpectedly. Thus, most died on the seventh or ninth day of internal fever, though their strength was not exhausted; or, if they survived, then the disease descended into the bowels and there produced violent lesions; at the same time diarrhea set in which was uniformly fluid, and at a later stage caused exhaustion, and this finally carried them off with few exceptions. For the disorder which had originally settled in the head passed gradually through the whole body and, if a person got over the worst, would often seize the extremities and leave its mark, attacking the privy parts, fingers and toes; and many escaped with the loss of these, some with the loss of their eyes. Some again had no sooner recovered than they were seized with a total loss of memory and knew neither themselves nor their friends.

50. The character of the malady no words can describe, and the fury with which it fastened upon each sufferer was too much for human nature to endure. There was one circumstance in particular which distinguished it from ordinary diseases. Although so many bodies were lying unburied, the birds and animals which feed on human flesh either never came near them or died if they touched them. This is the evidence: there was a manifest disappearance of birds of prey, which were not to be seen either near the bodies or anywhere else; while in the case of the dogs, what happened was even more obvious because they live with man.

51. Such was the general nature of the disease: I

omit many strange peculiarities which variously characterized individual cases. None of the ordinary sicknesses attacked any one while it lasted, or if they did, they ended in the plague. Some died from want of care, but so did others who were receiving the greatest attention. No single remedy was established as a specific; for what did good to one did harm to another. No constitution was noticed of itself strong enough to resist or weak enough to escape the attacks; the disease carried off all alike and defied every mode of treatment. Most appalling was the despondency that seized upon anyone who felt himself sickening; for he instantly abandoned his mind to despair and, instead of holding out, was much more likely to throw away his chance of life. Equally appalling was the fact that men died like sheep, catching the infection if they attended on one another; and this was the principal cause of mortality. When they were afraid to visit one another, the sufferers died in solitude, so that many houses were empty because there had been no one to take care of the sick; or if they ventured, they perished, especially those who made any claim to be good men. Out of a sense of honor, they went to see their friends without thought of themselves at a time when their own relations were at last growing weary and ceasing even to make lamentations over the dead, overwhelmed by the vastness of the calamity. But more often the sick and the dying were tended by the pitying care of those who had recovered, because they knew the course of the disease and were themselves free from apprehension. For no one was ever attacked a second time, or not with a fatal result. All men congratulated them, and they themselves, in the excess of their joy at the moment, had an idle fancy that they could never die thereafter of any other sickness.

52. The crowding of the people out of the country into the city aggravated the misery, and the newly arrived suffered most. They had no houses of their own but inhabited stifling huts in the height of summer and perished in wild disorder. The dead and the dying lay one upon another, while others hardly alive rolled in the streets and around every fountain craving water. The

temples in which they lodged were full of the corpses of those who died in them; for the violence of the calamity was such that men, not knowing where to turn, grew reckless of all law, human and divine. The customs which had hitherto been observed at funerals were universally violated; and they buried their dead, each one as best he could. Many, for lack of what was proper because the deaths had been so numerous already, lost all shame in the burial of the dead. When one man had raised a funeral pile, others would come, put their own dead on it first and set fire to it; or when some other corpse was already burning, they would throw on top the body they brought and be off.

53. There were other and worse forms of lawlessness which the plague first introduced at Athens. Men who had hitherto concealed that they acted on the dictates of pleasure now grew bolder. They saw the rapid vicissitudes of fortune—how the rich died in a moment, and those who had nothing immediately inherited their property—reflected that life and riches were alike ephemeral, and thought it right to enjoy themselves without a pause and to think only of pleasure. None was eager to exert himself first for an honorable reputation when he esteemed it uncertain if he would not perish before securing it. The pleasure of the moment and everything which conduced to it was established as both honorable and expedient. No fear of gods or law of man deterred. Those who saw all perishing alike thought that the worship or neglect of the gods made no difference; and as for offenses against human law, no one expected to live long enough to be called to account and pay the penalty; already a far heavier sentence had been passed and was suspended over a man's head; before it fell, why should he not take a little pleasure?

54. Such was the calamity which now afflicted the Athenians; within the walls their people were dying, and without, their country was being ravaged. In their troubles they naturally called to mind a verse which the older men among them declared was current long ago: "A Dorian war will come and with it plague." There was a dispute about the word; some saying that *limos*,

a famine, and not *loimos,* a plague, was the original word. Nevertheless, as might have been expected, for men's memories reflected their sufferings, the argument in favor of *loimos* prevailed at the time. But if ever in future years they are in the grip of another Dorian war which happens to be accompanied by a famine, they will probably repeat the verse in the other form. The answer of the oracle to the Lacedæmonians when the god was askcd "whether they should go to war or not" and he replied "that if they fought with all their might, they would conquer, and that he himself would take their part" was not forgotten by those who had heard of it, and they quite imagined that they were witnessing the fulfillment of his words. The disease certainly did set in immediately after the invasion of the Peloponnesians and did not spread into the Peloponnese in any degree worth speaking of, while Athens felt its ravages most severely, and next to Athens, the places which were most populous. This was the history of the plague.[1]

55. After the Peloponnesians had wasted the plain, they entered what are called the coast lands and penetrated as far as Laurium, where the Athenians have their silver mines. First they ravaged the part of the coast which looks towards the Peloponnese and afterwards that situated towards Eubœa and Andros. But Pericles, who was general at this time too, continued to insist, as in the former invasion, that the Athenians should remain within their walls.

56. Before, however, the Peloponnesians had left the plain and moved forward into the coast lands, he had begun to equip an expedition of a hundred ships against the Peloponnese. When all was ready, he put to sea, having on board four thousand Athenian hoplites and three hundred cavalry, conveyed in horse transports which the Athenians then constructed for the first time out of their old ships. The Chians and Lesbians joined them with fifty vessels. The expedition did not actually put to sea until the Peloponnesians had reached the coast lands. Arriving at Epidaurus in Peloponnese, the Athenians devastated most of the country and attacked the city, which at one time they were in hopes of taking

but did not quite succeed.[1] Setting sail again, they ravaged the territory of Trœzen, Halieis, and Hermionè, all places on the coast of Peloponnese. They put off again and reached Prasiæ, a small town on the coast of Laconia, ravaged the country, and took and plundered the place. They then returned home and found that the Peloponnesians had also returned and were no longer in Attica.

57. All the time the Peloponnesians were in the country and the Athenians on their naval expedition the plague was raging both among the troops and in the city. The fear it inspired was said to have induced the enemy to leave Attica sooner than they intended; for they heard from deserters that the disease was in the city and also saw the burning of the dead. Still, in this invasion, they ravaged the whole country and remained about forty days, which was the longest stay they ever made. . . .

Pericles and His Successors

59. After the second Peloponnesian invasion, now that Attica had been once more ravaged, and war and plague together oppressed the Athenians, a change came over their spirit. They blamed Pericles because he had persuaded them to go to war, declaring that he was the author of their troubles; and they were anxious to come to terms with the Lacedæmonians. Accordingly, envoys were dispatched to Sparta, but they met with no success. Completely at their wits' end, they turned upon Pericles. He saw that they were exasperated by their situation and were behaving just as he had always anticipated that they would. As he was still general, he called an assembly, wanting to encourage them and to convert their angry feelings into a gentler and less fearful mood. At this assembly he came forward and spoke somewhat as follows:[1]

60. "I was expecting this outburst of anger against me, for I can see its causes. And I have summoned an assembly to remind you of your resolutions and reprove

you if you are wrong to display anger against me and want of tenacity in misfortune. In my judgment it is better for individuals themselves that the citizens should suffer and the state as a whole flourish than that the citizens should prosper singly and the state communally decline. A private man who thrives in his own business is involved in the common ruin of his country; but if he is unsuccessful in a prosperous city he is much more likely to be saved in the end. Seeing then that states can bear the misfortunes of individuals, but that no individual can bear the misfortunes of his state, let us all stand by our country and not do what you are doing now. Because you are stunned by your domestic calamities, you are abandoning the safety of the commonwealth and blaming not only me who advised the war but yourselves who consented to it. And yet what sort of man am I to provoke your anger? I believe that I am second to none in devising and explaining a sound policy, a lover of my country, and incorruptible. Now a man may have a policy which he does not clearly expound, and then he might as well have none at all; or he may possess both qualities but be disloyal to his country, and then he would not be so apt to speak in her interest; or again, though loyal, he may be unable to resist a bribe, and then all his other good qualities would be sold for money. If, when you determined to go to war, you even half-believed me to have somewhat more of the qualities required than others, it is not fair that I should now be charged with doing wrong.

61. "I allow that for men who are fortunate in other respects and free to choose it is great folly to make war. But when it is necessary either to yield and at once take orders from others or to hold out at the cost of danger, it is more blameworthy to shun the danger than to meet it. For my own part, I am unchanged and stand where I did. It is you who are changed; you repent in suffering of decisions you made when unhurt, and you think that my advice was wrong because your own judgment is impaired. The pain is present and comes home to each of you, but the good is as yet not manifest to any one; and your minds have not the strength to persevere in your

resolution, now that a great vicissitude has overtaken you unawares. Anything which is sudden and unexpected and utterly beyond calculation enthralls the spirit of a man. This is your condition, especially as the plague has come upon other hardships. Nevertheless, as the citizens of a great city, educated in a temper of greatness, you should not succumb even to the greatest calamities nor darken the luster of your fame. For men think it equally right to hate the presumption of those who claim a reputation to which they have no title and to condemn the faintheartedness of those who fall below the glory which is their own. You should put away your private sorrows and hold fast to the deliverance of the commonwealth.

62. "Perhaps you fear that the strain of the war may be very great and, after all, end in defeat. I have shown you already over and over again that this fear is groundless, and that should be enough. But I will make plain this further point. It seems to me that you yourselves have never reflected on one feature of your imperial greatness, which I too have never mentioned before; nor would I now, because the claim is rather arrogant, if I did not see that you are unreasonably panic-stricken. You think that your empire is confined to your allies; but I say that of the two divisions of the world plainly at man's service, the land and the sea, you are absolute masters of one, not only to the degree to which you now exercise mastery, but as widely as you please. Neither the great King nor any nation now on earth can hinder you with your naval resources from sailing where you choose. To this great power, the use of houses and lands, the loss of which seems so dreadful to you, is as nothing. We ought not to be troubled about them or to think much of them in comparison; they are only the garden of the house, the ornament of wealth; and you should realize that if we hold fast to our freedom and preserve it, we shall easily recover them, but that men who submit to others commonly lose all they have previously acquired. You must decide not to fall doubly short of your fathers. For they did not inherit the empire from others but won it by their exertions, and preserved it and bequeathed it to us. But to be robbed of what you

have is a greater disgrace than to be unfortunate in trying to acquire more. Meet your enemies therefore, not only with spirit, but with disdain. Even a coward may brag out of ignorance blessed by fortune, but a man can afford disdain when his confidence in his superiority over adversaries is grounded in judgment: that is our position. When luck is even, daring is rendered more reliable by intelligence and the sense of superiority it gives; intelligence trusts less to hope, the strength of men who have no other resource, than to judgment based on facts, from which is derived sounder foresight.

63. "It is reasonable for you to support the imperial dignity of your city in which you all take pride; you should not covet glory unless you will make exertions. And do not imagine that you are fighting about a simple issue, freedom or slavery; you have an empire to lose, and there is the danger to which the hatred of your imperial rule has exposed you. Neither can you any longer resign your power if, at this crisis, any timorous spirit is for playing the peace lover and the honest man. For by this time your empire has become a despotism, which it is thought unjust to acquire but unsafe to surrender. The men of whom I was speaking, if they could find followers, would soon ruin a city, and if they were to go and found a state of their own, would equally ruin that. The love of peace is secure only in association with the spirit of action; in an imperial city it is of no use, but it is suited to subjects who enjoy safety in servitude.

64. "You must not be led away by the advice of such citizens as these nor be angry with me, for the resolution in favor of war was your own as much as mine. What if the enemy had come and done what he was likely to do when you refused to submit? What too if the plague followed? That alone was an unexpected blow, but we might have foreseen all the rest. I am well aware that your hatred of me is aggravated by it, but how unjustly, unless you also ascribe to me the credit of any extraordinary success you may gain! The visitations of heaven should be borne as inevitable, the sufferings inflicted by the enemy with manliness. This has always

been the spirit of Athens, and should not die out in you now. You should recognize that our city has the greatest name in all the world because she does not yield to misfortunes, but has sacrificed more lives and endured severer hardships in war than any other; therefore she also has the greatest power of any state up to this day, and the memory of her glory will always survive. Even if we should some day weaken a little, for by nature all things decline—yet will the recollection live, that, of all Hellenes, we ruled over the greatest number of Hellenic subjects; that we withstood our enemies, whether single or united, in the most terrible wars; and that we were the inhabitants of a city endowed in every way with the most ample resources and greatness. The peace lover may indeed find fault, but every man of action will emulate us, and the powerless envy us. Hatred and unpopularity at the time have ever been the fate of those who have aspired to empire. But it is good judgment to accept odium in a great cause; hatred does not last long, and the brilliance of the moment and fame of afterdays remain forever in men's memories. Looking forward to future glory and present avoidance of dishonor, make the effort now to secure both. Send no more heralds to the Lacedæmonians, and do not betray to them that you are depressed by the present strain. For the greatest states and the greatest men are those which, when misfortunes come, are the least distressed in spirit and the most resolute in action."

65. By such words Pericles endeavored to appease the anger of the Athenians against himself, and to divert their minds from their terrible situation. In the conduct of public affairs they took his advice and sent no more embassies to Sparta but turned instead to prosecuting the war. Yet as individuals they felt their sufferings keenly; the common people had been deprived even of the little which they possessed, while the upper class had lost fine estates in the country with all their houses and rich furniture. Worst of all, instead of enjoying peace, they were now at war. The universal indignation was not pacified until they had fined Pericles;[1] but, soon afterwards, with the usual fickleness of the masses, they

elected him general and committed all their affairs to his charge. Their domestic sorrows were beginning to be less acutely felt, and for the needs of the city as a whole they thought that there was no man like him. During the peace while he was at the head of affairs, he showed moderation as a leader; he kept Athens safe, and she reached the height of her greatness in his time. When the war began he showed here too his foresight in estimating Athenian power. He survived two years and six months; and, after his death, his prescience regarding the war was even better appreciated. For he told the Athenians that if they were not restless, and would attend to their navy, and not seek to enlarge their dominion while the war was going on, nor imperil the existence of the city, they would come through; but they did all that he told them not to do; and in other matters which apparently had nothing to do with war, they adopted bad policies at home and in their empire because of private ambitions and private interests, policies whose success brought honor and profit chiefly to individuals, while their failure did harm to the city in the conduct of the war. The reason was that he was powerful in mind and public esteem and a man of most transparent integrity, and he controlled the people in a free spirit; he led them himself rather than followed them; for, not seeking power by dishonest practices, he did not speak to gratify the people, but, possessing power based on his high character, he would oppose them and even provoke their anger. Whenever he saw them inopportunely elated and arrogant, he would by his speeches strike them with fear and alarm; and when they were unreasonably apprehensive, he would reanimate their confidence. Thus Athens, though in name a democracy, was in fact coming to be ruled by her first citizen. But his successors were more on an equality with one another; as each was struggling to be first himself, they came to sacrifice the whole conduct of affairs to the gratification of the people. As was natural in a great and imperial city, this led to many errors, of which the greatest was the Sicilian expedition; here the chief error of policy did not lie so much in their decision to attack Sicily, but instead of consulting later for the interests of the expedition which they had sent out, they were occupied in private recriminations with a view to winning the leadership of the people, and not only hampered the operations of the army but became embroiled for the first time at home.[2] And yet after they had lost in the Sicilian expedition the greater part of their fleet, besides other resources, and were already distracted by revolution at home, still they held out eight[3] years, not only against their former enemies, but against the Sicilians who had combined with them, and against most of their own allies who had risen in revolt. Even when Cyrus, the son of the King, joined in the war and supplied the Peloponnesians with money to pay their fleet, they continued to resist and were at last overthrown only when they were ruined by their own internal dissensions. So that at the time Pericles was more than justified in the conviction at which his foresight had arrived, that the Athenians could very easily have the better of the unaided forces of the Peloponnesians.

Phormio's Naval Victories

[*The plague made Athens too weak to undertake an effective offensive for some years, though Potidæa was taken in the winter of 430, and a squadron of twenty ships was sent under Phormio to Naupactus to prevent enemy ships sailing into or out of the Corinthian gulf. In 429, instead of invading Attica, the Peloponnesians began the siege of Platæa, and a force was sent under Cnemus to attack Athens' allies in Acarnania, but was defeated at Stratus. The narrative which follows illustrates most clearly the superiority of the Athenians on the sea.*]

83. The fleet from Corinth and the other allied cities on the Crisæan Gulf, whose task was to support Cnemus and to prevent the Acarnanians on the seacoast from assisting those in the interior, never arrived, but was compelled, almost on the day of the battle of Stratus, to fight with Phormio and the twenty Athenian ships sta-

tioned at Naupactus. As they sailed by out of the gulf, Phormio was watching them, preferring to make his attack where there was plenty of searoom. Now the Corinthians and their allies were not equipped for a naval engagement but for the conveyance of troops into Acarnania, and they never imagined that the Athenians with twenty ships would venture to engage their own forty-seven. But, as they were coasting along the southern shore, they saw the Athenian fleet following their movements on the northern; they then attempted to cross the sea from Patræ in Achæa to the opposite continent in the direction of Acarnania when they again observed the enemy bearing down upon them from Chalcis and the mouth of the river Evenus. They had weighed anchor before it was light, but had been detected. So at last they were compelled to fight in the middle of the channel. The ships were commanded by generals of the cities which had furnished them; the Corinthian squadron by Machaon, Isocrates and Agatharchidas. The Peloponnesians arranged their ships in such a manner as to make the largest possible circle without leaving space to break through, turning their prows outwards and their sterns inwards; within the circle they placed the smaller craft which accompanied them and five of their fastest ships so that they might quickly row out at whatever point the enemy attacked.

84. The Athenians ranged their ships in line and sailed round and round the Peloponnesian fleet, which they drove into a narrower and narrower space, almost touching as they passed and leading the crews to suppose that they were on the point of ramming. But they had been warned by Phormio not to begin until he gave the signal; for he expected that the enemy's ships would not keep their formation, like a land army, but would run foul of one another; they would be embarrassed by the small craft, and if the usual morning breeze, for which he was waiting as he sailed round them, blew from the gulf, they would not be able to keep still for a moment. He thought that he could attack whenever he pleased because his ships were better sailers and that this would be the best time. When the breeze began to blow, the

ships, which were by this time crowded into a narrow space, were distressed at once by the force of the wind and by the small craft knocking up against them; ship dashed against ship, and they kept pushing one another away with long poles; there were cries of "keep off" and noisy abuse, so that nothing could be heard either of the word of command or of the coxswains' giving the time; and the difficulty which unpracticed rowers had in clearing the water in a heavy sea made the vessels disobedient to the helm. At that moment Phormio gave the signal; the Athenians attacked, began by sinking one of the admirals' vessels and then, wherever they went, disabled them; at last such was the disorder that no one any longer thought of resisting, but they fled to Patræ and Dymè in Achæa. The Athenians pursued them, captured twelve ships, and taking on board most of their crews, sailed away to Molycrium. They set up a trophy on Rhium; and after dedicating a ship to Poseidon there, retired to Naupactus. The Peloponnesians too, with the remainder of their fleet, proceeded quickly along the coast from Dymè and Patræa to Cyllenè, where the Eleans have their docks. Cnemus with the ships from Leucas, which should have joined them, arrived after the battle of Stratus at Cyllenè.

85. The Lacedæmonians at home now sent to the fleet three commissioners, Timocrates, Brasidas and Lycophron, to advise Cnemus. He was told that he must contrive to fight again and be more successful; he should not allow a few ships to keep him off the sea. The recent sea fight had been their first attempt, and seemed extremely unaccountable; they did not think that their own fleet was so inferior to that of the enemy but that there had been some cowardice, not considering that the Athenians were old sailors and that they were only beginners. So they despatched the commissioners in a rage. On their arrival they and Cnemus sent around to the allied cities for ships and equipped for action those which were on the spot. Phormio too sent home messengers to Athens to announce the victory and to inform the Athenians of the preparations which the enemy were making. He told them to send him immediately as large a reinforcement

as possible, as each day he was in constant expectation of a sea battle. They sent him twenty ships but ordered the commander of them to go to Crete first; for Nicias of Gortyn in Crete, who was the proxenus of the Athenians, had induced them to send a fleet against Cydonia, a hostile town which he promised to reduce. But he really invited them to please the Polichnitæ, who are neighbors of the Cydoniatæ. So the Athenian commander took the ships, went to Crete and joined the Polichnitæ in ravaging the lands of the Cydoniatæ; there, owing to bad weather, a considerable time was wasted.

86. While the Athenians were detained in Crete, the Peloponnesians at Cyllenè, equipped for a naval engagement, coasted along to Panormus in Achæa, where the Peloponnesian army had gone to co-operate with them. Phormio also coasted along to Molycrian Rhium and anchored outside the gulf with the twenty ships which had fought in the previous engagement. This Rhium was friendly to the Athenians; there is another Rhium on the opposite coast in Peloponnese; the space between them, about seven stades by sea, forms the mouth of the Crisæan Gulf. It was in Achæan Rhium that the Peloponnesians were anchored with seventy-seven ships, not far from Panormus where their land forces were stationed, when they saw the Athenians. For six or seven days the two fleets lay opposite one another and were busy in practicing and getting ready for the engagement. The Peloponnesians were resolved not to sail into the broad waters beyond the Rhiums, fearing a recurrence of their disaster; the Athenians, not to sail into the strait, thinking that the confined space was favorable to their enemies. At length, Cnemus, Brasidas and the other Peloponnesian generals determined to bring on an engagement at once and not wait until the Athenians too received their reinforcements. So they assembled their soldiers and, seeing that they were generally dispirited at their former defeat and reluctant to fight, encouraged them with such words as these:

87. "The late sea fight, Peloponnesians, may have made some of you anxious about the one which is impending; but it really affords no just ground for alarm. In that

battle we were, as you know, ill-prepared; and our whole expedition had a military rather than a naval object. Fortune was in many ways unpropitious to us; and as this was our first sea fight, we may possibly have suffered a little from inexperience. The defeat which ensued was not due to cowardice. Our spirit was not then mastered and beaten; it has an inherent quality which challenges the result, and it is not right that it should lose its edge from the accident which has occurred. You ought to think that though fortune may sometimes bring reverses, yet the spirit of brave men may rightly remain the same, and while they retain their courage, it would not be fair for them to make inexperience an excuse on any occasion for turning cowards. And whatever be your own inexperience, it is more than compensated by your superiority in daring. The skill of your enemies which you chiefly dread, if united with courage, may be able in the moment of danger to remember and execute the lesson which it has learned; but without courage no technique gives strength in the face of dangers. For fear makes men forget, and technique is useless to the fainthearted. And therefore against their greater experience, set your own greater daring; and against the alarm resulting from your defeat, set the fact that you were then unprepared. But now you have the advantages of a large fleet and of fighting close to a friendly shore guarded by hoplites. Victory is generally on the side of those who are more numerous and better equipped. So that we have absolutely no reason for anticipating failure. Even our former mistakes will be an additional advantage because they will be a lesson to us. Be of good courage, then, and let every one of you, pilot or sailor, do his own duty and maintain the post assigned to him. We will order the attack rather better than your old commanders, and so give nobody an excuse for cowardice. But, if any one should be inclined to waver, he shall be punished as he deserves, while the brave shall be honored with the due rewards of their valor."

88. Such were the words of encouragement addressed to the Peloponnesians by their commanders. Phormio too, fearing that his sailors might be frightened and observ-

ing that they were gathering in knots and were apprehensive of the enemy's numbers, resolved to call them together and inspire them by suitable encouragement. He had always been in the habit of telling them and training their minds to believe that no superiority of hostile forces could justify them in retreating. And it had long been the pride of the sailors themselves that, as Athenians, they were bound to face any number of Peloponnesian ships. When, however, he found them dispirited by the sight which met their eyes, he determined to remind them of their old confidence; and after assembling them together, he spoke somewhat as follows:

89. "Soldiers, I have summoned you because I see that you are alarmed at the numbers of the enemy, and I would not have you dismayed when there is nothing to fear. In the first place, the reason why they have provided a fleet so disproportionate is because we have defeated them already, and they do not think themselves a match for us; next, as to the courage which they claim as their special quality and on which they chiefly base their confidence in attacking us, their boldness is merely inspired by the success which their experience on land usually gives them, and will, as they think, equally ensure them by sea. But the superiority which we allow them on land will, on just reasoning, now be more likely ours by sea; for in courage we are their equals, and superior boldness in either case is really based upon greater experience. The Lacedæmonians lead the allies for their own glory; the majority of them are dragged into danger against their will, or they would never have ventured to fight again at sea after so great a defeat. So that you need not fear their daring; they are far more afraid of you and with better reason, not only because you have already defeated them, but because they cannot believe that you would oppose them at all if you were not about to do something worthy of note. Most antagonists, like these men, rely more upon their strength than upon their resolution in attack, but those who go into battle against far superior numbers and under no constraint possess in a high degree the firmness of mind which makes them dare to resist. Our enemies are well aware of this and are

more afraid of our surprising boldness than they would be if our forces were less out of proportion to their own. Many an armament before now has succumbed to smaller numbers owing to want of experience; some too through cowardice; and from both these faults we are certainly free.

"If I can help it I shall not give battle in the gulf, or even sail into it. For I know that where a few vessels which are handled with experience and are better sailers engage with a larger number which are ignorantly managed, the confined space is a disadvantage to them. Unless the captain of a ship see his enemy a good way off, he cannot come on to ram properly; nor can he retreat when he is pressed hard. The maneuvers suited to fast sailing vessels, such as breaking of the line or backing water, are impossible. The sea fight must of necessity be reduced to a land fight in which numbers tell. For all this I shall do my best to provide. Meanwhile you must keep order and remain close to your ships. Be prompt in taking your instructions, for the enemy is anchored near. In the moment of action, remember that silence and order are of prime importance; they are generally of advantage in war, especially at sea. Repel the enemy in a spirit worthy of your former exploits. There is much at stake, for you will either destroy the rising hope of the Peloponnesian navy or bring nearer to Athens the fear of losing the sea. Once more I remind you that you have beaten most of the enemy's fleet already; and, once defeated, men do not meet the same dangers with their old spirit." Thus did Phormio encourage his sailors.[1]

90. The Peloponnesians, when they found that the Athenians would not enter the gulf and the narrow waters, determined to draw them in against their will. So they weighed anchor at dawn, and, ranging their ships four abreast, stood in towards the gulf along their own coast, keeping the order in which they were anchored. The right wing, to which twenty of their fastest vessels were assigned, took the lead. These were intended to close round the Athenians and prevent them from eluding their attack and getting beyond the wing in case Phormio, thinking that they were sailing against Naupactus, should

himself sail along shore to its aid. When he saw them weighing anchor, he was alarmed, as they anticipated, for the safety of the town, which was undefended. Against his will and in great haste, he embarked and sailed along the shore; the land forces of the Messenians followed. The Peloponnesians saw that the enemy were coasting in line ahead and were already within the gulf and close to land, which was what they especially wanted. At a given signal they turned their ships; and the whole line faced the Athenians and bore down upon them, every ship rowing at the utmost speed; for they hoped to cut off the whole Athenian fleet. Eleven vessels which were in advance evaded the turn of the Peloponnesians and rowed past their right wing into the open water; but they caught the rest, forced them aground, disabled them, and killed all the Athenian sailors who did not swim away. They fastened some of the empty ships to their own and began to tow them away; one they had already taken with the crew; but others were saved by the Messenians,[1] who came to the rescue, dashed, armed as they were, into the sea, boarded them, and, fighting from their decks when they were already being towed away, finally recovered them.

91. While in this part of the engagement the Lacedæmonians had the victory and disabled the Athenian ships, their twenty vessels on the right wing were pursuing the Athenian eleven which had escaped from their attack into the open water of the gulf. In their flight, with one exception, they reached Naupactus before their pursuers. They stopped off the temple of Apollo and, turning their prows outwards, prepared to defend themselves in case the enemy followed them to the land. The Peloponnesians soon came up; they were singing a pæan of victory as they rowed, and one Leucadian ship far in advance of the rest was chasing the single Athenian ship which had been left behind. By chance a merchant vessel was anchored in the deep water; the Athenian ship rowed around her just in time, struck the Leucadian amidships and sank her. At this sudden and unexpected feat the Peloponnesians were panic-stricken; moreover, because of their success they were pursuing in disorder;

and now some of them, dropping the blades of their oars, halted, intending to await the rest, which was a foolish thing to do when the enemy were so near and ready to attack them, while others, not knowing the coast, ran aground in shallows.

92. When the Athenians saw what was going on their confidence revived, and at a single command they attacked their enemies with a shout. They did not long resist, for they had made mistakes and were all in confusion, but fled to Panormus, where they had put out to sea. The Athenians pursued them, took six of the nearest ships, and recovered their own ships which the Peloponnesians had originally disabled and taken in tow near the shore. The crews of the captured vessels were either killed or made prisoners. Timocrates the Lacedæmonian was on board the Leucadian ship which went down near the merchant vessel; when he saw the ship sinking, he killed himself; the body was carried into the harbor of Naupactus. The Athenians then retired and raised a trophy on the place from which they had just sailed out to their victory. They took up the bodies and wrecks which were floating near their own shore and gave back to the enemy, under a flag of truce, those which belonged to them. The Lacedæmonians also set up a trophy of the victory which they had gained over the ships disabled by them near the shore; the single ship which they took they dedicated on the Achæan Rhium, close to the trophy. Then, fearing the arrival of the Athenian reinforcements, they sailed away at nightfall to the Crisæan Gulf and to Corinth, all with the exception of the Leucadians. And not long after their retreat the twenty Athenian ships from Crete, which ought to have reached Phormio before the battle, arrived at Naupactus. So the summer ended. [*Other operations in 429 are omitted.*]

BOOK III

The Revolt of Mytilene

[*In early summer 428 Mytilene revolted from Athens. Except for Chios, Mytilene was the only city in the empire which still had a large fleet; she also enjoyed autonomy and was in fact under oligarchic rule. The revolt, planned no doubt in the belief that the plague had irreparably ruined Athens, was precipitated by denunciations at Athens on the part of some of Mytilene's neighbors and her own citizens. Of the four other cities on Lesbos, only Methymna remained loyal to Athens. The Athenians at once sent an expedition which blocked the harbors. The details of Thucydides' narrative show that the Mytilenæans did not venture to resist the Athenians by sea and that they soon lost control of their land, it is apparent that the government could not rely on its own people to fight hard for "freedom." Instead, they hoped to be saved by Sparta. A Mytilenæan embassy addressed the Peloponnesian league at Olympia in about August 428 "somewhat as follows."*]

9. "We know, Lacedæmonians and allies, the fixed practice of the Greeks: when men secede in time of war and desert an old alliance, their new allies are delighted with them, in so far as they profit by their aid; but they do not respect them, for they deem them traitors to their former friends. And this opinion is not undeserved, provided that the seceding party and those from whom they sever themselves entertain similar views and friendly sentiments and are equally matched in power and resources, and when there is no reasonable excuse for secession. But our relation to the Athenians was of another

sort, and no one should be severe upon us for seceding from them in the hour of danger, although we were honored by them in time of peace.[1]

10. "Since an alliance is our object, we will first address ourselves to the question of justice and honor. We know that no friendship between man and man, no league between city and city is permanent unless the parties to it believe in each other's honor and are similar in general character: the diversity of men's minds makes them act in differing ways. Now our alliance with the Athenians began when you abandoned the Persian War, and they stood by us to complete the work. But we did not enter the Hellenic alliance to enslave the Hellenes to Athens but to liberate them from the Persians. And while in the exercise of their command the Athenians claimed no supremacy, we were very ready to follow them. But our fears began to be aroused when we saw them relaxing their hostility against Persia and imposing slavery on their allies, who could not unite in resistance because of the multiplicity of their votes, and so all were enslaved, except ourselves and the Chians.[1] We fought at the side of the Athenians, and were actually called autonomous and free. But we no longer put any trust in them as leaders, judging from previous examples. For they had subjugated others to whom, equally with ourselves, they were bound by treaty; and how could we expect that they would not do the same to the rest, if ever they had the power?

11. "Had all the allies retained their autonomy, we should have had better assurance that they would leave us as we were; but when they had subjugated the majority but were dealing with us on a footing of equality, they were naturally likely to take offense, contrasting the equality we alone maintained with the submission already accorded by the majority, especially as their strength and our isolation were increasing proportionately. Fear based on equal power is the only guarantee for an alliance; men who would break faith are deterred from aggression if they lack superior strength. And why were we left autonomous? Only because they thought that it helped them in gaining their empire to seize control by

fair words and policy rather than by violence. They would cite it as evidence on their behalf that cities with equal votes would not willingly have shared in their expeditions unless those whom they attacked were in the wrong, and at the same time they would attack the weakest allies first and bring up the strongest in their support; these they would leave to the last, for when the lesser states had all been removed, they were likely to fall an easier prey. But if they had begun with us while the power of the allies was still intact, and we might have afforded a rallying point, they would not so easily have mastered them. Besides, our navy caused them some apprehension; they were afraid that we might join you or some other power and that the union would be dangerous to them. We also saved ourselves by paying court to the Athenian state and to the popular leaders of the day. But we were not likely to have survived long, judging by the conduct of the Athenians to the other allies, if this war had not arisen.

12. "What trust then could we repose in such a friendship or such freedom as this? Our mutual civilities were insincere; they courted us in time of war out of fear, and in peace we did the same to them. Other alliances are generally cemented by good will, but ours was guaranteed by fear, and it was more by fear than affection that we were constrained to be their allies, and whichever of us first thought that he could safely make the venture was sure to be the first to break the alliance. And therefore if any one thinks that because they delay the blow which we dread, we do wrong in being the first to break away and in not waiting ourselves to make quite sure if any such blow will fall, he is mistaken. If it were equally in our power to plot against them, then we ought to have delayed as they do before attacking; but the power of attack is always in their hands, and the right of anticipating attack should be in ours.

13. "Such are the motives and grievances, Lacedæmonians and allies, which made us break away, clear enough to prove to all who hear them that we acted reasonably, and strong enough to fill us with alarm and drive us to seek some means of safety. Long ago we wished to take

this course; before the war began, we sent envoys to consult you about secession; but you rejected our proposal and stopped us. Now, however, we at once obeyed the invitation of the Bœotians, and we thought that we would break away both from the league and from Athens; we would cease as members of the league to join the Athenians in injuring the Hellenes, but would assist in liberating them and avoid subsequent destruction upon ourselves at the hands of the Athenians by forestalling it. However, our secession has come too soon and without preparation; hence you are the more bound to receive us into alliance and to send us speedy help, thereby showing that you protect those who are entitled to protection and that you can simultaneously do your enemies damage. Never was there such an opportunity before. The Athenians are exhausted by pestilence and the expenditure of their money; some of their ships are cruising about your shores; the remainder are threatening us; so that they are not likely to have many to spare if you, in the course of this summer, make a second attack upon them both by land and by sea. They will not meet you at sea; or if they do, they will withdraw both from Lesbos and from the Peloponnese. None should think that he will be risking his own life for another's country. Lesbos may seem to be a long way off, but the help which it will give lies very near. For the war will not be decided in Attica, as some suppose, but in those countries by which Attica is supported. The revenues of the Athenians are derived from their allies, and, if they subdue us, will be greater than ever. No one else will break away, our resources will be added to theirs, and we should suffer more severely than those who are already their slaves. But if you show energy in assisting us, you will gain the alliance of a city with a large fleet, of which you stand most in need; you will draw away the allies of the Athenians, who will all be bolder in coming over to you; and you will more easily overthrow the power of Athens, and no longer incur, as in times past, the reproach of not helping those who secede from her. But if you are seen to be liberators, your success in the war will be more certain.

14. "Do not then for very shame frustrate the hopes

which the Hellenes rest on you or forget Olympian Zeus in whose temple we are virtual suppliants; protect the Mytilenæans by accepting us as allies, and do not abandon us; we are exposing our own lives to danger, but the benefit of our victory will accrue to all alike; and all alike, in a still higher degree, will suffer if you are inflexible and we fall in consequence. Prove yourselves worthy of your reputation in Hellas and of the hopes which in our fear we repose in you."

[*The Spartans decided on a second invasion of Attica in 428; but their allies, occupied with the vintage, were not ready to act; and the Athenians showed that they were not exhausted by manning a large fleet and descending on the Peloponnese. They also levied a property tax of two hundred talents, the first in the war, and completed the investment of Mytilene. The arrival of a Spartan officer, Salæthus, encouraged the Mytilenæans not to give in; in spring 427 the Peloponnesians actually sent a fleet of forty ships across the Ægean; it was utterly ineffective. In the meantime Salæthus armed the common people at Mytilene; but when they demanded a fair distribution of grain and threatened to surrender the city otherwise, the government decided that it would be better to surrender the city themselves at discretion. Salæthus was sent to Athens, and with him Mytilenæan representatives to plead for their people.*

I have also omitted here the story of the escape of part of the Platæan garrison.]

36. When the captives arrived at Athens, the Athenians instantly put Salæthus to death, although he promised among other things to procure the withdrawal of the Peloponnesians from Platæa, which was still blockaded. There was a debate about the Mytilenæans; and in anger the Athenians determined to put to death not only the men then at Athens but all the adult citizens of Mytilenè and to enslave the women and children on the ground that they had revolted, especially as they were not subjects like the rest; moreover, the fact that Peloponnesian ships had been so bold as to venture across to Ionia and

assist them contributed to increase their fury; for it appeared that their revolt was a long premeditated affair. So they sent a trireme to Paches announcing their decisions and bidding him put the Mytilenæans to death with all speed. But on the following day a kind of remorse at once seized them; they began to reflect that a decree which doomed to destruction a whole city rather than the guilty persons alone was cruel and monstrous.[1] The Mytilenæan envoys who were at Athens and the Athenians who collaborated with them perceived this and prevailed on the persons in authority to bring the question again before the people; they found it easier to persuade them because they saw themselves that the majority of the citizens wished to have an opportunity given them of reconsidering their decision. An assembly was summoned at once, and different opinions were expressed by each speaker. In the former assembly Cleon the son of Cleænetus had carried the decree condemning the Mytilenæans to death. He was in general the most violent of the citizens, and at that time the people found him far the most persuasive leader.[2] He now came forward a second time and spoke somewhat as follows:[3]

37. "On many other occasions in the past I have personally recognized that a democracy cannot manage an empire, and I see this most clearly in your repentance over the Mytilenæans. In your daily life you are free from mutual fears and intrigues, and you therefore deal with your allies on the same principle;[1] and you do not consider that whenever you are misled by their persuasive arguments or yield to them out of pity, you are guilty of a weakness dangerous to yourselves and receive no thanks from them. You fail to observe that your empire is a despotism exercised over unwilling subjects who conspire against you; they obey, not in return for any kindness which you do them, to your own injury, but in so far as you are their masters and hold them down by force rather than by good will. But it is worst of all if we do not stand firm by any of our decisions and fail to recognize that a state in which the laws, though imperfect, are always observed is better than one where they are good but ineffective, that it is more useful to have little

learning but sound sense than to be clever and undisciplined, and that the simpler sort of men generally administer cities better than the more astute.[2] For the latter desire to appear wiser than the laws and to get their own way in every discussion of public affairs, as though there were no more important occasions for them to display their judgment; and by such conduct they generally ruin their cities; whereas the others, mistrusting their own intelligence, admit that the laws are wiser than they, do not pretend to censure the argument of the fine speaker and, being impartial judges rather than contestants, usually prove right. This is the spirit in which we should act; we should not be so excited by our own cleverness in a war of wits as to advise the Athenian people contrary to our own better judgment.

38. "My own policy is unchanged; and I wonder at those who have brought forward the case of the Mytilenæans again, thus interposing a delay which is more in the interest of the wrongdoers, as the victim pursues the offender with passion dulled: vengeance which follows closest on the injury is most likely to exact retribution in equal measure. I wonder too who will answer me and claim to show that the crimes of the Mytilenæans are of benefit to us or that our disasters are harmful to the allies. Clearly, he must be one who has such confidence in his powers of speech as to contend that you never took the decision that you certainly did take, or one who is inspired by greed to elaborate specious arguments and try to lead you astray. In such rhetorical contests the city gives away the prizes to others while she takes the risk upon herself. And you are to blame, for you conduct these contests wrongly: you are accustomed to use your eyes when speeches are to be heard, but your ears when actions are concerned;[1] you estimate the possibility of future enterprises from the eloquence of an orator; but when you are considering accomplished facts, you do not rely so much on what you see has been done as on what is reported to you; and you judge actions from the censures of fine speakers. None are more easily duped by some novelty of expression, or less ready to follow well-tested advice. You are enthralled by every

paradox and contemptuous of the commonplace. Not a man of you but would be an orator if he could; when this is beyond you, you compete to avoid the appearance of being behind the rest in following the argument, and to gain that of being first to praise a clever point; you are eager to anticipate what is said and slow to foresee its consequences. You hanker after a world remote from that in which we live, and you do not even give adequate attention to what is right before you. In a word, you are at the mercy of what you like to hear and sit like spectators of sophists[2] rather than like men deliberating on affairs of state.

39. "I am trying to make you desist from these habits by proving that no single city has ever injured you so deeply as Mytilenè.[1] I am ready to pardon men who revolted because they found our rule too heavy to bear or because the enemy coerced them. But when men living in an island with walls, unassailable by our enemies except at sea and protected against them on that element too by a fleet of their own, men who were autonomous and treated by us with the highest regard, acted like the Mytilenæans, it cannot be said that they revolted (that word implies that they were oppressed); they conspired against us, they rose up against us, they entered the ranks of our bitterest enemies and sought to destroy us. And surely this is more atrocious than if they had taken up arms to secure power on their own account. They learned nothing from the misfortunes of their neighbors who had already revolted, and been subdued by us; nor did the prosperity they enjoyed make them hesitate to incur danger. Imbued with boldness for the future, they cherished hopes which, if less than their wishes, were greater than their power, and went to war, thinking that they should prefer might to right. At the moment when they thought they would win, they set upon us, although we were doing them no wrong. When great success comes very swiftly to a city, and takes it by surprise, it is apt to promote arrogance; it is generally safer for men not to enjoy more good fortune than they can reasonably expect, and it may be said that they find it easier to triumph over adversity than to preserve prosperity. The

Mytilenæans ought from the first to have been treated by us with no more honor than the rest of our allies, and then their arrogance would never have risen to such a height; for in general it is the nature of mankind to despise those who court them and to respect those who make no concessions. Let them now be punished as they deserve for their wrongdoing, and do not absolve the people while throwing the blame on the upper class. They were united in attacking us, the people no less than the rest, though *they* might have come over to us and have then secured reinstatement in their city; but they considered that their safety lay in sharing the dangers of the oligarchy, and they joined in the revolt. Reflect: if you impose no heavier penalties upon those of your allies who willfully rebel than upon those who have been coerced by the enemy, which of them will not revolt upon any pretext, however trivial, seeing that if they succeed, they will be free, and if they fail, no irreparable suffering will follow? But we shall have to risk all our lives and fortunes against every city in turn. When successful, we shall recover only a ruined city; and, for the future, the revenues which are our strength will be lost to us; but if we fail, the number of our adversaries will be increased, and the time we should spend in withstanding the enemies we already have will be occupied in fighting against our own allies.

40. "Do not then hold out a hope, which eloquence can secure or money buy, that they are to be pardoned for an error deemed human. The harm they did you was not involuntary: in plotting against you, they knew what they were doing—but pardon is accorded to involuntary acts. This was my original contention; and I still maintain that you should not repent of your former decisions and not be misled by pity, the charm of words and kindness, three things most prejudicial to the empire. Compassion is rightly shown to equals who reciprocate it, not to men who will show no compassion to us and who are of necessity our permanent enemies. The orators who charm us with their language will still find an arena in which the questions at stake will not be so grave, and when the city will not pay dearly for a brief pleasure,

while they get a good fee for a good speech. Kindness is better shown to men who are likely to be kindly disposed to us, even in times to come, rather than to those who will always remain what they were and will abate nothing of their enmity. In one word, if you do as I say, you will act with justice to the Mytilenæans and in your own interests; but if you take another decision, you will not win their gratitude, but rather you will be self-condemned. For if they were right in revolting, you must be wrong in ruling. But if, right or wrong, you still think fit to rule, then, even though equity forbids, they must be punished for your advantage: otherwise you may give up your empire and, with danger removed, play the honest man. Vindicate yourselves by imposing the same penalty as before, and do not let those who have escaped machinations appear more insensible than those who devised them. Consider what they might naturally have done, if they had conquered you, especially since they were the aggressors. Men who inflict harm on others without excuse are most apt to proceed to their annihilation; they suspect that it will be dangerous if their enemies survive; for after suffering unnecessarily at their hands and escaping, their victims are more bitter than enemies of equal status. Be true then to yourselves and recall as vividly as you can what you thought at the time when you were injured, how you would have given the world to crush them; and exact retribution now. Do not be softhearted at the sight of their present condition, and do not forget the danger which once hung over your heads. Punish them as they deserve, and make them a clear example to your other allies that rebellion will be visited with death. If this is your decision, your attention will be less diverted from your enemies by wars against your own allies."

41. Cleon spoke in this fashion; and after him Diodotus son of Eucrates, who in the previous assembly had been the chief opponent of putting the Mytilenæans to death, came forward again and spoke somewhat as follows:

42. "I do not blame those who invite us to reconsider the case of the Mytilenæans, nor do I approve of

the censure which has been cast on the practice of deliberating frequently on matters of the highest importance. In my opinion the two things most adverse to wise policy are haste and passion; the former generally goes with folly, and the latter with uninstructed and shortsighted views. When a man contends that words ought not to be our guides in action, either he lacks intelligence or he has some personal interest: he is not intelligent if he thinks that there is any other way in which we can throw light on the obscure future; and he has some interest of his own if he wishes to carry a discreditable measure and, believing that he would not be able to speak well in a bad cause, supposes that by well-devised slanders he can terrify opponents and audience alike. It is hardest to deal with those who accuse their adversaries in advance of hiring out their eloquence. If they were to charge a speaker with ignorance and he failed to win his case, he might escape with the reputation of lacking intelligence rather than lacking honesty; but when his honesty is impugned, he is suspect if he wins, and if he fails, he is thought to be both fool and rogue. And then the city suffers, for she is robbed of advisers by fear. The city would be most successful if such citizens were incapable of speaking, for then the people would less often be misled. The good citizen should prove his superiority as a speaker, not by intimidating those who are to speak on the other side, but in fair debate, and a city shows sense while not giving new honors to the man who generally tenders good advice, if it does not deprive him of honor he already enjoys, nor punish nor even reproach anyone for an error in judgment. It would then be least likely that the successful orator will speak contrary to his own judgment, to ingratiate himself and earn still greater rewards, and that the unsuccessful will also strive to win over the masses by the same practice of courting popularity for himself.

43. "*We* take the opposite course, and worse still, if a man is suspected of giving even the best advice for his own profit, the jealousy prompted by this unconfirmed belief makes us forfeit manifest advantages for the city. It has come to this, that the best advice offered in plain

terms is as much distrusted as the worst; as a result, just as the advocate of the most pernicious courses must inveigle the masses by deceit, so must the speaker in the better cause use lies to carry conviction. In this city alone, oversubtlety makes it impossible to do good openly and without deception; for when anyone confers a manifest benefit on you, he is requited with a suspicion that he is somehow, secretly, better off. Still, even in such circumstances it is right that when such great interests are at stake we who advise you should make some claim that we look further ahead than you do, for you have only a moment to consider, and, in particular, we are accountable for our advice, and you who listen are accountable to nobody.[1] If men who followed advice suffered as much as men who gave it, your decisions would have been sounder; but as it is, whenever you meet with a reverse, in the passion of the moment you punish the individual adviser for his error of judgment and condone your own because many shared in making it.

44. "I have not come forward as an advocate or as an accuser of the Mytilenæans. If we show good sense, we shall not debate their crimes but the policy that we should be wise to pursue. If I prove them ever so guilty, I shall not on that account bid you put them to death, unless it is expedient; and if I prove that their conduct was in some degree pardonable, what of that, unless I can show what the good of Athens requires? I conceive that we are deliberating about the future rather than about the present. Cleon insists that the infliction of the death penalty will be expedient and will secure you against revolts in time to come: I too take the ground of your future interest and stoutly maintain the contrary position. And I do not think that the plausibility of his speech should make you reject the utility of mine. You are angry with the Mytilenæans, and the superior justice of his argument might well attract you, but we are not at law with them and do not need to be told about our rights; we are deliberating on their fate, only to make them useful to us.

45. "Cities have affixed the punishment of death to many offenses not so serious as this but less heinous, and

yet, excited by hope, men risk their lives;[1] and no one has ever ventured on a perilous enterprise after passing a sentence of failure on himself. And what city has ever revolted when it thought that its own resources or those obtained from its allies were inadequate? It is in men's nature to err in personal and public affairs alike, and no law will prevent them. Men have gone through the whole catalogue of penalties, increasing their severity in the hope that they might suffer less at the hands of evildoers. Probably in early times punishments of the worst offenses were milder, but as time went on and men continued to transgress, they seldom stopped short of death. And still there are transgressors. Some more fearful deterrent has then still to be discovered; certainly, death is no restraint. But poverty produces daring by the pressure of necessity, and power produces ambition by its insolence and pride; while the other conditions of human life engendering passion, as men are held in the grip of some force varying with circumstances, for which no cure exists, also lead men into dangers. Hope and desire are never wanting; desire leads the way, and hope follows, for men think out an enterprise in desire and hope suggests that fortune will supply the means of its success. They do men the greatest harm; concealed in their minds, they prevail over dangers that are plain to see. And fortune too does play a part and contributes no less encouragement; she often presents herself unexpectedly and leads men on into perils, however inadequate their means—states even more than individuals, because they are throwing for the highest stakes, freedom or empire, and because each man, when he has a whole people acting with him, magnifies his own power out of all reason. In short, it is impossible and simply absurd to suppose that when human nature is under a strong impulse toward some action, it can be restrained either by the force of laws or by any other deterrent.[2]

46. "We ought not therefore to take a less prudent decision in reliance on the security that the penalty of death affords. Nor should we make rebels despair of repentance or think that they may not, in a moment, cancel their error. Consider: at present, if a city has actually

revolted and recognizes that defeat is certain, it may come to terms, while still able to pay an indemnity and tribute for the future; but in those conditions, do you suppose that any city will fail to make better preparations for revolt and to extend itself to the uttermost when besieged, if it is all the same whether it comes to terms early or late? And how can we fail to suffer? The siege will be costly because there is no capitulation; and if we capture the place, the city we have acquired will be in ruins; and we shall in future lose the revenue from it; but it is our revenue that makes us strong against our enemies. We should not then act as strict judges of offenders to our own hurt but rather have an eye to the future and impose moderate punishment, and then we shall have cities financially strong at our disposal. We should not expect security from the terror of our laws but from the vigilance of our administration. At present we do just the opposite; a free people ruled by force naturally revolt to obtain autonomy; and when we have put them down, we think that they should be harshly punished. But instead of inflicting strict penalties on free men who revolt, we should practice strict vigilance before they revolt and ensure by our precautions that such a thought never enters their minds, while after conquering them, we should place the blame on the narrowest circle.

47. "Consider: this is another error into which you would fall if you listened to Cleon. At present the common people in every city are friendly to us; either they do not join the upper class in revolt, or, if compelled to do so, they are from the very first hostile to the rebels; and in going to war, you have on your own side the masses of the city opposed to you. But if you destroy the people of Mytilenè, who took no part in the revolt and who voluntarily surrendered the city as soon as they got arms into their hands, you will, firstly, be doing wrong to your benefactors by killing them, and, secondly, you will give the magnates what they most desire; when they have secured the revolt of a city, they will at once have the people on their side, for you will have shown by example that the innocent and the guilty will share the same fate. Even if they were guilty, you should wink at their con-

duct, so that your only remaining allies may not be converted into enemies. I think this far more conducive to the maintenance of the empire—to condone the wrongs done to us than to stand on our rights and put to death men whom we had better spare. Cleon claims that retribution is both just and expedient; but you will find that in his proposal, the two cannot be combined.

48. "You must see then that what I advise is the better course, and without attaching more weight to pity or kindness—I too would not have you influenced by these motives—adopt my proposal on the basis of the arguments I have used: pass sentence at your leisure on the Mytilenæans whom Paches has sent here as guilty, but let the rest live. This will be good policy for the future and will strike present terror into your enemies. Wise deliberation is more potent against an adversary than attacks made in force and folly."

49. This was the substance of Diodotus' speech. When these proposals had been made, which had much the same effectiveness, the Athenians were involved in a conflict of opinion, the voting was close, but still the motion of Diodotus prevailed. The Athenians instantly dispatched another trireme in haste, fearing that as the first trireme had the start—it had left about twenty-four hours before—they might find the city destroyed. The Mytilenæan envoys provided wine and barley meal for the ship and promised great rewards if it arrived first. And such was the energy they showed on the voyage that they continued rowing while they ate their barley meal kneaded with wine and oil, and they slept and rowed by turns. By chance no adverse wind sprang up; the first ship was in no great hurry on her unwelcome mission, while the second pressed on as I have described; and though the first did arrive sooner, Paches had only read the decree and was about to execute it when the second put in and arrested the destruction of the city. Mytilenè had come so close to danger.

50. The captives whom Paches had sent to Athens as the men most to blame for the revolt were put to death on the motion of Cleon; they numbered a few more than a thousand.[1] The Athenians razed the walls of the Mytilen-

æans and took away their ships. Later, instead of imposing tribute on the Lesbians, they divided the whole island, exclusive of the territory of Methymna, into three thousand lots, dedicated three hundred to the gods and sent out their own citizens, chosen by lot, as colonists to the rest. The Lesbians undertook to pay them a yearly rent of two minæ for each lot and cultivated the land themselves.[2] The Athenians also took over the small towns on the mainland which the Mytilenæans held and which were henceforth subject to Athens.

[*About the same time the remnant of the Platæan garrison was starved into surrender; they agreed to submit to trial by the Lacedæmonians. Thucydides records at length their defense and the charges made against them by the Thebans. The Platæans relied in part on the services they had rendered at the time of the Persian invasion in 479 and on the guarantee of independence the Greeks had then given them and argued that as Athens had long protected them against Theban aggression, they were justified in taking Athens' side; they themselves had no quarrel with Sparta and had done her no wrong. The Thebans urged that Platæa had only taken the patriotic side against Persia out of attachment to Athens, that they had since been co-operating in the "enslavement of Greece" and that they should have accepted the offer made to them in 429 to remain neutral. The debate, unlike that held at Athens on the fate of the Mytilenæans, turns almost wholly on moral issues; right, rather than expediency, is in question. The sequel recorded below therefore makes a bitterly ironical commentary on the real importance of such arguments for practical men.*]

68. The Lacedæmonian judges thought that no objection could be made to their question, whether the Platæans had done them any service in the war; for besides other occasions when they had required them to stay out of the war, in accordance with the original treaty concluded with Pausanias after the defeat of the Persians (479), just before the siege they had made to them a proposal of neutrality under that treaty; but the

Platæans had refused. Considering that they had been injured by them, after their own fair proposals had released them from the obligations of the treaty, they brought up the Platæans one after another and again asked each of them separately whether he had done any service to the Lacedæmonians and their allies in the war. When he said "No," they led him away to death; no one was spared. They killed not less than two hundred Platæans, as well as twenty-five Athenians who had shared with them in the siege, and made slaves of the women. For about a year the Thebans gave possession of the city to certain Megarians, who had been driven out by a revolution, and to any surviving Platæans of their own party; but they afterwards razed the whole place to the ground and used the foundations to build an inn near the precinct of Herà, forming a square of two hundred feet; it had two stories and chambers all round. They used the roofs and the doors of the Platæans; and of the brass and iron articles of furniture found within the walls, they made couches, which they dedicated to Herà; they also built in her honor a stone temple a hundred feet long. They converted the Platæan territory into public land and let it out for terms of ten years; some of their own citizens occupied it. Throughout the whole affair the aversion shown by the Lacedæmonians to the Platæans was mainly promoted by a desire to gratify the Thebans, who, they thought, were useful allies in the war then just beginning. Such was the fate of Platæa in the ninety-third year after the Platæans entered into alliance with Athens (519).

Revolution at Corcyra

69. The forty Peloponnesian ships which had been sent to the aid of Lesbos were caught in a storm near Crete, as they fled through the open sea, pursued by the Athenians, and, making their way in a straggling condition from Crete to the Peloponnese, found at Cyllene thirteen Leucadian and Ambraciot triremes, and Brasidas the son of Tellis, who had come out as a commissioner to advise Alcidas. After the failure of their attempt on

Lesbos, the Lacedæmonians at home wished to increase their navy and sail to Corcyra, which was in a state of revolution. The Athenian squadron at Naupactus consisted of twelve ships only, and the Lacedæmonians wanted to reach the island before any more vessels could arrive from Athens. Brasidas and Alcidas made their preparations accordingly.

70. Now Corcyra had been in an unsettled state ever since the return of the prisoners who were taken at sea in the Epidamnian war and afterwards released by the Corinthians. They were nominally let out on bail for a sum of eight hundred talents[1] on the security of their proxeni, but in reality they had been induced to try and gain over Corcyra to the Corinthian interest. They went from one citizen to another and did their best with them to bring about a defection from Athens. On the arrival of an Athenian and a Corinthian vessel conveying ambassadors, there was a discussion in the assembly; and the Corcyræans voted that they would continue allies of Athens according to their agreement but would renew their former friendship with the Peloponnesians. A man called Peithias, who voluntarily acted as the proxenus of the Athenians and was the popular leader, was summoned by the partisans of the Peloponnesians to stand trial; they said that he was enslaving Corcyra to Athens. He was acquitted; and then he in turn summoned their five richest men, declaring that they were in the habit of cutting poles for vines in the sacred precinct of Zeus and Alcinous; for each pole the penalty was fixed at a stater.[2] They were condemned; but the fine was so heavy that they went and sat as suppliants in the shrines, begging that they might pay the money by installments. Peithias, who was also a member of the council, persuaded it to put the law in execution. As the law precluded their request and as they were also aware that, before he ceased to be a councilor, Peithias was likely to induce the people to make an offensive and defensive alliance with Athens, they conspired together and, rushing into the council chamber with daggers in their hands, killed him and other private persons and councilors to the number of sixty. A few of his

party took refuge in the Athenian trireme, which had not yet left.

71. The next step taken by the conspirators was to assemble the people and tell them that they had acted for the best and in order to secure them against subjection to Athens. For the future, they should receive neither Athenians nor Peloponnesians unless they came peaceably with only one ship; to bring more should be deemed a hostile act, and they compelled the people to ratify this proposal. They even sent envoys at once to Athens, who were to explain their conduct in a favorable light and to dissuade the refugees who had fled there from taking any inconvenient step which might lead to a counterrevolution.

72. When the envoys arrived, the Athenians arrested them as disturbers of the peace and deposited them in Ægina, together with any of the refugees they had gained over. In the meantime, the Corcyræans now in power, on the arrival of a Corinthian trireme and Lacedæmonian envoys, attacked the people and defeated them in battle. At nightfall the people took refuge in the Acropolis and the higher parts of the city and concentrated their forces there. They also held the Hyllaic harbor; the other party seized the market place, where most of them lived, and the adjacent harbor which looked towards the continent.

73. On the following day there were a few skirmishes, and both parties sent messengers round the country inviting the slaves to join them and promising them liberty; the greater number came to the aid of the people, while the other faction was reinforced by eight hundred mercenaries from the mainland.

74. After resting a day, there was more fighting; and the people, who had the advantage in numbers and in the strength of their positions, gained the victory. Their women joined boldly in the fray, hurling tiles from the housetops, and showing amid the uproar a fortitude beyond their sex. The conflict was decided towards evening; the oligarchs, fearing that the people might take the arsenal at the first blow and make an end of them, set fire to the private houses around the market place, as

well as to the larger blocks of buildings, in order to deny access to their enemies, sparing neither their own property nor that of any one else. Much merchandise was burned, and the whole city would have been destroyed if the wind had come up and carried the flame in that direction. Both parties now left off fighting and kept watch in their own positions during the night. When the popular cause triumphed, the Corinthian vessel stole away and most of the mercenaries crossed over unobserved to the continent.

75. On the following day, Nicostratus the son of Diitrephes, an Athenian general, arrived from Naupactus with twelve ships and five hundred Messenian hoplites. He tried to bring about a treaty; and on his suggestion they agreed to bring to trial ten of the most guilty persons, who were no longer to be found. The rest were to live together and to make peace with one another and an offensive and defensive alliance with Athens. After this success he was about to sail away when the leaders of the people urged him to leave five of his own vessels so that the enemy might be less inclined to stir: they promised to man five ships of their own and send them with him. He agreed, and they selected the crews of the ships from their enemies. Afraid of being sent to Athens, they sat as suppliants in the temple of the Dioscuri. Nicostratus sought to raise them up and reassure them, but they would not trust him; and on this pretext the people armed, arguing that their mistrust and unwillingness to sail was proof of their evil designs. They took their enemies' arms out of their houses and would have killed some of them whom they chanced to meet if Nicostratus had not interfered. The rest, not less than four hundred, when they saw what was going on, took refuge afresh in the temple of Herà. Fearing that they would resort to violence, the people persuaded them to rise and conveyed them at once to the island that lies in front of the temple of Herà; provisions were sent to them there.

76. At this stage of the revolution, on the fourth or fifth day after the suppliants had been conveyed to the island, the Peloponnesian ships from Cyllenè, which had

been in harbor there since the expedition to Ionia, arrived on the scene, fifty-three in number, still under the command of Alcidas. Brasidas was on board as his adviser. They anchored at Sybota, a harbor on the mainland, and when the morning broke, sailed against Corcyra.

77. The whole place was in an uproar; the people dreaded their enemies within the city no less than the Peloponnesian fleet. They hastened to equip sixty ships; and as fast as they were manned, they sent them out against the Peloponnesians, although the Athenians recommended that they should be allowed to sail out first, leaving the Corcyræans to follow as soon as they had got their fleet together. But when their ships approached the enemy in this straggling fashion, two of them at once deserted; in others the crews were fighting one another, and everything was in disorder. The Peloponnesians, seeing the confusion, employed twenty ships only against the Corcyræans and opposed the remainder of their fleet to the twelve Athenian ships, of which two were the Salaminia and Paralus.

78. The Corcyræans, coming up a few at a time in disorder, had trouble enough among themselves. The Athenians, afraid of being surrounded by superior numbers, attacked not the main body nor the center of those opposed to them but one of the wings and sank a single ship; then, as the enemy formed in a circle, they sailed round them and endeavored to throw them into confusion. But the Peloponnesians opposed to the Corcyræans, seeing this movement and fearing a repetition of what happened at Naupactus,[1] came to the rescue; the united fleet bore down on the Athenians. They were now backing water and withdrawing, with the aim of giving the Corcyræans as much time as possible to escape, while they withdrew slowly and the enemy were in line against them. The naval engagement ended at sunset.

79. The Corcyræans, who were afraid that the enemy would sail to the city as victors and take on board the prisoners in the island or strike some other blow, conveyed the men from the island back to the temple of Herà and guarded the city. But, although the Pelopon-

nesians had won the battle, they did not venture to attack the city but returned to their station on the mainland with thirteen Corcyræan ships which they had taken. On the next day, they were equally inactive, although there was great panic and confusion among the inhabitants. It is said that Brasidas advised Alcidas to make the attempt, but he was not his equal in command. So they only disembarked at the promontory of Leucimmè and ravaged the fields.

80. Meanwhile, in great apprehension of attack by the Peloponnesian fleet, the people of Corcyra entered into discussions with the other faction, especially with the suppliants, in the hope of saving the city; they even persuaded some of them to go on board the fleet, for they still contrived to man thirty ships. But after devastating the land until about midday, the Peloponnesians sailed away. And at nightfall the approach of sixty Athenian vessels was signaled to them from Leucas. These had been sent by the Athenians under the command of Eurymedon the son of Thucles when they heard of the revolution and of the intended expedition of Alcidas to Corcyra.

81. In the night, the Peloponnesians hastened homeward without delay, keeping close to the land, and returned safely by hauling the ships over the Leucadian isthmus, that they might not be seen sailing round. When the Corcyræans realized that the Athenian fleet was approaching while that of the enemy had gone, they took the Messenian troops, who had hitherto been outside the walls, into the city and ordered the ships which they had manned to sail round into the Hyllaic harbor. While they were on their way, they killed any of their enemies whom they caught in the city. On the arrival of the ships, they disembarked those whom they had induced to go on board and dispatched them; they also went to the temple of Herà, persuaded about fifty of the suppliants to stand their trial and condemned them all to death. The majority would not come out and when they saw what was going on, destroyed one another in the temple where they were; some hung themselves on trees, and the rest put an end to their own lives in any way that they could. And, during the seven days that Eurymedon re-

mained after his arrival with his sixty ships, the Corcyræans continued slaughtering those of their fellow-citizens whom they regarded as enemies; they charged them with designs against the democracy, but some were killed from motives of personal enmity, and some perished at the hands of their debtors because money was owing to them. Every form of death was to be seen; and everything, and more than everything, that commonly happens in revolutions, happened then. Fathers killed their sons, and suppliants were torn from the temples and killed near them; some of them were even walled up in the temple of Dionysus, and perished.

82. To such extremes of cruelty did revolution go, and this revolution seemed the worse because it was among the first. For afterwards the whole Hellenic world, one may say, was in commotion; in every city the leaders of the people were struggling to bring in the Athenians or the Lacedæmonians. Now in time of peace, they would have had no excuse for introducing either and no desire to do so; but when they were at war, and each party could obtain assistance to injure their opponents and simultaneously to gain new strength for themselves, interventions were easily procured by those with revolutionary designs. And revolution brought many calamities on the cities, which occurred and always will occur so long as human nature remains the same, but which are more or less aggravated and differ in character with every new combination of circumstances. In peace and prosperity both states and individuals act on better principles because they are not involved in necessities which allow them no choice; but war, stealing away the means of providing easily for their daily lives, is a teacher of violence and assimilates the passions of most men to their circumstances.

When civil strife had once begun in the cities, the later outbreaks, doubtless because men had learned of the earlier, far surpassed them in the novelty of the plans, the ingenuity of the enterprises and the enormity of the vengeance taken. And men changed the conventional meaning of words as they chose. Irrational daring was held to be loyal courage; prudent delay, an excuse for cowardice; sound sense, a disguise for unmanly weakness; and men who consider matters in every aspect were thought to be incapable of doing anything. Frantic haste became part of a man's quality; and if any one made safety the condition for conspiracy, it was a specious pretext for evasion. The lover of violence was always trusted, and his opponent suspected. If anyone succeeded in a plot, he was shrewd; if he detected one, even more clever; but if anyone took measures in advance to make plots or detection superfluous, he was regarded as a man who broke up his own party in terror of the opposition. In a word, it was praiseworthy to strike first, while your enemy was meditating an injury, and to incite a man to strike who was not thinking of it. Furthermore, the tie of party came to be closer than the tie of kinship because the partisan was more audacious and made fewer excuses. For party associations were formed, not for men's good under the existing laws, but in defiance of them, for sheer aggrandizement; and mutual pledges were sealed, not so much in accordance with the divine law as by collaboration in some breach of law. Fair proposals by opponents were received by the stronger party with precautionary actions and not in a generous spirit. Revenge was dearer than self-preservation. And if ever sworn treaties were agreed to, they were granted for the moment when no other course was open and lasted as long as neither party had support from outside; but when opportunity offered, whichever party took courage first, on seeing their adversaries off their guard, they were more delighted by perfidious than by open revenge; they reflected that it was taken in safety and that by a triumph of duplicity they had also gained a prize for superior intelligence. It has generally proved easier to call wicked men clever than to call foolish men good, and men are ashamed of folly and proud of cleverness.

The cause of all these evils was the love of power, originating in avarice and ambition; hence, once engaged in the struggles, men were unsparing of their efforts. The leaders on either side in the cities used specious catchwords; one party preferred "a fair share of political rights for the masses," the other, "the good sense of government by the best men"; they professed devotion to the public interest but rewarded themselves at the public cost. They stopped at nothing in their struggle for victory, did not shrink from the most monstrous crimes and proceeded to even more monstrous acts of revenge, observing no limits of justice or public expediency, but each bounded only by his own pleasure at the time. When an unjust sentence gave them the chance or when force gave them the mastery, they were eager to satiate the enmity of the moment. They had no use for scruples; but when they succeeded in effecting some odious purpose, they were more highly spoken of, if they found a plea that sounded well. The citizens who were of neither party were destroyed by both because they were neutral or because men grudged them survival.

83. Thus, revolutions gave birth to every form of wickedness in Hellas, and the simplicity which is so large an element in a noble nature was laughed to scorn and disappeared. An attitude of distrustful antagonism widely prevailed, for no words were strong enough and no oaths sufficiently terrible to reconcile opponents; all who obtained the upper hand reasoned that security was not to be hoped for, and were readier to think out precautions against injury than to show a capacity of trusting others. Men of inferior intellect generally succeeded best. Afraid of their own deficiencies and of the shrewdness of their adversaries, fearful that they would get the worst of argument and that the subtle policy of their enemies would find some means of striking at them first, they proceeded boldly to action, whereas the others arrogantly assumed that they would detect their opponents' plans and had no need to take by force what they could get by policy, and were more apt to be taken by surprise and destroyed.

84.[1] It was in Corcyra that most of these audacious acts were first committed and all the crimes that would be perpetrated in retaliation by men who had been governed tyrannically rather than with good sense and had the chance of revenge, or that would be unjustly designed by others who were longing to be relieved of their habitual poverty, and who above all were animated by a passionate desire for their neighbors' property; crimes too that men commit, not from greed, but when they assail their equals and are so often swept away by untutored rage into attacks of pitiless cruelty. In this crisis the life of the city was in utter disorder; and human nature which is accustomed to do wrong, even in defiance of the laws, now trampled them under foot and delighted to show that it is ungovernable in passion, uncontrollable by justice and hostile to all superiors. For they would not have set revenge above religion and profit above innocence, if envy had not exercised a fatal power. In revenging themselves on others, men claim the right to annul in advance those common laws of humanity to which every man trusts for his own hope of deliverance from calamities, and to leave no recourse against the day when he may be in danger and in need of their support.

85. Such were the passions which the citizens of Corcyra first of all displayed towards one another. After the departure of Eurymedon and the Athenian fleet, the Corcyræan refugees, of whom about five hundred had survived, seized forts on the mainland and became masters of the territory on the opposite coast which belonged to Corcyra; from this base they plundered the people on the island and did much harm, so that there was a severe famine in the city. They also sent ambassadors to Lacedæmon and Corinth to procure their return; but failing of their object, they obtained boats and mercenaries and passed over to the island about six hundred in all; then, burning their boats that they might have no hope but in the conquest of the land, they went up to Mount Istone and, building a fort there, became masters of the country to the ruin of the people in the city.[1]

86. At the end of the same summer, the Athenians sent twenty ships to Sicily under the command of Laches the son of Melanopus and Charœades the son of Euphiletus. Syracuse and Leontini were at war with one another. All the Dorian cities, except Camarina, were allied to Syracuse; it was these cities which at the beginning of the war were reckoned in the Lacedæmonian confederacy, but they had not actually taken part in the war. The Chalcidian cities and Camarina were allied to Leon-

tini. In Italy the Locrians sided with the Syracusans, and the Rhegians with the Leontines, in virtue of their kinship. The Leontines and their allies sent to Athens and on the ground, partly of an old alliance,[1] partly of their Ionian descent, urged the Athenians to send them ships; for they were driven off both sea and land by the Syracusans. The Athenians sent the ships on the plea of kinship: they really wanted to prevent the Peloponnesians obtaining corn from the west; they also meant to try what prospect they had of getting the affairs of Sicily into their hands. . . .

87. In the following winter, the plague, which had never entirely disappeared, although abating for a time, again attacked the Athenians. It continued on this second occasion not less than a year, having previously lasted for two years. Nothing else distressed the Athenians and damaged their power more than this; not less than 4,400 Athenian hoplites on the roll died[1] and a countless number of the common people. . . .

[*The narrative of other operations in the winter of 427 and in 426 is omitted. The most important were in the north. The Athenian general, Demosthenes, who figures largely in later events, tried from his base at Naupactus to attack Bœotia in the rear through Ætolia; but he was disastrously defeated in rough country by the lightly armed Ætolians. He later redeemed himself by successes in Acarnania, as a result of which the Corinthian colony Ambracia was forced into neutrality. Athens eventually obtained a grip on northwest Greece.*

The dispatch of a larger fleet to Sicily in 425 indicates that Athens had now somewhat recovered from the effects of the plague, and in 425-24 Athens took the offensive and forced Sparta to sue for peace, as will now be shown.]

BOOK IV

The Athenian Offensive: Pylos and Cythera

2. During the spring and about the same time, before the corn was in full ear, the Peloponnesians and their allies invaded Attica under the command of Agis the son of Archidamus, the Lacedæmonian king. They settled down and ravaged the country.

The Athenians sent to Sicily the forty ships, which were now ready, under the command of Eurymedon and Sophocles, the third general, Pythodorus, having gone thither beforehand. Orders were given to them as they passed Corcyra to assist the Corcyræans in the city, who were being plundered by the exiles on the mountains. The Peloponnesians had already sent sixty ships to the assistance of the exiles, expecting to make themselves masters of the situation with little difficulty, for there was a great famine in the city. Demosthenes, since his return from Acarnania, held no office; but now at his own request the Athenians allowed him to make use of the fleet, if he wished, around the Peloponnese.

3. When they arrived off the coast of Laconia and heard that the Peloponnesian ships were already at Corcyra, Eurymedon and Sophocles wanted to hasten there; but Demosthenes desired them to put in at Pylos and not to proceed on their voyage until they had done what he wanted. They objected, but it so happened that a storm came on and drove them into Pylos.[1] Instantly, Demosthenes urged them to fortify the place, this being the project which he had in view when he accompanied the fleet. He pointed out to them that there was abundance of timber and stone ready to their hand and that the position was strong and uninhabited, as was the country for a long way around. Pylos is about four hundred stades distant from Sparta and is situated in the territory which once belonged to the Messenians; by the

Lacedæmonians it is called Coryphasium. The other generals argued that there were plenty of desolate promontories in the Peloponnese which he might occupy if he wanted to waste the public money. But Demosthenes thought that this particular spot had exceptional advantages. There was a harbor ready at hand; the Messenians, who were the ancient inhabitants of the country and spoke the same language as the Lacedæmonians, would make descents from the fort and do the greatest damage; and they would be a reliable garrison.[2]

4. As the generals would not listen to him nor would the taxiarchs to whom he later communicated his idea, he did nothing until, as the weather was still unfit for sailing, the soldiers in their inactivity were themselves seized with an impulse to come around and fortify the place forthwith. So they put their hands to the work; and being unprovided with iron tools, they brought stones which they picked out and put together as they happened to fit; if they required to use mortar, having no hods, they carried it on their backs, which they bent so as to form a resting place for it, clasping their hands behind them that it might not fall off. By every means in their power, they hurried on the weaker points, wanting to finish them before the Lacedæmonians arrived. The position was in most places so strongly fortified by nature as to have no need of a wall.

5. The Lacedæmonians, who were just then celebrating a festival, made light of the news, being under the impression that they could easily storm the fort whenever they chose to attack it, even if the Athenians did not run away of their own will. They were also delayed in part by the absence of their army in Attica. In six days the Athenians finished the wall on the land side and in places where it was most required; they then left Demosthenes with five ships to defend it, and with the rest they hastened on their way to Corcyra and Sicily.

The Peloponnesian army in Attica, when they heard that Pylos had been occupied, quickly returned home, king Agis and the Lacedæmonians thinking that this matter was their special concern. The invasion had been made quite early in the year while the corn was still green, and they were in want of food for most of their soldiers; moreover, the abnormally severe weather distressed them, so that there were many grounds for their earlier withdrawal. This was the shortest of all the Peloponnesian invasions; they only remained fifteen days in Attica. . . .

[*Chapter 7 records minor operations against the Chalcidians in Thrace.*]

8. On the return of the Peloponnesians from Attica, the Spartiates and the Periœci nearest to Sparta went at once to attack Pylos; but the other Lacedæmonians, having just returned from an expedition, were slower in arriving. A message was sent around the Peloponnese bidding the allies assist the attack on Pylos as soon as possible; another message summoned the sixty Peloponnesian ships from Corcyra. These were carried over the Leucadian isthmus; and, undiscovered by the Athenian ships, which were by this time at Zacynthus, they reached Pylos, where their land forces had already assembled. While the Peloponnesian fleet was still on its way, Demosthenes dispatched unobserved two vessels to tell Eurymedon and the Athenian fleet at Zacynthus to come as Pylos was in danger.

While the Athenian ships were hastening to the assistance of Demosthenes in accordance with his request, the Lacedæmonians prepared to attack the fort both by sea and by land; they expected little difficulty in taking a work hastily constructed and defended by a handful of men. But as they anticipated the speedy arrival of the Athenian fleet, they meant to close the entrances to the harbor and prevent the Athenians from anchoring there, should they fail in taking the fort before their arrival.

The island which is called Sphacteria stretches along the land and is quite close to it, making the harbor safe and the entrances narrow; at one end by Pylos and the Athenian fort, it admits two ships abreast; at the other, next the rest of the mainland, eight or nine. The length of the island is about fifteen stades; it was wooded and, being uninhabited, had no paths.[1] The Lacedæmonians were intending to block up the mouths of the harbor by ships placed close together with their prows facing each other; but fearing lest the Athenians should use the island as a military base, they conveyed thither some hoplites and posted others along the shore of the mainland. Thus, both the island and the mainland would be hostile to the Athenians, and nowhere on the mainland would there be a possibility of landing. For on the shore of Pylos itself, outside the entrance of the strait, and where the land faced the open sea, there were no harbors; and the Athenians would find no position from which they could assist their countrymen. Meanwhile, the Lacedæmonians, avoiding the risk of an engagement at sea, could count on taking the fort, which had been occupied in a hurry and was not provisioned. Acting on this impression, they conveyed their hoplites over to the island, selecting them by lot out of each division of the army. One detachment relieved another; those who went over last and were taken in the island were 420 men, besides the Helots who attended them; they were under the command of Epitadas the son of Molobrus.

9. Demosthenes, seeing that the Lacedæmonians were about to attack him both by sea and by land, made his own preparations. He drew up on shore under the fort the three triremes remaining to him out of the five which had not gone on to Corcyra, and protected them by a stockade; their crews he armed with shields, but of a poor sort, most of them made of wickerwork. In an uninhabited place there was no possibility of procuring arms, and these were only obtained from a thirty-oared privateer and a light boat belonging to some Messenians who had just arrived. Of these Messenians about forty were hoplites, whom Demosthenes used with the others. He placed the greater part of his forces, armed and unarmed, upon the side of the place which looks towards the mainland, and was stronger and better fortified; these he ordered to repel any attack by land while he himself selected out of the whole body of his troops sixty hoplites and a few archers, and marched out of the fort to the seashore at the point where he expected that the Lacedæmonians would most probably attempt a land-

ing. The spot lay towards the open sea and was difficult and rocky, but he thought that the enemy would be attracted there because the Athenian fortifications were weaker. For the Athenians, not expecting ever to be inferior at sea, had left the wall just there less strong; and he thought that if the enemy could once force a landing, the place would easily be taken. Accordingly, marching down to the very edge of the sea, he posted his hoplites there to keep the enemy off if he could; and he addressed his men somewhat as follows:

10. "My companions in danger, let none of you desire in so critical a position to display his cleverness by reckoning up the sum of the perils which surround us; rather resolve to meet the enemy without much thought but with a lively hope that you will survive them all. In cases like these, when there is no choice, reflection is least useful; and the sooner danger comes, the better. I am sure that our chances are more than equal if we will only stand firm; and, having so many advantages, do not take fright at the numbers of the enemy and throw them all away. I think that the inaccessibility of the place is one of them; this, however, will aid us only if we maintain our position. If we retreat, the ground, though difficult in itself, will be easy enough to the enemy, with no one to oppose him; and even if we then press upon him, he will be more formidable; for his retreat will be next to impossible. On shipboard the Peloponnesians are easily repelled, but once landed they are on equal terms. Of their numbers too we need not be so much afraid; for, numerous as they are, only a few can fight at a time, owing to the difficulty of anchoring close in. We are not contending against an army on land, where superiority tells with other things equal, but one that fights from shipboard; many other circumstances must favor them before they can act with advantage on water. So that I consider their embarrassments counterbalance our want of numbers. You are Athenians and know by experience the difficulty of disembarking in the presence of an enemy; and you know that if a man holds his ground and does not give way in alarm at the splashing of oars and the threatening look of a ship bearing down upon him, no

force can move him. It is now your turn to be attacked, and I call on you to stand fast and fight where the breakers come in. Thus you will save yourselves and the place."

11. The Athenians, inspirited by the exhortation of Demosthenes, went down to the shore and formed a line along the water's edge. The Lacedæmonians now began to move and assaulted the fort with their army by land and with their fleet, consisting of forty-three ships, by sea. Their admiral Thrasymelidas son of Cratesicles, a Spartiate, was on board; he made his attack just where Demosthenes expected. The Athenians defended themselves both by sea and land. The Peloponnesians had divided their fleet into relays of a few ships, as more could not put in at once; and so resting and fighting by turns, they made their attack with great spirit, loudly calling to one another to force back the enemy and take the fort. Brasidas distinguished himself above all the rest; he was captain of a ship; and seeing his fellow captains and the pilots hesitating, even where a landing might seem practicable, and afraid of shattering their ships on the rocks, he shouted to them: "There is no sense in sparing timber when the enemy have built a fort in our country; wreck the ships to force a landing"; to the allies he said that "they should not hesitate at such a moment to make a present of their ships to the Lacedæmonians, who had done so much for them; they must run aground, and somehow or other land and take the fort and the men in it."

12. While thus spurring on the others, he compelled his own pilot to run his ship aground and stepped onto the gangway. But in attempting to disembark, he was struck by the Athenians; and after receiving many wounds, he swooned away and fell into the outrigger; his shield slipped off into the sea and, being washed ashore, was taken up by the Athenians and used for the trophy which they raised in commemoration of this attack. The Peloponnesians in the other ships made great efforts to disembark but were unable on account of the roughness of the ground and the tenacity with which the Athenians held their position. It was a singular turn of fortune

which drove the Athenians to fight on land, and Laconian land, against the Lacedæmonians, who were attacking them by sea, and the Lacedæmonians to fight on ships for a landing on their own soil, now hostile to them, in the face of the Athenians. For in those days it was the great glory of the Lacedæmonians to be a land power distinguished for their military prowess, and of the Athenians to be a nation of sailors and the first sea power in Hellas.

13. The Peloponnesians, having continued their efforts during this day and a part of the next, at length desisted; on the third day they sent some of their ships to Asinè for timber with which to make engines, hoping by their help to take the part of the wall by the harbor where the landing was easier, although it was built higher. Meanwhile, the Athenian ships arrived from Zacynthus; they had been increased in number to fifty[1] by the arrival of some guardships from Naupactus and of four Chian vessels. Their commanders saw that both the mainland and the island were full of hoplites and that the ships were in the harbor and were not coming out; so, not knowing where to find anchorage, they sailed away for the present to the island of Protè, which is close at hand and uninhabited, and bivouacked there. Next day, having made ready for a sea battle, they put out, intending, if the Peloponnesians were willing to come out against them, to give battle in the open water; if not, to sail into the harbor. The Peloponnesians did not come out, and had somehow neglected to close the mouths as they had intended. They showed no sign of moving but were on shore, manning their ships and preparing to fight if anyone entered the harbor, which was of considerable size.

14. The Athenians, seeing how matters stood, rowed in upon them at both mouths of the harbor. Most of the enemies' ships had by this time got into deep water and were facing them. These they put to flight and pursued them as well as they could in such a narrow space, damaging many and taking five, one of them with the crew. They rammed the remaining vessels even after they had reached the land, and there were some which

they battered while the crews were getting into them and before they put out at all. Others they began to tie to their own ships and to drag away empty, as the sailors had taken flight. At this sight the Lacedæmonians were in an agony, for their friends were being cut off in the island; they hurried to the rescue and, dashing armed as they were into the sea, took hold of the ships and pulled them back; it was a time when everyone thought that the action was at a stand where he himself was not engaged. The confusion was tremendous; and the two combatants in this battle for the ships had interchanged their usual manner of fighting; for the Lacedæmonians in their energy and alarm were virtually carrying on a sea fight from the land; and the Athenians, victorious and eager to push their good fortune to the utmost, were waging a land fight from their ships. At length, after giving each other much trouble and inflicting many wounds, they parted. The Lacedæmonians saved their empty ships, with the exception of those which were first taken. Both sides retired to their encampments; the Athenians then raised a trophy, gave up the dead, and took possession of the wrecks. They lost no time in sailing around the island and establishing a guard over the men who were cut off there. The Peloponnesians on the mainland, who had now been joined by all their contingents, remained in their position before Pylos.

15. At Sparta when the news arrived, it was resolved in view of the magnitude of the disaster that the magistrates should go down to the camp and see for themselves; they could then take on the spot any measures which they thought necessary. Finding on their arrival that nothing could be done for their soldiers in the island and not liking to run the risk of their being starved to death or overcome by force of numbers, they decided with the consent of the Athenian generals to suspend hostilities at Pylos, to send ambassadors and ask for peace at Athens, and to endeavor to recover their men as soon as possible.

16. The Athenian commanders accepted their proposals, and a truce was made on the following conditions:

"The Lacedæmonians shall deliver into the hands of

the Athenians at Pylos the ships in which they fought and shall also bring thither and deliver over any other ships of war which are in Laconia, and they shall make no assault upon the fort either by sea or land. The Athenians shall permit the Lacedæmonians on the mainland to send to those on the island a fixed quantity of kneaded flour, viz. about four pints of barley meal for each man and one of wine and also a piece of meat; for an attendant, half these quantities; they shall send them into the island under the inspection of the Athenians, and no vessel shall sail in by stealth. The Athenians shall guard the island as before but shall not land and shall not attack the Peloponnesian forces by land or by sea. If either party violate this agreement in any particular, however slight, the truce is to be at an end. The agreement is to last until the Lacedæmonian ambassadors return from Athens, and the Athenians are to convey them thither and bring them back in a trireme. When they return, the truce is to be at an end and the Athenians are to restore the ships in the same condition in which they received them." These were the terms of the truce. About sixty ships in number were given up to the Athenians. The ambassadors were sent off. On arriving at Athens, they spoke somewhat as follows:

17. "Men of Athens, the Lacedæmonians have sent us to negotiate a settlement concerning the men on the island, which we may convince you will be in your interest, as it is also most likely to be as honorable to us in our disaster as circumstances permit. If we speak at some length, this will be no long-winded departure from our custom. On the contrary, it is our local practice, not to say much where few words will suffice, but to be more liberal of speech whenever there is an occasion to give valuable instruction, and so to secure the action needed. Do not receive what we say in a hostile spirit or imagine that we are instructing you as if you lacked sense, but regard us simply as putting you in mind of what you know to be good policy. For you may turn your present good fortune to excellent account, not only keeping what you have won, but gaining honor and glory as well. Do not suffer the fate of men inexperienced in suc-

cess; when they obtain some advantage, the unexpectedness of their momentary good fortune makes them continually hope for and grasp at further gains. But men who have most often known the vicissitudes of both kinds of fortune ought to be least reliant on successes, and it would be most natural if experience should have taught this lesson to your city as well as to us.

18. "Make your decision only after reviewing our present calamities. We enjoy the greatest prestige of any Hellenic state but are now come to ask of you the favor which at one time we thought ourselves better able to grant. And yet our experience is not due either to want of power or to the pride which an increase in power fosters; but reckoning on our permanent resources, we made an error of judgment; and to such errors all men are equally liable in the same way. It is then not reasonable for you to suppose that because your city and the possessions you have acquired are strong at this moment, you will also have fortune perpetually on your side. Men are classed as wise who invest their gains safely against the uncertainty of the future; it is these men who might show more sagacity in disasters; and they would realize that men are involved in war, not within the limits in which they would wish to wage it, but under the dictates of their fortunes. None would be less likely to meet with reverses, because they are not puffed up by confidence bred of military success, and they would be most inclined to end the struggle in the hour of good fortune. It is now a fine occasion for you, Athenians, to act thus towards us. You may, without risk, leave to posterity a reputation for power and wisdom. And then the victories which you have gained already will not be attributed to chance, as they certainly will be if, rejecting our overtures, you should hereafter encounter disasters, a thing which is not unlikely to happen.

19. "The Lacedæmonians invite you to make terms with them and to finish the war. They offer peace and alliance and in general a friendly and close relation, and they ask in return for their men from the island. They think it better that neither city should run any further risk: you of the besieged, forcing their escape if some

chance of safety appears; we of their being compelled to surrender and passing absolutely into your hands. We think that great enmities may be most firmly reconciled, not when one side seek revenge and, getting a decided superiority, bind their enemies by enforced oaths and make a treaty with them on unequal terms, but when, having it in their power to do all this, they are moved by equity, conquer them in good deeds and surprise them by the moderation of the terms. For opponents who are under an obligation, not to seek revenge for violence, but to requite a benefit received, are the more ready, from a sense of honor, to abide by the compact. And men are more apt to make such a concession to more bitter enemies than to those with whom they have no very grave differences. Nature makes men take pleasure in counterconcessions to those who give way voluntarily, but face perils contrary to their own better judgment against overbearing claims.

20. "Now, if ever, is the time of reconciliation for us both, before an irremediable conflict intervenes between us. Then of necessity you will incur in perpetuity our hatred, based on our own as well as on the common grievances; and we shall have lost the benefits that we now invite you to confer. While the contest is still undecided, while you may acquire reputation and our friendship, and while our disaster can be repaired on tolerable terms and disgrace averted, let us be reconciled, choosing peace instead of war for ourselves, and give relief from ills to all the Hellenes. The chief credit of the peace will be yours. Which of us began the war is unclear; but it lies chiefly with you to give them peace; and if you do so, they will be grateful to you. If you decide for peace, you may secure the lasting friendship of the Lacedæmonians, proposed by them and freely granted by you rather than extorted by force. Consider the great advantages which this is likely to yield. If we both speak the same language, you may be certain that the rest of Hellas, which is less powerful, will pay to both of us the greatest honor."

21. This was the substance of the Lacedæmonian speech; they thought that the Athenians, who had former-

ly been desirous of making terms with them, and had only been prevented by their refusal,[1] would now gladly agree, when peace was offered to them, and would restore their men. But the Athenians reflected that, since they had the Lacedæmonians shut up on the island, it was at any time in their power to make peace; and they grasped at more.[2] They were chiefly urged on by Cleon the son of Cleænetus, a popular leader of the day who had the greatest influence over the multitude. He persuaded them to reply that the men in the island must first of all give up themselves and their arms and be brought to Athens; the Lacedæmonians were then to restore Nisæa, Pegæ, Trœzen, and Achæa—places which had not been taken in war but had been surrendered under the former treaty (446) in a time of reverses, when the Athenians were in greater need of peace. On these conditions they might recover the men and make a treaty of such duration as both parties should approve.

22. To this reply the Lacedæmonians raised no objection but requested only that the Athenians would appoint commissioners to discuss with them the details of the agreement and quietly arrive at a mutual understanding. This was the moment for Cleon to deliver a vehement invective: he had always known, he said, that they meant no good; and now their designs were unveiled; for they were unwilling to speak a word before the people but wanted to be closeted with a select few; if their intentions were honest, let them say what they wanted to the whole city. But the Lacedæmonians saw that, even if they decided to make any concession under the pressure of their calamity, they could not speak openly before the people (for if they spoke and did not succeed, the terms which they offered might injure them in the opinion of their allies); they saw too that the Athenians would not grant what was asked of them on tolerable conditions. So, after a fruitless negotiation, they returned home.

23. Upon their return the truce at Pylos instantly came to an end, and the Lacedæmonians demanded back their ships according to the agreement. But the Athenians accused them of making an assault upon the fort and of

some other petty infractions of the treaty which seem hardly worth mentioning. Accordingly, they refused to restore them, insisting upon the clause which said that if "in any particular, however slight," the agreement were violated, the treaty was to be at an end. The Lacedæmonians remonstrated and, protesting against the injustice of detaining their ships, went away and resumed the war. Both parties engaged in hostilities at Pylos with the utmost vigor. The Athenians had two triremes sailing around Sphacteria in opposite directions throughout the day; and at night their whole fleet was moored about the island, except on the side towards the sea when the wind was high. Twenty additional ships had come from Athens to assist in the blockade, so that the entire number was seventy. The Peloponnesians lay encamped on the mainland and made assaults upon the wall, watching for any opportunity which might present itself of rescuing their men. . . .

[*Chapters 24-25 record further minor operations in Sicily in the summer of* 425.]

26. At Pylos the Athenians continued to blockade the Lacedæmonians in the island, and the Peloponnesian forces on the mainland remained in their old position. The watch was harassing to the Athenians, for they were in want of both food and water; there was only one small well, which was in the acropolis of Pylos; and the soldiers were commonly in the habit of scraping away the shingle on the seashore and drinking such water as they could get. The Athenian garrison was crowded into a narrow space and, their ships having no regular anchorage, one half of the crews in turn took their meals on land, while the others lay at anchor in the open sea. The unexpected length of the siege was the greatest discouragement to them; they had hoped to starve their enemies out in a few days, for they were on a desert island and had only brackish water to drink. The reason was a proclamation issued by the Lacedæmonians offering large fixed prices, and freedom if he were a Helot, to anyone who would convey into the island

meal, wine, cheese and any other provisions suitable for a besieged place. Many braved the danger, especially the Helots; they started from all points of the Peloponnese and, before daybreak, bore down upon the shore of the island looking towards the open sea. They took special care to have a strong wind in their favor, since they were less likely to be discovered by the triremes when it blew hard from the sea. It was then impracticable for ships to lie at anchor around the island, and the crews of the boats were reckless in running them aground, for they had been valued, and Lacedæmonian hoplites were waiting to receive them at the landing places of the island. All, however, who ventured when the sea was calm were captured. Divers too swam under water in the harbor, drawing after them by a cord skins containing pounded linseed and poppy seeds mixed with honey. At first they were not found out, but afterwards watches were posted. The two parties had all sorts of devices to send in food or to detect the importation.

27. When the news reached Athens that their own army was suffering while supplies were being introduced into the island, they were at a loss what to do and were apprehensive that the blockade might extend into the winter. They saw that the conveyance of necessaries around the Peloponnese would then be impracticable. Their troops were in a desert place to which, even in summer, they were not able to send sufficient supplies. Anchorage off a coast without harbors would be impossible. Either the blockade would be relaxed and the men would escape, or, awaiting a storm, they might sail away in the ships which brought them food. What alarmed them most of all was the conduct of the Lacedæmonians, who no longer made overtures to them; they supposed that they must now be on strong ground, and they regretted having rejected the peace. Cleon, knowing that he was an object of mistrust because he had stood in the way of the treaty, challenged the reports of the messengers from Pylos, who advised that if their words were not believed, the Athenians should send some persons to inspect the position. Theagenes and Cleon himself were chosen. As he knew that he would be compelled to con-

firm the report of the messengers whom he was calumniating or would be convicted of falsehood if he contradicted them, and as he observed that the Athenians were now more disposed to an expedition, he advised them not to send inspectors nor to let slip the moment for action by prolonged delay but, if they themselves believed the report, to send a fleet against the island. Pointedly alluding to Nicias the son of Niceratus, who was one of the generals and an enemy of his, he declared sarcastically that if the generals were men, they might easily sail with a proper force to the island and take the garrison, and that this was what he would certainly have done, had he been general.

28. The Athenians were murmuring at Cleon, and asking "why he did not sail now if he thought the capture of Sphacteria to be such an easy matter"; and Nicias, observing his criticisms, told him that, as far as they, the generals, were concerned, he might take any force which he required and try. Cleon at first thought that the offer of Nicias was only a pretence, and was willing to go; but finding that he was really ready to hand over the command, he tried to back out and said that not he but Nicias was general. He was now alarmed, for he did not think that Nicias would have dared to give up his place to him. Again Nicias bade him take the command against Pylos and called the Athenians to witness this. And the more Cleon declined the expedition and tried to retract what he had said, the more the Athenians, acting as a rabble will, urged Nicias to resign and shouted to Cleon that he should sail. At length, unable to escape from his own words, he undertook the expedition and, coming forward, said that he was not afraid of the Lacedæmonians and that he would sail without taking a single man from the city but only the Lemnian and Imbrian forces now at Athens, the auxiliary peltasts from Ænus and four hundred archers from other places. With these and with the troops already at Pylos, he gave his word that within twenty days he would either bring the Lacedæmonians alive or kill them on the spot. There was some laughter among the Athenians at his boasting; but men of sound sense were pleased when they reflected

that of two good things they could not fail to obtain one —either they would be free of Cleon, which they rather expected, or, if they were mistaken, he would put the Lacedæmonians into their hands.[1]

29. When he had concluded the affair in the assembly and the Athenians had passed the necessary vote for his expedition, he chose one of the generals at Pylos, Demosthenes, as his colleague and proceeded to sail with all speed. He selected Demosthenes because he heard that he was intending to make an attack upon the island. For the soldiers, who were suffering much from the lack of supplies in a place in which they were rather besieged than besiegers, were eager to risk a decisive blow; and Demosthenes had been further encouraged by a fire on the island. It had previously been nearly covered with wood and was pathless, having never been inhabited; and he had feared that the nature of the country would give the enemy an advantage; for, however large the force with which he landed, the Lacedæmonians might attack him from a concealed position and do him much injury. Their mistakes and the character of their forces would not be so visible because of the wood; whereas all the errors made by his own army would be palpable; and so the enemy, with whom the power of attack would rest, might come upon them suddenly wherever they liked. And if they were compelled to go into the bush and fight at close quarters, a smaller force which knew the ground would be more than a match for the larger number who were unacquainted with it. Their own army, however numerous, would be destroyed without knowing it; for they would not be able to see where they needed one another's assistance.

30. Demosthenes was led to make these reflections particularly by his disaster in Ætolia, which had been in some measure due to the forest.[1]

However, while the Athenian soldiers were compelled by want of room to land on the extremities of the island and take their meals there with guards posted in advance, some one unintentionally set fire to a portion of the wood and a wind came on; and before they knew what was happening, the greater part of it was burnt.

Demosthenes, who had previously suspected that the Lacedæmonians, when they sent in provisions to the besieged, had exaggerated their number, saw that the men were more numerous than he had imagined; thus the prize the Athenians were seeking was more valuable. He also saw that a descent on the island was more practicable. So he prepared for the enterprise, dispatching messengers to the allies in the neighborhood for additional forces and putting all in readiness. Cleon had sent and announced to Demosthenes his approach, and now arrived at Pylos with the army which he had requested. On the meeting of the two generals, they first of all sent a herald to the Lacedæmonian force on the mainland, inviting them, if they would agree, to avoid any further risk by ordering the men in the island to surrender with their arms; they were to be placed under surveillance but be well treated until a general peace was concluded.

31. Finding that their proposal was rejected, the Athenians waited for a day; and on the night of the day following, they put off, taking with them all their heavy-armed troops, whom they had embarked in a few ships. A little before dawn, they landed on both sides of the island, towards the sea and towards the harbor, a force amounting in all to about eight hundred men. They then ran to attack the first guardpost on the island. Now the disposition of the enemy was as follows: This first post was garrisoned by about thirty hoplites, while the main body with Epitadas, the commander, was posted near the spring in the center of the island, where the ground was most level. A small force guarded the very extremity of the island opposite Pylos, which was precipitous towards the sea and which, on the land side, was the strongest point of all, being protected to some extent by an ancient wall made of rough stones, which the Spartans thought would be of use to them if they were overpowered and compelled to retreat. Such was the disposition of the Lacedæmonian troops.

32. The Athenians rushed upon the first garrison and cut them down at once, half asleep as they were and just snatching up their arms. The landing had been unobserved, the enemy supposing that the ships were only

gone to keep the customary watch for the night. When the dawn appeared, the rest of the army began to disembark. They were the crews of rather more than seventy ships, including all but the lowest rank of rowers, variously equipped. There were also eight hundred archers, and as many peltasts, besides the Messenian auxiliaries and all who were on duty about Pylos, except the guards on the walls. Demosthenes divided them into parties of two hundred more or less, who seized the highest points of the island in order that the enemy, completely surrounded and distracted, might not know whom they should face first, but might be exposed to missiles on every side from superior numbers. For if they attacked those who were in front, they would be assailed by those behind; and if those on one flank, by those posted on the other; and whichever way they moved, the light-armed troops of the enemy were sure to be in their rear. These were their most embarrassing opponents because they were armed with bows and javelins and slings and stones, which could be used with effect at a distance. Even to approach them was impossible, for they would secure victory by flight; and when the Lacedæmonians retreated, they would press close at their heels. Such was the plan of the descent which Demosthenes had originally made and which he now carried into execution.

33. The main body of the Lacedæmonians on the island under Epitadas, when they saw the first guardpost cut to pieces and an army approaching them, drew up in battle array. The Athenian hoplites were right in front; and the Lacedæmonians advanced against them, wanting to come to close quarters; but having light-armed adversaries both on their flank and rear, they could not get at them or profit by their own experience; for they were impeded by a shower of missiles from both sides; and the Athenians, instead of going to meet them, remained in position. Whenever the light-armed ran up and attacked more closely, the Lacedæmonians drove them back; but though compelled to retreat, they still continued fighting, as they were lightly equipped and easily got the start of their enemies as they fled; the ground was

difficult and rough, the island having been uninhabited; and the Lacedæmonians, who were incumbered by their arms, could not pursue them.

34. For some little time these skirmishes continued. But soon the Lacedæmonians became too weary to rush out quickly upon their assailants, who became aware that their resistance grew more sluggish. The sight of their own number, which was many times that of the enemy, encouraged them more than anything; they soon found that their losses were trifling compared with what they had expected; and familiarity made them think their opponents much less formidable than when they first landed, cowed by the fear of facing Lacedæmonians. They now despised them and with a loud cry rushed upon them in a body, hurling at them stones, arrows, javelins, whichever came first to hand. The shout with which they accompanied the attack dismayed the Lacedæmonians, who were unaccustomed to this kind of warfare. Clouds of dust arose from the newly burnt wood; and there was no possibility of a man's seeing what was before him, owing to the showers of arrows and stones hurled by large numbers of men which were flying amid the dust. And now the Lacedæmonians began to feel the difficulty of their task, for their helmets did not protect them against the arrows, and the points of the javelins broke off where they struck. They were at their wits' end, not being able to see out of their eyes or to hear the word of command, which was drowned by the cries of the enemy. They were encompassed by danger on every side, and they had no means or hope of deliverance.

35. As they were always facing about on the same ground, many were already wounded; so at length they closed their ranks and fell back on the last fortification of the island, which was not far off, where their garrison was stationed. From the very moment when they gave way, the light-armed troops pressed upon them with fresh confidence, redoubling their cries. The Lacedæmonians who were caught by them during the retreat were killed, but the greater number escaped to the fort and ranged themselves with the garrison to defend the whole length of the wall wherever it was assailable. The Athe-

nians followed, but the strength of the position made it impossible to surround and encircle it, and so they attacked frontally and tried to force them back. For a long time, and indeed during the greater part of the day, both armies, although suffering from the battle and thirst and sun, persisted in endeavoring either to thrust their opponents from the high ground or not to give way. But the Lacedæmonians now defended themselves with greater ease because they were not liable to be taken in flank by an encircling movement.

36. There was no sign of the end. At length the general of the Messenian contingent came to Cleon and Demosthenes and told them that the army was throwing away its pains; but if they would give him some archers and light-armed troops and let him find a path by which he might get round in the rear of the Lacedæmonians, he thought that he could force the approach. Having obtained his request, he started from a point out of sight of the enemy; and making his way wherever the rocky ground afforded a footing and where the place was so strong that no guards had been set, he and his men with great difficulty got around unseen and suddenly appeared on the summit in the rear of the astonished enemy, striking panic into them and redoubling the courage of their own friends who were watching for their reappearance. The Lacedæmonians were now assailed with missiles on both sides, and to compare a smaller thing to a greater, were in the same case with their own countrymen at Thermopylæ.[1] For as they perished when the Persians found a way around by the path, so now the besieged garrison was between two fires and no longer resisted. The disparity of numbers and the failure of bodily strength arising from want of food compelled them to fall back, and the Athenians were at length masters of the approaches.

37. Cleon and Demosthenes saw that if the Lacedæmonians gave way one step more, they would be destroyed by the Athenians; so they stopped the engagement and held back their own army; for they wanted, if possible, to bring them alive to Athens. They were in hope that when they heard the offer of terms, their courage

might be broken, and that they might be induced by their desperate situation to yield up their arms. Accordingly, they proclaimed to them that they might, if they would, surrender themselves and their arms at discretion to the Athenians.

38. Upon hearing the proclamation, most of them lowered their shields and waved their hands in token of their acceptance of the terms. A truce was made, and then Cleon and Demosthenes on the part of the Athenians and Styphon the son of Pharax on the part of the Lacedæmonians held a parley. Epitadas, who was the first in command, was already dead; Hippagretas, who was next in succession, though still alive, lay among the corpses for dead; and Styphon had been appointed to command, as the law prescribed, in case anything should happen to them. He and his companions expressed their wish to communicate with the Lacedæmonians on the mainland as to the course which they should pursue. The Athenians allowed none of them to stir, but themselves invited heralds from the shore; and after two or three inquiries, the herald who came over last from the body of the army brought back word, "The Lacedæmonians bid you act as you think best, in your own behalf, but you are not to dishonor yourselves." So they consulted together and then gave up themselves and their arms. During that day and the following night, the Athenians kept guard over them; on the next day they set up a trophy on the island and made preparations to sail, distributing the prisoners among the trierarchs to guard. The Lacedæmonians sent a herald and conveyed away their own dead. The number of the dead and the prisoners was as follows: 420 hoplites in all passed over onto the island; of these, 292 were brought to Athens alive, the remainder had perished. Of the survivors the Spartiates numbered about 120.[1] But few Athenians fell, for there was no regular engagement.

39. Reckoned from the sea fight to the final battle on the island, the time during which the blockade lasted was seventy-two days. For about twenty days the Lacedæmonians were supplied with food while the ambas-

sadors were away treating for peace, but during the rest of this time they lived on what was brought in by stealth. Some corn and other provisions were captured on the island; for the commander Epitadas had not served out rations to the limit of his means. The Athenians and Peloponnesians now withdrew their armies from Pylos and returned home. And the promise of Cleon, mad though it was, was fulfilled; for he did bring back the prisoners within twenty days as he had undertaken.

40. Nothing which happened during this war caused greater amazement in Hellas; for it was held that the Lacedæmonians would never give up their arms, under either the pressure of famine or any necessity, but would fight as best they could and die sword in hand. No one would believe that those who surrendered were men of the same quality as those who perished. There is a story of a reply made by a captive taken on the island to one of the Athenian allies who had insultingly asked, "Where were their brave men—all killed?" He answered, "The spindle [meaning the arrow] would be indeed a valuable weapon if it picked out the brave," He implied that the destruction caused by the arrows and stones was indiscriminate.

41. On the arrival of the captives, the Athenians resolved to put them in bonds until peace was concluded, but if in the meantime the Lacedæmonians invaded Attica, to bring them out and put them to death. They placed a garrison in Pylos; and the Messenians of Naupactus, regarding the place as their native land (for Pylos is situated in the territory which was once Messenia), sent thither some of their own men, the best suited for the service, who ravaged Laconia and did most harm because they spoke the same language with the inhabitants.[1] The Lacedæmonians had never before experienced this kind of predatory warfare; and finding the Helots desert and dreading some more serious internal revolt, they were in great trouble. Although reluctant to expose their condition before the Athenians, they sent envoys to them and endeavored to recover Pylos and the prisoners. But the Athenians only grasped at greater

gains[2] and, at last, after they had made many journeys, dismissed them unsuccessful. Thus ended the affair of Pylos.

[*Chapters 42-52 include some minor incidents, particularly a landing in Corinthian territory and the fortification of Methone between Epidaurus and Trœzen, in pursuance of the same strategy as the occupation of Pylos and of Cythera (below). In his account of operations in 424, after recording the solar eclipse of March 21, Thucydides proceeds:*]

53. During the same summer the Athenians with sixty ships, two thousand hoplites and a few cavalry, taking also Milesian and other allied forces, made an expedition against Cythera, under the command of Nicias the son of Niceratus, Nicostratus, the son of Diïtrephes, and Autocles the son of Tolmæus. Cythera is an island which lies close to Laconia off Cape Malea; it is inhabited by Lacedæmonian Periœci, and a Spartan officer called the Judge of Cythera was sent there every year. The Lacedæmonians kept there a garrison of hoplites, which was continually relieved, and took great care of the place. The merchant vessels coming to them from Egypt and Libya commonly put in there; the island protected the Lacedæmonians against privateers from the sea, the only quarter from which they were exposed to depredation, for the whole of Laconia runs out toward the Sicilian and Cretan seas.

54. The Athenian fleet put in to Cythera and, with ten ships and two thousand Milesian hoplites, took Scandea, the city on the seaward side. The rest of their army disembarked on the side of the island looking towards Malea and moved on to the city of the Cytherians; there they found all the inhabitants encamped in force. A battle was fought in which the Cytherians held their ground for some little time; and then, betaking themselves to flight, they retired to the upper city. Thereafter they surrendered to Nicias and his colleagues, placing themselves at the disposal of the Athenians but stipulating that their lives should be spared. Nicias had already contrived to

enter into communication with some of them, and in consequence the negotiations were speedier, and lighter terms were imposed upon them both at the time and afterwards. Else the Athenians would have expelled them because they were Lacedæmonians and their island was close to Laconia. After the capitulation they took into their own hands Scandea, the city near the harbor, and secured the island by a garrison. They then sailed away, made descents upon Asinè, Helos, and most of the other maritime parts of Laconia, and, encamping wherever they found it convenient, ravaged the country for about seven days.

55. The Lacedæmonians, seeing that the Athenians had got possession of Cythera and anticipating similar descents on their own shores, nowhere opposed them with their united forces but distributed a body of hoplites in garrisons through the country where their presence seemed to be needed. In other ways too they kept strict watch, fearing lest some domestic revolution should break out. Already a great and unexpected blow had fallen upon them at Sphacteria; Pylos and Cythera were in the hands of the Athenians, and they were beset on every side by an enemy against whose swift attacks precaution was vain. Contrary to their usual custom, they raised a force of cavalry numbering four hundred, and archers. Never in their history had they shown so much alarm in their conduct of war. They were caught in a conflict at sea, for which their own kind of armaments did not prepare them, and against the Athenians, who always thought that when they neglected an enterprise, they had lost a chance of success. Fortune too was against them, and they were panic-stricken by the many incalculable reverses which had befallen them within so short a time. They feared lest some new calamity like that of the island might overtake them; and therefore they were less bold in seeking battle and thought that they would prove to be wrong, whatever action they took, since their policy had not guaranteed safety, and they were not used to misfortune.[1]

56. While the Athenians were then ravaging their coasts, they hardly ever stirred; for at the places where

they happened to land, each garrison considered, in their depressed state of mind, that they were too few to act. One of them, however, which was in the neighborhood of Cotyrta and Aphroditia, did, by a sudden rush, put to flight a scattered rabble of light-armed troops; but, being encountered by the hoplites, they again retired with the loss of some few men and arms. The Athenians, raising a trophy, sailed back to Cythera. Thence they coasted around to Epidaurus Limera and, after devastating some part of its territory, to Thyrea, which is situated in the country called Cynuria, on the border of Argolis and Laconia. The Lacedæmonians, who held the town, had settled there the Aeginetan exiles, whom they wished to requite for services rendered to them at the time of the earthquake and the Helot revolt,[1] and also because they had always been partisans of theirs, although subjects of the Athenians.[2]

57. Before the Athenian ships had actually touched the shore, the Aeginetans quitted a fort there which they were just building and retired to the upper city, where they lived at a distance some ten stades from the sea. One of the country garrisons of the Lacedæmonians which was helping to build the fort was entreated by the Aeginetans to enter the walls, but refused, thinking that to be shut up inside them would be too dangerous. So they ascended to the high ground, considering the enemy to be more than a match for them, and remained quiescent. Meanwhile, the Athenians put in, marched straight upon Thyrea with their whole army, and took it. They burnt and plundered the city and carried away with them to Athens all the Aeginetans who had not fallen in the battle and the Lacedæmonian governor of the place, Tantalus the son of Patrocles, who had been wounded and taken prisoner. They also had on board a few of the inhabitants of Cythera, whom they had decided to remove as a precaution. These the Athenians determined to deposit on the islands; at the same time they allowed the other Cytherians to live in their own country, paying a tribute of four talents. They resolved to kill all the Aeginetans whom they had taken, in satisfaction of their

long-standing hatred, and to put Tantalus in bonds along with the captives from Sphacteria.

The Congress of Gela

58. During the same summer the people of Camarina and Gela in Sicily made a truce, in the first instance with one another only. But after a while, all the other Sicilian states sent envoys to Gela, where they held a conference in the hope of effecting a reconciliation. Many opinions were expressed on both sides, and the representatives of the different cities wrangled and put in claims for the redress of their several grievances. At length Hermocrates the son of Hermon, a Syracusan, whose words chiefly influenced their decision, addressed the conference somewhat as follows:

59. "Sicilians, I shall speak for a city which is not the least in Sicily and not the chief sufferer in the war; I want to lay before you all the policy which seems to me best for Sicily as a whole. You well know, and therefore I shall not rehearse to you at length, all the misery of war. Nobody is under the necessity of fighting because of his ignorance of it, and no one who thinks that he will gain anything from it is deterred by fear. In practice, some think the advantages outweigh the dangers and others are ready to run risks rather than suffer any immediate loss. But when either party is acting in this way at the wrong time, it is useful to offer counsels of peace; and such counsels, if we will only listen to them, will be at this moment invaluable to us. Why did we go to war in the first place? Simply from a consideration of our own individual interests; and with a view to our interests, let us now try by means of discussion to obtain peace; and if, after all, before we separate, we do not each succeed in getting a fair settlement, we shall go to war again.

60. "But at the same time, if we show sense, we must see that this conference is not solely concerned with our individual interests but with those of all Sicily; in my opinion, it is imperiled at this moment by the designs of the Athenians, and the question is whether we can still

save the island. You ought to regard the Athenians as a much more convincing argument for reconciliation than any words of mine can be. They have the greatest power in Hellas; they come here with a few ships[1] to watch out for our mistakes; they use the name and pretext of a lawful alliance to turn natural enmity to their own advantage. We go to war and invite their assistance (though they are fond of coming whether they are invited or not); we harm ourselves at our own cost, and at the same time we pave the way for the advance of their empire; it is likely that when they see that we are exhausted, they will come again with a larger armament and attempt to bring all Sicily under their yoke.

61. "And yet if we must call in allies and involve ourselves in dangers, as men of sense we should each be aiming at an increase of dominion rather than damaging what we already have. We should consider that internal quarrels are, more than anything else, the ruin of Sicily and her cities; we Sicilians are divided city against city when we are all threatened in common. Knowing this, we should be reconciled man to man, city to city, and make an united effort for the preservation of all Sicily. Let no one think, 'The Dorians among us are enemies to the Athenians, but the Chalcidians, being Ionians, are safe because they are their kinsmen.'[1] For the Athenians do not attack us because we are divided into two races, of which one is their enemy, but because they covet the good things of Sicily which we all share alike. Is not their reception of the Chalcidian appeal a proof of this? They have been zealous in fulfilling their obligations, beyond the terms of the agreement, to those who up to this hour have never aided them as required by the alliance. It is altogether pardonable that the Athenians should display such long-sighted aggressiveness. I blame not those who wish to rule but those who are too willing to serve. It is the nature of mankind to rule wherever no resistance is offered but also to ward off attacks.[2] And if, knowing all these things, we do not plan correctly for the future, and have not all come decided that, first and foremost, we must all deal wisely with the danger which threatens all, we are in error.

"Now a mutual reconciliation would be the speediest way of deliverance from this danger, for the Athenians are not based in their own country but in that of the Sicilians who have invited them. Instead of finishing one war only to begin another, we should then quietly end our differences by peace. And those who came at our call and had so good an excuse for doing wrong will have a good reason for going away, having accomplished nothing.

62. "Such is the great advantage which we obtain by sound policy as against the Athenians. And why, if peace is acknowledged by all to be the greatest of blessings, should we not make peace among ourselves? Whatever good or evil is the portion of any of us, is not peace more likely than war to preserve the one and to alleviate the other? And has not peace honors and splendors less attended by dangers than war? But it is unnecessary to dilate on all the blessings of peace. Consider them closely, and instead of despising my words, may every man look ahead and seek his own safety in them! And should there be some one here present who thinks that either right or force will give him the certainty of success, I would have him avoid a serious reverse from the disappointment of his hopes. He should realize that many a man before now has sought a righteous revenge and, far from obtaining it, has not even saved himself; and many another has pursued his aggrandizement in the consciousness of power and, instead of achieving it, has ended by losing his own possessions. Revenge of a wrong is not favored by fortune merely because it is sought by the victim; nor is strength most assured of victory when it is most full of hope. The inscrutable future is the controller of most events; it is the most treacherous of all things, and the most beneficient; for when men all fear it equally, they think twice before they attack one another.

63. "And now, the undefined fear of the hidden future and the immediate danger of the presence of the Athenians should both inspire us with alarm; policy fails us, and we ought to think these sufficient barriers to have prevented us from fulfilling our several aims. Let us send

out of the country the enemies who threaten us and make peace among ourselves, if possible, forever, but if not, for as long as we can; and let us postpone our private differences to another day. In sum, if you take my advice, we should decidedly maintain the freedom of our several cities, from which we may go forth our own masters, and recompense, like true men, the good or evil which is done to us.[1] But if you will not believe me and we submit to others, the punishment of our enemies will be out of the question. Even supposing we succeed in obtaining vengeance to our hearts' content, we should of necessity become the friends of our greatest enemies and adversaries of those with whom no quarrel should subsist.

64. "As I said at first, I am the representative of the greatest city, which is more likely to act on the aggressive than on the defensive; and yet, as I foresee these dangers, I think it right to come to terms and not to injure my enemies in such a way that I shall doubly injure myself. Nor am I so foolishly bent on victory as to think that, because I am master of my own will, I can control fortune, of which I am not master; but I am disposed to make reasonable concessions. And I would ask the other Sicilians to do the same of their own accord and not to wait until the enemy compels them. There is no disgrace in kinsmen yielding to kinsmen, whether Dorians to Dorians, or Chalcidians to the other Ionians. Let us remember too that we are all neighbors, inhabitants of one island home, and called by the common name of Sicilians. When we see occasion, we will fight among ourselves and will again negotiate and come to terms among ourselves. But we shall always, if we show sense, unite as one man against invaders of another race; for when a single state suffers, all are imperiled. We will never again introduce allies from abroad, nor mediators. This policy will immediately secure to Sicily two great blessings: she will get rid of the Athenians and of internecine war. And for the future we shall keep the island free and our own, and men will be less tempted to attack us."

65. This was the substance of Hermocrates' speech.[1]

The Sicilians took his advice and agreed among themselves to make peace, on the understanding that they should all retain what they had; only Morgantinè was handed over to the Camarinæans, who were to pay in return a fixed sum to the Syracusans. The cities in alliance with Athens sent for the Athenian generals and told them that a treaty was about to be made which would include Athens too. They approved; the treaty was concluded, and the Athenian ships then sailed away from Sicily. When the generals returned, the Athenians at home punished two of them, Pythodorus and Sophocles, with exile and imposed a fine on the third, Eurymedon, on the grounds that they might have conquered Sicily but had been bribed to go away. For in their present good fortune, they were indignant at the idea of a reverse; they expected to accomplish everything alike, possible or impossible, with any force, great or deficient.[2]

The Spartan Counteroffensive: Brasidas

[Besides minor incidents, Thucydides now tells how the democrats at Megara tried to betray the city to Athens. The Athenians did seize the port of Nisæa on the eastern coast of the Isthmus and the long walls connecting it with Megara; but Megara itself was saved by the Spartan general, Brasidas, then on his way to Thrace; in addition to his own small army, he mobilized the forces of Corinth, Bœotia and other neighboring cities; and the Athenians would not risk battle with an army of some eight thousand men. The Athenians then planned a concerted attack on Bœotia from Attica and the west, to be synchronized with a democratic rising in Bœotia. This plan ended with the disastrous defeat of the Athenians at Delium in winter 424; over one thousand Athenians were killed. The most important land engagement in the war before 421, this proved for the first time that the Athenians, with their manpower reduced by the plague, were inferior by land to the Bœotians alone.

What follows is earlier than the Delium campaign and concerns Brasidas' expedition to Thrace. This was the only successful offensive operation by Sparta before 421. It was very risky, as the lines of communication could be and were cut; and Brasidas had no secure base in the north; Perdiccas, king of Macedon, who had invited him, proved unreliable as he always did. Thucydides' narrative is of particular interest because he was personally concerned. He does not fail to do justice to the great qualities of the Spartan general, whose success led to his own political ruin. The events also cast further light on the relations of Athens and her allies. Acanthus revolted only under pressure and feared that Sparta might interfere with her democratic freedom; in some other cities revolts were engineered by oligarchic coteries. On the other hand, many of the cities which revolted, Acanthus herself and Amphipolis, never again returned to Athenian allegiance. It is, however, impossible to say whether they later fell under oligarchic rule, despite the promises made by Brasidas.]

78. During this summer (424), and about the same time, Brasidas set out on his march to the Thraceward region with seventeen hundred hoplites. When he arrived at Heraclea in Trachis,[1] he dispatched a messenger to his friends at Pharsalus with a request that they would conduct him and his army through Thessaly. Accordingly, he was met at Melitia in Achæa Phthiotis by Panærus, Dorus, Hippolochidas, Torylaus, and Strophacus, the proxenus of the Chalcidians. Under their guidance he started. Other Thessalians also conducted him, in particular Niconidas, a friend of Perdiccas from Larissa. It was not easy to cross Thessaly without an escort, especially for an armed force; to go through a neighbor's country without his consent was a proceeding which excited suspicion anywhere in Hellas. Besides, the common people of Thessaly were always well disposed towards the Athenians. Hence, if the local Thessalian in-

stitutions had not tended toward narrow oligarchy rather than equality of rights, Brasidas could never have gone on; even as it was, some of the opposite party met him on his march at the river Enipeus and tried to stop him, saying that it was wrong for him to proceed without the consent of the whole nation. His escorts replied that they would not conduct him if the others objected, but that he had suddenly presented himself and they were doing the duty of hosts in accompanying him. Brasidas himself added that he came as a friend to the Thessalian land and people and that he was making war upon his enemies the Athenians, not upon them. He had never heard that there was any ill-feeling between the Thessalians and Lacedæmonians which prevented either of them from passing through the territory of the other; however, if they refused their consent, he would not and indeed could not go on; but they would not be right to hinder him. Upon this they departed; and by the advice of his escort, fearing that a large force might collect and stop him, he marched on at full speed and without a halt. On the same day on which he started from Melitia, he arrived at Pharsalus and encamped by the river Apidanus. Thence he went on to Phacium and then to Perrhæbia. Here his Thessalian escort went home again; and the Perrhæbians, who are subjects of the Thessalians, brought him safe to Dium in the territory of Perdiccas, a little city of Macedonia which is situated under Mount Olympus on the Thessalian side.

79. Thus Brasidas hurried through Thessaly before any measures were taken to stop him and reached Perdiccas and Chalcidice. Perdiccas and the Thracian rebels from the Athenians,[1] alarmed at their recent successes, had invited the Peloponnesians. The Chalcidian rebels were expecting that the first efforts of the Athenians would be directed against them; the other Chalcidian cities in the neighborhood which had not revolted also joined secretly in the invitation. Perdiccas was not a declared enemy of Athens but was afraid that the old differences between himself and the Athenians might revive, and he was especially anxious to win over Arrhibæus, king of the Lyncestians.[2]

80. It was fortunate for them that the Lacedæmonians were the more willing to send an army from the Peloponnese owing to the gravity of their position at the time. The Athenians were pressing home their attacks on the Peloponnese and especially their own territory; and they hoped that a diversion would be best effected if they could retaliate on them by sending troops to the Athenian allies, especially as these were ready to maintain them, and were asking for assistance from Sparta with the intention of revolting. They were also glad of a pretext for sending out of the way some of the Helots, fearing that they would take the opportunity of rising afforded by the occupation of Pylos. In general, Spartan policy was always especially intended to secure them against this source of danger. In their fear of the number and vigor of the Helot youth, they even did this: they proclaimed that a selection would be made of those Helots who claimed to have rendered the best service to the Lacedæmonians in war, and promised them liberty. The announcement was intended to test them; it was thought that those among them who were foremost in asserting their freedom would be most high-spirited and most likely to rise against their masters. So they selected about two thousand, who were crowned with garlands and went in procession round the temples; they were supposed to have received their liberty; but not long afterwards, the Spartans put them all out of the way, and no man knew how any one of them came by his end. And so they were only too glad to send with Brasidas seven hundred Helots as hoplites.[1] The rest of his army he hired from the Peloponnese.

81. The Lacedæmonians sent Brasidas, as he himself wanted to go, and the Chalcidians too desired to have him, and at Sparta he was considered a man active in every way. And on this expedition he proved invaluable to the Lacedæmonians. At the time, he displayed justice and moderation in his behavior to the cities, which induced most of them to revolt, while others were betrayed into his hands. Thus, the Lacedæmonians lightened the pressure of war upon the Peloponnese; and if they desired to negotiate, as they actually did, they had places

to give in return for those they sought to recover. And at a later period of the war, after the Sicilian expedition, the honesty and sagacity of Brasidas which some had experienced and of which others had heard the fame, did most to attract the Athenian allies to the Lacedæmonians. For he was the first Spartan to command abroad, and he had a thoroughly good reputation; this made men confidently expect that the others would be like him.

82. The Athenians, hearing of the arrival of Brasidas in Thrace and believing that Perdiccas was the instigator of the expedition, declared war against the latter and kept a closer watch over their allies in that region.

83. Perdiccas, at once uniting the soldiers of Brasidas with his own forces, made war upon his neighbor Arrhibæus the son of Bromerus, king of the Lyncestian Macedonians; for he had a quarrel with him and wanted to subdue him. But when he and Brasidas and the army arrived at the pass leading into Lyncestian country, Brasidas said that before appealing to arms, he should like to try in person the effect of negotiations and see if he could not make Arrhibæus an ally of the Lacedæmonians. He was partly influenced by messages from Arrhibæus expressing his willingness to trust to the mediation of Brasidas; and the Chalcidian ambassadors who accompanied the expedition recommended him not to remove from Perdiccas' path all his difficulties, so as to have more energetic help from him in their own affairs. Besides, the envoys of Perdiccas when at Sparta had said something to the Lacedæmonians about his making many of the neighboring places their allies; and on this ground Brasidas claimed to act jointly with Perdiccas in the matter of Arrhibæus. But Perdiccas answered that he had not brought Brasidas there to arbitrate in his own quarrels; he had meant him to destroy his enemies when he pointed them out. While he, Perdiccas, was maintaining half the Lacedæmonian army, Brasidas would be wrong to consort with Arrhibæus. But in spite of the opposition and reluctance of Perdiccas, Brasidas communicated with Arrhibæus, and was induced by the discussion to withdraw his army without invading the country. From that time Perdiccas thought himself ill-

treated and paid only a third instead of half the expenses of the army.

84. During the same summer without delay Brasidas, reinforced by Chalcidian troops, marched against Acanthus, a colony of Andros, a little before the vintage. The inhabitants of the city were not agreed about admitting him; he had been invited by men who were in concert with the Chalcidians and opposed to the people. So he asked them to receive him alone and hear what he had to say before they decided; and to this request the multitude were induced to consent, partly out of fear for their fruits still outside the walls. Coming forward to the people (for a Lacedæmonian he was not a bad speaker), he addressed them somewhat as follows:

85. "Men of Acanthus, the Lacedæmonians have sent me out at the head of this army to substantiate the reason we gave publicly for war at the beginning—that we were going to fight the Athenians for the liberties of Hellas. If we have been long in coming, the reason is that we were disappointed in the result of the war nearer home; for we had hoped that, without involving you in danger, we might ourselves have made a speedy end of the Athenians. And therefore let no one blame us; we have come when opportunity occurred, and with your help will try to overthrow them. But I am surprised that you close your gates against me and do not seem to welcome my arrival. We Lacedæmonians thought that we should find you, even before we actually came, our allies in spirit, and that you would wish to see us; we have braved the greatest danger, marching for many days through a foreign country, and have shown the utmost zeal in your cause. And now, for you to be of another mind and to set yourselves against the liberties of your own city and of all Hellas would be monstrous! The evil is not only that you resist me yourselves; but wherever I go, people will be less likely to join me; they will take it amiss if you, the first I approached, representing a city of note and reputed to be men of sense, did not receive me; and it will be thought that I have no convincing explanation but that the liberty I bring is spurious or that I have come without strength and ability to protect

you against any Athenian attack. And yet, this is the very army with which I brought assistance to Nisæa, and which the Athenians, though more numerous, refused to engage;[1] and they are not likely now, when their forces must be conveyed by sea, to send an army against you equal to that which they had at Nisæa. And, for my own part, I am come here, not to injure, but to free the Hellenes. I have bound the government of Lacedæmon by the most solemn oaths to respect the autonomy of any states which I may bring over to their side. I do not want to gain your alliance by force or fraud, but on the contrary to give you ours, that we may free you from the Athenian yoke. I think that you ought not to doubt my word when I offer you the most solemn pledges, nor should I be regarded as incapable of protecting you, but you should join me with confidence.

86. "Perhaps some of you are hanging back because you have a personal fear of others, and are afraid that I might hand over the city to a party. If so, you ought to put the fullest trust in me. For I have not come to act with a faction, nor do I think that I should be bringing you freedom beyond question if I were to neglect tradition and to enslave the majority to the few or the minority to the masses. Such freedom would be harder to bear than the dominion of the foreigner; and we Lacedæmonians should receive no thanks in return for our trouble, but reproach rather than honor and reputation. We should lay ourselves open to the charges on which we are fighting the Athenians, and in a more detestable form than men who never gave a glimpse of honor. For to men with a reputation, there is more disgrace in seeking aggrandizement by specious deceit than by open violence; in one case men go to work with a justification in the strength which fortune has given, in the other with intrigue in a spirit of injustice. We show great circumspection in regard to our principal interests; and not to speak of our oaths, you could not have a better guarantee than we can give; inspect our actions in the light of our words, and you cannot escape the view that they actually conform to our advantage, as I have described it.

87. "But if you plead that you cannot accept my pro-

posals and claim that you ought not to suffer for rejecting them because you are our friends, if you are of opinion that liberty is perilous for you and should not in justice be forced upon any one but offered to those who are really able to receive it—I shall first call the gods and heroes of the country to witness that I have come hither for your good and that you would not listen to me; I shall then ravage your country and try to coerce you without any more scruple. I shall deem myself justified by two overpowering arguments. In the first place, I must not permit the Lacedæmonians to suffer by your friendship, and suffer they will, if you do not join me, through the revenues which the Athenians derive from you; and in the second place, the Hellenes must not be denied liberation by your fault. We would not act in this way without fair cause. Nor have we Lacedæmonians any right to free men who do not desire it except for the sake of the common good. It is not empire we seek; we are striving instead to end the empire of others; and we should do injustice to the majority if, while offering autonomy to all, we tolerated opposition from you. Consider these points carefully in your deliberation. Strive to take the lead in liberating Hellas and to lay up a treasure of undying fame, to save your property as individuals, and to crown your whole city with glory."

88. This was the substance of Brasidas' speech. The Acanthians, after much had been said on both sides, partly because of the plausibility of his words and partly because they were afraid of losing their vintage, determined by a majority, voting secretly, to revolt from Athens. They pledged Brasidas to stand by the engagement to which the government of Sparta had sworn before they sent him out, to respect the autonomy of all whom he brought over to the Lacedæmonian alliance. They then admitted his army; and shortly afterwards Stagirus, a colony of the Andrians, revolted also. Such were the events of the summer (424).

[*The narration of the Delium campaign follows; see summary following Chapter* 65.]

102. During the same winter (424-23), Brasidas and his Thracian allies made an expedition against Amphipolis upon the river Strymon, an Athenian colony. The place where the city now stands is the same which earlier Aristagoras of Miletus attempted to colonize when he was fleeing from King Darius; he was driven out by the Edonians (496). Thirty-two years afterwards, the Athenians made another attempt; they sent a colony of ten thousand, made up partly of their own citizens, partly of any others who liked to join; they were destroyed by the Thracians at Drabescus (464). Twenty-eight years later, the Athenians came again, under the leadership of Hagnon the son of Nicias, drove out the Edonians, and built this town which was formerly called "The Nine Ways" (436). Their base of operations was Eion, a market and seaport which they possessed at the mouth of the river, about twenty-five stades from the site of the present town. The Strymon flows round it on both sides, and Hagnon built a long wall across from one stream to the other and called it Amphipolis because it strikes the eye both by sea and land.

103. Against Amphipolis, Brasidas now led his army. Starting from Arnæ in Chalcidice, towards evening he reached Aulon and Bromiscus at the point where the lake Bolbe flows into the sea; having there supped, he marched on during the night. The weather was wintry and somewhat snowy; and so he pushed on all the quicker, with the aim of surprising the inhabitants of Amphipolis except the traitors. They included settlers from Argilus (a town which was colonized from Andros) and others instigated of Perdiccas or by the Chalcidians. The town of Argilus is not far off, and the inhabitants were always suspected by the Athenians, and were always conspiring against Amphipolis. For some time past, ever since the arrival of Brasidas had given them an opportunity, they had been most active in concerting measures with their countrymen who enjoyed citizenship at Amphipolis for its surrender. The Argilians now revolted from the Athenians on that very night and received him into their town; and before dawn they conducted the army to the bridge over the river, which is at some distance from the

town. At that time no walls had been built down to the river, as they have since been; a small guard was posted there. Brasidas easily overcame the guard, owing partly to treason, partly to the severity of the weather and the suddenness of his attack; he crossed the bridge and at once was master of all the possessions of the Amphipolitans outside the walls. For they lived scattered about in the country.

104. The passage of the river was a complete surprise to the citizens within the walls. Many who happened to be outside were being taken. Others were fleeing into the town. The Amphipolitans were in great consternation, especially as they suspected one another. It is even said that Brasidas thought that if, instead of allowing his army to plunder, he had marched directly to the place, he would have captured it. But he merely occupied a position and overran the country outside the walls; finding that his confederates within failed to do what he expected, he took no further step. Meanwhile, the opponents of the conspirators, who were superior in number, prevented the immediate opening of the gates; and acting with Eucles, the general to whose care the place had been committed by the Athenians, they sent for help to the other general in the Thracian region, Thucydides the son of Olorus, who wrote this history; he was then at Thasos, an island colonized from Paros, and distant from Amphipolis about half a day's sail. As soon as he heard the news, he sailed quickly to Amphipolis with seven ships which happened to be on the spot; he wanted to get into Amphipolis if possible before a surrender, or, at any rate, to occupy Eion first.

105. Meanwhile Brasidas, fearing the arrival of the ships from Thasos and hearing that Thucydides had the right of working gold mines in the neighboring district of Thrace and consequently had influence as one of the leading men of the country, did his utmost to get possession of the city before his arrival. He was afraid that if Thucydides once came, the people of Amphipolis would no longer be disposed to surrender. For their hope would be that he would bring in allies from the islands or maritime towns or from Thrace and keep them safe. He there-

fore offered moderate terms, proclaiming that any Amphipolitan or Athenian might either remain in the city and have the enjoyment of his property on terms of equality; or, if he preferred, he might depart, taking his goods with him, within five days.

106. When the people heard the proclamation, they began to waver; for very few of the citizens were Athenians: the greater number were mixed in origin, and many were relatives of those who had been captured outside. In their alarm they thought the terms fair; the Athenian population, because they were glad to withdraw, reflecting how much greater their share of the danger was and not expecting speedy relief; the rest of the people, because they were to retain all their existing rights, and to be unexpectedly freed from danger. The partisans of Brasidas now proceeded to justify his proposals without disguise, for they saw that the mind of the people had changed and that they no longer paid any regard to the Athenian general who was on the spot. So the agreement was made and his terms were accepted. Thus, the city was surrendered; and on the evening of the same day, Thucydides and his ships sailed into Eion, but not until Brasidas had taken possession of Amphipolis, missing Eion only by a night. For if the ships had not come to the rescue with all speed, he would have taken it at dawn.

107. Thucydides now put Eion in a state of defense, desiring to provide not only against any immediate attempt of Brasidas but also against future danger. He received the fugitives who had chosen to move there from Amphipolis according to the agreement. Brasidas suddenly sailed with a number of small craft down the river to Eion, hoping that he might take the point which runs out from the wall and thereby command the entrance to the harbor; at the same time he made an attack by land. But in both these attempts he was foiled. He then took measures for the settlement of Amphipolis. Myrcinus, a city in the Edonian country, joined him, Pittacus the king of the Edonians having been assassinated by the children of Goaxis and Brauro his wife. Soon afterwards Galepsus and Oesymè (both colonies from Thasos)

came over to him. Perdiccas too arrived shortly after the taking of Amphipolis and assisted him in settling the newly acquired towns.

108. The Athenians were seriously alarmed at the loss of Amphipolis, especially because the place was very useful to them in supplying revenue and timber for shipbuilding, and because as far as the Strymon the Lacedæmonians could always have found a way to the allies of Athens, if the Thessalians allowed them to pass; but until they gained possession of the bridge, they could have proceeded no further; above, the river forms a large lake for a long distance and below, towards Eion, there were triremes on guard. But now they thought all difficulty had been removed, and they feared that their allies would revolt.[1] For Brasidas showed himself moderate in all his actions, and whenever he made a speech would declare that he was sent to emancipate Hellas. When the cities which were subject to Athens heard of the taking of Amphipolis and of his promises and mild conduct, they were more impatient than ever to rise, and secretly sent embassies to him, asking him to come and help them, every one of them wanting to be first in revolt. They thought that there was actually no danger, for they had underestimated the Athenian power to an extent that later became apparent. They tended to believe without proof what they wished, instead of exercising foresight which saves men from mistakes. (It is common for men to rely for the fulfillment of their desires on unreflecting hope and only when they are averse to some course, to give reason full power to reject it.) Moreover, the Athenians had lately received a blow in Bœotia, and Brasidas told the allies what was likely to attract them but was untrue—that at Nisæa the Athenians had refused to fight against his unassisted forces. And so they grew bold and were confident that no army would ever reach them. Above all, they were influenced by the pleasurable excitement of the moment; they were now for the first time going to find out of what the Lacedæmonians were capable when their passion was aroused, and therefore they were ready to risk anything. The Athenians were aware of their disaffection; and as far as they could, at short

notice and in wintertime, they sent garrisons to the different cities. Brasidas also dispatched a message to the Lacedæmonians requesting them to let him have additional forces, and he himself began to build triremes on the Strymon. But they would not second his efforts because their leading men were jealous of him and also because they preferred to recover the prisoners taken in the island and bring the war to an end.

[The Spartan government therefore negotiated a year's truce (423), as a preliminary to peace. Meantime Brasidas won over Toronè (betrayed by oligarchs), Scionè and Mendè, as well as other cities in Thrace. Both Scionè and Mendè revolted after the truce; and the Athenians naturally resumed operations in the north, with a good chance of success, since Brasidas had quarreled with Perdiccas, and Perdiccas used his influence in Thessaly to prevent reinforcements reaching him. In 423 the Athenian general, Nicias, recovered Mendè with the help of most of the citizens, who were left to punish the authors of the revolt. In 422 he was replaced by Cleon, who had already carried a decree that the citizens of Scionè should be massacred, a decree that was put into effect later, when the town fell. Cleon recaptured Toronè and gained other successes minimized by Thucydides. He then prepared for an attack on Amphipolis from Eion.]

BOOK V

Brasidas

6. Cleon had now sailed around from Toronè against Amphipolis; and making Eion his headquarters, he attacked Stagirus, a colony of the Andrians, which he failed to take. He succeeded, however, in storming Galepsus, a Thasian colony. He sent an embassy to Perdiccas, requesting him to come with an army, according to the terms of the alliance, and another to Polles, the king of the Odomantian Thracians, who was to bring as many Thracian mercenaries as he could; he then remained quietly at Eion waiting for these reinforcements. Brasidas, hearing of all this, took up a counterposition on Cerdylium. This is a place high on the right bank of the river, not far from Amphipolis, belonging to the Argilians. From this spot he commanded a view of the country around, so that Cleon was sure to be seen by him if—as Brasidas fully expected—despising the numbers of his opponents, he should go up against Amphipolis without waiting for his reinforcements. At the same time he prepared for a battle, summoning to his side fifteen hundred Thracian mercenaries and the entire forces of the Edonians, who were peltasts and horsemen; he had already one thousand Myrcinian and Chalcidian peltasts, in addition to the troops in Amphipolis. His hoplites, when all mustered, amounted to about two thousand, and he had three hundred Hellenic cavalry. Of these forces about fifteen hundred were stationed with Brasidas on Cerdylium, and the remainder were posted under Clearidas in Amphipolis.

7. Cleon did nothing for a time, but he was soon compelled to make the movement which Brasidas expected. For the soldiers were disgusted at their inaction and drew comparisons between the generals; what skill and

daring might be expected on the one side, and what ignorance and cowardice on the other. And they remembered how unwilling they had been to follow Cleon when they left Athens.[1] Observing their murmurs and not wanting them to be depressed by too long a stay in one place, he led his army forward. He acted in the same way as at Pylos; his good fortune there had convinced him of his own wisdom. That any one would come out to fight with him he never even imagined; he said that he was only going to look at the place. If he waited for a larger force, this was not because he was reckoning with the security that superior forces would give, if he were forced to fight, but that he might completely surround and storm the city. So he stationed his army upon a steep hill above Amphipolis, whence he surveyed with his own eyes the lake formed by the river Strymon, and the lie of the city on the side towards Thrace. He thought that he could go away without fighting whenever he pleased. For indeed there was no one to be seen on the walls, nor passing through the gates, which were all closed. He thought that he had made a mistake in coming up against the city without siege engines; had he brought them he would have taken Amphipolis, for there was no one to prevent him.

8. No sooner did Brasidas see the Athenians in motion than he himself descended from Cerdylium and went into Amphipolis. He did not go out and draw up his forces in order of battle; he feared too much the inferiority of his own troops, not in their numbers (which were about equal to those of the enemy), but in quality; for the Athenian forces were the flower of their army, and they were supported by the best of the Lemnians and Imbrians.[1] So he determined to use a stratagem in attack, thinking that if he showed the Athenians the real number and meager equipment of his soldiers, he would be less likely to succeed than if he came upon them before they had had time to observe his forces and to view them with a contempt based on the facts. Selecting 150 hoplites and handing over the rest to Clearidas, he resolved to make a sudden attack before the Athenians retired, considering that if their reinforcements should arrive,

he might never again have such an opportunity of catching them by themselves.

[*In a speech here omitted, Brasidas outlines the plan he was to follow.*]

10. When Brasidas had thus spoken, he prepared to sally forth with his own division and stationed the rest of his army with Clearidas at the so-called Thracian gate, that they might come out and support him in accordance with his instructions. He had been seen descending from Cerdylium into Amphipolis and then offering up sacrifice at the temple of Athene within the walls and engaged in these activities; for the interior of the city was visible from the surrounding country; and a report was brought to Cleon, who had just gone forward to reconnoiter, that the whole army of the enemy could plainly be seen collected inside the town and that the feet of numerous men and horses ready to come out were visible under the gate. He went to the spot and saw for himself; and not wishing to fight it out until his allies arrived and thinking he could get away soon enough, he gave a general signal for retreat, at the same time ordering his forces to make a left turn, the only possible maneuver, and retire gradually towards Eion. They appeared to linger, whereupon he caused his own right wing to face round; and so with his unshielded side[1] exposed to the enemy, he began to lead off his army. Meanwhile Brasidas, seeing that the Athenians were on the move and that his opportunity was come, said to his companions and to the troops: "These men do not mean to face us; look at the movement of their spears and their heads. Men who act in this way seldom withstand attack. Open the gates there as I ordered, and let us boldly attack them at once." Thereupon he went out himself by the gate leading to the palisade and by the first gate of the long wall which was then standing, and ran at full speed straight up the road, where, on the steepest part of the hill, a trophy now stands. He then attacked the center of the Athenians, who were terrified at his audacity and their own disorder, and put them to flight. Then Clearidas, as he

was bidden, sallied out by the Thracian gate with his division, and charged the Athenians. The sudden attack at both points created a panic among them. Their left wing, which had proceeded some way ahead and was near Eion, was at once cut off and fled. They were already in full retreat when Brasidas was wounded, attacking the right wing in its turn; the Athenians did not observe his fall, and those about him carried him off the field. The right wing of the Athenians was more disposed to stand. Cleon indeed, who had never intended to stand, fled at once, and was overtaken and killed by a Myrcinian peltast. But his soldiers rallied where they were on the top of the hill and repulsed Clearidas two or three times. They did not yield until the Chalcidian and Myrcinian cavalry and the peltasts hemmed them in and put them to flight with a shower of darts. And so the rout became general, and those of the Athenians who were not destroyed at once in close combat by the Chalcidian horse and peltasts, made their way with difficulty back to Eion after wandering by many paths over the hills. Brasidas was carried safely by his followers out of the battle into the city. He was still breathing and knew that his army had conquered, but soon afterwards he died. The rest of the army, returning with Clearidas from the pursuit, spoiled the dead and erected a trophy.

11. Brasidas was buried in the city with public honors in front of what is now the Agora. The whole body of the allies in military array followed him to the grave. The Amphipolitans enclosed his sepulcher; and to this day they sacrifice to him as to a hero,[1] and have also instituted games and yearly offerings in his honor. They dedicated their colony to him as their founder, pulling down the buildings of Hagnon and obliterating any memorials which might have remained to future time of his foundation. For they considered Brasidas to have been their deliverer, and under the present circumstances the fear of Athens induced them to pay court to their Lacedæmonian allies. That Hagnon should retain his honors, now that they were enemies of the Athenians, seemed to them no longer in accordance with their interests and likely to be displeasing to him. . . .

The Peace of 421 B.C.

14. After the battle of Amphipolis and the return of Rhamphias from Thessaly,[1] neither side undertook any further military operations. Both alike were more inclined to peace. The Athenians had been beaten at Delium and shortly afterwards at Amphipolis; and so they had lost that hopeful confidence in their own strength which had indisposed them to treat before, when they thought that they would gain the upper hand, because good fortune was then on their side.[2] They were afraid too that their allies, elated at their disasters, would revolt still more; they repented that after the affair at Pylos, when they had a fine opportunity, they had not come to terms. The Lacedæmonians, on the other hand, inclined to peace because the course of the war had disappointed their expectations. They had thought that if they devastated Attica, they would crush the power of Athens within a few years;[3] they had received a blow at Sphacteria such as Sparta had never experienced until then; their country was continually ravaged from Pylos and Cythera; the Helots were deserting, and they were always fearing lest those who had not deserted, relying on foreign help, should seize their opportunity and revolt, as they had done before.[4] Moreover, the truce for thirty years which they had made with Argos was on the point of expiring;[5] the Argives were unwilling to renew it unless Cynuria were restored to them,[6] and the Lacedæmonians thought it impossible to fight against the Argives and Athenians combined. They suspected also that some of the Peloponnesian cities would secede and join the Argives, which proved to be the case.

15. Upon these grounds both governments thought it desirable to make peace. The Lacedæmonians were the more eager of the two because they wanted to recover the prisoners taken at Sphacteria, for the Spartiates among them were of high rank and related to men of high rank. They had negotiated for their recovery immediately after they were taken; but the Athenians, in the hour of their prosperity, would not as yet agree to fair terms. After their defeat at Delium, the Lacedæmonians

were well aware that they would be more compliant; and therefore they had at once made a truce for a year, during which the envoys of the two states were to meet and consult about a longer term. When Athens had received a second blow at Amphipolis and after the death of Brasidas and Cleon, who had been the two greatest enemies of peace—the one, because the war brought him success and reputation and the other, because he thought that in quiet times his misdeeds would be more manifest and his slanders less credible—the two chief aspirants for political power at Athens and Sparta, Pleistoanax the son of Pausanias, king of the Lacedæmonians, and Nicias the son of Niceratus the Athenian, who had been the most fortunate general of his day, became more eager than ever to make an end of the war. Nicias desired, while he was still immune from reverses and held in repute, to preserve his good fortune, to rest from his own exertions for the moment, to give the people rest, and to leave behind him to other ages the name of a man who in all his life had never brought disaster on the city; he thought that the way to gain his wish was to trust as little as possible to fortune and to keep out of danger, and that danger would be best avoided by peace. Pleistoanax wanted peace because his enemies circulated slanders about his return and were always stirring up the scruples of the Lacedæmonians against him, attributing any misfortunes to his illegal return from exile. For they accused him and Aristocles his brother of having induced the priestess at Delphi, whenever Lacedæmonian envoys came to inquire of the oracle, constantly to repeat the same answer: "Bring back the seed of the hero son of Zeus from a strange country to your own; else you will plough with a silver ploughshare," until, after a banishment of nineteen years, he persuaded the Lacedæmonians to bring him home again with the same kind of dances and sacrifices, as when they first established their kings at the foundation of Lacedæmon. He had been banished on account of his withdrawal from Attica, when he was supposed to have been bribed.[1] While in exile at Lycæum, he had occupied a house half within the sacred precinct of Zeus, through fear of the Lacedæmonians.

17. He was vexed by these accusations; and thinking that in peace, when there would be no misfortunes and when the Lacedæmonians would have recovered the captives, he would himself be less open to attack, whereas in war leading men are always of necessity subject to accusation on the occasion of disasters, he was very anxious to come to terms. Negotiations went on during the winter. Towards spring the Lacedæmonians sent around to the allies for contingents to build a fort in Attica; they thought that by such menaces the Athenians would be induced to listen to them. At the conferences many demands were simultaneously urged on both sides; but an understanding was arrived at that peace should be made, both parties giving up what they had gained by arms. The Athenians, however, were to retain Nisæa; for when they demanded the restoration of Platæa, the Thebans protested that they had obtained possession of the place, not by force or treachery, but by the capitulation of the inhabitants, to which the Athenians rejoined that they had obtained Nisæa in the same manner. The Lacedæmonians then summoned their allies; and although the Bœotians, Corinthians, Eleans, and Megarians were dissatisfied, the rest voted for peace. And so the peace was concluded and ratified by oaths and libations, the Lacedæmonians binding themselves to the Athenians and the Athenians to the Lacedæmonians in the following terms:[1]

18. *The Athenians and Lacedæmonians and their allies made peace upon the following terms, and swore each city separately:*

I. Touching the common temples, anyone who pleases may sacrifice in them and inquire at them on behalf either of himself or of the state, according to the ancestral customs, and go to them both by land and sea, without fear.

II. The precinct and the temple of Apollo at Delphi and the Delphian people shall be autonomous and shall retain their own revenues and their own courts of justice, both for themselves and for their territory, according to the ancestral customs.

III. The peace between the Athenians and their allies

and the Lacedæmonians and their allies shall endure fifty years, both by sea and land, without fraud or hurt.

IV. They shall not be allowed to bear arms to the hurt of one another in any way or manner, neither the Lacedæmonians and their allies against the Athenians and their allies, nor the Athenians and their allies against the Lacedæmonians and their allies; and they shall determine any controversy which may arise between them by oaths and legal means in such sort as they may agree.

V. The Lacedæmonians and their allies shall restore Amphipolis to the Athenians.

VI. The inhabitants of any cities which the Lacedæmonians deliver over to the Athenians may depart whithersoever they please and take their property with them. The said cities shall be autonomous but shall pay the tribute which was fixed in the time of Aristides. After the conclusion of the treaty, the Athenians and their allies shall not be allowed to bear arms against them to their hurt so long as they pay the tribute. The cities are these —Argilus, Stagirus, Acanthus, Scolus, Olynthus, Spartolus:[2] *these shall be allies neither of the Lacedæmonians nor of the Athenians; but if the Athenians succeed in persuading them, having their consent, they may make them allies.*

VII. The Mecybernæans, Sanæans and Singæans shall dwell in their own cities on the same terms as the Olynthians and Acanthians.

VIII. The Lacedæmonians and the allies shall restore Panactum to the Athenians. The Athenians shall restore to the Lacedæmonians Coryphasium,[3] *Cythera, Methonè, Pteleum and Atalantè.*

IX. The Athenians shall surrender the Lacedæmonian captives whom they have in their public prison or in any other within the Athenian dominions, and they shall let go the Peloponnesians who are besieged in Scionè and any other allies of the Lacedæmonians who are in Scione and all whom Brasidas introduced into the place and any of the allies of the Lacedaemonians who are in the public prison at Athens or in any other within the Athenian dominions. The Lacedæmonians and their allies in the same manner shall restore those of the Athenians and their allies who are their prisoners.

X. Respecting Scionè, Toronè and Sermylè[4] *or any cities which are held by the Athenians, the Athenians shall do with the inhabitants of the said cities, or of any cities which are held by them, as they think fit.*

XI. The Athenians shall bind themselves by oath to the Lacedæmonians and their allies, city by city; and the oath shall be taken by seventeen persons and shall be that which in the several cities of the contracting parties is deemed the most binding. The oath shall be in the following form: "I will abide by this treaty and by this peace justly and without fraud." The Lacedæmonians and their allies shall bind themselves by oath in the same way to the Athenians. This oath shall be renewed by both parties every year; and they shall erect pillars at Olympia, Delphi and the Isthmus,[5] *at Athens in the Acropolis, at Lacedæmon in the temple of Apollo at Amyclæ.*

XII. If anything whatsoever be forgotten on one side or the other, either party may, without violation of their oaths, alter the treaty by lawful negotiations in such manner as shall seem good to the two parties, the Athenians and Lacedæmonians.

[*The official dating and names of signatories follow:*]

20. This treaty was concluded at the end of winter, just at the beginning of spring, immediately after the festival of Dionysus held at Athens in the city. Ten years, with a difference of a few days, had passed since the commencement of the war. This can be seen by reckoning according to natural divisions of time and not by relying on the lists kept in each city of the holders of offices or dignities by which past events are dated: it is not accurate to date events by such lists as they may occur in the beginning or middle or at any time within a year of office. But if the count is made by summers and winters as they are here set down, each amounting to half a year, it will be found that ten summers and as many winters passed in this first war.[1]

[The prisoners were exchanged; and to guard against the danger from Argos and discontent elsewhere in the Peloponnese, the Spartans also concluded a treaty of alliance with Athens. Thucydides proceeds to explain that the peace was not durable and that the first ten years' war forms part of a struggle for twenty-seven years which embraced also a period of nominal peace between Athens and Sparta (421-14) and a second decade of open war. This is one passage that must have been written after 404. It is a matter for speculation how soon Thucydides realized that the peace of 421 had not ended the struggle which he began to describe in 431 and decided to continue his work.]

25. The treaty and the alliance which terminated the ten years' war were made in the Ephorate of Pleistolas at Lacedæmon and the Archonship of Alcæus at Athens. Those who accepted the treaty were now at peace; but the Corinthians and several of the Peloponnesian cities did what they could to disturb the arrangement; and at once a new cause of quarrel set the allies against the Lacedæmonians, who also, as time went on, incurred the suspicion of the Athenians because in certain particulars they would not execute the provisions of the treaty. For six years and ten months the two powers abstained from invading each other's territories, but abroad the cessation of arms was intermittent, and they did each other all the harm which they could. At last they were under the necessity of breaking the treaty made at the end of the ten years and engaged once more in open war.

26. Thucydides of Athens also wrote of these events following their order, by summers and winters, up to the destruction of the Athenian empire and the taking of Piræus and the Long Walls by the Lacedæmonians and their allies. Altogether the war lasted 27 years; for if anyone argue that the interval during which the truce continued should be excluded, his claim will be wrong. In distinguishing this period, let him look at the facts and he will see that the term *peace* can hardly be applied to a state of affairs in which neither party gave back

or received all the places stipulated; moreover, in the Mantinean and Epidaurian wars and in other matters, there were violations of the treaty on both sides: the Chalcidian allies maintained their attitude of hostility toward Athens, and the Bœotians merely observed an armistice terminable at ten days' notice. So that, including the first ten years' war, the doubtful truce which followed and the later war, anyone who reckons by the seasons will find that I have rightly given the exact number of years with the difference only of a few days. He will also find that this was the solitary instance in which those who put their faith in oracles were justified by the event. For I well remember how, from the beginning to the end of the war, there was a common and often repeated saying that it was to last thrice nine years. I lived through the whole of it as a man of mature years and judgment, and I took great pains to make out the exact truth. For twenty years I was banished from my country after I held the command at Amphipolis; and as an exile I associated with both sides, with the Peloponnesians quite as much as with the Athenians, and was thus enabled to watch quietly the course of events. I will now proceed to narrate the quarrels which after the first ten years broke up the treaty, and the events of the later war.

The Mantinea Campaign

[*The following events are highly intricate. In brief, Corinth and Bœotia were opposed to the peace out of enmity to Athens; Elis and Mantinea, two members of the Peloponnesian league, had private disputes with Sparta; and the truce between Argos and Sparta was due to run out in early 420. Corinth tried to organize these and other cities into a new confederacy to counterbalance Sparta and Athens, who were now allied. But the negotiations broke down, fundamentally because Corinth and Bœotia were seeking a common front against Athens, while Argos, Elis and Mantinea had no quarrel with Athens but only with Sparta. At the same time the entente between Sparta and Athens did not prove lasting.*

The Spartan garrison had evacuated Amphipolis, and Sparta was unable to fulfill her obligation under the treaty to restore the place to Athens. In fact, the cities in the Thracian region which had revolted and not been recovered by Athens in the war did not return to Athenian allegiance, in accordance with the treaty. As a reprisal Athens held on to Pylos and Cythera. Eventually in 420 Athens entered into a defensive alliance with Argos, Mantinea and Elis, without formally denouncing either the peace or the defensive treaty of alliance with Sparta. Sparta was, however, at war with these three cities; and Athenian forces took part in military operations against Sparta. This was not regarded as a breach of the peace so long as the Athenians abstained from a direct attack on Spartan territory. The architect of the new alliance at Athens was Alcibiades, who for the first time at the age of about thirty became important in Athenian politics. Thucydides explains his influence by his patrician descent and says that he genuinely preferred the Argive alliance but acted partly out of pique because the Spartans had neglected him, despite his family connections with them, when negotiating the peace of 421. By reading between the lines of Thucydides' narrative and from other evidence, we can see that in these years Athens was hampered by the rivalry between Nicias, who preferred a rather pacific policy, and Alcibiades, and by the jealousy between Alcibiades and other radical leaders [ct. II:65]. Alcibiades' policy was not followed wholeheartedly, and Athens gave no very effective aid to her Peloponnesian allies and made no determined effort to seize the opportunity of destroying Sparta's power in the Peloponnese. At the same time the new alignment brought Corinth and Bœotia firmly back on to Sparta's side. In 418, in the absence of Athenian forces, Argos was all but forced to surrender to Sparta; but King Agis, the Spartan general, was content to make a truce for four months. Alcibiades persuaded the Argives that the truce was not binding; the allied forces, now including one thousand hoplites and three hundred horse from Athens, but deserted by the Eleans, prepared to attack Tegea; and the Spartans under Agis marched out in full force, relieved the pressure on Tegea and encamped in Mantinean territory. (Tegea and Mantinea were in Arcadia, immediately to the north of Sparta, on a high plateau.)]

65. When the Argives and their allies saw the enemy, they took up a steep and hardly assailable position and arranged themselves in order of battle. The Lacedæmonians instantly advanced upon them, and had proceeded within a javelin or stone's throw when one of the elder Spartans, seeing the strength of the ground which they were attacking, called out to Agis that he was trying to mend one error by another, showing that his present inopportune eagerness for battle was intended to repair the discredit of his retreat from Argos. And either in consequence of this exclamation or because some new thought suddenly struck him, he withdrew his army in haste without actually engaging. He marched back into the district of Tegea and proceeded to turn the water into the Mantinean territory. This water is a source of war between the Mantineans and Tegeans on account of the harm which is commonly done to one or other of them according to the direction in which it flows. Agis desired that the Argives and their allies, when they heard of this, should come down and try to prevent the diversion of the water and fight on level ground. Accordingly, he stayed by the water during the whole day, diverting the stream. The Argives and their allies were at first amazed at the sudden retreat of their enemies when they were so near, and did not know what to conjecture. But when the Lacedæmonians had retired and disappeared from view, and they found themselves standing still and not following, they once more began to blame their own generals. Their cry was that they had already let the Lacedæmonians slip when they had them at a disadvantage close to Argos, and now they were running away and no one pursued them; this inactivity was saving the Lacedæmonians and betraying their own cause. The commanders were at first bewildered; but later they quitted the hill and, advancing into the plain, encamped in a position to attack the enemy.

66. On the following day, the Argives and their allies drew themselves up in the order in which they intended to fight, should they meet with the enemy. Meanwhile, the Lacedæmonians returned from the water to their old encampment near the temple of Heracles. There they saw quite close to them the Argive army, which had moved on from the hill, and was already in full order of battle. Never within the recollection of men were the Lacedæmonians more dismayed than at that instant; not a moment was lost in preparation: immediately they hurried every man to his own place, King Agis directing every movement in accordance with custom. For when the king is in the field everything is done under his orders; he himself gives instructions to the polemarchs, which they convey to the commanders of *lochoi;* these again to the commanders of pentecosties; the commanders of pentecosties to the commanders of enomoties; and these to the enomoty. Special instructions, if wanted, are passed down through the army in the same way, and quickly reach their destination. For almost the whole Lacedæmonian army are officers who have officers under them, and the responsibility of executing an order devolves upon many.

67. On this occasion the Sciritæ[1] formed the left wing, a position in the Lacedæmonian army to which they have a perpetual and exclusive right. Next to them were placed the troops who had served in Thrace under Brasidas and with them the Neodamodes.[2] Next in order were ranged the several *lochoi* of the Lacedæmonian army, and next to them the Heræans of Arcadia; then the Mænalians, and on the right wing the Tegeans, and a few Lacedæmonians at the extreme point of the line; the cavalry were placed on both wings. This was the order of the Lacedæmonians. On the right wing[3] of the enemy were placed the Mantineans because the action was in their country, and next to them such of the Arcadians as were their allies. Then came the select force of a thousand Argives, whom the city had long trained at the public expense in military exercises; next the other Argives; and after them their allies, the Cleonæans and Orneatæ. Last of all, the Athenians

occupied the left wing, supported by their own cavalry.

68. Such was the order and composition of the two armies: that of the Lacedæmonians appeared to be the larger; but what the number was of the several contingents or the total on either side, I could not state with accuracy; for the secrecy of the government did not allow the strength of the Lacedæmonian army to be known, and the numbers on the other side were thought to be exaggerated by the vanity natural to men when speaking of their own forces. However, the following calculation may give some idea of the Lacedæmonian numbers. There were seven *lochoi* in the field, besides the Sciritæ who numbered 600; in each division there were 4 pentecosties, in every pentecosty 4 enomoties, and of each enomoty 4 men fought in the front rank. The depth of the line was not everywhere equal, but was left to the discretion of the commanders of *lochoi;* on an average it was 8 deep. The front line consisted of 448 men, exclusive of the Sciritæ.[1]

69. The two armies were now on the point of engaging, but first the several commanders addressed exhortations to their own contingents. The Mantineans were told that they were not only about to fight for their country, but would have to choose between dominion or slavery; were they to be deprived of the dominion they had tasted, or to avoid a further taste of slavery?[1] The Argives were reminded that in old times they had possessed hegemony and, later, parity in the Peloponnese; they should not tolerate the loss of this forever but should revenge themselves upon neighbors who were hateful and had wronged them again and again. The Athenians were told that it was glorious to be fighting side by side with a host of brave allies and to be found equal to the bravest. If they could conquer a Lacedæmonian army in the Peloponnese, they would both extend and secure their dominion, and need never fear an invader again. Such were the exhortations addressed to the Argives and to their allies. But the Lacedæmonians, both in their war songs and in the words which a man spoke to his comrade, only reminded one another as brave men of what they had learned. For they knew

that more safety was to be found in long previous training than in eloquent exhortations uttered when they were going into action.

70. At length the two armies met. The Argives and their allies advanced with fury and determination. The Lacedæmonians moved slowly to the melody given by many flute players, who were stationed in their ranks, and played, not as an act of religion, but in order that the army might march evenly and in time, and that the line might not break, as often happens in great armies when they go into battle.

71. Before they had actually closed, they decided on the following action. All armies, when engaging, are apt to thrust outward their right wing, and both opposing forces tend to outflank the enemy's left with their right, because every soldier fears for his exposed side and keeps as near as he can to the shield of his comrade on the right in the belief that the closer he draws in, the better he will be protected. The first man in the front rank of the right wing is originally responsible for the deflection, for he is always anxious to withdraw from the enemy his own exposed side; and the rest, from the same fear, follow his example. In this battle the line of the Mantineans extended far beyond the Sciritae; and still further, in proportion as the army to which they belonged was the larger, did the Lacedæmonians and Tegeans extend beyond the Athenians. Agis was afraid that the Lacedæmonian left wing would be surrounded; and thinking that the Mantineans outflanked them too far, he signaled to the Sciritæ and the old soldiers of Brasidas to make a lateral movement away from their own army, and so cover the Mantineans. To fill up the space thus left vacant, he ordered Hipponoidas and Aristocles, two of the polemarchs, to bring up two *lochoi* from his right wing, thinking that he would still have more troops there than he wanted and that he would thus strengthen the line opposed to the Mantineans.

72. He had given the order at the last moment, when the charge had already begun, and Aristocles and Hipponoidas refused to make the movement. On this ac-

count they were later charged and banished from Sparta, as it was thought that they had shown cowardice. The enemy were upon him before he was ready; and as the two divisions did not advance into the place left by the Sciritæ, Agis ordered the Sciritæ themselves to close up again; but they also were now unable to fill the vacant space. Thus Lacedæmonian experience utterly failed; yet never did they more clearly show that in courage they were just as superior. When they were at close quarters with the enemy, the Mantinean right put to flight the Sciritae and the soldiers of Brasidas. The Mantineans and their allies and the thousand chosen Argives dashed in through the enclosed gap; the Lacedæmonians suffered heavily; they were surrounded, put to flight and driven back to their wagons, where some of the older men who had been appointed to guard them were killed. In this part of the field the Lacedæmonians were beaten; but elsewhere, and especially in the center of the army, where King Agis was posted with the three hundred so-called horsemen,[1] they charged the older Argives, the five *lochoi* as they are termed, the Cleonæans, Orneatæ, and those of the Athenians who were ranged with them, and put them to flight. Most of them never even struck a blow but gave way at once on the approach of the Lacedæmonians; some were actually trodden under foot in the fear of being overtaken by them.

73. When the Argives and their allies had given way in this quarter, they were now cut off from their comrades to the left as well as to the right of the line; meanwhile the extended right wing of the Lacedæmonians and the Tegeans threatened to surround the Athenians. They were in great danger; their men were being hemmed in at one point, and were already defeated at another; and but for their cavalry, which did them good service, they would have suffered more than any other part of the army. Just then Agis, observing the distress of the Lacedæmonian left wing, which was opposed to the Mantineans and the thousand select Argives, commanded his whole forces to go and assist their own defeated troops. Whereupon the Athenians,

when their opponents turned aside and began to move away from them, quietly made their escape, and along with them the defeated Argives. The Mantineans and their allies and the select force of Argives, seeing their army conquered and the Lacedæmonians bearing down upon them, gave up all thoughts of pressing hard their opponents and fled. Many of the Mantineans were killed, most of the select Argive force escaped. In their retreat the fugitives were not far or fiercely pursued, for the Lacedæmonians fight long and refuse to move until they have put an enemy to flight; but, having once defeated him, they do not follow him far or long.

74. This was roughly the course of the battle, by far the greatest of Hellenic battles which had taken place for a long time, and which was fought by the most famous cities. The Lacedæmonians exposed the arms of the enemies' dead and at once erected a trophy and plundered the bodies; and taking up their own dead, they carried them away to Tegea, where they were buried; the enemies' dead they gave back under truce. Of the Argives, Orneatæ and Cleonæans there fell seven hundred, of the Mantineans two hundred, and of the Athenians, including their settlers in Ægina, two hundred, and both their generals. As to the Lacedæmonians, their allies were not hard pressed and therefore incurred no notable loss; their own dead are reported to have numbered about three hundred, but the truth was hard to ascertain. . . .

75. Thus, by a single action, the Lacedæmonians wiped out the charge of cowardice (which was due to their misfortune at Sphacteria and in general due to lack of judgment and slowness to act) then current against them in Hellas. They were now thought to have suffered from a mischance but to be the same as ever in character.

The Melian Dialogue

[*Mantinea and Elis abandoned the fight, and even Argos made peace and alliance with Sparta. This was the work of the oligarchic party there, but it was soon overthrown, and the war resumed. Thucydides records various other desultory operations in the Peloponnese and elsewhere in 417 and 416.*]

84. The Athenians next made an expedition against the island of Melos with thirty ships of their own, six Chian, and two Lesbian, twelve hundred hoplites and three hundred archers and twenty mounted archers of their own, and about fifteen hundred hoplites furnished by their allies in the islands. The Melians are colonists of the Lacedæmonians who would not submit to Athens like the other islanders. At first they were neutral and passive. But when the Athenians tried to coerce them by ravaging their lands, they were driven into open hostilities.[1] The generals, Cleomedes the son of Lycomedes and Tisias the son of Tisimachus, encamped with the Athenian forces on the island. But before they did the country any harm, they sent envoys to negotiate with the Melians. Instead of bringing these envoys before the people, the Melians desired them to explain their errand to the minority who held the magistracies. They spoke as follows:

85. "Since we are denied a public audience on the ground that the multitude might be deceived by hearing our seductive arguments without refutation if they were set forth in a single uninterrupted oration (for we are perfectly aware that this is what you mean in bringing us before the select few), we ask you who are seated here to proceed with even further caution, to reply on each point, instead of speaking continuously yourselves, and to take up at once any statement of ours of which you do not approve, and so reach your decision. Say first of all how you like our proposal."

86. The Melian representatives answered: "The quiet interchange of explanations is reasonable, and we do not object to that. But at this very time you are actually engaged in acts of war, which obviously belie your words. We see that you mean to decide the discussion yourselves and that at the end of it, if (as is likely) the justice of our cause prevail and we therefore refuse to yield, we may expect war; if we are convinced by you, slavery."

87. *Ath.* "Of course, if you are going to base your calculations on conjectures of the future or if you meet us with any other purpose than that of looking your circumstances in the face and thinking how to save your city, we might as well have done; but if this is your intention, we will proceed."

88. *Mel.* "It is natural and excusable that men in our position should resort to many arguments and considerations. But we admit that this conference has met to consider the question of our preservation; and therefore let the argument proceed in the manner which you propose, if you think that best."

89. *Ath.* "Well, then, we Athenians will use no fine words; we will not say at length, without carrying conviction, that we have a right to rule because we overthrew the Persians or that we are attacking you now because we are suffering any injury at your hands. And you should not expect to convince us by arguing that, although a colony of the Lacedæmonians, you have taken no part in their expeditions or that you have never done us any wrong. You must act with realism on the basis of what we both really think, for we both alike know that in human reckoning the question of justice only enters where there is equal power to enforce it and that the powerful exact what they can and the weak grant what they must."

90. *Mel.* "Well, then, since you thus set aside justice and make expediency the subject of debate, in our judgment it is certainly of advantage that you respect the common good, that to every man in peril fair treatment be accorded, and that any plea which he has urged, even if failing of the point a little, should help his cause. Your interest in this principle is quite as great as ours, since if you fall, you might incur the heaviest vengeance and be an example to mankind."

91. *Ath.* "The end of our empire, even if it should fall, does not dismay us; for ruling states such as Lacedæmon are not cruel to their vanquished enemies.[1] But we are not now contending with the Lacedæmonians; the real danger is from our subjects, who may of their own motion rise up and overcome their masters. But this is a

danger which you may leave to us. We will show that we have come in the interests of our empire and that in what we are about to say, we are only seeking the preservation of your city. We wish to subdue you without effort and to preserve you to our mutual advantage."

92. *Mel.* "It may be your advantage to be our masters, but how can it be ours to be your slaves?"

93. *Ath.* "By submission you would avert the most terrible sufferings, and we should profit from not destroying you."

94. *Mel.* "But must we be your enemies? Would you not receive us as friends if we are neutral and remain at peace with you?"

95. *Ath.* "No, your enmity does not injure us as much as your friendship; for your enmity is in the eyes of our subjects a demonstration of our power, your friendship of our weakness."

96. *Mel.* "But do your subjects think it fair not to distinguish between cities in which you have no connection and those which are chiefly your own colonies, and in some cases have revolted and been subdued?"

97. *Ath.* "Why, they believe that neither lack pleas of right, but that by reason of their power some escape us and that we do not attack them out of fear. So that your subjection would give us security, as well as an extension of empire, all the more as you are islanders, and insignificant islanders."

98. *Mel.* "But do you not think that there is security in our proposal? For, once more, since you drive us from the plea of justice and urge us to submit to you our interest, we must show you what is for our advantage and try to convince you, if it really coincides with yours: Will you not be making enemies of all who are now neutrals? When they see how you are treating us, they will expect you some day to turn against them; and if so, are you not strengthening the enemies whom you already have and bringing upon you others who, if they could help it, would never dream of being your enemies at all?"

99. *Ath.* "We consider that our really dangerous ene-

mies are not any of the peoples inhabiting the mainland who are secure in their freedom and will defer indefinitely any measures of precaution against us, but islanders who, like you, are under no control, and all who are already irritated by the necessity of submission to our empire; for without calculating, they would be most likely to plunge themselves, as well as us, into a danger for all to foresee."

100. *Mel.* "Surely then, if you and your subjects will brave all this danger, you to preserve your empire and they to be quit of it, how base and cowardly would it be for us, as we are still free, not to do and suffer anything rather than be your slaves."

101. *Ath.* "Not if you deliberate with sound sense; you are in an unequal contest; not about your good character and avoiding dishonor: you must think of saving yourselves by not resisting far superior forces."

102. *Mel.* "But we know that the fortune of war is sometimes impartial and not always on the side of numbers. If we yield, hope is at once gone, but if we act, we can still hope to stand unbowed."

103. *Ath.* "Hope comforts men in danger; and when they have ample resources, it may be hurtful, but is not ruinous. But when her spendthrift nature has induced them to stake their all, they see her as she is only in the moment of their ruin; when their eyes are opened, and they would at last take precautions, they are left with nothing. You are weak, and a single turn of the scale may be your ruin: do not desire to be deluded; or to be like the common herd of men; when they still, humanly speaking, have a chance of survival but find themselves, in their extremity, destitute of real grounds for confidence, they resort to illusions, to prophecies and oracles and the like, which ruin men by the hopes which they inspire in them."

104. *Mel.* "You may be sure that we think it hard to struggle against your power and against fortune if she does not mean to be impartial. But still we trust that we shall not have the worst of the fortune that comes from heaven because we stand as righteous men against your injustice, and we are satisfied that our deficiency in

power will be compensated by the alliance of the Lacedæmonians; they are bound to help us, if only because we are their kinsmen and for the sake of their own honor. And therefore our confidence is not so utterly unreasonable."

105. *Ath.* "As for the gods, we expect to have quite as much of their favor as you: for we are not claiming or doing anything which goes beyond what men believe of the gods and desire in human relationships. For we believe of the gods by repute, and of men by clear evidence, that by a necessity of nature, wherever they have the power, they will rule. This law was not made by us, and we are not the first who have acted upon it; we did but inherit it, and shall bequeath it to all time; we obey it in the knowledge that you and all mankind, with our strength would act like us. So much for the gods; we have no reason to fear any lack of their favor. And then as to the Lacedæmonians—when you imagine that out of very shame they will assist you, we congratulate you on your blissful ignorance, but we do not admire your folly. No men do each other more services, by their own local standards, than the Lacedæmonians; but as for their conduct to the rest of the world, much might be said, but it could be most clearly expressed in a few words—of all men whom we know, they are the most conspicuous for identifying pleasure with honor and expediency with justice. But how inconsistent is such a character with your present unreasonable hope of deliverance!"

106. *Mel.* "That is the very reason why we are now particularly reliant on them; they will look to their interest, and therefore will not be willing to betray the Melians, their own colonists, lest they should be distrusted by their friends in Hellas and play into the hands of their enemies."

107. *Ath.* "Then you do not think that the path of expediency is safe, whereas justice and honor involve action and danger, which none are more generally averse to facing than the Lacedæmonians."

108. *Mel.* "No, we believe that they would be ready to face dangers for our sake, and will think them safer

where we are concerned. If action is required, we are close to the Peloponnese; and they can better trust our loyal feeling because we are their kinsmen."

109. *Ath.* "Yes, but what gives men security in joining in a conflict is clearly not the good will of those who summon help but a decided superiority in real power. To this none look more keenly than the Lacedæmonians; so little confidence have they in their own resources that they only attack their neighbors when they have numerous allies; and therefore they are not likely to find their way by themselves to an island, when we are masters of the sea."

110. *Mel.* "But they might send others; the Cretan sea is a large place, and the masters of the sea will have more difficulty in seizing vessels than those who would elude detection in making their escape. And if the attempt should fail, they might invade Attica itself and find their way to allies of yours whom Brasidas did not reach; and then you will have to make efforts, not for the conquest of a land which is not yours, but nearer home, for the preservation of your confederacy and of your own territory."

111. *Ath.* "Some of this may happen; we have actually experienced it, and you are not unaware that never once have the Athenians retired from a siege through fear of others. You told us that you would deliberate on the safety of your city; but we remark that, in this long discussion, you have uttered not a word which would justify men in expecting deliverance. Your strongest grounds are hopes deferred; and what power you have, compared with that already arrayed against you, is too little to save you. What you have in mind is most unreasonable, unless you ultimately come to a sounder decision after we have withdrawn. For surely you will not fall back on a sense of honor, which has been the ruin of so many, when danger and dishonor were staring them in the face. Many men with their eyes still open to the consequences have found the word *honor* too much for them and have let a mere name lure them on, until with their own acquiescence it has drawn down upon them real and irretrievable calamities; through their

own folly they have incurred a worse dishonor than fortune would have inflicted upon them. If you are wise, you will not run this risk; you will think it not unfitting to yield to the greatest of cities, which invites you to become her ally on reasonable terms, keeping your own land and merely paying tribute; you will find no honor, when you have a choice between two alternatives, safety and war, in obstinately preferring the worse. To maintain one's rights against equals, to be politic with superiors and to be moderate toward inferiors is generally the right course. Reflect once more when we have withdrawn, and say to yourselves over and over again that you are deliberating about your one and only country, which a single decision will save or destroy."

112. The Athenians left the conference; the Melians, after consulting among themselves, resolved to persevere in their refusal and gave the following answer: "Men of Athens, our resolution is unchanged; and we will not in a moment surrender that liberty which our city, founded seven hundred years ago, still enjoys; we will trust to the good fortune which, by the favor of the gods, has hitherto preserved us, and for human help, to the Lacedæmonians; and we will endeavor to save ourselves. We are ready, however, to be your friends and the enemies neither of you nor of the Lacedæmonians and we ask you to leave our country when you have made such a peace as appears to be in the interest of both parties."

113. This was the substance of the Melian answer; the Athenians said as they quitted the conference: "Well, we must say, judging from the decision at which you have arrived, that you are the only men who find things to come plainer than what lies before their eyes: your wishes make you see the secrets of the future as present realities; you put your faith in the Lacedæmonians, in fortune and in your hopes; none have more than you at stake, and none will be more utterly ruined."

[*Melos fell after a siege. The adult males were massacred, the women and children enslaved, an atrocity long remembered against Athens. There is nothing even in the arguments ascribed above to the Athenians to justify this inhumanity; indeed they approve moderation to inferiors (V:111). It is doubtful whether Thucydides could have known what went on in a secret conference, and the Athenian case bears all the marks of his own interpretation, not only of Athenian imperialism, but of the general truth about interstate relations (cf. Introduction). It may also be regarded as an ironic commentary on the character of the Athenian empire, on the very eve of its collapse; hence, the emphasis laid on an incident which in itself had no effect on the course of the war.]*

BOOK VI

The Athenian Decision to Invade Sicily

1. During the same winter (416-15) the Athenians conceived a desire of sending another expedition to Sicily, larger than those commanded by Laches and Eurymedon,[1] to conquer the island if they could. Most of them were unaware of its great size and numerous population, barbarian as well as Hellenic, and did not know that they were entering on a struggle almost as arduous as the war with the Peloponnesians. The voyage in a merchant vessel around Sicily takes up nearly eight days; and this great island is all but a part of the mainland, divided from it by not much more than twenty stades of water.

[*Thucydides inserts here a description of the inhabitants of Sicily which I omit. In brief, the island was divided between barbarian and Greek settlers. Of the former, the Sicanians and Elymians lived in the west; Egesta, which sought Athenian help under an old alliance, was an Elymian city. There were also in the west some Phœnician settlements under the protection of Carthage. (Thucydides never mentions that between 409 and 405 Carthage temporarily subdued most of the Greek cities; the great power she then showed makes it even more unlikely that Athens could have effected a permanent conquest.) The Sicels, an Italian people, lived mainly in the north and center; some were subject to Syracuse, others still independent. Greek colonization had begun in the late eighth century. By 415 the number of cities had been reduced to nine. Of these the Athenians could count on the help of the Chalcidian cities, Naxos and Catana; their former ally, Leontini, had been destroyed by Syracuse between 424 and 422. The others were mainly Dorian by race; viz., Syracuse, Camarina, Gela, Acragas, Selinus, Himera* and *Messene. Syracuse, a*

Corinthian colony, was much the strongest; it was as large as Athens (VII:28) and always threatened to dominate the island. As the sequel showed, Athens had some hopes of winning over Messene and Camarina, which proved abortive; Acragas, the chief rival of Syracuse, like Messene, remained neutral; the other cities, including Camarina, eventually helped Syracuse.]

6. These were the powerful peoples, Hellenic or barbarian, who inhabited Sicily; and this the great island on which the Athenians were determined to make war, under the pretense of wishing to assist their own kinsmen and the allies they had gained there, but, to adopt the truest explanation, from a desire to rule the whole of it. They were principally instigated by an embassy which had come from Egesta, and was urgent in requesting aid. The Egestæans had gone to war with the neighboring city of Selinus about certain questions of marriage and about a disputed piece of land. The Selinuntians summoned the Syracusans to their assistance, and their united forces reduced the Egestæans to great straits both by sea and land. The Egestæan envoys reminded the Athenians of the alliance which they had made in the time of Laches and the former war, and begged them to send ships to their relief. Besides other arguments, they urged in brief that if the Syracusans were not punished for the expulsion of the Leontines, and destroyed the remaining allies of the Athenians and got the whole power of Sicily into their own hands, there was a danger that one day they would come with a great army—Dorians to assist their Dorian kinsmen, and colonists to assist their Peloponnesian founders—and would unite in overthrowing Athens herself. It was good sense for the Athenians to combine with the allies who were still left to them against the Syracusans, especially since the Egestæans would themselves provide money sufficient for the war. These arguments were constantly repeated in the ears of the Athenian assembly by the Egestæans and their partisans; at length the people passed a vote that they would first send envoys to Egesta to investigate whether the Egestæans really had the money which they

professed to have in their treasury and in their temples, and to learn the state of the war with Selinus. . . .

8. Early in the spring of the next summer (415), the Athenian envoys returned from Sicily. They were accompanied by Egestæans who brought about sixty talents of uncoined silver, a month's pay for sixty vessels which they intended to ask Athens to send. The Athenians called an assembly; and when they heard both from their own and from the Egestæans envoys, among other inviting but untrue statements, that there was abundance of money lying ready in the temples and in the treasury of Egesta, they passed a vote that sixty ships should be sent to Sicily; Alcibiades the son of Cleinias, Nicias the son of Niceratus, and Lamachus the son of Xenophanes were appointed commanders with full powers to assist Egesta against Selinus and, if this did not demand all their military strength, to restore the Leontines and generally to further the Athenian interests in Sicily in such manner as they deemed best. Four days afterwards, another assembly was called to consider what steps should be taken for the immediate equipment of the expedition and to vote any additional measures which the generals might require. Nicias, who had been appointed general against his will, thought that the people had come to a wrong conclusion and that it was upon slight and specious grounds that they were aspiring to the conquest of all Sicily, which was no easy task. So, being desirous of diverting the Athenians from their purpose, he came forward and admonished them somewhat as follows:

9. "We are assembled here to discuss the preparations which are required for our expedition to Sicily, but in my judgment we ought still to examine the question whether we ought to go there at all; we should not be hasty in determining a matter of so much importance nor allow ourselves to enter into an impolitic war at the instigation of foreigners. Yet to me personally war brings honor, and I am less fearful than others for my own life: not that I think the worse of a citizen who shows a little forethought for his life or property; such men are most apt to desire the city's success in their own interest. But I have never in my life been induced by the high

honor in which I am held to say a single word contrary to what I thought; neither will I now: I will say simply what I believe to be best. If I recommended you to take care of what you have and not to risk the possessions of which you dispose for uncertain gains in the future, my words would be powerless in view of your character. But I shall show that your enterprise is inopportune and that you will find it hard to hold down the peoples you have attacked.

10. "I tell you that in going to Sicily you are leaving many enemies behind you and are bent on bringing new ones here. You are perhaps relying upon the treaty you have made. If you remain quiet, it will still be a treaty in name, for to a mere name the activities of certain persons both here and at Lacedæmon have reduced it. But if you meet with any serious reverse, your enemies will be upon you in a moment in considerable force. In the first place, they made it because of their disasters, under necessity; and it was more dishonorable to them than to us; and secondly, in the treaty itself there are many disputed points. And even this treaty several cities have not yet accepted, and very powerful cities too.[1] Some of these are at open war with us already; others may resume war at ten days' notice, and are only restrained because the Lacedæmonians are still inactive. And very possibly, if they find our power divided (and such a division is precisely what we are striving to create), they may eagerly join the Sicilians, whose alliance in the war they would previously have given much to obtain. We should examine these points. The city is far from the desired haven, and we should not take it upon us to run her into danger and seek to gain a new empire before we have fully secured the old. The Chalcidians in Thrace[2] have been rebels all these years and remain unsubdued, and there are other subjects of ours in various parts of the mainland who are uncertain in their allegiance. Yet we cannot lose a moment in avenging the wrongs of our fine allies, the Egestæans, while we still defer the punishment of our revolted subjects, whose offenses are of long standing.

11. "And yet if we subdue the Chalcidian rebels, we

may retain our hold on them; but even if we conquer the Sicilians, they are so distant and numerous that we could hardly rule them. And how foolish it is for anyone to select for attack a land which no conquest can secure, when failure leaves him weaker than he was before the attempt.

"In my view the Sicilian cities are not to be feared in their present condition and even less if they were to fall under Syracusan rule (and this is the prospect with which the Egestæans try, most of all, to alarm us). Some of them might cross the sea out of friendship for the Lacedæmonians now, but not in the situation envisaged; it is not natural for one empire to march against another. If they were to wrest from us our empire in concert with the Peloponnesians, the Peloponnesians would naturally overthrow theirs in just the same way. The Hellenes in Sicily would be most terrified of us if we were never to go there; in a less degree, if we were to display our strength and speedily depart; but if we were to suffer any reverse, they would very soon despise us and join our enemies in attacking us here. We all know that men marvel most at what is farthest off, whose reputation has been least tested; and this, Athenians, you have verified by your own experience with the Lacedæmonians and their allies. Your unexpected triumph over them, so different from your original apprehensions, has now made you despise them and cast your eyes on Sicily. But you ought not to be elated at the chance mishaps of your opponents; before you can be confident, you should have gained the mastery over their minds. Remember that the Lacedæmonians are sensitive to their dishonor and that their sole thought is how they may even yet find a way of inflicting a blow upon us which will retrieve their own disgrace; all the more because they have labored so earnestly and so long to win a noble reputation. If we show good sense, we shall not enter a contest for the Egestæans, mere barbarians, in Sicily; we shall take sharp precautions against a city whose oligarchy threatens us.[1]

12. "We must remember also that we have only just recovered in a small measure from a great plague and

war and thereby increased our resources in men and money. It is our duty to spend them upon ourselves at home and not upon these exiles begging aid,[1] who have an interest in successful lies, who only contribute words, and who let others fight their battles and then are less grateful than they should be in success, though in failure they may involve their friends in a common ruin.

"I dare say someone[2] delighted at his election to command will recommend you to sail, looking only to his own interest, all the more because he is too young for his post; he wants to win admiration for his stud of horses and to make something out of his command to maintain him in his extravagance. But do not give him the opportunity of private splendor at the city's risk. Remember that men of his stamp injure the public and impoverish themselves, and that an expedition to Sicily is a serious business and not one which mere youths can plan and carry into execution offhand. When I see these youths here today, seated by the very same person who has spurred them on, I am alarmed; and I appeal against them to the older citizens among you. If any of you should be placed next to one of his supporters, I would not have him ashamed, or afraid of being thought a coward if he does not vote for war. They may feel a perverse longing for things beyond their reach; you should be free of it; you know that most successes are gained by foresight, but few or none by passion. On behalf of our country, which is now making the most dangerous throw in her history, hold up your hands against them. Vote that if the Sicilian Greeks adhere to their present frontiers with us, which are satisfactory, the Ionian gulf for anyone coasting and the Sicilian sea, if you cross the open water, they should enjoy their own country and negotiate on their own differences by themselves; and that the Egestæans in particular be informed that, as they originally went to war with the Selinuntians on their own account, they must make peace on their own account. Let us have no more allies such as ours have too often been, to whom we are expected to render aid when they are in misfortune, but from whom we ourselves get no help when we need it.

14. "And you, Prytanis,[1] as you wish to be a good citizen and believe that the welfare of the state is entrusted to you, put my proposal to the vote; and lay the question once more before the Athenians. You should realize that if you hesitate to submit it a second time, you would not be culpable of overriding our normal procedure with so many witnesses to your defense, and that you would be the physician of the state when it has been ill-advised. A magistrate acts with honor if he does the very best which he can for his country or, at least, no harm of his own volition."

15. This was the substance of Nicias' speech. Most of the Athenians who came forward to speak were in favor of war and against rescinding the vote which had been already passed, although a few took the other side. The most enthusiastic supporter of the expedition was Alcibiades the son of Cleinias; he was determined to oppose Nicias, who was always his political opponent and had just now spoken of him in disparaging terms; but an even stronger motive with him was his desire to command and hope that he might be the instrument for conquering Sicily and Carthage and that success would enhance his personal wealth and glory. He had a great position among the citizens and was devoted to horse racing and other expenses which outran his means. And later nothing contributed more to the ruin of the Athenian state. For the people feared the extremes to which he carried the lawlessness of his personal habits, and the far-reaching purposes which invariably animated him in all his actions. They thought that he was aiming at a tyranny and set themselves against him. And therefore, though in public affairs none conducted the war better, they entrusted the administration of the war to others because as individuals they objected to his private habits; and so they speedily shipwrecked the state.[1] He now came forward and spoke somewhat as follows:

16. "I have a better right to command, men of Athens, than another (for as Nicias has attacked me, I must begin by praising myself), and I consider that I am worthy of it. The actions for which I am so much cried out against are an honor to myself and to my ancestors

and a solid advantage to my country. In consequence of the distinguished manner in which I represented the state at Olympia, the other Hellenes formed an idea of our power which even exceeded the reality; they were previously hoping that we were exhausted by war. I sent into the lists seven chariots—no other private man ever did the like. I was victor and also won the second and fourth prize, and I ordered everything in a style worthy of my victory. Such successes customarily bring honor, but the activity involved also creates an impression of power. At home, again, whenever I gain distinction by providing choruses[1] or in any other way, although the citizens are naturally jealous of me, here too foreigners find evidence of our strength. There is some use in the folly of a man who, at his own cost, benefits the state as well as himself. And where is the injustice, if such a man is conscious of his greatness and will not admit an equal? Men who do badly are unequal in misfortune to others. We are not recognized by our acquaintance when we are down in the world; and on the same principle why should any one complain when treated with disdain by the successful? A man should treat others as equals if he claims like treatment for himself. I know that men of this lofty spirit and all who have been in any way illustrious are hated while they are alive, by their equals especially, and also by others who have to do with them, but that they leave behind them to after-ages a reputation which leads even those who are not of their family to claim kindred with them, and that they are the pride of their country, which regards them, not as aliens or wrongdoers, but as her own children, who have acted nobly. These are my own aspirations, and these are the private acts for which I am assailed; but consider carefully whether in the management of public affairs any man surpasses me. Did I not, without involving you in great danger or expense, combine the most powerful states of the Peloponnese against the Lacedæmonians and compel them to stake at Mantinea all that they had upon the fortune of one day? And even to this hour, although they were victorious in the battle, they have hardly recovered full confidence.

17. "With all my youth and supposedly unnatural folly, I found arguments appropriate for these negotiations with the Peloponnesian power and won conviction by passion which inspired trust. Do not then be afraid of my youth now; but while I am still young and therefore in my prime and Nicias enjoys a reputation for good fortune, use the services of us both to the full. After determining to sail, do not change your minds under the impression that Sicily has great power. For although the Sicilian cities are populous, their inhabitants are a mixed rabble; and men readily lose and secure citizenship there. For this reason no one feels that he has a city of his own; and so the individual is ill-provided with arms and the country with the ordinary installations. Their resources consist only of what men think they can personally appropriate by persuasive oratory or party faction and peculation from the treasury, and of what in the event of failure they think they can carry off to another land. It is not likely that such a medley should be of one mind in counsel, or capable of concerted action.[1] Every man is for himself, and would readily come over to anyone who makes an attractive offer—the more readily if, as report says, they are in a state of internal discord. Nor have they as many hoplites as they boast, just as the rest of the Hellenes proved to have less than each city claimed; this was the greatest self-deception, for Hellas hardly had enough hoplites in this war. Such then will be the situation there, to judge from the information which I have heard; indeed, it will be easier for us, for there will be many barbarians, whose hatred of the Syracusans will make them join us in attacking them.[2] And at home there is nothing which will hinder us if you take the correct decision. Our forefathers had the same enemies whom we are now told that we are leaving behind us, and the Persian besides; but they won the empire, simply by superior naval strength. Never were the Peloponnesians more hopeless of success against us than at the present moment; and let them be ever so confident; they will only invade our land, which they can do even if we do not go to Sicily. But on the sea they could

not hurt us, for we shall leave behind us a navy equal to theirs.

18. "What reason can we give to ourselves for hesitation? What excuse can we make to our allies for denying them aid? We have sworn to them, and ought to protect them and not to argue that they never assisted us. We did not attach them to us in order that they should come and help us here, but that they should harass our enemies in Sicily and prevent them from attacking us. Like all other imperial powers, we have acquired our dominion by our readiness to stand by anyone, whether barbarian or Hellene, who invoked our aid. If we are to sit and do nothing or to draw distinctions of race when our help is requested, we should add little to our empire but rather run a good risk of losing it altogether. For men are not content to repel the attack of a superior power: they anticipate it. We cannot regulate at pleasure the extent of our empire: in our position it is necessary for us, while not relaxing our hold on our subjects, to plan attacks on the rest; for if we do not ourselves rule over others, we should be in danger of falling under their rule. You cannot afford to regard inaction in the same light as others, unless you change your habits to conform with theirs.

"Let us then calculate that we shall be likely to increase our power here if we attack in Sicily, and sail. Thus we should humble the pride of the Peloponnesians when they see that scorning the repose we now enjoy, we have actually sailed to Sicily; and by adding Sicily to our empire, we shall probably become masters of all Hellas; at any rate we shall injure the Syracusans, and that will benefit ourselves and our allies. Whether we succeed and remain, or depart, our navy will ensure our safety; for at sea we shall be more than a match for all the Sicilian Greeks. Nicias must not put you off by his talk of the virtue of peacefulness and by setting young and old at variance; you should follow the traditional order; and in the same way as our fathers in their youth made plans in common with their elders and raised the city to its present state, you should try to advance it further. You must consider that youth and age have no power unless united, but that simplicity, mediocrity and great acumen of mind should be most effective when blended and combined; that the state, if at rest, like anything else, will wear itself out by internal friction, and that knowledge of all kinds will grow old, whereas in unceasing struggles the city will gain fresh experience and the habit of defending herself, not in theory, but in practice. In general it is my judgment that a state which is not peaceful would most rapidly be ruined—or so I think—by changing over to a peaceful attitude, and that the people who enjoy the greatest security are those whose policy is most consistent with their existing character and customs, even though these may not be the best."

19. This was the substance of Alcibiades' speech. After hearing him and the Egestæans and certain Leontine exiles who came forward and earnestly entreated assistance, reminding the Athenians of the oaths which they had sworn, the people were far more than ever resolved upon war. Nicias, seeing that his old arguments would no longer deter them but that he might possibly change their minds if he insisted on the magnitude of the force which would be required, came forward again and spoke somewhat as follows:

20. "Men of Athens, as I see that you are thoroughly determined on the expedition, I hope our wishes may be fulfilled, but I will indicate what I judge proper in the circumstances. The cities which we are about to attack are, according to the information I hear, powerful, independent of one another and not in need of internal change, unlike peoples who might welcome a change to an easier condition from servitude imposed by force; and they are unlikely to accept our rule in exchange for liberty. As regards numbers, although Sicily is but one island, it contains a great many Hellenic states. Not including Naxos and Catana (which, I hope, will be our allies from kinship with the Leontines), there are seven other cities fully provided with means of warfare similar to our own, above all Selinus and Syracuse, the cities against which our expedition is particularly directed.[1] They have numerous hoplites, archers and javelin men, many triremes and a multitude to man them; besides their private wealth,

they have the treasures of the Selinuntian temples; and the Syracusans receive a tribute from some barbarians. Moreover, they have a numerous cavalry and grow their own corn instead of importing it: in the two last respects especially they have an advantage over us.

21. "Against such a power, more is needed than a fleet with a small land force; if we mean to do justice to our design, and not to be kept within our lines by the numbers of their cavalry, we must embark a great force of infantry. For what if the Sicilians in terror combine against us and we make no friends, except the Egestæans, who can furnish us with horsemen capable of opposing theirs? It would be disgraceful to be forced to go home or to send for reinforcements because we were wanting in forethought at first. We must take a powerful armament with us from here, in the knowledge that we are going to a distant land and that the expedition will be of a kind very different from any which you have hitherto made among your subjects under an alliance against some power in this part of the world, when a friendly country is always near and you can easily obtain supplies from it. There you will be dependent on a country which is entirely strange to you, and during the four winter months a messenger can hardly reach Athens.

22. "I think, therefore, that we must take with us many hoplites, Athenian and allied, our own subjects or Peloponnesians whom we can persuade or attract by pay to our service; also many archers and javelin men to act against the enemy's cavalry. Our naval superiority must be overwhelming, that we may also have no difficulty in bringing in supplies. Grain must be carried from home, wheat and parched barley, in merchant vessels; we must also have bakers, conscribed in a certain proportion from each mill, who will receive pay in order that, if we should be detained by bad weather, the army may not want supplies; for it is not every city that will be able to receive so large a force as ours. We must make our remaining preparations as complete as possible and not be dependent on others; above all, we must take out with us as much money as we can; for as to the

money of the Egestæans which is said to be awaiting us, we had better assume that it is imaginary.

23. "Even supposing we leave Athens not only prepared to sail with a hoplite force equal to the army of the enemy but superior in every way, still it will be no easy task to conquer Sicily or indeed to preserve ourselves. You ought to consider that we are like men going to found a city among foreigners and enemies, who on the very day of their disembarkation ought to have command of the country in the knowledge that if they meet with a disaster, they will have no friends. And this is what I fear. I know that we shall have much need of prudence, still more of good fortune. But who can guarantee this to mortals? I would trust myself and the expedition as little as possible to fortune and would not sail until I had taken such measures as will be likely to ensure our safety. This I conceive to be the course which gives the best guarantee to the whole state and is a condition of safety for us who are sent upon the expedition. If any one thinks otherwise, I resign the command to him."

24. This was the substance of Nicias' speech. He thought that he would either put the Athenians off by the vastness of the undertaking or provide, as far as he could, for the security of the expedition if he were compelled to proceed. Far from losing their enthusiasm for the expedition because it would be a burden to fit it out, they were far more determined than ever; and he achieved the opposite of his intention; they approved of his advice and thought that every chance of danger was now removed. All alike were seized with a passion to sail. The older among them were convinced that they would achieve the conquest of Sicily; at any rate such an armament could suffer no disaster; the youth were longing to see with their own eyes the marvels of a distant land and were confident of a safe return; the main body of the troops expected to receive pay for the present and to win new power which would be an inexhaustible source of pay for the future. Although some disapproved, the excessive passion of the majority made them afraid of being thought unpatriotic if they voted on the other side; and they therefore held their peace.

25. At last an Athenian came forward and, calling upon Nicias, said that they would have no more excuses and delays; he must speak out and say what forces the people were to vote him. He replied unwillingly that he would prefer to consider the matter at leisure with his colleagues but that, as far as he could see at present, they ought to have at least a hundred triremes of their own: of these as many as they thought fit should be troop transports, and they must send for more triremes from their allies. They would require in all, including Athenians and allies, not less than five thousand hoplites, and more if they could possibly have them. The rest of the armament, which must be in proportion—archers from home and from Crete, and slingers, and whatever else seemed to be required—would be organized and taken with them by the generals.

26. The Athenians then at once voted that the generals should be given full powers and should act as they thought best respecting the numbers of the army and the whole expedition. Then the preparations began. Lists for service were made up at home and orders sent to the allies. The city had newly recovered from the plague and from the continuous war; a large new population had grown up; money had been accumulated during the peace, so that everything was easily procured.

27. While they were in the midst of their preparations, the Hermæ[1] of stone in the city, carved quadrangular blocks of which by local custom there are many both in temples and private portals, in one night nearly all had their faces mutilated. The offenders were not known, but great rewards were publicly offered for their detection; and in addition a decree was passed that anyone, whether citizen, foreigner or slave, might without fear of punishment disclose this or any other profanation of which he was cognizant. The Athenians took the matter greatly to heart: it seemed to them ominous of the fate of the expedition, and they ascribed it to conspirators who wanted to effect a revolution and to overthrow the democracy.

28. Some metics and servants gave information, not indeed about the Hermæ, but about the mutilation of

other statues which had shortly before been perpetrated by some young men in a drunken frolic; they also said that the mysteries[1] were repeatedly profaned by the celebration of them in private houses; Alcibiades was one of the accused. The persons who disliked Alcibiades because he hindered them from establishing themselves as leaders of the people, thought that if they could expel him, they would be supreme; they took this up and exaggerated it, clamorously insisting that both the mutilation of the Hermæ and the profanation of the mysteries were part of a conspiracy against the democracy and that he was implicated in all these affairs. In further proof they spoke of the general and undemocratic lawlessness of his habits and the excesses of his ordinary life, which were unbecoming in the citizen of a free state.

29. He strove to clear himself of the charges then and there and offered to be tried before he sailed (for all was now ready), in order that, if he were guilty, he might be punished and, if acquitted, might retain his command. He adjured his countrymen to listen to no calumnies against him in his absence but to put him to death at once if he was guilty, and he protested that they would be wiser in not sending a man under so serious a charge on a command so important before deciding on it. But his enemies feared that if the trial took place at once, he would have the support of the army, and that the people would be soft and indulgent to him and would not forget that he had induced the Argives and some Mantineans to join in the expedition. They therefore exerted themselves to postpone the trial and suborned fresh speakers, who proposed that he should sail now and not delay the expedition, but should return and stand his trial within a certain number of days. Their intention was that he should be recalled, brought home and tried when they had aggravated their slanders against him, which they could better do in his absence. So it was decided that Alcibiades should sail.

30. About the middle of summer, the expedition finally started for Sicily. Orders had been previously given to most of the allies, to the corn ships, the smaller craft, and generally to the vessels in attendance on the arma-

ment that they should muster at Corcyra; from there the whole fleet was to strike across the Ionian gulf to the promontory of Iapygia. At dawn on the day appointed for their departure, the Athenian forces and such of their allies as had already joined them went down to the Piræus and began to man the ships. Almost the entire population of Athens went down with them, citizens and strangers alike. The citizens were each sending off their own people—friends, relatives or sons—and as they passed along, they were full of hope and full of tears: hope of conquering Sicily, tears because they might never see them again, when they thought of the long and distant voyage on which they were sending them.

31. The hour had come when they were at last to part, with dangers in view; and they were now more conscious of the perils than when they voted for sailing. Nevertheless, their spirits revived at the sight of the armament in all its strength and of the abundant provision which they had made. The foreigners and the rest of the rabble came, out of curiosity, to witness an enterprise of which the greatness exceeded belief. No armament so magnificent or costly had ever been sent out by any single Hellenic power, though in mere number of ships and hoplites, that which sailed to Epidaurus under Pericles and afterward under Hagnon to Potidæa was not inferior.[1] For that expedition consisted of a hundred Athenian and fifty Chian and Lesbian triremes, conveying four thousand hoplites, all Athenian citizens, three hundred cavalry, and a multitude of allied troops. Still the voyage was short and the equipment poor, whereas this expedition was intended to be long absent and was thoroughly provided both for sea and land service, according to need. On the fleet, the greatest pains and expense had been lavished by the trierarchs and the state. The public treasury gave a drachma a day to each sailor and furnished empty hulls for sixty fast vessels and for forty transports carrying hoplites and the best officers for them. The trierarchs added bonuses to the pay given by the state to the upper ranks of rowers and the petty officers. The figureheads and other fittings provided by them were of a costly description. Everyone strove to the utmost that

his own ship might excel both in beauty and swiftness. The infantry had been selected by careful levies. There was the keenest rivalry among the soldiers in the matter of arms and personal equipment. The effect was that while the Athenians were competing with one another in the performance of their several duties, to the rest of Hellas the expedition seemed more like a display of their power and greatness than a preparation for war. If anyone had reckoned up the whole expenditure, both of the state and of individual soldiers, not only what the city had already laid out, but what was entrusted to the generals, and what, either at the time or afterwards, private persons spent upon their outfit, or the trierachs upon their ships, and besides all this, the provision for a lengthy expedition which every one may be supposed to have carried with him over and above his public pay, and what soldiers or traders may have taken for purposes of exchange, he would have found that, altogether, many talents were taken out of the city. The expedition was constantly on men's lips, no less for its astonishing boldness and brilliant appearance than for its superiority in armed power to the peoples whom it was to attack, and because none had ever sailed in such force so far from home and none with such high hopes for the future, based on their actual strength.

32. When the ships were manned and everything required for the voyage had been placed on board, silence was signaled by the sound of the trumpet; and they offered the prayers customary before setting sail, not in each ship separately, but by a single herald, the whole fleet accompanying him. On every deck both the officers and the marines, mingling wine in bowls, made libations from vessels of gold and silver. The multitude of citizens and other well-wishers who were looking on from the land joined in the prayer. The crews raised the pæan and, when the libations were completed, put to sea. After sailing out at first in line ahead, the ships raced with one another as far as Ægina. They then hastened to Corcyra, where the allies who formed the rest of the army were assembling.

Meanwhile, reports of the expedition were coming in

to Syracuse from many quarters, but for a long time nobody gave credit to them. At length an assembly was held.[1] Even then different opinions were expressed, some affirming and others denying that the expedition was coming. At last Hermocrates the son of Hermon, believing that he had clear knowledge on the subject, came forward and warned the Syracusans somewhat as follows:

33. "I dare say that, like others, I shall not be believed when I tell you that the expedition is really coming; and I am well aware that those who say or report what seems incredible not only fail to convince others but are thought fools for their pains. Yet, when the city is in danger, fear shall not stop my mouth; for I am convinced in my own mind that I speak from clearer knowledge than others. The Athenians, much to your surprise, are coming against us with a great fleet and army, professedly to assist their Egestæan allies and to restore the Leontines. But the truth is that they covet Sicily, and especially our city. They think that if they can conquer us, they will easily conquer the rest. They will soon be here, and you must consider how with your present resources you can make the most successful defense. You should not let them take you off your guard because you despise them, or neglect everything in disbelief. But anyone who actually believes what I say must not be dismayed at their audacity and power. They will not be able to do more harm to us than we can do to them; the very greatness of their armament may be an advantage to us; it will have a good effect on the other Sicilian cities, who in their panic will be the more ready to assist us. Then, again, if in the end we overpower them or drive them away baffled in their aims (for I have not the slightest fear of their succeeding in their expectations), we shall have achieved a truly noble triumph. And of this I have good hope. Rarely have great expeditions, whether Hellenic or barbarian, met with success far from their own country. They are not more numerous than the inhabitants and their neighbors, who all combine through fear, and if owing to scarcity of supplies in a foreign land they miscarry, although their ruin may be chiefly due

to themselves, they confer glory on those whom they meant to overthrow. It was in this way that these very Athenians rose to greatness, on the great and unexpected defeat of the Persians, who were said to have directed their expedition against Athens; and we can hope for a similar event.

34. "Let us take courage then and put things here into a state of defense; let us also send to the Sicels, confirm the allegiance of some and try to gain the friendship and alliance of others. Let us dispatch envoys to the rest of Sicily to point out that the danger is common to all, and to Italy in the hope that they may either become our allies or refuse to receive the Athenians. And I think that we should send to the Carthaginians; the idea of an Athenian attack is no novelty to them; they are always living in apprehension of it.[1] They may very possibly think that if they leave us to our fate, they too may be in trouble; and they may be inclined in some way or other, secretly, if not openly, to assist us. If willing to help, of all existing states they are the best able to do so; for they have abundance of gold and silver, the means to success in war and in policy generally. Let us also send to the Lacedæmonians and Corinthians and entreat them to come to our aid speedily and to revive the war in Hellas.

"I have a plan which in my judgment is the best suited to the present emergency, although it is the last which in your habitual indolence you would readily embrace. Let me tell you what it is.[2] If all the Sicilian Greeks, or if we and as many as will join us, would launch all our available ships with two months' provisions, meet the Athenians at Taras and the promontory of Iapygia, and show them that before they fight for Sicily, they must fight for the passage of the Ionian Sea, we should be most likely to strike a panic into them and to make them reflect that our base for defense is in friendly country, as Taras[3] is ready to receive us, but that they have a wide sea to cross with their whole armada; they would know that after a long voyage their ships will find it hard to keep station and, coming up slowly and few at a time, will be easy for us to attack.

On the other hand, if they lighten their vessels and meet us, using oars, in a more compact body with the faster ships, we might attack them when they are exhausted; or if we should prefer not to fight, we can retire again to Taras. Having come over with slender supplies and prepared for a naval engagement, they would not know what to do on desolate coasts. If they remain, they would find themselves blockaded; if they attempt to sail onward, they would leave the rest of their armament behind and be discouraged by uncertainty whether the cities would receive them. In my opinion this line of reasoning would bar them from even leaving Corcyra. Instead they would consult and send out spies to discover our number and exact position and find themselves stopped by the onset of winter; or else in dismay at the unexpected opposition, they would break up the expedition; especially if, as I am informed, the most experienced of their generals has taken the command against his will, and would gladly make any considerable demonstration on our part an excuse for retreating. I am quite sure that reports would exaggerate our strength. The minds of men are apt to be swayed by what they hear; and they are more afraid of those who are first to take the offensive or who, at any rate, show in advance that they will resist an offensive, for they suppose them equal to the danger. And so it would be with the Athenians. They are now attacking us because they do not believe that we shall defend ourselves; and in this condemnation of us, they are justified by our failure to join with the Lacedæmonians in putting them down. But if they were to see us venturing on something they had not thought of, they would be more dismayed at our unexpected resistance than at our real power. Take my advice; best of all, resolve on this bold step; but if not, adopt other measures of defense as quickly as possible. It should be in the minds of all that contempt of an invader is shown by actual resistance but that at the moment it would be the most advantageous course to act as if danger were upon us, in the consciousness that preparations made in fear give most security. The Athenians are coming; I am certain that they are already on the sea and are all but here."

35. Hermocrates spoke in this way. Great was the contention which his words aroused among the Syracusan people, some asserting that the Athenians would never come and that he was not speaking the truth, others asking, "And if they should come, what harm could they do to us nearly so great as we could do to them?" Still others were quite contemptuous and made a jest of the whole matter. A few only believed Hermocrates and feared the future. At last Athenagoras, the popular leader who had at that time the greatest influence with the masses, came forward and spoke somewhat as follows:

36. "A man who would not rejoice to hear that the Athenians are so mad as to come here and deliver themselves into our hands is either a coward or a traitor. The audacity of the people who alarm us with such reports does not surprise me, but I do wonder at their folly if they cannot see that their motives are transparent. Having private reasons for being afraid, they want to strike terror into the whole city that they may hide their own alarm under the shadow of the common fear. This is now the meaning of the current reports. They do not grow of themselves; they have been got up by persons who perpetually disturb the state. If you are well advised, you will not measure probabilities by examining their reports but by what shrewd and experienced men would do, such as I conceive the Athenians to be. They are not likely, with the Peloponnesians in their rear and the war at home not yet ended with certainty, to come here and undertake a war of equal magnitude. In my opinion they are only too glad that we are not attacking them, considering the number and power of our states.

37. "Even if the rumor of their coming should turn out to be true, I am sure that Sicily is better fitted than the Peloponnese to carry through a war. The whole island is better supplied in every way; and our own city is herself far more than a match for the army which is said to be coming against us, and even for another as great. I know that they will not bring horses with them and will procure none here, except some few from Egesta.

They cannot provide a force of hoplites equal to ours, for they have to cross the sea; and to sail all this distance, even with the ships unladen, is a large task. I know too that they will lack the other equipment requisite against so great a city as ours, which will be immense. I am absolutely convinced that if they came here with another city as large as Syracuse at their command, and could settle there on our border and carry on war against us, they would still be destroyed utterly to a man; how much more when the whole country will be their enemy (for Sicily will unite) and when they must go from ships into camp and live from little tents with the minimum of equipment, not moving far afield because of our cavalry. Indeed I do not think that they could effect a landing at all, so far superior, in my judgment, are our forces to theirs.

38. "The Athenians, I repeat, know all that I am telling you and do not mean to throw away what they have got: I am perfectly sure of that. But some of our people are fabricating reports which neither are, nor are ever likely to be, true. I know, and have always known, that by words like these and others still more mischievous, if not by acts, they want to intimidate you, the Syracusan people, and make themselves rulers of the state. And I am afraid that if they persevere, they will succeed at last. We are bad at taking precautions and at detecting and punishing them before any damage has been done. This is the very reason why our city is usually in a state of unrest and brings upon herself internal disorders and struggles, more frequent than foreign wars, and is sometimes subjected to tyrants and to narrow and wicked oligarchies. If you will only support me, I shall endeavor to prevent any such misfortunes happening in our day; I shall seek to persuade you, the majority, to punish such intriguers, not only when they are caught in the act (for who can catch them?), but also for intentions which they lack power to fulfill. In resisting enemies, we should anticipate not only their actions but their plans; if a man does not strike first, he will be the first struck. As for the oligarchs, I shall resort to refutations, to precautions, even to instruction; that, I think, is the way by which

I may best deter them from their evil courses. Come now, young men, and answer me a question which I have often asked myself. What do you want? To hold office now? The law forbids it. And the law was passed because you lack the capacity, not to deprive you of civic rights for which you possess the capacity. But you would rather not be on an equality with others? But when there is no real difference between men, how can they justly claim differing rights?

39. "I shall be told that democracy is neither wise nor just and that those who have the money are most competent to govern best. To which I answer, first of all, that the people is the name of the whole, oligarchy of a part; secondly, that the rich are the best custodians of money, the wise the best counselors, and the majority, when they have heard a matter discussed, the best judges; and that in a democracy each and all of these classes have a fair share. Whereas an oligarchy gives the majority a full share of dangers, and does not simply take too much of the profits but absolutely monopolizes them. And this is what the powerful and young men among you would like to have and what in a great city they will never obtain.

"You are the most senseless of all the Hellenes I know if you do not see how wicked your schemes are, or the most unscrupulous if your audacity is accompanied by knowledge.

40. "Yet even now if you would learn or repent, you will promote the common good of all classes in the city. Remember that those among you who do good service will have an equal or larger share in this common good than the masses, but that if you want more, there is a danger of your losing everything. Make no more of these reports; we know all about them, and will not admit them. Let the Athenians come, and Syracuse will repel her enemies in a manner worthy of herself; we have generals who will look to the matter. But if, as I believe, none of your tales are true, the city will not choose you to rule her in a moment of panic and voluntarily impose slavery on herself; we shall inquire independently and judge your speeches as if they were actions. We shall not

be talked by you out of the liberty we enjoy, but try to preserve it, by real precautions against any surrender to you."

41. Athenagoras spoke in this way. One of the generals rose, and letting no one else come forward, spoke himself somewhat as follows:

"There is no wisdom in exchanging abuse or in sitting by and listening to it; let us rather, in view of the reports, see how the whole city and every man in it may take measures for honorably resisting the invaders. Why should not the city be richly furnished with arms, horses, and all the pride and pomp of war; where is the harm even if they should not be wanted? We shall be responsible and review the preparations, and we will send messengers to the other cities in order to obtain information and for any other purpose which may be necessary. Some measures we have taken already, and we will bring before you whatever we discover." When the general had spoken in this way, the assembly dispersed.

The Operations of 415 B.C.

42. The Athenians and their allies were by this time gathered at Corcyra. There the generals began by holding a final review of their forces and disposed them in the order in which they were to anchor and encamp. They divided the ships into three squadrons, and each took one by lot in order to avoid a shortage, if they sailed together, of water, anchorage and provisions where they touched; they also thought that with a general to each division, they would be in better order and easier to command. They then sent before them to Italy and Sicily three ships, to find out what cities in those regions would receive them, with orders to meet them again on their way, that they might know before they put in.

43. At length the great armament proceeded to cross from Corcyra to Sicily. It consisted of 134 triremes in all, besides two Rhodian vessels of 50 oars. Of these, 100 were Athenian, 60 being fast ships and the remainder transports: the rest of the fleet was furnished by the Chians and other allies. The hoplites numbered in all

5,100 of whom 1,500 were Athenians taken from the roll, and 700 who served as marines were thetes. The remainder of the hoplites were furnished by the allies, some by the subject states, 500 by Argos, besides 250 Mantinean and other mercenaries. The archers were in all 480, of whom 80 were Cretans. There were 700 Rhodian slingers, 120 light-armed Megarians who were exiles, and one horse transport which conveyed 30 cavalry.

44. Such were the fighting forces with which the first expedition crossed the sea. For the transport of provisions there were thirty merchant ships carrying grain and also bakers, masons, carpenters, and tools required in sieges; and a hundred small craft, which like the merchant vessels, were pressed into the service. Other merchant vessels and small craft in great numbers followed of their own accord for purposes of trade. The whole fleet now struck across the Ionian Sea from Corcyra. They arrived at the promontory of Iapygia, at Taras and at other points, wherever a favorable course had taken them, and passed along the coast of Italy. The cities did not admit them within their walls or open a market to them, but allowed them water and anchorage; Taras and Locri refused even these. At length they reached Rhegium, the extreme point of Italy, where the fleet reunited. As they were not received within the walls, they encamped outside the city at the temple of Artemis; there they were provided by the inhabitants with a market; and drawing up their ships on shore, they took a rest. They held a conference with the Rhegians and pressed them, as Chalcidians, to aid the Chalcidians of Leontini. The Rhegians replied that they would be neutral and act only in accordance with the decision of the other Italian Greeks. The Athenian commanders now began to consider how they could best commence operations in Sicily. Meanwhile, they were awaiting the ships which had sailed ahead and were to meet them from Egesta; for they wanted to know whether the Egestæans really had the money of which the messengers had spoken at Athens.

45. At Syracuse, meanwhile, confirmation was now coming from their spies and many quarters that the

Athenian fleet was at Rhegium. They now no longer doubted but put heart and soul into their preparations. To some of the Sicel towns they sent troops, to others envoys; they also garrisoned the forts in their territory and within the city inspected the horses and arms to see if they were in good condition and in general organized in the belief that war was rapidly approaching, and almost at their gates.

46. The three ships which had sailed ahead to Egesta now returned to the Athenians at Rhegium; they reported that of the money which had been promised thirty talents only were forthcoming and no more. The spirits of the generals fell at once on receiving this, their first discouragement. They were also disappointed because the Rhegians would not join the expedition; they were the first whom they had tried to persuade, who might most naturally have been expected to join them because they were kinsmen of the Leontines, and had always hitherto been in the Athenian interest. Nicias had expected that the Egestæans would fail them; to the two others this was even more incomprehensible. When the original envoys came from Athens to inspect the treasure, the Egestæans had practiced a trick upon them. They brought them to the temple of Aphrodite at Eryx and showed them the offerings—bowls, flagons, censers, and a good deal of other plate. As it was of silver, it made a show quite out of proportion to the value. They also gave private entertainments to the crews of the triremes: on each of these occasions the hosts produced, as their own, drinking vessels of gold and silver, not only collected in Egesta itself, but borrowed from the neighboring towns, Phœnician as well as Hellenic. All of them exhibiting much the same vessels and making everywhere a great display, the sailors were absolutely amazed; and on their arrival at Athens, they told everyone what heaps of wealth they had seen. When the news spread that the Egestæans had not got the money, great unpopularity was incurred throughout the army by these men, who had been deceived themselves, and had then convinced the rest.

47. The generals now held a council of war. Nicias

was of the opinion that they should sail with the whole fleet against Selinus, the place against which they had chiefly been sent. If the Egestæans provided pay for all their forces, they would shape their course accordingly; if not, they would demand maintenance for sixty ships, the number which the Egestæans had requested, and remain on the spot until they had brought the Selinuntians to terms either by force or by negotiation. They would then pass along the coast before the eyes of the other cities and display the power of Athens, prove her zeal in the cause of her friends and allies, and return home, unless a speedy way of helping the Leontines or winning over any of the other cities should unexpectedly present itself. But they should not imperil Athens, at their own expense.

48. Alcibiades urged that it would be a disgrace after setting out with so great an armament to return without achieving anything. They should send envoys to every city of Sicily, with the exception of Selinus and Syracuse; they should also negotiate with the Sicels, making friends of the independent tribes and persuading the rest to revolt from the Syracusans. They would thus obtain supplies and troops. They should first appeal to the Messenians, whose city lay on the straits and the principal approach to Sicily and who possessed a harbor and anchorage from which they could most conveniently watch. Finally, as they won over the cities and knew who would be on their side in the war, they should attack Selinus and Syracuse, unless the Selinuntians would come to terms with the Egestæans and the Syracusans would permit the restoration of the Leontines.

49. Lamachus said that they ought to sail direct to Syracuse and fight as soon as possible under the walls of the city while the inhabitants were unprepared and the consternation was at its height. He argued that all armies are most terrible at first; if time passes before they are seen, the spirits of men revive, and the sight of them tends to awaken contempt. If the Athenians could strike suddenly, while their opponents were still in fear and suspense, that would be the best chance of victory. Not only the sight of the armament which would never

seem so numerous again, but the expectation of sufferings to come, and above all the immediate peril of battle, would all combine to create a panic among the enemy. Many of the Syracusans would probably have been cut off in the fields outside, not believing in the approach of an invader; and while they were trying to enter the city, their own army, if it were in control, encamped close under the walls, would have no lack of provisions. In such conditions, the other Sicilian Greeks would tend not to join the Syracusan alliance but to come over to them, and would not hesitate and look about them to see which side would conquer. He said that on withdrawal they should make Megara their naval station and keep watch from an anchorage there; the place was deserted and was not far distant from Syracuse either by land or by sea.

50. But after speaking in this way, Lamachus gave his own voice for the proposal of Alcibiades. Alcibiades then sailed across in his own ship to Messenè and proposed an alliance to the inhabitants. He failed to convince them; for they refused to receive the Athenians into the city, although they offered to open a market for them outside the walls. So he sailed back to Rhegium. The generals at once manned sixty ships from the entire fleet; and taking the necessary provisions, they coasted along to Naxos; one of them was left with the rest of the armament at Rhegium, The Naxians received them into their city, and they sailed on to Catana; but the Catanæans, who had a Syracusan party within their walls, denied admission to them; so they moved to the river Terias and encamped there. On the following day, they went on to Syracuse in line ahead with all their ships, except ten, which they had sent forward to sail into the Great Harbor and see whether there was any fleet launched. On their approaching the city, a herald was to proclaim from the decks that the Athenians had come to restore their allies and kinsmen—the Leontines—to their homes and that therefore any Leontines who were in Syracuse should join the Athenians without fear, as their friends and benefactors. When the proclamation had been made and

they had taken a survey of the city and harbors and of the ground which must be their base for operations, they sailed back to Catana.

51. The Catanæans now held an assembly; and although they still refused to receive the army, they told the generals to come in and address them if they wished. While Alcibiades was speaking and the people of the city had their attention occupied with the assembly, the soldiers unobserved broke down a postern gate which had been badly walled up; and finding their way into the town, they began to walk about in the market place. Those of the Catanæans who were in the Syracusan interest, when they saw that the army had entered, at once took alarm and stole away. They were not numerous, and the other Catanæans voted for alliance with the Athenians and told them to bring up the rest of their armament from Rhegium. The Athenians then sailed back to Rhegium and with their entire force moved to Catana, where on their arrival they began to establish their camp.

52. News came from Camarina that if they would go there, the Camarinæans would join them. They also heard that the Syracusans were manning a fleet. So they sailed with their whole force first to Syracuse; but when they found that no fleet was being manned there, they passed on to Camarina and, putting in to the open beach, sent a herald to the city. The citizens would not receive them, declaring that their oath bound them to receive only one Athenian ship, unless they themselves sent for a greater number. So they sailed away without effecting their purpose. They then disembarked on a part of the Syracusan territory and ravaged it. But the Syracusan horse intervened and killed some stragglers of their light-armed troops. They then returned to Catana.

53. There they found that the vessel *Salaminia* had come from Athens to order Alcibiades home to defend himself on charges brought by the state, as well as some other soldiers, who had been denounced with him of profaning the mysteries or of mutilating the Hermæ. For after the departure of the expedition, the Athenians prosecuted both inquiries as keenly as ever. They did not investigate the character of the informers but in their

suspicious mood listened to all manner of statements, seized some very respectable citizens on the word of scoundrels and put them in bonds; they thought it better to sift the matter and discover the truth rather than let even a man of good character, against whom an accusation was brought, escape without a thorough investigation merely because the informer was a scoundrel. For the people knew by report that the tyranny of Pisistratus and his sons ended in great oppression and, further, that their power was overthrown, not by Harmodius or any efforts of their own, but by the Lacedæmonians; and they were in a state of incessant fear and suspicion.

54. The *coup* of Aristogeiton and Harmodius (514) arose out of a love affair, which I will narrate at length and show that the Hellenes and the Athenians themselves give quite an inaccurate account of their own tyrants and of the incident in question. Pisistratus died at an advanced age in possession of the tyranny, and was succeeded in his power not by Hipparchus, as is generally thought, but by Hippias, his eldest son. Harmodius was in the flower of youth, and Aristogeiton, a citizen of the middle class, became his lover. Hipparchus made an attempt to gain the affections of Harmodius, but he would not listen, and denounced him to Aristogeiton. As a lover he was tormented at the idea and, fearing that Hipparchus in view of his power would resort to violence, at once formed such a plot as a man in his station might for the overthrow of the tyranny. Meanwhile, Hipparchus made another attempt; he had no better success, and thereupon he determined not indeed to take any violent step but to insult Harmodius in a way which would not reveal his motive. For in the rest of his government,[1] he was not oppressive to the majority, but had ruled without incurring unpopularity; in fact these tyrants displayed merit and capacity for a longer period than any others. The tax on produce which they exacted amounted only to five per cent; they improved and adorned the city, carried on successful wars and sacrificed in the temples. In general, the city retained her ancient laws; but the family of Pisistratus took care that one of their own number should always be in office. Among others who

thus held the annual archonship at Athens was Pisistratus, a son of the tyrant Hippias, named after his grandfather Pisistratus; and during his term of office, he dedicated the altar of the Twelve Gods in the market place and that in the temple of the Pythian Apollo. The Athenian people afterwards added to one side of the altar in the market place and so concealed the inscription upon it; but the other inscription on the altar of the Pythian Apollo may still be seen, although the letters are nearly effaced. It runs as follows:

> "Pisistratus the son of Hippias dedicated this memorial of his archonship in the sacred precinct of Pythian Apollo."

55. That Hippias was the eldest son of Pisistratus and succeeded to his power I positively affirm from more accurate oral tradition than others possess.[1] But anyone could discover it from what follows. It is evident that of the legitimate sons of Pisistratus, he alone had children; this is indicated by the altar just mentioned and by the column which the Athenians set up in the Acropolis to commemorate the oppression of the tyrants. For on that column no son of Thessalus or of Hipparchus is named, but five of Hippias who were born to him by Myrrhinè the daughter of Callias son of Hyperochides; now the eldest son naturally married first. Moreover, his name is inscribed on the same column immediately after his father's; this again is natural as he was the eldest son and tyrant. I think, moreover, that Hippias would have found a difficulty in seizing the tyranny at once if Hipparchus had been tyrant at the time of his death and he had tried to step into his place the same day. As it was, owing to the habitual dread which he had previously inspired in the citizens and to the strict discipline among his mercenaries, he held the government with a large margin of security and had no such difficulty as a younger brother, who had not in the past been continuously associated in the government. But Hipparchus became famous because of the misfortune he suffered and

also obtained the reputation with posterity of having been the tyrant.

56. When Hipparchus found his advances repelled by Harmodius, he carried out his intention of insulting him. There was a young sister of his whom Hipparchus and his friends first invited to come and carry a sacred basket in a procession; and then they rejected her, declaring that she had never been invited by them at all because she was unworthy. Harmodius was very angry and Aristogeiton, for his sake, more angry still. They had already laid their preparations with those who were to share in their *coup,* but were waiting for the festival of the great Panathenæa, when the citizens who were to take part in the procession assembled in arms; for to do so on any other day would have aroused suspicion. Harmodius and Aristogeiton were to begin the attack, and the rest were immediately to join in and engage the guards. The plot had been communicated to a few only, the better to avoid detection; but they hoped that, however few struck the blow, even those not in the secret, as they were armed, would at once be ready to assist in the recovery of their own liberties.

57. The day of the festival arrived, and Hippias went out of the city with his guards to the place called the Ceramicus, where he was occupied in marshalling the procession. Harmodius and Aristogeiton, who were ready with their daggers, stepped forward to do the deed. But seeing one of the conspirators in familiar conversation with Hippias, who was readily accessible to all, they took alarm and thought that they had been betrayed and were on the point of being seized. They therefore determined to take their revenge first on the man who had offended them, on whose account they were putting everything in peril. So they rushed, just as they were, within the gates. They found Hipparchus near the Leocorium, as it was called; and then and there falling upon him with all the blind fury of an injured lover or of a man smarting under an insult, they struck and killed him. The crowd ran together, and so Aristogeiton for the present escaped the guards; but he was afterwards taken and not very gently handled. Harmodius perished at once on the spot.

58. The news was carried to Hippias at the Ceramicus; he went at once, not to the place, but to the armed men who were to march in the procession and, being at a distance, were as yet ignorant of what had happened. Betraying nothing in his looks of the calamity which had befallen him, he bade them leave their arms and go to a certain spot which he pointed out. Supposing that he had something to say to them, they obeyed; and then bidding the mercenaries seize the arms, he at once selected those whom he thought guilty and all who were found carrying daggers; for the custom was to march in the procession with spear and shield only.

59. Such was the conspiracy of Harmodius and Aristogeiton, which began in the resentment of a lover; the reckless attempt which followed arose out of a sudden fright. To the people at large, the tyranny became more oppressive afterwards; Hippias became more apprehensive, put many citizens to death and also began to look abroad in hope of securing an asylum should a revolution occur. An Athenian himself, he married his daughter Archedicè to a Lampsacene, Æantides son of Hippoclus the tyrant of Lampsacus; for he observed that the family of Hippoclus had great influence with King Darius. Her tomb is at Lampsacus and bears this inscription:

"Here Hippias' child, of all his peers the best,
Archedicè beneath this dust doth rest;
Though father, husband, brethren, sons all bore
Rule absolute, to sin she did not soar."

Hippias ruled three years longer over the Athenians. In the fourth year (510), he was deposed by the Lacedæmonians and the exiled Alcmæonidæ.[1] He retired under an agreement, first to Sigeum and then to Æantides at Lampsacus. He then went on to the court of Darius (the Persian king). In his old age he returned in the twentieth year with the Persian army in the expedition to Marathon (490).

60. The Athenian people, reflecting on these things and recalling what they knew of them from report, were suspicious and savage against the supposed profaners of the mysteries; the whole affair seemed to them to indi-

cate some conspiracy aiming at oligarchy or tyranny.[1] In their resulting anger, they had already imprisoned many men of note. There was no sign of returning quiet; but day by day the movement became more furious, and the number of arrests increased. At last one of the prisoners, who was believed to be most deeply implicated,[2] was induced by a fellow prisoner to make a confession—whether true or false I cannot say; conjectures are made on both sides; and no one knew at the time, or knows to this day, who the offenders were. His companion convinced him by saying that even if he were not guilty, he ought, by obtaining immunity, to save his own life and at the same time to deliver Athens from the prevailing state of suspicion. His chance of escaping would be better if he obtained immunity by confession than if he denied it and stood his trial. So he gave evidence both against himself and others in the matter of the Hermæ. The Athenians were delighted at finding out what they supposed to be the truth; they had thought it monstrous that the conspirators against the democracy should not be known, and they immediately liberated the informer and all whom he had not denounced. The accused they brought to trial and executed such of them as had been taken into custody. Those who had fled they condemned to death and promised a reward to anyone who killed them. It was unclear whether the sufferers were unjustly punished, but the beneficial effect on the rest of the city at the time was conspicuous.

61. The enemies of Alcibiades, who had attacked him before he sailed, continued their machinations; and popular feeling was deeply stirred against him. The Athenians now thought that they knew the truth about the Hermæ; and they were more than ever convinced that the violation of the mysteries which had been laid to his charge was done by him with the same purpose, and was a part of the conspiracy against the democracy. It so happened that while the city was in this state of excitement, a small Lacedæmonian force proceeded as far as the Isthmus, having something to do in Bœotia. It was supposed that they had come, not in the interest of the Bœotians, but by a secret understanding with Alcibiades, and that if they

had not struck first themselves in arresting the accused persons, the city would have been betrayed. For one whole night the people lay in arms in the temple of Theseus within the walls. About this time too, the friends of Alcibiades at Argos were suspected of conspiring against the Argive democracy and accordingly the Argive hostages who had been deposited in the islands, were now given up by the Athenians to the vengeance of the Argive people. From every quarter, suspicion had gathered around Alcibiades; and the Athenian people were determined to have him tried and executed; so they sent the ship *Salaminia* to Sicily bearing a summons to him and to others against whom information had been given. They were told to instruct him to follow the officers home and defend himself but not to arrest him; the Athenians were careful not to cause excitement among their own soldiers in Sicily or among the enemy; and above all they wished not to lose the Mantineans and Argives, who, they thought, had been induced by his influence to join in the expedition. He left Sicily in his own ship, along with those who were accused with him and sailed for Athens in company with the *Salaminia.* When they arrived at Thurii, they followed no further but left the ship and disappeared, fearing to return and stand trial under prejudice. The crew of the *Salaminia* searched for them for a time but, as they were nowhere to be seen, sailed away home. Alcibiades, now an exile, crossed not long afterwards in a small vessel from Thurii to the Peloponnese; and the Athenians on his nonappearance sentenced him and his companions to death.

62. The two Athenian generals who remained in Sicily now divided the fleet between them by lot and sailed with the whole of it towards Selinus and Egesta; they wanted to know whether the Egestæans would give them the money and also to ascertain the condition of the Selinuntians and the nature of their quarrel with the Egestæans. Sailing along the north coast of Sicily, which looks towards the Tyrrhenian Gulf, they touched at Himera, the only Hellenic city in this part of the island. But they were not admitted, and passed on. On their voyage they took Hyccara, a city on the seashore which, al-

though of Sicanian origin, was hostile to the Egestæans. They enslaved the inhabitants and handed the place over to the Egestæans, whose cavalry had now joined them. The Athenian troops then marched back through the country of the Sicels until they arrived at Catana; the ships with the slaves sailed round the coast. Nicias had sailed straight from Hyccara to Egesta, where he did his business, and, having obtained thirty talents of silver, rejoined the army. The Athenians sold their slaves; the sum realized was about 120 talents. They next sailed round to their Sicel allies and bade them send reinforcements. Then with half of their army, they marched against Hybla Geleatis, a hostile town, which they failed to take. And the summer ended.

63. Early in the ensuing winter, the Athenians made preparations for an attack upon Syracuse; the Syracusans likewise prepared to take the offensive. For when the Athenians did not assail them at once, as they had expected in their first panic, day by day their spirits rose. And now the Athenians, after cruising about at the other end of Sicily, where they seemed to be a long way off, had attacked Hybla; and their attempt to take it by force had failed. So the Syracusans despised them more than ever. They behaved as a rabble will when it has plucked up courage, and they insisted that since the Athenians would not attack them, their generals should lead them against Catana. Syracusan horsemen, who were always riding up to the Athenian army to watch their movements, would insult them, particularly by asking whether they had come to settle down themselves with them in a foreign land rather than to resettle the Leontines in their own.

64. The Athenian generals were aware of the state of affairs. They wished to draw the whole Syracusan army as far away from the city as possible and then in their absence to sail along the coast by night and, unmolested, occupy a convenient position for a camp. They knew that it would be less practicable to disembark their men in the face of an enemy prepared to meet them, or to march by land, when they would be discovered; for they had no cavalry of their own, and the numerous Syra-

cusan horses would do great harm to their light-armed troops and the mass of attendants. But by this plan they would occupy a position in which the cavalry could do them no serious harm. The exact spot near the temple of Olympian Zeus which they afterwards occupied was indicated by Syracusan exiles who accompanied them. To realize their object, the generals devised the following stratagem. They sent to Syracuse a man of whose fidelity they were assured but whom the Syracusan leaders believed to be a friend of theirs. He was a Catanæan and professed to come from adherents of their party whose names were familiar to them and who, they knew, were still left in Catana. He told them that the Athenians were bivouacked within the city away from their arms, and if the Syracusans with their whole force would attack the camp at dawn on a set day, their partisans in Catana would themselves shut up the Athenians in the town and fire their ships; meanwhile, the Syracusans might assault the palisade and easily take the camp—many of the Catanæans were in the plot and were already prepared; and they had sent him.

65. The Syracusan generals were already in high spirits, and even before this proposal reached them, had made up their minds to march against Catana. So they trusted the man with much too little consideration and at once fixed the day on which they would arrive. They then sent him back and issued orders for all the Syracusans to march out *en masse:* the Selinuntians and some other allies had now arrived. When their preparations were complete and the appointed day drew near, they marched towards Catana and encamped by the river Symæthus in the Leontine territory. The Athenians, aware of the approach of the Syracusans, took all their own army and Sicels or others who had joined them on board their ships and small craft and sailed by night to Syracuse. At dawn they disembarked by the temple of Olympian Zeus, intending to seize a place for their camp. At the same time the Syracusan horse who had ridden before the rest to Catana discovered that the whole Athenian army had put out to sea, turned back and told the infantry: then all together returned to protect the city.

66. The march from Catana to Syracuse was long; and in the meantime the Athenians had established a camp unmolested in an advantageous position, where they could give battle whenever they pleased and the Syracusan horse were least likely to harass them either before or during the engagement. On one side they were protected by walls, houses, trees and a marsh; on another, by cliffs. They felled the trees near and, bringing them down to the sea, made a palisade to protect their ships; on the shore of Dascon too they hurriedly raised a fortification of rough stones and logs at a point where the ground was most accessible to the enemy and broke down the bridge over the river Anapus. No one came out from the city to hinder them in their work. The first to the rescue were the Syracusan cavalry; after a while the whole body of infantry mustered. They at first marched right up to the Athenian position, but the Athenians did not come out to meet them; so they retired and encamped on the other side of the Helorine road.

67. On the next day the Athenians and their allies prepared to give battle. Their order was as follows: the Argives and Mantineans formed the right wing, the Athenians the center, the remaining allies the left wing. Half of their army which formed the van was ranged eight deep. The other half was also drawn up eight deep close to their sleeping places, in a hollow oblong. The latter were told to watch the engagement and to move up to the support of any part of the line which might be most distressed. In the midst of the reserve thus disposed were placed the baggage bearers. The Syracusans drew up their hoplites sixteen deep; the army consisted of the whole Syracusan people and their allies, chiefly the Selinuntians; they had also two hundred horsemen from Gela, and twenty horsemen, with about fifty archers, from Camarina. The cavalry, numbering not less than twelve hundred, were placed upon the right wing, and beside them, the javelin men. When the Athenians were on the point of beginning the attack, Nicias went up and down and addressed some such words to all and each of the various peoples:

68. "What need, soldiers, is there of a long exhorta-

tion when we are all united here in the same cause? The very character of our force is, I think, better able to put courage into you than an eloquent speech and a weak army. We are Argives and Mantineans and Athenians and the best of the islanders; and must not the presence of so many brave men fighting together inspire every one of us with a good hope of victory, especially when we reflect that our opponents are not like ourselves, picked soldiers, but a mass levy? They are Sicilians too, who despise us, but will not withstand us; for their skill is not equal to their courage. It should also be in your minds that we are far from home and that there is no friendly land near, except that which you can win by fighting. The generals of the enemy, as I know well, are appealing to very different motives. They are saying, 'You are fighting for your own country', but I say to you that you are fighting in a country which is not your own, and from which, if you do not conquer, retreat will be hard, for swarms of cavalry will follow at your heels. Remember your own reputation, and attack with vigor; you have no choice, no way out; and you must therefore regard the enemy as less formidable."

69. After thus exhorting his men, Nicias advanced at once. The Syracusans did not expect that they would have to fight just at that moment; and some of them had even gone away into the city, which was close at hand; others came running up as fast as they could and, although late, joined the main body one by one at the nearest point. For they showed no want of enthusiasm or daring in this or any other engagement; they were not inferior in courage when their skill was adequate; but when skill failed, they were compelled to abandon their purpose. On this occasion they were forced to make a hasty defense, for they did not think that the Athenians would begin the attack; still they took up their arms and immediately went forward to meet them. At first the throwers of stones, slingers and archers skirmished in front of the two armies, driving one another before them as light-armed troops are expected to do. Then the soothsayers brought out the customary victims, and the trumpets sounded and called the hoplites to the charge. The

two armies advanced; the Syracusans to fight for their country, and every man for life now, and liberty hereafter; on the opposite side the Athenians to make a foreign country their own, and to save their own from the danger of defeat; while the Argives and the independent allies were eager to share in the conquests for which they had come and, if they were victorious, to see their own fatherland once more. The subject allies were ready to fight, most of all because at that moment they had no hope of saving their lives except by victory, and then in less degree from the feeling that if they were to assist in making any new conquests, their own subjection would be lighter.

70. The armies met hand to hand, and for a long time neither gave way. During the battle thunder and lightning came on and a deluge of rain; these added to the terror of men who were fighting for the first time and had least acquaintance with war, but more experienced soldiers ascribed the storm to the time of year and were much more alarmed at the stubborn resistance of the enemy. First the Argives drove back the left wing of the Syracusans; next the Athenians, the force opposed to them. The rest of the army too now began to give way and were put to flight. The Athenians did not pursue them far, for the Syracusan horsemen, who were numerous and undefeated, interposed; and wherever they saw hoplites advancing in pursuit from the ranks, they attacked and drove them back. The Athenians followed in a body as far as they safely could and then retired once more and raised a trophy. The Syracusans rallied on the Helorine road and did their best to re-form after their defeat. They did not neglect to send some of their forces as a guard to the Olympium, fearing that the Athenians might remove the treasures of the temple. The rest of the army retired within the city.

71. The Athenians, however, did not attack the temple; but collecting their dead and laying them on a pyre, they bivouacked where they were. On the following day, they gave back the Syracusan dead under truce and gathered from the pyre the bones of their own dead. About 260 had fallen of the Syracusans and of their

allies not more than 50 of the Athenians and their allies. The Athenians, taking with them the spoils of their enemies, sailed back to Catana. Winter had now set in; and they thought that before they could do anything more at Syracuse, they must send for horsemen from Athens and collect others from their allies in Sicily; without them they would be dominated by the Syracusan cavalry. They also wanted to obtain both in Sicily and from Athens a supply of money, to gain over some of the cities, which, they hoped, would be more willing to listen to them after the battle, and to procure grain and everything else requisite for attacking Syracuse in the spring. Accordingly, they sailed away to Naxos and Catana to winter there.

Diplomacy and Preparations, Winter 415-14 B.C.

72. The Syracusans, after burying their dead, held an assembly. Hermocrates the son of Hermon, a man of unsurpassed sagacity and competent military experience, distinguished for his courage, came forward and encouraged them. He told them not to give in as a result of the battle, for their spirit had not been vanquished, but they had suffered from want of discipline. Yet they had proved less unequal to the Athenians than might have been expected; especially as they had been contending against the most experienced people in Hellas; they were, so to speak, unskilled workmen, and the Athenians masters in their craft. Another great source of weakness had been the number of generals (there were fifteen of them) and the lack of organization and discipline among the troops. If they had a few experienced generals, and during the winter organized their hoplite force, providing arms for those who had none and so raising the number of their forces to the utmost, and were more severe in drilling them, he said that they would have a good chance of victory; for they had courage already, and only wanted discipline in action. Both qualities would improve together; they would learn discipline in the school of danger, and their natural courage would be re-

inforced by the confidence which experience gives. The generals whom they elected should be few in number and should be entrusted with full power, the people taking a solemn oath to them that they would be allowed to command according to their own judgment. Necessary secrets would then be better kept, and in general they would be prepared to act in an orderly way with no excuses made.

73. The Syracusans listened to him and voted all that he proposed. They chose three generals and no more: Hermocrates himself, Heraclides the son of Lysimachus, and Sicanus the son of Execestus. They also sent ambassadors to Corinth and to Lacedæmon to request aid as allies and urge the Lacedæmonians to make war openly and more decidedly against the Athenians on their behalf, thus they would either draw them away from Sicily or at any rate prevent them from sending reinforcements to the army which was there already.

74. No sooner had the Athenians returned in the fleet to Catana than they sailed to Messenè, expecting that the city would be betrayed to them. But their intrigues came to nothing. For Alcibiades, when he was recalled and gave up his command, foreseeing that he would be an exile, communicated to the Syracusan party at Messenè the plot of which he was cognizant. They put to death the persons whom he indicated; and on the appearance of the Athenians, the same party, rising and arming, prevented their admission. The Athenians remained there about thirteen days, but the weather was bad, their provisions failed, and they were having no success. So they withdrew to Naxos, and after surrounding their camp with defenses and palisades, began to pass the winter there. They also dispatched a trireme to Athens for money and cavalry, to arrive at the beginning of spring.

75. The Syracusans employed the winter in various defensive works.[1] Close to the city they built a wall, which took in the shrine of Apollo Temenites and extended all along that side of Syracuse which looks toward Epipolæ; their aim was to enlarge the area of the city and increase the difficulty of investing it in case of defeat. They fortified and garrisoned Megara and also

raised a fort at the Olympium, besides fixing stockades at all the landing places along the shore. They knew that the Athenians were wintering in Naxos; and so, marching out with their whole army to Catana, they ravaged the country and burnt the tents and the camp of the Athenians; they then returned home. They heard that the Athenians were sending an embassy to gain over the Camarinæans on the strength of their former alliance, which had been made under Laches (427); and they dispatched a counterembassy of their own. They suspected that the Camarinæans had not been enthusiastic in sending their contingent to the first battle, and would not be willing to assist them any longer now that the Athenians had done well in the battle; old feelings of friendship would revive, and they would be induced to join them. Accordingly, Hermocrates went with an embassy to Camarina, and Euphemus went with another embassy from the Athenians. An assembly of the Camarinæans was held, at which Hermocrates, hoping to raise a prejudice against the Athenians, spoke somewhat as follows:

76. "We are not here, Camarinæans, because we suppose that the presence of the Athenian army will overwhelm you with fear; we are more afraid of the speeches they will make, to which you may too readily lend an ear if you hear them without first hearing us. You know the pretext on which they have come to Sicily, but we can all guess their real intentions. If I am not mistaken, they want not so much to restore the Leontines to their city as to drive us out of ours. Who can believe that men who desolate the cities of Hellas mean to restore those of Sicily or that the enslavers and masters of the Chalcidians in Eubœa care from a feeling of kindred for the colonists of these Chalcidians in Leontini? In their conquests at home and in their attempt to conquer Sicily, is not their principle the same? The Ionians and other colonists of theirs who were their allies, wanting to be revenged on the Persians, freely made them their leaders. But soon they charged them with desertion or with making war upon each other or with any plausible accusation which they could bring against each city, and re-

duced them to subjection. It was not for the liberties of Hellas that Athens fought against the Persians; nor did the Hellenes fight for their own; the Athenians fought to enslave Hellas to themselves instead of Persia, the Hellenes to get a new master, of mind equally acute but more maleficent.

77. "But it is easy to indict Athens; you know the wrongs she commits, and we are certainly not here to set them forth but rather to accuse ourselves. We have had a warning in the fate of the Hellenes elsewhere; we know that they were reduced to slavery because they did not stand by one another; and when the same tricks are practiced upon us and we hear of the restoration of 'our kinsmen the Leontines' and the succor of 'our allies the Egestæans,' why do we not all combine with enthusiasm and show them that here they will find, not Ionians, nor Hellespontians and islanders, who must always be the slaves, if not of the Persian, of some other master; but Dorians and free inhabitants of Sicily, sprung from the independent soil of the Peloponnese? Are we waiting till our cities are taken one by one when we know that this is the only way in which we can be conquered? We see what their policy is: they set some of us at variance by their speeches; they stir up others to internecine war by the hope of alliance; or they resort to soothing language with each particular city, as best they can, before doing them injury. And does any one suppose that if his countryman at a distance is ruined first, the danger will not finally reach him, or that the first victim is likely to be alone in his misfortune?

78. "If it has occurred to anyone that the Syracusans are enemies of the Athenians and he is not, and asks indignantly, 'Why should I risk myself for you?' he should consider that he will not so much be fighting for my country; he will be fighting in my country, but his own too is equally concerned. This will be less dangerous, with Syracuse not already destroyed; he will not carry on the struggle alone, for Syracuse will be his ally. He should consider that the Athenians are not punishing Syracuse as an enemy but under pretense of attacking her desire rather to secure the bonds of friendship

with him. And if anyone from envy or possibly from fear (for greatness is exposed to both) would have Syracuse suffer, that we may receive a lesson, and yet survive for his own security, his wishes and hopes are more than human power can compass. For a man may regulate his own desires, but he is not equally the dispenser of fortune; the time may come when he will find himself mistaken; and while mourning over his own ills, he may very possibly wish that he might once more have our prosperity to envy. But this cannot be when he has once abandoned us and has refused to take his share in dangers, which are not nominally but really the same for all. For though in name you may be saving our power, in reality you will be saving yourselves. You, Camarinæans, are our neighbors and next in the line of danger; and you have most reason to foresee all this and not to fight so feebly on our side. Instead of our coming to you, you should have come to us. Suppose the Athenians had gone to Camarina first, would you not at this moment be begging and praying for assistance? Then why did not you equally present yourselves at Syracuse and encourage us in the present hour not to give in? But, hitherto, neither you nor any of the Sicilians have shown this spirit.

79. "Perhaps from cowardice you will profess respect for justice between us and the invaders and plead that you have an alliance with the Athenians. But that alliance was made, not against a friend, but in case you were attacked by an enemy; and you promised to assist the Athenians if they were wronged by others, not when, as now, they are doing wrong themselves. Even the Rhegians who are Chalcidians are unwilling to join in the restoration of their Leontine kinsmen. And yet how monstrous that they, suspecting the real meaning of this fine claim, should display prudence with no excuse to give; and that you with a reasonable explanation for acting differently should be ready to assist your natural enemies and to combine with them for the destruction of those who are still more naturally your kinsmen. This should not be. You should make a stand against them and not be afraid of their armament. There is no danger

if we all hold together; on the contrary, the danger is in disunion; and they are trying to disunite us. Even when they engaged with our unaided forces and defeated us in battle, they failed in their main purpose and quickly retired.

80. "If then we once unite, there is no reason for discouragement. But there is every reason for you to show more enthusiasm for our alliance, especially as help will come to us from the Peloponnesians, who are superior to the Athenians at all points in war. Let no one think that the caution which consists in helping neither side because you are allies of both is fair to us or safe for you. The plea sounds fair, but it is not so in fact. Suppose that you do not fight on our side; when one party has suffered defeat and the other is victorious and master, what will you have gained by this very neutrality? You will not have effected our preservation, and you will not have hindered the Athenians from iniquity. It is the nobler course to join the victims of injustice who are your own kinsmen, to preserve the common interests of Sicily and to prevent these Athenian friends of yours from doing wrong.

"To sum up, we Syracusans say that it is no use for us to read you or the other Sicilians lessons or to demonstrate what you know as well as ourselves. If you are deaf to our arguments, we entreat you and call you to witness that we are exposed to aggression from Ionians, our inveterate enemies, and to betrayal by you, our fellow Dorians. If the Athenians subdue us, they will triumph by your decisions but gain the honor for themselves; and the prize they will obtain for victory will be none other than the authors of it. But if we win through, you will incur vengeance because it was you who were responsible for our dangers. Reflect then and take your choice: will you have slavery and escape danger for the moment, or will you, with the chance of victory at our side, refuse the dishonor of taking these men as your masters and escape our hostility, which would not be short-lived?"

81. Hermocrates spoke in this way; and Euphemus, the Athenian envoy, replied somewhat as follows:

82. "We have come to renew our former alliance, but

the attack made upon us by the Syracusan envoy renders it necessary for us to vindicate our title to empire. He himself bore the strongest witness in our favor when he said that Dorians and Ionians are inveterate enemies. And so they are. We Ionians, dwelling in the neighborhood of the Peloponnesians (who are Dorians and more numerous than ourselves), considered how to secure as much independence from them as we could. After the Persian War, we were delivered by the navy we had acquired from the rule and leadership of Lacedæmon; they had no more title to give orders to us than we to them, except in so far as they were temporarily stronger. We then assumed the leadership of the King's former subjects, which we still retain; we thought that with the means of self-defense we should be least likely to come under Peloponnesian control. It is inaccurate to say that we acted unjustly in subjugating the Ionians and the islanders, those kinsmen of ours whom the Syracusans say that we have enslaved. For Athens is their mother city, and they joined in the Persian attack upon us. They had not the courage to revolt and to destroy their homes as we did when we left our city. But they chose slavery for their own portion, and would have imposed it upon us.

83. "We rule then because we deserve to rule; for we provided the largest navy and showed alacrity, without making excuses, in the cause of Hellas, while those who became our subjects were ready to act in the Persian cause and did us injury. And secondly, we were anxious to gain strength against the Peloponnesians. We use no fine words: we do not tell you that our rule is reasonable on the ground that we alone overthrew the barbarians or that we risked our lives for the liberty of our allies, and not equally for the general liberty and for our own. None can be blamed because he makes the appropriate provision for his own safety. The same care of our safety has brought us here, and we see that our interests and yours are the same. This we will prove to you, from the calumnies of the Syracusans and from the suspicions which tend to make you fear us. For we know that those who are timorous and mistrustful enjoy fine oratory at

the moment but that when the time of action comes, they follow their own interests.

84. "We have told you already that fear makes us maintain our empire at home; and we assert that a like fear brings us to your shores to secure our position in Sicily by the help of our friends, not to enslave you, but to save you from being enslaved. Let no one suppose that your welfare is no business of ours; he should recognize that if you are preserved, and are strong enough to hold out against the Syracusans, they will be less likely to send a force to aid the Peloponnesians, and so to injure us. Thus, you become at once our first concern. And we are quite consistent in restoring the Leontines, not to be subjects, like their kinsmen in Eubœa, but to be as strong as ever we can make them, in order that they may harass the Syracusans from their position on the border and do our work. In Hellas we are a match for our enemies singlehanded; and as to our subjection of the Chalcidians at home, which Hermocrates finds so inconsistent with our emancipation of the Chalcidians here, it is for our advantage, on the one hand, that the cities of Eubœa should have no armed force and contribute money only, and, on the other hand, that the Leontines and our other friends in Sicily should be as independent as possible.

85. "To a tyrant or to an imperial city nothing is inconsistent which is expedient, and there is no kinship where there is no trust. In every case we must make friends or enemies according to circumstances; and here our interest requires, not that we should weaken our friends, but that our enemies should be powerless because our friends are strong. Do not mistrust us. In Hellas too we manage our allies as the services they can each render us suggest; the Chians and Methymnæans (on Lesbos) furnish us with ships and are autonomous; the majority are subject to more coercion and pay a tribute; other allies, although they are islanders and might be easily conquered, enjoy complete freedom because they are situated conveniently for operations round the Peloponnese.[1] So that in Sicily too our policy is naturally determined by our interest and, as I was saying, by our

fear of the Syracusans. For they desire to rule you and wish first to unite you in a common suspicion of us and then, either by force or through your isolation, when we have failed and retired, to be rulers of all Sicily. This is inevitable if you unite with them. Your united power will not be easy for us to manage; and the Syracusans, when we are gone, will not lack strength against you.

86. "Anyone who thinks otherwise is refuted by the facts. You originally invited us here, brandishing before us this very fear—if we allowed you to fall into the hands of the Syracusans, we should incur danger ourselves. You ought not now to distrust the argument which you thought good enough for us. Nor should you suspect us because we have brought a force larger than before, for we have to contend against the power of Syracuse. They are much more to be distrusted. Without your aid we cannot even remain here; and if we behaved so badly as to make conquests, we should be unable to retain them; for the voyage is long; and we lack the means to garrison great cities whose resources are those of a mainland power. But the Syracusans are your neighbors and dwell not in a camp but in a city far more powerful than our forces; they are always scheming against you and never miss a chance, as they have often shown, especially in their conduct towards the Leontines. And now they have the audacity to invite your aid to stir you up against those who hinder their policy, and have thus far kept Sicily from subjection to them. As if you had no eyes! Far more real than the security offered by them is that to which we invite you, a security which is reciprocal, and we beseech you not to throw it away. Reflect: the Syracusans are so numerous that with or without allies they can always find the way to attack you, but you will not often have the chance of defending yourselves with the aid of an army like ours. And if from any suspicion you allow us to depart unsuccessful, or even defeated, the time will come when you will desire to see but a fraction of our army, although then no assistance will be of effect.

87. "But we would not have either you, Camarinæans, or the rest moved by Syracusan calumnies. We have told

you the whole truth about the suspicions which are entertained of us; we will again sum up our arguments, and we think that they ought to convince you. We rule over the cities of Hellas in order to maintain our independence, and we emancipate the cities of Sicily to avoid injuries at their hands. We are under the necessity of constant activity because we have many interests to defend. We come now as we came before, to assist those of you who are suffering wrong; we were not uninvited, but an appeal was made to us. It is not for you to sit in judgment on our actions or to impose discipline on us. Do not try to divert us from our purpose; that would now be difficult. In so far as the constant activity characteristic of us is conducive to your interests as to ours, avail yourselves of it; and remember that it is not injurious to all alike but beneficial to the great majority of Hellenes. In every place, however remote from our sphere, it affects those who expect and those who plan injustice; the former readily entertain a hope of succor from us to match the threat; while the latter are not free from the fear that if we come, they will be in danger; they are bound to practice involuntary prudence, and the others to obtain deliverance without effort. Do not reject the security which is common to all in need and now available to you, but follow the example of the rest and join us; and instead of having always to watch the Syracusans, change your attitude and threaten them as they have long been threatening you."

88. This was the substance of Euphemus' speech. The Camarinæans were swayed by opposite feelings; they were well disposed to the Athenians, except in so far as they thought they would enslave Sicily, whereas they were at perpetual variance with Syracuse as a power on their border. But they were not so much afraid of the Athenians as of their Syracusan neighbors, who, as they thought, might win without their assistance. This was why they had at first sent them the small body of horse and they determined that for the future they would rather give actual assistance to the Syracusans, but to the most moderate extent they could. For the present, however, in order that they might seem to pay the

Athenians no less respect, especially after their recent victory, they resolved to return the same answer in words to both. These considerations led them to reply that, as both were their allies and actually at war with each other, they thought that in the circumstances they were keeping their oaths by assisting neither. The two embassies departed.

The Syracusans proceeded with their own preparations for the war, and the Athenians who were encamped at Naxos tried by negotiation to gain over as many of the Sicels as they could. The Sicels who lived nearer the plains, as subjects of the Syracusans, mostly stood aloof; but the settlements in the interior (which had always been independent) with a few exceptions, joined the Athenians at once, and brought down food to the army and in some cases money too. The Athenians dispatched troops against those who were recalcitrant and forced some to submit, but others were protected by the Syracusans who sent garrisons to their aid. The Athenians changed their anchorage from Naxos to Catana and, reconstructing the camp which had been burnt by the Syracusans, passed the winter there. They sent a trireme to Carthage with a proposal of friendship, in case they might get some help there; and they sent too to Etruria, where some cities were offering of their own accord to join them in the war. They sent around to the Sicels and to Egesta orders to supply them with as many horses as possible. They further prepared bricks, iron and the other material required to build a wall around Syracuse, intending to prosecute the war when spring arrived.

The envoys whom the Syracusans had sent to Corinth and Lacedæmon endeavored on the voyage to persuade the Italian Greeks that they were equally threatened by the Athenian designs, and should not be indifferent to their activities. When they arrived at Corinth, they appealed to the Corinthians for aid on the ground of kinship. The Corinthians took the lead by voting at once that they would assist Syracuse with all possible energy. They sent with the Syracusans ambassadors of their own to the Lacedæmonians to join in persuading them to make war at home more openly against the Athenians and to send some help to Sicily. Along with the Corinthian ambassadors, Alcibiades and his fellow exiles appeared at Lacedæmon. He had crossed without delay from Thurii in a trading vessel to Cyllenè in Elis and proceeded to Lacedæmon later on the invitation of the Lacedæmonians themselves under a safe conduct, for he was afraid of them because of his activity in the Mantinean affair. The result was that in the Lacedæmonian assembly the Corinthians, Syracusans and Alcibiades addressed the same requests and arguments to the Lacedæmonians. The ephors and the magistrates were intending to send envoys to the Syracusans, telling them not to make terms with the Athenians; but they were not strongly disposed to assist them actively. But Alcibiades came forward and stimulated and excited the Lacedæmonians with a speech of the following kind:

89. "It is necessary for me first of all to address you on reports injurious to myself, in case suspicion of me makes you less attentive to considerations of public interest. My ancestors in consequence of some grievance renounced the office of Lacedæmonian proxenus; I myself resumed it and did you good offices, especially in connection with your disaster at Pylos. My zeal in your service did not cease; but when you made peace with Athens, you negotiated through my enemies, conferring power on them and dishonor on me. If then I turned to the Mantineans and Argives and opposed you in various other ways, I was justified in doing you harm; and anyone who was unreasonably angry with me while the wound was recent should now view the matter in the light of truth and change his mind. Or, again, if any one thought the worse of me because I was inclined to the people, he should not think even this a real ground of offense. Any form of government adverse to absolute power has got the name of democracy. Our family have always been opposed to tyrants and have therefore always retained the leadership of the people in our hands. Moreover, as the city is democratic, it has been in general necessary for us to conform to circumstances. However, we did our best to show more moderation than others in our political conduct, despite the prevailing license.

But there were others in the past, as there still are today, who led the rabble to adopt pernicious measures; and it was they who drove me out. Our family were leaders of the whole commonwealth, and we thought it right to agree in maintaining the form of government handed down to us, under which the city enjoyed the greatest power and freedom. Of course like all men of sense, we understood democracy; and I might abuse it better than anyone, as none have suffered greater wrongs at its hands. Its folly is admitted, and there is nothing new to be said about it. It did not seem safe to change it, with you as enemies at our gates.

90. "Such is the truth about the reports injurious to myself. And now I must inform you on the subjects on which you have to deliberate, and so far as I have more knowledge, to make proposals. We sailed to Sicily, first of all, to conquer the Sicilian Greeks if we could; then, to proceed against those of Italy; and lastly, to make an attempt on the Carthaginian dominions and on Carthage itself.[1] If all or most of these enterprises succeeded, we meant then to attack the Peloponnese, bringing with us the whole Hellenic power which we had gained in the west and hiring many barbarians—Iberians and others esteemed to be at present the most warlike barbarians of those parts. We should have built many triremes additional to our own, as Italy supplies timber in abundance. We meant to encircle and invest the Peloponnese, and at the same time by making inroads by land with our infantry, we hoped to storm some of your cities and blockade others and to crush you easily and to rule over the Hellenic world. To facilitate these aims, our newly acquired territory in the west was to supply money and grain in sufficient quantity, apart from the revenue from that part of the world.

91. "You have heard the objects of the present expedition from one with the most precise knowledge; the remaining generals will carry them out in much the same way if they can. And now I must show you that if you do not come to the rescue, Sicily will be lost. If the Sicilian Greeks would all unite, they might even now, notwithstanding their want of experience, resist with

success; but the Syracusans alone, whose whole forces have already been defeated and who cannot move freely at sea, will be unable to withstand the power which the Athenians already have on the spot. And Syracuse once taken, the whole of Sicily is in their hands, and Italy will follow at once; and the danger from that quarter of which I spoke just now would speedily descend upon you. So let none think that he is deliberating only about Sicily: the Peloponnese is at stake. No time should be lost. You must send to Sicily a force of men who will row their own passage and take the field as hoplites without delay. Even more useful, in my opinion, than such a force would be a Spartiate commander to organize the troops which are already available and to press the unwilling into service. Thus you will inspire more confidence in the friends you have, and the waverers will be less afraid to come over to you. Here too in Hellas you must make war more openly so that the Syracusans may think you have an interest in them and be more persevering to resistance, while the Athenians may have greater difficulty in reinforcing their army. You ought to fortify Decelea in Attica; the Athenians are always in particular dread of this and think it the only trial of war which they have escaped. The surest way of injuring an enemy is to strike where you realize from clear evidence that he is most apprehensive; every man is likely to know most accurately the dangers which he himself has most to fear. I will sum up the chief, though by no means all the advantages which you will gain by the fortification and of which you will deprive your opponents. Most of the country's equipment will fall into your hands by capture or desertion.[1] The Athenians will at once be deprived of their revenues from the silver mines of Laurium and of all the profits which they now make from land and workshops; above all, the revenue from their allies will be diminished; for when they think that you are at last carrying on the war with all your strength, they will treat them with contempt. How far any of these plans are executed and with how much speed and energy, Lacedæmonians, depends on you; I am absolutely confident that they are practicable, and I think that my judgment will not prove mistaken.

92. "I hold that none of you should think worse of me if I am now vigorously attacking my own country along with her worst enemies, despite my former reputation for patriotism; nor should you suspect what I say, attributing it to the impatience of an exile. An exile I am—banished from the wickedness of the men who drove me out, but not from your service if you would follow my advice. And because you once did Athens harm as your enemy, you are not worse enemies than those who have forced her friends to become her enemies. I cannot be a patriot when I am wronged, as when I enjoyed with security the rights of a citizen. The city I now assail is in my view no longer my fatherland: I am far more inclined to think that I am recovering a fatherland I do not possess. And truly considered, the patriot is not one who would not attack his own country when unjustly deprived of her, but one who in the warmth of his passion would try to win her back by every means in his power. Thus I hold that you, Lacedæmonians, should use me without fear in any service, however dangerous and laborious, recognizing that, according to the saying on all men's lips, if I did you much harm as an enemy, I might do you good service as a friend, all the more as I know the circumstances at Athens, while I only guessed at yours. You must believe that your deliberations affect your greatest interests, and you should not hesitate to send an expedition of your own to Sicily and to Attica. By dispatching a fraction of your forces to co-operate in Sicily, you may save what is of high importance and overthrow the power which the Athenians possess and hope to gain; and henceforward you may enjoy safety yourselves and the leadership of all Greece, given not under compulsion, but freely and from good will."

93. This was the substance of Alcibiades' speech; the Lacedæmonians, who had themselves been intending to send an army against Athens but were still hesitating and looking about them, were greatly strengthened in their resolution when they heard all these points urged by a man who, they thought, had the clearest knowledge.

Accordingly, they now began to consider the fortification of Decelea seriously, and determined to send immediate assistance to the Sicilians. They appointed Gylippus son of Cleandridas[1] commander for the Syracusans and ordered him to consult with the Syracusan and Corinthian representatives and arrange for aid to be sent to Sicily in the speediest and most effective manner which the circumstances admitted. Whereupon he told the Corinthians to dispatch immediately two ships to him at Asinè and to fit out as many more as they meant to send; the latter were to be ready for sea whenever opportunity came. With this understanding, the envoys departed from Lacedæmon.

About this time the trireme which the Athenian generals had dispatched from Sicily for money and cavalry arrived at Athens. The Athenians, hearing their request, voted to send the subsistence money and cavalry to the army. So the winter ended and with it the seventeenth year of this war of which Thucydides wrote the history.

The Siege of Syracuse (414 B.C.)

94. At the very beginning of spring in the following summer, the Athenians in Sicily quitted Catana and sailed along the coast toward the Sicilian Megara; this place, as I have already mentioned, in the days of Gelo the tyrant was depopulated by the Syracusans,[1] who still retain possession of the country. They disembarked and, after ravaging the fields, proceeded to attack a Syracusan fort without success; they then moved on by land and sea to the river Terias and, going up the country, wasted the plain and burned the corn. They encountered a few Syracusans, some of whom they killed, and, setting up a trophy, returned to their ships. They then sailed back to Catana; and having taken in provisions, they marched with their whole force against Centoripa, a Sicel town, which capitulated. They then returned and on their way burned the corn of the Inessians and the Hyblæans. Arriving at Catana, they found that the horsemen had come from Athens to the number of 250 with their equipment but without horses, which they were expected

to procure on the spot. Thirty mounted archers and three hundred talents of silver had arrived also. . . .

96. The Syracusans heard that the Athenians had received their cavalry and that they would soon be upon them. They considered that unless the Athenians gained possession of Epipolæ (which was a steep place looking down upon Syracuse), the city could not easily be walled off, even if they were defeated in battle; they therefore determined to guard the paths leading to the summit, to prevent the enemy getting up unobserved. At all other points, they thought, this would be impossible. Elsewhere, Epipolæ lies high and slopes right down to the city, from the interior of which it can all be seen; the Syracusans call it Epipolæ because it is above the level of the adjacent country. Hermocrates and his colleagues had now just entered upon their command. The whole people went out at break of day to the meadow skirting the river Anapus and proceeded to hold an arms inspection. A selection had previously been made of six hundred hoplites, who were appointed to guard Epipolæ and to combine quickly for the defense of any point at which they were needed. They were commanded by Diomilus, an Andrian exile.

97. But in the night preceding the morning of this inspection, the Athenians had come from Catana with their whole force, had put in unobserved near a place called Leon, six or seven stades from Epipolæ, and had disembarked their troops. Their ships cast anchor at Thapsus, which is a peninsula with a narrow isthmus, running out into the sea, not far from Syracuse either by land or water. The Athenian crews made a stockade across the isthmus and remained quietly at Thapsus, while the troops ran at once to Epipolæ and gained the summit by the way of the Euryelus before the Syracusans saw them or could come up to them from the meadow where the review was going on. Nevertheless, Diomilus with his six hundred went to the rescue with the rest of the army, each man as fast as he could; but the distance from the meadow which they had to traverse before they could engage was not less than twenty-five stades; consequently they were in disorder when they closed

with the Athenians. They were defeated in the engagement which ensued on Epipolæ, and retired into the city. Diomilus and about three hundred others were killed. The Athenians erected a trophy and gave up to the Syracusans the bodies of the dead under a flag of truce. On the following day, they went down toward the city itself; but as the Syracusans did not come out against them, they retired and built a fort upon Labdalum, at the edge of the cliffs of Epipolæ looking towards Megara, in order that when they advanced either to fight or to construct lines, the place might serve as a depository for their baggage and money.

98. Not long afterwards, the Athenians were joined by three hundred Egestæan horsemen and about a hundred more furnished by the Sicels, Naxians, and others. They had 250 of their own, for some of whom they received horses from the Egestæans and Catanæans; other horses they bought. The whole number of their cavalry was now raised to 650. They placed a garrison in Labdalum and advanced to Syce, where they took up a position and quickly built "the circle" there.[1] The Syracusans were panic-stricken at the celerity of the work. They planned to march out and fight rather than look on. The two armies were already drawn up against each other when the Syracusan generals, seeing that their forces had broken apart and were forming with difficulty, led them back into the city, all but a detachment of the cavalry, who, remaining on the spot, prevented their opponents from gathering stones for the wall and scattering widely. Advancing with one division of their hoplites and all their cavalry, the Athenians attacked the Syracusan horse, whom they put to flight, and killed some of them; they then erected a trophy for the cavalry engagement.

99. On the following day, some of the Athenians proceeded with the construction of the wall north of "the circle"; others collected wood and stones, and were engaged in laying them towards the place called Trogilus. This was on their shortest line, from the Great Harbor to the sea north of the city, for building a wall to cut Syracuse off from the land. The Syracusans by the ad-

vice of their commanders, chiefly of Hermocrates, determined to risk no more general engagements. They thought it better to raise a counterwall across the line on which the Athenians would take their wall and thus, if they were first, to bar its progress. They decided if they were attacked by the Athenians while thus engaged, to oppose them with a part of their army; they hoped that they would have time to forestall the Athenians in occupying the line with their stockades and that the Athenians would leave their work and turn their whole army against them. So they came out and began a crosswall, beginning at their own city, from a point below the Athenian "circle," cutting down the olive trees in the precinct and erecting wooden towers. As yet the Athenian ships had not sailed around from Thapsus into the Great Harbor; the Syracusans were still masters of their own coast, and the Athenians brought their necessaries from Thapsus by land.

100. The Athenians did not interfere with their work, for they were afraid of dividing their forces and finding it harder to fight a battle, and they were pressing forward with their own wall of circumvallation. So the Syracusans, when they had sufficiently completed their stockade and crosswall, leaving one division to guard the work, withdrew into the city with the rest of their army. The Athenians now destroyed the conduits, which were laid underground to bring drinking water into the city. Then, choosing their time at noon when the Syracusan guards remained within their tents (some of them had even gone off into the city) and when the vigilance of the men in the stockade was relaxed, they took a body of three hundred chosen hoplites of their own and some light-armed troops, picked soldiers, to whom they had given heavy arms, and ordered them to run quickly and suddenly to the crosswall. The rest of the army proceeded in two divisions under the two generals, one towards the city in case the enemy should come to save the wall, the other to that part of the stockade which adjoined the postern gate of the city. The three hundred attacked and captured the stockade; the guards abandoned it and fled inside the advance wall which enclosed Temenites. The

pursuers made their way in with them; but after a struggle inside, they were forced out again by the Syracusans; and some Argives and a few of the Athenians fell there. Then the whole army retired, destroyed the crosswall, tore up the stockades, carried the stakes to their camp and raised a trophy.

101. On the following day, the Athenians, beginning from the "circle," began to build their wall on the cliff above the marsh which on this side of Epipolæ looks towards the Great Harbor, intending to carry on the circumvallation by the shortest way to the harbor right through the level country and the marsh. Meanwhile, the Syracusans also came out and, beginning from the city, proceeded to carry another stockade through the middle of the marsh, with a ditch at the side, in order to prevent the Athenians from completing their line to the sea. The latter, having finished their work by the cliff, attacked the new Syracusan stockade and ditch. They ordered the ships to sail around from Thapsus into the Great Harbor of the Syracusans; with the first break of day, they themselves descended from Epipolæ to the level ground; and passing through the marsh where it was muddy and most firm to the feet, crossing on hurdles and planks which they laid down, they succeeded at sunrise in taking nearly the whole of the stockade and the ditch, and the remainder afterwards. A battle took place in which the Athenians were victorious; and the Syracusans on the right wing fled to the city, those on the left along the river. The three hundred chosen Athenian troops pressed on at full speed towards the bridge, intending to stop their passage, but the Syracusans, fearing this and having most of their horsemen on the spot, turned upon the three hundred, and putting them to flight, charged the right wing of the Athenians. On their attack the panic extended to the division at the extremity of the wing. Lamachus saw what had happened, and went to the rescue from his own place on the left wing, taking with him a few archers and the Argive troops; but pressing forward across a ditch, he was cut off from the rest with a few followers, and fell with five or six of his companions. The Syracusans at once hastily

snatched up their bodies and carried them across the river out of the reach of the enemy. But when the rest of the Athenian army then advanced towards them, they retreated.

102. Meanwhile, the Syracusans who had at first fled into the city, observed these events, took courage and, coming out again themselves, drew up against that part of the Athenian line which was opposed to them. They also sent a detachment against the "circle" on Epipolæ, supposing that it was undefended, and then they would take it. They did indeed take and demolish the outwork, which was about a thousand feet in length; but Nicias, who happened to have been left there because he was ill, saved the "circle" itself. He commanded the servants to set fire to the engines and to the timber which had been left lying in front of the wall; for, being without troops, he knew that there was no other way of success. The expedient succeeded; in consequence of the fire, the Syracusans did not come nearer but again retired. For the Athenians in the plain, who had pursued their enemies off the field, were now coming up towards the "circle" to help, while at the same times the ships, as they had been ordered, were sailing from Thapsus into the Great Harbor. The Syracusans on the heights saw this and quickly retreated, together with the rest of the army, into the city, thinking that with their present force they were no longer able to prevent the completion of the wall to the sea.

103. The Athenians then erected a trophy and restored the Syracusan dead under a truce. The Syracusans delivered to them the bodies of Lamachus and his companions. The whole Athenian forces, both naval and military, were now on the spot; and they proceeded to cut off the Syracusans by a double wall, beginning at the southern cliff of Epipolæ and extending to the sea. Provisions came to their army in abundance from all parts of Italy. Many of the Sicel tribes, who had hitherto been looking on, now joined the Athenians; and three penteconters came from the Etruscans. Everything began to answer to their hopes. The Syracusans despaired of saving the city by arms, for no help had reached them even

from the Peloponnese. Within the walls they were talking of peace; and they began to enter into communications with Nicias, who, now that Lamachus was dead, had the sole command. But no definite result was attained although, as might be expected with men who felt their own helplessness and were more nearly beleaguered than before, many proposals were made to him, and many more were discussed in the city. Their calamities even made them rather suspicious of one another; they deposed the generals, under whom all this had occurred, on the ground that their ill-luck or treachery was injurious to the city. In their place they chose Heraclides, Eucles and Tellias.

104. Meanwhile, Gylippus the Lacedæmonian and the ships from Corinth were already at Leucas and desirous of aiding Sicily without delay. Alarming reports were pouring in, all false, and all agreeing that the Athenian lines around Syracuse were now complete. Gylippus had no longer any hope of Sicily, but he wished to save Italy; so he and Pythen the Corinthian sailed across the Ionian Gulf to Taras as fast as they could, taking two Laconian and two Corinthian ships. The Corinthians were to man ten ships of their own, two Leucadian, and three Ambracian, and to follow. Gylippus on his arrival at Taras went on a mission to Thurii, as his father had formerly been a citizen there;[1] he failed to gain over the Thurians and then continued his voyage along the coast of Italy. He was caught in the Terinæan gulf by a wind which in this region blows violently and steadily from the north and was carried into the open sea.[2] After the storm he returned to Taras, where he drew up those of his ships which had suffered most in the gale and refitted them. Nicias heard of his approach but like the Thurians, regarded the small number of his ships with contempt. He thought that he had come on a mere privateering expedition, and as yet took no precautions.

105. During this summer, about the same time, the Lacedæmonians and their allies invaded Argolis and wasted most of the Argive territory. The Athenians assisted the Argives with thirty ships, which flagrantly violated their treaty with the Lacedæmonians. Hitherto

the Athenians had gone out on marauding expeditions from Pylos, directed not against Laconia but against other parts of the Peloponnese; and they had fought as the allies of the Argives and Mantineans. The Argives had often urged them just to land soldiers on Lacedæmonian ground and to waste some part of Laconia, however small, without remaining; and they had refused. But now, under the command of Pythodorus, Læspodias and Demaratus, they landed at Epidaurus Limera, Prasiæ and other places, and wasted the country. Thereby the Athenians at last gave the Lacedæmonians a better justification for complaining of them and retaliating.[1] After the Athenian fleet and the Lacedæmonians had retired from Argos, the Argives invaded Phliasia and, having ravaged the country and killed a few of the Phliasians, returned home.

BOOK VII

The Siege of Syracuse (414 B.C.)

1. Gylippus and Pythen, after refitting their ships, coasted along from Taras to Epizephyrian Locri. They now got clearer information that Syracuse was not as yet completely invested but that an army might still enter by way of Epipolæ. So they considered whether they should take Sicily on the right and risk sailing into Syracuse, or on the left and sail first to Himera, gather a force of the Himeræans and of any others whom they could induce to join them, and make their way by land. They determined to sail to Himera, especially as the four Athenian ships which Nicias sent off on learning of Gylippus' presence at Locri had still not yet arrived at Rhegium. So they sailed through the strait before these ships arrived and, touching at Rhegium and Messenè, reached Himera. There they persuaded the Himeræans to make common cause with them and to join in the expedition themselves and to supply arms to all their unarmed sailors, for they had beached their ships at Himera. They also sent to the Selinuntians and told them to come and meet them with their whole army at an appointed place. The Geloans and some of the Sicels promised to send them a small force; the latter were ready to join with the more alacrity because Archonides, a Sicel king in these parts who was powerful and friendly to the Athenians, had recently died, and because Gylippus had come from Lacedæmon with a reputation for energy. And so, taking with him about seven hundred of his own sailors and marines for whom he had obtained arms, about a thousand Himeræan infantry, both heavy- and light-armed, a hundred Himeræan horsemen, some light-armed troops and cavalry from Selinus, a few more from Gela, and about a thousand Sicels in all, Gylippus marched towards Syracuse.

2. The Corinthian ships had put to sea from Leucas, and were coming with all speed to the relief of the besieged. Gongylus, one of the Corinthian commanders, who started last in a single ship, arrived at Syracuse before the rest, and a little before Gylippus. He found the citizens on the point of holding an assembly at which the question of peace was to be discussed; he stopped them by the encouraging announcement that more ships, and Gylippus the son of Cleandridas, whom the Lacedæmonians had sent to take the command, were on their way. The Syracusans were reassured, and at once went forth with their whole army to meet Gylippus; they were informed that he was already close at hand. He had then captured the Sicel fort Ietæ on his march, and drawing up his men in readiness to fight, reached Epipolæ, which he ascended by the Euryelus, as the Athenians had originally done. He then marched against the Athenian lines with the Syracusans. He arrived just at the time when the Athenians had finished their double wall for a length of seven or eight stades, as far as the Great Harbor; there remained only a small portion towards the sea upon which they were still at work. In the other part, above the "circle," which extended towards Trogilus and the northern sea, the stones were mostly lying ready; a part was half-finished; a part had been completed and left. So near was Syracuse to disaster.

3. The Athenians, though at first disconcerted by the sudden advance of Gylippus and the Syracusans, drew up their forces in order of battle. He halted as he approached and sent a herald to them offering a truce if they were willing to quit Sicily within five days, taking what belonged to them. But they treated his offer with contempt and sent away the herald without an answer. Both armies then set themselves in order of battle. Gylippus, seeing that the Syracusans were in confusion, and could form only with difficulty, led back his troops to the more open ground. Nicias did not follow but remained inactive, close to his own wall. When Gylippus observed that the Athenians were not advancing, he led away his army to the height called Temenites; there they bivouacked. On the following day, he stationed the

greater part of his troops in front of the Athenians' wall to prevent them from sending out forces to any other point under attack, and then sent a detachment against the fort of Labdalum, which was out of sight of the Athenian lines. He took the place and killed everyone whom he found in it. On the same day, an Athenian trireme which was keeping watch over the mouth of the harbor was taken by the Syracusans.

4. The Syracusans and their allies now began to build a single line of wall starting from the city and running upwards across Epipolæ at an angle with the Athenian wall; this was a work which, unless it could be stopped by the Athenians, would make the investment of the city impossible. Towards the sea the Athenian wall was completed, and their forces had now gone up to the high ground. A part of their wall was weak, and Gylippus went by night with his army to attack it. But the Athenians, who were actually bivouacked outside the walls, detected this movement and marched to oppose him; he saw this and rapidly withdrew. They then raised the weak portion of their wall higher and guarded it themselves, while they now posted the allies on the other parts of the fortification in places severally assigned to them.

Nicias determined to fortify the place named Plemmyrium, a promontory opposite the city which juts out and narrows the entrance of the Great Harbor. He thought that this measure would facilitate the introduction of supplies. His forces would then watch the harbor of the Syracusans from a nearer point, instead of putting out from a corner of the Great Harbor, as hitherto, whenever a Syracusan ship threatened to move. He now paid more attention than before to naval operations; for he saw that since the arrival of Gylippus, the Athenian prospects by land were not so encouraging. Having therefore transferred his ships and a portion of his army to Plemmyrium, he built three forts in which the greater part of the Athenian stores was deposited, and the large boats as well as the ships of war were now anchored at this spot. The removal was a first and main cause of the deterioration of the crews. They had little water, and the source was not near; and in addition, whenever they went out to forage for wood, they were cut off by the Syracusan cavalry, who were masters of the country; for a third part of their force had been posted in a village in the Olympium in order to prevent the enemy at Plemmyrium from coming out and ravaging. About this time Nicias was informed that the rest of the Corinthian fleet was sailing, and he sent twenty ships to guard against them with orders to lie in wait for them off Locri and Rhegium and the approach to Sicily.

5. While Gylippus was building the wall across Epipolæ, employing the stones which the Athenians had previously laid there for their own use, he constantly led out the Syracusans and their allies and drew them up in front of the wall; and the Athenians on their part drew up against them. When he thought that the moment had arrived, he began the attack; the two armies met and fought hand to hand between the walls. But there the Syracusan cavalry was useless; the Syracusans and their allies were defeated, and received their dead under truce, while the Athenians raised a trophy. Gylippus then assembled his army and confessed that the fault was his own and not theirs; for by confining their ranks too much between the walls, he had rendered their cavalry and their javelin men useless. So he would lead them out again. He urged them to reflect that in material force they were equal to their enemies, while as for spirit it would be intolerable if they, as Peloponnesians and Dorians, did not think that they should master Ionians and islanders and a mixed rabble and drive them out of the country.

6. On the first opportunity afterwards he led them out again. Nicias and the Athenians thought that whether or not the Syracusans offered battle, they must not allow them to build the counterwall past their own. For already it had almost passed the end of the Athenian wall; and if it advanced any further, it would make no difference to the Athenians whether they fought and conquered in every battle or never fought at all. So they went out to meet the Syracusans. Gylippus, before engaging, led his heavy-armed further outside the walls than on the former occasion; his cavalry and javelin men he placed

on the flank of the Athenians in the open space where their respective lines of walls stopped. In the course of the battle, the cavalry attacked the left wing of the Athenians which was opposed to them and put them to flight; the defeat became general and the whole Athenian army was flung back within their fortification. On the following night, the Syracusans forestalled the Athenians by carrying their wall across and past the works of the enemy so that they could no longer be stopped by the Athenians; and the Athenians, whatever success they might gain in the field, were utterly deprived of all hope of investing the city.

7. Afterwards the remaining twelve Corinthian, Ambraciot and Leucadian ships sailed in, under the command of Erasinides the Corinthian, having eluded the Athenian guardships. They assisted the Syracusans in completing the crosswall. Gylippus went off to collect both naval and land forces in the rest of Sicily and also to bring over any cities which were not enthusiastic in the Syracusan cause, or had so far stood quite aloof from the war. More ambassadors, Syracusan and Corinthian, were dispatched to Lacedæmon and Corinth, requesting that reinforcements might be sent across the sea in merchant ships or small craft, or by any other available means, since the Athenians were sending for further assistance. The Syracusans also manned a fleet and began to practice, intending to try an attack on sea too. Altogether they were full of confidence.

8. Nicias on his side, observing this and seeing that the strength of the enemy and the helplessness of the Athenians was daily increasing, sent to Athens a full report of his circumstances, as he had often done before but never in such detail. He now thought the situation critical and that if the Athenians did not at once recall them or send another considerable army to their help, the expedition was lost. Fearing that his messengers might not report the facts from inability to speak or defect of memory, or because they would curry favor with the rabble in their speeches, he wrote a letter, thinking that the Athenians would thus learn his own opinion, with nothing concealed in the transmission, and deliber-

ate on the real facts. The messengers left with his letter and verbal instructions. He was now more careful to keep his army on the defensive and to run no risks which he could avoid. . . .

10. In the following winter, the messengers from Nicias arrived at Athens. They delivered their verbal instructions and answered any questions which were put to them. They also presented his letter, which the city secretary, coming forward, read to the Athenian people. It ran somewhat as follows:[1]

11. "Athenians, I have reported to you previous events in many other messages, but now there is greater need than ever that you should deliberate with knowledge of our present situation. After we had beaten the Syracusans, against whom you sent us, in most battles and had built the fortifications within which we are now stationed, Gylippus, a Lacedæmonian, arrived with a force from the Peloponnese and from some cities in Sicily. In the first engagement we defeated him; but on the following day we were overcome by numerous horsemen and javelin men, and retired within our lines. We have therefore desisted from the work of circumvallation, and remain inactive because of the superior numbers of the enemy: indeed we should not be able to bring our whole army into the field, for the defense of our walls absorbs a large part of our hoplites. The enemy has built a single wall which crosses ours, and we can no longer invest them unless a large army comes up and takes this cross-wall. The result is that though we are supposed to be the besiegers, we are to a greater extent besieged, at least by land; we do not even go far into the country, for we are prevented by their horsemen.

12. "They have also sent ambassadors to the Peloponnese, asking for reinforcements; and Gylippus has gone to the cities in Sicily, intending to induce those who are at present neutral to join him, and to obtain from his allies, if he can, fresh naval and land forces. For they purpose, as I learn by inquiry, to attack our walls by land and at the same time to make an effort at sea. And let no one be startled that they should act by sea too. Our fleet was originally in first-rate condition: the ships were dry, and

the crews were in good order; but now, as the enemy are well aware, the timbers of the ships, after being so long at sea, are soaked, and the efficiency of the crews is destroyed. We have no means of drawing up our vessels and airing them because the enemy's fleet is equal or even superior in numbers to our own, and we are always expecting an attack from them. We can see them exercising; they can attack us when they please, and they have far greater facilities for drying their ships since they are not engaged in a blockade.

13. "Even if we had a great superiority in the number of our ships, and were not compelled as we are to employ them all in keeping guard, we could hardly do this. For our supplies pass the enemy's city, and are conveyed to us now with difficulty; and if we relax our vigilance ever so little, we shall lose them altogether.

"It has been and continues to be the ruin of our crews, that the sailors, having to forage and fetch water and wood from a distance, are cut off by the Syracusan horse, while our servants desert us, since we have been reduced to an equality with the enemy. Of the foreign sailors, some who were pressed into the service run off to the Sicilian cities as they arrive; others, who were originally attracted by high pay, and thought that they were going to trade rather than to fight, see that, contrary to their belief, the enemy are resisting by sea, as well as elsewhere, and either find an excuse for desertion or for escape as best they can in different ways; Sicily is a large place. Others, again, have persuaded the trierarchs to put on board Hyccarian slaves in their place while they themselves are busy trading; and thus the efficiency of the fleet is gone.

14. "I am writing to you who know that the crew of a vessel does not long remain at its prime and that the sailors who set the ship under way and keep the rowing together are few. The greatest difficulty of all is that although I am general, I am not able to put a stop to these disorders; for the character of Athenians makes them hard to control. We cannot even fill up the crews, whereas the enemy can obtain recruits from many sources, but we have to man the ships and replace losses

from the men we brought with us, for the cities which are now our confederates, Naxos and Catana, cannot assist. There is only one advantage more which the Syracusans can gain over us: if the towns of Italy from which our provisions are derived see that we are in this position and that you do not send reinforcements, and go over to the enemy, we shall be starved out; and they will have made an end of the war without striking a blow. I might have sent you a different message more pleasant to hear, but it would not have been so valuable, for you need to deliberate in clear knowledge of our position. Moreover, I know your character; you like to hear the most pleasant news but afterwards lay the fault on those who tell them, if they are falsified by the event; therefore I thought it safer to make the truth plain.

15. "And now, do not imagine that your soldiers and their generals have failed in the fulfillment of the duty which you originally imposed upon them. But when all Sicily is uniting against us and the Syracusans are expecting another army from the Peloponnese, it is time that you should make up your minds. For the troops which we have here cannot hold out even against our present enemies; and therefore you ought either to recall us or to send another army and fleet as large as this, and plenty of money. You should also send a general to succeed me, for I have a disease in the kidneys and cannot remain here. I claim your indulgence; while I retained my health, I often did you good service when in command. But do whatever you mean to do at the very beginning of spring, and let there be no delay. The enemy will obtain reinforcements in Sicily without going far; and although the troops from Peloponnese will not arrive so soon, yet if you do not take care, some will elude your notice, as they did before, and others will forestall you."

The Expedition of Demosthenes (413 B.C.)

16. Such was the condition of affairs described in the letter of Nicias. The Athenians, after hearing it read, did not release Nicias from his command; but they joined

with him two officers who were already in Sicily, Menander and Euthydemus, until regular colleagues could be elected and sent out; for they did not wish him to bear the burden in his sickness alone. They also resolved to send a second fleet and an army of Athenians taken from the muster roll and of allies. As colleagues to Nicias, they elected Demosthenes the son of Alcisthenes, and Eurymedon the son of Thucles. Eurymedon was dispatched immediately to Sicily about the winter solstice; he took with him ten ships conveying 120 talents of silver, and was to tell the army in Sicily that they would receive assistance and would not be neglected. Demosthenes remained behind, getting ready for the voyage which he was to make in the spring. He sent to the allies for troops and procured money, ships and hoplites at Athens. The Athenians also sent twenty ships round the Peloponnese to prevent any vessels crossing to Sicily from the Peloponnese or Corinth. The Sicilian envoys had now arrived at Corinth, and the Corinthians had heard from them that affairs were looking better in Sicily. Seeing how opportune had been the arrival of the ships which they had already dispatched, they were more than ever encouraged, and themselves prepared to convey hoplites to Sicily in merchant vessels; the Lacedæmonians were to do the same from the rest of the Peloponnese. The Corinthians also proceeded to man 25 ships of war, intending to try a naval engagement against the Athenian squadron stationed at Naupactus; the Athenians there might be less able to stop their merchant vessels from sailing off if they were defending themselves against Corinthian triremes ready for battle.

18. The Lacedæmonians also prepared for their already projected invasion of Attica. They were urged on by the Syracusans and Corinthians, who had heard of the reinforcements which the Athenians were sending to Sicily, and desired they might be stopped by the invasion; and Alcibiades was insisting that they should fortify Decelea and carry on the war with vigor. Above all, the Lacedæmonians had been encouraged by the thought that the Athenians would be more easily overthrown now that they had two wars on hand, against themselves and

against the Sicilians. They considered also that this time the Athenians had been the first to violate the treaty, whereas in the former war the transgression had rather been on their own side. For the Thebans had entered Platæa in time of peace, and they themselves had refused arbitration when offered by the Athenians, although the former treaty forbade war in case an adversary was willing to submit to arbitration. They thought that their ill success was natural, and they took to heart the disasters which they had sustained at Pylos and elsewhere. But now the Athenians with thirty ships based on Argos had ravaged Epidaurus and Prasiæ, besides other places; marauding expeditions from Pylos were always going on; and whenever quarrels arose about disputed points in the treaty and the Lacedæmonians proposed arbitration, the Athenians refused it. The Lacedæmonians concluded that the disrespect of law of which they had been guilty before had shifted to the Athenians and taken the same form, and they were enthusiastic for the war. In this winter they bade their allies provide iron and got the other tools in readiness for the fortification of Decelea. They also furnished themselves and forced the other Peloponnesians to furnish the assistance which they intended to send in merchant vessels to the Syracusans. And so the winter ended, and the eighteenth year of this war of which Thucydides wrote the history.

19. At the very beginning of the next spring, and earlier than ever before, the Lacedæmonians and their allies entered Attica under the command of Agis son of Archidamus, the Lacedæmonian king. They first devastated the plain and its neighborhood. They then began to fortify Decelea, dividing the work among the cities of the confederacy. Decelea is about 120 stades from Athens, about as far or not much further from Bœotia. The fort was erected for the devastation of the plain and the richest parts of the country, and could be seen as far as Athens.

While the Peloponnesians and their allies in Attica were thus engaged, the Peloponnesians at home were dispatching the hoplites in the merchant vessels to Sicily. The Lacedæmonians selected the best of the Helots and

Neodamodes, numbering in all six hundred hoplites, and placed them under the command of Eccritus, a Spartiate. The Bœotians furnished three hundred hoplites, who were commanded by two Thebans, Xenon and Nicon, and by Hegesander, a Thespian. These started first and put out into the open sea from Tænarum in Laconia. Not long afterwards, the Corinthians sent five hundred hoplites, some of them from Corinth itself, others who were Arcadian mercenaries, under the command of Alexarchus, a Corinthian. The Sicyonians also sent with the Corinthians two hundred hoplites under the command of Sargeus, a Sicyonian. Meanwhile the twenty-five ships which the Corinthians had manned in the winter lay opposite to the twenty Athenian ships at Naupactus until the merchant vessels conveying the heavy-armed troops had sailed from the Peloponnese. So the design succeeded, and the attention of the Athenians was diverted from the merchant ships to the triremes.

20. At the beginning of spring, whilst the Lacedæmonians were fortifying Decelea, the Athenians sent thirty ships under the command of Charicles the son of Apollodorus around the Peloponnese. He was told to touch at Argos and to request the Argives to put hoplites on board under the treaty of alliance. Meanwhile, they dispatched under Demosthenes their intended expedition to Sicily: it consisted of sixty Athenian ships and five Chian, twelve hundred Athenian hoplites taken from the roll, and as many others as could possibly be obtained from the different islanders; they had also collected from their subject allies any supplies they had for the war. Demosthenes was told first of all to cooperate with Charicles on the coast of Laconia. So he sailed to Ægina and there waited until the whole of his armament was assembled and until Charicles had taken on board the Argives.

21. In Sicily, about the same time in this spring, Gylippus returned to Syracuse, bringing from each of the cities which he had persuaded to join him as many troops as he could obtain. He assembled the Syracusans and told them that they should man as large a fleet as possible and try their fortune at sea and that he hoped

to obtain a success in the war which would justify the risk. Hermocrates, particularly, joined Gylippus in urging them not to be fainthearted at the prospect of attacking with their ships. He said that the Athenians had not inherited their maritime experience and had not enjoyed it in all time past; they were once less of a naval people than the Syracusans themselves, but they had been made sailors from necessity by the Persian invasion. To daring men like the Athenians, those who emulated their daring would appear the most difficult to defeat. The same confidence which had often enabled the Athenians, although inferior in power, to strike terror into their adversaries might now be turned against them by the Syracusans. He said that he well knew that by unexpectedly daring to withstand the Athenian fleet, the Syracusans would be more likely to gain the advantage by the consternation they inspired than the Athenians to do them damage by the superiority of their knowledge to Syracusan inexperience. He told them, therefore, to try what they could do at sea and not to hesitate. Thus, under the influence of Gylippus, Hermocrates and others, the Syracusans, now eager for the conflict, began to man their ships.

22. When the fleet was ready, Gylippus, under cover of night, led forth the whole land army, intending to attack the forts on Plemmyrium in person. Meanwhile, the triremes of the Syracusans sailed out at a concerted signal, thirty-five from the greater harbor and forty-five from the lesser, where they had their dockyard. These latter sailed around into the Great Harbor, intending to form a junction with the other ships inside and make a combined attack on Plemmyrium, so as to disconcert the Athenians, assailed both by sea and land. The Athenians, however, quickly manned sixty ships and with twenty-five of them engaged the thirty-five of the Syracusans which were in the Great Harbor; with the remainder they encountered those which were sailing around from the dockyard. These two squadrons met just before the mouth of the Great Harbor: the struggle was long and obstinate, the Syracusans striving to force an entrance, the Athenians to prevent them.

23. Meantime, while the Athenians in Plemmyrium

who had gone down to the waterside had their minds occupied by the sea fight, Gylippus surprised them by making a sudden attack at dawn upon their forts. He captured the largest of them first, then the two lesser, their garrisons forsaking them when they saw the largest so easily taken. Those who escaped from the first captured fortress by getting into a merchant vessel and some boats which were moored at Plemmyrium, found their way to the Athenian camp, but with difficulty; for they were chased by a single fast trireme, the Syracusans at that time having the advantage in the Great Harbor. But when the two lesser fortresses were taken, the Syracusans were already losing the day; and the fugitives got past them with greater ease. For the Syracusan ships which were fighting in front of the mouth of the harbor, after overcoming the Athenian ships, entered in disorder and, falling foul of one another, gave away the victory to the Athenians, who routed them, and also the others by which they were at first worsted inside the harbor. They sank eleven Syracusan ships; the crews in most of them were killed, in three made prisoners. The Athenians themselves lost three ships. They now drew to land the wrecks of the Syracusan ships and, erecting a trophy on the little island in front of Plemmyrium, returned to their own camp.

24. But although the Syracusans were unsuccessful in the sea fight, still they had taken the fortresses of Plemmyrium. They erected three trophies, one for each fort. Two out of the three forts they repaired and garrisoned, but one of the two which were captured last they demolished. Many perished, and many prisoners were made at the capture of the forts, and the total of stores taken was large, for the Athenians had used them as an arsenal, and much corn and goods of traders were deposited in them; also much property belonging to the trierarchs, including the sails and other fittings of forty triremes fell into the enemy's hands, as well as three triremes which had been drawn up on the beach. But the greatest and severest blow to the Athenians was the capture of Plemmyrium. For now they could no longer even sail in safely with provisions, but the Syra-

cusan ships lay watching to prevent them, and they now had to fight for the passage. General discouragement and dismay prevailed throughout the army.

25. The Syracusans next sent out twelve ships under the command of Agatharchus, a Syracusan. One of them went to the Peloponnese conveying envoys who were to report their improved prospects and to urge more strongly than ever the prosecution of the war in Hellas. The remaining eleven sailed to Italy, hearing that ships laden with supplies were on their way to the Athenians. They fell in with most of these ships and destroyed them and burnt a quantity of ship timber which was lying ready for the Athenians in the territory of Caulonia. Then they came to Locri; and while they were at anchor there, one of the merchant vessels from the Peloponnese sailed in, bringing Thespian hoplites. The Syracusans took them on board and sailed homewards. The Athenians watched for them near Megara with twenty ships and took one ship with the crew, but the rest made their escape to Syracuse.

There was also some skirmishing in the harbor around the stakes which the Syracusans had fixed in the sea in front of their old dock houses so that their ships might ride at anchor in the enclosed space, where they could not be struck and damaged by the enemy. The Athenians brought up a merchant ship of ten thousand talents burden,[1] which had wooden towers and parapets; and from the little boats they tied cords to the stakes and wrenched and tore them up, or dived and sawed them through underneath the water. Meanwhile, the Syracusans kept up a shower of missiles from the dock houses, which the men in the merchant ship returned. At length the Athenians pulled up most of the stakes. Those which were out of sight were the most difficult of all, as some were so fixed that they did not appear above the water; and no vessel could safely come near. They were like a sunken reef; and a pilot, not seeing them, might easily cast his ship upon them. Even these were sawn off by men who dived for hire, but the Syracusans drove them in again. Many other contrivances were employed on both sides, as was very natural when two armies confronted each other at so short a distance. There were continual skirmishes and attempts of all kinds.

The Syracusans also sent to the cities in Sicily Corinthian, Ambraciot and Lacedæmonian ambassadors announcing the taking of Plemmyrium and explaining that in the sea fight they had been defeated not so much by the superior strength of the enemy as through their own disorder. They were to show their great hopes of success and above all to ask for assistance both by land and sea, on the ground that the Athenians too were expecting reinforcements; if they could succeed in destroying the army then in Sicily before these arrived, there would be an end of the war. Such was the course of events in Sicily.

26. Demosthenes, when the expeditionary force which he was to take to Sicily had mustered, sailed from Ægina to the Peloponnese and joined Charicles and his thirty ships. They embarked the Argive hoplites and, proceeding to Laconia, first devastated some part of Epidaurus Limera, next landed in the district of Laconia opposite Cythera, where there is a temple of Apollo, ravaged parts of the country and fortified a sort of isthmus, so that the Helots of the Lacedæmonians might desert and find a refuge there and that privateers might make the place, like Pylos, a base for marauding expeditions. Demosthenes assisted in the occupation and then at once sailed for Corcyra to collect additional forces from the allies in that region and to sail with all speed to Sicily. Charicles waited until he had completed the fort; and then, leaving a garrison, he sailed home with his thirty ships, accompanied by the Argives.

27. During the same summer there arrived at Athens thirteen hundred Thracian peltasts of the Dian race, armed with short swords; they were to have sailed with Demosthenes to Sicily, but came too late; and the Athenians determined to send them back to their native country. Each soldier was receiving a drachma per day; and to keep them appeared expensive, in view of the operations conducted from Decelea.

The occupation of Decelea, at first by the whole Peloponnesian army and afterwards by a succession of garrisons sent from the allied cities which made incursions into the country, did the Athenians great damage; the destruction of property and life did as much as anything to impair their position. Previously, the invasions had been brief, and did not prevent them from getting something from the soil in the interval; but now the Peloponnesians were continually on the spot; sometimes they were reinforced by additional troops, and the regular garrison inevitably overran and despoiled the country. The Lacedæmonian king, Agis, was present in person and devoted his whole energies to the war. Great damage was done. For the Athenians were dispossessed of their entire territory; more than twenty thousand slaves had deserted, most of them workmen; all their flocks and draft animals were lost; and now that the cavalry had to go out every day and make sallies toward Decelea or keep guard all over the country, their horses were wounded by the enemy or lamed by the roughness of the ground and the incessant fatigue.

28. Provisions, which had been formerly conveyed by the quicker route from Eubœa to Oropus and thence overland through Decelea, were now carried by sea around the promontory of Sunium at great cost. Athens was obliged to import everything from abroad, and came to be a fort rather than a city. In the daytime the citizens guarded the battlements by relays; during the night every man was on service except the cavalry, some at their places of arms, others on the wall; their fatigues lasted summer and winter alike. But the pressure was most severe because they had two wars to fight at once, and their appetite for war was so enormous that until these events none would have believed it on report. At home they were besieged by the Peloponnesians in their fort; yet even so they did not withdraw from Sicily; there they responded by besieging Syracuse in the same way, a city not at all inferior, taken by herself, to their own. Their power and daring so far exceeded the calculations of the Hellenes—at the beginning of the war, some thought that they would last out for a year, others for two, none for longer than three years, if the Peloponnesians were to invade their country—that in the seven-

teenth year after the first invasion, they attacked Syracuse, when they were already exhausted in every way by the war,[1] and undertook a fresh war, as great as that in which they were already engaged with the Peloponnesians.[2] As a result, with Decelea now doing them so much damage and other expenses falling heavily upon them, they came to lack funds. It was about this time that they imposed upon their subjects, instead of the tribute, a duty of five per cent on seaborne trade, thinking that this would be more productive of money. For their expenses had become far heavier than ever before, in proportion to the extension of the war; and their revenues were vanishing.

29. And so, from a desire to economize when money was so short, they at once sent away the Thracians who came too late for Demosthenes, ordering Diitrephes to convey them home and also, as their route lay through the Euripus, to employ them in any way which he could against the enemy. He landed them at Tanagra and there made a hasty raid; in the evening he sailed from Chalcis in Eubœa through the Euripus and, disembarking in Bœotia, led them against the town of Mycalessus. He passed the night unobserved near the temple of Hermes, about 16 stades from Mycalessus, and at dawn assaulted and captured the city, which is not large. The inhabitants were taken off their guard, for they never imagined that an enemy would come and attack them at so great a distance from the sea. The walls were weak, and in some places had fallen down; in others they were built low; while the citizens, in their security, had left their gates open. The Thracians dashed into the town, plundered the houses and temples and slaughtered the inhabitants. They spared neither old nor young, but killed, one after another, all whom they met, the women and children, the very beasts of burden and every living thing which they saw. (The Thracians, like the worst barbarians of their kind, are most bloodthirsty when they have nothing to fear.) On this occasion there was great turmoil and destruction in every form. They even fell upon a boys' school, the largest in the place, which the children had just entered, and cut them all down. No

calamity could be worse than this, touching as it did the whole city; none was ever so sudden or so terrible.

30. When the news reached the Thebans, they went to the rescue. Coming upon the Thracians before they had gone far, they took away the spoil and, putting them to flight, pursued them to the Euripus, where the ships which had brought them were moored. Of those who fell, the greatest number were killed in the attempt to embark; for they did not know how to swim; and the men on board, seeing what was happening, had anchored their vessels out of bowshot. In the retreat itself, the Thracians made a very fair defense against the Theban cavalry which first attacked them, running out and closing in again, in accordance with the tactics of their country; and their loss at that time was trifling. Some who remained in the city for the sake of plunder were killed there. The whole number who fell was 250, out of 1,300. They killed, however, some of the Thebans and others who came to the rescue, in all about 20 horsemen and hoplites, including Scirphondas, one of the Theban Bœotarchs. A large proportion of the Mycalessians perished. Such was the fate of Mycalessus; considering the size of the city, no calamity more lamentable occurred during the war.

31. Demosthenes, who, after helping to build the fort on the Laconian coast, had sailed away to Corcyra, on his way destroyed a merchant vessel anchored at Phea in Elis, which was intended to convey some of the Corinthian hoplites to Sicily. But they escaped and sailed in another vessel. He went on to Zacynthus and Cephallenia, where he took on board some hoplites, and sent to the Messenians of Naupactus for others; he then passed over to the mainland of Acarnania and touched at Alyzia and Anactorium, which were at that time occupied by the Athenians. While he was in these regions, he met Eurymedon returning from Sicily, where he had been sent during the winter with the money for the army; he reported, among other things, the capture of Plemmyrium by the Syracusans, of which he had heard on his voyage home. Conon too, who commanded at Naupactus, brought word that the twenty-five Corinthian ships which were

stationed on the opposite coast were not dispersing, and clearly meant to fight. He requested the generals to send him ships, since his own ships—eighteen in number—were not able to give battle against the twenty-five of the enemy. Demosthenes and Eurymedon sent ten ships, the best they had, to the fleet at Naupactus, while they themselves completed the muster of the expedition. Eurymedon, sailing to Corcyra, ordered the Corcyræans to man fifteen ships, and himself levied a number of hoplites. He had turned back from his homeward voyage, and was now holding the joint commands with Demosthenes, to which he had been appointed. Demosthenes, meanwhile, had been collecting slingers and javelin men in the neighborhood of Acarnania.

32. The ambassadors from Syracuse who had gone to the cities of Sicily after the taking of Plemmyrium and had persuaded them to join in the war, were now about to bring back the army which they had collected. Nicias, having previous information, sent word to the Sicel allies of Athens who commanded the road, such as the Centoripes and Halicyæi, and told them not to let the forces of the enemy pass but to unite and stop them; they would not even try a different route, since the people of Acragas had refused them a passage through their country. So when the Sicilian Greeks were on their way, the Sicels, complying with the request of the Athenians, set an ambush in three divisions and, falling upon them suddenly when they were off their guard, destroyed about eight hundred of them, and all the envoys except the Corinthian; he brought the survivors, numbering fifteen hundred, to Syracuse.

33. About the same time arrived a reinforcement from Camarina of five hundred hoplites, three hundred javelin men and three hundred archers. The Geloans also sent five ships with four hundred javelin men and two hundred horsemen. For now almost the whole of Sicily, with the exception of Acragas, which was neutral, including the cities which had previously watched events, united with the Syracusans against the Athenians. After their misfortune in the Sicel country, the Syracusans deferred their intended attack on the Athenians for a time.

The forces which Demosthenes and Eurymedon had collected from Corcyra and the mainland were now ready, and with their whole force they crossed the Ionian Sea to the promontory of Iapygia. Proceeding from there, they touched at the Iapygian islands called Chœrades, and took on board 150 Iapygian javelin men of the Messapian tribe. After renewing an ancient friendship with Artas, a prince who had furnished the javelin men, they went on to Metapontium in Italy. They persuaded the Metapontians, under their alliance, to let them have two triremes and three hundred javelin men; with these they sailed to Thurii. At Thurii they found that the party opposed to the Athenians had just been driven out by a revolution. There they wished to hold a muster and inspection of their whole army to be sure that no one was missing and to induce the Thurians to join their expedition with the utmost energy and, as events had taken this turn, to make an offensive and defensive alliance with Athens; so they stayed at Thurii, occupied in these ways.

34. About the same time the Peloponnesians in their fleet of twenty-five ships, which was stationed opposite the Athenian fleet at Naupactus to protect the passage of the merchant vessels going to Sicily, made ready for action. They manned some additional ships, which raised their number nearly to that of the Athenians, and anchored at Erineus off Achæa, in the territory of Rhypæ. The shore off which they were stationed has the form of a crescent; and the infantry of the Corinthians and their allies, which had come from the country on both sides to co-operate with the fleet, was disposed on the projecting promontories. The ships under the command of Polyanthes the Corinthian formed a close line between the two points. The Athenians sailed out against them from Naupactus with thirty-three ships, under the command of Diphilus. For a while the Corinthians remained motionless; when they thought the due time had come, the signal was raised; and they rushed against the Athenians and engaged them. The battle was long and obstinate. Three Corinthian ships were destroyed. The Athenians

had no ships absolutely sunk, but about seven of them were rendered useless; for they were struck full in front by the beaks of the Corinthian vessels, which had the projecting beams of their prows built thicker for this very purpose; and their bows were stoven in. The engagement was undecided, and both sides claimed the victory, but the Athenians gained possession of the wrecks because the wind blew them towards the open sea and the Corinthians did not put out again. The two fleets parted, and there was no pursuit, nor were any prisoners taken on either side; the Corinthians and Peloponnesians were fighting close to the land and thus their crews escaped, while on the Athenian side no ship was sunk. As soon as the Athenians had returned to Naupactus, the Corinthians set up a trophy as victors, because they had disabled more of the enemy's ships than the enemy of theirs, and thought that they had not been worsted on the same grounds which made the Athenians not regard themselves as victors. For the Corinthians considered themselves conquerors if they were not severely defeated, but the Athenians thought that they were defeated because they had not gained a signal victory. When, however, the Peloponnesians had sailed away and the land army was dispersed, the Athenians raised another trophy in Achæa, at a distance of about twenty stades from the Corinthian station at Erineus. Such was the result of the engagement.

35. When the Thurians were prepared to join them with seven hundred hoplites and three hundred javelin men, Demosthenes and Eurymedon commanded the ships to sail towards the territory of Croton and, after reviewing it at the river Sybaris, led the whole infantry force in person through the territory of Thurii. On their arrival at the river Hylias, the people of Croton sent them a message that they would not consent to the army marching through their country. So they went down to the sea and bivouacked at the mouth of the river, where they were met by their ships. On the following day, they re-embarked the army and coasted along, touching at the cities which they passed, with the exception of Locri, until they came to the promontory of Petra near Rhegium.

36. The Syracusans, hearing of their approach, desired to try out their ships again, and to use the army which they had collected with the express purpose of bringing on an engagement before Demosthenes and Eurymedon arrived. In their naval preparations they took all the measures which experience in the earlier sea battle suggested they would gain some advantage from; above all, they cut down the prows in length and so made them more solid and made the beams which projected from them massive; these latter they supported underneath with stays of timber extending from the beams to and through the sides of the ship a length of nine feet within and nine without, in the same way as the Corinthians had refitted their prows before they fought with the squadron from Naupactus. For the Syracusans expected thus to gain an advantage over the Athenian ships, which were not comparably constructed but had slender prows, because they were in the habit of rowing around an enemy and striking the side of his vessel rather than meeting him prow to prow. They also thought that it would be in their favor that they were going to fight in the Great Harbor, where many ships would be crowded in a narrow space. They would ram the enemy prows which were hollow and weak with their own massive and solid beaks, while the Athenians, confined as they were, would not be able to sail around them or break their line before striking, maneuvers to which they mainly trusted—the want of room would make the first impossible, and the Syracusans themselves would do their best to prevent the second. What had hitherto been considered ignorance on the part of their pilots, the practice of ramming prow with prow, would now be their chief advantage, to which they would have constant recourse; for when the Athenians were forced back, they could only back water towards the land, which was too near and of which but a small part, that is to say, their own encampment, was open to them. The Syracusans would be masters of the rest of the harbor; and if the Athenians were hard pressed at any point, they would all be driven together into one small place, where they would run foul of one another and fall into confusion. In fact

nothing was more damaging to the Athenians in all these sea fights; they could not back water, as the Syracusans could, to any part of the harbor. Again, they themselves could advance from the open sea and back water into it, but the Athenians would be unable to use the open water for their turning movements, especially as Plemmyrium was hostile to them and the mouth of the harbor was narrow.

37. Thus, the Syracusans adapted their plans to the degree of naval skill and strength which they possessed; and even more encouraged by the result of the previous engagement, they attacked the Athenians both by sea and land. A little before the fleet sailed out, Gylippus led the land forces out of the city against the part of the Athenian wall which faced Syracuse, while the heavy-armed troops, cavalry and light infantry stationed at the Olympium approached the wall from the opposite side. Immediately afterwards, the ships of the Syracusans and their allies sailed out. The Athenians at first thought that they were going to make an attempt by land only; but when they saw the ships as well suddenly bearing down upon them, they were disconcerted. Some mounted the walls or prepared to meet their assailants in front of them; others went out against the numerous cavalry and javelin men, who were coming up quickly from the Olympium and the outer side of the wall; others manned the ships or prepared to give support on the beach. When the crews had got on board, they put out with seventy-five ships; the number of Syracusan ships was about eighty.

38. During a great part of the day, the two fleets continued advancing and backing water and skirmishing with one another. Neither was able to gain any considerable advantage; only the Syracusans sank one or two ships of the Athenians; so they parted, and at the same time the infantry retired from the walls. On the following day, the Syracusans remained quiet and gave no sign of what they meant to do next. Seeing how close the conflict had been, Nicias expected another attack; he therefore compelled the trierarchs to repair any damaged ships, and anchored merchant vessels in front of the

stockade which the Athenians, for lack of a harbor that could be closed, had driven into the sea in front of their own ships; these he placed at a distance of about two hundred feet from one another, in order that any ship which was hard pressed could retreat safely and sail out again unmolested. These preparations occupied the Athenians for a whole day from morning to night.

39. On the next day, at an earlier hour, the Syracusans advanced on the Athenians both by sea and land as they had done before. Again the ships faced one another in the same way, and again a great part of the day was passed in skirmishing. At length Ariston the son of Pyrrhichus, a Corinthian, the ablest pilot with the Syracusan fleet, persuaded their commanders to send a message to the proper authorities in the city telling them to have the provisions market transferred as quickly as possible to the shore, and to compel anyone who had food for sale to bring it all there. The sailors would thus be enabled to disembark and take their midday meal by the ships and, after a short interval, without waiting until the next day, unexpectedly renew the attack upon the Athenians.

40. The generals agreed and sent the message, and the market was brought down to the shore. Suddenly the Syracusans backed water and rowed toward the city; disembarking at once, they took their meal on the spot. The Athenians, regarding their retreat as a confession of defeat, disembarked at leisure and, among other matters, set about preparing their own meal, taking for granted that there would be no more fighting that day. Suddenly the Syracusans manned their ships and again bore down upon them; in great uproar the Athenians, most of whom had had no food, went on board in no kind of order and finally got under weigh. For some time the two fleets looked at one another and did not engage; after a while the Athenians thought they had better not delay until they had tired themselves out, but attack at once. So, cheering one another on, they bore down on the Syracusans and began the battle. The Syracusans remained firm, and meeting the enemy prow to prow, as they had resolved, stove in a great part of the bows of

the Athenian ships by the strength of their beaks. Their javelin men on the decks also did much damage; and still more was done by Syracusans who rowed about in light boats and dashed in under the blades of the enemy's oars or ran up alongside and threw darts at the sailors.

41. At last in this way the Syracusans, who made a great effort, gained the victory; and the Athenians, retreating between the merchant vessels, took refuge at their own moorings. The Syracusan ships pursued them as far as the merchant vessels, but they were stopped by the beams suspended from the vessels over the entrances between them which carried heavy weights. Two Syracusan ships, in the exultation of victory, approached too near, and were disabled; one of them was taken with its whole crew. When the Syracusans retired, they had damaged many of the Athenian ships and sunk seven; a large number of men were killed or taken prisoners. They raised trophies of the two sea fights and were now quite confident that they were actually far superior to the Athenians at sea, and they thought that they would gain the victory on land as well. So they prepared to renew the attack on both elements.

42. But in the midst of their preparations, Demosthenes and Eurymedon arrived with the Athenian reinforcements, about seventy-three ships including foreign ships, about five thousand hoplites, Athenian and allied, numerous javelin men, both Hellenic and barbarian, slingers and archers and abundant supplies of every kind. The Syracusans and their allies were, for the time, thrown into great consternation. It seemed to them as if their perils would never have an end when they saw that notwithstanding the fortification of Decelea, another army had arrived nearly equal to the former, and that Athens was displaying great strength on all fronts, while the first Athenian army regained a certain degree of confidence after their disasters. Demosthenes at once saw how matters stood; he thought it impossible to delay and repeat Nicias' experience. For Nicias inspired terror at his first arrival; but, when, instead of at once attacking Syracuse, he passed the winter at Catana, he fell into contempt; and his delay gave Gylippus time to come with

an army from the Peloponnese. If he had struck hard at first, the Syracusans would never even have sent for it; thinking their own forces adequate, they would have discovered their inferiority only when the city had been invested, and then even if they had sent for reinforcements, they would not have found them so useful. Demosthenes, reflecting on all this and aware that he too would never again be in a position to inspire such terror as on the day of his arrival, desired to take the speediest advantage of the panic caused by the appearance of his army. Accordingly, seeing that the crosswall of the Syracusans which had prevented the Athenians from investing them was but a single line, and that if he could gain the command of the way up to Epipolæ and then of the camp there, the wall would be easily captured, for no one would so much as stand his ground against them, he was in a hurry to make the attempt. He thought this the shortest way of putting an end to the war. If he succeeded, Syracuse would fall into his hands; if he failed, he meant to bring away the forces and not to wear out the Athenians on the expedition and the whole state to no purpose.

The Athenians began by ravaging the fields of the Syracusans about the Anapus and regained their former superiority both by sea and land. The Syracusans did not oppose them on either element, except with their cavalry and javelin men from the Olympium.

43. Before he attacked Epipolæ, Demosthenes decided to try what could be done with engines against the counterwall. But the engines which he brought up were burnt by the enemy, who fought from the wall; and other assaults at several points were repulsed. He now determined to delay no longer and persuaded Nicias and his colleagues to carry out the plan of attacking Epipolæ. To approach during the daytime and ascend the heights undetected appeared to be impossible. He ordered provisions for five days and took with him all the masons and carpenters in the army and also a supply of arrows and of everything which would be required for siege works if he were victorious. At the first watch he, Eurymedon, and Menander led out the whole army and marched

towards Epipolæ. Nicias was left in the Athenian fortifications. Reaching Epipolæ at the Euryelus, where their first army had originally ascended, and advancing, undiscovered by the garrison, to the fort which the Syracusans had erected there, they took it and killed some of the guards. But the greater number at once made good their escape to the three fortified camps on Epipolæ, which constituted the outworks of the defense, one of the Syracusans, one of the other Sicilian Greeks and one of the allies; they gave the news of the attack and also told the six hundred Syracusans who were stationed on this part of Epipolæ as an advanced guard. They went to the rescue at once, but Demosthenes and the Athenians came upon them and, in spite of a vigorous resistance, drove them back. The Athenians immediately pressed forward so as not to lose their dash or delay in achieving their objectives. Others captured in the first moment the Syracusan counterwall as the garrison took to flight, and began to drag off the battlements. The Syracusans and their allies, and Gylippus with his own troops, were hurrying from the outworks. The boldness of this night attack had surprised them; they had not recovered from their consternation when they met the Athenians, and at first they were forced to give ground. But now the Athenians began to fall into greater disorder in their advance; they felt themselves victorious and wanted to cut as quickly as they could through all the enemy force which had not yet fought; and they were afraid that if they relaxed their impetus, the Syracusans might re-form. The Bœotians were the first to make a stand: they attacked the Athenians, turned them and put them to flight.

44. At this moment the Athenians were in such great confusion and perplexity that it was hard even to find out from either side exactly how things went. In daytime combatants see more clearly, though even then only what is going on immediately around them, and that imperfectly—nothing of the battle as a whole. But in a night engagement—this was the only one in which great armies were engaged during this war—how could any one have known anything clearly? The moon was bright; and as

men naturally would in the moonlight, they saw the figures of one another before them, but were unable to distinguish with certainty who was friend or foe. Large bodies of hoplites on both sides were moving about in a narrow space; of the Athenians some were already worsted, while others, still unbeaten, were carrying on the original attack. A great part of their army had just mounted the heights, or were making the ascent; so that they did not know what movement to make. Their foremost ranks, where the defeat had occurred, were already in utter confusion and in the clamor were hard to identify. The Syracusans and their allies, who had no other means of communication in the darkness, cheered on their comrades as victors with loud cries, while meeting the enemy's charges. The Athenians were looking about for each other; and everyone who met them, though he might be a friend who had already turned and fled, they imagined to be an enemy. They kept constantly asking the watchword (for there was no other mode of recognizing each other), and thus they not only made much noise among themselves by all asking it at once but revealed it to the enemy. The watchword of the Syracusans was not discovered in a similar way because they were victorious and kept together and had less difficulty in recognizing each other. Thus, if some combatants encountered superior enemy forces, the Syracusans escaped because they knew the Athenian watchword; but the Athenians perished if they could not answer a challenge. But nothing caused so much harm as the pæans. On both sides they were much the same, and this was a source of perplexity. Whenever the Argives, Corcyræans and the other Dorian partisans of Athens raised the pæan, they inspired the Athenians with terror, rather as the enemy did. Thus, in the end, in many parts of the army, where confusions had once begun and friends were colliding with friends and citizens with fellow citizens, they not only inspired each other with alarm but actually came to blows and were parted with difficulty. And in the pursuit many flung themselves down the cliffs and perished, for the descent from Epipolæ is by a narrow path, while of those who got down safely to the level ground, although the majority, including those who had served in the first army and knew the neighborhood better, escaped to the camp, some of the newly arrived missed their way, and, wandering about until daybreak, were then killed by the Syracusan cavalry who scoured the country.

45. On the following day, the Syracusans erected two trophies, one on Epipolæ on the side of the ascent, the other at the spot where the Bœotians made the first stand. The Athenians received their dead under truce. A considerable number of them and of their allies had fallen; there were, however, more arms taken than there were bodies of the slain; for those who were compelled to leap from the cliffs, whether they perished or not, had thrown away their arms.

The Athenian Disaster at Syracuse

46. The confidence of the Syracusans was again restored by their unexpected success; and they sent Sicanus with fifteen ships to Acragas, then in a state of revolution, to win over the place if he could. Gylippus went off again by land to collect a new army in the other parts of Sicily, hoping after the victory of Epipolæ to carry the Athenian fortifications by storm.

47. Meanwhile, the Athenian generals, in view of their recent defeat and the utter discouragement which prevailed in the army, held a council of war. They saw that their attempts were all failing and that the soldiers were weary of remaining. They were distressed by sickness, proceeding from two causes: it was the season of the year when men are most liable to disease; and the place in which they were encamped was marshy and unhealthy. And they felt that the situation was in every way hopeless. Demosthenes was against remaining longer; in accordance with his intention, when he made the venture on Epipolæ, he voted for immediate departure in view of its miscarriage, while it was still possible to cross the open sea and while, with the help of the ships which had recently joined them, their fleet was the stronger. It was more expedient for the city, he said, that they should make war upon the Peloponnesians,

who were raising a fort in Attica, than against the Syracusans, whom they could now scarcely conquer; and there was no sense in carrying on the siege at vast expense to no purpose. Such was the opinion of Demosthenes.

48. Nicias in his own mind took the same gloomy view of their affairs, but he said that he did not wish to disclose their weakness or to have them vote for withdrawal publicly with many persons present; this would reach the enemy's ears and they would then find it much harder to escape observation when they wished to withdraw. He had, moreover, still some hope that the Syracusans, of whose condition he was better informed than the other generals, were likely to be worse off than themselves if they would only persevere in the siege; they would be worn out by the exhaustion of their resources, especially as the Athenians with the ships at their disposal now had much greater command of the sea. There was a party in Syracuse itself which wanted to surrender the city to the Athenians, and they kept sending messages to Nicias and advising him not to depart. Having this information, he was actually still wavering and considering, and had not made up his mind. But in his public speech at the time, he refused to withdraw the army; he knew, he said, that the Athenian people would not forgive their departure if they left without an order from home. The men upon whose votes their fate would depend would not, like themselves, have seen with their own eyes the state of affairs; they would only have heard the criticisms of others, and would be convinced by any accusations which a clever speaker might bring forward. Indeed many or most of the very soldiers who were now crying out that their case was desperate would raise the opposite cry when they reached home and would say that the generals were traitors, and had been bribed to depart. Therefore, knowing the character of the Athenians, for his own part he would rather fall, if he must, by his own decision, at the post of danger and by the hands of the enemy, than die unjustly on a dishonorable charge at the hands of the Athenians. And, after all, the Syracusans were in a condition worse than their own; they

had to maintain mercenary troops; they were spending money on garrisons, and had now kept up a large fleet for a whole year; some of their perplexities would become insuperable; they had expended two thousand talents, and owed far more still; and if they were to withhold pay and lose any part of their present forces as a result, their affairs would be ruined. For they depended on mercenaries rather than on men like the Athenian troops, bound to serve. Therefore, he said, they ought to persevere in the siege and wear the Syracusans down and not leave as if they were inferior in financial resources, in which they were far better off.

49. Nicias was obstinate in expressing these views because he knew exactly how matters stood in Syracuse, their want of money, and the existence there of a large party which wished well to the Athenians and was continually sending word to him not to depart; moreover, in the superiority of the fleet at least, he had more confidence than in the past. But Demosthenes would not hear for an instant of persisting in the siege; he said that if the army should not be removed without a vote of the assembly but should wear the Syracusans down, then they should retire to Thapsus or Catana, and do this; there they might overrun much of the country with their land forces, maintaining themselves by plundering the enemy, and do them damage. As for their ships, they would then fight, not cooped up in the harbor, which gave an advantage to the enemy, but in the open sea, where their experience would be of service to them and they could advance and retreat without being circumscribed by the narrow space which now hampered their movements whenever they put in or out. In a word, he wholly disapproved of the Athenians' continuing in their present position; they should now break up the siege as soon as possible and not delay. Eurymedon took the same side. Still Nicias resisted; there was hesitation and delay, and a suspicion that some private knowledge made him so obstinate. The Athenians continued to delay in this way and stayed on where they were.

50. Meanwhile, Gylippus and Sicanus returned to Syracuse. Sicanus had not succeeded in his design upon

Acragas; for while he was at Gela on his way, the party inclined to friendship with the Syracusans had been driven out. But Gylippus brought back another large army from Sicily, together with the hoplites who had been sent in merchant vessels from the Peloponnese in the spring, and had come by way of Libya to Selinus. They had been driven to Libya by stress of weather, and the Cyrenæans had given them two triremes and pilots. On their voyage they had made common cause with the Evesperitæ,[1] who were besieged by the Libyans. After defeating the Libyans, they sailed on to Neapolis, a Carthaginian trading station and the nearest point to Sicily, the passage taking only two days and a night; they crossed from there and reached Selinus. On their arrival, the Syracusans immediately prepared to renew their attack upon the Athenians both by land and sea. Seeing that their enemy had been reinforced by a new army and that their own affairs, instead of improving, were daily growing worse in every respect, and were especially aggravated by the sickness of their troops, the Athenian generals regretted that they had not gone before. Even Nicias now no longer objected so much but only made the condition that there should be no open voting. So, maintaining such secrecy as they could, they gave orders for the departure of the expedition by sea; the men were to prepare themselves for a given signal. The preparations were made; and they were on the point of sailing, when the moon, then at the full, was eclipsed.[2] Their scruples made the mass of the army call upon the generals to stop. Nicias himself, who was too much under the influence of divination and such like, refused even to discuss the question of their removal until they had remained thrice nine days, as the soothsayers prescribed.[3] This was the reason why the departure of the Athenians was finally delayed.

51. As soon as the Syracusans heard what had happened, they were more eager than ever to allow the Athenians no respite; they saw in the intention of the Athenians to depart a confession that they were no longer superior to themselves either by sea or land; furthermore, they did not want them to settle down in

some other part of Sicily where they would be more difficult to fight, but sought to compel them to fight at sea without delay under the disadvantages of their present position. So they manned their ships and exercised for as many days as they thought sufficient. When the time came, on the first day they began by attacking the Athenian wall. A small number of the hoplites and cavalry came out by some of the gates to meet them; but they cut off a portion of the hoplites, took some prisoners, put them to flight and pursued them closely. The entrance was narrow, and the Athenians lost seventy horses and a few hoplites.

52. On that day, the Syracusan army retired. On the next day their ships, seventy-six in number, sailed out, while at the same time their land forces marched against the walls. The Athenians on their side put out with eighty-six ships; and the two fleets met and fought. Eurymedon, who commanded the right wing of the Athenians, desiring to surround the enemy, extended his line too far towards the land, and was defeated by the Syracusans and their allies, who, after overcoming the Athenian center as well, cooped him up in the bay of the harbor. There he and the vessels which followed him were lost. The Syracusans now closely pursued the rest of the Athenian fleet and began to drive it ashore.

53. Gylippus, observing that the enemy ships were being defeated and driven to land outside their own stockade and the lines of their camp, tried to assist by taking part of his army to the causeway, intending to kill all who landed, and to make it easier for the Syracusans to tow the Athenian ships away if the shore was in the hands of their friends. The Etruscans, who were guarding this part of the Athenian lines, seeing Gylippus and his forces advance in disorder, sallied out, attacked the foremost, put them to flight and drove them into the marsh called Lysimelea. But soon the Syracusans and their allies came up in greater numbers. The Athenians, in fear for their ships, advanced to the support of the Etruscans and joined in the engagement; the Syracusans were overcome and pursued, and a few of their hoplites killed. Most of the Athenian ships were

saved and assembled at the camp. Still the Syracusans and their allies took eighteen, and killed all their crews. Then seeking to burn the remainder of the fleet, they loaded an old merchant vessel with faggots and brands, lighted them and let the ship go; the wind was blowing right on the Athenians. They contrived means to extinguish the fire and keep the fireship at a distance. Thus the danger was averted.

54. The Syracusans now raised a trophy for their naval victory and another marking their interception of the hoplites on the higher ground close to the wall at the place where they took the horses. The Athenians raised a trophy for the victory over the land forces whom the Etruscans drove into the marsh and another for that which they had gained themselves with the rest of the army.

55. The Syracusans, who up to this time had been afraid of the reinforcements of Demosthenes, had now gained a brilliant success by sea as well as by land; the Athenians were in utter despair. Great was their surprise at the result and still greater their regret that they had ever come. They had never before attacked cities similar in character to their own, which had the same democratic institutions as well as ships, cavalry and large populations. They were not able, by holding out the prospect of a change of government, to introduce an element of discord among them which might have gained them over; nor could they master them by a decided superiority of force. They had failed at almost every point, and were already in great perplexity; and now the defeat at sea, which they could not have thought possible, had increased it by far.

56. The Syracusans at once began to sail around the shore of the harbor without fear and planned to close the mouth so that the Athenians might not be able, even if they wanted, to sail out unobserved. For their concern was no longer to achieve their own deliverance but to prevent that of the Athenians; they considered that their position was now far superior, as indeed it was, and that if they could conquer the Athenians and their allies by sea and land, their success would be glorious in the

eyes of all the Hellenes, who would at once be set free, or relieved of fear; for what was left of the Athenians' power would no longer be able to sustain the war subsequently to be waged upon them. And they themselves would have the credit and would enjoy great admiration from the rest of mankind, even in ages to come. The struggle was still further ennobled by the fact that they were conquering not only the Athenians but a host of their allies. And they themselves were not alone, but many had come to their support; they were taking the command in a war by the side of Corinth and Lacedæmon; they had placed their own city in the forefront of danger, and they had made an immense advance in naval power. More peoples met at Syracuse than at any single city, although not so many as the whole number of peoples involved in this war under the Athenians and Lacedæmonians.

57. I will now enumerate the various peoples who came to share either in the conquest of Sicily or in the defense of the country and fought at Syracuse, choosing their side not so much from a sense of right or from obligations of kinship as from varying circumstances of self-interest or necessity.

The Athenians who were Ionians themselves of their own free will attacked the Syracusans who were Dorians; they were followed by the Lemnians and Imbrians and the then inhabitants of Ægina and also by the Hestiæans living at Hestiæa in Eubœa: all these were their own colonists, retaining the same language and institutions.

Of the rest who joined in the expedition, some were subjects, others independent allies, some again mercenaries. Of the subjects and tributaries, the Eretrians, Chalcidians, Styreans and Carystians came from Eubœa; the Ceans, Andrians and Tenians from the islands; the Milesians, Samians and Chians from Ionia. Of these, however, the Chians were autonomous and, instead of paying tribute, provided ships. All or nearly all were Ionians and descendants of the Athenians, with the exception of the Carystians; they are Dryopes. They were subjects and forced to follow, but still they were Ionians fighting against Dorians. There were also Æolians;

namely, the Methymnæans, who furnished ships but were not tributaries, and the Tenedians and Ænians, who paid tribute. These Æolians were compelled to fight against their Æolian founders, the Bœotians, who sided with the Syracusans. The Platæans were the only Bœotians opposed to Bœotians, a natural result of mutual hatred. The Rhodians and Cytherians were both Dorians; the Cytherians, although Lacedæmonian colonists, bore arms in the Athenian cause against the Lacedæmonians who came with Gylippus; and the Rhodians, though Argive by descent, were compelled to fight against the Syracusans, who were Dorians, and against the Geloans, who were actually their own colonists and sided with the Syracusans. Of the islanders around the Peloponnese, the Cephallenians and Zacynthians were autonomous; still, as islanders, they followed under a certain degree of constraint; for the Athenians were masters of the sea. The Corcyræans, who were not only Dorians but actually Corinthians, were serving against Corinthians and Syracusans, although they were the colonists of the one and the kinsmen of the other; they followed under a decent appearance of compulsion, but quite readily, because they hated the Corinthians. The people now called Messenians from Naupactus and Pylos, which was at that time held by the Athenians, were taken by them to the war. A few Megarian exiles, as a result of their misfortune, were fighting the Selinuntians, who were Megarians like themselves.

The service of the rest was more voluntary. The Argives, not so much because they were allies of Athens, as owing to their hatred of the Lacedæmonians and the desire of each man among them to better himself at the moment, followed the Athenians, who were Ionians; though Dorians, they fought against Dorians. The Mantineans and other Arcadian mercenaries were accustomed to attack any enemy who from time to time might be pointed out to them; and profit made them no less ready to regard the Arcadians in the service of the Corinthians as their enemies. Cretans and Ætolians also served for hire; the Cretans, who had once joined with the Rhodians in the foundation of Gela, consented for pay to fight, not with, but against their own colonists. Some Acarnanians came to aid their Athenian allies, partly from motives of gain, but much more out of friendship for Demosthenes and good will to Athens. All these lived on the eastern side of the Ionian Gulf.

Of the Hellenes in Italy, the Thurians and Metapontians, constrained by the necessities of revolutions, joined in the enterprise; of the Hellenes in Sicily, the Naxians and Catanæans. Of barbarians, there were the Egestæans, who invited the expedition, and the greater part of the Sicels; and beyond Sicily, some Etruscans who had a quarrel with the Syracusans and Iapygian mercenaries. These were the peoples who followed the Athenians.

58. The Syracusans, on the other hand, were assisted by the Camarinæans, on their borders, and by the Geloans, who adjoined them, and then (as Acragas was neutral) by the still more distant Selinuntians. All these inhabited the region of Sicily which faces Libya. On the side looking towards the Tyrrhenian Gulf, the Himeræans, the only Hellenic people in those parts, were also their only allies. These were the Hellenic peoples in Sicily who fought on the side of the Syracusans; they were all Dorian and autonomous. As for barbarians, they had only such Sicels as had not gone over to the Athenians.

Of Hellenes who were not inhabitants of Sicily, the Lacedæmonians provided a Spartiate general; the Lacedæmonian forces were all Neodamodes and Helots. The Corinthians alone furnished both sea and land forces. Their Leucadian and Ambraciot kinsmen accompanied them; from Arcadia came mercenaries sent by Corinth; there were also Sicyonians who served under compulsion; and of the peoples outside the Peloponnese, Bœotians. This external aid, however, was small compared with the numerous troops of all kinds supplied by the Sicilian Greeks themselves; for their cities were large, and had mustered many ships, horses and hoplites, besides a vast number of other troops. And again, the proportion furnished by the Syracusans themselves was greater than that of all the rest put together; their city was the largest, and they were in the greatest danger.

Such were the forces who were assembled on both sides.

59. The Syracusans naturally thought that it would be a glorious success for them if, after having defeated the Athenian fleet, they captured the whole of their great armament and did not allow them to escape either by sea or land. So they at once began to close the mouth of the Great Harbor, which was about eight stades wide, by means of triremes, merchant vessels, and small boats placed broadside, which they moored there. They also made every preparation for a naval engagement, should the Athenians dare to fight another; and all their thoughts were on a grand scale.

60. The Athenians, seeing the closing of the harbor and inferring the other intentions of the enemy, decided to hold a council. The generals and taxiarchs met and considered the difficulties of their position. The most pressing of all was the want of food; they were already short, for they had sent to Catana, when they intended to depart, and stopped further supplies; and they would get no more in the future unless they had the command of the sea. They resolved, therefore, to quit their lines on the higher ground and to wall off a space close to their ships, no greater than was absolutely required for their baggage and for their sick. After leaving a guard there, they meant to put on board every other man from the rest of their army and to launch all their ships, whether fit for service or not; they would then fight a decisive battle, and, if they won, go to Catana; but if not, they would burn their ships and retreat by land in good order, taking the quickest way to some friendly place, barbarian or Hellenic. This design they proceeded to execute; they withdrew gradually from the upper walls and manned their whole fleet, compelling every man of age to embark if he was at all fit for service. Crews were found for about 110 ships in all. They put on board numerous archers and javelin men provided by the Acarnanians and other foreigners, and made such preparations for action as the exigencies of their situation and the nature of their plan allowed. When all was nearly ready, Nicias, perceiving that his men were de-

pressed by their severe defeat at sea, which was so new an experience to them, while at the same time the want of provisions made them impatient to risk a battle with the least possible delay, called the whole army together and, before they engaged, exhorted them somewhat as follows:

61. "Soldiers of Athens and of our allies, we all have the same interest in the coming struggle; every one of us as well as of our enemies will now have to fight for his life and for his country; for if we win in the impending sea fight, anyone may once more see his native city, wherever it may be. But we must not be fainthearted nor behave like the merest novices, who after defeat in their first battles never cease to fear and expect that their disasters will be repeated. You who are here from Athens already have experience of many wars; and you, allies, are always fighting at our side; remember the incalculable turns of war; let your hope be that fortune may yet come over to us; and prepare to renew the fight in a manner worthy of the greatness of your own army which you see before you.

62. "We have consulted the pilots about the improvements which, we saw, would assist against the crowding of ships in the narrow harbor, as well as against the force on the enemy's decks, which in previous engagements did us so much harm; and we have now adopted them all as far as we have the means. Many archers and javelin men will embark, and a great number of other troops, whom we should not employ if we were going to fight in the open sea, because they increase the weight of the ships and therefore impede our skill; but here, where we are obliged to fight a land battle on shipboard, they will be useful. We have thought of all the changes which are necessary in the construction of our ships; and in order to counteract the thickness of the beams on the enemy's prows, for this did us more damage than anything else, we have provided iron grapnels, which will prevent any ship that strikes us from backing water if the marines then do their duty. This course we are positively compelled to adopt to fight a land battle on shipboard. Our best plan is neither

to back water ourselves nor to let the enemy do so, especially as the shore is in their hands, except so far as our land forces extend.

63. "Recollecting all this, you must fight to the last with all your strength, and not be driven ashore. When ship strikes ship, refuse to separate until you have swept the enemy hoplites from their decks. I am speaking to the hoplites rather than to the sailors, for this is the special duty of the men on deck. Our infantry still preserves, on the whole, its superiority. I recommend the sailors, and in the same breath, I implore them not to be paralyzed by their disasters; for they will find the arrangements on deck improved and the numbers of the fleet increased. Some among you have long been deemed Athenians though you are not;[1] ponder on this as a joy well worth preserving; for you were admired in Hellas because you spoke our language and adopted our manners; and you shared equally with ourselves in the substantial advantages of our empire, the dread inspired in subject states and still more your security against wrong. You alone have been free partners in that empire; you ought not to betray it now. And so, despising the Corinthians, whom you have beaten again and again, and the Sicilians, none of whom would even confront us when our fleet was in its prime, repel them and show that your skill even amid weakness and disaster is superior to the strength of others which fortune favors.

64. "Let me appeal once more to you who are Athenians and remind you that there are no more ships like these in our dockyards and that you have no such hoplites of age for service at home. In any event but victory, your enemies here will instantly sail against Athens, while our countrymen at home, who are but a remnant, will be unable to defend themselves against the attacks of their enemies over there reinforced by the new invaders. You would instantly fall into the hands of the Syracusans (and you know how you meant to deal with them), and our countrymen into the hands of the Lacedæmonians In this one struggle you have to fight for yourselves and them. Therefore, stand firm now, if ever, and remember one and all of you, who are embarking, that you are the

fleet and army of your country, and all that remains of the city and the great name of Athens: if any man excel another in skill or courage, he should display them in this cause; he will never have a better opportunity of serving himself and saving his country."

65. Nicias, as soon as he had done speaking, gave orders to man the ships. Gylippus and the Syracusans could see clearly enough from the preparations which the Athenians were making that they were going to fight. But they had also been told in advance of the iron grapnels, and they took precautions against this as against all the other devices of the Athenians. They covered the prows and much of the upper parts of their vessels with hides so that the grapnels might slip and find no hold. When all was ready, Gylippus and the other generals exhorted their men somewhat as follows:

66. "That our actions so far have been glorious and that in the coming conflict we shall be fighting for a glorious prize, most of you, Syracusans and allies, seem to be aware: what else would have inspired you with so much energy? But if any one has failed to understand our position, we will enlighten him. The Athenians came here intending to enslave, first of all, Sicily and, then, if they succeeded, the Peloponnese and the rest of Hellas; and they already had the largest dominion of any Hellenic power, past or present. But you set mankind the example of withstanding the navy to which they owed all their power and which you have already defeated in several engagements at sea, and you will probably defeat in this. For when men are worsted at the point where they claim superiority, any vestige of self-respect is more completely lost than if they had never believed in themselves at all; as the downfall of their pride exceeded their expectation, their readiness to yield exceeds the strength they still command. And this is likely to be the condition of the Athenians.

67. "But with us the natural courage, which even in the days of our inexperience made us show such daring, now has a firmer basis; and as it is supported by the belief that we are the strongest since we have overcome the strongest, the hopes of every one are redoubled. And

in most enterprises the highest hopes infuse the greatest enthusiasm. As for their imitation of our fighting methods, what they propose to do is natural and familiar to us; and we shall be equipped to deal with each of their devices. But to them it is a novelty to have on their decks crowds of hoplites and crowds of javelin men, Acarnanians and others, who are mere awkward landsmen put into a ship, and, seated, will not even know how to discharge their darts. Will they not be the ruin of the ships? And as they will not be able to move as they are accustomed, will they not all collide and fall into utter confusion? The greater number of the enemy ships will be the reverse of an advantage to them, should any of you fear your inequality in that respect; for so many ships in a small space will be slower in movement and far more likely to suffer from our devices. And I would have you know the simple truth, which we think we have on the clearest information. Their calamities are too much for them and they are driven by their present perplexity to a desperate decision to risk a last venture, as best they can, relying on fortune rather than on strength; they would either force a way out to sea or, in the last resort, retreat by land; for they know that they cannot in any case be worse off than they are.

68. "Against most hateful enemies, so disorganized and abandoned by fortune, let us advance with fury in the belief that men are treating their adversaries with a strict regard for law when they seek vengeance upon an aggressor and claim a right to satiate their heart's animosity, and that retribution on our enemies is proverbially the sweetest of all things, and will soon be within our grasp. That they are our enemies, and our worst enemies, you all know. They came against our land to enslave us; and if they had succeeded, they would have inflicted the greatest sufferings on our men and the worst indignities upon our wives and children, and would have stamped a name of dishonor upon our whole city. Therefore let no one's heart be softened towards them. Do not think it your advantage that they should leave without a fight. Even if they conquer, they can only depart. But supposing that we obtain, as we most likely shall, the fullness of

our desires in the punishment of the Athenians and in the confirmation to all Sicily of the liberties which she now enjoys, how glorious will be our prize! Seldom are men exposed to hazards in which they lose little if they fail and gain most if they succeed."

69. When Gylippus and the other Syracusan generals had, like Nicias, encouraged their troops, noticing that the Athenians were manning their ships, they did the same. Nicias, overwhelmed by the situation, and seeing how great and how near the peril was (for the ships were on the very point of rowing out), feeling too, as men do on the eve of a great struggle, that all which they had done was insufficient and that he had not said enough, again addressed the trierarchs; and calling each of them by his father's name and his own name and the name of his tribe, he entreated those who had made any reputation for themselves not to be false to it, and those whose ancestors were eminent not to tarnish their hereditary fame. He reminded them that they were the inhabitants of the freest of cities, and how in Athens there was no interference with the daily life of any man, and said all that in so grave a crisis men would say; they do not care if men think that they are using outworn phrases, but on all occasions they make the old appeals to their women and children and their fathers' gods, thinking them all of use in the terror of the hour. When he thought that he had exhorted them not enough but as much as the scanty time allowed, he retired and led the land forces to the shore, extending the line as far as he could so that they might be of the greatest use in encouraging the combatants on board ship. Demosthenes, Menander and Euthydemus, who had gone on board the Athenian fleet to take the command, put out from their camp and proceeded straight to the bar at the mouth of the harbor, intending to force their way to the open sea where a passage was still left.[1]

70. The Syracusans and their allies had already put out with nearly the same number of ships as before. A detachment of them guarded the entrance of the harbor; the remainder were disposed all around it in such a way that they might attack the Athenians from every side

at once; their land forces came to assist them, wherever their ships might retreat to the shore. Sicanus and Agatharchus each commanded a wing of the Syracusan fleet; Python and the Corinthians occupied the center. When the Athenians approached the bar, at the first impact of attack they overpowered the ships which were stationed there and began to try to loosen the chains. But then the Syracusans and their allies came bearing down upon them from all sides; and the conflict was no longer confined to the bar, but extended throughout the harbor. No previous engagement had been so fierce and obstinate. Great was the vigor which the rowers on both sides showed in bringing up their ships whenever the word of command was given, and keen was the contest between the pilots as they maneuvered one against another. The marines too made sure that when ship struck ship, their conduct on deck did not fall short of the skill shown by the rest. Everyone in the place assigned to him was eager to be foremost among his fellows. Many vessels were engaged in a small space; never indeed did so many fight in so small a space, for the two fleets together amounted to nearly two hundred, and there was little regular ramming because they had no opportunity of backing water or breaking the line; they generally fouled one another as ship dashed against ship in the hurry of flight or pursuit. All the time that another vessel was bearing down, the men on deck poured showers of javelins and arrows and stones upon the enemy; and when the two closed, the marines fought hand to hand and endeavored to board. In many places, owing to the want of room, those who had struck another ship found that they were struck themselves; often two or even more vessels were unavoidably jammed with one another; the pilots had to make plans of attack and defense, not against one adversary only, but against several coming from different sides. The violent crash of so many ships dashing against one another took away the wits of the crews and made it impossible to hear the boatswains on both sides who were constantly crying out directions to the rowers or encouragements in the excitement of the struggle. On the Athenian side they were shouting to their men that they must force a passage and seize the opportunity of now or never returning in safety to their native land; on that of the Syracusans and their allies, that it was a fine thing to prevent the escape of their enemies and to win a victory by which every man would exalt the honor of his own city. The commanders too on each side, when they saw any ship backing without necessity, would call the captain by his name and ask, of the Athenians, whether they were retreating because they expected to be more at home on the land of their bitterest foes than upon the sea, which by the labor of years they had made their own; on the Syracusan side, whether, when they knew perfectly well that the Athenians were only eager to find some means of flight, they would themselves flee from the fugitives.

71. While the naval engagement hung in the balance, the two armies on shore were in great mental conflict and tension; they were passionate for victory, the Syracusans in the hope of increasing the glory they had already won, the invaders in the fear that their fortunes might sink lower still. The last chance of the Athenians lay in their ships, and their fear of the issue was unparalleled. The fortune of the battle varied, and the spectators on the land inevitably received a varying impression of it. Being quite close and having different points of view, they would some of them see their own ships victorious in one quarter; their courage would then revive, and they would call upon the gods not to take deliverance from them. But others, who saw part of their line worsted, cried and shrieked aloud and were more utterly unnerved by the sight of the action than the men engaged in it. Others again who had fixed their gaze on some part of the struggle which was still in the balance were in the worst state of all; even their bodies swayed to and fro in an agony of fear as their expectations changed with the course of the obstinate and undecided conflict, for at every instant they were all but saved or all but lost. And while the event of the battle was in doubt, in the Athenian army alone you might have heard at once lamentation, shouting, cries of victory or de-

feat, and all the various sounds which would be wrung from a great army in extremity of danger. The men on board were subject to similar feelings, till at last the Syracusans and their allies, after a protracted struggle, put the Athenians to flight and, triumphantly bearing down upon them with loud cries and encouragements to each other, pursued them to the shore. Then that part of the fleet which had not been captured at sea beached their ships in different places and rushed out of them into the camp. The land forces, no longer divided in feeling but united by a single impulse in groans and laments at a defeat that was so hard for them to bear, moved to rescue the ships or to guard what remained of the wall; but the greater number began to look to themselves and some way of saving their lives. Never had there been a greater panic in all past history than at that moment. The Athenians now suffered more or less what they had done to others at Pylos; for when the Lacedæmonians had lost their ships, their men who had crossed over into the island were lost along with them; and so now the Athenians had no hope of saving themselves by land unless something incalculable occurred.

72. Thus, after a fierce battle and a great destruction of ships and men on both sides, the Syracusans and their allies gained the victory, gathered up the wrecks and corpses and, sailing back to the city, erected a trophy. The Athenians, overwhelmed by their misery, did not even think of asking leave to recover their wrecks and their dead: their intention was to retreat that very night. Demosthenes went to Nicias and proposed that they should once more man their remaining vessels and force their passage at daybreak, if they could, saying that they still had more ships fit for service than the enemy. (They had sixty left, and the enemy less than fifty.) Nicias agreed with his proposal, and they would have manned the ships, but the sailors refused to embark; they were paralyzed by their defeat and had no further belief in their chance of success. So the Athenians, one and all, made up their minds to retreat by land.

73. Hermocrates the Syracusan suspected their intention; and, dreading what might happen if so large

an army withdrew by land, settled somewhere in Sicily and chose to renew the war, he went to the authorities, told them his own opinion and represented to them that they should not allow the Athenians to retreat by night, but that all the Syracusans and their allies should go out at once, wall up the roads and occupy the passes with garrisons in anticipation. For their own part, they entirely shared his views and thought that they should carry out his plan, but doubted whether their men who had just finished a great sea battle with jubilation and were celebrating a festival—for there happened to be a sacrifice to Heracles on that very day—would readily comply. Most of them, in the exultation of victory, were drinking and keeping holiday, and would, they expected, be least of all likely to obey an order to take up arms and go out on an expedition at such a time as this. These reflections made the generals think Hermocrates' proposal impracticable. As he had failed to win them over, and feared that the Athenians might gain an undisturbed start in the night and pass the most difficult places, he resorted to a stratagem of his own. He sent some of his partisans with a few horsemen to the Athenian camp when it was growing dark. They rode up within earshot and, pretending to be friends of the Athenians (for there were men in the city who gave information to Nicias), called to some of the soldiers and bade them tell Nicias not to withdraw his army during the night, as the Syracusans were guarding the roads; he should make preparations without hurry and retire by day. Having delivered their message, they departed; and those who had heard them reported to the Athenian generals.

74. In view of this message, which they supposed to be genuine, they stopped for the night. And since they had not started immediately, they decided to remain for the next day too, so that the soldiers might pack up the most useful baggage, so far as circumstances allowed; they would take all the supplies which men could carry for their own subsistence and leave everything else behind. But the Syracusans and Gylippus went out before them with their army, blocked the

roads in the country by which they were likely to pass, put guards at the fords of the streams and rivers, and posted themselves at the best points for meeting and stopping them. With their ships they rowed up and dragged away the Athenian ships from the beach. The Athenians themselves had burnt a few of them as they had intended; but the rest the Syracusans towed away to the city, unhurried and unhindered, from the different places where they had run aground.

75. After this, when Nicias and Demosthenes thought that they had made sufficient preparations, the army at last began to move on the third day from the sea fight. Their condition was dreadful in many ways; they were retreating after they had lost all their ships; and instead of the great success they had hoped for, they and their city were in danger; and in addition the sights which presented themselves as they quitted the camp were painful to every eye and mind. The dead were unburied; and when anyone saw a friend lying on the ground, he was filled with sorrow and fear, while the survivors who were left behind because they were wounded and sick caused still more sorrow to the living and were more to be pitied than the dead. Their prayers and lamentations drove their companions to distraction; they claimed to be taken along and called by name on any friend or relation whom they saw passing; as the men who had shared their tents were already leaving, they would hang upon them and follow as far as they could; and when their strength and limbs failed them and they were abandoned, it was not without a few last laments and appeals to heaven. The whole army was in tears; and such was their perplexity that they hardly made up their minds to stir, although they were leaving a hostile country, had suffered calamities too great for tears already and dreaded miseries yet greater in the unknown future. A feeling of shame too and of self-reproach was heavy upon them. Indeed they resembled nothing so much as fugitives from a city that had been taken by siege, and a great city too. For the whole multitude on the march numbered not less than forty thousand. Each of them took with him anything

he could carry which was of use. Even the hoplites and the cavalry, contrary to their practice, carried for themselves their own food in addition to their arms because they had no attendants, or none they could trust; for they had long been deserting, and most of them had gone off just at the present crisis. But even the food they carried was not sufficient as there was a shortage in the camp. Their sufferings in general and the fact that their miseries were shared by all alike, although there was some consolation in "community of woe," were, even so, in their condition hard to bear, especially as they had sunk from such pride and splendor to such final humiliation. Never had an Hellenic army experienced such a change. They had come to enslave others, and in the result they were going away in the fear that they would themselves be enslaved. Instead of the prayers and pæans with which they had put to sea, they were once more setting out amid ominous cries altogether different. They were no longer sailors but landsmen and were concerned with their hoplites more than with their fleet. Yet, in face of the great danger which still hung over them, all these things appeared endurable.

76. Nicias, seeing the army disheartened and greatly changed, went along the ranks and encouraged and consoled them so far as circumstances allowed. In his fervor he raised his voice louder and louder as he passed from one part of the army to another, desiring that the benefit of his words might reach as far as possible.

77. "Even now, Athenians and allies, we must still hope; men have been delivered from even worse straits than ours, and you must not blame yourselves too severely for our disasters or for our present undeserved miseries. I too am as weak as any of you—you see how I am reduced by my disease—and although I have a reputation second to none, I suppose, for good fortune in my private and public life, I am now in the same danger and suspense as the meanest. Yet, throughout my life I have been assiduous in worshipping the gods and in just and blameless conduct to men. Therefore, I am still bold in hope for the future; and though I am alarmed

at our disasters, I know that they are undeserved, and perhaps may cease; our enemies have enjoyed enough good fortune; and if our expedition incurred the jealousy of any of the gods, by this time we have been sufficiently punished. Others before now have doubtless been aggressive; they have done as men will do and have suffered what can be borne. We too may now reasonably hope that heaven will be kinder to us, for pity rather than jealousy is what we now deserve from the gods. And look at your own ranks; see how many brave hoplites are massed for the march, and do not give way to excessive fears, but bear in mind that you constitute a city in yourselves from the moment that you take up your position anywhere and that no other city in Sicily would find it easy to resist your attack or to dislodge you, wherever you have settled. As for the march, you must yourselves ensure that it is conducted safely and in good order; and every man must entertain only one thought: whatever the place where he may be forced to fight, by victory he will make it his fatherland and fortress. We shall press forward day and night alike on our journey, for our supplies are short. The Sicels still adhere to us through fear of the Syracusans; and if we reach any of their places, we shall be among friends; and you may then consider yourselves secure. We have sent to them, and they have been told to meet us and bring food. In a word, soldiers, you must realize that you have no choice but to acquit yourselves as brave men; there is no place near in which cowards might find safety. And if you now escape your enemies, the rest of you will succeed in seeing once more all that you long to see; and the Athenians will restore the great power of their city, fallen as it is. For a city consists in its men, not in walls or unmanned ships."

78. Thus exhorting his troops, Nicias passed through the army; and wherever he saw any gap in the ranks or men dropping out of line, he set them in close order. Demosthenes did the same for the troops under his command and gave them similar exhortations. The army marched disposed in a hollow oblong, the division of Nicias leading and that of Demosthenes following; the

hoplites enclosed within their ranks the baggage bearers and the great mass of the army. When they arrived at the ford of the river Anapus, they found a force of the Syracusans and their allies drawn up to meet them; they put them to flight and, getting command of the ford, proceeded on their march. But the Syracusans continued to attack with their horse, who rode alongside, and with their light-armed troops, who hurled darts at them. On this day they proceeded about forty stades and bivouacked next to a hill. On the next day they started early and proceeded twenty stades; they then descended to a plain and encamped there. The country was inhabited, and they wished to obtain food from the houses, and water to carry with them, as there was little to be had for many stades in the country ahead, where they were to march. Meanwhile, the Syracusans had gone forward, and were blocking up the pass ahead with a wall; there was a steep hill, called the Acræan height, with a precipitous ravine on either side. On the next day the Athenians advanced, although impeded by the numbers of the enemy cavalry who rode on each side and of their javelin men who threw darts at them. For a long time the Athenians maintained the struggle but at last retired again to the same camp. They now had more difficulty in obtaining supplies because the horsemen circumscribed their movements.

79. In the morning they started early and resumed their march. They forced a passage to the hill where the way was barred, and found in front of them the Syracusan infantry drawn up to defend the wall, in deep formation, for the pass was narrow. The Athenians attacked and tried to take the wall, but they were exposed to a rain of missiles from the hill, which was steep; and as these were hurled from higher ground, they tended to strike home; and so, not being able to force their way, they again retired and rested. During the conflict, as is often the case in the fall of the year, there came on a storm of thunder and rain; and this made the Athenians yet more disheartened, for they thought that everything was conspiring to their destruction. While they were resting, Gylippus and the Syracusans dispatched a division of

their army to raise another wall behind them across the road by which they had advanced; but the Athenians sent some of their own troops and frustrated the plan. They then retired with their whole army in the direction of the plain and bivouacked there. On the following day, they began to advance; and the Syracusans surrounded them and attacked on every side and wounded many of them. If the Athenians advanced, they retreated, but charged when they retired, falling especially upon the hindermost, in the hope that if they could put to flight a few at a time, they might strike a panic into the whole army. In this fashion the Athenians struggled on for a long time and then, after moving forward five or six stades, rested in the plain. The Syracusans then left them and returned to their own encampment.

80. The army was now in a bad condition: it was in want of every necessary; and by the continual assaults of the enemy, great numbers had been wounded. Nicias and Demosthenes therefore resolved during the night to light as many watchfires as possible and to lead off their forces by a route different from that which they had intended to take, and to march toward the sea in the direction opposite to that where the Syracusans were watching for them. Now their whole line of march lay not towards Catana but towards the other side of Sicily, in the direction of Camarina and Gela, and the cities, Hellenic or barbarian, of that region. So they lit numerous fires and moved off in the night. And then, just as all armies, especially very great ones, are subject to panic fears, they fell into confusion, all the more as they were marching by night in hostile country with the enemy not far distant. The army of Nicias, which was leading the way, kept together and got on considerably in advance; but that of Demosthenes, which was the larger half, was detached from it, and marched in worse order. At daybreak, however, they reached the sea; and striking into the road called Helorine, they marched along it, intending as soon as they arrived at the Cacyparis to follow up the course of the river through the interior. For they hoped that the Sicels for whom they had sent would meet them on this route. When they reached the

river, they found there a guard of the Syracusans cutting off the passage by a wall and palisade. They forced their way across and began to march on to another river, the Erineus, this being the direction in which their guides led them.

81. When daylight broke and the Syracusans and their allies realized that the Athenians had departed, most of them blamed Gylippus for having let them go on purpose. They easily found the line of their retreat and, quickly pursuing, came up with them about the time of the midday meal. The troops of Demosthenes were last; they were marching more slowly and in greater disorder as a result of the confusion in the night, when they were overtaken and attacked; in the battle the Syracusan cavalry had less difficulty in encircling them, as they were separated from the others, and in driving them into a narrow space. Nicias' division was now as much as fifty stades in advance; for he moved faster, thinking that their safety at such a time depended not on remaining and fighting, if they could avoid it, but in retreating as quickly as they could and fighting only when they were compelled. But Demosthenes was generally under more continuous stress because he was bringing up the rear in the retreat and was first to be attacked by the enemy; and now, when he saw the Syracusans in pursuit, instead of moving forward, he ranged his army in order of battle; and thus lingering, he was surrounded. He and his forces were in great confusion; for they were crushed into a walled enclosure, with a road on both sides, planted thickly with olive trees; and missiles were hurled at them from all around. The Syracusans naturally preferred this mode of attack to a regular engagement; to risk everything against desperate men would now favor the Athenians more than them. Moreover, no one wished to lose his own life before victory when their success was already clear; and they thought that, even so, they could overpower the Athenians by this mode of fighting and capture them.

82. And so when they had gone on all day assailing the Athenians and their allies with missiles from every

quarter, and saw that they were quite worn out with wounds and all their other sufferings, Gylippus and the Syracusans and their allies made a proclamation first of all to the islanders that any of them who pleased might come over to them and have their freedom. But only a few cities accepted the offer.[1] At length an agreement was made for the entire force under Demosthenes. Their arms were to be surrendered, but no one was to suffer death from violence or imprisonment or want of the bare means of life. In all, six thousand men surrendered and deposited all the money they had in the hollows of shields; they filled four of them. The captives were at once taken to the city.

83. On the same day, Nicias and his division reached the river Erineus, crossed it and halted his army on rising ground. On the following day, he was overtaken by the Syracusans who told him that Demosthenes' forces had surrendered and bade him do the same. He did not credit this and procured a truce while he sent a horseman to go and see. Upon his return with confirmation of the fact, Nicias sent a herald to Gylippus and the Syracusans, saying that he would agree, on behalf of Athens, to repay the expenses which the Syracusans had incurred in the war on condition that they would let his army go; until the money was repaid, he would give Athenians as hostages, a man for a talent. The Syracusans and Gylippus would not accept these proposals, but attacked and surrounded this division too and hurled missiles at them from all sides till evening. They too were grievously in want of food and necessaries. Nevertheless they meant to wait for the dead of the night and then to proceed. They were just taking up their arms when the Syracusans discovered them and raised the pæan. The Athenians, perceiving that they were detected, laid down their arms again, except for about three hundred men who broke through the enemy's pickets and went off in the night, wherever they could.

84. When the day dawned, Nicias led forward his army; and the Syracusans and their allies assailed them as before on every side with javelins and other missiles. The Athenians hurried on to the river Assinarus. They

thought that they would gain some relief if they forded the river, for the mass of horsemen and other troops were pressing them with attacks on every side, and their haste was also due to fatigue and thirst. No sooner did they reach the water than they lost all order and plunged in; every man wished to cross first, and the enemy pressed upon them and made the crossing harder. As they were compelled to keep close together, they fell upon one another and trampled each other under foot; some were killed at once by their own spears and equipment; others were entangled and carried down stream. The Syracusans were in line upon the further bank of the river, which was steep, and hurled missiles from above on the Athenians, most of whom were drinking greedily and huddled together in confusion in the deep bed of the stream. The Peloponnesians came down the bank and slaughtered them, chiefly those in the river. The water was fouled at once with mud and blood, but still they went on drinking though most of them had to fight for the chance.

85. At last, when the dead bodies were lying in heaps in the river and the army had been destroyed, partly in the stream and any fugitives by the cavalry, Nicias surrendered himself to Gylippus, in whom he had more confidence than in the Syracusans. He urged him and the Lacedæmonians to do what they pleased with himself but not to go on killing the other soldiers. Gylippus then at last gave the word to take prisoners. The survivors, except for a large number whom the soldiers concealed, were collected together; and the Syracusans sent a force to pursue the three hundred who had got through the pickets in the night and seized them. The total of the army surrendered to the state was not great, for many were stolen away by their captors; and the whole of Sicily was full of them, since there had been no capitulation as when Demosthenes' troops had been captured. A large number also perished, for no slaughter equal to this ever took place in this Sicilian war, and many had fallen in the previous attacks frequently made upon the Athenians during their march. Still, many too escaped, some at the time, others by running away later after they had been in slavery. They found refuge at Catana.

86. The Syracusans and their allies collected their forces and returned to the city with the spoil and as many prisoners as they could take with them. They deposited the other Athenians and allies in the quarries, which they thought would be the safest place of confinement; but they executed Nicias and Demosthenes against the will of Gylippus; he thought that it would be a brilliant triumph for him, over and above his other successes, to carry home with him to Lacedæmon the generals of the enemy. In fact, one of them, Demosthenes, was the greatest enemy of the Lacedæmonians because of the events at Pylos and Sphacteria; and the other, their greatest friend for the same reason, as Nicias had been most active in persuading the Athenians to make the peace which set at liberty the Lacedæmonians taken on the island. The Lacedæmonians were well disposed to him for this service, and this was the main reason why he trusted Gylippus and surrendered to him. But according to report, some of the Syracusans, who had been in communication with him, were afraid that he might be put to the torture for some such reason and make trouble for them in the hour of their success, while others, and especially the Corinthians, feared that, being rich, he might escape by bribery and cause them further difficulties. So they won over the allies and killed him. It was for these or the like reasons that he suffered death. No one of the Hellenes in my time was less deserving of so miserable an end, for he had invariably conformed to the rules of good conduct.

87. The men in the quarries were at first harshly treated by the Syracusans. There were great numbers of them crowded in a deep and confined place. At first the sun by day was scorching and suffocating, for they had no roof over their heads, and by contrast the nights came on autumnal and cold and engendered sickness by the change of temperature. They were cramped for room and had to do everything in the same place. The corpses of those who died from wounds, change of temperature and the like were also heaped one upon another; and the smells were intolerable. They were afflicted too by hunger and thirst, for during eight months

they were each given only about half a pint of water and a pint of food daily. In addition they suffered every other kind of misery without exception which men in such a place would naturally experience. This was the life that all of them lived for some seventy days; then the Syracusans sold all except the Athenians and any Sicilian or Italian Greeks who had sided with them in the war. The whole number of the prisoners is hard to state with accuracy, but they were not less than seven thousand.

Of all the actions which took place in this war or indeed, as I think, of all Hellenic actions reported and known, this was the greatest—the most brilliant for the victors, the most miserable for the vanquished; they were utterly defeated at all points, and their sufferings were terrible in every way. Fleet and army perished from the face of the earth; nothing was saved; and of many who set out, few returned home. These were the events in Sicily.

BOOK VIII

Revolution at Athens

1. The news was brought to Athens; but for long the Athenians absolutely disbelieved that the armament had been so completely annihilated, even when they had clear information from the soldiers who had escaped from the scene of action. When they recognized the truth, they were hard on the orators who had joined in promoting the expedition—as if they had not voted it themselves—and furious with the soothsayers and prophets and all who by the influence of religion had at the time inspired them with the belief that they would conquer Sicily. Whichever way they looked, there was trouble; in view of what had happened, they were encompassed by fear and unutterable consternation. Every family was affected with grief, and so was the city, by the loss of many hoplites and cavalry, and the flower of their youth, who could not be replaced. And when they saw an insufficient number of ships in their docks and no crews to man them, nor money in the treasury, they despaired of deliverance. They supposed that their enemies in Sicily, especially as they had already gained such a great victory, would at once sail against the Piræus; and their enemies in Hellas, with all resources then doubled, would set upon them with all their might both by sea and land, and would be assisted by their own revolted allies. Still they determined, so far as their situation allowed, not to give in. They would procure timber wherever they could, and money, and fit out a navy. They would make sure of their allies and above all of Eubœa. In the city a sounder policy of economy was to be adopted; and older men chosen for a new office, whose function should be to give prior consideration to measures required from time to time.[1] Acting as a populace will, the Athenians were ready, in their immediate panic, to submit to

discipline. They proceeded to carry out these resolutions. And so the summer ended.

2. During the following winter, all Hellas was at once excited by the great disaster of the Athenians in Sicily. The states which had been neutral determined that the time had come when, invited or not, they should no longer stand aloof from the war; they must, of their own accord, attack the Athenians. They all considered that if the Sicilian expedition had succeeded, they would sooner or later have been attacked by them. The war would not last long, and it would be fine to take part in it. The Lacedæmonian allies were all alike more eager than ever to make a speedy end of their great hardships. But above all, the subjects of the Athenians were ready, even beyond their power, to revolt; for they judged the situation by their excited feelings, and would not admit a possibility that the Athenians could survive the next summer. To the Lacedæmonians themselves, all this was most encouraging, especially the prospect that their allies from Sicily would probably join them at the beginning of spring with a large force, now that they had of necessity built up their fleet. Everything looked hopeful, and they determined to prosecute the war without evasions. They considered that by its successful termination they would in future be delivered from dangers such as would have surrounded them if the Athenians had become masters of Sicily. Athens once overthrown, they would assure to themselves the undisputed leadership of all Hellas.

[*In 412 Persia entered the war on Sparta's side to recover the Greek cities liberated by Athens in the 470's; and many of Athens' subjects revolted, notably Chios, still autonomous and oligarchic, and democratic Miletus. The government of Chios seems to have been unable to depend on the loyalty of her citizens, but the Milesians fought well against Athens, an exception to the general rule that democrats supported her. With some help from Sicily, the Peloponnesians gradually built and put to sea a large fleet. The Persians gave no naval and little military aid, but they subsidized the Peloponnesian fleet.*

Athens too equipped a series of squadrons, but her financial strength was greatly impaired. Revolts meant less revenue from the empire; she had to draw on an iron reserve of one thousand talents, and increased burdens on the richer citizens paved the way for revolution. The naval operations of 412 were desultory.

The relations between Sparta and the Persian satrap in eastern Asia Minor, Tissaphernes, were uneasy. Sparta had once professed to be aiming at the liberation of Greek cities from Athenian rule; and though now obliged to admit Persian suzerainty over some of them in return for Persian subsidies, she tried to limit Persian claims as far as possible. Alcibiades, who had done much to bring the Spartans and Tissaphernes together, had then quarreled with King Agis and fled to Tissaphernes in fear of his life; he began to advise Tissaphernes to keep the Peloponnesian fleet short of money and let both belligerents wear each other out. Tissaphernes did adopt this policy and hence the Peloponnesians could not take full advantage of Athenian internal dissensions in 411. (In what follows I omit the record of minor naval operations and of the negotiations between Tissaphernes and the Spartans.) Alcibiades even tried to persuade Tissaphernes to go over to the Athenian side; he hoped that if he were successful, he could obtain his recall to Athens as the price of Persian help.]

47. In giving this advice to Tissaphernes and the Persian king, now that he was under their protection, Alcibiades did what he really thought to be most in their interests. But he had another motive; he was intriguing for his own return from exile. He knew that if he did not destroy his country altogether, the time would come when he would persuade his countrymen to recall him; and he thought that his arguments would be most effectual if he were seen to be on intimate terms with Tissaphernes. The result proved that he was right. The Athenian forces at Samos saw that he had great influence with Tissaphernes; and he sent messages to their most powerful men, whom he begged to remember him to the best people, and to let them know that he would

be glad to return and be their fellow citizen and win over Tissaphernes, but only under an oligarchy, not under the villainous system which had driven him out. Partly moved by these messages, but still more of their own inclination, the trierarchs and most powerful Athenians at Samos were eager to overthrow the democracy.

48. The movement began in the camp and reached the city afterwards. A few persons went over from Samos to Alcibiades and conferred with him: to them he held out the hope that he would make, first of all, Tissaphernes and, secondly, the king himself their friend if they would put down democracy; the king would then be better able to trust them. And so the most powerful citizens, on whom the heaviest burdens are apt to fall, conceived great hopes of getting the government into their own hands and overcoming the enemy. Returning to Samos, the envoys combined all suitable persons into a conspiracy, while telling the masses publicly that the king would be their friend and would supply them with money if Alcibiades was restored and democracy given up. Now the rabble, even if at first displeased with the action in hand, remained quiescent in the hope of abundant Persian pay; and the oligarchic organizers, after they had broached the idea to the people, once more considered the proposals of Alcibiades among themselves and the greater part of their faction. Most of them thought them easily practicable and safe. Phrynichus, who was still general, opposed them at every point.[1] He maintained, and rightly, that Alcibiades cared no more for oligarchy than he did for democracy and, in seeking to change the existing form of government, was only considering how he might be recalled and restored to his country by the faction; whereas their chief care should be to avoid disunion. Why should the king go out of his way to join the Athenians whom he did not trust when he would only get into trouble with the Peloponnesians, who were now as great a naval power and held some of the most important cities in his dominion, when they had never done him any harm and he might make friends with them? As to the allies, to whom they had promised the blessings of oligarchic government on the ground

that their own too was not to be democratic, he said that he knew perfectly well that there would be no better chance of the revolted cities returning to them or of their remaining allies being more loyal. The allies did not wish to be slaves under democracy or oligarchy so much as to enjoy freedom under either form of government. And as for the so-called men of honor and virtue, in his view the allies thought that they would be quite as troublesome as the Athenian people; it was they who prompted and proposed to the people the measures injurious to the allies and profited most from them. The allies thought that as far as it rested with these persons they would be more liable to violence and death without trial, whereas the people brought the oligarchs to their senses and were their own refuge. Phrynichus said that he was clearly aware that the cities had been taught by actual experience to think in this way. He was, therefore, himself altogether opposed to the proposals of Alcibiades and the current actions.

49. But the conspirators who were present were not at all shaken in their opinion. They accepted the plan and prepared to send Peisander[1] and others to Athens to obtain the recall of Alcibiades and the overthrow of the democracy and to make Tissaphernes a friend of the Athenians. . . .

[*After describing abortive intrigues of Phrynichus against Alcibiades, and Tissaphernes' continual indecision, Thucydides proceeds:*]

53. Peisander and the other envoys who had been sent from Samos arrived at Athens and made speeches in the assembly, summing up many arguments by insisting above all that if the Athenians restored Alcibiades and modified their democracy, they might secure the alliance of the king and gain the victory over the Peloponnesians. Many spoke against any change in the democracy, and the enemies of Alcibiades were especially loud in protesting that it would be a dreadful thing if he were to return when he had violated the laws. The Eumolpidæ and Ceryces[1] called heaven and

earth to witness that the city must never restore a man who had been banished for profaning the mysteries. Amid much opposition and indignation, Peisander came forward; and having up the objectors one by one, he pointed out to them that the Peloponnesians had a fleet at sea ready for action as large as their own, that they numbered more cities among their allies, and that they were furnished with money by Tissaphernes and the king; whereas the Athenians had spent everything. He then asked each of them whether he had any hope of saving the country unless the king could be won over. They all acknowledged that there was none. He then said to them plainly that this alliance was impossible unless there was more good sense in their government, unless office was confined to a smaller number, to win the king's trust, and unless in this crisis they thought less about the constitution than about survival; they would be free later to make further changes in the constitution if anything done now was unpopular. And they must restore Alcibiades, who was the only man living capable of saving them.

54. The people were very angry at the first suggestion of an oligarchy; but when Peisander proved to them that they had no other solution, partly in fear and partly in hope that it might be changed later, they gave in. So a decree was passed that Peisander himself and ten others should go out and negotiate to the best of their judgment with Tissaphernes and Alcibiades. Peisander also denounced Phrynichus, and therefore the people dismissed him and his colleague Scironides from their commands and appointed Diomedon and Leon to be admirals in their place. Peisander thought that Phrynichus would stand in the way of the negotiations with Alcibiades; and for this reason he calumniated him, alleging that he had betrayed Iasus and Amorges.[1] Then he went, one after another, to all the clubs which already existed in Athens for the management of trials and elections, and exhorted them to unite and by concerted planning to put down the democracy.[2] When he had completed all the preparations which the situation

required to avoid further delay, he and his two colleagues proceeded on their voyage to Tissaphernes. . . .

[*Besides minor operations, Thucydides now describes how negotiations between the Athenian generals and Tissaphernes broke down and how Tissaphernes made a new agreement with Sparta.*]

63. Peisander and his fellow envoys, on their return to Samos after their visit to Tissaphernes, had strengthened their interest in the army and had even persuaded the most powerful men of Samos to join them in trying to set up an oligarchy, although they had lately risen against their own countrymen in order to avoid oligarchy.[1] At the same time conferring among themselves, the Athenian leaders at Samos came to the conclusion that since Alcibiades would not co-operate,[2] they had better leave him alone; for indeed he was not the sort of person who was suited to an oligarchy. But they determined, as they were already compromised, to proceed by themselves and to take measures for carrying the movement through; they meant also to persevere in the war and to contribute readily money or anything else which might be wanted from their own property, since it would no longer be in the interest of others, but in their own, that they would bear such burdens.

64. Having thus encouraged one another in their purpose, they sent Peisander and half the envoys back to Athens. They were to carry out the scheme at home and had directions to set up oligarchies in the subject cities at which they touched on their voyage. The other half were dispatched different ways to other subject cities. Diitrephes, who was then at Chios, was sent to assume the command in the Thracian region, to which he had been previously appointed. On arriving at Thasos, he put down the democracy. But within about two months of his departure, the Thasians began to fortify their city; they had no further need of an aristocracy dependent on Athens when they were daily expecting to obtain their liberty from Lacedæmon. For there were Thasian exiles with the Peloponnesians who had been driven out by the

Athenians; and they, with the assistance of their friends at home, were exerting themselves vigorously to obtain ships and effect the revolt of Thasos. The recent change was exactly what they desired; for the government had been reformed without danger to themselves; and the democracy, which would have opposed them, had been overthrown. Thus the result at Thasos and also, in my view, in many other states was the opposite of what the Athenian oligarchs had intended. For the subject cities, having secured governments with good sense, and having no fear of being called to account for their proceedings, aimed at absolute freedom; they scorned the pretense of "orderly government" proffered by the Athenians.

65. Peisander and his colleagues pursued their voyage and, as they had agreed, put down the democracies in the cities. At the same time, from some places, they also obtained the assistance of hoplites, whom they took with them to Athens. There they found the revolution more than half accomplished by the oligarchical clubs. Some of the younger citizens had conspired and secretly assassinated Androcles, one of the chief leaders of the people, who had been foremost in procuring the banishment of Alcibiades. Their motives were twofold: they killed him because he was a demagogue, but more because they hoped to gratify Alcibiades whom they were still expecting to return, and to make Tissaphernes their friend. A few others who were inconvenient to them they made away with in the same secret manner. Meanwhile, they declared in their public program that no one ought to receive pay who was not on military service and that not more than five thousand should have a share in the government; namely, those who were best able to serve the state in person and with their money.

66. This was only intended to look well in the eyes of the people, for the authors of the revolution meant to be masters of the city. The popular assembly and the council chosen by lot were still convoked, but decided nothing of which the conspirators had not approved; the speakers were of their party, and the things to be said had been all arranged by them beforehand. No one else any longer raised his voice against them, men were

afraid and saw the strength of the conspiracy; and if any one did utter a word, he was at once killed in some convenient way. No search was made for the assassins; and if they were suspected, no prosecution took place; the people were quiescent and so terrified that a man who escaped violence thought himself fortunate, even though reduced to silence. Their minds were cowed by the supposed number of the conspirators, which they greatly exaggerated, having no means of discovering the truth, since the size of the city prevented them from knowing one another. For the same reason anyone who was indignant could not even complain to others, with a view to combining in revenge; he could not speak to a stranger, nor trust his acquaintances. For the members of the popular party all approached one another with suspicion; any of them might have a hand in what was going on, as some were concerned whom no one would ever have thought likely to turn oligarchs; their adhesion created the worst mistrust among the masses and, by making it impossible for them to rely upon one another, contributed most to the security of the oligarchs.

67. At this juncture, Peisander and his colleagues arrived and immediately set to completing their task.[1] First, they called an assembly and proposed the election of ten commissioners with full powers to draft a constitution; after doing so, they were to lay proposals before the people on a fixed day for the best government of the city. When the day arrived, they enclosed the assembly at Colonus, where there is a temple of Poseidon about ten stades from the city. But the commissioners only moved that any Athenian should be allowed with impunity to propose whatever resolution he pleased—nothing more; they imposed severe penalties on anybody who should indict the proposer for unconstitutional action or otherwise injure him. Then at last it was said without concealment that no magistracy should any longer be held in accordance with the old system, and no pay given and that five presidents should be chosen; these five were to choose a hundred, and each of the hundred was to co-opt three others. The Four Hundred thus selected were to meet in the council chamber; they were to have

absolute authority, and might govern as they deemed best; the Five Thousand were to be summoned by them whenever they chose.

68. The mover of this proposal was Peisander, and throughout none had shown more energy in helping to overthrow the democracy; but the man who had conducted the whole business to this point and had been longest in charge of it was Antiphon, a man inferior in virtue to none of his contemporaries and unexcelled in forming plans and in expounding his views. He did not like to come forward in the assembly or in any other public arena: he was suspect to the masses because of his reputation for cleverness; but when men were engaged in controversy in the courts and the assembly, there was no single man who could do more for any who consulted him. And when the government of the Four Hundred was later overthrown and became exposed to the vengeance of the people, and he was accused on account of his actions at this time, for taking part in its establishment, his defense was clearly the best ever made by any man tried on a capital charge down to my time.[1] Phrynichus also showed extraordinary energy in the interest of the oligarchy. He was afraid of Alcibiades and knew him to be cognizant of his intrigue at Samos with Astyochus,[2] and he thought that no oligarchy would ever be likely to restore him. Once he had set his hand to the work, none appeared more trusty in the hour of danger. Theramenes the son of Hagnon was also prominent among the party who overthrew the democracy, a man of eloquence and judgment. No wonder, then, that in the hands of many shrewd men, the attempt, however arduous, succeeded. For it was hard, about one hundred years after the fall of the tyrants, to deprive the Athenian people of liberty when they were not only free, but for more than one half of this time had been accustomed to ruling others.

69. The assembly passed all these measures without a dissentient voice, and was then dissolved. And now at a later stage, the Four Hundred were introduced into the council chamber. The manner was as follows: the whole population was always under arms either manning the

walls or in battle order, for the enemy was at Decelea. On that day those who were not in the conspiracy were allowed to go home as usual, while the conspirators were quietly told to remain, not actually by their arms, but at a short distance; if anybody opposed what was doing, they were to arm and prevent them. There were also on the spot some Andrians and Tenians, three hundred Carystians, and some of the Athenian colonists from Ægina, who received similar instructions; they had come from their homes armed for this very purpose. Having disposed their forces, the Four Hundred arrived, everyone with a dagger concealed on his person, and with them 120 youths whose services they used for any act of violence. They broke in upon the councilors chosen by lot in the council chamber and told them to take their pay and begone. They had brought with them the pay for the remainder of their term of office, which they handed to them as they went out.

70. In this manner the council went off without offering any remonstrance, and the rest of the citizens kept quiet and made no countermovement. The Four Hundred then installed themselves in the council chamber; for the present they elected by lot Prytaneis of their own number and did all that was customary in the way of prayers and sacrifices to the gods at their entrance into office. Soon, however, they wholly changed the democratic system, although they did not recall the exiles because Alcibiades was one of them, and governed the city by force. Some few whom they thought would be better out of the way were put to death; others, imprisoned or exiled. They also sent heralds to Agis, the Lacedæmonian king, who was at Decelea, saying that they desired to conclude a peace with him and that it was reasonable for him to be more ready to treat with them than with the untrustworthy people.

71. But as he thought that the city was in an unsettled state, and that the people would not at once yield up their ancient liberty and that the appearance of a great Lacedæmonian army would unsettle them, and was far from convinced in the circumstances that confusion had ceased, his answer to the envoys of the Four Hun-

dred held out no prospect of agreement. He sent to the Peloponnese for large reinforcements and, soon afterwards, with the garrison at Decelea and the newly arrived troops, came down in person to the very walls of Athens. He hoped that the Athenians in their distraction would probably fall into the hands of the Peloponnesians, just as they wished, or that as a result of the confusion likely to arise both from within the city and outside it, he would succeed, even without a blow, in capturing the Long Walls, deserted in the confusion. But when he drew near, there was not the slightest movement within; the Athenians, sending out their cavalry and a part of their hoplites, light-armed troops and archers, struck down a few of his soldiers who had come in close, and obtained possession of some arms and dead bodies; whereupon, having found out his mistake, he withdrew his army. He and the garrison remained at their post in Decelea, but he sent home the newly arrived troops after they had continued a few days in Attica. The Four Hundred thereafter resumed negotiations, and Agis was now more ready to listen to them. At his suggestion they sent envoys to Lacedæmon in the hope of coming to terms.

72. They also sent ten men to Samos, who were to pacify their forces and to explain that the oligarchy was not established with any design of injuring Athens or her citizens but for the preservation of the whole state. The change, they said, was the work of five thousand, not just four hundred; and yet, owing to the pressure of war and of business abroad, so many as five thousand Athenians had never before assembled to deliberate even on the most important questions. They instructed them to say anything else that was appropriate and sent them on their mission as soon as they themselves were installed in the government. For they were afraid of what actually occurred, that the naval rabble would be impatient of the oligarchical system and that disaffection would begin with them and end in their own overthrow.

73. At the very time when the Four Hundred were establishing themselves at Athens, at Samos there was a change affecting the oligarchical party. The Samians of

the popular party, who had originally risen up against the upper class, had changed sides again when Peisander came to the island and, persuaded by him and his Athenian accomplices at Samos, had formed a body of three hundred conspirators and prepared to attack the rest as democrats. There was an Athenian, Hyperbolus, a scoundrel, who had been ostracized,[1] not for any fear of his power and influence, but because his villainy was a disgrace to the city. This man was assassinated by them with the help of Charminus, one of the generals, and of some Athenians at Samos, to whom they pledged their faith. They also joined these Athenians in other deeds of violence and were eager to attack the masses. But the latter discovered the plan and gave information to the generals Leon and Diomedon, who were opposed to the oligarchy because they were respected by the people, to Thrasybulus, a trierarch, and Thrasyllus, a private soldier, and to others who were thought to be the steadiest opponents of the conspirators. They entreated them not to allow the Samian people to be destroyed and the island of Samos, without which the Athenian empire would never have lasted until then, to be estranged. On hearing this, these men went to the soldiers one by one, begging them to interfere, especially to the crew of the Paralos, all freeborn Athenians who were at any time ready to attack oligarchy, even when it did not actually exist. Leon and Diomedon, whenever they sailed to any other place, left some ships for the protection of the Samians. And so, when the three hundred began the attack, all the crews, especially of the Paralos, hastened to the rescue; and the popular party gained the victory. Of the three hundred, they killed about thirty, banished the three chief culprits, and forgave the rest; and henceforward all lived together under a democracy.

74. Chæreas the son of Archestratus, an Athenian, who had been active in the movement, was quickly dispatched in the Paralos by the Samians, and the fleet to Athens, to report what had occurred; for as yet they did not know that the government was in the hands of the Four Hundred. No sooner had they arrived than the Four Hundred imprisoned two or three of the crew and,

taking away their ship, transferred the rest to a troop-ship which was ordered to keep guard around Eubœa. Chæreas, seeing promptly how matters stood, contrived to steal away and get back to Samos where he told the fleet the news from Athens, exaggerating the whole story: they were punishing everybody with stripes; no one might speak a word against the government; their wives and children were being outraged; the oligarchy was going to take the relatives of all the men serving at Samos who were not of their faction and imprison them, intending, if the fleet did not submit, to put them to death. And he added a great many other falsehoods.

75. When the army heard his report, they instantly rushed upon the chief oligarchs and their confederates and tried at first to stone them. But they were prevented by the moderates who warned them not to ruin everything while the enemy were lying close to them, prow threatening prow. So they desisted. Thrasybulus the son of Lycus, and Thrasyllus, the chief leaders of the reaction, now desired to make the change to democracy at Samos absolutely clear; and they bound the soldiers, more especially those of the oligarchical party, by the most solemn oaths to maintain a democracy and be of one mind, to prosecute vigorously the war with the Peloponnesians, to be enemies to the Four Hundred and to hold no parley with them by heralds. All the Samians of age took the same oath, and the Athenian soldiers made the Samians partners in all their affairs and in the consequences of their dangers. They considered that neither the Samians nor themselves had anywhere else to turn for safety but that, whether the Four Hundred or their enemies at Miletus gained the day, they were doomed.

76. There was now an obstinate struggle between those who were forcing democracy on the city and those who were forcing oligarchy on the fleet. The men in the fleet held an assembly at once, at which they deposed their former generals and any trierarchs whom they suspected, and chose new trierarchs and generals, including Thrasybulus and Thrasyllus. They rose up and encouraged each other, particularly by saying that there was

no need for despondency because their own city had revolted; the deserters were inferior to them in numbers and in resources of all kinds. They had the whole navy, and could compel the remaining cities of the empire to pay money, just as well as if Athens were their base; for they still had a city in Samos and one that was not weak; in the war it had all but wrested from Athens the dominion of the sea.[1] They would resist the enemy from the same place as before and, with the ships in their hands, would be better able to obtain supplies than the Athenians at home. Indeed the reason why the Athenians had previously commanded the sea passage into the Piræus was that they were stationed at Samos and protected it; and in the present situation, if the oligarchs refused to restore to them their old constitution, they were better able to keep them off the sea than the oligarchs could deny it to them. The help the city gave them in overcoming the enemy was small and valueless; and they had lost nothing, as the Athenians at home no longer had any money to send, but they were supplying themselves. Nor could they help by wise policy, the reason for which states exercise authority over their armed forces; here too they had gone astray by overthrowing the ancestral laws, which they themselves were preserving, and would try to force the oligarchs to accept. Thus they were not even inferior in sound advisers; and Alcibiades, if they granted him pardon and recall, would gladly secure for them the king's alliance. Above all, if they failed in everything else, their great fleet permitted them to retire to many places where they would find cities and land.

77. After meeting and encouraging each other with such appeals, they were equally active in preparations for war. The commissioners whom the Four Hundred had sent to Samos, hearing when they reached Delos how matters stood, went no further. . . .

[*Some minor operations are now recorded, including the revolt of Byzantium, which endangered Athens' grain supplies from south Russia.*]

81. The Athenian leaders at Samos and particularly Thrasybulus, who from the time when he restored the democracy at Samos never deviated from the opinion that Alcibiades should be recalled, at last obtained the consent of the mass of the men at an assembly which voted his return and pardon. Thrasybulus then sailed to Tissaphernes and brought Alcibiades to Samos, convinced that there was no solution for the Athenians unless he were to draw Tissaphernes away from the Peloponnesians. An assembly was called, at which Alcibiades complained pathetically of his personal calamity in being banished; he then spoke at length of the political situation, inspired them with great hopes for the future and magnified to excess his own influence over Tissaphernes. He meant thereby to frighten the oligarchy at home and promote the dissolution of their clubs, to exalt himself in the eyes of the army at Samos and fortify their confidence, and to widen the breach between Tissaphernes and the enemy, and to blast the hopes of the Lacedæmonians. He therefore carried his boastful assurances to the utmost. Tissaphernes, he said, had actually promised him that if he could trust the Athenians, they should not want for maintenance while he had anything to give, not if he were driven at last to turn his own bed into money; that he would bring up the Phœnician ships (which were already at Aspendus) to assist the Athenians instead of the Peloponnesians; but that he could not trust the Athenians unless Alcibiades were restored, and became surety for them.

82. Hearing all this, and a great deal more, the Athenians immediately appointed him a colleague of their other generals and placed everything in his hands; no man among them would have given up for all the world the hope at once aroused of deliverance and of vengeance on the Four Hundred; they were ready on the spot under the influence of his words to treat the Peloponnesians with contempt and to sail for the Piræus. But he absolutely stopped them from sailing there and leaving behind them enemies nearer at hand, though many pressed for this. Having been elected general, he said he would make the conduct of the war his first care and sail

at once to Tissaphernes. And he went straight from this assembly in order that he might be thought to be acting in entire conjunction with Tissaphernes; at the same time he wished to gain honor in his eyes and to show him that he had now been chosen general, and could do him a good or a bad turn. Thus Alcibiades succeeded in frightening the Athenians with Tissaphernes, and Tissaphernes with the Athenians. . . .

[*Meantime, relations between Tissaphernes and the Peloponnesians were deteriorating. Alcibiades returned to Samos.*]

86. The envoys whom the Four Hundred had sent to pacify the army and give explanations left Delos and came to Samos when Alcibiades was present, and an assembly was held at which they endeavored to speak. At first the soldiers would not listen to them, but shouted, "Death to the subverters of the democracy." When quiet had been with difficulty restored, the envoys told them that the change was not meant for the destruction but for the preservation of the state and that there was no intention of betraying Athens to the enemy, which might have been effected by the new government already if they had pleased during the recent invasion. They declared that all the Five Thousand were in turn to have a share in the administration and that the families of the sailors were not being outraged, as Chæreas slanderously reported, or in any way molested; they were living quietly, each in their own homes. They defended themselves at length; but the more they said, the more furious and unwilling to listen the masses became. Various proposals were made; above all they wanted to sail to the Piræus. And in my view Alcibiades was then foremost in doing as eminent a service to the state as any man ever did. For if the Athenians at Samos had sailed against their fellow citizens in their excitement, the enemy would beyond all question instantly have obtained possession of Ionia and the Hellespont. This he prevented, and at that moment no one else could have restrained the rabble: but he stopped them from sailing and with sharp

words protected the envoys from those who were personally inflamed against them. He then dismissed them himself with the reply that he would not stop the Five Thousand from governing but that the Four Hundred must be got rid of and the old council of Five Hundred restored. If they had reduced the expenditure in order that the soldiers on service might be better maintained, he highly approved. For the rest he urged them to stand firm and not give in to the enemy; if the city was preserved, there was good hope of an agreement amongst themselves; but if once disaster occurred either to the army at Samos or to their fellow citizens at home, there would be no one left to be reconciled with.

There were also present envoys from Argos, who proffered their aid "to the Athenian people at Samos." Alcibiades complimented them, requested them to come with their forces when they were summoned, and dismissed them. These Argives came with the Paralos crew who had been ordered by the Four Hundred to cruise off Eubœa in a troopship; they were employed in conveying to Lacedæmon certain envoys sent by the Four Hundred, Læspodias, Aristophon, and Melesias. But when they were near Argos on their voyage, the crew seized the envoys, and, as they were among the chief authors of the revolution, delivered them over to the Argives; instead of returning to Athens, they went themselves from Argos to Samos, and brought with them in their trireme the Argive ambassadors. . . .

[*Chapters 87-88 concern mainly Tissaphernes' relations with the Peloponnesians.*]

89. The envoys sent by the Four Hundred returned from Samos to Athens and reported that Alcibiades had told them to stand firm and not give in to the enemy and that he entertained great hopes of reconciling the army to the city and overcoming the Peloponnesians. The greater number of the oligarchs, who were already dissatisfied, and would have gladly got out of the whole affair if they safely could, were now much encouraged. They began to come together and to criticize the conduct

of affairs. Their leaders were some of the chief oligarchs and office holders; for example, Theramenes the son of Hagnon, and Aristocrates the son of Scelias, and others with a principal share in the government who now alleged that they were very seriously afraid of the fleet at Samos and Alcibiades and also of the envoys at Sparta who might act without authority from the majority and do the city injury. They did not yet avow that they would gladly be rid of extreme oligarchy but said that the Five Thousand should be established in reality and not in name and the constitution made more equitable. This was the political system of which they spoke, but the truth was that private ambitions made most of them incline to practices which are more fatal than anything to an oligarchy succeeding a democracy. (The instant an oligarchy is established all disdain mere equality, and each claims to be far above everybody else; but in a democracy, when an election is made, a man is less disappointed at the result; he does not feel that he is worsted by his peers.) Most clearly, they were incited by the great power of Alcibiades at Samos and their belief that the oligarchy would not be permanent. This made every one of them struggle hard to be the first champion of the people himself.

90. The leading men among the Four Hundred most violently opposed to democracy were Phrynichus, who had been general at Samos and had there come into antagonism with Alcibiades, Aristarchus, a man who had long been the most thoroughgoing enemy of the people, Peisander, and Antiphon. At the first establishment of the oligarchy and again when the forces at Samos separated from them in the cause of the democracy, these and the other most powerful men sent envoys of their own number to Lacedæmon and were anxious to make peace; they also began to build the wall on what is called Eetionea. They were confirmed in their purposes after the return of their own ambassadors from Samos; for they saw that not only the people but even those who had appeared steadfast adherents of their own party were now changing. So, fearing what might happen both at Athens and Samos, they sent Antiphon, Phrynichus, and

ten others in great haste, authorizing them to make peace with Lacedæmon upon anything like tolerable terms; at the same time they proceeded with still more energy to build the wall on Eetionea. The design was (so Theramenes and his party averred) not to bar the Piræus against the fleet at Samos from forcing an entry but rather to admit the sea and land forces of the enemy whenever they pleased. Eetionea is the mole of the Piræus, and ships enter right alongside; the new wall was to be so connected with the previously existing wall, which looked toward the land, that a handful of men stationed there might command the approach from the sea. For the old wall looking toward the land and the new inner wall in process of construction facing the water ended at the same point in one of the two forts which protected the narrow mouth of the harbor. They also walled off the largest portico in the Piræus and the nearest to the new fortification; they controlled this themselves and forced everyone to deposit his corn there, not only what came in by sea, but what was on the spot, and to take from it grain to sell.

91. For some time Theramenes had been circulating reports of their designs; and when the envoys returned from Lacedæmon without having effected anything in the nature of a treaty for the Athenian people, he declared that this fort was in danger of being the ruin of Athens. Further, just at this time at the invitation of the Eubœans, 42 ships, including Italian vessels from Tarentum and Locri and a few from Sicily, stationed at Las in Laconia, were making ready to sail to Eubœa under the command of Agesandridas the son of Agesander, a Spartan. Theramenes said that these ships were intended not for Eubœa but for the party who were fortifying Eetionea and that if precautions were not taken now, they would be ruined before they knew where they were. In fact something of the kind was meditated by the men he accused, and there was more than simple slander in his words. For they most of all desired to keep the oligarchy and rule the allies too; failing this, to keep their ships and walls and to be autonomous; if this too proved impracticable, at the worst they would not see democracy

restored and themselves fall the first victims but would rather bring in the enemy and come to terms involving the loss of walls and ships and hold the city in any way they could, provided that they could save their own lives.

92. So they worked energetically at this wall of theirs, which had entrances and postern gates and facilities for introducing the enemy, and sought to finish the building in time. As yet the murmurs of discontent had been generally secret and confined to a few when suddenly Phrynichus, after his return from the embassy to Lacedæmon, was treacherously struck by one of the Peripoli[1] in the market place which was filling up; he had taken only a few steps away from the council chamber. The blow was immediately fatal; the man who dealt it escaped; his accomplice, an Argive, was seized and put to the torture by the Four Hundred, but did not disclose the name of any who had instigated the deed. He only admitted to knowing that a number of persons used to assemble at the house of the commander of the frontier guard and in other houses. No further measures followed this incident; and so Theramenes and Aristocrates and the other citizens, whether members of the Four Hundred or not, who were of the same mind, were emboldened to take decided steps. For the Peloponnesians had already sailed round from Las and, having cast anchor at Epidaurus, had overrun Ægina; and Theramenes said that if they were on their way to Eubœa, it was not natural for them to have gone up the gulf to Ægina and then returned and anchored at Epidaurus, but that someone had invited them for the purposes which he was always alleging; it was impossible therefore to be any longer inactive. Finally after many insinuations and factious harangues, the people now began to take active measures. The hoplites who were at work on the wall of Eetionea in the Piræus, among whom was Aristocrates with his own tribe, which, as taxiarch, he commanded, seized Alexicles, an oligarchical general who had been most concerned with the clubs, and shut him up in a house. Others too joined in the act, especially one Hermon, who commanded the Peripoli stationed at Munychia; above all, the rank and file of the hoplites heartily ap-

proved. The Four Hundred, who were assembled in the council house when the news was brought to them, were ready to take up arms at once, except for those who disapproved of their proceedings; they began to threaten Theramenes and his associates. Theramenes in defense said that he was ready to go with them at once and help rescue Alexicles. So, taking one of the generals who was of his own way of thinking, he went down to the Piræus. Aristarchus and certain young men in the cavalry also came to assist. Great and bewildering was the tumult, for in the city the people thought that the Piræus was already in the hands of the insurgents and that their prisoner had been killed, and the inhabitants of the Piræus thought that they were on the point of being attacked from the city. The older men with difficulty restrained the citizens, who were running up and down and flying to arms. Thucydides of Pharsalus, the proxenus of Athens in that city, happening to be on the spot, kept throwing himself in every man's way and loudly entreating the people not to destroy their country when the enemy was lying in wait so near. At length they were pacified, and refrained from laying hands on one another. When Theramenes, who was himself a general, reached the Piræus, in an angry voice he pretended to berate the soldiers, while Aristarchus and the party opposed to the people were really furious. The mass of the hoplites were for going to work at once without any regrets. They began asking Theramenes if he thought that the wall was being built for a good purpose and whether it would not be better demolished. He answered that if they thought so, he agreed. Immediately the hoplites and a crowd of men from the Piræus climbed up and began to pull the fort down. The cry addressed to the rabble was, "Let anyone who wishes the Five Thousand to rule and not the Four Hundred come and help us." For they still veiled their real plan under the name of the Five Thousand and did not say outright, "Anyone who wishes the people to rule": they feared that the Five Thousand might actually exist and that one man speaking in ignorance to another might get into trouble. For this reason the Four Hundred did not wish the Five Thousand either to exist or to be known not to exist, thinking that to give so many a share in the government would be downright democracy, while on the other hand, the mystery would make the people afraid of one another.

93. The next day the Four Hundred, although much disturbed, met in the council chamber. Meanwhile, the hoplites in the Piræus who had seized Alexicles let him go and, after demolishing the fort, went to the theater of Dionysus near Munychia; they piled arms there, held an assembly and resolved to march at once to the city, which they accordingly did and again piled arms in the temple of the Dioscuri. Presently deputies appeared sent by the Four Hundred, who conversed with them singly and tried to persuade any reasonable persons they saw to keep quiet themselves and restrain the rest, saying that they would publish the names of the Five Thousand and that the Four Hundred should be drawn from them in turn in such a manner as the Five Thousand might decide. In the meantime they begged them not to ruin everything and drive the city into the arms of the enemy. The discussion became general on both sides, and the whole body of soldiers grew calmer and turned their thoughts to the danger which threatened the whole commonwealth. They finally agreed that an assembly should be held on a fixed day in the theater of Dionysus to deliberate on the restoration of harmony.

94. When the day arrived and the assembly was on the point of meeting in the theater of Dionysus, news came that Agesandridas and his forty-two ships had crossed over from Megara, and were sailing along the coast of Salamis. Every man of the popular party thought that this was what they had been told in the past by Theramenes and his friends and that the ships were sailing to the fort, happily now demolished. Perhaps Agesandridas was hovering about Epidaurus and the neighborhood by agreement; but it is likely that he lingered there of his own accord, with an eye to the agitation which prevailed at Athens, hoping to be on the spot at the critical moment. Instantly upon the arrival of the news, the Athenians rushed down to the Piræus *en masse*, thinking that a conflict with their enemies

more serious than their domestic strife was now awaiting them, not at a distance, but by the harbor. Some embarked in the ships which were lying ready; others launched fresh ships; others manned the walls and prepared to defend the entrance of the Piræus.

95. The Peloponnesian squadron sailed past, doubled the promontory of Sunium, anchored between Thoricus and Prasiæ and finally proceeded to Oropus. The Athenians in their haste were compelled to employ crews not yet trained to work together, for the city was in a state of revolution, and they wished to protect their most important possession without delay; Eubœa was all in all to them now that they were shut out from Attica. They dispatched a fleet under the command of Thymochares to Eretria; these ships, added to those which were in Eubœa before, made up thirty-six. No sooner had they arrived than they were compelled to fight; for Agesandridas, after his men had taken their midday meal, brought out his own ships from Oropus, sixty stades by sea from the city of Eretria, and bore down upon them. The Athenians at once began to man their ships, thinking that their crews were close at hand; but in fact they were getting their provisions not in the market, for the Eretrians intentionally sold nothing there, but from houses at the end of the town, so that the men might lose time in embarking; the enemy would then come upon them before they were ready, and they would be compelled to put out as best they could. A signal was also raised at Eretria telling the fleet at Oropus when to put out. Thus the Athenians put out to sea ill-prepared; and though in the battle off the harbor of Eretria, they held out for a little while in spite of this, before long they fled and were pursued to the shore. Those who took refuge in the city of Eretria, relying on the friendship of the inhabitants, fared worst, for they were butchered by them; but those who gained the fortified position which the Athenians held in Eretria escaped, and so did the ships which reached Chalcis. The Peloponnesians, who had taken twenty-two Athenian ships and had killed or made prisoners of the crews, erected a trophy. Not long afterward, they induced all Eubœa to revolt, except

Oreus which Athenian settlers held, and set in order the affairs of the island.

96. When the news from Eubœa was brought to Athens, there was the greatest panic yet known. Neither the Sicilian disaster, great as that had seemed at the time, nor any other previous event caused so much alarm. The fleet at Samos was in insurrection; they had no ships in reserve or crews to man them; there was revolution at home—civil war might break out at any moment; and by this new and terrible misfortune, they had lost not only their ships but what was worst, Eubœa, which was of much more use to them than Attica itself. Had they not reason to despair? But they were most disturbed by the immediate danger; that the enemy, emboldened by victory, would at once attack the Piræus, where no ships were left; indeed they thought that they were all but there. And had the Peloponnesians been bolder, they could easily have executed such a plan, and either have anchored near and aggravated the divisions in the city or, by remaining and carrying on a blockade, have compelled the fleet in Ionia, although hostile to the oligarchy, to come and assist their kindred and the whole city, and then the Hellespont, Ionia, all the islands between Ionia and Eubœa, in a word, the whole Athenian empire would have fallen into their hands. But on this occasion, as on so many others, the Lacedæmonians proved themselves to be the most convenient enemies that the Athenians could possibly have had. For the two peoples were of very different tempers; the one quick, the other slow; the one enterprising, the other deficient in daring; and this was of the greatest service to the Athenians, the more so because their empire was maritime. The Syracusans proved this; they were most like the Athenians in character and fought best against them.

97. When the news came, the Athenians still contrived to man twenty ships and immediately summoned an assembly (the first of many) in the place called the Pnyx, where they had been in the habit of meeting at other times; there they deposed the Four Hundred and voted that affairs should be in the hands of the Five Thousand; this number was to include all who furnished

themselves with arms. No one was to receive pay for holding any office, on pain of falling under a curse. In the numerous other assemblies which were afterwards held, they appointed commissioners to draft laws and voted the other constitutional measures required. This government during its early days was manifestly the best which the Athenians ever enjoyed in my time; the rights of the few and the many were blended with moderation; and after the miserable state into which affairs had fallen, it was this which first revived the city. The people also passed a vote recalling Alcibiades and others with him from exile and sent him and the fleet in Samos directions to act vigorously.

98. When this transformation began, Peisander, Alexicles and the other leaders of the oligarchy stole away to Decelea, all except Aristarchus, who, being one of the generals at the time, gathered round him hastily a few archers of the most barbarous sort and made his way to Oenoè. This was an Athenian fort on the borders of Bœotia which the Corinthians, after calling the Bœotians to their aid, were now besieging on their own account in order to revenge an overthrow inflicted by the garrison of Oenoè upon a party of them who were going home from Decelea. Aristarchus entered into communication with the besiegers and deceived the garrison by telling them that the Athenians at home had come to terms with the Lacedæmonians and that by one of the conditions of the peace, they were required to give up the place to the Bœotians. Trusting him as a general and entirely ignorant of what had happened because they were closely invested, they capitulated and came out. Thus Oenoè was taken and occupied by the Bœotians, and the oligarchy and revolution at Athens came to an end. . . .

Epilogue

Thucydides' narrative breaks off in the midst of operations in the Hellespont in late 411. The following events are known from the continuation of his work by Xenophon of Athens, born about 430, in his Hellenica *and from other sources.*

It was vital for the Athenians to keep control of the grain route from south Russia, and in the spring of 410 Alcibiades achieved this by destroying the Peloponnesian fleet off Cyzicus. It took years to rebuild, and in the meantime Alcibiades was able to raise revenue and consolidate Athens' hold on the cities of the Hellespontine and Thracian regions. His victory also encouraged the Athenians at home to abolish the moderate government so highly praised by Thucydides (VIII:97) and to restore full democracy. The democrats made the mistake of rejecting a Spartan offer to make peace on the basis that each side should retain what it held. If this had been accepted, Athens would have kept much of her old empire. Moreover, many moderates concerned in the revolution of 411 now suffered from the rancor of the democrats. Even Alcibiades did not venture to return home till 407, and only then did his brilliant successes lead the Athenians to entrust him formally with the chief command. But he remained suspect to the democratic leaders, and a minor reverse incurred by one of his subordinates at Notium in 406 gave them the opportunity to remove him once more from the command, with results that were ultimately fatal. Most scholars think that Thucydides has this in mind in VI:15.

Persian subsidies had now enabled the Peloponnesians to rebuild and man a large fleet, and it was only with great difficulty that the Athenians defeated it at Arginusæ in 406; this was the bloodiest battle of the war. It is possible that Athens then once more rejected a compromise peace. But the end was now near. The king's son, Cyrus, had taken over the government of the western provinces of Asia Minor and the Spartan admiral, Lysander, established such cordial relations with him that he reversed Tissaphernes' policy of letting Athens and Sparta wear each other out and placed his purse freely at Lysander's disposal. Athens could hardly have held out for long in these circumstances, but in 405 her whole fleet was destroyed almost without a blow in the Hellespont as a result of the incompetence or treachery of the commanders. In April 404, she was starved into surrender. Sparta rejected the proposal made by Thebes and Corinth that she should be destroyed (cf. perhaps V:91), but made her a satellite state under an oligarchy, which enjoyed considerable support from well-to-do citizens disgusted by the follies of the democratic leaders and the heavy burdens imposed on themselves. This oligarchy proved intolerably oppressive, and was overthrown in 403; in another decade Athens recovered her independence and something of her old strength. But this is another story.

The last period of the war goes far to bear out Thucydides' judgment in II:65. Despite the heavy losses in Sicily, the devastations from Decelea (VII:27-28), the help Persia supplied to Sparta, and the numerous revolts in the empire in and after 412, Athens still had the strength to hold out, and could still have made a reasonable peace if she had not been weakened by internal factions and unwisely guided by the democratic leaders.

GENERAL NOTES

[1] MONEY

Greek cities coined in silver on varying standards. The most common coins were drachmas and obols (six to the drachma). It is misleading to give modern monetary equivalents, but the ordinary daily wage at Athens was from three obols to one drachma. The mina (one hundred drachmas) and talent (six thousand drachmas) were terms of account. It probably cost about a talent to build a trireme and as much to maintain it for a year in service; the crew, if paid at a drachma *per diem*, cost another talent each month.

[2] ARMIES AND FLEETS

The Greeks made relatively little use of archers or other light infantry or of cavalry; except in Sicily the land was too poor to provide sufficient fodder for horses, and few Greeks were rich enough to raise them. The strength of a Greek army consisted of *hoplites*, heavy-armed infantry drawn from citizens who could furnish equipment at their own cost, who fought in close formation; battles were decided at push of pike. Thucydides sometimes mentions *peltasts*, soldiers who carried a much smaller shield and a javelin and had little defensive armor. Greek armies could hardly ever take fortified cities by assault; they could be captured only by treason or blockade; and Athens, for instance, was invulnerable, as she was connected with the sea, commanded the water and could import necessary supplies. Most other cities could be starved out if denied use of their own land and home-grown food.

Merchant ships used sail; but the standard warship, or *trireme*, was propelled by 180 oarsmen on three banks; the exact arrangement is controversial. Some Greeks still relied on boarding tactics and carried many soldiers on their ships, but the Athenians had only a few marines; their ships were finely built and fast, and, thanks partly to the long training of the rowers, easily maneuverable. They were expert in backing water, and in breaking the enemy line or rowing round it. In breaking the line, they hoped to smash the enemy oars, while lifting their own at the crucial moment; and in any event they could afterward ram the enemy ships in their defenseless sides or sterns, and, in these ways, sink or disable them. These tactics required plenty of sea room, which the Athenians lacked in the harbor of Syracuse; moreover, the Syracusans made their own prows much stronger than the Athenian and rammed head on.

There was insufficient space on a trireme to sleep or to eat with comfort. It was the practice to beach the ships each night, if possible. Hence, triremes preferred to hug the coast; they were also not well constructed to meet storms on the open sea. Merchantmen could more easily cross the open water.

[3] THE ATHENIAN CONSTITUTION

All decisions of policy were made by the council and assembly. The council consisted of five hundred citizens, chosen annually by lot, who could not hold the office more than twice and not in successive years. Their tasks were to co-ordinate the administration and prepare business for the assembly. In the assembly every citizen could speak and make motions. A simple majority was decisive, though decrees could be annulled as illegal by appeal to the courts. Most of the administration was minutely subdivided between officials or boards chosen by lot. Criminal and civil cases were normally heard by large juries chosen by lot; there were no professional judges. Councilors, jurors and most officials were paid so that even the poor could serve. When special competence was required, officials were elected. This applied to, for instance, ambassadors and some curators of public works, and above all to the generals. They were ten in number, elected annually and re-eligible; they commanded fleets as well as armies, and were often charged with important civil business. There were no comparable financial officials. The council supervised finance (advised, no doubt, by leading politicians), and the assembly itself voted monies for particular purposes; to make this possible, accounts were published on stone inscriptions.

[4] THE SPARTAN CONSTITUTION

The official name for the Spartan state is "the *Lacedæmonians.*" They included (i) the *Spartiates* and (ii) the *Periœci* (dwellers-round). The latter enjoyed limited rights of municipal self-government and were liable to all the duties of citizens, eg., serving in the army, but had no part in the government of the state. The Spartiates were the full citizens, a small minority of the inhabitants, who owed their privileges to birth, property and a sort of education; they forfeited their rights if they failed to go through a severe discipline from the age of seven, designed to make them good soldiers, or to maintain Spartan standards of honor thereafter. Even the assembly consisting of the Spartiates seems to have had little power: it could answer "Yea" or "Nay" to motions put to it by the magistrates. The kingship survived at Sparta; there were two kings, chosen from two different hereditary lines. One of the kings normally commanded the Spartan army; but the kings had little other power, though they might enjoy great influence, depending on their talents. A council of elders could even try them and condemn them to death; its other powers are ill-known. Five annually elected *ephors* watched over the kings, mobilized the army and conducted civil administration. In particular, they policed the *Helots,* serfs owned by the state who worked on the domains of the individual Spartiates. Some Helots were freed as a reward for service in the army (*Neodamodes*).

[5.] DORIANS, IONIANS ETC.

Although the Greeks were conscious that they were a single people to be contrasted with "barbarians" whose language was unintelligible, they were themselves divided not only into many cities but also into more primitive ethnical units, such as the Aeolians, Arcadians, Dorians,

Ionians etc., which to some extent corresponded to differences in dialects. These units had no kind of political organization, but Thucydides indicates that in his time there were still some sentimental ties linking Dorians or Ionians together, especially perhaps in Sicily. Sparta and most of her Peloponnesian allies, as well as Syracuse, were Dorian, while Athens claimed to be the mother-city of the Ionian cities, scattered principally over the islands and shores of the Aegean, which comprised the majority of her "allies" or subjects. Such common sentiment as existed never seems to be decisive in determining the policy of a city.

[6] OTHER TECHNICAL TERMS (NOT EXPLAINED IN 1-4)

AGORA. The civic center (e.g., at Athens).

ATTICA. Athenian territory.

THE (GREAT) KING. The king of Persia, whose empire extended westward to western Asia Minor, to the coast of Syria and Palestine and to Egypt.

LACONIA. Spartan territory.

LACONIAN. Spartan.

METICS. Persons permanently resident in a foreign city.

PAEAN. A war chant.

PARALOS. A fast Athenian ship employed on state missions.

PROXENUS. A citizen who represented the interests of some foreign city, rather like a consul.

PRYTANIS (PLURAL, PRYTANEIS). Member of an executive standing committee of the Athenian council; one of them, chosen by lot, presided over the assembly.

SALAMINIA. As for Paralos.

STADE. About two hundred English yards.

THETES. Very poor citizens.

TRIERARCH. Commander of a trireme, who at Athens had to pay for the running costs, other than crew's pay, while he was in command; this was a form of taxation, and trierarchs came from the propertied class.

TYRANT. An unconstitutional monarch, not necessarily an oppressive ruler.

TYRANNY. Rule by a tyrant.

FOOTNOTES ON THE TEXT

BOOK ONE

Chapter 1

1. The notes are numbered separately for each chapter. (The division of the text into books and chapters is not due to Thucydides.) Readers are advised first to look at the General Notes on p. 336-339 for explanation of some technical points. All dates are B.C.

2. On Thucydides' method of reconstructing early history, see Introduction (p. xx).

Chapter 3

1. Like all ancient writers, Thucydides did not distinguish between what we regard as historical and legendary periods; he assumes not only that the Trojan War took place but that figures of Greek legend, Hellen, Minos, etc., were historical, though he submits the details of legends to critical scrutiny.

Chapter 4

1. The sea power of Minos is taken as a prototype of Athenian and depicted in the light of Thucydides' own experience.

Chapter 9

1. *Iliad,* II:108.

Chapter 12

1. Greek writers dated the Trojan War *c.* 1200.

2. Thucydides himself (VI:2 ff., not printed here) implies that Greek colonization in Sicily began *c.* 730. This is usually accepted.

Chapter 13

1. Cf. I:25.

2. The modern Marseilles.

Chapter 14

1. See I:74 n.1.

Chapter 15

1. This ill-recorded war has been variously dated by modern scholars between *c.* 700 and 570.

Chapter 16

1. King of Lydia in western Asia Minor, overthrown by Cyrus *c.* 546.

Chapter 17

1. There were tyrants in, e.g., Corinth c. 650-580 and in Athens c. 560-510. In Sicily tyrants were very powerful at Syracuse c. 485-465.

Chapter 18

1. Few modern scholars would accept the view that the Spartan government was unchanged, and untroubled by internal dissensions, from *c.* 800.

2. The Spartans overthrew tyranny at Athens in 510, but this is the only clear case known to us.

3. In and after 479, most of the Greeks in Asia and the islands revolted from Persia and eventually became allies and then subjects of Athens; cf. I:94 ff.

Chapter 19

1. See Introduction (pp. xvi, xxv).

2. After 439, when Samos lost her fleet and autonomy.

Chapter 20

1. See VI:54-59.

2. Herodotus fell into these errors.

Chapter 22

1. See Introduction (p. xxii).

Chapter 23

1. In 446 a truce was made between Athens and Sparta to last thirty years; Athens surrendered certain possessions on the mainland (IV:21) but retained her maritime empire; both parties agreed not to receive the allies of the other into their own confederacies but were free to accept other Greek cities (e.g., Corcyra) as allies. Athens guaranteed the autonomy of Ægina, a former ally of Sparta, which she had forced into her own league. Any disputes were to be settled by arbitration.

2. In the speeches recorded by Thucydides, Spartan fear of Athens is often mentioned, and the inevitability of war sometimes assumed. Thucydides may mean that Sparta could not make formal complaint of Athens' growing power, but had to allege breaches of the treaty as grounds for making war.

Chapter 26

1. Ambracia and Leucas were Corinthian colonies and (unlike Corcyra) very much under Corinthian control.

Chapter 34

1. Relations between metropolis and colony were usually good, though the colony was nominally independent.

Chapter 36

1. Corcyra is on the route between Greece and Italy which involves the shortest voyage across the open Adriatic Sea. The Corcyræans assume that Athens might wish to send a fleet to the west and that the Greek cities in the west might send triremes to help her enemies in Greece; cf. II:7. See General Note 2 (p. 336).

Chapter 37

1. It was common for Greek cities to conclude treaties with each other providing that the citizens of one city could sue and be sued in the courts of the other under an agreed procedure; cf. I:77.

Chapter 40

1. 440. It seems probable that Corinth had resisted a Spartan proposal to help the Samian rebels.

Chapter 41

1. About 487, before Athens had built a large fleet.

Chapter 42

1. This refers either to the Megarian decree, for which see I:67, or to an incident about 460, when Athens saved Megara from Corinthian attack and first incurred the bitter hatred of Corinth.

Chapter 67

1. See I:23, note 1.
2. This decree has been variously dated to 433-32 or to some years earlier; for its pretext, see I:139. Some think that Athens was trying to force Megara to rejoin her own confederacy, as in 460-46; control of Megara would enable Athens to bar the Peloponnesian army from invading Attica. Other ancient writers represent this decree as the chief cause of the war.

Chapter 69

1. The walls connecting Athens with the Piræus, built in the 450's, which made it impossible for the Peloponnesians to invest Athens and starve her out.

Chapter 70

1. The contrast drawn between Athens and Sparta represents Thucydides' own views. Cf. IV:14, 55; VII:28; VIII:96 and many passages in other speeches.

Chapter 71

1. One of the rather rare allusions to an "idea of progress" in antiquity.

2. See summary following I:44.

Chapter 72

1. This implausibly unconciliatory speech contains many ideas which seem to be those of the historian; see Introduction (p. xxviii).

Chapter 74

1. Herodotus gives 378 Greek triremes of which 200 were Athenian. In 480 the Athenians had to evacuate Attica, and almost all men of military age went on board the ships for the battle of Salamis.

Chapter 77

1. See note on I:37. The translation and interpretation of this passage are controversial. Some think that Athens almost monopolized for her own courts suits between Athenians and subjects.

2. See I:94-95.

Chapter 80

1. A fleet was costly (cf. General Note 1, p. 336) and the Peloponnesians had small revenues.

Chapter 82

1. Chiefly the Persian king.

Chapter 87

1. Probably July 432.

Chapter 96

1. Another object was to free Greek subjects of Persia; cf. III:10.

2. The word is usually translated "tribute"; this is appropriate from the time when Athens had converted the confederacy into an empire, but at first we have to think of contributions made by common consent for a common cause.

3. This was transferred to Athens in 454.

Chapter 97

1. See III:10-11. By 432 these councils had ceased to meet.

2. His work is lost.

Chapter 99

1. See Introduction (p. xxix).

Chapter 118

1. Within the period of 477-65, Sparta had to put down a movement for secession from her league in Arcadia, which had some support from Argos (at war with Sparta *c.* 470-50); and in about 465 there was a serious Helot revolt in Messenia.

Chapter 119

1. The Corinthians answer Archidamus' speech.

Chapter 121

1. The Peloponnesians did not act on this advice. The temples were very rich; but it would have been regarded as impious to raid their funds, with little prospect of repayment.

2. Compare I:143. Perhaps two-thirds of the crews of Athenian ships were usually non-Athenian.

Chapter 125

1. The invasion took place in May 431; the congress, probably in August 432.

Chapter 139

1. Land on the border between Athens and Megara consecrated to Demeter and Persephone.

2. Thucydides makes Pericles refute the Corinthian speech which he could not have heard. These two speeches, together with that of Archidamus and II:13, fulfill the purpose of showing us something of the resources and prospects of the belligerents.

Chapter 141

1. Greeks were reluctant to pay direct taxes, though they were occasionally levied at Athens; and the idea of a national debt was unknown. Athens paid for the war partly from tribute, partly from a reserve accumulated earlier; see II:13. cf. V:17.

Chapter 142

1. It was not till 413 that the Peloponnesians built a fort in Attica (cf. VI:91; VII:27-28) and so made their

strategy of devastating Attica more effective, though not decisive. Perhaps it did not seem safe to do so till the Bœotians, who were sufficiently near to relieve the fort at any time if it were invested by the Athenians, had shown their ability to do so by defeating the Athenians at Delium in 424.

Chapter 143

1. The Peloponnesians had overwhelming numerical superiority by land.

Chapter 146

1. Heralds were employed for communications between belligerents.

BOOK TWO

Chapter 2

1. Probably March 431. See Introduction (p. xxi).

2. The Bœotians formed a league dominated by Thebes; the Bœotarchs were the chief magistrates. Platæa had always refused to enter this league and had been under Athenian protection since about 519.

Chapter 7

1. The number, absurdly high, may be wrongly transmitted. In fact, the western Greeks gave Sparta no help till after 413.

Chapter 9

1. Sparta had conquered the Messenians c.700 B.C. and made them Helots. They never acquiesced. After a great revolt c.465, Athens settled some Messenian refugees at Naupactus. See IV: 3 and 80.

Chapter 13

1. See summary following I:126.

2. The figure apparently includes some two hundred talents from external possessions which was not strictly "tribute." Athens' internal revenues perhaps amounted to another 400 talents.

3. On another reading, the reserve had never exceeded 6,000 talents and 5,700 were left. Between 431 and 424 the greater part of this reserve was spent as we know from inscriptions, and in 424 the tribute was raised to about 1,000 talents, an important measure on which

Thucydides is silent. The siege of Potidæa, which fell in 430, cost 2,000 talents.

4. The interpretation of these figures is very hard; "16,000" seems too high, and Thucydides has at least expressed himself with too little care.

5. See I:69, note 1.

Chapter 15

1. For Thucydides' method, compare notes on I:1 and 3.

2. This commemorated the union or "synœcism" of Attica.

3. They ruled within the period 560-10.

4. Similarly, the oldest part of London is the "City."

Chapter 17

1. Thucydides rationalizes. Compare II:54; V:26.

Chapter 19

1. The townships or parishes into which Attica was divided.

Chapter 20.

1. The number is probably wrongly transmitted.

Chapter 21

1. Cf. I:74, note 1.

Chapter 22

1. The generals probably had this power when the enemy were in the country.

Chapter 34

1. The Greeks practiced cremation.

2. Ten artificial units among which the citizens were distributed.

Chapter 36

1. Compare I:2.

Chapter 39

1. Compare I:144.

2. The Spartans were subjected to a rigorous training from boyhood.

Chapter 43

1. They were like men who brought contributions to a banquet.

Chapter 48

1. Scholars are still divided about the identification of the disease. Typhus is most probable.

Chapter 54

1. See III:87.

Chapter 56

1. Compare VI:31. Thucydides fails to explain Pericles' aim. Argos had claims on Epidaurus, and perhaps Pericles hoped to bring Argos into the war by offering the place to her. Her entry into the war might have transformed the strategic situation; see V:14.

Chapter 59

1. See Introduction (pp. ix-xi).

Chapter 65

1. The formal charge was perhaps embezzlement; if so, Thucydides implies that it was incredible. On Pericles' position, see Introduction (pp. xi-xii).

2. Thucydides apparently refers to Alcibiades' removal from command and perhaps to the refusal of the Athenians to relieve Nicias; his narrative shows that in other ways the Athenians gave all possible support to their forces in Sicily.

3. The manuscripts give "three" which cannot be right.

Chapter 89

1. This speech in which Phormio refutes that of the Peloponnesian commanders is surely invention. Since Phormio could not and did not avoid an action in the straits, his analysis of the disadvantages of fighting there was not likely to encourage his men in the action. Thucydides uses the speech to explain Athenian naval tactics.

Chapter 90

1. See II:9, note.

BOOK THREE

Chapter 9

1. As the Spartans professed to be fighting for the liberation of Athens' allies from unjust rule, the Mytilenæans are implausibly apologetic. It seems likely that Thucydides has simply made this speech the occasion to expound the views of Athens' discontented subjects on Athenian imperialism and to state a case on the justice of the revolt which Cleon is later made to answer.

Chapter 10

1. Here and in III:11 it is apparently implied that many of the Athenian aggressions against her allies had been taken with the formal consent of the allied council (I:97), in which the numerous members, each with one vote, could not unite against Athenian proposals.

Chapter 36

1. The real motives, surely, for the Athenians' changing their mind, though they are excluded from the subsequent debate, as described by Thucydides.

2. Aristophanes, especially in the *Knights,* and also in allusions in the *Acharnians, Wasps* and *Peace,* gives a hostile picture of Cleon.

3. In my view the two speeches which follow are largely invented (cf. note 1). Note that Cleon echoes not only the sentiments of Pericles and other spokesmen for Athenian imperialism, in the extreme form in which Thucydides puts the imperialist case, but also ideas found elsewhere, as noted below.

Chapter 37

1. Cf. I:68.

2. Cf. I:84.

Chapter 38

1. Cf. VII:48.

2. Sophists: traveling lecturers on ethics, politics, etc.

Chapter 39

1. Cleon is made to answer the Mytilenæan speech, an obvious artifice by Thucydides.

Chapter 43

1. Cf. Thucydides' own judgment in VIII:1.

Chapter 45

1. Cf. IV:108 (Thucydides' opinion).

2. Cf. III:84 (Thucydides' opinion).

Chapter 50

1. The figure has been amended to "thirty."

2. The colonists were *rentiers,* and do not seem to have remained as residents on the island.

Chapter 70

1. Too much: probably the manuscripts are wrong.

2. About two Attic drachmas.

Chapter 78

1. Cf. II:83-84.

Chapter 84

1. The authenticity of this chapter has been unjustly suspected.

Chapter 85

1. In IV:46-48 (not printed here) Thucydides recounts how the democrats with Athenian help treacherously massacred the remaining oligarchs in 425; this was the end, he says, of the revolution "in this war." In fact, it broke out again in 410; Thucydides was perhaps writing earlier or distinguishing the ten years' war (431-21) from the war of 413-04; cf. V:26.

Chapter 86

1. Athens had made alliances with Leontini and Rhegium in the 440's and renewed them in 432.

Chapter 87

1. Perhaps a third, if this figure is comparable with the 13,000 hoplites of II:13.

BOOK FOUR

Chapter 3

1. Pylos is the promontory jutting southward into the bay of Navarino, which Thucydides calls the "harbor." He does not seem to have known that it is an arm of the sea, a perfect harbor for modern ships but not for triremes. In 425 the waters of the bay washed the east side of Pylos, where there is now a shallow lagoon, cut off from the bay by a sandbar which connects the southern tip of Pylos with the land. The Athenian fort could therefore be attacked by land only along one narrow path to the north.

2. See II: 9 note, and IV:80.

Chapter 8

1. Thucydides' description of the island which protects the bay of Navarino is accurate, except that it is 24 stades long. The northern strait, between Pylos and the island, could have been blocked by two triremes; but the southern strait, 1,400 yards wide and 200 feet deep, could not have been blocked even by the whole Pelopon-

nesian fleet. It is clear that Thucydides had not visited Navarino. The explanation of his error is controversial.

Chapter 13

1. Manuscripts are not agreed on the figure.

Chapter 21

1. Cf. II:59.
2. Cf. IV:41; V:14. Thucydides probably thought that Athens should have made peace now, in conformity with Pericles' policy of seeking no aggrandizement during the war (I:144; II:65). But he cannot, consistently with his own judgment in I:23, have believed that Spartan friendship would be durable; and in 421-20 the alliance of Athens and Sparta proved ephemeral.

Chapter 28

1. Cf. IV:39. Thucydides held that Cleon's promise was foolhardy and that Athens would have been well quit of him. Yet Cleon probably knew that Demosthenes intended an attack and that if it could be made successfully, it could be made at once; and he took out the troops needed (cf. IV:29). The capture of the island's garrison put an end to the annual Peloponnesian invasions of Attica and gravely diminished Spartan prestige. It is hard to acquit Thucydides of bias.

Chapter 30

1. See summary following III:87.

Chapter 36

1. Here in 480 a Spartan force was surrounded and annihilated by the Persians.

Chapter 38

1. As there were only 2,500 Spartiates in all, this number was significant; hence Spartan anxiety for their captives' lives.

Chapter 41

1. See II:9, note.
2. See IV: 21, note 2.

Chapter 55

1. Cf. I:70.

Chapter 56

1. About 464, when Ægina was still an ally of Sparta.
2. Cf. I:67 and note. The Athenians had expelled the

Æginetans and settled their own citizens in Ægina in 431.

Chapter 60

1. Sixty ships—"few" only in comparison with the armada of 415. Cf. Introduction (p. xxv).

Chapter 61

1. Cf. III:86.
2. See Introduction (p. xxviii).

Chapter 63

1. See Introduction (p. xxix).

Chapter 65

1. The whole speech is full of Thucydidean ideas, and was probably composed after 415, when Thucydides could find out little of what had been said, and had to resort to much invention. Hermocrates' success at Gela then seemed important, as it foreshadowed the failure of Athens to win support in Sicily in 415-13.
2. Athenian ambitions had grown since 427; cf. III:86.

Chapter 78

1. Sparta had founded a colony here in 426 to command the pass into Thessaly and prepare for just such an expedition as Brasidas'; though the expedition became practicable only when Perdiccas, king of Macedon, offered a base in the north and facilitated the Spartan march through Thessaly. Later, when Perdiccas turned against Sparta, no reinforcements could get through Thessaly to Brasidas.

Chapter 79

1. Cities which had rebelled along with Potidæa in 432; see summary following I:44.
2. A rebellious vassal of Perdiccas.

Chapter 80

1. Discontent among the Helots was probably concentrated in Messenia; other Helots often fought loyally for Sparta. Probably the latter were Laconians and had no memory of independence.

Chapter 85

1. A lie; cf. IV:108 and summary following IV:65.

Chapter 108

1. Especially in the Hellespontine region, vital for control of Athens' grain supplies from south Russia.

BOOK FIVE

Chapter 7

1. The hoplites were middle-class citizens and perhaps opposed politically to Cleon (cf. IV:28); alternatively, they had no confidence in his military capacity.

Chapter 8

1. Colonists from Athens.

Chapter 10

1. His right flank; soldiers carried shields on their left arms. Cf. V:71.

Chapter 11

1. Dead men or women who were supposed to have shown superhuman qualities sometimes received quasi-divine honors at their tombs as "heroes."

Chapter 14

1. Prevented from taking reinforcements to Brasidas by the Thessalians.

2. Cf. IV:17, 21, 41, 65.

3. Despite Archidamus' warnings (I:81). Cf. VII:28.

4. For example, in a great revolt *c.* 464.

5. From V:40 (not printed here) it appears that the truce expired in the spring of 420.

6. A border district which Sparta had wrested from Argos by the middle of the sixth century; Argos had never recognized Sparta's right to it.

Chapter 16

1. Pleistoanax had commanded the Spartan forces which invaded Attica in 446 and compelled Athens to accept the thirty years' truce; his enemies apparently thought that the terms then granted to Athens were too favorable.

Chapter 17

1. The document is given here as a specimen of several treaties Thucydides inserted in his work.

Chapter 18

1. The Athenian statesman who fixed the first monetary assessments of Athens' allies, with their consent, in 477.

2. Cities which had revolted in 432 or in 424-23.
3. The Spartan name for Pylos.
4. Other cities which had revolted to Brasidas.
5. Places where all the Greeks celebrated common festivals.

Chapter 20

1. See Introduction (p. xxi).

Chapter 67

1. One of the peoples subject to Sparta (periœci).
2. Helots who had received freedom.
3. The post of honor.

Chapter 68

1. An army of 3,584 Lacedæmonians plus 600 Sciritæ is implied.

Chapter 69

1. Sparta had interfered with the attempt of Mantinea to reduce some other Arcadians to subjection.

Chapter 72

1. A title of honor; they fought on foot.

Chapter 84

1. Athens had previously tried to reduce Melos in 426 and in 424 had assessed her for tribute, though there is no evidence that she ever paid.

Chapter 91

1. In 404 many Athenians feared punishment for their treatment of Melos, but Sparta refused to destroy Athens (see Epilogue, p. 335). Some think that this passage betrays knowledge of these events and that the dialogue was written after the war.

BOOK SIX

Chapter 1

1. In 427-24. Cf. III:86; IV:59-65.

Chapter 10

1. Corinth and Thebes.
2. Cities which had rebelled in 432 or in 424-23 and which had not been reduced.

Chapter 11

1. Sparta.

Chapter 12

1. Leontines.

2. Alcibiades. See General Note 5 (p. 338).

Chapter 15

1. Some think this a reference to Alcibiades' removal from command and banishment later that year; but it is generally thought to relate to events in 411-06; see Epilogue (p. 334). Thucydides discusses Alcibiades' private life only because of its impact on the war.

Chapter 16

1. The cost of providing choruses for the dramatic festivals and other occasions fell on rich citizens, who might discharge their duties with more or less care and liberality.

Chapter 17

1. Revolutions, often involving great changes in the composition of the citizen bodies, had been a marked feature of Sicilian politics.

2. In the event the Athenians had considerable but not unanimous support from Sicels who were independent or subject to Syracuse.

Chapter 20

1. The other five cities were Camarina, Gela, Acragas, Himera and Messenè; of these Acragas and Messenè remained neutral.

Chapter 27

1. "Hermæ" because associated with the cult of Hermes; their origin lay in magical practices.

Chapter 28

1. A secret cult in honor of Persephone and her mother, the earth-goddess Demeter, which held out hope of a future life to initiates. To reveal the rites was a capital offense.

Chapter 31

1. See II:56.

Chapter 32

1. Syracuse had a moderate democracy.

Chapter 34

1. Carthage, a Phœnician colony in Africa near the modern Tunis, controlled western Sicily and dominated the western Mediterranean with her naval power. In

409-05 she conquered most Greek cities in Sicily and nearly took Syracuse. Alcibiades probably exaggerated in speaking of Athenian designs against her (VI:90), but Athenian success in Sicily would have been contrary to her interests.

2. Probably it was too late to adopt this plan.

3. A Spartan colony.

Chapter 54

1. Thucydides knew that Hippias was ruler and expresses himself carelessly.

Chapter 55

1. Herodotus agreed. Thucydides' arguments against the inferior tradition are an interesting specimen of his critical methods.

Chapter 59

1. A noble clan, to which Pericles and Alcibiades were related.

Chapter 60

1. Probably Thucydides underrates strictly religious concern. But people may have suspected that the profanations were the work of men who were giving "mutual pledges . . . by collaboration in some breach of law" (III:82). Many of those implicated belonged to aristocratic clubs.

2. Andocides, whose mendacious speeches *On His Return* (*c.* 409) and *On the Mysteries* (399) supply much additional information.

Chapter 75

1. In regard to the topography of the siege of Syracuse, see the map.

Chapter 85

1. Corcyra, Cephallenia and Zacynthus. But VII:57 indicates that they were virtually under Athenian control.

Chapter 90

1. Cf. VI:34 note.

Chapter 91

1. Desertion of slaves.

Chapter 93

1. Cleandridas, the adviser of King Pleistoanax in 446

and exiled like him (cf. V:16 note), had served Thurii in local wars; his son probably had good knowledge of affairs in the west.

Chapter 94

1. *c.* 483. Cf. VI:3, not printed here.

Chapter 98

1. Most scholars think that this was a circular fort as marked on the map; this view requires an emendation in the manuscript text of VII:2. Alternatively, the "circle" means the lines of circumvallation; in that case some passages would be translated differently.

Chapter 104

1. Cf. VI:93 note. Thurii, a colony founded by Athens in 444 with a mixed population, had at first remained neutral, but now began to give a little help to Athens.

2. If text and translation are sound, Thucydides must have been ignorant where the gulf of Terina (on the southwest coast of Italy) was; Gylippus can hardly have sailed round there.

Chapter 105

1. See summary following V:26.

BOOK SEVEN

Chapter 10

1. Thucydides' composition, but probably authentic in substance.

Chapter 25

1. About 250 tons, very large for that time.

Chapter 28

1. Compare VI:12 but contrast VI:26, which is nearer the truth.

2. Strictly, Athens was not at war with the Peloponnesians in 415, when the first Sicilian expedition was sent.

Chapter 50

1. Near Benghazi.

2. August 27, 413.

3. In II:28 Thucydides records the solar eclipse of August 3, 431, and adds that apparently such eclipses

occur only at the beginning of a lunar month (which is true); he evidently thought that eclipses were not omens but susceptible of a natural explanation. It is alleged that some Greek scientists had already predicted the occurrence of an eclipse.

Chapter 63

1. Metics.

Chapter 69

1. This opening between the ships moored at the entrance to the harbor (VII:59) was apparently blocked by chains (VII:70).

Chapter 82

1. The loyalty of subjects who are so often said to have resented Athenian rule is noteworthy.

BOOK EIGHT

Chapter 1

1. Aristotle regards such "probouloi" as characteristic of an oligarchy, and they may have done something to prepare the way for the oligarchic revolution.

Chapter 48

1. Phrynichus' objections were justified in the event; but though a former demagogue, he himself joined the oligarchic plot as soon as the conspirators gave up the idea of restoring Alcibiades, of whom he was a personal enemy.

Chapter 49

1. Another former demagogue.

Chapter 53

1. Great priestly families.

Chapter 54

1. A rebel Persian satrap, whom Athens had helped.
2. Such oligarchic clubs had been implicated in the mutilation of the Hermæ.

Chapter 63

1. An incident in 412 which I have omitted. The present leaders of the oligarchic faction at Samos had previously been popular leaders.
2. He had failed in fact to bring Tissaphernes over to the Athenian side.

Chapter 67

1. The divergent account in the *Constitution of Athens* ascribed to Aristotle can conveniently be consulted in the translation by K. von Fritz and E. Kapp (Hafner Library of Classics, New York, 1950); see Chapters 29 to 33.

Chapter 68

1. Some of his speeches are extant, but not this.
2. The Spartan admiral.

Chapter 73

1. Ostracism was a procedure by which the Athenians banished a citizen for ten years. It was originally intended to eliminate men whose power made them dangerous to democracy but was later used by leading politicians to get rid of their rivals. Hyperbolus, an extreme demagogue of the same kind as Cleon, had been ostracized in 417 by the combined influence of Nicias and Alcibiades.

Chapter 76

1. An allusion to the great revolt of Samos in 440-39.

Chapter 92

1. Some sort of mobile guards.

ABOUT THE EDITORS

Hugh R. Trevor-Roper, general editor of *The Great Histories Series,* is the distinguished Regius Professor of Modern History at Oxford University. He is probably most well known to American readers for his book *The Last Days of Hitler,* which is a classic in the field of modern German history and was the result of official investigations carried out by Professor Trevor-Roper at the behest of British Intelligence in an attempt to unshroud the mystery surrounding the dictator's fate. The book has already been translated into nineteen foreign languages. Professor Trevor-Roper is a specialist in sixteenth- and seventeenth-century history and has published several other notable works: *Archbishop Laud, Man and Events.* He has contributed numerous articles on political and historical subjects to the journals and is familiar to American readers of *The New York Times Magazine* and *Horizon.*

Peter Astbury Brunt, Fellow and Tutor of Oriel College, Oxford University, is a distinguished scholar in the field of Classical Greek and Roman historical studies. He is a graduate of Oxford and prior to his joining the faculty of his *alma mater,* was a Lecturer in Ancient History at the University of St. Andrews (1947-51). He has a considerable number of reviews and articles concerned with Greek and Roman history.

Index

Index

INDEX